D1542167

THE HUGUENOT
CHRONICLES
TRILOGY
COMPLETE IN ONE VOLUME

PAUL C.R. MONK

A BLOOMTREE PRESS Book.

First published in 2018 by BLOOMTREE PRESS.

Copyright © Paul C. R. Monk 2020

ISBN 978-1-9164859-1-4

www.paulcrmonk.com

Cover design by David Ter-Avanesyan.

The moral right of Paul C.R. Monk to be identified as the author of this work has been asserted by him in accordance with the Copyright, Designs and Patents Act 1988.

All rights reserved. No part of this publication may be reproduced, stored in a retrieval system or transmitted in any form or by any means, without the prior permission in writing of the publisher, nor to be otherwise circulated in any form of binding or cover other than that in which it is published without a similar condition, including this condition, being imposed on the subsequent purchaser.

MERCHANTS OF VIRTUE

(Based on a true story)

Book One of
THE HUGUENOT CONNECTION
Trilogy

PAUL C.R. MONK

The death of Charles II in February 1685 enabled the Duke of York to accede to the throne as a Roman Catholic king. He became James II of England and Ireland, and James VII of Scotland.

The Duke's friend and cousin, Louis XIV of France, welcomed the news. It encouraged the French king to hasten his plans to complete the purge of non-Catholic subjects from his court, kingdom, and colonies, especially the Protestants, known in France as Huguenots.

These Huguenots had enjoyed freedom of worship, as well as political and civil rights guaranteed by the Edict of Nantes, which had been signed eighty-seven years earlier by Louis XIV's grandfather. Louis's plan to revoke the edict would consolidate France under one faith, one law, and one king.

Indeed, slowly but surely, Louis had already stripped the heretics of civil rights, ordered the destruction of their temples and schools, and restricted their fields of professional activity.

While James embarked on his Catholic kingship, Louis and his entourage perfected plans for the last push to persuade resisting Protestants to reconvert to the true religion. The final dragonnades were soon to be put into action.

1

19 August 1685

JEANNE DELPECH DE Castanet took a sip from the exquisite Chinese teacup. Suzanne was telling her about the arrival of Monsieur de Boufflers, which had been the talk of the town since yesterday.

'I wondered why there were so many carts travelling out from Montauban,' said Jeanne.

'Were there really?' said Suzanne with a hint of concern. Then, helping herself to another biscuit, with her usual merriment she said, 'These ones are flavoured with vanilla, you know.'

Jeanne could not help but notice that her sister had not only put on a little weight, she had aged slightly around the eyes. Jeanne wondered if she, too, would look the same in nine years' time, for that was how many years separated them.

Suzanne was past childbearing age already, which was not a bad thing. While Jeanne suffered her pregnancies with a certain facility, Suzanne had many times lost the baby before its term. But she was happy, and she had her 'miracle child,' as she called him. She had also married well, even though her husband, Robert Garrisson, was twenty-five years her senior. He was nonetheless good company, doted on his wife and son, and did not look at all his age.

'I was telling Robert only yesterday that it was high time I paid you a visit,' said Suzanne. 'Really, you ought to have stayed put, dear sister. And I am not so sure your husband will be happy about you returning.'

'Well, I am not happy about him leaving me on my own. His business concerns seem to be his only preoccupation of late. Wife and children in the country, and Monsieur can do as he pleases.'

'Worry not your pretty head, my dear. He has been meeting with Robert.'

'And that Maître Satur, I suspect, soliciting more money for his unscrupulous ventures, no doubt. Anyway, I am here now, and I am certainly not going all that way back, whether Monsieur de Boufflers chooses to stay or not.'

'Robert fears he has plans to stay,' said Suzanne, pouring out more tea. 'And now Robert wants me to leave. But if you are staying, then so shall I! Besides, I got a glimpse of Monsieur de Boufflers yesterday: he did not look at all like the person he is made out to be. In fact, he was all frills and colour, most becoming to the eye.'

'Clothes do not make the man, Suzanne!'

'Quite. And did you know, he even showed off his undergarment ruffles!' said Suzanne with a ring of laughter. 'I believe it is the fashion in Versailles. But tell me, my dear sister, what is the news from Verlhac?'

Jeanne related the recent tidings from the country: the children's playacting in the barn, the drought, the lengths to which farmers had to go to irrigate the land, the daily ritual of leading the cows to water, and the proliferation of mosquitoes after the recent storm.

Two pots of tea later, Suzanne showed Jeanne down the flagstone steps to the carriage entrance where a sedan chair was waiting. A bearer stood at either end.

'Really, my sister, I can walk.'

'You know what they say: by mid-August, the hazelnut has a full belly!' Suzanne had a way with words, and would always make them sound like they were chiming inside her. 'Now, in you get. And send for me as soon as the pangs begin.'

'I cannot sit in that box.'

'Well, you must. You are in no condition to cross the filthy streets in this heat. You might slip over. I shall not be responsible for a tragedy! In you go. You, your hazelnut, and all,' said Madame Garrisson.

Ever since Jeanne could remember, Suzanne won her way in the most mirthful fashion, and always attracted a smile. Jeanne, on the other hand, most often displayed a little thought-pleat across her brow.

'All right, if you want me to feel like Madame de Maintenon. But I shall send it back so that you can visit when the time comes.'

'I will, dear sister. I am in haste to meet little Pierre's new cousin!'

No sooner had Jeanne Delpech sat on the chair than the bearers lifted the poles, and the valet opened the smaller of the front doors. Amid amused rings of laughter from the ladies, the bearers stepped through the door into the sunny street. Then they marched westward across town.

'Take the market route, would you? I would like to call at

Monsieur Picquos's,' said Madame Delpech, feeling very much like a Parisian marquise.

*

With a flourish of his lace-cuffed hand the Marquis de Boufflers put the question of conversion to the intendant of Montauban, Urbain Le Goux de La Berchère.

'Swearing allegiance to the king is not enough,' said de Boufflers. 'The king's policy of one faith and one law must be enforced throughout the entire kingdom! There can be no more exceptions. We need to make this town entirely Catholic. However, it would be most disagreeable to our divine sovereign if we had to resort to the arrest and castigation of his own subjects. But can we avoid it? I have heard Montauban will be the hardest nut to crack.'

They were sitting in the sumptuous oak-panelled chamber of the town hall. Intendant de la Berchère sat back in his barley twist chair behind his walnut desk, arching together his lean fingers. Within the short time since he had taken up office in Montauban, he had come to know what made people here tick.

He said: 'The Huguenots preach about the individual's right to decide matters of spirituality, my Lord, but they are in truth like all bourgeois. They aspire to pre-eminence and a title. And they will stand in one block behind their prominent members whom they will follow like sheep.'

'Ah. So if we win over the Huguenot leaders we win the whole town,' said the marquis with false candour. As commander of the Sun King's dragoons he had to find out to what extent he could count on the intendant's complicity. And in fact, de la Berchère was turning out to be sharper and more sophisticated than his solemn and somewhat stoic appearance would have one believe, much more to the marquis' liking than Dubois, the previous administrator.

'Undoubtedly, my Lord, if not the whole *généralité*.' With a wry smile, de la Berchère reached over and served his illustrious visitor some more of his best Fronton wine.

The Marquis de Boufflers said: 'Then our first task, before we put forth our propositions, will be to acquire some substance for negotiation.'

'Indeed, my Lord,' said the intendant. And to show he not only grasped but also subscribed to the marquis' allusion to a dragonnade, he added: 'It will be wise to first remind them that their soft hands and soft bellies will not help them if their heads are too hard!'

'I could not have put it better myself,' said de Boufflers. 'Your name will go down in history, Sir, as the one who saved a multitude from torment and brought the fold back from the precipice of spiritual ruin.'

'I only seek to avoid unnecessary strife, my Lord, and desire what sits well with our good king . . .'

'Quite,' said de Boufflers, thoroughly satisfied, and he raised his glass. 'To king and country!'

'To king and country . . . and God!'

*

The pretty backdrop of peachy brick walls appeased Jeanne Delpech, and reassured her of her decision to return to Montauban. This was her home, the provincial town she so loved. Even animal muck and litter from the recent Catholic procession did not put her out. She was so looking forward to the year's gatherings.

Elizabeth would be eleven this year, Lulu was coming up for three, and little Paul was seven. He had clearly manifested a penchant for structure and order by his observances of God's tiny creatures that he pinned into his collection. She hoped her mother-in-law would not interfere too much in his upbringing. She hoped too that the Lord would help the king see clearly how the divine design did not advocate idolatry and forced ceremony, but freedom of thought and worship. However, for the time being, she banished such shadows from her brow.

Her bearers came to a halt under the brick arcades of the royal square peopled with shoppers, and then lowered her chair to the ground. She got out and ambled into the spacious, vaulted boutique, its deep shelves packed with rolls of colourful fabric and swathes of drapery.

She had known Monsieur Picquos since her late father arranged financing for him to purchase his boutique. He sold the finest textiles in the generality. But she had not stopped by for cloth. She had dropped in for a rare and expensive edible indulgence that came from Guadeloupe, where he possessed interests in a plantation. She had come to purchase some chocolate, a treat for Jacob, her husband, to sweeten the taste of her defiance.

'Madame Delpech,' said the draper with a bow after leaving a customer in the hands of his assistant.

Monsieur Picquos was a co-religionist who had suffered from the restrictions imposed by Louis XIV and his advisers—even if retail was the least affected of occupations, given its direct impact on the royal treasury. Monsieur Picquos, like most Huguenots, had learnt to battle on in the hope that the storm would pass and things would become re-

6

established according to the Edict of Nantes.

'How nice to see you looking so well,' Monsieur Picquos continued.

Being in the country for so long had made her quite disregard her physical metamorphosis. It suddenly occurred to her how enormous she must look. But any embarrassment was quelled by experience—this was not her first pregnancy.

She gave him her thanks with a polite smile, and, glancing around, she was reassured to find the shop surprisingly quiet. But it was Sunday, a day when Huguenots, like Catholics, would normally be in church, if it were not for the fact that their Protestant temples had been demolished.

'When is the happy event due?'

'As soon as possible, I hope,' said Jeanne, fanning herself.

'You won't be leaving town, then.' Monsieur Picquos lowered his voice. 'Many say they are, because of de Boufflers. I have sent my wife and children to my cousin's, you know.'

'Oh? But do you really think such a man can cause a whole town to convert in one fell swoop? Just like that, on a whim?' said Jeanne, half in jest.

The draper looked blankly back at her.

*

Jacob Delpech de Castanet looked out into the street from the bourgeois comfort and coolness of his ground-floor study. He was standing in his tall townhouse in Rue de la Serre. The thick wooden shutters had been left ajar; the windows were closed. Distant church bells announced a quarter to noon as behind him the discussion continued.

'We are condemned, I am telling you,' said Maître Pierre Satur, a stout man in his early fifties.

7

'The king's intention is to eradicate all forms of religion, except Catholicism, naturally,' added Robert Garrisson, Jacob's friend and brother-in-law. Messieurs Satur and Garrisson were court attorneys and former members of the now banned Huguenot consistory.

Turning to face the room, Jacob said, 'That would constitute a grave transgression of the law. Would our king be unlawful? Why, article seven of the Edict of Nantes stipulates, does it not, that it is—'

Maître Satur held up his hand, and in the cavernous voice usually reserved for the courtroom, he said, 'It is permitted to all lords, gentlemen, and other persons making profession of the said religion called Reformed, to exercise the said religion in their houses . . .' Satur lowered his hand and continued in a more conversational tone of voice. 'I know it, we all know it by heart, my dear Monsieur Delpech. However, it does not alter the fact that he wants every one of his subjects to convert.'

Robert, who had been seated, stood up with surprising energy for his age, unfurling his lean, tall person made taller by his periwig and heels. 'Then, tell me, gentlemen,' he said, 'would you leave or abjure?'

Maître Pierre Satur tilted his head from side to side as if weighing up the odds, which made his periwig wobble. Then he took a sip from his goblet of Armagnac.

'For my part,' said Jacob, 'forsaking my faith is beyond me. I would rather leave for pastures new if I could.'

'Indeed, many are preferring exile,' said Robert.

Jacob continued, 'But, I cannot. I have my properties and my land. Not to mention my dear wife, who is on the verge of her labours, and who is justifiably against the idea anyway. Our roots are in this soil.'

Maître Satur said, 'Moreover, it will soon be impossible to leave the town, let alone traverse the frontier. Get caught leaving the country nowadays, and it's off to the galleys!' Then, in a graver tone, he announced, 'Boufflers has declared that his men-at-arms are at but a day's march. And when they get here, they are to be billeted in Huguenot homes.'

'Outrageous, surely not!' said Jacob.

'You have read the reports from Bearn, have you not?' said Maître Satur.

'Yes, yes. I find it hard to believe, though.'

'And the dragonnades of sixty-one, you believe those, do you not?'

'Yes, but . . .'

'They will be here tomorrow, Jacob,' said Robert solemnly.

With determination, Jacob declared, 'We are by far the majority here. We shall just have to stand together.'

Jacob's guests did not react with the same vigour. Instead, lowering his voice, Robert said, 'And what of our mutual investment? Any news?'

'None, I fear,' said Satur. 'But remember, gentlemen, the higher the stakes, the greater the risk . . .'

'But you are the one who advised us to pay into it, Maître,' said Jacob.

'And I stand to lose a good deal more than anyone.'

Jacob was about to respond when footsteps compelled him to glance out onto the street. He caught sight of two bearers sweating under their felt hats, and between them a sedan chair with the curtains drawn back. His heart quickened with both discontent and contentment now that, along with his children whom he had greeted at home earlier, he once again had a full house.

'It is Jeanne,' he said. 'She need know nothing of this; I do not want to worry her in her condition.' Jacob rang the little brass bell on his desk and called out to Anette, the maid.

Turning back to his visitors with renewed optimism, he said, 'But come, gentlemen, the heat has abated, this year's yield promises to be excellent, we have bread and wine, and we have our faith. Will you do me the honour of joining us for our midday repast?'

*

After evening prayer, Elizabeth, Paul, and Louise Delpech kissed their parents goodnight.

They were sleeping when, two hours later, Jacob looked in on each of them, holding his chamberstick. Sensing his father's presence, Paul awoke. Jacob put down the bronze candleholder, sat on the boy's bed, and held him to his bosom for a full minute.

What was to become of him and his sisters in this world gone mad? Should he take them and their mother away to a safer country? But how would they cope with a different language? How would they fit into a new culture? Or ought he to remain and pray to God that the winds of folly would soon blow over? What if the king died? What if the future belonged to those who waited patiently? He laid the boy back down onto his bed, and covered him up with just a sheet of linen that smelt of lavender.

The seven-year-old turned over. Contented, he slipped back into sleep.

By the time Jacob entered his bedroom, Jeanne was lying in bed, propped up on pillows, with the shutter half-open for air, and a window gauze inserted into the frame to keep out the mosquitoes. Her candelabra flickered beside her on the wooden marriage chest. Jacob stepped round the rocking cot made ready for the new baby, put down his chamberstick on the washstand, and then sat down on the edge of the high bed, placing a heavy hand on the carved wooden post. Heartened though he was to see his wife and children, their presence did not take away any of his anxiety—quite the contrary.

Jeanne knew better than anyone in the world when her husband had doubts. She had seen it when he had been obliged to sell his practice, when he had ventured into a new occupation, when their second daughter was called to heaven after a short illness at the age of five. She placed her hand on his temple and brushed back his hair over his ear.

The young lady he had married twelve years earlier had grown to love him. Her devotion shone through in the way she had made his house their home. It shone through when he saw their children.

Turning to her, he grasped her hand to arrest its caress, and said, 'Jeanne, you really ought not to have travelled in your condition.'

'I told you, Jacob, I want the baby to be born in Montauban, like our other children.' She tugged her hand free, ran it down his arm, and slipped it around his wrist. 'I am the one who is carrying it.'

There was no rational case against that. He would have to try to force his wishes upon her.

'I am not going to argue with you, Jeanne. My decision is final.'

She let his hand drop onto the bed, and said, 'I am not

one of your farmhands, Jacob . . . I suspect you want me out of the way so that you can put together another moneymaking venture with your lawyer friend.'

'No, it is not that. I told you, there is little risk there. And besides, Maître Satur takes care of everything: he is the one in relation with the shipowners.'

'But doesn't the Bible say it is wrong to lend money for money's sake? And you know what my father used to say, that money put into New World ventures is more often than not employed to purchase slaves.'

'Jeanne, I would do no such thing.'

'I know you would not, Jacob, but I am not so sure about Maître Satur.'

'Well, if it will reassure you, I am not planning another moneymaking venture, as you call it. I shall have enough on my plate with the harvest.' He took her hand in both of his, and softening his tone, he pleaded, 'Please, Jeanne, you must leave first thing tomorrow morning with the children.'

'I cannot . . .'

'My dear Jeanne, listen. I . . . I fear the immediate future does not bode well.'

Jeanne sat immobile as she studied the gravity of her husband's expression. 'Monsieur Picquos was not exaggerating when he told me the soldiers are coming then.'

'I fear not.'

Taking hold of his right hand again, she said, 'All the more reason to stay together, Jacob, as we always have. We are a family, are we not?' She pressed his hand against the tight mound of her belly, and she said, 'Come, let us pray.'

12

2

20 August 1685

AN HOUR AFTER sunrise, two raps of the doorknocker made Jacob and Jeanne look up from their draught of chocolate.

Jeanne, holding her belly with one hand, pushed back her chair, then made her way from the panelled dining room to the spacious vestibule. She began to climb the wide dark-wood staircase to the upper rooms where her children still lay sleeping.

Jacob had hurried to the window in the adjoining study that looked onto the street. He now peered between the wooden shutters that had been pulled ajar to screen the room from the day's heat. The maid, with fear in her eyes, had moved into the vestibule and now stood at the front door, waiting for the signal.

'It is one of Robert's servants,' said Jacob with a sigh of relief. 'Open the door, Anette, and let him in.'

It was that time of day when a large number of chamber pots were emptied out of upper-floor windows and, in his precipitation, the lackey had trodden on a turd. He was scraping his shoe on the wrought-iron boot scraper when the massive green door opened. He stepped inside the entrance hall which led to the study, the rear corridor, and the staircase. Inside the door stood a wooden bench where people could remove their street footwear and garments, but the lackey remained standing.

'Speak up, my boy,' said Jacob from the study doorway.

'Monsieur, my master has sent me to tell you that soldiers are entering through Moustier gate. They are in great numbers, some on foot, some on horseback. Even greater numbers, some say thousands, are entering through the gate of Villebourbon.'

Despite her imminent labour, Jeanne, who had paused on the intermediate landing, hurried up the stairs. She was normally of a calm and rational disposition and not subject to panic; however, these days, it was every Huguenot mother's fear that her children would be taken away from her. She knew how easy it was for powerful men to amend and interpret the law as it suited them. When Madame Larieux's husband died, the authorities took the opportunity of her mourning to assign her three daughters to a convent, so that they could be brought up in the religion of the state, according to a new law.

Jacob sent word to his own lackey to forewarn his mother and widowed sister, who resided in the west part of town, a stone's throw away from the recently demolished temple. In this way, word spread from family to family, and in its wake marched de Boufflers's army, an army made up for the most part of Swiss and German mercenaries.

*

The bells of Saint Jacques chimed the hour. Today might be the day the Huguenot safe haven would become Catholic again, thought intendant de la Berchère. It gave him a real sense of virtue and piety to win over the heretics and rid the generality of heresy, for the sake of national unity, once and for all.

Unfurling a scroll that lay on his desk, he turned his head to the Marquis de Boufflers, who was standing at his side with the Bishop of Montauban.

The intendant said: 'In accordance with your instructions, my Lord Marquis, with Monseigneur Jean-Baptiste-Michel, we have drawn up a list of Protestant homes to be billeted, here.' His forefinger ran down a long list of names. 'Along with the number of troopers they are to accommodate.'

The Right Reverend Bishop Jean-Baptiste-Michel Colbert, a large-shouldered and pot-bellied man in his mid-forties, gave a little cough. And in his beautiful tenor voice, he said: 'The numbers have been carefully pondered, my Lord, in relation to the type of house and the, shall we say, potential resistance that is likely to be encountered.'

'Excellent, Your Grace,' said the marquis, who proceeded in opening a leather pouch he was holding. While pulling out bundles of printed billets, he continued: 'All you do now is write the name of the owner on a billet with the corresponding number of soldiers, and sign it.' The last wad of printed billets fell onto the desk. 'The simplest plans often make for the most effective results,' he said with a flourish of the wrist.

The billets were filled out, signed, then passed on to the commanding officers of small sections of troops. This took some time, and it was not until past lunchtime that many sections were informed of their quarters which they then had to locate.

*

After taking note of his billet, Lieutenant Didier Ducamp glanced at the sun from the northern double-vaulted arcade of the main square, where he and his men—four Germans, two French, two Swiss—had settled after the march into town. He cast his eyes to his left towards a cobbled lane. 'Right, men, Rue de la Serre is that way, I wager. We'll be needing a townsman to guide us, preferably a Catholic,' he said in his dry humour, as much to himself as to his men, half of whom could barely understand him anyway.

In truth, though, the lieutenant really did not care what religion his guide belonged to, so long as he led them to their destination. He knew from experience that every man was made of the same stuff inside; he had seen men of every religion slaughtered on the battlefield. They all spilled their guts the same when their bellies were sliced. They all bled red blood, and shat through their arses in a like manner. Besides, he was beginning to dislike this dragonnade business. It had been amusing in Pau at first, traipsing through bourgeois' homes, but now it was becoming tedious. It was not what the army was made for. That said, duty was duty, and in another three years, he might even retire with enough money to get a tavern and a new wife.

There happened to be a crowd of onlookers on the corner. They had stopped to witness the scene of a Huguenot grandee flapping around at his townhouse, where soldiers were piling in through the large carriage door.

'You there,' called the lieutenant, designating a bourgeois who looked like he was enjoying the show. Ducamp, who was over six feet tall, strode the few yards that separated them. He had to raise his voice above the ambient din of bawled commands, Germanic grunts, marching boots, the clank of steel, and horses stamping and snorting. He said: 'Do you know Rue de la Serre? I'm looking for a tall house with a large green door. Belongs to a certain Jacob Delpech.'

'I do indeed, Sir,' said the bourgeois, proud to be of service. He took a few strides away from the din and said: 'It so happens I live opposite. It is a spacious townhouse. Monsieur Delpech is of a long line of nobles of the robe, you know, except for his father, who was a physician, I believe. I am sure you will find all the comforts you require there.'

Ducamp liked jurists' homes: they were well-organised, and most of them were well-stocked. Things were picking up. He was looking forward to a decent night's kip in a good bed. And he wondered if his new host had any worthy maids, or daughters.

'If you would be so kind as to show us the way there, we shall find comfort all the sooner, shall we not?' said Ducamp as a quip, though the humour in his voice was hardly perceptible.

Over the next few hours, the clamour of four thousand men of war gradually spread out in small sections like Ducamp's from the epicentre of the town. Some lanes were made of dark-grey pebbles shaped like pork kidneys that marchers cursed; others were hard-earth thoroughfares made dusty in the high-noon sun.

*

The sickening ruckus of hobnailed boots on cobbles grew louder in Rue de la Serre, as the banging of iron knockers on doors proliferated. Inside the tall house with the green door, Jacob, Jeanne, and their three children came to the last verse of a favourite psalm as the doorknocker rapped with authority.

The song always helped Jacob Delpech fight panic in times of uncertainty. And he must remain in charge of his emotions. He was, after all, responsible for the safety and well-being of his family and household. And he could not deny they were all probably about to suffer, unless he put his faith to one side.

Jeanne sensed his inner turmoil. She pressed his forearm with silent and soulful determination, as on other occasions during their married life. But they were ready to confront the soldiers, even though they had both secretly hoped their house would be passed over, given Jacob's status.

He was a landowner and wealthy merchant now, had been so since the decree five years earlier that had forced Huguenot notaries to either sell their practices or abjure. His organisational skills had served him well in managing his farms and selling their produce of fruit, cattle, and cereal. He was one of the first to plant maize, the versatile crop from the New World, in the great fertile plain that surrounded the town. He had also become quite a botanist, and studied water usage and plant requirements for more efficient growth. This resulted in recent yields being consistently higher than average, and his conversion from records of law to record yields had not transpired without some envy.

God had come to try them before; if it pleased Him to try them again, then so be it, Jeanne had told him. They would face up to this hurdle in the same way that they had confronted Jacob's professional reconversion, with unwavering resolve but without straying from the road of God's love and ultimate reward.

She ushered the children up the stairs to their first-floor rooms. That was the plan.

The doorknocker hammered again.

'King's men, open the door!' hurled a soldier's voice.

Jacob gave the nod to Anette to open up as he joined her in the vestibule, where she stood at the front door, speechless and mouse-like.

'This the house of Jacob Delpech?' said the tall, rugged figure that dwarfed her, even though she was standing two steps higher

'Yes, Sir, I am he,' said Jacob, stepping into view. 'Who do I have the pleasure of . . .'

Lieutenant Ducamp had no time for bourgeois talk. He had a job to do. He held out his billet and read. 'Conforming with the law, Monsieur Jacob Delpech shall give quarter to nine soldiers and will give to these soldiers light, board, and lodging.'

In times of conflict, soldiers were lodged with the lower classes for a specified number of days.

'You must be mistaken,' said Jacob, feigning not to understand what was happening. 'I am Jacob Delpech de Castanet.'

'Read for yourself, Jacob Delpech de Castanet!' growled the lieutenant, holding up the billet in Jacob's face.

Didier Ducamp had seen the same mock incomprehension before in Bearn. It was becoming a bore. Did the bourgeois really think they were dealing with morons? He had to admit, though, he had fallen for the comedy the first couple of times. On those occasions, he had marched back to his commanding officer to check his information. However, now with experience, not to mention a right rollicking from his commander, he had learnt to disregard any theatricality and get on with the mission at hand.

When he thought about it now, it made him laugh to think that he, who feared neither God nor the devil, had become a better missionary than the Bishop of Bearn.

He pushed his way into the premises. His men followed suit without a thought for the boot scraper, and soon smells of sweat, oil, powder, leather, and horse shit filled the largest reception room of the house.

It was always an eye-opener to see how the upper crust lived. Useless ornaments on carved and embroidered furniture, paintings and tapestries on walls, and books, rows of them, all leather-bound, always a good sign of prosperity. Oh yes, money had left its mark here. It was a reassuring thought because he and his men could eat a stableful of horses. This, he sensed, would be better than the last billet in Pau which was barren as an old hen. And it had turned out messy too.

The slip of a hand had accidentally popped the proprietor's neck while they were helping him drink a 'restorative' to give him courage to abjure. Of course, the lieutenant had learnt since that you had to be extra careful how you handled pen-pushers, who were soft as young pigeons.

As the eight mercenaries in the pay of the king traipsed into the room, Didier Ducamp turned to his second in command, and gave him a hardly perceptible nod of appreciation. It meant there was no point in rushing this one, at least not while the storehouse was full and their bellies empty.

'Bring us bread, meat, cheese, and wine,' said Lieutenant Ducamp.

'Listen here, Sir, you really ought to check with the

intendant. I am a gentleman—'

'And we are the king's men!' said Ducamp. 'And hungry men with it. Now, do you love and respect your king?'

'I do.'

'Do you respect the law of this land?'

'Yes, Sir.'

'Then fetch us our grub and grog, unless you prefer we help ourselves.'

Jacob could but agree to do as was required of him.

'We'll find our quarters ourselves,' said Ducamp.

The next moment, the wooden staircase was trembling under the footfalls of nine massive men-at-arms. Jeanne was on her way down, with her children in tow, having considered it would be better to keep them with her.

'Gentlemen,' she said boldly and with an empathetic smile. She managed not to let the organic stench of manure and body fluids overpower her nerve. 'We have prepared a large room for you on the second floor, where you will be comfortable, I am sure.'

The soldiers laughed out loud and barged past her without a thought for her condition. Indeed, it was fortunate she was standing, with her children filed behind her like goslings, on the wide intermediate landing. Otherwise, she may well have been flattened against the wall.

'My mother is with baby, Sirs, please have some respect!' said a determined little voice. It belonged to Paul, Jeanne's son of seven.

A soldier leered back over the banister with an amused jeer. But he was not staring at the boy. He was looking at his elder sister, Elizabeth. The soldier seemed to be sizing her up; then he looked away in exasperation.

'Bah, flat as a battledore!' he grumbled.

His marching partner behind him then quipped: 'Give it another six months. If it bleeds, it breeds; that's what my ol' man used to say.'

By now, Jacob was standing at the foot of the stairs. 'Gentlemen, I protest,' he said firmly. 'Not under my roof will thou speak foul.'

He took his wife's hand and led her down into the vestibule and into the dining room while the soldiers continued into the first-floor corridor.

The bedroom doors upstairs could be heard being rattled, and forced open one by one. This was invariably followed by the clang of metal landing on the floor, which was in turn followed by the creak of bed ropes.

The harassment, though not physical, had shattered Jacob's sense of justice. It harked back to the day when he was told he would have to give up his practice. Then, too, he had felt that his world was about to cave in. However, as then, he still had his faith, and the love of his wife. She placed a hand on his shoulder as they knelt down to pray.

*

A good thing his uninvited guests missed the scene, busy as they were with their installation upstairs.

Jacob had got to his feet by the time the soldiers reappeared. They were visibly satisfied with the self-attributed quarters and now were ready for food.

They had been marching from Bearn since Friday. Bakers, who had been commissioned to produce bread in abundance, had not been able to provide enough for four thousand extra mouths. And by the time Ducamp had entered the town, albeit early in the morning, there was not a quignon of bread to be found. Was this the way to treat men who risked their lives in war? They had finished their own provisions of dried sausage and were now so ravenous they would put raw flesh between their teeth.

On seeing nothing served, panic, a sense of injustice, and then the fire of wrath consumed the pits of their bellies, where only hunger had previously growled. One soldier grabbed Jacob by the lapels, slammed him against the panelling. The thick-set man brought Jacob's face level with his own, and, in a Germanic accent, he bellowed: 'Food, where's the bloody food! You want me ask your fat wench?'

'Easy, Willheim, man!' said Ducamp with the stamp of authority. 'Remember what happened last time.'

Between gritted teeth, the dragoon growled something in German, and let Jacob drop to the floor. A second later, Monique, the old cook, thankfully shuffled in with a leg of ham, bread, cheese, a wicker-covered jug of wine, and pewter tankards. Ducamp's soldiers lunged for the table with their knives and sat down astride the benches.

'Thank you,' said Jacob, wiping the soldier's saliva from his face.

Didier Ducamp stood tall and stoic, in spite of the scare that reminded him he was responsible for containing these savages and would have to be vigilant at all times. He said to Jacob: 'If you want us out of here, you know what to do. Abjure, man!'

3

21 August 1685

UNDER THE EDICT of Nantes which ended the wars of religion in France, Protestants had been granted safe havens in the form of towns in which they could freely practice their faith.

However, Louis XIV craved to unify his kingdom under one religion, which meant stamping out reformist hotbeds. Slowly at first, but surely, Protestant rights were ground down, protective city walls were destroyed, temples and schools were demolished, and government and judicial offices became restricted to Catholics only.

The most versatile among the Huguenot population of Montauban seeking employment in a royal office became Catholic. Nonetheless, despite the discrimination and the influx of Catholic clerks and suchlike, Montauban families had remained largely Protestant, especially those who wanted to get on in business.

So all about the town, thousands of well-to-do families were undergoing a similar degree of intimidation and ill treatment. It seemed to them, as it did to Jacob, that the very men paid through their taxes to protect them were treating the town like a vanquished enemy city, and were bent on destroying its very fabric with no respect for its past.

Most of these troopers were in fact mercenaries of Germanic stock. They cared little for the tradition and culture of the French generality, which made them ideal candidates for the job. They had no emotional ties; all they wanted was to earn money to send back to their homeland, or to squander as they saw fit.

Gentlemen's homes became crowded with belching, farting, snoring men whose libido was quickened by the southern skies. The most audacious invariably grabbed inside their breeches whenever a lady of the house passed by.

✳

Jacob looked as though he had aged ten years in a single night, harassed as he was by the demands of nine ruffians.

He had insisted on waiting on them himself to save his household any further humiliation and to keep the soldiers from temptation. Besides, he would not have slept anyway, what with his harvest plans in turmoil—and no news from Maître Satur of their latest venture. At least he had managed to negotiate with the lieutenant to take repossession of his bedroom so that his wife and children could rest. In return, he agreed to generously provide the men with as much food and wine as they could put down their gullets. A costly compromise for sure, but it meant the soldiers slept the afternoon away in a drunken torpor, which enabled Jacob and his family to regroup and reinforce their unity and conviction through prayer.

On this same day, the intendant sent out a party of conciliatory officers to heretics' homes. It was crucial for him to strike while the iron was hot to win the town back over to Roman Catholicism, and to avoid as many 'spillages' as possible.

Bertrand Nolen—a well-mannered man with a white philosopher's beard, wearing a dark-leather doublet with a folded-down ruff from a previous decade—was one of these missionary officers. He had spent the morning pounding the cobblestones, trying to talk some sense into the Protestant patriarchs. He bore witness time and again to ransacked homes in complete disorder. The dishevelled Huguenots saw his coming as a link to the higher spheres that could perhaps put an end to their sufferance. Nine times out of ten, Bertrand Nolen had to first hear out their remonstrances, their rage, and the accusations of wrongdoing. Bertrand's strategy was to let them empty their bag of grievances so they would be in a better disposition to hear his arguments. Of course they were right: they were victims of higher affairs of state, out of his control. Of course they deserved compensation.

At present, he was standing, with his tall beaver hat under his arm and an abjuration certificate in his hand, in the entrance hall of the large house in Rue de la Serre. He had known Monsieur Delpech from when Jacob worked as a notary.

'It is up to you,' said Monsieur Nolen, brandishing the blank certificate. 'You can make it cease now, right this minute, with a simple signature. That is all it takes for you to recover your household, Sir. Not only that, but as a Catholic, you may take up your former profession, if you so wish. Our king only wants his kingdom to be united again, as it once was not so long ago. Is that so wrong?'

'You ask of me to betray my very soul,' said Jacob, palming his straggling hair from his forehead. 'My innermost convictions which make me the man that I am, Sir.'

'Then if not for the sake of your livelihood, do it for the sake of your family. For is not vanity a sin? I believe your wife is soon to bear her child. Will she not fare better in a quiet room in a tranquil house?'

Jacob knew this argument had some substance, that he could be accused of taking his family hostage for his personal concerns. It even presented a respectable pretext for him to forsake his religion. But Jeanne, who had been standing by the stairs, raised her skirts slightly and stepped into the vestibule.

'No, Sir,' she said, to Monsieur Nolen's regret. 'I for one could never live with myself if we abjured our spiritual heritage, our simple and pure faith in God as our Saviour preached it, without artifice. It is what keeps us strong against adversity and injustice, Sir. It is the very fibre of our being. I would rather go without earthly possessions than be deprived of our Lord and His eternal promise.'

'You have my answer,' said Jacob, who felt the force of righteousness behind him again. 'We shall not abjure: we shall endure.'

'Then I am afraid endure you shall,' said Monsieur Nolen, placing his certificate with grave regret back into his leather shoulder pouch. 'You have been given the opportunity to save yourselves from the imminent storm. I have tried my best; our elite have tried and will continue to do so despite your obstinacy.' He turned and made for the door. 'But let me leave you in the hope that our conversation will stay with you, that you may see reason yet. May you know, Sir, Madame, that it will never be too late to abjure and bear allegiance to your king once again. May God be with you.'

Bertrand Nolen gave a prolonged bow, sweeping his tall hat before him. He knew his sincerity had at least touched their hearts, and he felt better in the knowledge that he had done all he could to bring these poor souls back into the fold. He stepped back into the street, positioned his hat on his head, and continued on his crusade.

4

23 August 1685

'MY LORDS, GENTLEMEN,' said intendant Le Goux de La Berchère, 'dare I say there has been some heated debate this afternoon.' He paused with the solemnity of one used to public speaking.

Intendant Le Goux de La Berchère was standing— immaculately attired in black breeches and stockings, a velvet doublet with white cuffs, and silver-buckle shoes that gave him extra poise— before an assembly of Huguenots in the large bureau in the town hall. The bishop was to his left, and on his right stood Louis Lefranc de Lacary, the president of the election bureau, who was indeed his right-hand man. Monsieur de Boufflers was absent. Impatient as he was to get the job done, he had taken a battalion of dragoons on a preliminary excursion to convert surrounding towns and villages from Albias to Realville and Caussade to Negrepelisse.

The intendant continued in his measured style. 'But we have made progress, gentlemen. Indeed, may I venture to say that we all agree that we are on the same side. We are all of Christian faith who believe in Jesus Christ, our Saviour. Are we not?'

The intendant again punctuated his irrefutable statement with a pause to take in the nods from the handpicked delegation. He had invited about thirty leading Huguenots—two aristocrats, eleven lawyers, seven bourgeois, and a handful of merchants—to a conciliatory debate at the town hall after lunch. This was always a good time to negotiate with the local population, so thought the intendant. However, today, despite the drowsy heat of the closed room and the organic mixture of sweat and fading perfume, his guests had kept up their guard with gravity. They demanded more time for deliberation, and to enlarge the assembly to embrace more of their fellow Huguenots.

De la Berchère knew they were now expecting a few words in his closing speech on the regiments of soldiers quartered throughout the town. However, he was not going to oblige. Instead, with a certain satisfaction, he said: 'I invite you all to examine your conscience, to weigh the reasons that have driven you from your natural church, the church of your king and country. I would like you to see if the minor differences proclaimed by a minority of reformists are truly worth the risk of losing your livelihood. I pray the night will bring good counsel, that tomorrow, we shall be united once again here for the common good. I propose we meet tomorrow morning at eight o'clock. That will be all.'

An instant of immobility fell upon the assembly. It was broken when, as the intendant turned to the bureau president to close the session, an incredulous voice rose up from the Huguenot ranks.

'But, my Lord, what of the soldiers in our homes?'

A rumble of 'hear hears' and shuffling feet on the polished parquet seconded Maître Pierre Satur's objection.

De la Berchère turned back to face the assembly, and in

all simplicity, he said: 'As I stated earlier, let us hope we can reach a satisfactory conclusion tomorrow.'

'With all due respect, Your Honour,' said one merchant, standing a few yards to the side of Satur, 'my home is like a pigsty, and my poor wife is about to go into labour. The men go about the place with no regard whatsoever for her privacy. I found one of them urinating in a vase this morning. There was another, in full view in the dining room, trying to burst a boil on his posterior. I pray you make this cease, that common sense will prevail!'

'What is your name, Sir?' said de la Berchère above the mutterings of empathy and remonstration.

'Delpech, my Lord. Jacob Delpech.'

'Well, Monsieur Delpech, I unfortunately cannot vouch for every one of the four thousand men of arms billeted around town. And no doubt they lack your refinement.' He left a beat for the complaisant chuckling from his sympathisers, then continued, 'But they are warriors after all, battle-hardened through years of protecting the king's subjects from the enemy. However, our Most Reverend bishop here will, I am sure, be only too glad to offer you absolution, and your hardships will cease. It is as simple as that, Monsieur Delpech.'

The bishop stepped up to speak, his fine voice resounding high and sober above the remonstrations of the errant flock.

'Indeed, gentlemen, if you would rather rid your homes of the king's men today, you only need to come and see the intendant or myself directly after this meeting.'

Intendant de la Berchère then turned to the bureau president, who closed the session. All in all, it had gone better than expected.

*

Urbain Le Goux de La Berchère found himself, if not alarmed, then surprised at his own lack of feeling towards the suffering of his fellow citizens.

Indeed, he would be the first to admit he would not make a very sympathetic Samaritan; he simply had neither the patience nor the disposition. However, as the assembly evacuated the bureau, he found comfort in the knowledge that every character type serves a purpose in God's design, and that he had been put on earth to administer, and there was nothing wrong in that. There had to be unemotional types; otherwise, who else would be able to make amends in a crisis?

He recalled once in his younger days seeing an old woman collapse in a Parisian thoroughfare after being brushed by his coach. Instead of advising his driver to find a physician, he had thought it more appropriate to summon a priest and an undertaker directly. Anyone with a clear head could see that the old lady's goose was cooked, for she did not look very well at all. A short time after the incident, he received a letter from the woman's son, who thanked him for his presence of mind and for not incurring unnecessary expense for the family. Thanks to the then-young Urbain's detached demeanour, the old lady was saved from being laid to rest in the communal grave due to lack of coinage.

The whole incident had since given Urbain Le Goux de La Berchère the courage to be his natural self. After all, was it not thanks to people of his fibre that humanity had been able to forge ahead in the face of adversity? Such was the tenor of his thoughts when, as the last of the Huguenots evacuated the room, he turned to the bishop and said, 'How much longer, do you think?'

'Not long now, I hope, my Lord,' said Bishop Jean-Baptiste-Michel, as genuinely concerned as a father waiting for his newborn baby. 'Deep down, they are all desperate to convert, but no one dares take the first step.'

The intendant said, 'The fact is they have been living in denial. They know how much easier life would be if they embraced the will of our king.'

'I pray the night will draw out their inhibitions,' said the bishop.

'Well put,' said the intendant. 'I dare say another night with the soldiers will work wonders.'

Then, turning to Lefranc de Lacary, the bureau president, he said, 'However, it might be a good idea to send an agent to Monsieur Satur's house, to reiterate our proposition and comfort him that the others are simply waiting to follow his lead.'

'As you wish, my Lord,' said Lefranc with a bow.

'Moreover,' continued de la Berchère, glancing at the bishop, 'to save time in the long run, it may well be worthwhile to set up a budget for the most prominent conversions.'

The bishop said, 'A small price to pay to bring back the lost sheep into the fold.'

He was determined to embrace the wayward lambs with dignity and pardon, and lead them on dutifully as their spiritual father should. Abjuration certificates were indeed at that very moment being pressed in their thousands. With secret excitement, the bishop took his leave to continue preparations for the imminent absolutions of the multitude.

*

Lieutenant Ducamp had fallen asleep on the comfortable divan in the study. He dreamt of fields, sun, war, and of a frayed black cloak gradually falling over him, slowly blotting out the living light. This was the succession of visions that often came to haunt his dreams. Was the cloak the shadow of death? Did it mean he was struck off God's list and would fall into nothingness?

He awoke.

A distinct smell filled his nostrils, and in his confusion, he sat bolt upright, searching his body in case he was on fire. Still groggy-headed from drink and dejected by his dream, he scanned the floor near an empty bottle of red wine. Beside it, a half-smoked cigar roll had burnt itself out, leaving a black burn mark on the waxed parquet. Yet, the distinct smell was still very present and getting stronger. It was the smell of war.

Most of his men were lying around like barrels over the floor, snoring from excess booze. The lieutenant quickly pulled on his boots. He sniffed around the fireplace that had not been used since April, then climbed the stairway three steps at a time.

At the same time, Jeanne Delpech, who had finally dozed after a sleepless night, awoke in her bedroom with a feeling of insecurity, a feeling worsened by concerns for the harvest at Verlhac. Had she known about the dragonnade, she would have stayed behind; indeed, she would have left the realm as her husband had once suggested. But such worries were wiped away when she saw that two of her children were missing.

A knocking and rolling sound, accompanied by a burning smell, seemed to be coming from the room across the corridor where her son, Paul, normally slept. She pushed herself up from the bed, and, holding her bump, she hurried across the room.

She opened her door and stepped into the corridor just as Lieutenant Ducamp appeared at the top of the stairs, a dozen yards to her right. He stopped and stared at her as she swept across to the opposite room.

She burst in. Her son was squatting in front of the chimney, where a soldier was pouring liquid lead into a mould to make musket balls. The boy held a clutch of them. The place looked like an army camp with a bedroll half-unfurled on the floor and the contents of a knapsack scattered all around. A tinderbox, flint and steel, and a tin cup, spoon, and bowl lay around the hearth. In the fire, the remains of the legs of a chair had burned into embers.

'Come here, Paul!' she said, firmly but not in anger. She seized the boy, who rolled the lead balls into the green dragoon bonnet lying on the floor, and she pulled him out of the room.

Lieutenant Ducamp no longer focused on the familiar smell. Instead, his attention turned to two voices counting alternately in German in the bedroom in front of him: '*Funf, funf, sechs, sechs, sieben, sieben, acht, acht, nein, nein.*' One was the deep voice of a soldier, the other that of a child.

Ducamp opened the door and found the girl in her room, bouncing on a German trooper's knee. The soldier stopped. He looked frankly at the lieutenant, then back to the girl with a smile. He stroked her fair head and let her slide off his knee. Ducamp snatched her by the hand, which made her squeal. He pulled her out of the room, then dragged her the length of the corridor to where her distraught-looking mother was standing with her son.

'For Christ's sake, keep 'em out of sight!'

*

Jeanne sat upon the four-poster, her back cushioned with a bolster against the carved wooden headboard, and her two eldest children nestled around her. Lulu was asleep in the rocking cot which was almost too small for her now. It had been brought down from the storage room for her new brother or sister.

'But he said he had a daughter my age,' said Elizabeth, with her head on her mother's lap. 'He said she was pretty just like me.'

'Do as I tell you, children. Never leave my sight. You must promise to God.'

'Yes, Mother, we promise,' said Paul.

'Why is the French soldier so nasty to us?' said Elizabeth.

'He is not,' said Jeanne, realising that he had probably saved her child from a calamity. 'Now sing with me, children, quietly.'

The children joined her as she softly sang, 'Call upon me in the day of trouble. I will deliver thee . . .'

Hurried footsteps on the stairs interrupted their psalm. Jeanne anxiously listened to the sound of someone pacing up the corridor. Her face expressed relief when her husband burst into the room.

After a pause to take in the scene of his family huddled together, he said, 'The delegation stood firm.'

'Thank goodness,' said Jeanne.

By force of habit, he strode over to the cot, placed between the bed and the tall wardrobe with carved lozenge panels, where Louise was still sleeping. Then he continued in a more controlled voice, 'Only one abjured. Tomorrow's meeting at eight o'clock is open to more of us.'

'How much longer must we endure?' said Jeanne in a

lower voice. 'I long to bathe, or at least—'

At that instant, the bedroom door was thrust open, and the soldier from Paul's room opposite looked inside. He said in his thick Germanic accent: 'Abjure, and we leave you in peace!' Then he withdrew and marched off down the corridor, and down the stairs. This was nothing new: soldiers kept bursting in with the same message.

'They will not let us rest,' said Jeanne. 'I dare not even change—'

Before Jacob could answer, there came the ringing of a brass bell from downstairs. Moving to the door, he said, 'I hope that with more of us present tomorrow, we can persuade them that we stand as one, and that will be enough to discourage them in their villainy, and give them every reason to leave us in peace. Bear up a little longer, my dear wife. United, we will stand strong.'

The bell rang again, this time with more urgency. In a perpetual bid to keep his family out of harm's reach, Jacob hurried back downstairs.

5

24 August 1685

DUCAMP'S SOLDIERS KEPT Jacob up most of the night.

He was a walking wreck when, the next morning, he made his way to the town hall, as did one hundred and seventy-nine other co-religionists. Yet he looked forward to this meeting more than any other he could remember in the annals of Montauban. He was confident it would allow the Protestant city to affirm its identity. He looked forward to getting on with his harvest preparations which he cherished more than ever, as he did having his family around him in the gathering season. He regretted quarrelling with Jeanne over Maître Satur.

How right she had been to warn him against making money for money's sake. It would have been more Christianly to use it to work new land, and to employ more people. Lending money, as Calvin stated, was a fine mechanism when put to the good of others, but was plain usury when it was for pure personal profit. And to think he had knowingly turned a blind eye as to its application in Satur's shipping ventures. He had not wanted to know the details because he knew deep inside that it could well be used to finance not only the purchase and transport of New World produce to Europe, but the transport of slaves to America. For he well knew that a cargo ship could not leave for the Americas with an empty hold. He decided he would pull out of Satur's moneylending schemes and New World ventures.

Presided over by Lefranc, the debate centred on why the people of Montauban had slipped away from the religion of their ancestors. Were their differences not merely the relic of religious upheaval that had swept through northern Europe during the previous century? And yet, that upheaval of long ago had no place in today's society, had it not? Moreover, were they not each and every one of them Christians? Did they not share the same values? Did they not love their king, their country, and their children?

Even Delpech could not refute that certain points appeared to tip the balance in favour of a return to the established church. But then, what about the papal artifices, the sacraments, the unchristian worship of artefacts?

It was not until four hours had passed that intendant de la Berchère stood once again before the assembly to conclude with his characteristic gravity.

He said: 'So, my Lords and gentlemen, this morning, we have mutually identified that there is not sufficient difference between our religious values for you to remain separated from the fold. With God's grace and in the name of Christ, who died for us all on the cross, we would willingly embrace you back into our spiritual family here now. But, it is for you to decide: your future lies with your conscience. Let me remind you, however, that you will be rewarded if you adhere to our king's will. On the other hand, if you do not, you will expose yourselves, by your own obstinacy, to the rigours of our soldiers. In which case the winter will be long, I can assure you.'

The Marquis de Boufflers, who had been standing with one foot on his chair, stepped forward. He had ridden back to Montauban the previous evening. He did not want to miss this rendezvous with history. And he did not want history to take a wrong turn. For he knew full well he was not only defending his glorious majesty, he was acting for the good of the nation, of generations to come, and for the sake of future civil peace in France. Had the past not already shown there could only be one religion?

He cleared his throat, and spoke with his characteristic flourish of the hand, though his words were no less uncompromising.

'Indeed, my Lords and gentlemen, if you elect not to reciprocate our embrace, and so do not desire to side with our king, then you shall not be his friends. And you know what soldiers can be like when lodged at the expense of the enemy.'

The intendant continued: 'So, I invite you to step forward now and sign the declaration. You will then be led to the bishop's palace, where you will be given absolution, after which you will recover your status and the full rights of your station.'

The intendant's eyes fleetingly fell upon the respected lawyer and leading member of the assembly, Maître Pierre Satur, standing near the front. After so much heated debate, an intense silence now filled the room. Even for the intendant, it was a tense moment.

De Boufflers, however, knew from experience that the hush that followed meant that the assembly was collectively bordering on the ledge of their conscience. In other words, they were making up their minds.

At last Maître Satur bowed his head solemnly, then stepped forward. The marquis and the intendant were about to greet him at the register as if he were a friend who had just made it across a ravine on a dangerous footbridge, when a voice rose up from amid the assembly. It was Jacob Delpech who, waving his felt hat, called out: 'Maître, you of all people cannot surely abjure your religion so easily. You are letting down your fellow townsmen.'

The intendant frowned, but it was the marquis who was quickest to react. He said: 'Sir, is it intolerance that prompts you to place your own choice above Maître Satur's conscience?'

'It is common sense and our mutual faith,' said Jacob, who now found himself standing in a little isle of space in the middle of the assembly. 'And with all due respect, my Lords, would you accept someone who so easily renounces his religion for another? If so, then should you not fear that the same person might forfeit your religion just as easily for that of an infidel aggressor?'

This time, it was the intendant, remaining calm and collected in his black satin jerkin, who said: 'We are neither Turks nor Saracens. Your townsman is as much a Christian as we are.'

Jacob beseeched, 'Maître Satur, Sir, have you decided to betray yourself, your fellows, and God?'

The intendant could hardly believe his ears: the impertinent man was going to ruin everything. He was tempted to summon a guard to throw the imbecile out. Thankfully, however, Pierre Satur, in his ill-fitting periwig, at last turned and answered.

'On the contrary, Sir,' he said, 'the well-being of the

people I represent weighs heavy on my conscience. Does it yours?' Excellent answer, thought the intendant. The lawyer continued sternly: 'Even if I had to live with my own betrayal, as you put it, I would not stand here and knowingly risk being responsible for another Saint Bartholomew!'

That was not so good, thought the intendant. Especially as today was the one hundred and thirteenth anniversary of the Protestant massacres by Catholics. However, putting the finger on some people's unspoken fear in fact turned out to be a clincher. To Jacob's dismay, other high-ranking members of the assembly stepped forward in support of Satur.

The balance was thus tipped. In twos and threes, the Huguenots advanced to sign the declaration and their subsequent conversion. Over one hundred and sixty-three abjurations were registered in one fell swoop.

A coup de grace for Protestant resistance in France. Any remonstrance from the likes of Jacob Delpech would thereon be met with scolding stares, disapproving frowns, and scathing words, borne of a sentiment of guilt and bourgeois clannism.

Lefranc de Lacary declared the session closed. With de Boufflers in high spirits and the intendant suppressing a secret smile at the corners of his mouth, the bureau president led the procession of new Catholics to the episcopal palace.

His Eminence the bishop greeted the converts with solemnity and benevolence befitting such a moment of reunification. He gave them absolution in the chapel, and then wisely sent them home for a lunch respite before the afternoon celebrations.

*

News of the conversions spread even before the bells of Saint Jacques could finish their celebratory chimes. The intendant took pleasure once again in his detached observations and superior knowledge of human nature. As he had predicted, after the conversion of the top business and juridical individuals, there came a surge of abjurations which continued throughout the afternoon and all through the ensuing days.

Bishop Jean-Baptiste-Michel was obliged to recruit extra priests from the countryside to cope with the thousands of abjurations. It could only be an act of God. To prove his devotion and to consolidate the new sheep into the flock, he orchestrated a great procession which meandered through town singing a Te Deum in thanksgiving.

All reformist obstructions having thus been removed, Montauban could breathe again and resume business as before. It was in general a time of relief, and one that came with the perspective of renewed prosperity. Printers could print, journalists could report, and solicitors and clerks could return to their offices. The time of persecution had ended that Friday, 24th August. Except, that is, for the recalcitrant, as the intendant labelled them. He would now be able to focus on weeding them out.

6

25 August 1685

MONSIEUR BOUDOIN, A red-faced, portly man in his late forties, was one Montalbanais who had welcomed the dragonnade.

Every day since it began, he had given thanks in prayer for God's mysterious ways that had brought him out of the clutches of debt and ruin. He had lost much of his wife's inheritance investing in slaves for the New World, whose ship had sunk off the coast of Barbados. He had spent many a night bent over, worrying how he could avoid the shame of selling his house, and having to take rented accommodation at the age of forty-eight.

Was the dragonnade a godsend?

At any rate, he would certainly not miss such windows of opportunity so close to home. He knew he had to get in quick, though; hesitation would only lead to picking up the leftovers. He had been diligently busying himself across town by purchasing Huguenot furniture from soldiers so they could buy victuals. In this way, Monsieur Boudoin also had the moral satisfaction of defusing a potentially explosive situation which could put the Huguenots in mortal danger, for there was nothing more hazardous than lodging angry men of war.

He had nonetheless been shy if not embarrassed about helping his wealthy heretic neighbour—a neighbour who also happened to be one of his creditors. However, with the recent abjurations en masse, those windows of opportunity throughout the town were now closing with surprising rapidity. Nobody would have guessed in a thousand years that catholicisation could be achieved so quickly in the Protestant stronghold. It just went to show what little mettle this generation of Protestant bourgeois was made of. Soldiers were relinquishing their quarters at a horrendous rate, and with a dwindling number of Huguenots, Monsieur Boudoin had no choice but to endeavour to put his scruples to one side with regard to his neighbour, Monsieur Delpech.

Jacob's pantry had been emptied of food three times by the fifth afternoon of the soldiers' arrival. To pay for present and future upkeep, Lieutenant Ducamp resolved to sell the dining-room suite, four walnut armchairs with a matching low table in the latest fashion, an escritoire handed down from Jacob's grandfather, a fine Venetian cabinet, and a beautiful leather-topped ministerial desk. The lieutenant had no idea where to sell the bourgeois junk, and only had a rough idea of what it was worth. Thankfully, Monsieur Boudoin from across the road was at hand with ready cash, which would save Ducamp's men from having to lug furniture across town to the auction room.

*

When they saw the thick-armed soldiers envisaging how to carry the furniture outside, Monsieur and Madame Delpech voiced their outrage.

'Sir, you are breaking the law,' said Jacob to Lieutenant Ducamp, who was pulling up his brown-leather thigh boot. He had been giving his feet a breather. Jacob continued, 'If you insist in your endeavours, then I shall have no other choice than to inform the authorities!'

'Not my onions, pal,' said Ducamp, stamping his heel to the bottom of his boot. He turned and barked another order at his men, who were passing the large table through the dining-room door that led to the entrance hall. 'Easy, boys,' he said, 'that's good stuff; we don't wanna scratch it.'

Didier Ducamp proceeded to carry out his plan as if the owners were of no consequence, a delicious tactic he had picked up in Bearn as part of the strategy to pressure the Huguenots into submission and abjuration. It usually worked wonders, far better than any string of insults, although insults did generally have to come first as a preamble since they set the tone.

Madame Delpech, who had staggered to a seat among her children, was promptly lifted up by her underarms so that the soldier could carry the embroidered armchair outside. Jacob protested, and took his wife's shaking hand.

Ducamp turned to them, and in his deep baritone voice, he said calmly: 'Abjure. And we will put everything back, and leave you in peace.'

'Intimidation will not get you what you want,' said Jacob, staring back with determination in his eyes.

Jeanne, with new courage, said, 'What God gives, no man can take away.'

Ducamp wondered for a moment if they feigned a lack of common sense. Or were they just being plain arrogant because of his station as a lowly lieutenant? He decided to raise the stakes and told a soldier to fetch the carved oak crib from the master bedchamber. Ducamp knew it was customary to lay infants in the ancestral cot passed down through the ages, and by the looks of it, the one upstairs was no exception.

Jeanne had laid all her children in that crib, and had prepared it for her new baby.

Ducamp looked straight into her eyes; he knew he had every chance of winning an abjuration if he could break the woman.

But she stood her ground with bourgeois dignity. She said, 'Naked came I out of my mother's womb, and naked shall I return: the Lord gave, and the Lord hath taken away.'

Ducamp was again struck in his pride. His game of one-upmanship had done nothing more than lock the Huguenots further into their stubborn defiance.

An hour later, most of the furniture was stacked in the street. Before accepting Boudoin's ludicrous offer, Ducamp decided he would give Delpech and his duchess one last chance.

'For God's sake, man,' he said to Jacob. There was a slight resonance now in the bare dining room where they stood. 'Why don't you just lie? Then you can have everything back. You are not signing away your life, you know.'

'But you see, Sir,' said Jacob, 'we would be doing precisely that. We would be signing away our values, our faith in God, and His promise of eternal life.'

Ducamp knew now for sure that the man would not be subjugated. It was a waste of time trying; he had seen the obstinate type before in Pau.

Jacob continued, 'If you go ahead with this travesty of

justice, which amounts to nothing less than pillaging, then I shall have to report it to your commander . . .'

Ducamp shrugged; he had heard it all before. He let the Huguenot rattle off his foolish protest while he strode outside, where a crowd of onlookers wes already admiring the fine furniture. Then he went ahead with the sale.

*

Jacob did not wish to leave Jeanne and their children at the mercy of ruthless hands, so he accompanied them most of the way to Jeanne's sister's on foot. Their coach had been rendered unusable, and their servants had fled. Given the ardent appetites of the men who would not have thought twice about taking even old Monique, neither Jacob nor Jeanne could blame the servants for leaving the house. It was, on the contrary, one worry less.

Once past Place des Monges, which led on to Rue Porte du Moustier where his sister-in-law lived, Jeanne let him head back towards the town hall, where he hoped to gain an audience with the Marquis de Boufflers.

The balmy streets were throbbing with bells chiming, drums thumping, processional singing, and most of all, the clopping and clatter of horses and soldiers departing. They were vacating their lodgements and joining their regiment across the river Tarn at their base camp in Villebourbon.

Jeanne had barely walked ten paces when she came upon a notice freshly pasted to a tree. It announced a fine of 500 livres to anyone found guilty of harbouring persons of the so-called Reformed religion.

From the corner of the street lined with elms, she saw soldiers on the steps of her sister's house. Her heart sank; she did not want to bring further distress upon her sister's household. Despite the discomfort of her load, she turned around, and with her children holding her skirts, she headed back towards her house, where she hoped Jacob would have returned by the time she arrived.

It was not, however, the distance that pained her most. She could take her time, and besides, she felt that the longer she could keep herself and her children from those dreadful soldiers, the better. No, it was not her breathlessness nor her aching back that gave her the most discomfort: it was the number of remarks directed at her from houses she passed along the way. Folk of the 'true' religion, now in the majority and with the tacit connivance of local authorities, openly vented their disapproval of nonconformists.

Jeanne, her three children now strung along behind her, entered Rue Larrazet, a quiet, narrow lane lined with tall houses that bypassed the pomp and procession now in Rue Soubirou on the north side of Place des Monges. It was a route she used to take in the hottest months of summer when she was younger.

*

In an upstairs room halfway up the narrow street, despite the late hour of the day, two young chambermaids were still doing the bedrooms.

'I heard the baron say we are living in an historic moment,' said the new girl from Toulouse while tucking in the bed linen. She had only been with the house since the beginning of summer. She had agreed to go there because of the extra pay for Catholic servants, and perhaps because the baron had a penchant for fair hair.

'That may be, Elise, but we've still got to change the linen, sweep the floors, and empty the pots,' said the other chambermaid, whose name was Yvette. She was not yet twenty, slightly younger than Elise, though more serious-minded under her mop of sauerkraut hair.

'I thought we'd never get through all that washing-up. And the mess . . .'

'After-procession festivities,' said Yvette, flopping the bolster pillow like a black pudding across the bed. 'Went on late into the night, you can be sure.'

'The baron was ever so tipsy,' Elise said coquettishly as she picked up the chamber pot. Moving to the window, she said, 'I heard him say good times are here to stay.'

She placed the pot on top of an oak chest of drawers and leaned out of the half-shuttered window. 'Quick!' she said, turning back to Yvette. 'Here comes that Delpech woman. Looks like 'er old man's gone and dumped her. Poor thing, she's red as a cardinal. Lovely dress, though.'

Yvette joined her at the window and said, 'I don't pity her at all, nor her sect. They all stick together like shit to a sheet. Huh, think they're more saintly than the pope, they do.'

Elise said, 'Not anymore they don't, though, do they, ha!'

'Glad they've banned it at last,' said Yvette.

'Took 'em long enough, didn't it?'

'But she still won't convert back, you know,' said Yvette. 'Thinks she's a cut above the rest. Huh, we'll soon see where her airs and graces get her now.'

'And what of her children? Has she a heart?'

'Her sort only thinks of themselves!'

'Huguenot nobs are no different from our lot, then,' said Elise with her characteristic little laugh.

50

'And they're the devil incarnate when it comes to affairs. You know Monsieur Boudoin, the odds and sods merchant, who fell on hard times?'

'Yeah.'

'Well, he says her husband offered to lend him money, at an exorbitant rate too. So much so that he ended up having to borrow more and more just to pay back the interest.'

'That's not very Christian like, is it?' said Elise. 'Glad there ain't no Huguenots in Toulouse: we kicked 'em all out. If you can't fit in, then ship out. That's what my gran says!'

'No,' said Yvette, 'you can't fit a square peg into a round hole, can ya?'

'The baron says the bishop has been so patient, and so forgiving.'

'He's a saintly man,' said Yvette, 'a bon vivant but saintly. Yet the likes of her will show him no gratitude. They ought to send her to the nunnery.'

Elise pushed open the shutter another few inches with one hand and took up the chamber pot with the other. 'Take that, heretic bitch!' she yelled out and threw the pot's contents out of the window. She pulled the shutter flap back with a playful but guilty little giggle.

'Elise, you didn't!' said Yvette, stepping away from the window.

'I did, right on her bonce too.'

'That's rotten.'

'No, it i'n't, it's patriotic. And don't look so glum, it's only a bit of fun. Won't be able to do it when she turns Catholic, will we!'

'Good shot, though,' conceded Yvette, who suddenly

realised that the new girl was capable of anything, and wondered if she had already obliged the baron.

*

Jeanne walked on without showing her disgust, thankful that the chamber pot water had splashed her coif, not her children.

She made it back to her house as the church bell struck four o'clock. But Jacob was not there, and neither were the soldiers. So she now stood outside her own home with no key. She thanked God she had thought to take some *pain d'épices*, which she broke and shared among her children.

Her condition and her situation touched the heart of a neighbour, Madame Simon, a pious Catholic woman of fifty-six. It may have been forbidden to offer shelter to a Huguenot, but she was not about to watch a pregnant woman suffer from the arrogant stupidity of men. She brought her a chair and some fresh lemon juice, which Jeanne accepted with overflowing gratitude. Had she been obliged to stand anymore, her legs and back would have given way under the strain.

*

Jacob's venture to file a complaint had not met with greater success than Jeanne's attempt at finding refuge. De Boufflers, sensing that the wind of change was favourable, had lost no time in giving the order to a unit of troops to embark on another missionary tour of the neighbouring townships and villages. Lieutenant Ducamp and his dragoons were among these men. Now that the capital of the generality had fallen, the marquis was determined to convert the rest of Lower Quercy. And he could not wait to see the king's face, not to mention that of Madame de Maintenon.

In the absence of the marquis, Jacob had insisted on seeing the intendant. But de la Berchère refused him an audience. Instead, he sent Delpech an order to return to his house, to greet another dispatch of the king's soldiers.

On arriving back home, Delpech was astonished to discover his wife desperately fanning herself on a chair, and his children, Lizzie and Paul playing, Lulu sleeping, on the stone threshold of his front door. He deduced the soldiers must have left and taken the key.

He was contemplating how to break into his own premises when a magistrate appeared with the key and a note from Lieutenant Ducamp.

As they entered the spacious townhouse, even the magistrate was unable to hide his dismay at the disorder. They were met with the scattering of vermin and bottles rolling on floorboards, splashes of wine on every textile, broken glass and scraps of food trodden into the beautifully woven carpet, grease wiped on the curtains, and not a stick of furniture in the large dining room other than a two-seater sofa and a solitary crib.

'If you will, Sir,' said Jacob, determined to muffle his emotions, 'I would ask you to record the state in which you find my property.'

'I am sorry, Sir,' replied the magistrate, recovering his mask of stoicism. 'That is not within my remit.'

After the civil servant took his leave, Jacob opened the note from the lieutenant and read.

'I fear my men were lambs compared to your next guests. You will have been warned. If you love your children, ABJURE!'

*

The interval would no doubt be short, thought Jeanne. So she quickly assembled her children in her bedchamber, laid out fresh clothes for them, and did likewise for herself.

While changing her youngest daughter, she could not help asking herself why on earth she did not leave the country when she had been offered the chance. But she knew she must not give in to remorse, and besides, at least she was with her husband.

The sound of the door latch brought her out of her ponderings.

'Paul, where are you going?' she said to her seven-year-old boy, who was about to disappear into the corridor.

'To the privy, Mama,' he said, and she waved him on, telling him not to dawdle.

She refocused her attention on dressing Louise—barely three and already as chatty as a magpie—and tried not to think about the conditions under which she might have to go into labour. Instead, she forced herself to remain confident that God would light their lantern. Be it through feminine intuition or God's grace, she then turned her mind to preparing a small leather travel bag with the bare necessities.

*

Downstairs, the boy trundled through the kitchen towards the courtyard where the new latrine pit was housed. Jacob was dipping a finger into the copper basin of water he had been heating up for Jeanne. It was the first time the boy had seen his father in front of a stove, and he concluded that he looked perfectly odd in a kitchen. But with the house now empty of servants, Jacob had been given no choice. At least it had allowed him time to mull over his harvest plans, which he hoped to send to his overseer in Verlhac.

He was about to stoke the fire again when a heavy rapping at the front door announced the dreaded new arrivals.

'Come here, my boy,' he said to Paul. He had grabbed a leather jug which he now only partially filled so it would not be too heavy. With one hand around his son's shoulder, he carried the jug to the foot of the stairs, where he handed it to the boy.

'Take it up to your mother quick as you can,' he said. The boy took the leather jug with both hands. 'Think you can manage?'

'Yes, Papa,' said Paul.

Of course he could manage, and he made it his personal mission to deliver it to his mother. He heaved the receptacle up the stairs, letting it rest just an instant on every third step.

The soldiers were now banging on the front door with a hard instrument, probably the butt of a musket.

'Open up, by order of the king!' yelled a deep voice through the three-inch oak door. Jacob could no longer stall and soon found himself face to face with the soldier who introduced himself as Lieutenant Godefroi Rapier. Despite being a doorstep lower, the lieutenant looked square into Jacob's eyes as he handed him a billet.

He said: 'You are Monsieur Delpech, merchant and proprietor of this house?'

'I am,' said Jacob.

'You are to give full board and lodging to eight soldiers now, and six more this evening,' said the lieutenant as Jacob perused the billet. Jacob glanced back at the rugged, unshaven face, and the soldier said: 'Unless you have decided to abjure.'

'I have not,' said Jacob. 'I am afraid I shall have to let you in.'

The soldier pushed his way into the house, closely followed by a rabble of men of arms. They were not amused to find the storeroom bare of meat, and the most movable furniture gone.

'Sir,' said Jacob, 'the previous soldiers took everything I had; I cannot be made responsible for their pillaging. There is not much left I can give you.'

At that moment, the sound of a jug clunking on the floorboards upstairs alerted the lieutenant.

'Bertrand, Lecoq, go see upstairs!'

Jacob explained that the noise was only his son taking water to his pregnant wife, but the lieutenant continued as if he had not been interrupted.

'Monsieur Delpech, I am in possession of an inventory of your properties. I do declare that we shall have no choice but to proceed in the sale of the livestock from your farms.'

*

Paul was desperately trying to carry the jug with two hands down the long, high-ceilinged corridor towards his parents' bedroom.

'You, boy, stop there!' ordered the soldier named Bertrand. Paul halted a second, but then carried on, straight as a post and tightening the muscles in his buttocks. He realised, however, that he was not going to make it. And there was something else. He let drop the jug and still kept walking with a stiff gait, tears welling in his eyes.

'Pwah,' said Lecoq, as he approached the boy. 'Little tyke's gone and shit himself.'

This gave cause for much laughter among the soldiers. Lecoq grabbed the jug and threw the contents at the boy's lower body, where soft poo was running down his leg.

The banging at the front door had prompted Jeanne to make herself decent. She was passing her robe battante over her bump when she heard the ruckus outside her room. The next instant, two soldiers burst in, one holding her son by the scruff of the neck.

'Looks like the lady's been bitten by a mosquito, Henri,' said Lecoq, nudging his brother in arms, who looked sternly at Jeanne and said forcefully, 'We are requisitioning this room by order of the king. So, lady, take your heretic brats downstairs before we chuck 'em out the window!'

'Unless you'd care to abjure,' added Lecoq in a show of civility.

*

Scuttling from storeroom to dining room, Jacob was at pains to accommodate his visitors, who wanted feeding at once.

'What will you give us to sell to procure more food?' demanded Lieutenant Rapier, angry with hunger.

'I told you, I can give you nothing but what is left in the pantry.'

'What, stinking cheese?' roared the lieutenant. 'If you're trying to be funny, I am not laughing! Where d'you keep your money?'

'I have none here, Sir.'

'You lie,' said Rapier, who then motioned for Jacob to follow him into the study, and to a subordinate, he pointed out the bookcase which contained no fewer than two hundred and sixty-three leather-bound books. From experience, he knew Huguenots could be deceitfully devious. 'Guillaume,' he blasted, 'look inside them books, then tear every one of 'em apart!'

Jacob protested that there were no hollowed books for hiding coins in his collection; it would be a sacrilege to destroy them.

'The Huguenot has a point: they're worth more in one piece,' said the lieutenant. 'Once you've checked them, stack 'em outside where people can buy 'em. They'll fetch enough to keep us in grub and grog till we sell his cattle.'

Jacob's further protestations fell on deaf ears.

Rapier went to continue his tour of the premises, but then turned back to Delpech and said: 'Oh, nearly forgot: given that Monsieur de Molinier, our previous host, abjured, you'll notice your billet's been dated to include payment for our time spent at his residence.'

*

Monsieur Boudoin had strategically placed his favourite armchair in front of a first-floor window so that he could observe any comings and goings at the big house—a house which he no longer saw as a source of debt anxiety, but as a beacon of hope—in case he had to step in to temper any potentially volatile situation.

He had heard of how obnoxious men of war could become on empty stomachs. It was neighbourly help of a kind, he thought to himself; it saved them from physical suffering, and you could not take your possessions with you to the next world, could you? Such was the purport of Monsieur Boudoin's musings when he saw beautiful leather-bound books being piled up outside the house.

They did not have to wait there long before Monsieur Boudoin appeared with a ready cash offer, so that the soldiers could fetch some venison and bread and fill their cups with wine. Boudoin was only too glad to be able to help facilitate the cohabitation, despite the fact that his ground-floor storage space was seriously running out of room, which was worrying. He would have to rent somewhere to harbour his growing stock of household items and furniture. The soldiers soon became busy with their book-delivery task, which, upon Boudoin's suggestion, was extended to Jacob's collection of paintings and tapestries.

Jeanne took advantage of the brief hiatus to clean Paul down in the courtyard. Jacob had managed to retrieve some fresh breeches for the boy. While dressing him, Jeanne whispered to her husband that she could not have her baby in her home now, filled as it was with such callous individuals.

'I am unworthy,' said Jacob, who had taken his youngest daughter from the arms of Elizabeth. He kissed her forehead, then turned back to his wife. 'I am a wretch who cannot even offer protection to his children, nor comfort to his wife in her greatest hour of need.'

'You have done all you can, Jacob,' said Jeanne, and, preferring to make a joke out of their predicament, she said, 'I mean, you did heat up the water!'

Jacob's face momentarily lost all sign of strain when he said, 'Yes, it was quite an operation.' The children half-giggled at the thought of their father in the kitchen.

In a graver tone, Jeanne then said, 'The truth is, it is not your fault, Jacob. It was I who insisted on coming to town, against your wishes.'

Jacob said in a lower voice, 'They are requisitioning the farms and the country house. Where will you go?'

'God will show us a way,' said Jeanne.

'But you have no means of transport. And how will you

get past the soldiers?'

'Keep your faith, Jacob,' said Jeanne softly. 'I simply sense it would be dangerous for the children to remain here much longer.'

It was not like Jeanne to use exaggerated language, and Jacob was suddenly struck with horror at the unspecified danger. He wanted them to remain close by him where he could at least try to protect them, with his life if necessary. But then what? However, before they could reach the outcome of their whispered conversation, it was rudely curtailed when the lieutenant stepped into the yard and stood before them.

He said: 'There's no place for pregnant women in a soldier's quarters. Your wench and her sprats will have to go!' He strode on towards the privy at the opposite side of the courtyard.

'But, Sir,' said Jacob, almost unable to process the barbaric command. Handing his daughter back to Lizzy, he continued, 'My wife is on the verge of childbirth. This is her lawful home.' Rapier halted in his stride and turned back to Jacob, who was saying, 'Is this no longer a state of law where an honest man can live in peace in his own home?'

'Not for you, it ain't,' said the lieutenant. 'This is a Catholic country. You've got five minutes, or I'll kick 'em out myself. And by the way, you're coming with me to sell your livestock.'

Rapier continued to the privy. At the door, he turned back and shouted: 'Where's your god now, eh? Five minutes.' Then, after a beat, he added: 'Unless you abjure!' before disappearing inside the brick outhouse.

Jeanne looked at her husband with courage. 'At least we

are settled,' she said. Jacob took her in his arms, and they reached for their three children, who had huddled around them.

Feeling inside his jacket, in a whisper Jacob said: 'Take this, conceal it.'

Jeanne took the pouch of gold coins he had furtively unhitched from his inner pocket and slipped it inside her dress.

A few minutes later, she felt a twinge of fear and despair as she led her children over the threshold of their home. However, she plucked up the instant she perceived her neighbour, who feigned to be engrossed in a book. She would not, for the life of her, let him believe she was beaten.

*

Jeanne's back, hips, and pelvis ached continuously, and stabbing pains in her abdomen had her reaching for a wall or a tree.

She had walked first to the west side of town to the house of her mother-in-law, the widow of a respected physician. But a neighbour had told her that the old lady had taken her coach with her daughter and had not been seen since.

She had wended her way back across town, avoiding the busiest thoroughfares. In Rue Porte du Moustier, she laid down a blanket over a stone bench just twenty yards from her sister's house, where troopers were still quartered.

Paul, in spite of his years, could not bear the indignity and shame of his mother having to give birth in the open street. He still remembered the screams from the birth of the last baby called Jérôme, who went to heaven not long after his baptism. When the church bell chimed seven o'clock, the boy took up all his courage—which was greater than his recent embarrassment and fear—and ran to his aunt's house, despite his mother calling him back. He hoped the soldiers would be eating and that a servant would come to the door.

Instead of a servant, it turned out to be an old man with cropped grey hair who resembled his kind-hearted uncle, Robert.

'Paul, my lad,' said the man, keeping his voice down. It was obvious to the boy now that this old man was his uncle, whom he had never seen without his big hair. And how much older he looked compared to the other day when they were playing at swords in the garden.

Robert Garrisson needed no explanation. A glance across the street to his left told him everything he needed to know.

'Step inside, my lad,' he said.

'We have nowhere to go, Mother can no longer walk about, and my little sister keeps crying,' said Paul, standing inside the carriage entrance where a sedan chair was parked.

Robert made a sign for his nephew to stay put. Then he climbed the flagstone steps, and disappeared through a first-floor door into a room filled with the tumult of men of war, eating, grunting, hollering, drinking, burping, and laughing.

Five minutes later, the boy was chomping into a chicken drumstick while telling his aunt Suzanne how they had been told to leave their own house.

'She must come inside, Robert,' said Suzanne, holding a clenched hand to her lips.

'Not yet, my dear, the soldiers here will send her away too. Then where will she go?'

'But she cannot have her baby in the street like an animal!'

'God forbid, no. There is only one way, Suzanne, and may

God forgive what I am about to do.' Robert then turned to his nephew. 'Paul, I want you to tell your mother to endeavour to move further up the street, a few houses past our own in that direction,' he said, pointing the way. 'Do you understand?'

'Yes, my uncle,' said the boy.

'Tell her to wait there until the soldiers have left this house. Your aunt will let her know when you can come inside.'

*

It took all of Jeanne's strength to move the thirty yards up the street, where she was able to place her blanket on a convenient tree stump.

There, she prayed to God that her labour pains would not intensify until she had found a refuge. She stroked her son's hair (his head was on her lap) and rocked her three-year-old daughter, who had fallen asleep now that she had been given food and drink from the basket of provisions that Paul had brought from their aunt Suzanne's.

At that hour of the day, most folk were having their supper; only a handful of passers-by walked the street. Of those who did, only a few gave a look of surprise at the sight of a well-clad family huddled there without the father. They mostly went on their way as if nothing were there at all. Others crossed the road, grumbling their disgust at the thought that some deserters still dared give resistance to the king and the church of Rome.

The clock had scarcely struck quarter past eight when the door opened. An officer stepped out of the Garrissons' house. On his heels came Robert, who was in turn followed by half a dozen red-faced dragoons, some put out at having to leave their comfortable quarters. Robert pointed to his left to detract the officer's attention away from Jeanne and her children, waiting further up the street to the right. The section of soldiers went marching down the road.

As soon as the last bonneted head turned the corner, Suzanne came running out of her house. Jeanne managed to get to her feet on her approach. Then, for the first time since the overt persecution began, she let her emotions get the better of her, and she wept in the arms of her sister.

*

'I know what Robert has done,' said Jeanne, once within the safety of the house.

However, for the time being, Suzanne was not open to discussion and focused on getting her sister up the second flight of stairs and into bed. Elizabeth was given instructions to prepare whatever she could find to eat for her siblings. Antoine, the valet, was sent to fetch Madame Gauberte, the midwife.

'Robert has abjured, hasn't he?' said Jeanne.

'Do not worry your sweet soul, my dear sister,' said Suzanne in her characteristic mirthful tone, despite her uncharacteristically ruffled appearance. 'Yes, Robert has abjured; I have not, though. The soldiers have gone, and you, my dear, are safe now.'

'But it is my doing . . .'

'Nonsense. Robert wants me to tell you that he did it not only so that you could have your baby in appropriate surroundings, but because he is not a young man anymore. He could not have endured the chaos and suffering from the soldiers much longer.'

'But if I had not come—'

'No buts, just listen. He wants you to know that your coming has liberated him. It has given him an honest reason to abjure, at least on paper, though not in his soul. So, my sister, I implore you to rest: you must focus all your strength on the baby and the work at hand. I shall make the preparations.'

7

26 and 27 August 1685

WITH RESTRAINED FERVOUR, de la Berchère said: 'I shall send a note to Versailles with the news that Montauban is once again a Catholic city.'

'Nine thousand six hundred and ninety conversions,' said the bishop, sitting back in his leather-padded armchair, thoroughly sated. 'And not a drop of blood spilled!'

'The method is simply ingenious.'

'A miracle.'

'Yes, quite. A miracle,' said the intendant. Indeed, it was as though the good Lord had smiled down upon them. He would say just that in his letter to the king. Although, as he then pointed out, it was true that they did have the advantage of an army behind them.

'Guided by the grace of God,' intoned the bishop, whose prayers had been answered completely. There could not have been a greater reward for his relentless struggle against heresy, and he inwardly praised the Lord every minute of the day. All his doubts had been dispelled.

They were sitting on either side of the long, polished oak table in the middle of the intendant's chamber. It might have seemed like they were enjoying a hearty meal, but in fact they were busy totalling the piles of signed abjuration certificates against the number of absolutions performed. This meant tallying the totals given by the country priests who had been assigned to churches, and strategic points throughout the town, to meet the staggering demand.

Their conversation was interrupted by a knock at the door. On the intendant's command, the clerk entered. 'I thought you should know that the Delpech woman is reported to have been taken in by her sister, Sir,' he said servilely. 'Yet, the sister's husband, Maître Robert Garrisson, is a newly converted Catholic.'

'Then we shall have to fine Monsieur Garrisson five hundred livres as dictates the law,' said de la Berchère with a resolute frown. 'If he insists on putting her up, he must be imprisoned, and the woman thrown out by force.'

'Yes, my Lord.' The clerk gave a slow, deliberate bow.

'If I may, my Lord,' said the bishop. Lifting his hand from its natural resting place on his belly, he propped himself up squarely in his wide armchair and said, 'It might ignite public feeling if we did not allow her off the streets to have her child. Indeed, I have been led to believe that some of the new Catholics are already regretting their conversion. An incident of this sort could well kindle a feeling of indignation and cause some of them to rebel, or worse, to revert back to their sect.'

'Hmm, you have a point, Monseigneur,' said the intendant, arching his long, spindly fingers towards his nose in a pose of contemplation. 'Indeed, my informants tell me that some are already endeavouring to leave the realm.'

'What is more, my Lord, there have been more male than

female converts. Women are easily given to their emotions and could rally to her side, which could create further imbalance.'

'In that case, let her have her baby,' said the intendant to the clerk. 'Then do as the law dictates.'

The clerk bowed once more and left the room.

*

Jacob had been relegated to manservant in his own home. He was allowed only to sit in the entrance hall, where every time he closed his eyes, a soldier belched out his name, or an insult, followed by a command.

'Jacob, more wine!'

'Jacob, more chicken!'

'Shit-face Jacob, fetch the pisspot!'

However, it was night-time and the tall house had fallen into relative silence. Even his guard had overindulged in the excellent wine, and was at present slouched over, snoring heavily on the wooden bench in the hall beside him.

Jacob sat there a moment longer, his thoughts with his wife and children, but also with his production and his trade. Should he tell Jeanne that he had invested a large sum of money in Satur's last venture? That they were without news, that quite likely the ship had sunk with his debtor in it? There again, did it matter now that he was on the verge of losing everything anyway?

It was two days since his wife and children had been turned out of their own home. Word had reached him that it had pleased God to give Jeanne a refuge. And the previous evening, Robert Garrisson had sent him word of the birth of a baby girl.

All was peaceful; he could even hear mice in the next room, rummaging over the venison carcass parts and sleeping bodies of soldiers. At last the time had come for him to slip out.

Under a crescent moon, he hurried through the empty streets of Montauban to the Garrissons' house, where he found a welcome respite from servitude. He immediately recovered some human warmth, and some of the dignity that the soldiers had been steadily grinding away.

He lost no time in kissing his children, all four of them, and his wife, before letting her close her weary eyes while he held her hand.

Before falling deep into slumber in the soft four-poster bed, Jeanne recalled the first birth, how he held her hand until she slept, and how he was still holding it when she awoke two hours later for the feed. She remembered how he marvelled at the endless supply from her breasts, nature's fountain, she remembered him calling it.

Tonight, however, his visit would have to be brief. The soldiers might stir at any moment, even though he had taken the precaution of lacing the barrel of his best wine with sweet oil of vitriol, a strong sedative that he had found in the medicine chest inherited from his father.

'A simple signature on a piece of paper will not take away my religion,' said Robert at the dining-room table, which was lit up by a twelve-candle chandelier. Jacob had noticed the room was missing silverware and candelabras, but at least the lawyer had saved his furniture. And his paintings of family members still hung on the four walls above the oak panelling.

'Quite so,' said Jacob, spreading smooth duck pâté over a crust of bread. 'But you have abjured all the same. Indeed, with all due respect, Robert, I believe you have made yourself a wealthier man by your simple signature.'

'You could do the same, Jacob,' said Robert, who sat without eating. 'Abjure and lie low until the time is right to leave. Or until the king dies, upon my soul!'

'I cannot.'

'A lie to gain time. That is all.'

'I cannot put aside my faith as you put aside your convictions inside a court of law!'

'That is unfair. I have never defended anybody I thought unworthy of a second chance.'

'Well, now I am the one who risks losing everything, while you and Satur sign your abjurations and benefit from the exoneration of this year's tithe.'

'My signature also means your wife did not give birth in the street, Jacob.'

'And I am eternally grateful, Robert. Perhaps I am being unfair. But if everyone in the country has the same response, there will officially be no more Protestants in France, then I fear the worst.'

'The revocation of the Edict of Nantes, you mean. I am sure that is what the king has intended. In which case you must flee, my dear friend, to a more clement country. And do not be surprised if I join you. Many have already fled to Geneva, Amsterdam, Berlin, and even to London.'

'I doubt my seafaring legs would get me across Lake Geneva, let alone the Channel. Nevertheless, it is also my view that we should flee. But the realm is sealed, never mind the city gates . . .'

A commotion in the corridor cut their conversation short. Then Suzanne swept into the room.

'Robert, Jacob, soldiers are coming!'

'So be it,' said Robert, now standing calm but resolute. Being a lawyer, he knew better than anyone the price to pay for harbouring a Huguenot. 'I will gladly pay the fine.'

'That is not all, if I may, Sir,' said a broad-shouldered man now standing, holding his dented hat in his hands, in the doorway behind Madame Garrisson. His name was Abel Rostan. A few years earlier, Robert had defended his innocence upon a salt- smuggling charge, so saving him from being sentenced to five years on a galley ship. He worked as a caterer, and had been busy with his wife, serving the king's officers in their quarters.

'Do come in, Monsieur Rostan,' said Robert.

'I am your servitor, Sir,' said Rostan with a bow. 'I came as soon as I overheard soldiers grumbling about having to go out at this hour. They are coming here to throw Madame Delpech out of your house, Sir, and yourself in prison if you refuse.'

'So help me God, is there no reprieve from their monstrosities?' said Jacob, standing with his fists on the table.

'I thought this would come,' said Robert. 'In truth, I have been half expecting it.'

He thanked Abel Rostan for his presence of mind and let his valet show him out. Turning back to Jacob, he said, 'I have been thinking about it: we must endeavour to send Jeanne to the country.'

'My properties have been requisitioned, down to the smallest farm.'

'Then she and the children must go to Villemade,' said Suzanne.

'Exactly,' said Robert. 'The farmhouse there, barring the

milkmaid, has remained vacant since the farmer and his wife fled the country.' Robert paced to the doorway and called to his valet, who was already on the stairs. 'Antoine, make ready the carriage!'

'I will wake the children,' said Suzanne, who then hurried up the stairs with Jacob behind her.

*

Alerted by the disturbance, Jeanne was already sitting up in the high bed as Jacob walked into her room.

'They are coming, aren't they?' she said calmly.

'Robert is going to take you where you will be safe,' he said, holding her hand.

'You must come as well, Jacob.'

'Yes,' seconded Robert, who had walked in behind his brother-in-law. 'Then as soon as you are fit to travel, you must all leave the country.'

'I cannot go anywhere yet, or they will come looking for me,' said Jacob. 'I must return to our house and pray that by doing so, you and the children may be left in peace.'

Before either Jeanne or Robert could protest, there came a banging at the door downstairs.

'There is no time,' said Suzanne, now standing in the doorway with the three children, still sleepy-eyed in their improvised night clothes.

'Jacob, you'd better leave,' said Robert, who then stepped onto the landing, leaned over the parapet of the stairway, and called to Antoine to join them.

Hurriedly, Jacob kissed his wife and embraced his children while the soldiers banged on the door. He was glad he had not troubled Jeanne with the probable failure of his latest venture. It no longer mattered. And in that confused moment, it occurred to him that he may never see his family again. Yet the urgency of the situation meant he could not dwell.

'Put the children back in their beds,' said Robert to his wife. 'If they are not seen, they will not be missed.' Turning to Jacob, he said, 'Antoine will show you a back way I used to take as a boy; I will vouch for Jeanne. Go now, my friend, before your soldiers wake and find you gone.'

An instant later, Jacob was leaping behind the valet from a rear window onto the stable roof. In the white light of the moon, he then edged along a dividing brick wall to the end, where he jumped down into the alley that led to an adjoining street.

Robert, meanwhile made much ado out of lighting the candles of the wrought-iron sconces and unlocking the coach entrance door to attend to the unwanted visitors. He then tried to stall the soldiers further by discussing the legality of the operation.

'Sir,' he said, still holding his candlestick dripping with wax, 'tell me where the law stipulates that one is not permitted to welcome a close relative into one's house. Madame Delpech is my wife's sister.'

'I don't care if she's the bloody countess of Toulouse. She's a Huguenot, and I have my orders,' said the officer, who bowled past the ageing lawyer, almost knocking him to the ground.

Further into the spacious hall at the bottom of the stairs, he was met by Jeanne Delpech, slowly descending the dimly lit stairway that led to the first-floor living quarters, cradling her baby in her arms.

'Sir,' she said calmly and with dignity. 'I believe you would like me to end my social visit to my sister's.'

'Madame Delpech, I presume,' said the officer, never impressed by high–minded bourgeois manners. 'You should know that heretics are no longer permitted to mingle with true-blooded French folk faithful to their king. You have brought a hefty fine upon this household. You must leave these premises immediately, or this man will face prison.'

'That is ridiculous, man,' said Robert. 'Can't you see she has a newborn infant in her arms?'

'Sir, you yourself have seen sense and have abjured, have you not? Then answer me this: is it not ridiculous, indeed scandalous, to obstinately choose hardship over comfort for one's loved ones? Especially when your child's life is at stake?' It could have been Robert's argument to Jacob. The officer turned to Jeanne. 'You, Madame, you know what you need to do for your hardships to cease. You simply have to sign the abjuration form; that is all. Is that really so hard?'

'Sir, I would rather die in my faith than find momentary comfort in deceit.'

Though he knew her answer was not aimed at him in any way, Robert nonetheless felt its sting of truth. He would have that minute reconverted had it not been for the fact that the only way he could help Jeanne out of the godforsaken city was as a free-moving subject of the king. And that evidently meant adhering to the Roman Catholic Church.

Jeanne continued, 'My soul I surrender to God alone; to our king, I do swear my allegiance.'

The officer, seeing there was no point in trying to make this Huguenot see reason, directed two of his men to accompany her to the open front door.

Jeanne was marching calmly before a line of five soldiers when her sister came scuttling down the stairs.

'Sir,' she said. 'I beseech you to allow Madame the decency of privacy. Please will you allow her to sit in the sedan chair, in which she may at least be sheltered from the night? Or would you rather have the baby's death on your conscience?'

The soldier showed no signs of relenting. Robert followed up, 'Sir, the writ has no mention that Huguenots are not permitted to shelter in a sedan chair, has it not?'

'Please, officer,' implored Suzanne, who then approached the soldier and pressed two gold coins into his palm. This had the desired effect. He gave the command to carry the chair a good few blocks from the house, despite Suzanne's insistence that it be deposited at Place des Monges, which was just a stone's throw away at the end of the street.

Jeanne took leave of her sister in their secret satisfaction that the commanding officer had not made any reference to the other children. No one but the soldiers was allowed to accompany her.

Once in the dark street, they did not progress more than ten paces when one of the men put down the sedan chair, provoking the other soldier to do likewise. 'No one told us to carry the bleedin' Hugo, did they?' he said to his counterpart. Then, pulling back the flap, he said to Jeanne: 'You can get out and walk, you lazy bitch!'

Jeanne, without a word and suppressing her fear, climbed out of the chair, which started the baby off.

'Shut your brat up 'n' all before I bash its brains against the wall,' said the other soldier, manifestly proud to go one up on the previous rant.

It was under such harassment that Jeanne walked three

paces behind the dragoons across Place des Monges, now dark and secret, through the silent lanes where only cats' eyes shone, and on to the main square, where the uneven cobbles were empty and glistening in the moonlight.

This was where she would spend a sleepless night. But she was nonetheless relieved when her tormentors left the moment they set down the chair. She had been worried that, under the influence of their perverse diversion, their threats might spill into action just to goad each other on. Instead, while pursuing their conversation about the lack of proper whores in Montauban, they marched back the way they had come. It was already a quarter to the hour, and soldiers were not permitted out after nine o'clock. Moreover, all street lighting would soon be extinguished.

Jeanne now sat inside the sedan chair, gave her baby her breast, and prayed in the darkness, thanking God for their deliverance.

8

28 August to September 1685

THE COLD PALE light of early morning brought with it the smell of fresh bread from a nearby bakery.

Alone in the sedan chair on the market square, Jeanne woke from her intermittent sleep. Slowly, she eased herself into a different position, her thoughts turning again to the looming shame of being on public display. Especially since below the chair, a puddle on the cobbles, tainted with blood, still betrayed an unavoidable call of nature.

The creak and slap of wooden shutters being pushed open, and secured against the brick facades of upstairs apartments, announced the imminent opening of the gallery shops that surrounded the royal square. And soon, the first market sellers would be carting in their produce and poultry from the country.

But she was not alone, she kept telling herself. She knew from experience that there are a great many horrid storms in life to bear up to, which, once overcome, inevitably lead to more clement days. Besides, she had her beautiful baby, whose warmth and smell was better than bread, and she had God.

No, she was not alone, but she would still have to make a move before the bells chimed six o'clock, when shoppers would start pouring onto the square. Where would she go, though? Place des Monges? The stone bench of her childhood was still there on the west side of the square; it had the advantage of receiving the sun's warmth at the start of the day. She remembered travelling in the post office coach as a young girl and it hitting a bollard there and damaging a wheel. She had huddled with her sister on that bench, grateful for the pool of early- morning sunlight, until help had been sent for and the wheel repaired. What would that little girl have thought at seeing herself now on that same stone bench, a lone woman with a baby in search of warmth?

But she was not alone, she kept telling herself as the neighing, mooing, and clucking of animals and the chattering of country folk grew louder outside her modest wooden refuge. Again she prayed to God to give her strength to leave it before the crowds began to gather, before inquisitive heads started to peep in through the curtain. But after a sleepless, unclean night, she simply could not muster the courage to take the first, degrading step out. She could not face the shame.

Suddenly the flap was pulled aside, letting in a stream of light.

'Oh, my God!' said a man's voice. 'What in God's name have they done?'

Jeanne looked up through silent tears. Monsieur Picquos, the draper, discreetly closed the flap and said, 'Madame Delpech, please, forgive me, I had no idea you would be inside. I sent word to Madame, your sister, thinking the chair had been stolen. She has sent Antoine here.'

He called out to David, his lackey, then said to Jeanne, 'I fear I cannot take you in, but do not worry, Madame Delpech. Antoine knows where to take you. David will help carry you there.'

Jeanne had by now calmed her emotions. 'Thank you, Monsieur, you are most kind,' she said as the sedan chair was lifted. A splash of water chased away the bloody residue left behind her.

'Madame,' said Antoine after a few moments, 'I have been instructed to take you to Place des Monges. Once the guards have left the house, Monsieur Garrisson will come to collect you.'

*

Elizabeth loved being at Aunt Suzanne's. Aunt Suzanne treated her like a proper lady. Elizabeth liked to speak to her about all the things that passed through her mind, especially since her little sister Lulu had taken up more and more of her mother's time, and now there was the baby to contend with.

'Why can we not be like everyone else?' she said to her aunt on the morning after her mother had been taken away. She was perched, prim and proper, on the large bed the children had shared in the third-floor bedroom. The curtains had been drawn back from around it, and grey morning light filled the room. 'Lots of my friends have become Catholics, and they are still the same as before. I mean, they have not grown boils on their faces or grown devil's horns or become mad or anything, except for mad Rose, but she was already mad, deaf and dumb, and now she is gone to the nunnery anyway.'

'It is a question of faith, my darling,' said her aunt as she finished dressing Lulu in her son Pierre's murrey robe. 'Your faith is your most precious gift from God. It is what carries your immortal soul to heaven when you die. If you lose it, then so, too, will your soul be lost.'

'But Uncle Robert has forsaken the religion,' said Elizabeth.

'No, my dear, you must never say that,' said Suzanne, a little taken aback. 'He signed a piece of paper; that is all.' Her voice then wavered with an emotion that contrasted with her natural cheeriness when she said, 'It is true, though, he has resolved to make a sacrifice to keep all of us out of harm's reach, even though I fear it will prey heavy on his soul. But it may well be that God has chosen your uncle so that he may help your mama.'

Suzanne, having finished dressing Louise, clapped her hands to get everyone's attention and said, 'Come now, children, remember the plan.'

'I'd much rather stay here, my aunt,' said Elizabeth. 'Travelling makes me feel awfully sick at the best of times.'

'No buts, Lizzy, my dear, you know your mother needs you. Remember, you must hide in . . .?'

'The horrible trunk!' said Elizabeth.

'Yes. Only until you get through the gate. Your mother will give you the baby to look after while she takes Lulu on her knees.'

'Why can't Paul go in the trunk and me under the blanket?'

'Your brother cannot be expected to look after a baby, now, can he, darling angel?'

Lulu tottered over to her big sister. Elizabeth picked her up like a proper little mother, then turned her round, sinking her face into the crook of the child's neck.

'Lulu, you look like a boy. Are you a boy, Lulu?' she said to the child with a laugh.

'Not boy, no,' said the toddler pouting.

'You look splendid, my Lulu,' said Suzanne. 'Lizzy is only teasing; do not take any notice of her,' she said, frowning at Elizabeth to indicate she should be more compliant.

'I was only playing, Lulu. You look splendid.'

'Spendid,' said little Pierre to his cousin. He and Lulu were the same age, give or take a month. It was a good job he was not yet breeched; otherwise Louise really would have looked like a boy.

'Let me put on your hat for you,' said Aunt Suzanne, catching the child's head with a bonnet that had a sausage of cloth around it for protection against bumps. 'There,' she said as she attached it beneath her niece's chin. 'Now, Lulu, if you really love Pierre, you will be glad to wear his clothes for a while, just for a while. You do love him, don't you?'

Lulu responded by scrambling down from the high mattress, jumping off the bed step, and giving chase to her cousin with lips puckered. Everyone laughed, even Paul, who was slumped in the armchair. He had been down in the mouth without his mother.

Suzanne had to tell them to hush for fear of alerting the guards three floors below at the *porte cochère*. Then she clapped her hands again and gave the three children one last rundown of what they must do: stay hidden in the coach either inside the trunk or under the blanket, except for Lulu, who would sit on her mother's lap and say nothing.

'But what if the baby cries?' said Elizabeth.

'It is a risk, but we shall get word to your mama to make

sure baby has had her fill before going through the gate.'

Elizabeth knew exactly what her aunt meant; she had seen her mother giving her breast before. She wondered how long it would take for her breasts to grow. She hoped to God they would not be as small as Anette's.

'That way she will be contented and sleep through,' said Suzanne.

They heard steps on the landing. Pierre instinctively ran to his mother, Lulu to her sister. Then the door was pushed open.

'They are gone at last,' said Robert. He looked haggard, but managed a bright smile at the children. Turning back to his wife, he said, 'I gave them my word Jeanne would not come back and a louis d'or to each so they would leave us in peace early.'

He read love and gratitude in his wife's eyes that needed no words. He took the hands she and Pierre held out to him as she said, 'You'd better get going, Robert, before it gets too hot on the road. With the help of the Lord, you will be there by lunchtime. I only hope your back bears up and that dear Jeanne will be able to endure the bone-shaking.'

'Last week's rain will have moistened the ground. The road will not be quite so hard. I just hope we make it through the gate.'

*

It was approaching eight o'clock when a coach, drawn by a magnificent pair of horses, stopped at Montmurat gate, east of the town.

It contained a lawyer, his wife, and a little boy wearing a pudding hat and not yet in breeches, and was driven by a valet. Robert pulled down the window and told the guard he was taking his spouse and son to his country house. His eyes then stared in dismay before he quickly regained his composure; he had recognised one of the soldiers, who had been quartered at his house before his conversion. The soldier approached the lawyer's carriage which he fleetingly admired before looking inside.

'I know him,' he said, then glared at the woman and the child. Suzanne and Jeanne were from the same mould; apart from their age, it would be difficult to tell them apart in broad daylight, let alone in the shadows of a bourgeois carriage. The children did not cough; the baby did not cry. After a moment's pause which seemed to last an eternity, the guard said: 'A new Catholic, he can pass.'

It was all Jeanne could do to keep from fainting, such was the flush of relief. 'Thank God,' she sighed as they rolled into the Bordeaux road that followed the river Tarn, glorious and luxuriant at this time of year. But Jeanne's thoughts were already elsewhere: they were with Jacob.

*

The Marquis de Boufflers was exquisitely dressed as always. His blue damask just-au-corps with gold trim reflected his high spirits. And his beautifully flowing periwig quivered dashingly whenever he moved his head.

He was having luncheon at the bishop's palace and enjoying the chance to relate the news again of the king's jubilation over the miraculous abjurations. The nation was no longer plagued by a state within a state, and Louis could reign proudly over a kingdom united in one faith. Both the bishop and the intendant solemnly agreed, reintegrating those who had been deprived of their Roman Catholic heritage for so long had made the kingdom whole again. They had at last found the right method, harsh but not violent. More humane and less costly than bloodletting, the dragonnades were the way to go.

For the bishop, the conversions constituted the summit of years of relentless hard work, repairing the spiritual foundations of the city. He had not only carried out missionary forays throughout the diocese, but governed the construction of the Hotel Dieu Hospital, the episcopal palace, and the Jesuit College.

He was filled with inner satisfaction that his labours had so pleased His Majesty, not to mention Rome, where the conversions of Montauban were the talk of the Quirinal Palace. He could not have prayed for a better reward. Now, to cap it all, he just needed a proper seat for his diocese brimming with new converts. He needed a cathedral.

'I should strike while the iron is hot,' said de Boufflers, sitting on the opposite side of the great oaken table, 'while the king is still under the exultation of having a thorn removed from his royal side!'

'Actually,' said the bishop, feeling his chin, 'I was thinking of asking the question as soon as that abject edict is fully nullified. There is hardly a Huguenot in the kingdom, so it should not take long, should it?'

'Now that the best part of the reformists has embraced the true faith, you can be sure the wording is being finalised as we speak,' said de Boufflers, who dabbed the corners of his mouth before drawing from his glass.

'If I had any say in the matter,' said intendant le Goux de La Berchère from the end of the table, 'I should have it built not in brick, but in stone.' He paused for two beats for those present to seize the full measure of his statement. Everyone knew that churches in Montauban were traditionally built of brick, which was the natural building resource of the generality. It was what gave the town and surrounding villages their cheerful peachy hue. The intendant continued: 'It would stand as a statement of royal power.'

'Indeed,' said the bishop fervently, brandishing a chicken wing, 'and a reminder of Catholic prevalence over the Protestant congregation, now defunct!'

'Defunct but not quite eradicated,' said the intendant. 'Alas, there are still a few recalcitrant bourgeois who think themselves above the rest. Honestly, they are a thorn in *my* side: they are spoiling my conversion rate!'

'Hmm, quite a predicament, I dare say,' said the marquis with a quiver of the periwig. 'The rabble, one can easily dispose of, but the bourgeois are a bit awkward, I must admit.'

Between two bites of chicken, the bishop said: 'It is such a shame, especially when everything else is going so well.'

'Would you believe,' said the intendant, 'that Delpech fellow had the audacity to come knocking at my door, complaining of ill treatment? Honestly, is the man completely naive?'

'What did you say?' asked de Boufflers, sucking a quail leg bone.

'I ordered him to regain his house to receive another eight soldiers,' said the intendant. Then, delicately raising a long finger, he added: 'And their horses!'

'Hah. Outrageous!' said the marquis, who burst out in an extravagant laugh, making his wig tremble.

'I then had a notice pinned to his door, stating that soldiers will find food and lodging at this inn.'

'Ho, ho, ingenious!'

'Not really; the philistine still won't see reason. He is becoming a perfect pest. Not only does he have nothing left to sell for the subsistence of his guests, I fear he is in danger of becoming a dissenter, or worse, a martyr.'

'We can't have that,' said the bishop, nearly choking on a morsel of chicken.

'I know what,' said the marquis, with the nonchalant flourish of another quail leg. 'We'll send him to prison for a spell. That should knock the stuffing out of him.'

'Yes, and I'll have everyone say prayers to facilitate his return to the fold.' The bishop gave a bovine-eyed glance to the marble Virgin Mary on the mantle, and then held out his glass for more of the excellent 'blood' of Christ.

'That might do the trick,' said the intendant, rubbing the stubble on his chin. 'It cannot hurt; at the very least, it will send out a strong message to those thinking of converting back.'

'And what about the man's wife?' said de Boufflers.

'We let her go. She is staying at one of her brother-in-law's farms near Villemade with her children. At least, this way, she is out of sight and out of mind.'

'Quite,' said the bishop. 'There is nothing worse than a mother and infant to soften public opinion.'

'But I shall deal with her once her baby is weaned,' said the intendant.

Taking up his glass, the marquis said: 'I give you the king, the church, and our continued success!'

'Amen,' said the bishop.

9

November 1685 to April 1686

JEANNE WAS SITTING on a three-legged stool, tossing a long-handled copper chestnut pan over the kitchen fire.

The maid had gone to milk the goat. Lizzy, Lulu, and Paul were chasing hens in the farmyard. The baby, having been given the breast, gurgled contently in her cot. It struck Jeanne that the cries and cackles outside were louder now that the surrounding trees had dropped their leaves with the first frost.

The resonant rasping of jays in the oak thicket roused her from her fire-gazing. The children's cries then ceased; she turned to the window that looked over the farmyard. A squat man was walking away down the earthen track; it could only be the weaver from the cottage near the river. Paul and his sisters were running back to the farmhouse.

A moment later, pushing open the stiff door, the boy said, 'Mama, a letter for you.'

'It must be from Papa,' said Elizabeth, holding Lulu against her hip.

Jeanne handed the chestnut pan handle to Paul and took the folded paper. She stepped into the light of the south-facing window by the solid stone sink. Then, hastily, she broke the seal, unfolded the letter, and read to herself.

'*My dear wife,*

'*Once the soldiers had sold all the livestock of our farms, I was escorted here to the Château Royal one morning by the marshal, Monsieur Castagne, and three archers. The marshal gave orders that I am to see no one, but rest assured, I am not alone in this otherwise dark and forlorn cell. I am with our Lord, and every day, I give praise to Him for shedding His light on my poor existence. As you have time and again reminded me during our previous hardships, we are nothing without God. My dear wife, without His hope and love, there can be no rightfulness, no morals, no conscience.*

'*I have been told unendingly by the guards that I am to be hanged or sent to America. But abjure, I will not. On the contrary, such barbarism only strengthens my spirit and determination to follow my conscience. I am resolved to die rather than be my own betrayer. Indeed, I am filled with a deep joy that every day, God gives me strength I never thought I had, and helps me get through all sorts of ordeals.*

'*One of the guards, the one to whose heart God sent pity and who brought this quill with which I write, tells me I am to be transferred to the prison of Cahors, where prisoners are assembled to join a convoy to the galley ships at Marseille. Even if I am condemned to the life of a galley slave, I will not abjure.*

'*If you could get some straw to me, at least I will have bedding, and a quilt would be most welcome during these cold months. But, my love, you must stay away yourself and try to find a passage out of the realm as soon as the warmer weather comes. I only hope and pray our children will bear up to the long journey. I have left instructions with Robert concerning my affairs, our home, and Verlhac, though I wonder if we shall ever see them again.*

'You can imagine that I would like with all my heart to see you before my imminent transfer, but please stay away, my love. It pains me truly to say I fear our next rendezvous may well be in heaven. I wish you many blessings, my dear, beloved wife.'

Jeanne closed her eyes. She needed to empty her mind so that she would not be overwhelmed by emotion when she explained to her children that their father was in prison, but alive and well.

*

Robert Garrisson knew that signing the abjuration certificate and receiving the bishop's absolution would not suffice.

New Catholics were expected to make an appearance at Sunday Mass. This in turn meant partaking in the Holy Communion—which, for a Protestant, was like asking a Saracen to eat pork—or risk being considered a bad Catholic. Robert knew what that meant.

Being a bad Catholic brought with it the same punishment as being a Huguenot fugitive trying to leave the country. Garrisson knew if he did not play along, it could mean being condemned to a life on a galley ship, and his status and fortune would make no difference at all, and neither would his age. He had seen young men and old, the labourer and the master, the merchant and the thief, indiscriminately sent to the galleys, some for three years, others for ten, some never to return.

Posing as a good Catholic, on the other hand, brought exoneration of taxes for the year past, the right to continue his law practice, and to retain his houses, farms, and fortune. To a man approaching seventy, this was nonetheless little reward compared to the ruin of his soul. Robert at times felt miserable and increasingly weighed down with guilt over his conversion.

One day, sensing her husband beginning to withdraw into himself, Suzanne said, 'Once you have helped Jacob and Jeanne out of the country, we shall join them and live our faith in peace.'

It was delivered with such mirth and simplicity, and Robert did appreciate his wife's thoughtfulness. But he knew deep down that starting a new life in another country at his age, even if he could get over the border as a Catholic, would be infinitely difficult. Besides, now that he had a son, his family name would survive despite the present crisis.

So he resolved to try to live with his conscience. He would defend Jacob and watch over Jeanne, not to mention his dear wife. She had not abjured. His conversion as the chief of the household had sufficed to rid his house of the dragoons. Nobody had yet said anything against her. As long as she did not overtly proclaim her faith or partake in any clandestine Protestant gathering, she would be able to withstand the hostile climate until reason prevailed again in France, he thought. By that time, he might no longer be part of this world, but the satisfaction of safeguarding her person and soul and those of his descendants gave a sense to his life which always cheered him up. And what if God had meant for him to be an instrument of His grace to help his fellows? Then should he not rather rejoice?

Robert knew he was walking on thin ice by taking on the defence of his friend and brother-in-law. Jacob Delpech was not only determined to stick to his faith, but had resolved to plead his innocence against whatever motive it was that had put him in jail.

The soldier's prediction of Jacob's imminent transfer turned out to be wrong, no doubt partly due to the impracticalities of travelling in harsh weather. The earth roads would be deeply rutted, and getting stuck in the Causses du Quercy on the way to Cahors could mean dying of cold or hunger.

Delpech had nonetheless managed to win the trust of the youngest of the guards. His name was Francis, an average-sized man with bovine eyes who confessed to thinking as little as possible about God.

One day, through the bars of his cell, Jacob said to the soldier, 'You do realise you are going to die?'

The soldier quipped that at least he wouldn't have to endure the 'excitement' of a life standing in front of prison cells anymore.

'But then what?' said Jacob. 'Where will your soul go?'

'Don't know, don't care. Besides, heaven's a place for bourgeois and priests, far as I'm concerned.'

'You are wrong, my good man. Eternal life is promised to all those who persevere in God's love until the end.'

The soldier knew what God's love meant for some priests, but he kept it to himself. Instead, he just let the bourgeois rattle on about how anyone could save their soul, be they born in the Château de Versailles or the *cour des miracles*. At least it passed the time of day, and made a change from thinking about what he would do once he had saved up enough coin to get a wife. He had his eye on the fruit and veg seller's third daughter. She might be boss-eyed, but she had a fair-enough nature, wide mothering hips, and a generous pair of jugs.

Since that day, conversations between Francis and Jacob

had been discreet and few, but there had been enough of them to sow seeds of faith where once the soldier's soul had been a barren field. After all, what if all that God stuff really was true? So the soldier thereafter agreed to pass correspondence to and from Robert, in exchange for a fee for the risk taken.

*

Throughout his detention in Montauban, only once did Jacob sway.

He was sharing his cell with a new inmate, a certain Monsieur Edmond Galet, a loquacious tailor. Galet had been caught trying to reach Bordeaux via the post boat that ran from Toulouse via Agen. On the boat, he had entered into cordial conversation with a young, well-spoken gentleman named Boisset. To distinguish himself from the rabble of labourers, Edmond became congenial with the younger man to the point of inadvertently giving away one or two details of his and his wife's intentions, which were to go on a trip to London. It turned out that the young man had nothing to his name but the clothes on his back and the title of third son to a lesser lord near Toulouse. Seizing the occasion, he informed the authorities the moment the boat moored in Agen to let the passengers get some refreshment. Edmond Galet was questioned and arrested; his wife abjured. In accordance with the king's declaration of August 1685, Boisset was able to walk away with half of the value of Galet's wealth as reward for the denunciation.

Monsieur Galet could no longer suffer the vermin, the insalubrity, and the dampness of winter. Through teeth chattering with cold, he told Jacob his plan.

'I will sign this confounded paper if it will free me of this intolerable dungeon,' he said in whispers, so that the other prisoners, mostly common villains and thugs, could not hear and thus denounce him in exchange for a reduced sentence.

'Abjure?' said Jacob in a voice equally low.

'Abjure, no, or if that is what it is, then I will do it only for the time it takes for me to leave the country. For my plan is to escape to Brandenburg, where I have heard that Huguenots are welcome to practice their employ and religion freely. You should think about it, Monsieur Delpech.'

'I cannot forsake my faith, not even for ten minutes,' said Jacob. 'I cannot become that imposture.'

'Life, is it not a game of charades? Do you not play a role when you are buying and selling? When you want to seduce your wife? And you do not act the same to a lowly pauper as to a lordly buyer, do you not?'

'Not I,' said Jacob. 'And I believe it has been the reason for my past success. My produce is guaranteed, and my word is good. My clients know that they will not be deceived.'

'Suit yourself. But if you dig in your heels like a donkey does its hooves, then I fear the future bodes not well for you, my friend.'

Shortly after their conversation, Monsieur Galet was released from the abominable prison. On handing Jacob his sack of straw, the tailor whispered, 'It pains me to leave you, good Sir. But I would argue that the Lord gave me the inspiration, and I have chosen not to be shy of his grace. Think on it.'

Monsieur Galet left the dismal dungeon and, from what Jacob could gather, he lost no time in carrying out his project.

The conversation left Delpech torn between two minds for the next week, the first penetratingly cold week of winter.

Could signing the declaration really be a means sent by God to help the faithful to pastures new? But despite all the toing and froing in his mind, Jacob also knew that he himself constituted, as did the first martyrs, an example to his fellows. If he abjured, then any moral resistance would end in the hearts of his fellow co-religionists. And his self-esteem and credibility, even if he recovered his faith elsewhere, would be shattered. He knew he represented something greater than himself now: he had become a moral touchstone. He could not convert; he could not betray God or himself for a single minute.

*

Robert had found an angle of attack, even though he still did not know on what legal grounds Jacob had been incarcerated. He had built up a defence based on the very edict of October that had revoked and replaced the Edict of Nantes. Article XII of the Edict of Fontainebleau gave a glimmer of hope to Jeanne and Jacob because it clearly stated that '*liberty is granted to persons of the so-called Reformed Religion, pending the time when it shall please God to enlighten them as well as others, to remain in the cities and places of our kingdom, lands, and territories subject to us, and there to continue their commerce, and to enjoy their possessions, without being subjected to molestation or hindrance on account of the so-called Reformed Religion.*'

Robert had tried to use his influence and relations to find out if and when Jacob would stand before the judges. Each time he addressed the consuls, he was fobbed off with some excuse about the backlog of judicial cases due to the new context brought about by the Edict of October. In short,

Jacob could very well be left to rot as far as the authorities were concerned.

Robert reformulated letter after letter to the intendant during the winter months to reiterate his concerns and to try to extract answers. He knew full well he was in danger of becoming a nuisance.

In January, a close source to de la Berchère who had known Robert for forty years advised him to ease off for a while, or risk causing a calamity for Delpech's family, not to mention his own. He told Robert he would receive an answer in due course.

*

Late February, there was already a feeling of spring in the air. The exceptional weather over the past few days now induced the first daffodils on the esplanade to unravel their yellow heads under the plane trees. Windows throughout the city had been flung open to let in the clean, warm air.

Robert was in good spirits. He was at his desk, writing another note to Jacob. The intendant had at last informed him he would receive knowledge of Jacob's charge very soon. This meant Garrisson could shortly begin Jacob's defence and challenge his detention. Robert was dripping hot wax onto the note when there was a loud knock at the front door.

Antoine entered the downstairs study and handed his master a note with no seal. It was from Robert's town hall contact. Robert read: '*Transfer to Cahors planned for Wednesday, by lettre de cachet.*'

He had to sit down before his legs failed him. It was a double blow. Jacob's transfer to Cahors would create jurisdiction and coordination difficulties, but worst of all, the

95

order had been given through a lettre de cachet.

A lettre de cachet with the king's seal enforced judgements that could not be appealed, the king being above the law. Robert knew well how easily it had been used as a tool to mute so-called agitators, and even disobliging wives. He remembered the case of one man who, having converted several years earlier, had demanded that a lettre de cachet be made out for his wife in order to shut her up once and for all in a convent, so she could be 'instructed' in the Catholic religion.

In short, all of Garrisson's efforts in building a case for Jacob's defence were dashed. He would be sentenced without a trial. Robert scribbled another note which he arranged to be sent to Jeanne.

*

Towards the end of March, the wind of Autan blew for six days solid, enough to drive anyone insane.

It could blow so hard that one's face grew numb, then drop to a whisper, before cunningly whisking up again. It kept townsfolk cloistered with fear of falling tiles, and farmhands busy with fallen trees. Not far from Villemade, a tall lime tree had cracked at midpoint, and the top part had gone crashing onto the roof of a barn.

Jeanne's maid, Marie, was milking the goat at the time. The animal had obstinately shifted to the opposite end, out of the draft and away from the rattling bar of the barn door. With an appalling crack, a cluster of tiles smashed to the ground where she usually pulled up her milking stool. Jeanne dashed out of the house fearing the worst, but the girl stood up on the other side of the rubble, unscathed. The goat's move had saved her life. It was one of those moments that made Jeanne reflect on the fragility of life on earth compared to the eternity of heaven.

April was the gambolling season. The grass was now lush and plentiful, and the spring lambs would soon be weaned from their mothers. Jeanne's baby, a happy, gurgling child, was already sitting up on her own and chewing on a quignon of bread.

Now that the baby no longer needed breastfeeding, Jeanne was able to dedicate more time to her other children's education. Just because they had fallen upon hard times, that did not mean their spiritual and academic instruction should be neglected. Elizabeth and Paul could be taught together. Lulu required more attention, especially since Jeanne had been half-amused, half-horrified to hear her utter words in patois. This was due to the influence of Marie, who was more fluent in the local dialect than in the national language.

Even though she had fallen to living beneath herself, Jeanne was well aware that it was breeding and instruction that distinguished one class from another. She was determined that her children would retain the bourgeois values in hand with the religious doctrine taught by Calvin.

It had always been an ancestral satisfaction that her family had been in the law or in the cloth. Her grandfather had been a second consul of Montauban and member of the now-abolished Huguenot consistory, whose job it was to oversee people's moral attitudes and behaviour. Oh, if he could see them now, she often thought.

There had been whispers and fears that the new Catholics would revert to their former religion and rise up against state repression, drawing in surrounding support of Protestant countries into another bloody war of religion. Jeanne did not want war, no more so than anyone else. There had been enough horrid tales of butchery from the last century which were still within living memory from when she was a child.

But the king had been clever enough to make the Edict of Fontainebleau appear to state that Protestants were still tolerated in France, and their rights to property protected. Surrounding states would thus not be officially offended, and their heads of state would be able to save face against their detractors. What was more, England now had a Catholic king.

April was also the time for a good spring cleaning and to beat out the bedbugs. Jeanne had kept them at bay through the winter by dabbing wine vinegar onto the skin of her children. But of late, Paul had developed a rash.

Now that she had recovered her figure, Jeanne was sprightly as ever. With the help of Marie, she had managed to wash all the bed linen in vinegar and lavender, and then leave it out to dry and to bleach before the sun turned cold. Despite the fatigue of the long day's work, she felt an appeasement within that she had not experienced since before the soldiers rapped on her door in Rue de la Serre. The farmhouse felt much nicer, and the children's clothes that her sister had managed to retrieve were neatly folded away, in anticipation of the change of season.

Jeanne sat at the kitchen table opposite the south-facing window. It looked onto the little courtyard and barn, where Marie and the children were rounding up the chickens into their pen. Nowadays, she much preferred to write in the light of day, and in less than an hour, it would be dark.

Glancing out of the window had become a habit now that

Lulu was more often outside than in. Jeanne always directed her eyes first at the water well which she had warned Lizzy and Paul time again not to let Lulu go near. Reassured to see the girls together chasing the last chickens, she fell back to perusing her short account of life on the farm. She knew it would bolster her husband to know they at least were well. It would also soften the blow of her sister's abjuration, she thought, as again she dipped her quill in the oak gall ink.

Suzanne had recently announced her conversion in a letter in which she also related her inner turmoil. The growing fear of a Protestant revolt had led the authorities to increase their vigilance towards new Catholic households. The penalty for clandestine meetings or even being caught reading from a reformist Bible was severe. One such case had recently come to light at a chateau where both lord and male servants were given life on a galley ship, and the ladies and maids a life sentence in prison. The poor children were sent to convents, the rich to be raised by Catholic foster parents using the proceeds of the sale of their parents' properties, the best part of which went to the royal treasury.

Fearing for his wife, his son, and his heritage, Robert had given Suzanne an ultimatum. Either she would have to sign the abjuration certificate, or she would have to leave the country as soon as possible. Papers could be obtained, but if caught at the frontier, the penalty would be no less than life. Suzanne chose to stand by her husband.

The worst was when she had been obliged to perform what the authorities termed as the Easter duty, which meant taking the sacrament. Was it not an insult to Christ to read in the scriptures of the necessity of such superfluous rituals when what was really taught was love and faith?

Jeanne looked up again from her writing. She immediately noticed a hen strutting proudly along the ledge of the well, and Lizzy and Paul with Marie. But where was Lulu? She pushed away the wooden stool from under her and called out through the open window.

'Lizzy, Marie. Where's Lulu?'

Immediately, everyone started searching and calling out. Marie ran to the well. But before Jeanne could reach the back door, a patting on the other side of it brought her instant relief. Jeanne opened the door, scooped up her young daughter, embraced her, and said, 'Louise, there you are, my little angel. Go see Lizzy, darling.'

From the doorsill, she stepped into view of the others near the barn. 'Found her!' she sang out. And to her eldest daughter, she said, 'Lizzy, I told you not to let her out of your sight; you know how fast she can run now.'

'But I boarded over the well, Mother,' said Paul in defence. It wasn't the first time Lulu's disappearance had sent them all into a panic.

'Never mind, do as I say, please, children. Keep together at all times: you must always stay together. Now, I must finish my letter to your father.'

'Yes, Mother,' said Paul and Elizabeth.

'Come on, Lulu, come and feed the *conilhs*,' said Marie, using the patois for *rabbits*.

*

After supper, with the children asleep in the room next door, the maid ironed the last of the fresh linen. While making up a parcel for her husband, Jeanne tried out some patois on Marie. It was an amusement to them both.

Marie had been in awe when Jeanne first arrived at the farm, not knowing what to expect from such a lady. But awe quickly turned to admiration on witnessing how Jeanne retained her dignity in adversity, despite having fallen so low.

The maid, a plain-thinking, plain-faced girl of twenty, no longer regretted not leaving the farm with the previous tenants, a Huguenot farmer and his wife, who had fled to Geneva, the previous spring to keep their religion. It was not often that a peasant girl could observe the ways of a lady so closely. Despite her abjuration, Marie's Protestant faith was stronger than ever, and the frequent evening readings of the Bible with Jeanne comforted her. It was satisfying that, despite their condition, God's law had the same resonance with them both. In this, they were equal.

It had even bemused the girl to see Jeanne getting her hands into the washing, though she would not allow her to fetch the water, nor the milk; it simply was not right and did not respect the established order of things. A lady of quality could not pretend to be a peasant or vice versa. Nevertheless, Jeanne's attempt at speaking words in patois really did make her laugh out loud like a donkey.

'What is the word for *acorn?*' said Jeanne, smiling at the acorn faces that Paul had made for the parcel. Each acorn had been carefully selected from big to small to represent a member of their family. There were six of them.

'*Aglan*,' said Marie.

Jeanne repeated the word and added the happy acorns to the writing material contained in a wooden case, along with a blanket, the previous one having been stolen.

The peasants and crofters in the surrounding farmsteads who had taken on the cultivation of Robert's fields were mostly converted Huguenots. But like Marie, they were Huguenots to the core all the same. Despite some marginal jealousy, Jeanne was nonetheless mostly among people of her faith.

Some of them offered her produce from their winter store. Spontaneous generosity? Or was it to appease their own mortal souls for their lack of resistance? Jeanne neither condemned nor condoned. Some wanted to justify their abjuration, but nobody could look her in the eye and explain they had converted through fear of losing their livelihood, their heritage, their children, when she, a well-born lady, had already given up so much more.

Whatever their reasons, Jeanne accepted their produce as a manifestation of God's grace, though she always insisted on paying. No, she would not accept charity so easily. It would be like profiteering on poor souls in turmoil, and besides, there may come a time when she would truly need it.

Jeanne slipped her letter inside the parcel, which she fastened with some string for it to be ready when the weaver arrived.

Monsieur Cordelle, who was in his mid-thirties, travelled to Cahors once every few weeks to sell his cloth at the market, there being fewer weavers in Cahors than in and around Montauban, where the famous *cadis* and the *gros* de Montauban were produced.

A specific rap at the door announced the weaver. He deliberately used the same codified knock every time he came, and the maid opened the door without a second thought. She had to suppress a scream, however, when she saw not the squat, jovial figure of Monsieur Cordelle, but a tall, stooping frame that filled the doorway. Noticing the weaver standing behind, she then realised it was Monsieur Robert Garrisson, the owner whom she had seen close-up only a few times during her life at the farm.

'Robert! What is it?' said Jeanne as he doffed his hat and walked into the room. Cordelle followed behind. With Robert's presence, Jeanne noticed that the chairs and the table, indeed the entire room, suddenly looked drab and confined. She dared not think how she must look; probably like a farmer's wife.

'I came as soon as I could.'

'It is Suzanne, isn't it?'

'No, dear Jeanne, it is not Suzanne,' said Robert in earnest. 'I have come to save you from prison. They are coming here at first light to arrest you and take the children.'

He was relieved to get it out quickly; there was no point in beating about the bush. But he had been wondering how he would tell her since his contact at the town hall gave him the information that very afternoon. He was relieved, too, that the flash of alarm that darted through her eyes immediately turned to steely determination.

'They cannot!'

'Alas, they can, Jeanne,' said Robert. He wanted to console her in his arms, but his upbringing forbade it. He continued compassionately. 'They can, since the decree of January which states that children under sixteen are to be brought up as Catholics, which means removing them from their Huguenot parents. I am so sorry, Jeanne. I am powerless.'

Powerless. The syllables hammered through her brain and seemed to flatten all hope. She brought her hands together in prayer, but her knees buckled beneath her. Robert and Monsieur Cordelle were able to catch hold of her in time and ease her into the spindle-back chair by the oak trestle table.

'Poor, poor woman,' said Monsieur Cordelle. ''Tis too much for her to bear. I don't know how she's managed to take so many setbacks.'

'Because she's a saint woman, Monsieur,' said Marie, who then brought her lady round by dabbing salt and vinegar on her cheeks.

After a moment, Robert spoke. 'Jeanne, my dear Jeanne, you must leave. You must let Monsieur Cordelle take you to safety, or they will lock you up in prison.'

'My children, my babies,' said Jeanne, muffling her outburst with her hand so she did not wake up her children.

'I promise I will arrange to take them into my care. Suzanne will look after them until we can get them to you.'

'You are a good man, Robert, but you also promised to free Jacob. He is still in that foul dungeon after five months of captivity. I know it is beyond your control . . . but, no, I cannot leave my children. Please, do not ask that of me . . .'

'Listen, dear Jeanne, here is a letter from your sister. Suzanne and I already spoke about this eventuality when the decree was published last January. As a new Catholic, I will have the power to take them under my wing. We have both taken the Easter sacrament. There is no reason for the priest to put us on his list of bad Catholics.'

'Don't tell me that is why Suzanne abjured.'

'No, not only. But she knew you would not. And there were other reasons I imposed, too, I confess.'

Jeanne clasped her hands and closed her eyes. She said, 'I will take them with me away from here.'

'They will never survive the journey,' said Robert, 'not on the run.'

'And what with the lambing season well underway,' said Cordelle, 'the wolves are hungrier than ever—they smell blood. You'd need a good guide.'

Robert knew about the human mind; he knew the sacrifice Jeanne was capable of for her children's well-being. He said, 'I am sorry I have been unable to prepare you for this calamity; I have only just found out myself. I came immediately. But alas, you cannot help your children in prison, Jeanne, nor Jacob for that matter. You must go into hiding. Please, Jeanne, I know how hard this must be, but it is the only way to spare Lizzy of the convent and Paul of the Jesuits.'

Jeanne held her face in her hands. Robert was right: she could not expect her children to go into hiding, let alone flee into the wilderness. And if she stayed, she would be imprisoned, which would be of no good to anyone.

'They are afraid, Jeanne, that all those who refuse to abjure will stir up Protestant feeling, and cause a revolt. They won't let you stay here any longer.'

At length, Jeanne began to gather a few essential effects.

She had found refuge here in her cosy retreat. From here, she had been able to relieve some of her husband's misery. She felt it must have been a happy home the farmers had made. It smelt and felt wholesome, like freshly baked bread and clean linen and lavender. Why, oh why had this injustice fallen upon their community? Why this persecution when Catholics and Protestants had lived in peace together, traded together? Except for the odd spurt of aggression from high-blooded students, their lives had been good, the plain was fertile—indeed, there could not be a plain more fertile on God's earth. Why did men have to ruin it all?

She spent the whole night preparing to go. Every time, ten, twenty times perhaps, she was on the verge of leaving when she put down her sack of effects, and went quietly back to the bedroom to kiss her sleeping children: Lizzy, her little lady; Lulu, her sweet precious; Paul, such a responsible little boy; and her youngest, whom she time and again plucked from Marie's arms and cradled through the night. as She went from one child to the next, touching their arms, kissing their foreheads as they slept.

Despite Robert's reassurances, as the night began to grow pale, she still could not bring herself to leave them. It was like having her heart wrenched from her chest.

'We really must go now, Madame Delpech,' said the weaver. The cockerel would soon crow; the soldiers would soon come.

Weighed down with fatigue and heartache, to Robert's relief, at last she passed her baby to the maid, and pulled herself away from the farmhouse.

Robert gave instructions to Marie. He then accompanied Jeanne in Monsieur Cordelle's cart as far as the weaver's cottage, where, to avoid arousing suspicion, he had left his own coach. Robert reiterated his reassurances and rode back to Montauban to prepare a case to take custody of the children.

The sky was already half-lit over the furrowed field bordered with hedging; there was no need for the weaver to take a lamp to lead Jeanne to a small farm building where he sometimes worked. It contained a workshop with a spinning wheel, a loom, a table, and a bed ingeniously flattened upright against the wall. He pulled down the bed and removed the wooden partition behind it. This revealed a recess—

containing a stool and a bucket—of about three yards wide and two yards deep.

'I am sorry, Madame Delpech: this is where you will have to stay during the day. No one must see you. No one must suspect you are here. You must only come out at night.'

Jeanne thanked him. She knew he would be tortured and publicly hanged if caught harbouring a Huguenot.

10

August and September 1687

ON THE EVENING of 25 August, a bedraggled company of prisoners rode their pack donkeys into the fortified Mediterranean city of Aigues-Mortes.

Jacob's hands were blistered from the rough cord of the primitive bridle, and his body ached. His clothes had become three sizes too large, and he could feel his bones with the donkey's every stride. He and the rest of the detainees had ridden without stirrups from Montpellier to the walled city, under the escort of fusiliers on foot and archers on horseback.

At their head rode the subdelegate of the intendant of Languedoc. The fourteen captives, men and women of every age and rank, did not look like criminals at all. In fact, despite their visible signs of fatigue and wear, they resembled the townsfolk who watched them pass, mostly in silence, through the crowded lanes of the newly confirmed papist town. And yet, by law, criminals they were. Guilty of favouring their conscience over the king's divine will.

They were the *resistants*, secretly envied by those who

looked on, by those who, for whatever reason, lacked strength of faith to remain Protestant.

'Look at the poor wretches,' said a stocky man with burly forearms, unable to keep his thoughts to himself. He had paused with his handcart at the sight of the procession. The man, whose name was Jean Fleuret, secretly said a prayer asking for forgiveness for his own sins, and to give strength to these righteous convicts.

'Aye, I wager 'tis another load for the great crossing,' said the dapper grey-haired man standing next to him. Jean knew the man to be the haberdasher who twice took to the sea in his younger days, but had long since taken over his father's boutique. The man continued in a reminiscent tone of voice, ''Tis soon the season to be leaving. We used to get to the Canaries by mid-November, then crossed at Christmastide. Best time for avoiding the hurricanes.'

'See what you become, eh?' said a rotund man with a pot belly from good living.

'I ask you, Sir,' said Jean Fleuret, pointing to one convict, 'should we not be prouder riding with that poor fellow there than watching this procession of true faith like they were miscreants?' He doffed his hat respectfully to the ragged Huguenot in question, then wheeled his cart full of carpentry tools alongside the company, a short distance towards his home.

Jacob Delpech endeavoured to remain as dignified as possible to show the onlookers he was not a broken man, for he rode with God. It nevertheless came as no small relief to see, at the end of the lane, a bridge over a moat that led to the round Tour de Constance, an impressive and impenetrable vestige of medieval times, and his new prison.

The massive stone tower, walls six yards thick and thirty yards high, housed two dim vaulted chambers, one on each floor. The prisoners were divided into two groups according to their sex. The women and girls were placed downstairs where only a feeble light entered through the arrow slits, but at least they were out of the still-sweltering evening sun. The men were conducted to the vast room above. In each room, they were welcomed by a dozen or so prisoners who had previously arrived.

The intendant's subdelegate had thoughtfully arranged for the reformists to be handed abjuration certificates before the next leg of their long and perilous voyage, a voyage which would take them to America. A woman with a baby at her breast, and an old peasant woman in clogs who wanted to die on the French mainland, signed their conversions. They were instantly set free, at least in body, for their hearts would be bound in the prison of self-reproach.

Jacob was glad that, by the grace of God, Jeanne had not been made to endure such a soul-destroying place. However, the conversions did not trigger a wave of signatures as the subdelegate had hoped. Instead, despite imminent exile and possible death, one lady broke into a psalm and was joined by the other women.

The well of light that ran through the centre of the building carried the soft voices to the upper chamber. The sweet music could not fail to lift the men's hearts, and Jacob broke into song himself. Other men joined in the psalm until the whole tower, to the indignation of guards and officials, resonated like a cathedral of singing parishioners.

It occurred to Jacob that he, like every one of them there, may sometimes feel downhearted, but mostly they were happy in themselves in that they had remained faithful to their conscience. They were suffering for the highest reward. They were the *resistants*.

*

Their song could be heard across the walled city and had the power to move many new Catholics to pity and envy.

'We cannot sit here and carry on our work with falseness in our hearts as if we were not affected,' said Jean Fleuret to his wife when the singing started. His voice was stern but searching. 'It's as if we never had a conscience in the first place . . . What god would want such hollow souls in his great kingdom?'

They were seated around a sturdy timber table with their three children—two boys, eight and thirteen, and a girl of eleven—and were halfway through their meal. The windows were wide open, with a mosquito gauze placed in the frame, and the land breeze was a welcome refreshment. But the bread had stayed soft, which meant a storm was brewing. However, if it came, at least it would clear the air, and the southern sun would become more clement than before.

The Fleurets thanked the Lord every day at mealtime for their pleasant climate, their modest two-storey stone dwelling, the bread on the table, and the ham in the larder. But what was the sun or the rain to a man who had sold his soul for life's comforts? Too well had they come to know death and had learnt to accept it as an integral part of their short existence. They had lost three children, two of whom had reached the age of ten.

'I feel like I let mine fly out of me like a butterfly,' said Madame Fleuret, a robust woman with a natural generosity in her round face and smiling eyes. 'But like a butterfly, it keeps coming back to the same spot; then off it flies again before I can catch it.'

Jean stood up. He strode to the sink, pulled out the gauze above it, and closed the windows. He turned around, and in a grave voice, he said, 'I think you were right, my Ginette; I think we ought to leave. I don't want to look back with remorse at my life when the time comes. I want to trust in the future of His kingdom.' He strode back to his chair and sat down. Gesturing with his large, leathery hands, he said, 'Listen, Gigi, I think I can find work in Geneva. In fact, I'm sure of it. Monsieur Grosjean is doing well, I've heard, and he would need a good carpenter.'

'Jeannot, oh, my Jeannot,' said Ginette, clasping her hands. 'I can feel my butterfly coming back!'

'You mean you don't mind?'

'Don't mind? I've been praying so hard for you to change your mind about staying that I've got blisters on the palms of my hands.'

'Hah,' chuckled Jean Fleuret, 'and I've been praying every night for the Lord's enlightenment, and for you to tell me you wanted to leave!' They laughed together, content in their new resolution.

The family made their secret plans. Then the carpenter said, 'Let us pray for our brothers and sisters in the tower, who endure and set the example for us all of true religious fervour and trust in our Lord. And for them was laid in store the crown of life, which God has promised to those who love Him. Amen.'

Such manifestations of faith as the song of the Tower of Constance did not create a rebellion, but did cause many to seek exile rather than live the sham of a false Catholic.

*

Jacob had only ever made two return journeys over water.

Once, as a young man to London with his father, who attended medical lectures there, and more recently, for business on the post-boat which carried passengers from Toulouse to Bordeaux. He had detested every moment of the two-day trip along the river Garonne and was sick travelling both there and back. How would he fare on the great seas? Until this day, he dared not even think about it; he had put it all to the back of his mind, instead focusing on prayer, psalms, and thoughts of his wife and children.

While in his dungeon in Cahors the intendant of Montauban had visited him with a blank abjuration certificate and news of his children's removal. Though the intendant had willingly used Delpech as an example to would-be bourgeois *resistants*, Jacob's dispossession and imprisonment had been nonetheless a niggling source of bitterness in the otherwise resounding victory of the state over the so-called Reformed Church. His conversion would be the cherry on the cake.

But prior to the visit, Jacob had already received a message about Jeanne's misfortune. The note had been handed to him by an old woman—the same old woman who brought him articles of need such as a blanket, writing material, and fresh straw, and who had passed him a brazier to warm him on the coldest nights.

He knew at least his children would be in safekeeping with his friend and brother-in-law until it pleased God for him to reunite with them. There was no way he could become a Catholic, no more than he could turn lead into gold. Visiting priests, false converters, and other merchants of virtue had not made him convert; neither would the intendant.

The week after the intendant's visit, Jacob was on his way to Montpellier, then to Aigues-Mortes, and now, two days after his incarceration in the round tower, he was about to embark on a tartan. The small, single-mast ship, rigged with a lateen sail and a jib, was to ferry him and the other prisoners to Marseille.

For the crew, it was a lucrative activity, more constant than fishing, and less dangerous than carrying merchandise across the pirate-infested waters of the Mediterranean Sea. Some of the sailors were indifferently cordial in their behaviour towards the prisoners. Others used them to vent all the bitterness of their existence.

One seasoned seafarer in particular looked forward to these little voyages. He unrestrainedly aimed his witty discourse at the vulnerable prisoners while achieving self-gratification by entertaining his fellows with his endless verve. It began the very minute the captives were placed in the hold, when a young lady, no more than sixteen, had the misfortunate of asking this sailor with a benevolent grin and an epicurean twinkle where they were bound. Then he showed his true colours when, in a melodious southern accent, he said: 'From Marseille to Toulon, me lass, then through the treacherous straits of Gibralter to Cadix. That's if you don't get taken by Algerian pirates. Then it be a true and wondrous seafaring voyage that awaits you, my dear, all the way to the other side of the world. That's if you get through the raging winds they call *hurricane*, that whips up the waves as tall as houses, mark my word!

'Oh, aye, I been and seen with me own eyes, see. And I escaped with me life, I did. Then, if you don't get gobbled up by the great creatures that lurk 'neath the ocean waves, they'll set you down on a desert island so you can think of home. That's if you don't get eaten by the cannibals and the giant insects as big as my hand!' He held out his hands as if clutching pears and burst into a pirate-like chuckle. The girl looked squarely at the sailor with pity, as the crew members standing nearby held their bellies in unashamed laughter.

Neither savages nor creatures worried Jacob as he endeavoured to steady himself with every crack of the ship's timbers. Already the gentle sway was brewing a storm in his belly. No, what really worried him was the appalling feeling of seasickness.

The two days and nights that ensued were, for Jacob, worse than the damp, dark, cold two years he had spent behind bars. Under the mistral wind, the vessel pitched and rolled. While the captain and his crew fought to control the ship in the raging sea, all the captives could do was kneel amid the creaking timbers and pray that they would survive the terrifying battering.

Jacob was not the only one to hold his belly in spasms of vomiting. Nearly all of the prisoners became sick. Anyone who was not ill from the swell, soon became so from the stench of vomit and diarrhoea.

It was a harsh baptism of by the sea for most. But the seaworthy among them gave reassurance that the passage to the Americas in this season was rarely so rough, and that, contrary to what the sailors might say, the Caribbean hurricane season would be over by the time they left Cadix. Jacob gave praise to the Lord for this preparation, which nonetheless had strengthened his courage now that he had been put to the test once.

Two days after leaving Aigues-Mortes, the tartan sailed

between the impressive forts of St Jean and St Nicolas, and over the massive defensive chain that assured the protection of the Mediterranean port of Marseille.

(ii)

Throughout her husband's confinement in Cahors, Jeanne remained hidden in her recess near Villemade.

In this way, she could arrange for him to receive items for his rudimentary comfort, and was able time and again to exhort him to perseverance, despite his solitude and estrangement from loved ones.

The proximity to Montauban also meant she could receive regular news of her children, who, after an arduous administrative procedure, were now in the care of her sister and brother-in-law. She missed them terribly, and desperately endeavoured every day to keep their faces vivid in her memory.

But one day—it was a Sunday because Marie was not chatting at her spinning wheel—she could no longer see her baby's face. She could only vaguely recall that first smile when she held her in her arms after her birth, and which had helped her bear up to the terrible circumstance of her persecution. But she could no longer call to mind Isabelle's face.

And what of her other children? Would her face fade from their memory as Isabelle's had slipped from hers? Shut away in her recess, she sobbed with visceral pain and thrust her fist in her mouth to keep herself from wailing out. Anyone wandering near the little mud-brick farm building at that time would have heard muffled animal-like howls, but thankfully, there was no one. And no one expected to find

Jeanne Delpech de Castanet anywhere in the country, let alone in the countryside of Montauban.

Once it had been assumed that Jeanne had fled the realm, Cordelle had found a pretext to employ Marie at his workshop, and she often stayed there late into the night so that she could pass on his lessons in weaving to Jeanne.

'Ô *boudiou*, tongues may wag, but at least it keeps their minds off me lady,' she had said to Jeanne one night. 'And besides, the weaver i'n't such a bad catch neither!' They had both laughed.

Marie went to church that Sunday, as she did every Sunday according to the law, more to avoid unwelcome attention than through love of the Roman church. That evening, when she closed the shutters, drew down the bed, and pulled away the panel of the recess, it was a drawn and distraught lady who greeted her, the very opposite of the woman Marie had come to admire. Complaining over one's lot was not in Jeanne's breeding, but Marie's forthright questioning soon brought out what had been preying on her lady's mind.

'Have you ever had a portrait done, Madame?' she said, perched on her spinning chair.

'I have,' said Jeanne, seated on the edge of the bed, 'five years ago. My husband insisted on it for posterity. Family, past, present, and future, means everything to him, you see.'

'And a good job too,' said Marie, who spoke in patois, as did Jeanne more and more often nowadays—you never knew who might be listening outside in the dark. 'Then they won't forget you if your sister hangs it somewhere they can see it every day, will they?'

Marie's bright idea gave Jeanne new wings and instantly

brought the colour back to her cheeks. She took up her seat at the loom for another lesson in threading.

When, the following week, Suzanne received news of Jeanne's anxiety, she managed to retrieve her sister's portrait, which she hung up on the wall at the top of the stairs. Then she came up with her own idea that would help bring Jeanne's children back to her, at least in thought. Robert immediately took it up and commissioned an artist to make sketches of the children.

A few weeks after Jeanne's horrid realisation of the passing time, the weaver handed her the scrolls. He politely turned his head away as tears of joy rolled down her cheeks. Marie, who was 'working late,' touched her shoulder. What joy to behold her children again, albeit on paper. How they had changed.

*

It was these drawings that she treasured most when the time came for her to make a move out of the kingdom.

She folded them carefully and slipped them into a leather wallet. Jacob's transfer from Cahors meant her presence in Villemade was no longer indispensable, and she realised it would create unnecessary risks for her host if she remained, especially in light of the punishment that awaited anyone found harbouring a Huguenot.

Not only that, but she sensed a nascent romance between Monsieur Cordelle and Marie which the kind-hearted man felt visibly awkward about, given the difference in age. But Marie seemed available and willing, and he had been an heirless widower for long enough. Jeanne was gladdened by the thought that at least her stay had brought hopes of marriage to the girl who had given her so much of her time.

On a star-studded night in August, after a tearful farewell to Marie, who was working late, Jeanne left the Quercy plain for the first time in her life.

(iii)

The harbour was hardly a sight for sunken spirits, even though it lay still as a millpond.

As Jacob climbed down to the water's surface, where a rowboat was waiting, he saw it was in fact the most nauseating broth, thick with human sludge, floating matter of all sorts, and drowned rats.

The little Phocean town sprawled out westward of the port and up the hillside called Colline des Accoules. It was made up of a quaint confusion of three- and four-storey dwellings, where cords ran between upper-floor windows to accommodate row upon row of washing above the streets. The windmills, posted like white sentinels along the high ground, confirmed the wind was well up, which thankfully swept away the insalubrious pong.

But as Jacob took his place in the boat that faced east, his eyes were met with a coordinated display of grandeur in the form of the recently built galley arsenal, lit up by the westering sun. The immaculate buildings, some still under construction, stood as a stark contrast to the chaotic urbanisation of the town, and as a testimony to the king's magnificence.

The arsenal, purposely built for the construction of the king's galley fleet, was a pool of activity with carpenters, rope makers, joiners, sail makers, riggers, caulkers, riveters— a host of tradesmen and labourers required to build a galley ship. Once ferried to shore, Jacob was marched with the cortege of prisoners towards the white arsenal building.

Along the way, he saw with his own eyes a galley ship with its rows of great oars. He counted twenty-six on one side, which made fifty-two in all. The port harboured over twenty such vessels, whose slaves, if near enough, glanced at the newcomers, some with envy. For they knew that these Protestants were going to the New World, where they would at least be allowed to roam about unshackled; a galley slave could not.

There were Turks and common convicts whose complicit laughter expressed camaraderie. And then there were the downcast ones who looked on with a silent longing. There was always someone worse off than oneself, thought Jacob and, while continuing his march onward, closed his eyes just for two seconds. The moment he opened them again, they were seized by a familiar face on the greatest galley ship of all, la *Grande Réale*. The huge ship was manoeuvring only twenty yards from where Jacob was passing. The face stared back at him, and he recognised Monsieur Galet.

He was about to call out when the convert he met in his prison in Montauban gave a stern shake of the head. Delpech then realised there was no point in attracting unnecessary attention which would be beneficial to neither of them. Even from this distance, Jacob could read in the man's demeanour expressions of pity, shame, and remorse. He must have got caught trying to cross the frontier, he thought.

As Delpech marched past the galley ship, both men gave a hardly perceptible sign that bade each other God's grace and good fortune. They both knew they would probably never meet in this life again.

The cortege passed through the arsenal gates, over the impeccable courts strewn with cordage and sails, and past the workshops and depots stocked to the rafters with masts and timber.

They continued until they reached a large building which housed the galley slave hospital. They were then ushered into a large room already abuzz with two hundred men and women. They all constituted the next shipment for Saint Domingue, a French territory in the Caribbean Sea.

*

Jacob was exhausted from the voyage but glad to be able to rest on firm ground.

He wanted to mingle amid the strangers of every age, rank and condition, in the hope of hearing the unmistakable accent of his home town. But he had hardly the strength to stand up straight, and besides, he soon found himself in conversation with some fellow detainees from the tartan. He would go for a saunter tomorrow.

The guards were already lighting the night lamps, and sheeting was being drawn down across the middle of the ward to divide it into separate male and female sleeping quarters. The newcomers were given shabby straw mattresses, previously used by sick galley slaves, and ordered to find a place to settle or risk a hiding.

'Well, then, I shall bid you goodnight, Madame,' said Jacob to a lady of some distinction, with whom he had been sharing his first impressions. The vast room had just a few high windows and was scarcely less dismal than the round tower of Aigues-Mortes. But at least he had good company.

'May the Lord bring you rest, Sir,' said the lady.

Her name was Madame de Fontenay, seventy years old and fit as a fiddle. She was chaperoning Mademoiselle Marianne Duvivier, the demoiselle who had courageously held the sailor's gaze on board the tartan. Madame de Fontenay had literally fallen into conversation with Jacob during the voyage after he caught her as she stumbled. He had since taken it upon himself to watch over her and her granddaughter, although in truth, she had been more comfort to him during his seasickness than he to her.

Jacob said, 'I pray you find some sleep too, Madame.'

'Oh,' replied Madame de Fontenay with merriment in her voice, 'I have learnt to sleep with one eye open, for I shall have plenty of time to catch up on lost nights where I am headed.' She gave a fleeting glance upward as if she were peeping into heaven.

Jacob smiled, then bade goodnight to Mademoiselle Duvivier.

He set out his straw mattress against the wall and knelt in preparation for his evening prayer.

'Be careful when you pray here, my friend,' said a gentleman in a low voice next to him. The man, in his late fifties, could see that his new neighbour was one of the newcomers.

For his part, Jacob wondered if the man was a Huguenot or a common prisoner, for he did not look as though he was going to say his prayers. But then, on looking around, Delpech realised that no one else was either. The man flicked his eyes up at the approaching guard, doing his rounds and carrying a hard wooden club.

'I see,' said Jacob, 'I shall wait till they extinguish the lights.'

'They don't,' said the man. 'And they don't let up doing their rounds neither . . .'

As they spoke, an old man with his back to them, ten yards in front, rose up on his knees in prayer. The guard bounded forward and cracked the man's joined knuckles with his long club. Jacob could not abide such a display of needless cruelty. Forgetting his fatigue, he stood up and shouted, 'How dare you, Sir!'

The guard turned. He strode swiftly with a limp towards Delpech and, holding his long truncheon with two hands, he thrust it under Jacob's chin, driving him against the whitewashed wall. Jacob was forced up onto his toes, which virtually left the ground, a testimony to how much weight he had lost.

In a low growl, the guard said: 'Don't you dare try to impede a king's guard from doing his duty. Try it again, and I'll have you seated in one of our galleys, quicker than you can say Pope Innocent XI! You got that?'

The old man who had been rapped on the knuckles was now standing a short distance behind the guard, gesturing to Jacob to let it drop, that it was not worth risking being sent to the galleys. But it was the guard's informal use of you that made Delpech see there was no point in arguing over an injustice with a man who lacked social etiquette.

Jacob had just met Arnaud Canet, chief guard, mid-thirties, a quick eye, powerful neck, and thick forearms.

*

Arnaud Canet had been a sailor on the high seas before losing a leg, crushed by a cannon when he was twenty-seven. He had since worked up through the ranks at the arsenal where he had guarded some of France's most treacherous villains, at least, the ones who had escaped the executioner's talents.

He had guarded a broad range of delinquents from petty thieves to infidels, and clandestine salt sellers to Algerian pirates. Criminals of every race, class, and colour had been paraded before Canet's unblinking eye, especially nowadays, what with the king's policy to enlarge his galley fleet. Indeed, the galley slave ships had grown in numbers from ten to thirty since he had started at the arsenal. The new trend was recruiting Protestants, though this batch was lucky: they were going to the American islands. But whatever his crime, a criminal was a criminal, and by far, the best and safest way to deal with criminals was to treat them all as scoundrels.

Canet knew from experience at sea that the only way to prevent mutiny was to nip it in the bud. So his guards, through fear of revolt or cocky courage, did their rounds in search of opportunities to brandish their clubs on man or woman, young or old, in order to stamp out potential firebrands and demagogues. If allowed to flourish, such hotheads could incite a movement of riot.

One such opportunity arose when the reformist convicts prayed on their knees to their Protestant god. Such an act had been banned and their god banished from the realm by the king himself. But for Jacob, like for every other Huguenot, prayer was the spiritual staple that kept him going. Being without it was like living without God, and that was every bit as insufferable as the dreadful conditions in scenes from Dante's *Inferno*.

So it presented the perfect occasion for the guards to lay down their authority.

However, these Protestants were not martyrs, and the

group reflex was to discreetly gather round the kneeling co-religionists so forming a human screen. When one group went down, those standing around them tacitly moved close together to create a random ring three or four people deep.

By the second day, Jacob and the other newcomers had cottoned on. In this way, only rarely did the guards get a clean swipe at the recidivist worshippers.

But Canet was an old hand: it did not take long for him to suss out their tactics. He was nobody's fool.

'They're pissing in my boots, they are!' he said to his crew one day. Did these bourgeois really think they could pull the wool over the eyes of a battle-seasoned veteran and son of a tinker? So he told his guards to lie low for a few days, lead the lambs into a false sense of security.

'Then the wolves will pounce!' he said, punctuating his rallying talk in the guardroom with a gruff, vengeful growl.

*

Because of his altercation just after his arrival, Jacob had kept a sharper-than-usual eye on the guards, whose demeanour seemed to have changed slightly. He noticed they appeared to swagger more, and even turn a blind eye when people congregated.

'It may well be they were just setting down their law,' said Monsieur Blanchard, the gentleman who had warned Jacob about praying in the open.

'Yes,' said Jacob, scratching his six-day beard, 'I suppose their argument could be that it is always easier to begin with a tight rein, then loosen it, rather than the contrary.'

'They have tested us,' said Madame de Fontenay. 'Now they realise we are not to be treated as criminals.'

'Perhaps. Or perhaps not,' said Jacob musingly as he turned to eye an approaching guard, slapping his club in one hand in double time to his step.

*

The following morning, Canet told his guards the time had come to reap the rewards of the successful application of his plan.

'Prohibited action means punitive re-action!' he said, smashing his big, square fist into the wooden staff table.

He was looking forward to it: he had not cracked his stick over anyone's shoulder blades for two full days, and it was making him bearish, even to his wife. But she ought to know by now not to go on at a man when he was uptight. She would just have to avoid going out uncovered for a few days. He nonetheless regretted his slip of the hand, and even had to stifle a desire to blame the state for sending so many soft bourgeois pigeons through Marseille. As if he hadn't enough work with the usual crowd of galley slaves to break in. They, at least, put up a decent fight and had the mettle to take a fair battering for it.

So this morning, he was really looking forward to letting out the cats among the pigeons.

Their chosen tactic was to bide their time for a large round of people to form. 'The more the merrier,' said one of the guards called Durand, a slim man of medium stature with a goatee beard.

After the Huguenots' meagre slops, and black bread from the arsenal bakery, Canet went on the prowl. He had to be extra careful to keep a little malicious smile from pleating the corners of his mouth. He must give nothing away; the surprise must be total.

Now that he had taken time to observe their little circus, he was easily able to identify a screen forming, despite their attempt at discretion. He did not have to wait for long before a large group was beginning to cluster near the middle of the ward. It was perfectly placed, allowing him and his guards to slowly surround it, and probably offered a good-size group of Huguenots to bash. He chuckled to himself at their naive attempt to conceal their manoeuvres. Some of them had even forgotten their prudence now that they had been given some leash, probably imagining that he and his guards were deliberately turning a blind eye to their law-breaking.

He gave the sign to Durand, who was ten paces away. It consisted of three slaps of the club in his hand, repeated twice. Durand signalled likewise to the next guard, and suddenly, Canet could feel a new tension in the air.

Within thirty seconds, he knew his guards would be in place. On the other side, the two guards began to centre on the group, and instinctively, Huguenots from Canet's side began to shuffle round to where the agitation was coming from. It was the cue. Now that the human wall on his side had thinned, he could bowl in. With authority and the stern use of his club, he quickly blazed a trail through the protesting crowd to the epicentre.

There, his eyes were met not with ten or fifteen suppliant Huguenots in the act of their crime, but with old Madame de Fontenay squatting over a bucket.

After the initial shock, Arnaud Canet roared his frustration through gritted teeth. 'So this is how you honour your god, is it, old woman?' he said as the other two guards pushed through to join him. They instinctively shielded their eyes in disgust. Canet continued. 'It does not surprise me your god accepts offerings of crap!'

'As you well observe, Monsieur, this is not a call of God; it is a call of nature,' corrected the old woman. 'Now, if you will excuse me. It is demeaning enough for a lady to the manor born to find herself squatting on the throne amid her brethren, let alone in the company of her jailers!'

The sham was the talk of the ward for the rest of the week, and guards became less inclined to break through the crowd, unnerved as they were by what they might find. Would those at the centre be kneeling or squatting? There were limits to even the coarsest sensibilities.

*

'I am not familiar with these ports of Midi,' said Jacob. 'I usually ship via Bordeaux or the northern ports. They present less of a risk of capture.'

'Indeed, Sir,' said Monsieur Blanchard, 'and I only hope we shall sail under good escort, for as you well know, the sea offshore is infested with Barbary pirates. I do not want to end up in the prisons of Mulay Ismail.'

'Goodness gracious, neither do I,' said Mademoiselle Duvivier, who shuddered at the thought of losing her virginity to a dark infidel.

They were talking about their imminent departure for America. They had been informed they would set sail on 18 September, in less than a week. It was held in higher spheres that letting them know in advance would make them more susceptible to conversion as the fateful date approached. But the high hopes of conversion only fed Canet's frustration: so far, the Huguenots had remained infuriatingly steadfast.

A little before lunchtime, Jacob was standing near the wall at the imaginary dividing line where both sexes mingled by day. He was in the company of his usual circle of new acquaintances which included Madame de Fontenay, Mademoiselle Duvivier, Monsieur Blanchard, and a few others. It was certainly a comfort to be among like-minded people as opposed to the solitude of his imprisonment in the dungeon of Cahors. To pass the time, they had each told their story, how their brutal fall from their station was like the earth trembling beneath their feet. Monsieur Blanchard had been a master periwig maker to the king before having to turn his hand to buying and selling, as did many a Huguenot deprived by law of their livelihood. Madame de Fontenay's deceased husband, landowner and aristocrat, had served the king in arms. She had been caught praying at a clandestine assembly with her granddaughter, Marianne Duvivier. Mademoiselle Duvivier's mother died in childbirth; her father fell at the Battle of Entzheim a few years later. Her grandmother was her only family.

The beating of a drum interrupted their conversation and silenced the chatter of the ward.

'Jacob Delpech de Castanet of Montauban, you are asked to manifest yourself,' called out Canet's voice above the crowd.

A rush of anxiety sped through Jacob's veins, causing him to become almost out of breath. Could Robert have managed a last- minute reprieve?

'Over here, Sir,' Jacob called out.

Arnaud Canet limped through the parting crowd with a bounce in his step and a malicious rictus.

'Sir,' he said, 'are you the father of one Louise Delpech?'

The name of Jacob's daughter seemed to take him back an eternity. He had not seen her for two full years, since Jeanne escaped through the gate of Montauban with Lulu on her lap. Robert had recounted to him in a letter the whole episode of Jeanne's determination to protect her children. Now, life before the dragonnade seemed like a dream. He had never forgotten that poor Jeanne and his children had also been living a nightmare, and he had prayed every day for their safety and well-being. *Of course they are well. Of course they are all right*, he would constantly repeat in his mind between conversations, before his prayers, and before sleep, to chase away morbid thoughts of their suffering, suffering which he could not witness or temper.

'I am, Sir,' said Jacob with a sudden sickness in his heart. Canet loved to see a bourgeois deflate with fear.

'I am to inform you she's dead.'

Jacob turned white. 'Sir, please,' he said before the guard turned on his heels, 'are you certain?'

'Can you read the king's French?'

Jacob could only find the strength to nod.

'Cop that, then; keep it as a souvenir from Marseille.'

Canet turned with total satisfaction, and continued on his round.

Jacob's eyes fell on the note. Then he collapsed.

(iv)

By 1687, the passion for Protestant persecution had abated a little, which made Jeanne's escape more feasible, though it was not without risk. It was a time of exodus for thousands of converts who could no longer bear to live as impostors, and who often gave up their worldly possessions for the sake of a free conscience.

Since the Revocation, a network had sprung up along the roads of exile. A multitude of guides offered their services to fleeing Huguenots. And although the authorities were as keen as ever to prevent tradesmen and academics from leaving the country, they simply did not have the policing resources to do so.

Nonetheless, if Jeanne was to stand a chance of escaping to Geneva, she had to have a good guide, Robert had concluded, even if it cost the astronomic sum of two thousand livres. It was a small fortune, the price of the farmhouse where Jeanne first found refuge. But it could later be taken out of the children's inheritance, which the state would legally have to one day honour. And anyway, if the money could not be recovered, Robert considered it a small price to pay for appeasing his own conscience.

Jeanne followed the weaver on mule-back. It was a long and scary night journey to Villefranche in Rouergue. But the warm night air and her newfound freedom after sixteen months in hiding helped her overcome her fears of capture. They rode over flat country to Caussade, before passing into the limestone hills of Quercy. Then on they travelled by Caylus, and along the gorges of the province of Rouergue.

They arrived at Villefranche on schedule, an hour after daybreak. Outside the bastide city, they stopped at an inn run by a former Huguenot, where a guide, a thickset man of average height and few words, was waiting at a table near the window with two other evacuees who sat in silence. His wide-brimmed hat still obscured his weather-worn face. And beneath an aquiline nose, Jeanne noted his bushy moustache was beginning to turn grey. The name he gave was David Trouvier.

Jeanne had learnt enough patois to pass for a peasant; nevertheless, something compelled her to speak to her new guide in French, as if to assert her true status. Despite having occupied many a night learning how to spin thread and weave cloth to make herself useful to Monsieur Cordelle, she had not lost her ingrained sense of social rank.

It at first surprised her to discover how insignificant she had become, dressed as she was in Marie's clothing: a blue skirt, white blouse, laced bonnet, and a shawl for night travel. Nobody among the departing voyagers and travelling merchants had given a second turn of the head when she had walked into the inn.

Yet she had grown as a woman, become more worldly in her lower-class garb, even though her gait was still one of a manor-born lady, poised and erect, and without the stoop of the peasant. She had conditioned herself not to give in to melancholy or doubt, but to be strong and determined to bring her family back together. This was what fuelled her resolution to get to Geneva, where there would be hope.

She had developed such a deep understanding of the peasant's way of life that when the other two evacuees first set eyes on her, they must have wondered how in the world a country woman could pay the price of the passage to Geneva. Only when she lowered her shawl to reveal her head carriage and they heard her talk did they realise her true condition. Jeanne gave a discreet smile and nodded at the two young people. He was a cabinetmaker by the name of Etienne Lambrois, and was accompanied by his sister, whom he introduced as Mademoiselle Claire. It gave both ladies reassurance to find another woman among their little party, and they sat down together on the bench.

However, few words were exchanged between them. It was the advice given by Trouvier, so that if anyone got caught, they would reveal little or nothing of their fellow travellers.

Monsieur Cordelle took refreshment with the party. Then he headed back to Villemade, saddened but relieved that he had done his duty by Monsieur Garrisson, and with a rush of blood to be going back to Marie.

*

Jeanne and her new companions travelled by night, taking refuge come morning in a landscape of deep valleys and steep gorges.

On three occasions, they were able to halt at a remote inn or a safe house owned by resolute Huguenots determined to remain in the rocky range. But mostly, they sheltered by day in barns, granaries, shepherd's huts, and in the woods off the beaten track of patrolling soldiers. There, they would pray, take refreshment, and rest their aching bones. It was the right season to travel, and if all went well, they would be in Geneva well ahead of the first snowfall.

The talents of the cabinetmaker were put to good use, building a temporary shelter on the rare times it rained. It quickly became clear to Jeanne by their furtive gestures that Etienne and Claire were not siblings: they were lovers, she was sure. What drama had they left behind them? No doubt they wondered the same about her, but all persons present had vowed only to speak of the task at hand, which sometimes made Jeanne almost feel as young as Claire again.

One mid-September morning, Jeanne let out a gasp of surprise as they emerged from a dim mountain pass and halted at a gap in the vegetation. The sun was rising brightly over an expanse of softly rolling hills abounding with terraced vineyards and fields of lavender. Claire, though exhausted, gave a wheeze of delight. They had reached the Rhone valley.

'Halfway there,' said the guide, breaking the silence in his slow country accent. The ladies admired the clear view while Trouvier raised his arm and pointed to the left of the sun. 'From here, we follow the river to Seyssel,' he said.

Etienne Lambrois, who had been keeping up the rear, halted his mule and said, 'I was given to understand that we could pass into Orange country by crossing the bridge at Saint-Esprit. That is to the right of the sun, is it not?'

'If you have a passport, you can cross,' said Trouvier.

'Can't we slip a guard a louis d'or?'

'Some you can, some you can't, some you never know. I prefer not to take the risk.'

'Seyssel is only a few days from Geneva, is it not?' asked Jeanne, who had heard the name before, no doubt during dinner conversations with her husband's customers.

'Yes, it be that, Madame,' said Trouvier.

'But that would mean another three weeks on French soil,' said Etienne.

There was indulgence in Trouvier's voice when he turned in his saddle and said, 'Which is better than a lifetime on a galley ship, is it not?'

'As long as we do not get caught now that the terrain is more open,' said Jeanne, to soften the guide's natural ascendancy over the young man.

But the young cabinetmaker was still visibly wrestling

with a dilemma. After a moment, he said, 'Don't get me wrong, but how can we be sure we are not being led astray, into the hands of the king's men? There is a good reward for delivering Protestants.'

'If I were that way inclined,' said the guide, 'I'd have taken you over the bridge at Saint-Esprit. It's where they catch many an unwary traveller. Now, we'd better get to a safe house before we're seen by all the world and his wife.'

The guide dug in his heels and rode on down the track. Jeanne and the clandestine couple followed behind.

11

Mid to Late September 1687

LATE AFTERNOON ON 18 September, Jacob squinted as he stepped into the daylight.

He was being led out of the obscure hospital ward with nineteen other Protestant prisoners. His body felt stiff and his face still twinged from his fall onto the stone floor the week before. But the deep blue sky was like a therapy for the eyes. And he was relieved that his group included his small cast of friends.

Port activity was resuming, following the afternoon siesta imposed by the sultry heat. The group shuffled through the arsenal yards to the harbour, where two galley ships were still in construction. Jacob remarked how they had progressed since he first saw them. One was already being fitted with its ornate figurehead, which meant it was almost ready for its crew of two hundred and fifty slaves whose living, eating, and toilet quarters would be the bench they were assigned to.

Around the animated port, seasoned slaves were already knitting or sewing in the long galley ships. A few trustee convicts were busy at small stalls posted mostly on the west side of the harbour, where their galleys were moored. Apart from the shaved heads topped with red bonnets, these men were recognisable by the limp caused by the ball chained to their ankle, or by the chain that attached them to their stand. They were, however, the lucky ones, allowed to serve out their time by offering their wares and know-how to port visitors by day, and returning to their galley bench come evening-tide.

They exercised a multitude of trades from cobbler to wig maker, and made anything from straw boxes to small pieces of furniture, pipes, wood sculptures, and figurines made of shells. Some offered an astonishing assortment of services from letter writing to producing certificates stamped with fake seals, all under the knowing eye of the king's police.

But there were no Protestants among these privileged few; even in servitude, Huguenots were deprived of any sort of relief. Not only had their personal fortunes been added to the king's treasury, they were given worse treatment than the basest of criminals.

The group continued past horses pulling winches, dockers unloading Caribbean cargo, and officers barking commands. Well-heeled ladies and gentlemen who must have recently disembarked were directing their effects onto carts that waited among wine baskets and barrels of sugarloaf, cocoa, tobacco, and ginger. The port water was thronged with boats, galleys, tall ships, and seagulls pecking into sludge. But the windmills on the crest of land above the harbour stood motionless, and the place stank of fish, salt, seaweed, horses, and humanity.

It was nonetheless a stirring sight, though one which induced an anxious silence among the prisoners as they neared their embarkation point. In the calm water that shimmered like a silken lake, Jacob saw a pink—a square-rigged merchantman—and a larger ship, both anchored a short distance from the foreshore. He could make out that the smaller vessel was called La Marie, the larger one *La Concorde*.

'One of those, I believe, is to be our home for the coming months,' he said, turning to Mademoiselle Duvivier. She instinctively placed her hand on her chest as the notion sunk in that they really were about to embark on a voyage to the other side of the world.

They had walked out of the dim hospital ward together. Mademoiselle Duvivier and Madame de Fontenay had been angels to Jacob since the terrible shock which caused him to collapse. The young girl had nursed his brow, cut in the fall on the flagstone floor, and they had comforted him with prayer to mend his broken spirit.

They were standing in the middle of the line; behind them were Madame de Fontenay and Monsieur Blanchard.

'I wonder which,' said the girl.

'The bigger the ship, the better she sits in the sea, I have heard it said,' said Monsieur Blanchard.

'Well, the closest is *La Marie*,' said Madame de Fontenay. 'I am sorry to say—'

'Oy!' roared Canet. 'No talking in the ranks!' he bayed, limping back down the file. 'Unless you wanna feel my stick!'

A minute later found them at the embarkation point, where the head of the line began boarding a longboat. It was soon Jacob's turn to place a foot on the gangplank, slippery with sludge. With her bundle of effects strapped to her back, the girl lifted her skirts above her shoes, took his hand over the gangplank, then lowered herself into the boat. He then held out his hand for Madame de Fontenay.

By now Canet, standing three yards away, was losing patience; such gentility made him want to puke. And besides, he still hadn't had the last laugh on the old duchess. So he lunged forward and held out his stick like a turnstile in front of her.

'Halt there,' he commanded. Then with a snarl of triumph, to Jacob he said: 'You. Get in!'

While detaining Madame de Fontenay and Monsieur Blanchard, he told the prisoners behind to proceed into the longboat.

It took a moment for Jacob and Marianne to realise what was happening. Then the girl called out in a tone of voice that conveyed her sudden anxiety. 'Grandmother!'

Against the flow of the incoming prisoners, she hoisted herself back onto the gangplank. Madame de Fontenay still looked confused and reached out her hand to her granddaughter.

'Put her in the boat!' called Canet to a subordinate guard, while pushing back the old lady with his stick, held in two hands.

'Get back in the boat!' hurled the guard, whose deep bark would make any man shake in boots. But Marianne Duvivier persisted. Jacob reached her before the guard could use his stick. He placed himself in front of the girl.

'Sir,' he said to Canet, trying to keep his voice reasonable and calm. 'The lady is the child's grandmother.'

'That, you Protestant ponce, is why we are separating them,' roared Canet, spraying his bitterness into Jacob's face. 'Now do as you're soddin' told!'

Before Jacob could answer back, a sharp pain on his right upper arm made him cow down. He turned in time to see the second guard, raising his stick to carry out a correction commonly known as a *bastonnade*, which was a series of blows normally inflicted on obstinate galley slaves. But Jacob retreated down the plank, forcing the girl back behind him.

'Grandmother!' she cried in a fit of hysteria. However, Madame de Fontenay, being of a practical nature, understood that the scene could quickly degenerate. She pushed out her palms as if to push the girl away, and cast an imploring look at Jacob which needed no words.

She knew she might not survive the voyage herself anyway— then what would become of the girl? Monsieur Delpech was a good man; he would take care of her, give her protection day and night in the den of vigorous sailors. Was this not then God's intention? In return, she was sure that taking care of the girl would take his mind off the dark thoughts he had been having since the death of his child.

'Stay with Monsieur Delpech,' she called to Marianne.

Jacob gave the old lady a nod to confirm he would take good care of her granddaughter, though he secretly wondered how. He took hold of the girl's arms before she could battle with the guard to get past. With a firm grip, he turned her back towards the boat.

'Come, Marianne, there is no use fighting them; you will only make things worse,' he said. 'We will see your grandmother again when we arrive, on the other side.' Jacob realised the ambiguity of his words, but did not try to correct them.

It was a cruel and needless separation, designed to cripple more than any blow of the stick. The intention was to wrench a conversion from either grandparent or grandchild, even though it was widely accepted that once a Huguenot had come this far, there was very little chance of them abjuring.

Mademoiselle Duvivier suddenly seemed so frail, and she let him guide her. She looked back over her shoulder as her grandmother stood dignified on the foreshore. Madame de Fontenay stared back with passion in her eyes in a last effort to impress her obstinate resolution onto her granddaughter.

They continued into the longboat. 'Keep by me, my girl,' said Jacob. It was best to make the longboat crew assume they were related in some way. A lass on her own was always easy prey, and some shipmen would not think twice about trying it on. Catching on, she gave him a nod and pressed herself closer to him. But this did not impress the handsome sailor leaning against his punt, and he instinctively ogled the young female as she passed.

The longboat was soon breaking the silky film on the water's surface as it ferried the forlorn passengers to the place they would inhabit for the next five months.

*

La Marie was a three-mast vessel of two hundred tons.

Jacob did not know much about ships, but he did know that this type of vessel with its shallow draught was more commonly used for transporting cargo around the Mediterranean coast than for crossing the great ocean sea. She was smaller than La Concorde, the tall ship that Madame de Fontenay and Monsieur Blanchard were to board.

The space below deck was partitioned into five rooms. At the stern was the captain's and officers' cabin. Next came the sailors' and the soldiers' quarters. The third room was where common prisoners were kept chained. This was followed by a room that housed seventy galley slaves, men of every colour,

Turks as well as Christians, also cuffed in heavy chains. Too old or too ill for service, these broken men were sent to America to be sold.

The last compartment was situated under the kitchen at the front of the vessel. This was reserved for the Huguenots. It was so small that twenty people would have been pushed for space, yet there were close to eighty Protestant prisoners. Two-thirds men, one-third women, all were driven into the hole barely high enough to stand up in. Neither was there room to stretch out the length of one's body without lying on someone else.

Calling to mind how the hospital ward was divided at night, Jacob took the precaution to settle in the middle along one side so that he and the girl could remain within whispering distance. He noticed that the portholes were their only direct outlet to daylight, and realised the crossing would be more insufferable than any hole he had been made to suffer so far. He nevertheless thanked God for his previous preparation. He knew he would have stood little chance of surviving this scabrous den without it.

As he settled into his thoughts, with his back against the timber, there came screams and reports of rats crawling among the buckets placed at either end of the room. *How many months can we endure in this squalor and sickness?* he wondered.

But he vowed for the love of Jeanne and his children he would not give up, for the love of Christ he would not doubt. And he would not let Mademoiselle Duvivier abandon herself to defeat either. As she sat beside him, looking distant and downcast, he took her small hand, placed it like a small bird in his large palm, and gave it a pat of encouragement.

'There is one consolation,' he said. 'Things can only get better from now on.'

She put on a brave smile, but she knew as well as he did that in truth, their crossing the wilderness had only just begun.

*

Thudding, scuffing, and rolling sounds were heard well into the night as the last of the provisions were hoisted aboard and stored.

With her belly full and her load carefully balanced, La Marie set sail the following day with *La Concorde* for Toulon, which was a day's voyage eastward along the coast. This was the rendezvous of their escort, two warships, without which they would be easy pickings for Barbary pirates.

The heat generated by eighty people crammed like sardines in a barrel did nothing to help Jacob find his sea legs. He spent most of the time trying to slumber, in the hope of waking to find his body had become accustomed to the constant roll of the ship. But sleep, too, eluded him.

Nevertheless, the run into Toulon, gruelling though it was, passed without incident. Come nightfall, the calm port waters that gently rocked the pink made a welcome change from the commotion of the previous nights. And the Huguenot hole soon resounded with the sounds of sleepers snorting and snoring, some coughing, tossing, and turning, among the audacious rats rummaging for anything to sink their teeth into.

Late into the night, the clouds dissipated, letting white moonlight shine in through the portholes. And the cooler air that whisked round the room took the edge off the stifling heat, not to mention the stench.

One old man was still trying to sleep with his palm on his ear to block out the intolerable noise of sleepers, when he felt something nip his finger. He gave a yelp, and swiped the rat on the end of it. The obnoxious creature landed on Jacob Delpech's thigh, glared its annoyance at its aggressor, and then scampered off in search of another opportunity.

Whisperings at the door, a dimly lit oil lantern, and the turn of a key announced the late-night round of a guard. He found the Protestants sleeping top and tail, mostly. There was hardly any space for him to put his feet without treading on parts of their anatomy, which he was very careful to avoid. He stepped from one space to another like on stepping stones in a quagmire of bodies. At last he reached the object of his midnight jaunt.

He stared down at the young girl who had caught his eye in the longboat two days earlier. He had since been eyeing her movements, her mannerisms, smiling at her when it was his turn to take away the buckets, and had decided she was too sweet to suffer being squashed against these smelly bodies every night.

The old geezer did not fool him either; anyone could tell they were not that close, probably not even related. This sailor was not born with the last tide: this sailor had seen such a charade before. Why was it that some pompous codgers thought young girls wanted locking away when what they truly craved was to be properly loved? So he would do her the honour of taking her on deck for some clean air. The night was perfect, quite warm and starry now, and the captain was on shore.

He bent down and touched her arm gently, almost so as

not to wake her. How beautiful she was, how nice it felt to touch a tight-skinned young woman. He had been longing for this, and now imagined cupping her firm breasts in his hands like plump little birds. At that instant, he felt love. He had to be careful though; he had to gain her trust first, then he would be able to tame her, make her his little lady for the duration of the cruise.

He now clasped the ball of her shoulder and shook her a little more firmly, brushing her warm jaw with his index finger with every nudge forward.

'Mademoiselle,' he whispered. 'Mademoiselle.'

She moved her head slightly, which brought a crafty smile to the corner of his mouth. Clearly, she was making the most of it. Then she opened her eyes wide. She turned, let out a short gasp.

'Shhh, Mademoiselle,' he whispered before any sound came out of her. 'Don't alarm yourself; I've come to take you to somewhere nicer.'

She looked wide-eyed, astonished, and speechless at the handsome face lit up by the yellow glow of the lamp. She did not want to disturb her co-religionists, exhausted as they were from the short voyage. The first days were always the worst until one found one's sea legs, she remembered her grandmother saying.

'I beg your pardon, Sir,' she said.

The fact that she kept to an intimate whisper gave the young man all the more confidence to proceed with his plan.

'Come, Mademoiselle,' he said with gentle authority and a handsome smile that showed his white teeth. 'I will show you the deck. The sky is beautiful tonight. Come.' He held out his hand to her. 'You will be perfectly safe with me.'

The young man was no stranger to her anymore. She had remarked on previous occasions that he was well-mannered, nice to look at, and inspired confidence, quite the opposite of the vulgar sailor on that tartan. Not quite knowing what else to do, she took his hand, and got to her feet.

'Be careful where you tread,' he said considerately, and led her gently over the piles of bodies. She was already receptive; it would not take him long to take her under his wing, though he had to admit, he never expected her to come round so quickly.

Jacob was snoring loudly on the gentlemen's side of the room. But then a twinge of pain from the arm that had received the blow from Canet's guard interrupted his sleep. He woke vaguely, turned around, and saw it was only the old man poking him. No doubt to stop Jacob's snoring; Jeanne used to do it all the time. But the old man nudged him again with insistence. Turning over, Jacob saw he was stabbing the darkness with his index finger.

'What is it, Sir?' he said in a whisper and glanced in the direction the man was pointing. It took a moment for Jacob to realise that the dark shapes moving a few yards in front of him were that of the girl following a guard. He quickly got to his feet. Striding with difficulty towards them, he said:

'Where are you going?'

'None of your business, pal,' said the sailor nonchalantly. 'You get back to sleep now.'

'Sir, I ask you to leave the girl; she is under my responsibility.'

'No, she ain't, you only just met her.' He took hold of the girl's hand. 'Take no notice of him,' he said to her gently.

But the girl stopped; the sailor tugged her forward.

'No you don't, young man,' said Jacob, raising his voice. 'Any further and I shall call for the captain!'

By now people were beginning to stir; two or three of them were sitting up on their elbows, trying to fathom out what was going on. More people began to groan as Jacob stepped hurriedly towards the door to intercept the young guard. The girl was now struggling to get her hand free.

The magical moment, that window of serenity, was quickly closing for the sailor, all because of an interfering Huguenot. What an old codger, standing in the way of youth! The sailor let go of the girl, and put down his lantern.

He then lunged forward, seizing Jacob by the shirt front with one hand, and clobbering him on the side of the face with the other. He was strong and vigorous, and furious now that the Huguenot had messed everything up. Jacob could not fight back without the risk of being sent to the room next door for the remainder of the voyage. Besides, his hands were more used to turning the smooth pages of a ledger than gripping rough rope as were the sailor's. Another blow sent him stumbling backwards, and he tripped on someone lying behind. Sleepers woke and scattered. The sailor followed through with a boot in the ribs as Jacob endeavoured to protect himself by crawling into a ball.

By now the whole room had twigged the scene that was being played out in the darkness. There was a collective uproar of protest which was as loud as it was sudden, as if everyone in the room understood what was going on at the same time.

'Any more of your lip, pal, and I'll throw you next door!' hurled the sailor, who had taken up his lantern. He edged backwards the few yards to the barred timber door where a fellow guard was waiting for him.

Before Jacob could reply, the sailor slipped out, and a key was clunking in the door lock.

Mademoiselle Duvivier rushed to help Jacob back to his feet.

'What got into you, girl?' he said, still panting from the assault.

'I am sorry. I—I don't know,' she stuttered, 'I—I did not know what to do.'

How senseless she had been, like she was caught in a trance, like some sovereign force was compelling her forward, disabling her to think for herself. But now she knew what to do if any man tried to lead her away again. She would resist and scream at the top of her voice, she told Jacob.

'Yes, do that, my girl,' said Jacob. By now several people were around him, arms helping him back to his place.

'We must get word to the captain,' said one man, an aging surgeon named Bourget.

'It is simply outrageous!' said Madame Fesquet, a middle-aged matron, who was comforting the girl.

'We will not be treated as animals,' said another man.

But what could they do? The captain was hardly sympathetic to their cause; on the contrary. He visibly allowed his men to hurl the most obscene language at them, as if it were a contest to string together the most melodious and injurious insult.

'We shall have to set up a night watch,' said Jacob. 'They will not try to carry out their detestable designs if we all stand together.'

*

Come morning, Joseph Reners, merchant and master of *La Marie* after God, was on his way back to the ship after spending the night in Toulon.

He had met with the captain of *La Concorde* and the commander of the two warships that were to escort them to Cadiz via Gibraltar. Then they would sail on to the Canaries to pick up the trade winds that would take them across the ocean to the Caribbean Sea. It had been agreed they would set sail the day after tomorrow. But a tragedy came about later that morning that would delay their plans.

The wind had picked up slightly, and blew fresh air into the Huguenot cabin, which was much appreciated. The buckets still had not been emptied, and the place stank of sick, excrement, and gruel.

'I say,' said Madame Fesquet, who was looking out of a porthole, 'that looks like the scoundrel from last night.' She beckoned Mademoiselle Duvivier over to see.

'Yes, that is him,' said Marianne, peering at the longboat as it approached on the lee side of the pink out of the blustery wind.

The culprit was rowing with another sailor behind Captain Reners. Marianne Duvivier could see that he had not changed at all: he looked just as robust and confident as before his outrageous behaviour of the previous night.

As the boat came closer, the young man looked up at the front of the pink, where the Huguenot cabin was situated, and he blew a kiss to the porthole. Shocked and shamefaced, the girl brought her head out of view and stood with her back pinned against the timber wall. Her heart was racing. She was suddenly petrified of the man's audacity.

The first officer changed places in the longboat with the

captain. It had been agreed that the second in command would go ashore after the master.

Marianne said nothing of the kiss. Instead, she lingered near the porthole, grateful for the change of air. The next time she looked out, the longboat was already halfway to shore.

Jacob was trying to think how he could tell the captain about the incident of the night before, when a sudden gust kicked into the ship's starboard, causing the vessel to tilt to one side slightly. It did nothing to ease Jacob's aching head or his unstable belly; in fact, he nearly threw up.

Mademoiselle Duvivier, who was still peering out of the porthole, suddenly gasped. 'Oh, my God!' she shrieked in spite of herself.

At the same time, a sailor's voice from the deck above shouted: 'Man overboard!' This was surprising, given that they were anchored, and the sea, though not still, was not rough. Above deck, the sound of scurrying feet rumbled through the timber on the port side of the ship that looked onto the quay. Despite his aching body, Jacob managed to lift himself up and get a peek through the porthole at the longboat that had just keeled over. It had turned turtle under the force of a freak wave, and there was nothing anyone could do.

It became evident that the first mate and the two sailors could not swim. It was of the general opinion among seafarers that it was better to drown quickly than to suffer cold and a prolonged agony at the mercy of sharks and other creatures of the deep. However, in this case, it would have saved their lives had they known how to swim just a few yards to the floating oars. After a short struggle, under the eyes of both crew and prisoners, one after the other, the three men slipped under.

Was it maternal instinct, was it her faith, or was it something else? For some strange reason which she preferred not to understand, the girl felt deeply grieved for the handsome sailor who would surely have tried to abuse her innocence again had he lived. She prayed that he may rest in peace, if it so pleased God.

Stupid way to die, thought Jacob. How treacherous was the sea, even in mild weather. However, he felt no remorse for the young sailor who had tried to steal the girl away to satisfy his own illicit lust, and who had given him a hiding for interposing. For the first time, Jacob could not bring himself to pray for forgiveness for a man's sins. Nor could he pray that God Almighty would enable the young man's soul to receive His light if it so pleased Him. Instead, he gave thanks for their deliverance from malice.

The tragic accident meant that replacements had to be found, which delayed the departure.

After ten long days in Toulon harbour, *La Marie* and *La Concorde*, escorted by the king's warships, at last set sail on their voyage to America.

12

October 1687

JEANNE RODE UP with her travelling companions to the right-bank hillside that overlooked the village of Seyssel.

Being the last upstream village on the navigable stretch of the Rhone, it was both a landing dock and an embarkation point. Passengers travelling from Geneva could continue their journey by boat downstream as far as Marseille. Those travelling upstream could disembark on the left bank and carry on by land to Geneva.

The October sky had turned purple; local folk knew that as soon as the wind dropped, the low clouds would shed their load. Boat people on the far bank were frantically unloading parcels, crates, and barrels that were tightly packed on a boat towed by horse from Lyon.

Jeanne cast her gaze over the nearest bank of the village, with its medieval church spire, tall stone buildings, and warehouses along the quay where a cargo ferry was being loaded. Trouvier explained that the old wooden bridge that joined the village had not yet been rebuilt following its recent collapse into surging waters. The ferry was at present the only means to get to the other side. By consequence, although excise was still carried out on the other side, customs checks on travellers were not so stringent because anybody could walk around the checkpoint through the vegetation further downstream. All eyes then stared eagerly straight ahead.

'Savoyard country,' said Trouvier, nodding to the wooded hillside of fir trees and the distant mountain peaks. 'Once over the towpath on the other side, we'll be in the Duchy of Savoy. Then it's just a couple of days to Geneva.'

*

David Trouvier knew on first glimpse of the river that the visible urgency near the water was not only due to the imminent rainfall.

It was because the river had already risen by two yards, which was unusual for the time of year. He guessed there must have been torrential rainstorms further upstream, where fast-running water that fell from the mountainsides increased the river's volume and velocity.

He knew, too, that tree trunks and branches could cause natural barrages, and that when these barrages broke, they could release a surge of water capable of flooding a town in minutes.

The river at Scyssel had burst its banks in the past. Trouvier knew that when it did, it became too perilous to even consider a crossing. But worse than that, the *bac-à-traille*, the reaction ferry that carried goods from one side to the other, would inevitably be smashed to pieces by debris and tree trunks carried downstream by the coursing water.

The company sheltered with their mules in a barn, where they prayed. Then they drank watered-down wine and ate dry sausage, bread, and cheese, while waiting for night to fall. It was cold outside, the coldest it had been since Jeanne rode out from Villemade that warm August evening. She and her companions were thankful they had purchased warmer clothing and leathers for the change of season when they had passed through a small town outside Lyon.

At three o'clock, the clouds broke. Trouvier glanced out at the drizzle from the barn door. He looked north: a leaden ceiling blotted out the sky. To the east, the closest mountains were no longer visible behind the mist. He turned to the company, who were resting on a three-legged log stool, a broken barrel, and the shaft of a hay wagon. He said, 'If there's a flood, we might still be here when the first snows fall.'

Jeanne leaned over on her stool and glanced through the door that the guide held ajar. In all simplicity, she said, 'Why can we not cross now?'

'Guards patrol come rain or shine, Madame.'

'Surely they will be occupied elsewhere with the bad weather,' said Etienne, joining David at the door.

'Maybe. Maybe not,' the guide said, and turned his face dubiously back towards the sky. The penalty for guiding Huguenots through France was death by hanging. If caught, at least he would not have to suffer the misery of rowing with Turks and bandits for the rest of his life.

'But Monsieur Trouvier, we will certainly be denounced if we remain here too long,' said Jeanne, who suppressed a longing to plead with the man now that freedom was within eyeshot.

Half an hour later, Trouvier, who could not resist being spoken to as an equal by the fair lady, was down by the river. It was barely a hundred yards wide at this point. He was in conversation with the ferryman, whose flat-bottomed vessel was already loaded with tools, crates, and barrels of wine.

The *bac-à-traille* was attached by its mast to a single line that ran from bank to bank. This allowed the boatman to navigate across the river by angling the boat so it presented a slanted flank to the current which propelled the vessel forward.

The drizzle was nothing more than a nuisance to the ferryman, a big fellow in middle age with a large, weather-browned face under the wide brim of a leather hat.

'Ah, but there be four of us,' said David.

'Too risky, water's high, river's fast, can't take more than two,' said the boatman, handling a crate with his large hands.

David sensed the man was a Protestant sympathiser; otherwise, he would not have offered to take any at all. Trouvier said nothing, instead wheeled a barrel from the shore up the gangplank to the edge of the boat.

The boatman, having placed the crate, turned to catch hold of the barrel. 'I've another crossing yet before the day's done.' He nodded to a stack of tiles and more barrels of Seyssel wine waiting further back on the shore. 'I can ferry the other two on the next run.' He began rolling the barrel, then growled back, "Course, long as we don't get a surge!'

The guide went back to the group standing under an old plane tree with the mules. Jeanne suggested the young couple should embark first; it would be more sensible for the guide to be the last to leave. She would not hear of the cabinetmaker giving up his place to allow the two women to cross together; besides, their mules might need a man's strength to calm them in case of a swirl. And he could help the boatman unload and reload on the other side, the quicker the better.

The clandestine lovers boarded and crossed without mishap. The rain continued to fall softly, though thunder in the hills announced that the river might not be negotiable for very long.

As soon as the ferry came back, the boatman, a warehouse worker, and Trouvier unloaded the barrels that contained cheese, butter, and fruit from Savoy. Then they loaded the tiles, barrels of French wine, and wheat destined for Geneva.

Jeanne counted time, out of sight in the shelter of the barn. With no knowledge of loading boats, if she tried to help, she would only get in the way. And as Monsieur Trouvier pointed out, it would be suspect, to say the least, to see a woman loading barrels onto the *bac-à-traille*. She spent the time thinking of her children, of where Jacob could be now, and of her life before the Revocation. On the approach of footsteps, she quickly folded her drawings and placed them neatly into her leather wallet.

'We must make haste, Madame,' said Trouvier at the door. 'The ferry will soon be primed to leave.'

Daylight was beginning to fade by the time she and her guide led their mules onto the raft. As the ferryman pushed away from the shallows with his punt, Jeanne and Trouvier turned simultaneously at the sound of approaching hooves.

Soldiers. Two of them.

Jeanne's heart stopped. She was barely a hundred yards from freedom. How could she be caught after so much effort, having tried so hard?

Her anxious eyes met those of the guide, who said, 'Remember, you are my wife.' She gave a half nod. 'Let me do the talking,' he said, stroking his moustache to hide his speech. 'If they hear you, we're both done for.'

Jeanne quashed a desire to pay the ferryman to go faster, and a temptation to plead for mercy. Instead, she steeled her nerves and focused her thoughts on her role as peasant wife. She adopted a stooped stance, which wasn't difficult after six weeks on mule-back.

The soldiers approached the little wooden jetty and commanded the boater to stop punting. They rode into the water up to the flat-bottomed boat on the downstream side so that it protected them from the splash of the flow. Their stirrups were just twelve inches above the water's surface.

'What are you carrying?' said the younger of the horsemen.

'Usual, Sir,' said the ferryman, 'wheat, tiles, and barrels of wine.'

'Why are you taking passengers?'

'Been visiting family, Sir,' said David before the boater could answer. 'On our way home.'

'Your passport paper.'

Under the force of the current, the boat bobbed. David reached over the edge and passed his passport to the officer. It was a fake, but a good one, and the seal on the letter was genuine.

'Where you from?'

'Rumilly, Sir. Been visiting the wife's sister.'

'There is a bridge further downstream. Why are you crossing here?'

'To save time. It's only three leagues from Seyssel.'

'Huguenots have been found trying to cross, thinking we are too busy to patrol here,' said the soldier with a hint of sarcasm. Jeanne's heart pounded so hard, she could hear its pulse in her ears despite the rush of the river.

'Your wife's passport,' said the soldier, steadying his horse. Jeanne looked in bewilderment to Trouvier.

'Your papers. This!' snapped the guard, waving Trouvier's forged permit to travel. 'Where is your passport paper?'

What could she do? For a moment, her mind was numbed.

Trouvier suspected he was about to be arrested, which meant he would hang by the first snowfall. He stood, smiling up at the young soldier, wondering if he had a devil's chance of reaching his arm. No, he was not ready to swing yet. For ninety yards to freedom, he was prepared to kill a man, or be killed. It could not be much different from slicing a lamb's throat. He slowly placed his hand on his sheathed skinning knife tucked under his belt, and waited for the right moment.

Jeanne, meanwhile, opened her travelling sack. 'Boudiou, boudiou,' she said in Occitan, which in French meant Good God. She was not taking His name in vain. She was praying for a miracle.

Her hand fell upon her leather wallet. She had an idea.

She reached over to pass the wallet to the soldier's outstretched hand. Trouvier clasped his knife handle, but then a timely gust kicked into the stacked cargo and made the boat dip. Jeanne let slip the wallet. It was as if a wave had snatched her babies from her hands. Her cry of pain was genuine as she watched her precious drawings being whisked away by the rapid current.

She looked up at David, who had to suppress his surprise when she hurled in fluent patois, 'My God, my wallet, I've lost my wallet! It's your fault for bringing us here! Now what?' It was a risk, but she had noted that the soldiers had accents from the north. She speculated that they would probably not know which kingdom her patois was from, never mind which region.

The soldier turned to his superior, who said: 'Search her bag; if she's a fugitive, she'll be carrying a Protestant Bible.'

The lady has her wits about her, thought Trouvier, who loosened his clasp on his knife. Jeanne handed her bag to the soldier, confident in the knowledge that he would not find her Bible due to the simple fact that she wore it on her person. It was called a chignon Bible because it was small enough for ladies to hide in their hair.

The soldier rummaged around in the sack. Then he shook his head at his superior who had been half expecting to find a bourgeoise in disguise. But Huguenot ladies are not educated to speak patois. They are bred to speak the king's French. They would not lower themselves to speak the language of peasants.

Jeanne hurled more of her patois at David about the fading light. He stood there exactly like an embarrassed husband, gormless.

'Please forgive her insolence, Sir,' he said. But the senior guard had already held up a hand, laughed out loud, and waved them on. The young guard threw Jeanne's sack to the harassed 'husband.' They then turned their horses, rode back up the shore, and cantered away. The boatman pushed on his punt.

Half an hour later, they were standing in the Duchy of Savoy. Jeanne and Claire fell into each other's arms, rejoicing for their imminent freedom from persecution. Beneath the joy, however, Jeanne hid her grief at the loss of the precious drawings of her children.

*

By the second day's ride from Seyssel, they were easier about travelling by daylight. Now that the storm had passed, Jeanne even began to marvel at the spectacular mountainscapes, the lush alpine meadows, rocky ravines, and snow-capped crests high above.

Following the French king's example, Victor Amadeus II of Savoy had instigated a purge of Protestantism from his duchy. However, unlike their French counterparts, the Savoyard Protestants, known as Waldensians, were at least allowed to leave the dukedom if they did not wish to become Catholics overnight. Nevertheless, to avoid any unpleasant encounters with the duke's soldiers, who now had a licence to harass, David Trouvier kept his group off the beaten track.

Trouvier invariably marked the pace up front, Monsieur Lambrois kept up the rear, and Jeanne and Mademoiselle Claire rode alongside each other wherever the path permitted. Despite the fatigue from weeks of travel, and the shift to sleeping at night, the journey took on a more convivial mood. And now that they had left French soil, their conversation became less constrained, despite the guide's reminder that danger could still be lurking.

'To tell the truth, we were to wed two years ago,' said Mademoiselle Claire as she and Jeanne rode abreast along the mountain trail in the cool morning sun. 'But the Revocation put a stop to all our plans. I tried to convert, but I could not bring myself to marry before a Catholic altar.'

'So you decided to leave,' said Jeanne, who sensed the young woman's relief as she voiced her secret.

Claire simply nodded. It brought back scenes of farewell and the thought of perhaps never seeing her family again in this life. She needed an instant for the surge of emotion to subside.

Jeanne understood her agitation. She said with finality, 'You were right, my dear, to follow your conscience.'

After a moment, Claire said, 'It was Etienne who suggested we leave France; he could not bear us not being married. My dear father told the authorities I would be staying with my aunt in Bordeaux. Then we left with his blessing, though I cannot help feeling bad about it, like I'm running away.'

'You need not. You have followed your heart, and you were right,' said Jeanne. 'Listen to me: if I had left France when my husband first suggested it, we would both be together with our children now. And I would not be here today travelling without them like a lonely spinster.' Claire was pressing Jeanne's arm in sympathy when there was a movement above and then falling rubble ahead.

Two mountain men jumped down from a rock ledge with muskets at their belts. David raised a hand to halt the mules. Jeanne froze. Claire now pressed her hand to her mouth to stifle her fright as Etienne trotted up to join the guide.

'Where go you?' said one of the men, striding forward to meet them head-on. He wore a red neck scarf and a wide-brimmed hat similar to that of Trouvier.

'Geneva, if my life's worth living!' affirmed David in a raised voice. Jeanne thought it rather bold, perhaps too bold. The guide dismounted. But then both men's faces blossomed into a broad smile as they walked into each other's arms.

'Cousin, your timing is impeccable,' said the man. David then grasped the arm of the second man—ten years younger than his cousin—in a manifestation of friendship.

Jeanne smiled her relief. Claire let out a little laugh in appreciation of the caper. Lambrois jumped down from his mule.

David introduced his cousin, Thomas Trouvier, who was accompanied by a man named Jacques, who carried a cane and wore a brown knitted cap.

'Monsieur, Mesdames, fear not. You are among friends,' said Thomas. He then explained to the group that on this day, the Lord's Day, they were lookouts. For what, the party would soon hear and see for themselves.

The man named Jacques, a taciturn shepherd in his thirties, led them on. Towing his mule, David walked beside Thomas while exchanging news of high waters and impending snowfalls. Jeanne, Claire, and Etienne Lambrois followed on mule-back.

After a five-minute trek, they veered off the mountain path. Everyone dismounted to avoid the low branches. In a moment, they could hear singing. Then the rocky path developed into a clearing fringed by spindly spruce trees, and they were met with the heartening sight of a congregation of Waldensians who had just broken into beautiful song. Jeanne recognised the song 'Through the Desert of My Suffering.'

The preacher was standing on wooden steps. The congregation of about sixty souls of every age and condition was standing, kneeling, or sitting on rocks all around, like the first Christians persecuted by Romans, thought Jeanne. Today, however, it was Roman Catholics who were the persecutors. Clandestine services in the hills like this one were held throughout Savoy for Protestants no longer allowed to practice their faith in their villages.

Jeanne let fall the rein of her mule and walked into the assembly. She knelt down, and a feeling of rejuvenation inhabited her. It was as if a great burden were being lifted from her back as she thanked Christ for helping her keep her faith.

Claire and Etienne exchanged a loving smile, advanced together, then knelt beside Jeanne and joined in the last couplets of the song.

It assuaged the pain in Jeanne's heart to feel her warm tears stream down her cold cheeks as she prayed to God for her husband and her children. She resolved there and then that once she arrived in Geneva, she would spend the remainder of her money, if necessary, to bring at least Elizabeth to her side. Elizabeth was old enough to stand up to the rigours of the long and perilous journey. That was what she would do once she got to Geneva.

*

They passed over the drawbridge the following day, and entered through the south city gate, recently fortified. Labourers and builders on scaffolds were finishing reinforcement work along the stone ramparts.

Trouvier led his party on through the tall interior gate, porte de la Tartace, then to the lower city centre. The colourful hullabaloo of the bustling market with its savoury smells and unashamed abundance was a heartening sight indeed. People knew instinctively whence they had come, and as they filled their gourdes with water at a fountain, some folk doffed their hats in a sign of welcome, while a few others stared with curiosity, or was it disapproval?

Having stabled their mules, a short time later, they pushed the heavy door of a tavern, where they ordered food and sent a messenger to inform their contacts of their arrival. Soon, Claire and her cabinetmaker were met by the relative who had offered them board and lodging until they were properly married and settled. Jeanne was glad to see he was a very civil man, middle-aged and soberly dressed. Of course Jeanne would see them again; of course they would sit together in church. Etienne Lambrois and his bride-to-be took their leave in an effusion of thanks to both their guide and Madame Delpech.

The log fire crackled in the hearth. A dog sat scratching itself by their table, then yawned. Now alone with Trouvier, Jeanne seized the moment to ask him if he would bring her one of her children from Montauban. But the guide, whose usual job was shearing and shepherding, had thought a lot since the river episode in Seyssel. He had got out of a tricky spot, partly, it was true, thanks to Jeanne. But the fact remained that he had been close to either being arrested or committing murder. Both notions made him feel uncomfortable. His luck had held out until now, so maybe he ought not to push it any further. Besides, he had already made a handsome stash of money, much more than he could have earned in many years of herding and shearing sheep, and he hoped to be around long enough to enjoy it, maybe get himself a place of his own. He was not without sympathy for the lady, who was desperate to recover some of her children. But as a matter of principle, he tried never to get involved; it was a question of self-preservation. After all, it was his head that would be on the block should he get caught. He told her he could not.

A neatly dressed gentleman walked into the tavern, where people were drinking ale and smoking wooden pipes. He had a well-trimmed beard, and wore a dark tunic and white cloth collar under a black cloak. He scanned the noisy room twice before his eyes fell again upon a country woman with her flank to him. She was wearing a peasant woman's white bonnet and was deep in conversation with a man of rustic appearance. Could that possibly be Jeanne Delpech de Castanet? Surely not. Yet the poise of her head compelled him to walk over to the table, where earthen bowls of stew and wooden tankards of ale had been served. He had a difficult task.

Trouvier looked up on the approach of the gentleman, who doffed his felt hat, revealing his thinning grey hair. Jeanne turned to face him.

'Madame Delpech? Thank God you have arrived safely.'

She instantly recognised Samuel Duvaux, the former pastor of Montauban who had left France three years before the Revocation. He had aged but had retained his benevolent smile. After the introductions, he pulled up a stool to take the weight off his feet. He explained he had been expecting her.

'Indeed, I received another note from your dear sister,' said the pastor, who immediately regretted mentioning Suzanne's letter. He adroitly steered conversation into another direction. 'I thought you would be here last week, actually, and was beginning to worry. But your room is made up, and you must know, as a refugee, you are officially welcome to winter in Geneva until April, although if you need to stay longer, I am sure we shall be able to sort something out.' But his uncharacteristic quick succession of pleasantries did not go unnoticed by Jeanne.

She said, 'Thank you so much. What news has my sister?' The pastor's delayed response, and his expression that became more solemn, told her all was not well. 'Something is wrong,' Jeanne said, 'isn't there?'

'My dear lady, I fear this is perhaps not the place . . .'

'Tell me, please,' she said. She was prepared for Jacob's

passing, had been for so long. It would almost come as a relief, for it would perhaps mean she would no longer have nightmares of him being tortured.

Pastor Duvaux touched her arm and said, 'Your daughter. Louise.'

He did not need to say any more. Jeanne remained silent, dignified in her grief.

That evening, the soft bed and clean linen gave comfort to her body but no consolation to her mind. Her eyes were red and her face swollen from silently mourning the death of her daughter.

She reread the letter written by the hand of Suzanne. There was no signature, no mention of names either. It was a precautionary practice that gave protection in case the document got into the wrong hands. It told her that it was a fever that had taken her child away. The nurse said she had been playing near the latrines. She always was such an inquisitive child. Jeanne wrapped her arms around her belly, brought her knees up to the foetal position as she realised she would never be able to visit her child's grave. Could all this hardship have been for nothing? Was there no end to it?

Then she remembered that Jesus had said, 'Let the little children come to me.' She fell asleep.

*

Three days had passed since Jeanne's first night in Geneva.

The thin layer of snow that fell during the night had melted by morning. A little before noon, Monsieur Trouvier was shown into the pastor's parlour. He got to his feet when Jeanne entered. She had given up her peasant garb for a simple dress and shawl. Trouvier noticed she looked refreshed but pale. Jeanne noticed how much her guide looked out of place in the simple but elegant sitting room. She well knew what an astute man he was, and what mettle he was made of. And yet, standing there in his boots, holding his grubby hat, he looked more rural than ever, almost uncivilised. This was how she would have seen him before her hardships began. But now she knew different. Her struggles had made her a better person, she thought to herself. She smiled and sat down on the edge of an armchair.

She said, 'Thank you for your visit, Monsieur Trouvier. Please take a seat.'

'I've been thinking,' said the guide as he took a pew on the chair opposite. 'I'll go for you. I can bring back one of your children. Only one.'

'Thank you, thank you,' said Jeanne, holding her hands together.

'But you do realise that a young child under ten, unused to the wilds, might not survive the journey?'

'Yes, I have thought about that. Elizabeth shall go with you. She is thirteen years old.'

'Thirteen is good. All right, then. Though there is the added danger of winter. Although on the other hand, I s'pose the cold nights will keep the patrols away.'

13

December 1687 to February 1688

TWO MONTHS QUICKLY passed, during which Jeanne discovered she could earn a modest living from weaving.

She had used the best part of her remaining money to purchase a small loom. Church acquaintances tried to persuade her that artisan work was below her. But she would not accept charity from the refugee relief fund, and only continued staying at the pastor's residence because of his gentle insistence. Her clientele grew, thanks to the church, and to the reputation of Huguenot weavers whose techniques she had learnt from Monsieur Cordelle.

She had lost everything. She no longer cared for material things, so she found she could live on very little and put coin aside for when she would no longer just have her own upkeep to pay for. She looked forward to one day soon being reunited with her eldest daughter. Any spare time was used making for Elizabeth a set of winter clothes which she could alter accordingly when she saw her. Jeanne often wondered what she was like now. A proper little madam, knowing Lizzy.

Every day, she thanked the Lord for placing in her path a weaver and a shepherd, and considered how the humblest in society had given her self-sufficiency and filled her with hope to carry on.

A week before Christmastide, she received a note. Judging from the untutored handwriting, it could only be from Trouvier. She tore it open with trembling hands. It read: *'Your little lady wishes to stay with her friends. She refuses to leave her home town. I cannot wait anymore. I am very sorry.'*

*

January in Geneva was colder than anything Jeanne had ever experienced.

In the last week of that month, the lake froze around the port. Trees crystallised into fantastic ice sculptures, children played in snowdrifts heaped up by the north wind, and icicles formed under cornices of tall buildings that lined the steep streets leading up to the upper town and Protestant cathedral.

However, the lengthening days meant that Jeanne was able to work longer hours at her loom. The act of producing fabric, something physically useful, not only allowed her to earn a modest living, it kept her mind focused on creation rather than her own ruin. It also saved her from lingering in hope of a letter from Suzanne that never came. She deduced her sister's correspondence somehow must have been intercepted, unless there was another reason for the lack of tidings.

Of course there were times when she could not keep her mind from exploring ways of returning to Montauban to retrieve her children herself. She had not seen them for nigh on two years. However, those deliberations that sometimes came to frustrate her were quickly quashed by her economic reality. She simply had no more means to hire a guide.

But more than this, the extra daylight hours allowed her to invest herself further in her new occupation.

She was now living in third-floor rooms above a bakery that was situated on Place du Molard, a busy marketplace of the lower town that opened onto the lake harbour on the north side. She had wanted to be able to live through her sufferance in her own space, where she could choose to eat, sleep, work, and sometimes cry, as she pleased.

Pastor Duvaux had been supportive about the move. Together, they had found the rooms, which were well-heated thanks to the baker's oven, and she frankly did not mind the early-morning noise. On the contrary, it brought her comfort to hear the bakery in action and the daily rituals of family life going on beneath her.

She did, however, and gladly so, agree to retain her seat at the pastor's table every Sunday after church. Jeanne found the conversation during these meals helped her better understand Genevese society. And it was during one of these meals that she discovered her new raison d'être.

Jeanne was sitting at the end of the table in her usual place nearest the tiled stove, the place once occupied by the pastor's deceased wife. When a lady once pointed this out to her, at first Jeanne felt slightly awkward about it. But then her practical sense quelled any feelings of impropriety. The pastor's wife was dead, and she was cold, so that was where she continued to sit.

To her right sat the deacon, a wiry man with a full head of white hair. Next to him were Madame and Monsieur Tagliani, the latter a respected merchant and member of the Council of Two Hundred. The pastor presided at the opposite end of the table, and to his right sat the guests of honour, Monsieur Ezéchiel Gallatin and his wife. Gallatin was one of the four syndics elected to form the executive government of the Republic of Geneva. Jeanne noticed the dishes were well- garnished. She wondered if this was owing to the importance of the guests or to the extent of Monsieur the Syndic's prodigious belly. At any rate, the pastor was pulling out all the stops of the organ to get his special guest to rally to his cause.

Both she and the pastor had wanted to question him about the plight of Protestant refugees who would undoubtedly continue to flow into Geneva at a greater rate come spring.

'I really do not know how much longer we can open our gates to everyone,' said the syndic, who then shovelled a chunk of capon into his mouth using a fork, an unmanly utensil that he had nonetheless learnt to tame on diplomatic missions to Paris.

'With all due respect, Monsieur the Syndic,' said the pastor, chuckling cordially. 'May I remind us all what has in the past bolstered our economy and made our little city prosperous?'

'*I* certainly need no reminding,' said Monsieur Tagliani, seeing as Monsieur the Syndic had his face full. 'Protestant refugees during the governance of Jean Calvin. And I am proud to say that at least one of my forebears on my mother's side was among them.'

'Quite, quite,' said the syndic. 'And my great-great-great-great-grandfather was a clockmaker from Paris, as you well know. But come, Pastor Duvaux, that is beside the question.'

'Then what is the question, Monsieur the Syndic?' said Jeanne, with something of her sister's affable musicality.

Dinners with her husband and his clients had taught her that a contestation always had a better chance of hitting home when said with a smile.

'The question is, dear Madame,' returned the syndic, turning his head to gradually encompass the whole table. 'Where are we going to put them all? That is the question!' He gave a fine twirl of his fork, then brought it back to his mouth.

The pastor said, 'I realise that the relief fund is not inexhaustible; however, many of the refugees have means to rent or to acquire lodgings.'

Jeanne added, 'At the least, most of them have skills which will allow them to establish and sustain themselves in the long run.'

The pastor continued, 'Indeed, and those with means will inevitably create work. But if the local workforce cannot meet the demand, then such affluent individuals will move on to enrich Brandenburg and Holland instead.'

Monsieur Tagliani said, 'Put like that, I admit it does make sense for the town to grasp this opportunity as it did under Calvin. And I do not care if the French king's diplomat wants us to move them on.'

'You mean Monsieur Dupré. I confess, I am not overly keen on his manners either,' said the syndic, which gave some relief to Jeanne and Pastor Duvaux.

Otherwise known as the Résident de France, Monsieur Dupré was responsible for conveying to the Genevan authorities Louis XIV's desire to rid Geneva of Huguenots. Some high-ranking officials were beginning to fear a French invasion if the small Protestant republic did not comply.

As the syndic washed down his food with a quaff of wine,

Madame Tagliani, a mouse of a woman but with a certain pedigree, took advantage of the short silence to add her reasoning. She said, 'Makes me wonder if the king of France realises what a generous windfall he is giving to his rivals.'

'Well said, Madame,' said Jeanne, who was thinking exactly the same thing.

Indeed, during the short time Jeanne Delpech had been in Geneva, the pews of Saint Germain's church had swelled with tanners, shearers, lawyers, labourers, clockmakers, physicians, weavers, and more. No wonder King Louis had made up laws to prevent them from leaving his kingdom. The loss of income from taxes would be considerable, not to mention the drain of talent. That being said, to a certain extent, other laws shrewdly made up for the shortfall by allowing the king to confiscate the fortunes of wealthy Protestants who were sent to the galleys.

But Madame Tagliani was right. For the state capable of harnessing such an inflow of expertise, it was surely a windfall, even if not all Swiss cantons saw it that way. Indeed, the fact was, some of them were encouraging escapees to continue their path northward to the more accommodating pastures of Prussia and Holland.

The deacon, a sensible, calculating man and ageing bachelor, said, 'But the problem remains. Those without means will need time and shelter before they can stand on their own two feet. Or would you rather have them camp outside the city walls?'

'Certainly not,' said the syndic, 'it would look messy.'

It suddenly occurred to Jeanne that a role was waiting to be filled, and filled by her. She had been so centred on her own misgivings that she had not seen what must surely be the reason God had brought her to this cold refuge, pretty as it was. It now all made sense: she had come to serve her persecuted brethren.

She stood up, dropped the facade of affability, and with unshakable conviction, she said, 'Already these people are pushed away in Savoy and some Swiss cantons. We cannot push them away from the very capital of Protestantism, the city of Jean Calvin, the defender of the Reform, and our spiritual leader! We shall call upon the goodness of people's hearts. And I shall take care of finding the extra space required.'

There was no objection to that. On the contrary, the syndic let out a belch of approval. The pastor and the deacon gave her a doting smile, as if their prayers had been answered. She would in effect be removing a thorn from their side, what with the deacon lacking experience with the fairer sex and the pastor no longer able to call on his wife on account of her being dead.

What was more, Madame Delpech had first-hand experience as a refugee. She had a certain standing, possessed the gift of being able to speak with anyone of any social rank, and had become an active and respected member of Saint Germain's church. And of course, most of all, she knew about the secrets of womankind and motherhood.

Jeanne sat back down amid encouraging interjections, while the whole table clapped their hands.

Her first task would be to garner a list of addresses from churchgoers, where refugees could find a bed and a warm meal until they got settled or continued north.

*

Come February, Jeanne noticed a steady rise in the number of newcomers arriving through the city gates. Once again, the refugee issue was the main topic of conversation in the Genevese marketplace. The authorities were beginning to realise the amplitude of the situation and willingly directed refugees to organisations where they could find assistance.

Weaving on her loom one February morning, her thoughts turned to the grateful young couple—the wife with a baby in her belly—whom she had placed the day before with a church acquaintance.

The patter of footsteps followed by a knock on the door brought her out of her contemplation, and told her it was getting on for noon. Every day, little Denise, the baker's daughter, aged seven and very proper, delivered Jeanne's bread, for which the baker and his wife refused payment. It was their way of supporting the refugees, and hopefully kept Madame Delpech from asking if they could put up a foreigner. Jeanne finished passing the shuttle across the weft, squeezed the warp with the beater, and went to open the door.

'Oh, thank you, Denise, my sweet,' she said to the little girl, who stood in the doorway with a galette of bread and a gummy smile. 'And how are we this morning? Let me see your tooth.'

The child handed over the bread and showed her two gaps where the bottom front teeth had been.

'Well, well, what have we here, a little rabbit who has lost her teeth?'

'Oh no, Madame, not a rabbit,' said the child, who frowned at the thought of being compared to her grandma's favourite dish, a *civet de lapin*.

'Ah, but a pretty little rabbit, though,' Jeanne continued, and the child's frown turned into a polite smile. Of course, the lady was not expected to know about rabbit stew, even less about her grandma's delight in sucking rabbits' heads.

It struck Jeanne that Isabelle would have all her teeth by now, that she would have suffered teething without the love and patience of a mother. Jeanne had learnt to live with these impromptu flashes which popped into her head at any time of the day, during any activity or event.

She shook the anxiety from her mind as footsteps on the narrow wooden staircase announced another visitor. She recognised the constant and deliberate footfall of Pastor Duvaux.

'Off you run, my angel,' she said to Denise. The child ran off, passing the pastor as he came upon the landing.

'My dear Madame Delpech, I am sorry,' he said, doffing his hat as he arrived at the door. 'We have a father and a son this time. I was out when they called, but they left a message. And they asked for you. Your name knows no bounds, my dear. They are waiting at the tavern.'

Her new role, which had enabled her to recover some shreds of self-respect, had come as a blessing to the pastor. He now systematically passed onto her the charge of organising accommodation, food, and other requisites necessary for children, not to mention the female condition. This role he would have delegated to his wife, had she still been alive. Jeanne was careful not to let any misunderstanding creep into their relationship.

'Then please step inside, Pastor Duvaux, while I put on my coat,' said Jeanne, who crossed the room to her small bedroom. 'I shall be with you in a moment.'

With the increase of asylum seekers, the pastor was calling more often than before, to the extent of her having to delay some of her textile orders. But it was for the right cause, and it was bringing her attention and paradoxically more customers.

A few minutes later, she was standing before him, clad in her outdoor garments with a hat firmly pinned to her head and a heavy woollen shawl wrapped around her shoulders.

'You might have to take them in for just one night until I check if the captain's lodgers have vacated their room yet,' said Jeanne as they stepped out into the freezing street. She continued, 'A carpenter, his wife, and their children from Aigues-Mortes. They have found somewhere down by the river near the mills, a bit damp, but I believe it meets their requirements.'

'Yes, of course, whatever you say,' said the pastor.

The square was still bustling with shoppers, and barrows, baskets, and stalls whose vendors were stamping their feet and clapping half-mittened hands. The day was crisp: an icy chill swept off Lake Geneva, and horses and beasts of burden moved in shrouds of vapour that escaped from their muzzles. Jeanne and the pastor quickly wended through the busy lower town, past Madeleine church, where they bumped into acquaintances with whom they exchanged polite salutations, and into a wide, cobbled lane.

'I hope the syndic will see reason,' said Jeanne. 'We need his support for more temporary accommodation.'

'I hope so too,' said the pastor. 'I fear that, with the spring, the numbers will increase more quickly than we thought. It will be a difficult job to accommodate everyone. Thank goodness you have come to help, dear Madame Delpech.'

Jeanne gave a modest smile but hurried her step. However, her quickened pace did not stop his train of thought, and he said, 'You are, if I may say, a perfect . . . godsend!'

She had heard him say it before but was nonetheless flattered, though she made every effort to appear unmoved. She did not want to give him the wrong impression. Moreover, she noticed something new in the pastor's eyes that gave her a secret cause for alarm, and something more dramatic, too, in his speech, which had faltered uncharacteristically on the last syllables. Was the pastor falling in love? She shut out the notion from her mind as they arrived at their destination.

'Here we are,' he said, opening the sturdy wooden door for her. She then let him lead the way into the warm and smoky tavern.

They had entered the spacious room together many times over the past month, always for the same reason, and each time, the pastor had to overcome his natural reticence. Such places were often the refuge of corruption and vice, rarely visited by men of the cloth. However, given the present crisis, his presence was tolerated as long as his visit was short and he did not preach.

Jeanne had become familiar with the setting, which she found demystifying and which she would surely not have otherwise known in her life: the nonchalant dog, the blazing fire, the banter of patrons over a table scattered with playing cards, and the blended smells of ale, pipe smoke, and broth. A great iron cauldron sat permanently on the stove and was constantly topped up in the morning with meat, carrots, cabbage, onion, and dregs of red wine, all peppered with spices and herbs. She remembered how very good and heartening it was, especially after a long and exhausting trek. And every time she entered the place, she still felt the sense of comfort of that first time, when she had looked up and seen the pastor's benevolent smile.

Whatever her frame of mind, whatever her private sufferance, she always made a point of reserving the same welcome even when the stranger's face did not seem to register it. Nobody knew the inner battles a person was going through, the torments a person had already endured, and she would at least try to radiate a feeling of friendship while keeping a respectful distance. She knew as well as anyone how harrowing and confusing it was to be scornfully rejected in one land and find welcome in another.

As per their habit, they looked towards the barman, a middle-aged and barrel-shaped man with rugged features. He had a gash from his left cheek to his lip which gave him a grim rictus, a remnant of his soldiering days. But for all his roughness, he had heart; Jeanne sensed it.

She had become a familiar face to him now. He noted she was never ostentatious or pompous to the foreigners; she was never haughty or overbearing. He liked her for that, and appreciated her for sensing the kindness in his own soul.

He lifted his eyes, and jerked his head towards the table nearest the fire where the father and son were sitting in front of bowls of stew and a *quignon* of bread. The pastor and the lady directed their course towards them.

It was often the case during these times of religious persecution that young men would give a pretext for a visit to a distant French town for work, leaving the father with the mother to take care of the family business at home. In this way, the family heritage was not given up to the king's treasury, and the offspring would have the means to start a new life in a Protestant country without being missed.

But in the present case, the arrival of both son and father could only mean that the man must have lost his wife. And Jeanne could now see that the son, who had his back to her, was just a boy.

Halfway across the room, she had an awful premonition that shook her confidence. The man sitting in front of the lad looked up. It was Trouvier, the guide whom she had paid and on whom she had counted to bring her daughter to her.

A realisation struck.

'Oh, my God!' She held her hand over her mouth. The boy had looked around to face her.

The pastor stepped out of her path as she rushed forward to meet Paul. She let go of all restraint, hot tears streaming down her face.

'My son, my beautiful boy!' she cried as the young lad, now nearly as tall as she was, pushed back his stool, stood up with arms open wide, and then buried his cheek into his mother's bosom.

'Mama, Mama, dear Mama, I am here now,' he said.

VOYAGE OF MALICE

Book Two of
THE HUGUENOT CHRONICLES
Trilogy

PAUL C.R. MONK

1

FROM THE FOREMOST cabin of *La Marie*, Jacob Delpech steadied himself as best he could against the brine-splashed frame of the porthole. He stooped to avoid hitting his head on the coarse timber beam, so low was the cabin where he and his Huguenot brethren were incarcerated. But the view was certainly worth the effort, he thought, as the French pink, a three-masted cargo ship, pitched and rolled into the Bay of Cadiz.

'So this is the gateway to the ocean sea,' he said, almost to himself.

Mademoiselle Marianne Duvivier, standing next to him, made a comment on the pageant of colour growing nearer and bigger. Indeed, the Spanish port's importance was attested by the multitude of foreign merchant ships anchored here and there, flying their colours atop their main masts.

It occurred to Jacob that they were now only one stop away from their Caribbean island prison. That is, provided the ship, more apt for coastal ferrying than sailing the great sea, did not turn turtle en route—for she bobbed like a barrel.

The passage from Gibraltar, though short, had been rough enough to shake up the stomachs of the hardiest of seafarers.

In fact it had finished off two prisoners in the cabin next door, which housed galley slaves too old or too infirm for service. However, miraculously perhaps, the eighty or so Protestant prisoners were none the worse for wear despite being at the bow of the ship, that part which took the full brunt of the waves. But unlike the poor lame wretches next door, at least they bore no visible chains. And most of the Huguenot men and women seemed to be gaining their sea legs at last.

To Marianne Duvivier's great relief, they could now spy *La Concorde*, the great ship that had accompanied them much of the way from Marseille, and which carried a greater load of galley slave labour and Huguenot prisoners. More efficient and faster than *La Marie*, she had sailed ahead from Gibraltar and was already at anchor in the ancient Andalusian harbour. Significantly larger and built for the high seas, she was also more stable and seemed to sit in the port waters like an albatross among chicks, hardly bobbing amid the ripples.

La Marie dropped her anchors just a gunshot from *La Concorde*, but not close enough for prisoners to exchange words, nor parallel so that they could see each other. Nevertheless, Marianne Duvivier was still standing at the gun port an hour after their arrival, hoping for her grandmother to show her head through a porthole of the great ship.

She turned to Jacob, who had joined her again. In her resolute and selfless way, she said, 'I am so glad it was my grandmother and not I who was sent aboard the *Concorde*.' She was referring to the cruel separation from Madame de Fontenay at the embarkation point in Marseille. Jacob had since fathomed that separating grandmother and granddaughter was certainly a ploy between guards so that the girl could be more easily singled out and plucked from the crowd. However, her ravisher had ended up drowning with the first mate and another seaman when the longboat he was rowing capsized in the port of Toulon, the day after his failed abduction. And by a strange twist of fate, or Providence maybe, his death had granted her protection, for sailors were deeply superstitious.

'Yes, quite,' said Jacob, nodding towards the Spanish quay. 'Otherwise she may have been leaving the ship earlier than planned.'

The girl followed his eyes to where the dead prisoners, bound in hessian sacks, were being hoisted to quay from the longboat, then unceremoniously dumped like dead pigs onto a barrow. It was still early morning. The harbour was just beginning to stir in the grey light, and they could clearly hear the vociferations in French and Spanish about the stench emanating from the bodies. The Spaniard made several signs of the cross before taking up the shafts of the barrow, then wheeled the dead men away to God-knows-where.

Delpech felt a pang of injustice for the galley slave, whom he had known to have been a God-fearing shoemaker whose only crime had been the illicit purchase of salt. His wife and children would not even be able to mourn his passing properly without the body, he thought. He inwardly prayed for the man's soul to accept a place in heaven, if it so pleased God.

'I would willingly miss three days' worth of rations for a place on board the Concorde,' said one white-haired gentleman, a surgeon named Emile Bourget.

'Can't say you would be missing much,' said Madame Fesquet, the middle-aged matron who comforted Marianne after the attempted abduction.

'Let us not allow our regrets to undermine us, my dear Professor,' said Jacob, touching the man's arm. 'Instead let us spend our effort seeking God's grace in our misfortune.'

'Yes, you are right, Sir,' said Bourget. 'Forgive me my weakness.'

Madame Fesquet, in her matronly way, said, 'Praise be to God that we have arrived safely and have been granted this reprieve from the treacherous sea!'

Jacob thought she needn't be so loud; she might rouse the guards. But he bowed his head and said *Amen* anyway. After all, she was of goodwill and was only voicing her support of his remark.

Delpech had inadvertently become something of a moral touchstone among even these adamantly virtuous people. He had become their spokesman whenever their meagre rights of humanity needed to be reaffirmed to the captain, even though these demands were always made through the guards. The unsolicited honour no doubt had something to do with his forthright eloquence, his former position and fortune, and perhaps most of all, his standing up to the sailor who had one night tried to ravish the girl from the cabin.

Yet in truth, all Jacob Delpech really wanted was to lie low and get through this nightmare until he could find a way to escape the madness. And, with God's help, recover his wife and children.

The Huguenot ladies and gentlemen agreed to take advantage of the month-long stop in the Spanish port to swab the planks of their cabin, and to reduce the number of vermin. But undertaking the former required water and cloths, at the very least.

Jacob bravely accepted the task of go-between. He

decided, however, to wait for the most appropriate moment when the soil buckets had been emptied, and when the least volatile guard came on duty. So it was not until after their noon slops—a mix of pellet-like peas and half-boiled fish—that he was able to put the question to the guard through the iron slats of the half-timbered door.

GUARD: What now?

DELPECH: We desire to speak to the captain.

GUARD: Cap'ain's busy.

DELPECH: It is a matter of hygiene.

GUARD: Don't care what it's about, mate, I said he's busy. And when he's busy, it means he don't wanna be disturbed, savvy?

DELPECH: Then would you please be so kind as to ask him if we may be supplied with extra buckets and some rope so that we can haul seawater into the cabin.

GUARD: So you can escape more like, cheeky bugger!

DELPECH: Not at all. We would simply like to clean the cabin.

GUARD: I'll give you a bucket, all right, a bucket of heretic shit if you don't watch out!

DELPECH: Then would you kindly supply us with the water yourselves? And some sackcloth? I pray that you put my demand to the captain, or at least to the first mate, should the captain be unavailable. Will you do that?

GUARD: Pwah. All right, but woe betide you if I get my arse kicked!

Jacob Delpech had become as inured to threats as he had to the revolting stench of the cabin, full of unwashed people and buckets of excrement. Over the past two years, from one prison to another, he had been threatened with hanging, perishing in damnation, being burnt alive at the stake, having his balls stuffed into his mouth, and finally, being sent to America. Only the last threat had so far been carried out, which enabled him to take the guard's colourful language with a pinch of salt, and to pursue his demands calmly and collectedly.

An hour went by before the key clunked in the lock.

'Where's the prat who asked for water?' said the guard, peeking through the iron slats of the door.

'I am the one who asked for water. And rope,' said Jacob, who was still by the door, imperturbable.

'It's your lucky day, pal. The captain sends his blessings!'

The door was flung open, and three men with malicious grins stood in the doorway, each holding a pail. Delpech instinctively held up his hands to shield his head as three columns of water drenched him and those immediately around him from head to foot. The men laughed out loud. Then the guard pulled the heavy door shut and turned the key in the lock.

Jacob prayed inwardly for the strength to continue to suffer humiliation, torture, and even death for his faith. However, at least the guard's threat was only partially carried out. Thankfully, seawater was all that was in the buckets.

Nevertheless, to state that Delpech was becoming weary of the crew's scorn—scorn that he suspected was fuelled by a callous captain—was an understatement. But he kept it to himself, and prayed the day would come when he could escape to carry out his plan.

*

Captain Joseph Reners, thirty-nine, was a merchant. A strong leader and very proud of his person, he was as able with low life as he was with the elite, and he enjoyed the company in both the Old World and the New. He loved his occupation, buying and selling, which took him to places where a man could forget himself. What he disliked, though, were the bits in-between, the seafaring bits which were either extremely dangerous or downright boring.

He vaunted himself as being well travelled and delighted in thrilling the bourgeoisie in Cadiz, especially the ladies, with tales of peril at sea and man-eating savages called cannibals. Given his gregarious nature, he had acquired expert knowledge of parlour games and card playing. In short, he lived for the social life on land, and this latest venture transporting galley slaves and Huguenots gave him the means to indulge wholeheartedly in his passions, from Cadiz to the Spanish Main. Nevertheless, over the years he had traced a regular circuit and by consequence had a reputation to keep up, at least in Europe, if he were not to be shunned by his usual hosts.

Consequently, a day after the water-throwing incident, the crew's degree of crassness towards their prisoners slipped down a few notches, and their attitude became, if not respectful, at least more tolerable. The soil buckets were emptied before they were completely full, and the peas were cooked, so they no longer ended up in those buckets. The salted beef, however, remained as tough as boot leather, and the cold fish still resembled a kind of briny porridge. But most of all, the Huguenot detainees no longer ran the risk of being drenched by buckets of seawater whenever they knelt down to pray.

Jacob correctly supposed that this change was owing to the captain's desire to show a façade of respectability and humanity during his stay in the Spanish port town.

What is more, the shift in behaviour was sustained and even enhanced, thanks to a series of visits paid to the Huguenots during their stopover.

Dutch and English Protestant merchants who had settled in the Iberian port quickly got wind of the 'cargo' of Huguenots. It had become a normal occurrence to hear of lame slaves being transported to the New World. But how could respectable, devout Christians be stripped of their earthly possessions and dispelled from their homeland for simply remaining faithful to their religious conscience?

Despite Louis XIV's attempt to draw a veil over his religious purge and conceal it from the outside world, word had nevertheless percolated out of France. Tens of thousands of Huguenot escapees had taken with them to Geneva, Bearn, Brandenburg, Saxony, Amsterdam, and London tales of unfair trials, family separations, enslavement, and incarceration. French etiquette was quickly going out of fashion. It was losing its capacity to charm the breeches off the European bourgeoisie as the darker side of the Sun King was becoming apparent. And here in Cadiz was the chance to see the living proof.

The captains of neither *La Marie* nor *La Concorde* did anything to prevent visits to their ships. On the contrary, Reners for one was astute enough to give orders not to impede such visits, as proof that he himself had nothing to hide, that he was only carrying out the King's orders. When asked at his hosts' table about his cargo of Huguenots, he would make a point of stating that the poor wretches on his ship were treated with humanity, even allowed to pray to their God, in spite of their disloyalty to their King.

On the morning of 22 October 1687, the second morning after the French ships' arrival, Mr Izaäk van der Veen and his wife were the first of the Protestant merchants to visit *La Marie*. The Dutchman was an influential broker with links to counters in Holland and the West Indies. He had done business with the captain on numerous occasions, usually for the purchase of barrels of French wine which went down well with the multi-cultured population of Cadiz, as well as his Flemish buyers.

Mrs van der Veen, a straight-faced and well-endowed lady with mothering hips, climbed aboard *La Marie*, taking care not to dirty her dress in the rigging. The Dutchman knew the ship from previous visits, although this time neither he nor his wife was there to choose barrels of beverage. This was just as well, as the space normally given over to wine and spirits had been converted for the captain's human cargo.

Both Mr and Mrs van der Veen were dressed with sobriety in accordance with their reformist beliefs. They were greeted by the second in command. This did not disgruntle the visitors in the slightest, as they knew of the captain's legendary distaste for dwelling on board his ship. The remaining crew were busy offloading cargo destined for Cadiz. The visiting couple advanced carefully to avoid slipping on the wet decking, and continued past sailors swabbing the main deck.

Mr van der Veen followed the second mate down the scuttle hatch into the tween deck, and then turned to assist his wife. She immediately noticed that the open space that once spanned from the capstan to the windlass was now partitioned off into cabins. And thank goodness she had thought to perfume her handkerchief, which she now held to her nose. The savoury and sickly smell of food, urine, tar, and dank timber grew stronger as they advanced towards the galley slave cabin, where a large rat stood nibbling at a flat square of flesh—a prize stolen from an inmate's bowl. The rat had grasped that a man inside the cabin who carelessly placed his bowl on the ground had no chance of catching the rodent once it had scooted with the food under the door. But on the approach of the intruders, the hideous creature showed its teeth, jealously took up its prize, and indignantly scampered away.

Mrs van der Veen and her husband turned to each other with a look which said they were dreading to see the conditions in which their brothers and sisters in faith were being held captive.

Then the sound of a woman's voice rose up in song. It was spontaneously joined by a host of male and female voices, and the Dutch lady recognised a psalm that sounded beautiful, sung in the French language.

They hastened their step to the Huguenots' cell and stood to watch through the iron slats. The inmates nearest the door stopped their song, and for a suspended moment stood watching the couple staring back at them.

Mrs Van der Veen, who spoke some French, had prepared her introductory sentence in her head that morning. But it did not come out, so absorbed was she by the piteous sight of the scene before her. Instead she put her hands together in prayer. Her husband followed suit. Then gradually, like a wave leading from the door, the Huguenots also stood or knelt in silent prayer.

At last, the Dutch couple looked up, and their eyes met those of a slim gentleman with cropped hair who took a step from the crowd.

'Madame,' he said in French. 'Do not pity us but rather our persecutors. For we are the privileged few whom the Lord has graced with the chance to earn a place in heaven. There is no need to shed your tears for us.'

'Monsieur, please forgive us,' said Mrs Van der Veen. 'We were not prepared to see such injustice before our very eyes.'

The second mate who had accompanied them was standing sheepishly with the guard, three paces back. Mr van der Veen turned to them and asked in Spanish to open the door so that he and his wife could enter the cell. The second mate gave the nod to the guard, who opened the door, then locked it behind them.

The gaunt-looking man with the cropped head introduced himself. 'I am Jacob Delpech de Castanet,' he said. Other men and women huddled around them without thronging, and introduced themselves in the gentlest manner.

'Dear lady, your heart is noble and kind,' said one young lady who introduced herself as Mademoiselle Duvivier. 'But please do not be afraid to hold your handkerchief to your nose. We understand that the odours must be intolerable to someone unused to this despicable den.'

'Thank you for your consideration,' said Mrs Van der Veen, 'but allow me the honour of sharing a part of your humiliation and suffering with you. It will make me nobler.'

Mr van der Veen said slowly in Spanish, 'If we can bring you any comfort at all, we shall be eternally grateful.'

Mrs van der Veen said in French, 'I shall bring you vials of perfume, which will at least sweeten the air around you, as well as other provisions. Please tell us what you need most.'

'You are kind, my good lady,' said one Huguenot woman.

'A splendid idea,' said Madame Fesquet. 'It will distance the bad smells that breed disease.'

Mademoiselle Duvivier said, 'The disease is also brought by the vermin, I fear. As Jesus tells us to travel through life in a clean body, we should very much like to embark on our voyage in a clean cabin.'

'We have been enclosed in this cabin for the past four weeks,' said Jacob. 'Alas, in spite of our demands, we are deprived of water and rags for swabbing.'

'I will ask the captain to see to it that you are equipped,' said Mr van de Veen, who then let his wife translate.

*

By the following morning, not only was the Huguenots' wish for water and cloth granted, but more visits followed from other Dutch and English contingents, and continued throughout the Huguenots' stay in Cadiz harbour. Each visit uplifted their spirits, like a rag of blue sky in an otherwise murky firmament. They saw each visit as a ray of God's love that galvanised their faith and filled their souls with new courage. It meant He had not abandoned them. Now they could embark on the long, perilous voyage across the great sea, secure in the knowledge that their place in heaven was assured. What, after all, was earthly suffering compared to eternal life?

The visiting parties also brought very earthly provisions: dried sausage, cheese, bread, fruit, clothing, writing kits. They even managed to smuggle in miniature Bibles and a few other books for the voyage, one of which would shape the course of Jacob's destiny.

The book in question was at first given to Professor Bourget by a rosy-faced Englishman with sparse white hair for whom Jacob acted as interpreter. Delpech still possessed remnants of English, having learnt it as a young man when his father had taken a position there in 1663 to learn about medicine. However, the book was of no use to the professor, a surgeon who knew only his mother tongue, German, Latin, and Greek. Jacob's father had been a physician and herbalist, and during previous conversations with Bourget, it had come to light that Delpech had always nurtured a fond interest in the Lord's natural world. So it was without regret that the professor gave the book to Jacob.

It was an old book that the elderly Englishman had kept since his younger days. He had spent half his career as a ship's surgeon for the East India Company. The book was *The Surgeon's Mate*.

*

On the twenty-first of November, one month to the day of her arrival, the pink lowered her sails and turned her prow towards the open sea.

Jacob Delpech was eager to reach the New World. Before setting out from the Bay of Cadiz, he had been able to converse in his broken English with a Dutchman by the name of Marcus Horst, who was familiar with the West Indies. 'There are a great many islands, large and small,' he had said. 'You must hold firm. It would not be so difficult to escape to an English settlement by cargo ship. From there you can gain passage aboard a ship bound for London or Amsterdam.'

La Marie and *La Concorde* were escorted by *Le Solide*, commanded by Admiral Chateaurenaud, chief of the French fleet. As they left the Bay of Cadiz, Jacob knelt with a group of fellow inmates to give thanks to God for the reprieve before the storm, and for the rays of light that had brought them comfort, hope, and their Holy Bibles.

The sound of the key in the lock made Jacob look up in time to see the door swing open. Next thing, he saw two men, two buckets, and a shaft of seawater.

'Enough of yer jabbering to false gods!' bellowed one of the guards.

'Or we'll come in and search yer all for fake Bibles,' said his mate. 'And if we find any, it's twelve lashes for heresy!'

2

JACOB HAD KNOWN about the perils of sailing near the Barbary Coast for a long time—which was why, as a merchant, he had always shipped goods overseas from the west coast via Bordeaux.

He was sure that, should by misfortune they be captured, the King of France would find no reason to send his ambassador to Mulay Ismail to part with wealth or Muslim slaves in exchange for a few Huguenot bourgeois, no matter what their standing in society had once been.

Understandably, then, Jacob and those who knew anything about international affairs inwardly gave praise once they had sailed clear of the Gulf of Cadiz, unmolested by Barbary corsairs.

But the moment *Le Solide* veered northward towards the coast of Portugal, *La Concorde* put all sails to the wind southwestward, and *La Marie* was soon left alone amid the vast expanse of the Atlantic Ocean. They would not encounter land for six long weeks. Six weeks of being rocked and tossed about at the bow of the ship—the worst part, the part usually reserved for animals—with nothing to engage the eye but sea and sky.

Noah had endured a similar voyage, Jacob often philosophised; the Ark could not have been any more seaworthy than this pink. So he resigned himself to patience and prayer, and surreptitiously read books and his Bible whenever the light and the swell permitted. But even this was made impossible much of the time by the roasting heat of the sun, augmented by the heat of the kitchen stove only six feet above their heads. It was like sitting inside a furnace and so insufferable at times that the men were obliged to remove their shirts and tunics, drenched as they were in sweat. To compensate for their natural modesty, women were given the areas out of the direct sunlight and furthest away from the heat emanating from the stove above.

The only resort was to remain as still as possible, which became increasingly difficult given the atrocious proliferation of fleas that feasted on legs and other body parts come nightfall. And the itchiness the morning after was always more intolerable than the precedent.

One stifling afternoon, three weeks out of Cadiz, despite a constant urge to scratch his fleabites, Delpech sat, knees forming a *V*, perusing *The Surgeon's Mate*. With a steady wind in her sails, *La Marie* was able to hold an even keel, which made a change to the sporadic blasts of the night before. Most of the cabin was in slumber. Jacob was trying to decipher the chapter entitled *Of Salts and Their Virtues*—which gave him cause for a rare chuckle given that they were surrounded by the stuff—when a terrible cry of despair broke the creaking, snorting, catnapping silence. Lifting his head from the page, he saw a young woman jump up in a dim corner across the cabin and scream out: 'I cannot go on, I cannot. I am being devoured. Oh Lord, have pity! God help me, please!'

He recognised Madame Gachon, normally a quiet, obliging lady, whose two children had been taken from her to be raised in the 'true' religion back in France. She then flung off her bonnet, stripped off her dress from neck to waist, and dashed topless to the porthole opposite where Jacob was sitting.

Jacob sensed in his bones what she was about to attempt. But the surprise of seeing the poor woman half-naked and the horrible seeping carbuncles on her upper body had him mesmerized. And for an instant he was unable to react to the impending tragedy. Before anyone else had fathomed what all the fuss was about, she had hoisted herself through the square porthole in an attempt to reach the solace of the sea.

At last, throwing his book aside and heaving himself up, Jacob called out: 'Grab her!'

An old man dozing close to the gun port sprang up like a coiled snake and managed to latch onto her ankles before she disappeared completely through the hole. With the help of another man, he managed to pull her back inside the cabin as she drummed her fists wildly against the side of the hull.

They were laying her down on the rough timber boards, careful to avoid her arms lashing out, when two guards came bustling through the door, buckets at the ready, as if to put out a fire.

'She tried to jump out the porthole,' said Jacob, who was at present struggling to hold down her arms while Mademoiselle Duvivier and Madame Fesquet were trying to pull up her dress to cover her bare torso. The tortured soul was now in tears, writhing like a captured beast and tossing her head from side to side in a frenzy, crying out for the peace of Christ.

'Shut your bloody bone box and move over, unless you want another hiding!' said one of the guards. Jacob edged back a step, but stood ready to intervene even if it meant taking a beating.

'I'll give her a mouthful of sea all right, if that's what she wants!' said the other guard.

With deliberate, almost lascivious slowness, they poured the contents of their buckets up and down the length of Madame Gachon's body, reducing the flow to a trickle when they reached her open dress, her rash along her white belly, and her half-bare breasts.

'For the sake of common decency, that's enough, Sir, I beseech you!' said Jacob. Huguenot men had positioned themselves ready to pounce should the situation deteriorate. Sensing they may have gone too far, the guards more hastily finished emptying their buckets.

But the debasing punishment of pouring seawater in Huguenots' faces, which still kept the thugs amused, now seemed to instantly quell the woman's delirium. She stopped crying out, only snuffled now as the cool water splashed onto her skin. She let her arms lie limp, so that the unwavering ladies could thread them into her dress, and cover her torso.

'She does it again, we'll bound her up and leave her on Dominica with the savages!' bellowed one of the guards, puffing out his chest. Looking around with his hand on his scabbard, he backed out of the cabin with his mate.

Dominica was a Caribbean island inhabited by ferocious savages known as Caribs. It was one of the places the guards repeatedly said they would leave women who refused to attend the Catholic mass once on land. The men would simply be hanged, they said. These were ongoing threats they had concocted to put the 'fear of God' into their captives. But what can these heathens know about Christianity, let alone the fear of God? thought Jacob, who had previously told his fellows to dismiss their menaces as mere hogwash.

The women took over operations as Madame Gachon began to come back to her senses. They helped her return to her place. Jacob went back to his book.

But he could not help revisiting in his mind the neat bands of weals on the poor woman's torso where the fleas had eaten into her flesh, and the large weeping carbuncles that had formed here and there. The excruciating itching and pain they must have caused her, along with the intolerable heat and the confinement of her clothing, would have driven anyone to distraction, which was why the poor woman had sought comfort in the wide ocean.

But what gave Jacob the most matter for reflection was the effect of the seawater. It had seemed to bring her instant relief and had visibly quashed the distress and itchiness of her sores. No, her intention had not been to kill herself—for that was a crime in the eyes of the Lord—but to instinctively seek a cure from the ocean.

Jacob turned back to the page where the author was praising the virtues of salt. He read: *All those which are vexed with any disease, proceeding of grosse crudity, or unnatural humidity, as rheumes, itch, scurve, ring-worms, or the like noysome greefes: let them make a bath of common sea salt.*

Delpech sat in wonder as the confirmation of his deduction hit home. He then explained his theory to Professor Bourget and a few others who cared to listen.

'Salt has indeed been used since ancient times for its virtues,' said Bourget, who had been seasick throughout the voyage so far, and was only able to concentrate his thoughts for minutes at a time.

'And it is all around us,' said Jacob.

*

That night, after the buckets were emptied and returned to the cell, instead of using them all for their usual purpose, they kept one back for their experiment.

Men tied their shirts together to form a line. To the end of this line, Jacob tied the bucket, which he lowered through the porthole until it broke the water's surface. Then he hoisted it back up. In this way they were able to discreetly retrieve the providential brine.

Delpech and Bourget applied cloth soaked in seawater to the men's sores. Mademoiselle Duvivier and Madame Fesquet did likewise for the women. And indeed, to everyone's amazement, after the initial sting, the itchiness subsided, and the fleas did not bite so much during that night. 'Why, bless me soul,' said Bourget the next morning. 'Dear Delpech, you are right. Fleas are averse to salt!'

Every night thereafter, they carefully retrieved buckets full of ocean water. They doused their wounds and swabbed the planks, and some even soaked their clothes in it. Salt is not comfortable, but the discomfort it caused from dryness was but a small tithe to pay for the protection it gave against the evil of fleas, and the horrible pustules they caused on the skin.

Jacob linked the series of events which had led to his revelation: Madame Gachon exposing her sores; her uncontrollable attraction to the sea; Jacob reading the very pages that spoke about salt; having the book in the first place; saving the poor woman; her being soaked in seawater; and

Jacob falling upon the very paragraph that dealt with itching and the like.

Surely, then, the woman's momentary folly was a manifestation of God's grace, was it not? It had given them the cure to their greatest discomfort. And the ongoing voyage became more tolerable, or rather, less of a nightmare for it.

Whenever they were caught praying henceforth, they no longer felt humiliation at seawater being thrown into their faces. Instead they felt the grace of God.

*

The stench was intolerable at the best of times, what with the buckets of defecation seldom being emptied till evening. But at no time was it more asphyxiating than when the gun port flaps were closed, mostly due to big swells, but also due to the cruelty of the guards—although, in some ways, the dim light and the appalling smell were lesser evils than the blazing rays of the sun.

It was impossible to read once the wooden flaps were lowered, so Jacob found plenty of time for introspection.

He was going to die, no matter what, and so was everyone else. But where did the Christian soul go? He knew not; the Bible only gave a few lines in Revelation. Would the celestial city be anything like the one described in *The Pilgrim's Progress*? Since the stopover in Cadiz, John Bunyan's book had been passed round to the few who could understand English. Jacob had read it, and it gave him hope, especially when Christian was helped out of the Slough of Despond. Is that not where he and his fellow Huguenots found themselves now? Although their slough was an ocean!

Jacob Delpech often set to thinking about the coming of

Christ, the birth of Christianity, the gospel, and the inception of the Holy Roman Church. He reflected on the ungodly crimes to which the Church had turned a blind eye, and the assassinations it had sanctioned. He mulled over the wars of religion, and the Saint Bartholomew massacre where French Catholics had cold-bloodedly slaughtered thousands of Calvinists. He thought about how the pope had congratulated the French king by sending him a golden rose. Pope Gregory had even issued a medal to commemorate the event. When, as a young lad, Jacob first learnt of the horrific binge of killing, he could hardly believe his ears. Then one day he saw one of these medals with his own eyes. On one side it showed the head of Pope Gregory VIII, and on the other an angel brandishing a cross and a sword while standing over a group of slaughtered Protestants. It was struck with the words *Ugonottorum strages 1572*, which meant '*Slaughter of the Huguenots 1572.*' And so here was proof of the pope's benediction, and consequently of the Church's involvement.

How could such an institution have been allowed to breed hatred in the name of Christ and get away with it for centuries? How could it preach humility when it was adorned with gold? How could it be allowed to give Christendom such an appalling reputation for so long? Jacob was confused.

He prayed that God would enlighten him. As he was trying to put his thoughts into perspective, he began to doze off. A dark cloak of morbid matter seemed to encroach upon his mind like a black eagle folding its wings over him. Then he heard the high screech of a gull, and a distant human voice.

'Land ahoy! Land ahoy!'

Jacob roused from his slumber amid the general agitation. He shielded his eyes from the light as the wooden flaps were pulled open. He then hoisted himself onto his feet and staggered to the porthole, where he set his sight upon a faraway lump on the horizon. He was looking at the New World for the first time. It was the afternoon of January 2, 1688.

3

BY MORNING, ONCE the mist had lifted, Jacob and a few other porthole viewers perceived not a clump of vegetation but a full-blown island densely clad in rainforest. Its sheer mountain cliffs fell abruptly into the sea. This was the most mountainous island of the Lesser Antilles. This was Dominica, home to the warrior tribes of the Caribs, who had lent their name to the Caribbean Sea.

This was the island the guards had referred to time and again. The place where they threatened to maroon the women who would not stop singing psalms, where the insolent young ladies would be tamed by the savage men, and the old maids gutted, grilled, and eaten.

But *La Marie* sailed on past the spectacular landscape of lush woodland and waterfalls where nature still ruled in all its primal glory. She headed northward on the leeward side of Marie-Galante, the French-occupied island, flat as the galette that the natives called cassava bread. It sat like an antithesis of Dominica. Even from the gun port, Delpech could easily spy the ox-powered mills dotted here and there among the patchwork of flat, laboured fields.

His thoughts turned to the fields of his native Tarn and

Garonne: the waving wheat and the corn on the cob; the orchards of apples, pears, and plums; the peachy brick farm buildings that housed his farmhands; his ancestral home and his townhouse in Montauban. He wondered how the harvest had been over the past two years. Who was taking care of business now? Yet something told him he need not worry, that he would most likely never see his homeland again. But as long as he could recover his wife and his children, he knew he would still have the resilience and energy to build another patrimony, another home, wherever on earth that may be.

He had written to Jeanne when in Cadiz to inform her he ambitioned to escape from the Caribbean islands to London. He would send her word to join him when the time came. He had given one letter to a Dutchman and another to an Englishman to send on his behalf to the pastor in Geneva, where he knew his wife to have found refuge. By doing so he was increasing the odds twofold that his message would reach its destination.

Contrary winds made the going slow, though the many marvellous views at least broke the monotony—no more so than when a group of dolphins accompanied them a short distance by making arches over the clear, teal sea—and took their minds off their thirst.

By the twelfth of January, water was rationed to two cups per person. However, the following afternoon, even the guards thanked the Lord for the favourable wind that brought them relief, and pushed the pink into the bay of Guadeloupe for their first stop in the New World.

*

Guadeloupe is easily recognised on charts by its butterfly shape. The two wings were divided by a narrow channel that emerged on the south side into a large bay where French colonists from Saint Paul had established port villages.

The bay, consisting of a large south-facing inlet between these two areas of land, offered a natural harbour well sheltered from the easterlies, and well out of the way of the swell. From the gun ports on either side of the pink, Jacob could see that the shape is where all similitude to a butterfly ended, for the topographical features of the two wings were very different.

The land on the west side, Jacob was surprised to learn, was known as Basse-Terre, meaning lowlands. It actually offered splendid views of highlands covered in rainforest and gushing waterfalls. Delpech mused that given the clement climate and clear blue skies, the fresh water cascades and the luxuriant vegetation, it took no great leap of the mind to imagine this to be Paradise on earth.

Grande-Terre on the east side presented low rolling hills and flat land ideal for crop cultivation. Jacob remembered hearing this was the island where fortunes had been made cultivating sugar cane and distilling it into sugarloaves. He was curious to find out how the transformation was carried out.

But during the four-day stay, prisoners and slaves remained locked in their stifling cabins while cargos of pots, tools, and textiles were offloaded, and barrels of sugarloaves taken aboard. The captain may have been sozzled out of his mind on occasion during his forays on land, but he had certainly not lost his bearings when it came to trade, not by a long sea mile.

It was from their cabin in the natural harbour that many Huguenots saw black men for the first time. On Guadeloupe, the European colonists, many of whom were seeking a new life free from religious and political persecution, were building a tried and tested formula by which to make a fortune, and there were no scruples when it came to worldly wealth. Be you Protestant, Catholic, or a Jew, it was what made the world go round.

The men were rolling, humping, and hoisting barrels on the foreshore. One of them, a lad of seventeen as black as a frigate bird—turned to an older man who was securing a load of sugarloaves onto a boat. It was to be transported the short distance to the ship where white faces peered out from the holes in the hull.

In his native tongue, the lad said, 'Who are they to keep staring at us working?'

The older man, who knew better than to stop for a natter under a slave driver's nose, continued securing the barrels as he said in a low voice, 'They are slaves.'

The answer came as no small surprise to the young man. His name was Imamba Kan, and he had once been a prince of the Akwamu tribe in West Africa. The bulldoggish slave driver gave the lad a stroke of his whip for daring to dawdle.

'Gimme that black look again, boy,' bellowed the slave driver, 'and I'll whip your black ass till it turns so red you'll be beggin' me not to make you sit on it, boy, let alone shit!'

The young prince turned back to his chore. 'I will get away from this wicked oppression,' he said to himself. 'I will get away from here.' But for the moment, Imamba had no choice but to hurry his movements or else receive another lash of the whip.

*

Four days later, *La Marie* was leaving the sugar cane fields, the African huts, and the ox-driven mills of Guadeloupe. A steady southerly wind allowed her to make good headway, and in just two days, on the eighteenth of January, she dropped anchor in the roadstead of Saint Paul.

Jacob knew from conversations with Professor Bourget that the first Frenchmen to set foot on this island were Huguenots back in the 1620s. They had long since moved on to the island northwest of Hispaniola called Tortuga, where they formed a small colony. But the island of Saint Paul had nonetheless come a long way in sixty years. For a start, the gentle slopes of the volcano, and the low-lying plain at its foot, had been cleared and given over to the lucrative sugar cane.

And, as a testimony to its newfound importance and the size of its population, Catholic Jesuits had even built a monastery here. Jacob knew as well as anyone that those of this order were not known to settle in places of little interest. Such was their grandeur that when two of them set foot aboard the pink, they were given full honours.

However, these reverent clerics did not deign to visit the Protestant heretics. There was, of course, no point. Besides, they only had time to inspect the casks of wine they had come to procure and to settle the sale of sugarloaves before it was time for vespers. They had two thousand African slaves to hammer the true faith into, which was no small task, especially when you considered that many scholars were still arguing whether or not the wretches had a soul at all.

While negotiations were under way, Jacob noticed a cargo ship that flew the English flag. It was a normal occurrence in these waters, as the English occupied the central area of the island, and the two nationalities had found no better way to cohabit than by simply ignoring each other's company. It had been the modus vivendi ever since the French and English joined forces some decades back to wipe the rich, fertile island clean of its populations of trees and savages. Neither of these life forms was compatible with the white man's design. The vegetation was worthless, in spite of Carib complaints that replacing hundreds of healing plants with one crop was a senseless and disrespectful act against nature. But of course, these were savages who did not understand what made the world go round.

The Europeans' success had since enabled both nationalities to give themselves fervently to the intensive cultivation of their favourite crop, which the French called *white gold*.

The captain had manifestly found the discussions agreeable. On the departure of his venerable visitors, they were honoured with a three-gun salute, normally reserved for a governor.

On seeing the multitude of black slave workers going about their business on land, it suddenly occurred to Jacob that these islands that had once been the promised land for a few freedom seekers, had become a prison for so many. Surely this could not have been the intention of the first Huguenots, could it?

Nevertheless, the ease with which the English ship had come sailing past, without so much as a puff of animosity, bolstered his hopes that escape to an English territory was indeed a viable option.

*

After the nine-day stopover in the bay of Saint Paul, victualled and watered, *La Marie* continued her voyage towards the French territory on Hispaniola, the island of her destination.

The sea was dazzling and calm as they tacked north by northwest along the eastern side of Saint Eustache—a Dutch possession with lush volcanic slopes—and by the steep scarps of the little isle of Saba which belonged to the English. The Huguenots who were still eager and able took turns to huddle around the gun ports whenever they offered a new tableau of exotic vistas.

By the twenty-ninth of January, they were sailing eastward three sheets to the wind, past the even plains of the south coast of Saint Croix. The prevailing easterly kept the ship on a steady course, while giving her the advantage of manoeuvrability as she swept past the treacherous reefs of the southeast cape of Puerto Rico.

The south-facing coast of this island presented a profusion of settlements: more slave shacks and villages amid the fertile plains that sloped down from the timbered mountains. Jacob was becoming aware of the extent to which whole African populations had been transported to these new colonies. Be it Dutch, French, English, or Spanish, every island harboured settlements of African huts.

On rounding the southwest cape of Puerto Rico, they hit upon the tail end of a storm. The only safe place for non-crew members was lying flat on the floor on their canvas sacks. Even then Jacob and his eighty fellow inmates were often unable to keep themselves from rolling about like apples in a tub.

But the captain refused to tack back to the southern

coastline that provided numerous anchorage points away from the swell. Even if they did manage to negotiate the dangerous reefs, putting into a southwest inlet would be as good as stepping out of the briny broth onto a Carib barbecue. At least, so thought Captain Reners. Besides, the captain had no trading partners on Puerto Rico, and the odd sprain and bruise would not devalue the chattel. So he held the ship's course, shortened her sails, and rode through the tail end of the gale to the northeast cape of Hispaniola.

*

At daybreak, the coast of Hispaniola came into view. Jacob was surprised to see they were barely half a league from the shoals where clumps of rock jutted treacherously here and there out of the water. During the night, the beacons that had appeared on shore had seemed to indicate that the island was much further away. However, upon examination, Delpech could see that the lights must have been lit on the far side of a bay which was protected by a spit of land. And this spit reached a good deal further into the sea.

The mist rose, revealing a verdant landscape of singular beauty, and a ship wrecked on the rocks. Her sails had been struck. Debris was still dotted around her, which told Jacob the catastrophe must have happened recently, probably during the storm which the pink had met rounding the southwest coast of Puerto Rico. It was impossible to make out the ship's colours from the gun port, let alone her name, although what was left of the three masts made some of his fellow Huguenots fear the worst.

'Lord, let it not be *La Concorde*!' said Marianne Duvivier, clasping her hands together. The whole congregation prayed for the lost souls and could only hope the ship they had seen was not the one with which they had sailed out of Cadiz.

Realising that the men above deck did not share their concern, Jacob sent a message to Captain Reners, asking for a boat to be sent to investigate the wreckage. The captain, who until now had refused any moral, physical, or verbal contact with the prisoners, thought it best this time to meet their demand head-on. The whole voyage had gone incredibly well so far. He had only lost five galley slaves—two of whom had come aboard half-dead anyway—and no heretics, which was by far his personal best. It would be a pity to suffer any moral blight on his reputation so close to his port of delivery. And as for that wretched Huguenot chief, Reners did not doubt the man would not hesitate to make a nuisance of himself before the governor.

So, flanked by two guards, the captain bravely entered the Huguenot cell like the top dog he was to deliver his answer, despite the stench and the risk of contagion. Though slightly smaller than most would have imagined, he stood as large as life before them in all his fine glory, which made the Huguenot leader and his band of bedraggled brethren look ragged and pale in comparison. It was the first time the Huguenots had seen the captain of their ship close up. They all stood silent at first. Some doffed their hats, speechless and in awe.

Delpech, who had no hat to doff, levelled his eyes at the captain's when he said: 'But, Sir, are you not bound by Christian values, if not common decency, to investigate the tragedy? There might be survivors, by God.'

The captain remained calm and firm. He said: 'We are not a navy ship, and that wreck is in Spanish waters. My commission is to get you to port safe and sound, not for you to be captured by savages and Spaniards. I regret I cannot be held to account for other people's failures. You must realise this is a very dangerous coast.'

'But, Sir,' returned Jacob, 'have some humanity!'

'I have plenty of humanity within this ship,' said the captain, remaining the perfect master of himself. 'The place reeks of humanity, and I do not intend to lose any of it!' He thought that rather good and inwardly congratulated himself for his calmness and quick wit. Even his guards were infected by his superior reasoning and could not help their smug smiles. He continued, 'If there are survivors, they will have been picked up by Spaniards or savages by now, so there is nothing we can do anyway. Now, I suggest you bear up and examine your conscience in preparation for your new domicile.'

There, he thought, no one could accuse him of being dismissive or inhuman, or of failing to have a Christian heart. He was satisfied it would eventually sink into their scabby heads that he was acting for the good of all aboard. Moreover, he secretly looked forward to seeing the governor's face when he brought his pink to port ahead of *La Concorde*.

Despite Jacob's insistence, the captain stoically stepped out of the dank jail, and without so much as a glance towards the other unfortunate cabin, he made his way to his quarters for some fresh air.

Any captain ought to know to keep well away from that part of the island, he thought, not only because of the perilous rocks but because of Spanish wreckers who at night shone their lamps to provoke navigational errors. With a ship smashed and all aboard drowned or cut to shreds on the reef, they could tranquilly pick off the cargo that lay strewn along the shore. But Captain Joseph Reners, who well understood the practices and motivations of cruel people, never had trusted such lamps, even on his first voyage. He had always put double the usual distance between the shore and his ship.

The whingeing heretics should thank their Protestant God they had been transported under his command, he said to himself back in his cabin, as he poured himself another tot of rum to take away the foul taste of squalor.

*

A north-easterly wind filled the pink's sails as she bore westward along the north-facing coast of Hispaniola. This was the name Jacob knew Columbus had given to the island 196 years earlier. The French now occupied the western side which they called Saint-Domingue. Even a league from the shore, this, the longest Caribbean island Jacob had seen so far, was a spectacle of beauty. Dense forests of broadleaved trees that covered the foothills, palm trees that fringed the tracts of golden sand, and conifers that reached up the mountain sides gave it an aura of Eden.

The island's mountain ranges were some of the highest in the whole of the Spanish Main. Consequently, there were quick variations in climate. Sometimes a leaden mass of cloud would darken the horizon to such an extent that it seemed inevitable that the ship would be in for a deluge. But the threatening clouds yonder that flared up with great flashes of lightning invariably dissipated come nightfall, and more often than not, the waxing moon shone large and bright.

The wind direction was not always constant and sometimes followed the morning sun, then blew westward again. But come midday the sea often became very calm, and progress was slow. Thankfully, this was not the hurricane season, and the last leg of the voyage passed by without further incident.

On the eleventh of February, they dropped anchor between Saint-Domingue and Tortuga Island, where a contrary current and lack of wind obliged them to wait.

The following morning, the pink weighed anchor for the last time with the Huguenots aboard. She anchored at midnight off Port-de-Paix, where the governor of Saint-Domingue had his residence.

*

Jacob had lost weight, his body was drained, and his joints were stiff, but his chances of escape were better than ever. He was looking forward to standing with solid earth beneath his feet after five long months aboard the ship in abominable conditions.

However, the governor, Monsieur Tarin de Cussy, an orderly man of principle, only allowed sick Protestants and the galley slaves to disembark, the latter to be sold.

It was not until three days after their arrival in the roadstead of Port-de-Paix that the rest of the Huguenots were able to leave the detestable pink, but only to embark on another vessel, coincidentally called *La Maria*, which had not long dropped anchor. She was under the command of Monsieur de Beauguy, a newly converted Catholic and captain of the king's navy.

The governor gave the order to assign the Huguenots to Leogane, a port village sixty leagues from Port-de-Paix, which lay along the west coast in Gonâve bay. From experience, the governor knew it was wise to mix slaves, indentured workers, and prisoners throughout the territory rather than congregate them in tightly knit communities. A concentration of one type would only lead to friction and the need for rigorous repression, which was good for no one. The idea then was to build communities with a mixed bag of subjugated subjects. "Divide and rule" was the governor's motto. De Cussy was indeed a clever man, and what is more, well born. His excellent breeding and fine manners meant that his word was taken with solemnity, and it was so eloquently delivered that it was difficult for the commoner to contest his reasoning without seeming uncouth and coarse.

With simple elegance he stood on the middeck steps before the group of bedraggled Huguenots and said: 'This little voyage will last three or four days. I pray you will find some comfort at your port of destination, where you will live among many former Protestants who came here to start a new life. It is our hope that you will understand why they became Catholic, and that you too will become royal subjects once again.'

Jacob had heard it all before, but before the governor returned above deck, he raised his finger and asked: 'Sir, if I may. We are without news of *La Concorde*, which transported many of our brethren from Marseille. Would you be so kind as to light our lantern?'

'I am sorry, my good man,' said the governor, tactfully feigning to ignore the grubbiness of the well-spoken gentleman in front of him. How easily an individual could lose all trace of decorum and respectability, it was frightening, he thought to himself. Instinctively slipping a hand beneath the gold-braided edge of his red satin waistcoat, he continued:

'I am unable to divulge information of the whereabouts of your co-religionists, or any of the king's adversaries for that matter. I trust you will understand that I am under oath.'

'But, Sir, please,' said Mademoiselle Duvivier, taking a resolute step forward. She had more important things on her mind than the shame of her appearance. Besides, if she could face the embarrassment and humiliation of crossing the ocean with no privacy at all, she could jolly well stand up, albeit in rags, to a frilly-sleeved middle-aged nobleman. She said, 'We saw a ship wrecked on the rocks last week as we came into sight of this island. Our captain said it was too dangerous for him to investigate. We should very much like to know whether or not *La Concorde* has come safely to port, Sir.'

'I am sorry, Mademoiselle,' said the governor, with a pinch of impatience, 'I have no such information to impart to prisoners of His Highness.'

'But, Sir, please,' insisted the girl. 'My grandmother was on le Concorde!'

The governor calmly and in a lordly manner held up a hand, as one who was used to wielding authority and negotiating with rebels, slaves, and savages. 'If you desire the assistance of a king's officer,' he said with an indulgent, almost paternal smile, 'it goes without saying you must be a friend of the French state.'

The governor's time was counted, his mind crowded by a multitude of other concerns. The interview was thus curtailed with elegance, but curtailed all the same. He nodded to Captain de Beauguy, standing at the capstan for him to give the order to weigh anchor. Then he retired to his cabin.

4

'DON'T THANK ME, Madame Fleuret,' said Jeanne Delpech, handing the roll of fabric to the carpenter's wife. 'The loom does all the clever work!'

'True enough, but it wouldn't work at all without Madame's deft fingers and keen eye, and a good head on her shoulders, would it? my word!'

Jeanne smiled without reserve at Ginette Fleuret's way with words, typical of southern French folk and reminiscent of her own hometown. She was nonetheless glad that Madame Fleuret had learnt to lower the volume to a level more suited to Genevan manners—more restrained, more concise, and less exuberant than in the Mediterranean walled city of Aigues-Mortes. That being said, given her talent for dressmaking, few minded her Mediterranean vociferations, for Ginette would willingly fit out woman and child without taking a single *kreutzer* piece for her toil, provided she was given the fabric. And together, Jeanne and Ginette had made an unlikely match.

They were standing in Saint-Germain's church under the fine carved pulpit which, true to Calvinist tradition, was situated midway down the nave on one side. The church—

whose interior walls presented remnants of colour and empty statuette niches that bore witness to its Catholic past—was peopled mostly with women of all ages and rank, some chatting in clusters, some sipping hot soup around trestle tables. This was the midweek get-together where Huguenot refugees and local parishioners could exchange news and views, offer mutual assistance, and sing psalms together. Numbers had swollen since Jeanne's first visit in October, and these days French Protestants by far outnumbered Genevans.

The church had become an assembly point as much for establishing contacts as for bolstering faith. It was a favourite place for Jeanne where she could encounter God, refugees, and her customers all under the same roof. Here she could distribute her rolls of fabric to French fugitives who were able to pay, and to the needy who could not. People travelled great distances in harsh conditions to reach the walled city of Geneva, and more often than not, their first requirement, after food and lodging, was a new set of clothes. Ginette had unreservedly volunteered to help those without dressmaking skills. In this way, the mutual aid had brought people closer together, and their church had become a happy sanctuary—the ringing of laughter during such meetings bore testimony—despite its austere interior.

'How is your husband faring now?' said Jeanne, placing her empty earthenware beaker on the trestle table.

'He says he misses his bouillabaisse, which means he's recovered his appetite. Otherwise he's happy as a clam at high water now that he's helping down at the sawmill.'

Ginette Fleuret lived down near the river with her husband and three children. It was damp and penetratingly cold, but they had all recovered from their winter fevers, and they were not unhappy. Their lives might have radically changed in this colder climate, but now at least they were at one with their conscience. Wasn't that worth all the sun in the French Midi?

'Good. But we'll have to find you somewhere away from the damp.'

'Couldn't do that, Madame Delpech. We'd be all at sea if we didn't at least have a view over the water, my word; never lived without it. Anyway, I shall crack on with this little lot with Madame Lachaume.'

'I am so glad you were able to make space for her little family. It is becoming increasingly difficult to find accommodation within the city walls.'

'Difficult? Ironic, I'd say. Ironic, my word! My Jeannot volunteered to help build up the new floors on Taconnerie Square, but the guild won't have it, not without a work permit. Result, they've got too much on their hands, and my Jeannot ain't got enough. I don't know what we'd live on without the relief fund, I'm sure. So I'm only too glad to pay something back, Madame Delpech. Puts me on a level pegging, see? But if things don't move forward by the time the warm weather comes along, then we'll have to be moving on to pastures greener, where we are wanted!'

'You might have to be patient, dear Madame Fleuret. The Genevans do have a penchant for things done well, and unfortunately, that takes time . . .'

'Well, I call it stalling. Most of us would be working by now if it weren't for their licences for this and their permits for that.'

Jeanne had grown used to Ginette's little rants and was

not offended by what could have been taken as blatant ingratitude. After all, it wasn't the fault of Genevans if they were on the French king's doorstep. But there again, Ginette was only voicing what everyone else thought deep down. This was the centre of Protestantism, after all, and they deserved to be treated as all God's children, did they not?

'I'll leave you to your ponderings, Madame Fleuret, I am expected at the tailor's,' said Jeanne. 'Which reminds me, my coat. Where's my coat?' Jeanne stared blankly at the empty pew in front of her, where she had been sitting during the service. Her coat was there a minute earlier. For the first time, Ginette read anxiety in Jeanne's eyes. However, looking past Jeanne's shoulder, she saw the ragged-looking man whom she secretly called the pauper, walking up behind her.

'Madame Delpech, I believe this is yours,' said the ragged-looking man.

His name was Cephas Crespin. Of average height, in his mid-thirties, he usually helped the vicar out with putting away tables and chairs and such like. His distinguishing feature was mutilated thumbs, which he claimed had been placed in thumbscrews to persuade him to abjure.

Every time he went to a church service, Cephas Crespin felt amusement mixed with anger, but he kept it to himself. There he was amidst the niceties, trying to start over again, on par with everyone else, but try as he would, he could not get the coarseness out of his voice. It was just unfair. Any attempt at fancy language and fine manners just made him stick out, and whose fault was it if he had been earmarked from birth? Didn't God put paupers on the earth to test rich people's conscience? He never wanted to be a Lazarus, though, made to feed on leftovers. Yet when you were born as common as muck, that was all you could expect. However, at least the after-service soup made him feel better again. There was nothing better than a hot bowl of soup for spiritual comfort and peace within.

'Thank you, Monsieur Crespin,' said Jeanne, relieved to find her coat folded over the pauper's arm, though she tried not to show it.

'Let me hold it for you, Madame Delpech,' said Cephas, 'so you can put it on.' Cephas liked to hold coats for the ladies; the clumsiness caused by his disability always brought a smile of pity. As the pauper held out Jeanne's coat, his expression changed from one of polite obedience to one indicating an alarming realisation.

'Feels like you've got the family jewels in there, Madame Delpech, ha ha,' he joked.

'Ha ha, no, no,' said Jeanne with a level smile. 'I've weighted the hem with pebbles, Monsieur Crespin, that is all. It helps keep it from flapping in the wind, and I like to feel the benefit of the weight on my shoulders.' She remained high-minded, unflappable. But the pauper could have sworn it was a different kind of stone she had sewn inside the lining. He said no more about it as Jeanne's gaze turned to her nine-year-old son, running up to her with another boy, slightly older, southern-skinned with a forthright smile. Young Pierre, who most people called Pierrot, was a practical lad and clever with his hands.

'Mama,' said Paul, 'can I stay with Pierrot till lunchtime?'

'I am sure his mother has enough on her plate,' said Jeanne, who hated to see her son leave her side for five minutes, let alone a few hours.

'Get away, woman, he'll be no trouble,' said Ginette.

'They can help gather offcuts down at the mill for our fire!'

'Please, I never go anywhere,' said the boy. Jeanne could not dismiss the fact that he needed some leash after being cooped up in a room all winter long. Besides going to church, his only outings without her had been to fetch up water from the Molard Square fountain below their rooms, and even that he accomplished under her watchful eye.

'Youngsters do need their running-around time,' said Ginette, with a wink to the lads.

'I'll look after him, Madame, promise,' said Pierrot, who was a head taller than Paul.

'And I'll get Jeannot to walk him home safe and sound in time for his lunch.'

'Fair enough,' said Jeanne, trying her best not to sound too put out. 'I shall be off to the tailor's on my own then.' She could not resist the impulse of trying to make her son feel guilty for his momentary freedom. It was not envy but fear that put the words into her mouth. She had lost him once. She was petrified of losing him again.

'Then I shall accompany you!' said a mirthful voice.

Jeanne twisted her torso. 'Claire! I thought it was you I saw earlier,' she said as Ginette's boy tugged Paul's sleeve with a wink, and the lads shot off across the crowded church before Paul's mother could change her mind.

*

Wrapped up in woollen layers, booted and shawled for the season, the two ladies stepped into the sharp March morning from the vestry door. Despite the jaw-trembling cold, the sky seemed to be lifting, and patches of clear icy blue were widening. They walked briskly at first, to distance themselves from the stench of the noblemen's stables that stood opposite the church building.

Jeanne knew that Claire had some trouble on her mind, that she wanted a word in private. Why else would she have turned up late at church in her condition, only to leave ten minutes later? The young lady with whom Jeanne had escaped out of France now had a double hoop ring on her finger and a baby in her belly, having been sworn into wedlock shortly after her arrival in Geneva. Her cheeks were already fuller and her bump, despite the amplitude of her robes, was becoming visible. And she needed her mother. In her absence, Claire often sought guidance from Jeanne, who tacitly complied.

'Has the sickness passed at all?' she said as they emerged from the narrow passage that led into the busy Grand-Rue, lined with boutiques. The puddles that only yesterday crunched under foot now splashed muddy slurry which speckled ladies' hems and gentlemen's stockings.

'Yes. No, not quite, but I do feel less queasy,' said Claire, with an anxious but brave smile. 'I do not mind the sickness so much. It is the salivating I cannot abide. I keep wanting to empty my mouth. Now I know why a pregnant market woman I once saw kept spitting all the time like a trooper; I well recall how it verily put me off my purchases. I understand now how she must have felt. I cannot go anywhere without a pile of handkerchiefs.'

'It will pass, my dear Claire, or you will have to get Etienne to follow you about with a pillowcase!' Claire let out a jovial laugh and swiped her mouth with her handkerchief again. Jeanne continued. 'Unless you learn to spit like your market lady!'

'Oh, no, I could not do that,' said Claire, laughing mirthfully and momentarily losing her look of anxiety.

'How is Etienne progressing with his plans?'

'He is not,' said Claire, her face now etched anew with lines of worry. 'Formalities, endless formalities.'

'For a man of means, it is surely only a question of time,' said Jeanne, thinking to herself how impatient and demanding the younger generation were becoming. 'Once he has his licence and has been admitted into the guild, he will be settled for many years to come. For from what I gather, decisions made here are meant to last. It is why they take so long in making them.'

'But what about the resident?'

'Monsieur Dupré thankfully has no executive power here. This is not France.'

'Yet.'

'They cannot invade. If they try, the northern cantons will declare war.'

'The mere thought makes me shudder.'

'And Geneva is a republic. Besides that, the king's resident is not loved in Genevan circles, I can assure you.'

'Perhaps, but he can keep up the pressure to prevent us from being able to earn a livelihood.'

'Fear not, my dear Claire. You have enough to worry about with your baby.'

'That is the problem. I do wonder where I am going to have it, and who will be with me.'

'I shall, of course.'

In a more sombre tone, Claire said, 'Etienne is worried that he will not be allowed a permit to work. He wonders if we are wasting our time here.'

'He wants to move on?'

'Further away from France. We are seriously considering leaving next week, Jeanne.'

'I see.'

They turned right onto Rue du Soleil-Levant, a wide, well-to-do cobbled street of the upper town, where well-heeled ladies and gentlemen purchased their provisions and clothing. The tailor's boutique was at the top of the street. Remaining on the sunny side, they mutually slowed their pace to time their arrival with the end of their conversation.

Claire's announcement had roused Jeanne's own fears. In truth, she too had been anxious about residing in Geneva ever since she learnt about the French king's attempts, through the resident, to oblige Geneva magistrates to expel Huguenots from the republic, and send them packing back to their Catholic sovereign. Thankfully, the Swiss cantons of Bern and Zurich had responded by offering military support in case of imminent hostilities. And Geneva authorities had found pretext to reinforce the city's medieval fortifications. Consequently, Louis had tempered his tone, although his intentions towards fleeing French Protestants remained unchanged.

Prompted by false rumours—rumours spread by malevolent souls—tension in the crowded walled city was growing of late. More and more, Jeanne noticed hard stares from market wives, and ladies pursing their lips and flaring their nostrils as she passed them by. She overheard quips about Huguenots bringing the menace of war, complaints about the rise of the cost of living, and protests of the price of building more living space within the city walls by adding extra floors to the tall buildings of entire districts. The resident's strategy was worming its way slowly but surely into the thoughts of the population of the republican city. His informants and agents were doing a good job.

Jeanne's greater burden, however, was knowingly working illegally, even though half of her weaving was destined for the poor. The other half, which went to the moneyed church acquaintances, allowed her to pay her own way. She was not wronging local weavers, though; she did not poach on their clientele. And if she ceased to operate her loom, she would only constitute another strain on the already stretched Bourse Française, the Geneva refugee relief fund, which granted the poor two *batzen* a day to live on.

No, until she knew where in the world Jacob was, she would have to keep quashing her fears and stay put. Moreover, every step further north would be another step away from her children, taken away from her and now living in Montauban. Here, at least, she could receive news from her sister who, having converted to Catholicism, had been able to take them into her care.

'Etienne is keen to leave before the spring rush,' said Claire.

'Does he really think, despite having means, he would fail to secure a permit?'

'He is not sure, but both he and my uncle agree that the king has too strong a hold over Geneva. They believe the magistrates will not be able to stave off his demands forever. Then what would become of us? Etienne feels we would be safer and better off in the Duchy of Prussia where the grand elector is calling for Huguenot tradesmen to settle in Brandenburg.'

'But should you not wait till the baby is born?' said Jeanne.

'If the baby is born in October, we should not be able to leave until next spring. That means another year's wait,' said Claire, catching saliva from her mouth again with her handkerchief.

'I see.'

'Etienne says he does not mind going ahead without me first, and then fetching me once he is settled. I know not what to do, Jeanne.'

The two ladies were now standing at the roadside, letting an elegant carriage rattle by. Jeanne placed a gloved hand on the younger woman's forearm and said, 'He is a kind and considerate young man. But no, my dear Claire, you must not let him go without you. You must stay together for better and for worse. He will love you all the more for it.'

Claire laid her free mittened hand upon Jeanne's, and the two ladies crossed over the Rue du Soleil-Levant.

*

It was not yet eleven o'clock when Jeanne pushed the glass door and sailed into the spacious room of the master tailor's workshop. The conversation with Claire had allowed her not to dwell on the meeting with Maître Bordarier. But now, inside the muted room where cut cloth and an assortment of garments were hung up on rails, she suddenly became conscious of her nervousness. Claire followed her to the light-wood counter that stood eight yards into the boutique.

On the other side of it, three young seamstresses, who had glanced up at the pleasant ping of the doorbell, again buried their heads in their needlework. They were seated cross-legged on cushions, darning and sewing, on a very large table in front of the rear window that faced them. A well-endowed lady approaching middle-age, sitting on a stool by the stove, put down her work. Getting to her feet, she gave a professional smile and approached the counter. While passing her eyes from Jeanne's waist, up her shawl that had seen better days, and to her simple coif, in a superior voice she said, 'Madame?'

Jeanne knew full well the woman recognised her from a previous visit. Nothing put fire in her veins like being treated with scorn, and her apprehension quickly turned to steely determination. Holding her head high, she said, 'Madame. I have an appointment with Maître Bordarier.'

Jeanne had become acquainted with the master tailor after delivering fabric, made for a gentleman churchgoer for the master tailor to turn into a long coat and breeches to match. One thing leading to another, Bordarier, who appreciated the quality of Jeanne's weaving, asked her if she would care to produce the cotton fabric that was all the rage in Europe, including France, where it had been forbidden by French customs. This meant that there was a fortune to be made there with the right network.

Bordarier, a spindly, clean-shaven fifty-year-old, was busy measuring a gentleman from shoulder to thigh with the aid of his assistant, a certain Michel Chaulet. Chaulet, in his early thirties, stole a sly glance at the French ladies as Jeanne turned to face the tailor. She had noticed the young man's hard stare before when she once dropped off a roll of caddis, a coarse but robust fabric, from which the tailor had agreed to make capes for the poor. But this time she thought she saw the young man almost gloating, which sent a shudder down her spine. She knew full well from her church client that Chaulet's brother-in-law was also a weaver. But Jeanne had no intention of pinching someone else's work. She had agreed to produce the sample as a thank-you gift for the tailor's help with producing clothes for poor Huguenots at a discount which, nonetheless, also gave him access to their wealthier co-religionists.

On hearing Jeanne's voice, Maître Bordarier looked over his shoulder. Peering over his pince-nez, he called out, 'Ah, Madame Delpech.' He then left his customer in the hands of Chaulet so he could join her at the counter. 'Thank you, Madame Laborde.' The big-bosomed lady waddled back to her stool near the stove.

'This is what I came up with, Monsieur,' said Jeanne, spreading the square piece of fabric over the smooth surface of the counter, while trying not to let her words slip into her throat. She had spent hours threading the loom. But that was no reason to be nervous about the tailor's judgement, she told herself. It wasn't as if she owed him anything.

Perhaps it was not the thought of his judgement but the prospect of his approbation that made her nervous. And perhaps, though she expected nothing in return, she nurtured a secret hope—the hope of a woman bordering on poverty.

Claire, standing beside her, let out a gasp of admiration at the shimmering blue fabric. The tailor adjusted his pince-nez on the bridge of his nose, then touched the fabric with his open palm, spreading out his fingers wide to fully appreciate the texture. Jeanne was suddenly anxious about being found out that she was no more a weaver than Claire was a fishwife, or Ginette a countess.

She was suddenly fearful of being found out, of being labelled an impostor. How could she for one second dare to consider herself as good as a trained weaver, a seamstress, or even a spinner? The tailor glanced up with a raised eyebrow. She was regretting having accepted the offer to show off her handicraft. Surely any master tailor would see straight through her, she thought, as he now held up the cloth to the light to see how the threads interwove, and how evenly they were beaten.

He placed the cloth back down on the table, whipped off his pince-nez, and blinked at the French lady standing before him, oblivious to the turmoil going on inside her. He said, 'You are gifted, Madame.' Jeanne said nothing, instead emptied her mind of any thought that would cause her eyes to fill up. 'I should like to place an order, for twelve yards to begin with. Then we shall see how we can proceed.'

The woman on the stool, who had pricked up her ears, could not resist a secret smile from pleating the corners of her mouth. For a moment Jeanne thought she had maybe misread the woman's jealousy. Yet, it seemed so out of character.

*

'Why did you say you would think about it?' said Claire once they were back in the street, and had walked out of earshot from the boutique.

'Don't get me wrong, I am very flattered, but it puts me in a predicament. You see, if I refuse, the tailor might be offended. He might accuse me of only wanting to work with French Huguenots, and of remaining in my clan. And that is precisely what we do not want.'

'All the more reason to accept, then. It will put an end to your money worries. It might even be the debut of a successful business. That is how the Turrettinis made their fortune, you know.'

'Don't tease. Besides, if I accept, I will have the whole guild of weavers upon me.'

'Not if you don't tell them.'

'They are bound to find out sooner than later, especially in the present climate.'

'I know. Why don't you make a deal with a local weaver?'

'Actually, that is what I was thinking. But I do not know whether a weaver would take on a woman. I have to find out how to go about it first.'

'I dare say, if you bring profit . . .' said Claire, clapping her hands. 'Oh, Jeanne, how exciting for you!' They made their way across the cathedral square towards the Madeleine district, where Claire resided with Etienne and her great uncle. In her enthusiasm, she must have dropped her handkerchief along the way, and with nothing to hand, she now had the choice of either swallowing a mouthful of frothy saliva or discreetly spitting it out. 'Oh, my gosh, look away!'

'Claire!' said Jeanne with mirth in her eyes as the young woman spat out a blob of spittle onto the cobbles like a trooper.

'I am sorry,' she said in guilty giggles, and she brought out a spare white-lace handkerchief with which she wiped strands of drool from her mouth. 'I didn't see that coming.'

The ladies hurried along arm in arm into Rue de L'Eveché, cheerfully leaving their improper conduct behind.

'But wouldn't it be formidable?' said Claire.

'It is true, I would be able to put some money aside for when I recover my other children,' said Jeanne. Then in a lower voice, she said, 'Keep this under your bonnet, but my sister plans to leave France with her husband at the end of spring.' The instant her secret was out, she almost regretted divulging it. But she was glad to tell someone about the long-awaited letter she had received the day before, which Pastor Duvaux had passed on to her. Besides, she knew Claire would keep the news to herself. The two women had developed a trusting relationship, and Jeanne would be sorry to see her go.

'Jeanne, how doubly wonderful!' said Claire, who did not need to be told that it meant they would bring Jeanne's children with them.

'Shh.'

'So you must accept the tailor's offer. He did say you were gifted.'

'I had good teachers,' said Jeanne.

Claire knew from previous confidences that Jeanne was referring to her maid and a weaver in whose workshop she had hidden for a year and a half in France to escape imprisonment. 'I foresee a bright future for you.'

'I am not sure about that, but the extra will definitely not do any harm.'

'It is surely a godsend, Jeanne.'

'Is it, though? For I shall nonetheless be an illegal worker. Sometimes the difficulty is in knowing whether a thing is a godsend or a lure of the devil, is it not?'

'I do know what you mean,' said Claire with a sigh. 'Choices.' They had stopped before the large door of a tall, elegant building made of fine masonry.

Jeanne touched the younger woman's arm and said, 'Listen, Claire, as long as you do not overstretch yourself, there is no reason why you should not go on that journey. You are not ill.'

'Yes,' said Claire, emptying her mouth again into her damp handkerchief, 'you are right.'

'He will need your support; they all do. Our position, my dear, is to endear them to common sense. Otherwise there would be even less of it in this mad world, would there not!'

Jeanne declined Claire's offer to ask Etienne to accompany her back to her rooms. 'As I told Pastor Duvaux, I am perfectly capable of walking the streets on my own,' she said with a smile. 'And I want to stop off at the butcher's for a surprise lunch for Paul,' she said, hinting at the money the tailor had given her for her sample.

Jeanne left Claire to pass through the tall door and then wended her way back to Rue du Perron. She liked taking this route which sloped down steeply from Saint Pierre's hill into the lower town. From the top she could see the blue, shimmering water of Lake Geneva. Its proximity gave her comfort. For in the event of hostilities, she would only have to board a boat to flee to the northern Swiss cantons.

She was glad to be able to walk on her own and think everything through. How could she turn down such a lucrative offer? Could it really be pennies from heaven? However, her mind would soon be made up for her.

5

'THE KING OF France sees no harm in your reinforcing your fortifications, as long as you do not employ Swiss soldiers to do so,' said Monsieur Roman Dupré in his usual courteous, albeit condescending manner.

The French resident was sitting in his sumptuous office with the fat syndic, Monsieur Ezéchiel Gallatin, whose large buttocks comfortably filled the low, wide armchair on the other side of the ministerial desk.

Monsieur Dupré continued. 'Why, it would be defeating the object, for you would have your potential enemy inside the city walls even before hostilities began!'

'With all due respect, my Lord,' said Gallatin, 'our Swiss allies offered their support because they were afraid that His Majesty would invade Geneva and the republic.'

'Nonsense,' said Dupré with a dry laugh, 'mere fabricated rumours!'

Gently patting the edge of the polished desktop with his large, chubby fingers, the syndic said, 'Monsieur de Croissy did warn he would take action if we continued to harbour Huguenots, did he not?'

'A reaction of the moment, and I might add, only to be

expected. They are, after all, the king's subjects, are they not?' said the resident with a courteous, thin smile—a facial technique honed in Versailles which subtly suggested he had urgent business to attend to and had no time for pettiness.

However, the seasoned syndic, having often rubbed shoulders with the elite on missions to Paris, was not to be intimidated. For sure, his rotund appearance lacked the physical elegance of his French counterpart, but he had personality, patience, and a deceivingly smart sense of business—and what is more, any verbal blows seemed to bounce off him like little cherub fists punching into a bloated pig's bladder. So, remaining solidly seated, he said, 'We could hardly throw them out in the middle of winter, my Lord. As you are well aware, we make a point in Geneva of putting up any subjects of His Gracious Majesty, in spite of the cost.'

'I assure you we do understand the predicament, Monsieur the Syndic. And I am all the more pleased to inform you that His Majesty has found a means of dropping the tithe case lodged against you.' Gallatin gave a slow nod of his large head as a sign of deep gratitude. Dupré continued. 'It is thus hoped that our mutual understanding shall be rewarded, and that the tithes from the region of Gex will serve to replenish your coffers, emptied by the king's subjects who are outstaying their welcome.'

'Yes, my Lord. My colleagues, indeed the population of Geneva, are most grateful for your intervention in the matter.' He was referring to an attempt by the authorities of Gex to recover a tithe which was customarily paid to Geneva.

'What is more, His Majesty extends his affection to the people of Geneva and promises to provide continued protection against enemy invasion. And he insists, my dear

Sir, that he had no intention of invading. Fabricated rumours, that is all.'

'I am sure, my Lord.'

'However, he does advise you to be henceforth more cautious regarding the *good intentions* of your Swiss neighbours. For it is evident that Bern and Zurich are trying to lull you into letting their soldiers enter the city without any resistance at all, God forbid. His Majesty therefore warns you, with love and fervour, not to fall victim to their malicious ploy.'

'Yes, my Lord.'

'Otherwise he will have no choice but to take action in your defence. I am sure you will understand, Sir.'

'Yes, my Lord. Rest assured, as I said, the Council of Geneva are most grateful for our illustrious ally's continued support and protection.'

The resident gave another thin smile and got to his feet, which this time obliged the syndic to do likewise. The resident grinned condescendingly at Gallatin who, because of his cumbersome weight, did not wear heels, unlike Dupré, who was consequently able to tower over the fat syndic as he said, 'And you must keep your word regarding the Huguenots! And this time please remember to send them south, not north.'

'My Lord,' said Gallatin, bowing on the other side of the desk, 'you have our reassurances that they will be asked to leave come spring, as agreed. Moreover, it will ease our relief fund, which has been a bit stretched lately, as you well know.'

The resident showed the syndic to his door, both men satisfied with what they had achieved. The Genevans had gained the king's assurance his army would not invade, plus the unhoped-for tithes of Gex; they had also gained precious time, something the Genevans were inherently good at. The French had gained the imminent banishment of Huguenots from Geneva.

*

Five minutes later, the resident was standing in his private chamber, accessed by a door set in the panelling of his vast study. He was gloating over the mahogany serving table stacked with savoury dossiers, each contributing to his grand project—the exclusion of Huguenots from Geneva, thus removing one major route into Germany and Holland.

Roland Dupré had built his reputation on his diplomatic ability, and also on his methodical mindset that gave him the intellectual agility to pursue several channels of intelligence simultaneously. He had learnt from experience that it would be unwise, indeed counterproductive, to bank solely on the action of the magistrates for the success of his project. For magistrates in a republic required the driving voice of the people—in other words, bourgeois, merchants, and guilds. So he had been painstakingly building up a network of agents to fan the fire of discontent among the population.

It is something His Excellence, the Minister of Foreign Affairs, Monsieur Colbert de Croissy, surely failed to fully grasp, keen as he was to please the king. One had to coax the Genevans into submission on their own terms; any precipitation would inevitably backfire. And what in God's name had got into the minister to waive the threat of invasion? wondered Dupré. Now they were capable of bringing Bern and Zurich soldiers inside the very city, which would be awkward, to say the least, what with the Dutch crisis. No, he thought, gently does it with the Genevans, and that takes time, a good network, and a table full of dossiers.

He picked up the one concerning the trade guild which was slowly but surely being fired up against refugee carpenters taking work from the tax-paying native. Then there was the housing dossier which was coming along nicely, what with refugees pushing up the prices, which was a paradox because the weavers were complaining about illegal cheap labour driving the prices down. He had the situation in hand. All he had to do was to keep gently pushing, and the magistrates would have no choice but to carry out the terms of their agreement.

A scratching at the door brought Roland Dupré out of his projections. Without looking up from his desk, 'Entrez!' he said.

'My Lord, a message,' said the valet. Dupré held out his hand, eyes still glued to his table of dossiers. He brought the sealed letter into his field of view. He would normally lay it down at this point, but this one rumpled his brow.

'That will be all,' he said, taking a cutter to the seal.

He opened the message and read: *Job done, lady in for a surprise.*

With a smile of satisfaction, Roland Dupré placed the message in the dossier titled "Weavers."

*

Today, more than any other day, Jeanne Delpech enjoyed descending into the Rues Basses of the lower town. She now felt that she knew them as well as the alleyways of her natal Montauban. She admired the Genevan love for things well made, and their practical approach borne of necessity: the sheltered stalls on one side of the thoroughfare, the central carriageway for horse-drawn traffic, and the convenient *dômes*—protruding roofs or upper floors that advanced over the street, providing shelter to pedestrians come rain, shine, or snow.

The blue patches of sky put smiles on faces and joviality into banter despite the nip in the air. Jeanne too felt that a cloud was being lifted from over her. She had received professional approbation of her work; she would no longer feel embarrassed or unqualified about asking the small price she charged for her cloth. It even occurred to her that she could increase it in par with market rates. If Maître Bordarier thought her good enough to provide him with cloth, there was no reason why she could not aspire to become a fully-fledged weaver in the eyes of the guild, even if it meant working for a master weaver. Pity the council still would not authorise Huguenots to work for a living, she thought to herself with an inward sigh.

For now, though, she put the thought to one side as she purchased a choice piece of tournedos and a cabbage on Molard Square, where the vendors were beginning to pack away their wares. Dockers on the far end were stacking articles and merchandise from France by the lake harbour. The bakery below Jeanne's third-floor rooms was animated with late-morning customers. Commis were tidying up after the morning bake, and Madame Poulain was serving an old lady behind the large counter where wooden racks contained the last of the day's round loaves. As the baker's wife took the change, she lifted her head to see who had just walked in. Her commercial smile vanished, and her chubby jowls sagged as her eyes met Jeanne's.

'Whatever is the matter, Madame Poulain?' said Jeanne, taken aback by the woman's visible anguish.

'There's been an incident, Madame Delpech,' said the woman.

Jeanne felt weak in the stomach as she raised her free hand to her mouth. 'Lord, no, please, not my Paul,' she said, suddenly hot, pallid, and trembling.

'No, Madame, not Paul, not your family either.'

Jeanne nearly passed out with relief. Then, realising what could be the only other cause for such concern, she dumped her provisions on the counter, lifted her skirts, and hurried out to the stairway entrance before Madame Poulain could utter further explanation.

On the third-floor landing, she encountered Monsieur Poulain fixing a forced door, her door.

'We heard a banging noise and thought for a minute someone was moving furniture,' he said, standing aside to let her into the room. 'Then, before we realised what was up, a couple of blokes came bolting down the stairs, and off they went.'

Even before setting her eyes on the shambles inside, she knew it was her livelihood they had come to wreck. The frame of her loom was shattered—beaten by sledgehammers by the looks of the dents in the wood—smashed and rendered unusable.

Across the wall, an untutored hand had painted in red the words: 'Geneva For Genevans. Huguenots Get Out!'

6

'SO YOU SEE, my dear Delpech,' said Monsieur Verbizier, in whose home Jacob had taken quarters. 'Be you Protestant or Catholic, you're better off here than in the Old World, are you not? For there, as you well know, your livelihood can be taken away on the whim of a king!'

Monsieur Elias Verbizier was a self-taught, free-thinking convert whose heart swayed more to the balance of power than with religious fervour. But if one thing made him angry, it was a state-run monopoly, and he secretly hoped the French king would get his comeuppance for all the monies he had been made to pay in tobacco taxes.

Born into a Protestant family of rope makers, he had left his native La Rochelle as a young man in search of his fortune. He had been a planter in the early days of the buccaneers on Tortuga Island. Now in the force of age, he owned one of the largest plantations in Leogane.

Delpech had been listening to his host's update of events in Europe with one ear. The planter had been relating that a league of states neighbouring France had been set up on the suggestion of William of Orange—the champion of Protestantism and sworn enemy of Louis XIV—to counter potential French aggression. They called it the League of Augsburg. But even this might not suffice to contain the French king, as events in England were taking a surprising turn. William's father-in-law, James II, who was also Louis's cousin, had refused to join the league and was attempting to catholicise his country. Indeed, should James's pregnant Italian-born wife give birth to a boy, a Catholic dynasty would be established again in England.

However, neither Louis nor William nor James was among Jacob's concerns—that is to say, not yet. He said, 'I grant you that starting a life afresh in such a new world certainly has its advantages.' He took another sip of coffee and then continued, 'But as for myself, there is no place better on earth than with one's family. In a Christian home, which, I might add, is a home without slaves.'

They were sitting on the ground-floor balcony, finishing their breakfast of exotic fruits, dried sausage, bread, jam, and coffee. The planter's residence, one of a few made of stone, was built near a vigorous stream that ran down from the densely wooded mountain. It offered a splendid view over the township of Leogane on the backdrop of the beautiful teal-blue anchorage.

The large tract of land that stretched out before them was divided into fields of indigo, cotton, tobacco, and sugar cane. Especially sugar cane.

The present harvesting period was proving successful, and there was still a good month left of cutting cane and distilling the juices into sugarloaves. On a normal day, Negro slaves would have long since been hard at work. But today was Sunday. Instead of the usual animation of hacking, hauling, thrashing, grinding, and digging, the air was filled with blithe indolence and the laughter of children.

Jacob cast his eyes a hundred and fifty yards down the slope to the left, where trees screened the slave shacks. A headless chicken was running round with a bunch of slave sprogs dancing along after it.

Elias Verbizier contentedly scanned his possessions. He was at peace with the world, more so than ever before, now that the Black Code decreed by King Louis gave him an official framework by which to properly administer his black population. His conscience was clear. And now, with these free Sundays, the death rate had fallen, which meant fewer trips to the slave market, and the yield so far had made an extraordinary profit. He was so glad he had made the switch from tobacco to sugar cane. This is the life, this is how it should be, he thought. How could the gentleman sitting next to him want to go back to the Old World?

But there again, once the Huguenot had settled into the benefits of the Indies, Elias felt sure the man would come to his senses. Not only that, it did not sit well with the planter to see such a qualified gentleman having a social status hardly higher than that of a mere slave. It did not fit into his notion of social order. At least being allowed to pay Delpech for his expertise would enable him to properly establish his ascendance. But for that, the man would have to fall into step with current standards.

Verbizier gave another puff of his pipe, then turned back to Jacob. He said: 'You've seen for yourself, farming would not be viable without good slaves. All this wouldn't exist. What do you think the Code Noir is for?'

'It is unchristian, Sir,' said Jacob.

'It is in the Bible, Sir,' said the planter. 'Slavery has been around since man first walked the earth.' Here he held up his right hand solemnly and rolled off the cuff a quote he had learnt by heart. He said: 'Your male and female slaves are to come from the nations around you; from them, you may buy slaves. They will become your property!'

Jacob had never confronted slavery and at first was disconcerted by its overwhelming acceptance. He could not help feeling uncomfortable about it. He had prayed for enlightenment and had come upon a passage in the New Testament which he now used to respond to the planter's argument. He said, 'The teachings of Christ are thus: there is neither Jew nor Greek, there is neither bond nor free, there is neither male nor female, for ye are all one in Christ Jesus!'

'Hah, tit for tat, fair dos,' said Monsieur Verbizier, who was always game for a battle of wits. He lifted himself lithely out of his rattan chair. 'But come with me, Delpech,' he said. 'I have something to show you that might make you think twice about your movements of the soul.'

Verbizier had decided the time was right. He was ready to give Delpech some enlightenment, the same that had freed him from religious foreboding and such like so many years ago. Since that fateful day, he had been able to adapt his opinion and behaviour according to his own advantage. And today he was a successful man. As for Delpech, he was still imprisoned by his hopes of heaven which had made him so miserably poor. So Verbizier took it upon himself to free this poor man who deserved much more for his talents.

Jacob now found he could get up from his chair with hardly a crick or a crack. And he definitely felt that he had put on a bit of flesh. He no longer felt the sharpness of his bones on the seat. Life, it was true, was not so bad on the island. Small, perhaps. Remote, certainly. Impenetrable, without doubt. But apart from the wretched insect bites, he had become accustomed to its climate. And he had been working on Monsieur Verbizier, trying to make him realise the true Christian path. For in the short time he had been there, he had sensed the planter's want of spiritual direction.

Jacob followed into the cool and comfortable study where leather-bound books were displayed in a bookcase, and a series of sketches and paintings of Caribbean landscapes adorned the walls. A two-branched candelabrum was already lit on the acajou writing desk. Verbizier had displaced a brass telescope on a tripod and was pulling the shutters tight to completely shut out the morning sunlight.

'Do not fret, Delpech. I would just like to show you a little experiment of my own fabrication which I stumbled upon some time ago. I pray it will enable you to see some sense and help you out of your needless quandary. Now come, please.'

The planter closed the door and invited Jacob to the desk. He then pulled up a comfortable armchair and asked Jacob to take a pew on the one that was already positioned. Jacob sat down.

'Now, watch this,' said the planter, who brought out a three-sided mirror from a cabinet and placed it behind the candelabrum on the desk.

'There,' he said. 'What do you see?'

'I see a man who could do with a shave and a haircut,' said Jacob, trying to make a jest of the situation which was becoming a little strange.

'But how many faces can you see?'

'A great many, I suppose. Depending on how I sit and face the mirror.'

'I would venture to say that there is an incalculable number of faces. In fact, I would go as far as to say that it would prove that your theory of infinity really does exist, would it not?'

Verbizier was referring to a conversation they often had about the immortality of the soul and the infinity of heaven.

The planter had maintained that life is not infinite in any shape or form, neither in one's life nor in one's death. Once you are gone, you are gone. That was all there was to it, he had said. This was shocking to hear and something that was hardly ever even whispered. But the planter was a plain-speaking fellow who had seen life and death. And he knew one thing for sure: a dead man does not come back! Though of course, he also knew when and when not to share his private thoughts, as well as with whom, or else he could end up being roasted at the stake like a soulless savage.

'An astonishing observation, I grant you,' said Jacob, peering into the mirror so that his reflection appeared to recede in an endless stream of faces.

'Now, watch this,' said the planter, whose mischievous little chuckle announced one of his tricks. He then licked his thumbs, leant over the acajou desk, and snuffed the candle flames out simultaneously.

'And there is your proof of nothingness. No infinity, just plain nothing!' said the victorious voice of the planter from out of the darkness.

There was a moment's silence as Jacob, stumped for words, took in the abominable notion.

Then he said, 'But, Sir, I ask you. Who created this nothingness? What is this blackness in which we hear ourselves speak? It is part of God's creation! For if there were no darkness, how would we recognise the light? In the same way, if there were no sorrow, how could we appreciate happiness?'

'Hah, damn you! When a man don't want to learn, he won't learn!' said Verbizier, pushing away his chair with a forced chuckle. He then charged across the room to open the door as the Sunday mass bells began to chime. But his cordiality had returned by the time he turned back to Jacob.

'Will you come to church?' he said.

'As I have told you every Sunday since I came here, I do not need to visit a Catholic building to go to church.'

'A more stubborn one there never was. But even if you keep your infinity, and your heaven and hell, think over what I say. You only have to join in the ceremony to be a wealthy man again, Delpech.'

'That may be, but certainly not a happy one!'

This Huguenot was decidedly Protestant to the marrow.

'That is why, Sir, it is important to live for the day!' said the planter, who always liked to have the last word. He took his leave and met his wife with their children and her pretty slave girl, at the front of the grand house where a coach was waiting to take them to church.

*

Strolling down towards the village, Jacob contemplated the view over the bay. If only he could find a way to cut and run. However, the forest around was impenetrable, the mountain behind impassable. And as yet he had not seen a single foreign vessel come to anchor in the roadstead.

Upon arrival at Leogane, the governor had handed the Huguenots over to the lieutenant governor, Monsieur

Dumas, who had advised them to find lodgings among the inhabitants. They were assisted in this delicate undertaking by Catholic priests who acted as go-betweens. But the Protestants did not come without resources. Most of them had skills and expertise to offer in exchange for board and lodging.

Given his knowledge of farming and irrigation, Delpech was offered the room at the plantation, where Verbizier was glad to have a gentleman of quality with whom to converse, and who knew about farm management.

Jacob had been at Leogane for over a month already. He had established a cordial relationship with the Catholic clergy who, despite their numbers, had failed to convert him. On the contrary, he had become a popular speaker and defender of the Protestant contingent, one that the priests would rather have been without.

He rejected the Catholic Eucharist, impertinently questioning how the act of taking bread and wine could make you more righteous.

He asserted that praying to God through saints was another invention of the Catholic Church which had made it rich.

And he even went as far as insinuating that the Roman Catholic doctrine of the celibacy of the clergy was unwritten, unnatural, and misleading for its ministers.

Such was his heretic verve and foolhardy conviction that the poor priests ended up complaining to the lieutenant governor, a former Protestant himself, that Delpech was impeding them in their mission of conversion.

And as if all that were not bad enough, now he was teaching African slaves who—since the Code Noir had

251

granted them a human soul—were supposed to receive instruction in the Christian faith by their master. And there was no point counting on the likes of Verbizier to set his man on the right course. A moral compass he was not, more a weathervane. Everyone knew what he got up to when away buying slaves.

Even the other indentured workers were turning to Delpech for spiritual guidance, which he had the cheek to dispense in French instead of Latin. For the love of God, had the man really no sense of tradition?

Apart from the Huguenots themselves, many of these indentured workers had also been Protestant. Labourers for the most part, they had to give three years of their lives to a master for the right to a plot of land, a little cash, and their freedom at the end of their term. And they were the fortunate ones compared to the African slaves whose term only ended on the day they drew their last breath.

It is written in the Bible, the likes of Verbizier would say, then quote a learnt-by-heart extract such as: '*And ye shall take them as an inheritance for your children after you, to inherit them for a possession; they shall be your bondmen for ever.*'

But Jacob found the Bible also warned: *Masters, give unto your servants that which is just and equal; knowing that ye also have a Master in heaven.*

Treating someone *just* and *equal* is certainly not to whip and beat them like stubborn beasts, thought Delpech. Yet, for all his research and reasoning, he had to admit that slavery was the way of the world here, and perhaps something he might have to get used to.

*

An hour later, he was standing with Mademoiselle Duvivier. She had taken a room at the house of an old lady, Madame Grosjean, whom she had agreed to care for. Marianne had blossomed in the time Jacob had known her, which equated to eight months, and which seemed like half a lifetime. His paternal presence still bolstered her confidence, especially since he had asked her to organise their secret assemblies, which she did with relish and gusto.

They were at present quietly singing a psalm with as many Huguenots as could fit into Madame Grosjean's small downstairs parlour. It turned out that the old lady had only converted to Catholicism to be left in peace, but her heart was firmly Protestant. And the house was conveniently located at the opposite end of the village from the church. Secret assemblies like these took place throughout the township. In fact, Jacob was finding out that every other white person he met was of Protestant stock. Like Madame Grosjean, they had many a tale to tell of the days of the first buccaneers, who were not filibusters at all, but Protestant planters and hunters who initially settled on the northwest coast of Hispaniola, and on the island of Tortuga.

After the clandestine service, Delpech led a small party around the sugar works on the pretext of assessing the advancement of the new mill that he had been commandeered to oversee, along with the construction of wells. The works was located at a five-minute walk along the palm-lined track from the township, and gave a legitimate reason for them to meet in plain view.

The mill, the boiling area, and the drying room were situated near the river at the bottom of the plantation, where the first fields of sugar cane had been planted. A water-powered mill, like the ones made by the Dutch, was under construction to cope with the extra land to be freed up for the lucrative crop.

The party were at present speaking around the old ox-powered mill. Here, only last week, a slave had caught his hand in the vertical rollers that normally mangled the sugar cane. It only took a couple of ox strides for the columns to travel the equivalent of a yard, and before the ox driver could bring his animal to a halt, before Jacob could process the screams, the poor man's body had been drawn in and his head crushed like a pineapple.

Six days out of seven, from daybreak to dusk, the plant was busy with crushing cane, boiling juice, clarifying, thickening and crystallising the sugar, and drying it in sugar cones. But today the place was empty, except for the party of Huguenots. From afar, going by their gesticulating, it looked like they were discussing a feature of the mill construction. But they were not. Their conversation had turned, as always, to their favourite subject.

'I say we just take a rowboat,' said Monsieur Coulin, a master carpenter, while inspecting the wedge of a mortise and tenon joint.

'The problem,' said Professor Bourget, the surgeon, 'is what to do with it.'

'We hug the shoreline until we reach the south coast,' said Monsieur Roche, a stocky mason who spoke in a tenor voice.

'We would risk getting caught by Spaniards,' said a lanky solicitor by the name of Lautre.

'Then it's out of the rowboat and into the whale's mouth!' said the professor.

'No, no,' said Coulin, 'I've heard that English vessels

water there on their way to Jamaica.'

'Madame Grosjean told me they like to put in at a place called Cow Island,' said Mademoiselle Duvivier, who was not too shy to add to a predominantly male conversation. In fact, despite her prisoner status, ironically she had never experienced such freedom. She even enjoyed walking among Huguenot men without a chaperone. She continued. 'It is not far from the south coast, I am told.'

'That may well be, Mademoiselle,' said Monsieur Lautre. 'Nonetheless, I still think it safer and wiser to bide our time a while longer until a Dutch *fluyt* puts into the bay.'

'With all due respect,' said Monsieur Roche, 'we've been saying that for the past three weeks, and we've still seen neither yards nor prow of a cargo ship, have we?'

'I fear we are not likely to either,' said Jacob, 'given the current state of affairs back in Europe.'

'To look on the bright side,' said Monsieur Lautre, 'at least we have been able to send word home.'

'Did they go?' asked Jacob to Marianne.

'Yes, my uncle,' she said, 'they went this morning with the store keeper to Le Cap Français.'

The church bells began to chime, announcing the end of the long Catholic mass. The company instinctively took their leave from each other in twos and threes to avoid any risk of being accused of congregating, which was punishable by imprisonment.

'My dear niece,' said Jacob, 'will you walk with me a while?'

Marianne and Jacob had kept up their little ruse of being related to avoid rousing suspicions whenever they met to organise the assemblies, which they did often. It also let everyone know that the young lady was not alone in this strange, torrid, and colourful world. Even Huguenots, as she passed by alone in the street, would give their regards to her uncle.

*

The two of them headed in the direction of a newly dug well which was on the opposite side of the plantation, and barely a hundred yards from the slave shacks under the trees. Delpech had positioned it so that it would provide the most efficient water supply for Monsieur Verbizier's new fields of sugarcane.

'We must find another place to assemble,' said Jacob. 'I fear we are watched, and I suspect it is only a matter of time before Madame Grosjean's house is closed, and then where will the poor woman go?'

'She says she is fully aware of the risks,' said Marianne. 'But she says that it uplifts her to no end to feel the grace of God in her home again. And she says it will not be long now before she is taken to her husband and her son.'

'But I fear they could send you away too, Marianne. I promised your grandmother I would look after you.'

'You need not fret, I can look after myself,' said the young woman with an endearing laugh. 'Now, you said you would teach me how to find fresh water, do you remember?'

'Indeed, I do.'

'Heaven knows, I might need to know one day if I become marooned on an island.'

'We are marooned on an island, my dear,' said Delpech, with a chuckle which allowed him to disguise his smile at seeing her so grown up, and a fine figure of a woman at that.

Marianne, who had come to understand his moods, knew at that instant his mind was not preoccupied as it usually was by his family and the grief of losing Louise, his three-year-old daughter. It was one of those rare moments that relaxed his rather handsome features.

He opened his jacket and brought out the Y-shaped slender branch he used for locating water veins, a method dowsers used on his farms in Montauban.

'Oh, wonderful,' she said, clasping her hands together.

He handed her the foot-long dowsing stick as they approached the well.

Looking over her shoulder, she said: 'You are sure this is not witchery?'

'Bah, no,' said Jacob. 'Even Father Jeremy uses one. We had a good chuckle together when he saw me locating the other wells. Now, let us see if you have the gift.'

Black slaves were now walking, some running, back to their quarters in the Caribbean sunshine. They had been locked up inside the church for three long hours and were eager to spend what was left of their free day as they pleased.

A band of barefooted youngsters skipped past them.

'M'sieur, M'dame,' they hurled out as they ran excitedly towards their usual play area beneath the leafy trees.

To think that these young wretches would live their whole lives in servitude brought a frown to Jacob's brow. Then again, perhaps they would not be unhappy after all. Perhaps they would find comfort in God's grace, he thought. At least, this way, their daily objectives in life would be clear. They would not become beggars, and they would not be hindered by ambition. Moreover, their own civilisation was very rudimentary, was it not? So perhaps this was the life that was meant for them. Was it not a lesser evil than remaining in ignorance of the Lord?

'Forgive them. They are excited,' said Marianne, sensitive to his fleeting change of mood.

'Oh, it is not that,' he said, waving the thought away like a fly. 'Right, hold the forked end lightly at the extremities. That's it. Now walk slowly towards the well.'

After a few slow strides, she said, 'My word, I can feel it moving.'

'Keep walking slowly.'

'Oh, look, my uncle—incredible. It is working—it is dipping.'

'The water vein is right under your feet then, my niece!' laughed Jacob, both proud and touched by her wonderment. There was still the little girl beneath the veil of budding womanhood. 'Now you know what to do if you get marooned on a desert island!'

By now a little group of slave women and their children had gathered around them to marvel at the magic, which always gave cause for wonderment.

A child of three or four wriggled down the hips of its young mother. The young woman was engrossed in the spectacle of the white girl learning magic—the same magic performed by the elders of her village in west Africa, just half a day's walk from the Youbou River. The little girl tugged at her mother's dress and pointed towards the slave shacks near the trees. She was thirsty.

Marianne walked in zigzags, experimenting with her amazing new power.

Two minutes later, Jacob looked up to see how far they were from the well, so that he could trace the trajectory of the underground water vein with his eye. Then he saw a little girl in a short-sleeved dress, running barefoot towards the well. It should have been covered over. But Jacob could see that it was not.

'My God, no! Stop the child!' he cried out. The little girl gave a glance over her shoulder as she toddled on; the next instant, she was gone. There was a short scream. The mother, seeing her daughter disappear into the ground, let out an agonising cry as she sank to her knees, clasping her face in despair. Jacob wasted no time in dashing to the gaping hole in the ground, thirty yards ahead. It was a fourteen-foot drop to the bottom, which was still plugged for the interior walls to be sealed, so it contained no water.

He braced himself, then looked over the rim.

The child let out a wail of shock, fear, and pain on seeing the face of the white man looking down from above. But at least she had survived the fall.

Without a second thought, Jacob ripped off his jacket, stepped into the well, and descended the wooden ladder.

As he approached the bottom, he saw the whites of the child's large eyes, staring fearfully up at him. 'Don't be afraid, my girl,' he said in the same soft voice he used when his own children had hurt themselves. 'Good girl, there's my sweet,' he said as he managed to squat astride her.

She was sobbing. 'Legs,' she said. 'Legs hurtin'.'

In the dimness of the well, Jacob felt her legs. Her scream of pain when he touched the limp right foot told him the lower right leg was probably fractured. He only hoped that was all the poor child had broken. He felt the rest of her tiny body, her pelvis, her ribcage, her arms.

'I'm going to take you to your mama, my girl. To Mama,' he said.

'Mama,' said the child. 'Wanna go home,' she sobbed.

'Yes, Mama's waiting. Now, tell me your name, my sweet.'

'Lulu,' said the girl, bravely swallowing another sob.

It was the pet name of his daughter, his darling little Louise, who died while he was incarcerated in France for his faith.

Was it the words, the emotion, the adrenaline? Or was it something else that made him suddenly feel ashamed? Down in that dark pit, he now saw through the fallacy of the slaveholder society. How could he, even for a single instant, have fallen for the false normality of servitude?

'My God, I have been blind!' he said to himself as he ripped off his belt and, looking up, cupped his hand to his mouth. 'Marianne!' he called. 'Marianne, throw me something I can wrap around her legs. A belt, some string, whatever is closest to hand.'

Two seconds later, a white woman's shawl was falling towards him. He fastened the belt around the child's legs below the knee amid little yelps of pain. But Lulu was very brave. He tied the shawl around her calves just above her feet, so that the wounded leg was fastened to the good one. Then he scooped up her crumpled body in his big hands.

'Good girl, Lulu,' he said, trying to reassure her. 'Such a brave girl. Now hold on tight, there's a good girl. And don't let go.' The child held onto his neck as if for dear life. He could feel her shivering, her soft skin against his neck, her woolly hair on his cheek. How brave she was for such a mite.

It was a changed man that Mademoiselle Duvivier saw climb out of the well. The anguish etched on his face was the anguish of a father.

'Marianne,' he said, panting from the ascent, 'I want . . .

you to fetch Monsieur Bourget . . . fast as you can. Tell him a child has broken her leg.' He then looked at the nearest slave and said, 'Bono, you go with her and bring back anything the doctor needs.'

'But, M'sser . . .'

'Don't stand there, man, run!'

The mother's relief was palpable as she put her hand on her child's head and mumbled reassurances in her native tongue. But the child kept hold of the white man who had told her not to let go, and he was already striding in the direction of the slave quarters.

'Come, Madame, take me to your hut,' he said to the mother.

Five minutes later, he was standing in a windowless hut. Its roof was covered in palm leaves, its walls made of wattle. He lay the child down on a wooden board where the mother had laid a woven palm-leaf mat. The bone had not broken through the skin, but the fracture was evident from the swelling. The child looked alert while her mother bathed her grazed face; she must have hit the wooden ladder, which must have broken her fall.

Jacob was examining the splinter in her hand where she must have grabbed the ladder rung, when there came a sudden commotion from the gathering crowd outside, and a raised voice.

'What in God's name is going on here!' thundered Monsieur Verbizier, lowering his head through the doorway.

Jacob, who had never seen the man in such a wicked mood, told him what had happened. The planter said he would have the bastard who left the well uncovered stripped and whipped.

'There is really no need,' said Jacob. 'She will be all right . . .'

'I'm not talking about the brat. I am talking about discipline, Sir! Give them a loose rein, and the place will be like a savage village in no time!'

Verbizier looked about him in disgust at the shack, where small dead birds were strung up to be roasted on the spit that evening. Jacob continued his examination, but the child began to tremble with a new fear and reached for her mother.

The planter continued: 'And what if a mill worker had fallen in? Then what, eh? We are hard put to finish the harvest as it is!' Turning to the doorway, where a crowd stood at a respectful distance, he hurled: 'If no one owns up, I'll have the lot of you thrashed!'

Jacob got to his feet. 'It was me,' he said. 'I was showing the well to my niece. You will have to flog me instead! Now leave us, I beg you, you are frightening the child!'

'What?' said Verbizier, who stood as stunned as if he had received a slap on the face.

'You are frightening the child! Now leave us, I pray,' said Jacob, seething now, though keeping his voice down so as not to scare the patient further.

Verbizier knew when a man was beside himself. He knew too when to retreat in order to get what he could out of a person before the relationship ended. Pity, he thought. Delpech would have made an excellent plant manager.

He gave the Huguenot a stern once-over, turned, booted a chicken out of the doorway, and stomped out with orders to cover the well before someone else fell down it.

Professor Bourget arrived seconds later, followed by Mademoiselle Duvivier, who was carrying a leather bag. The slave named Bono was behind her, carrying a chest which he put down inside the hut. It had been presented to the doctor to enable him to carry out chirurgical and medicinal work in the colony. Given his past career as a surgeon in the king's army, Bourget had acquired vast experience and had quickly become a respected figure in Leogane.

It was a clean fracture. But the surgeon had to open the area to remove bone debris. He then set the fractured ends of the bone in place so that it could properly mend. Next, asking Jacob to hold the lower leg firmly, he wrapped it in a bandage, placed a wooden splint beneath it, and bound everything together with tape ligatures. Lastly, he thrust other splints beneath the tapes all the way around the dressing, and then made sure they were tightly in place. Throughout the operation, the mother, whose name was Monifa, tried to comfort her daughter while Mademoiselle Duvivier held the child's arms. She writhed in pain before falling unconscious.

At the end of two hours, Jacob stepped outside into the bright afternoon light. He reflected on the fascinating view into the world of medicine, and the powers of knowledge the Almighty had given to man. He was sitting in the shade of a tree when the young black man named Bono came up to him. Jacob knew his name because he was one of the well diggers. The man gave a bow. Jacob rose to his feet as Bono said, 'Thank you, M'sser.'

Jacob, seeing the young man had tears welling in his eyes, realised with mortification his blunder. He said, 'You are the child's father.'

The man nodded.

'I am sorry,' said Jacob, touching the man's shoulder. 'I should have asked and sent someone else with Mademoiselle

Duvivier. You should have gone with your daughter. Please forgive me.'

Bono gave a brief nod, and with dignity, he said, 'I forgive you, M'sser, and I thank you.' Then he went back into the hut.

Jacob reeled the sequence of events through his mind like a magic lantern. The child's fall—the mother's collapse—the child's fear—the father's gratitude. How could he have been tricked into believing, even for a wicked second, that these people were any less human in any way, shape, or form than the white man? How dare he have doubted, even for an instant. He would never let himself become so base again.

He let himself slump against the tree and soon found himself pondering the Code Noir that Verbizier had spoken of. There was one article which he was glad of, article 47. It forbade husbands and wives from being separated from each other and their offspring. Delpech saw this as a fundamental right for all men and women of honourable intent.

'Monsieur Delpech, are you all right?' said a soft and spirited voice. It was the voice of Mademoiselle Duvivier. Jacob looked up and felt tears water his eyes.

He was grieving not only over his shame, but for his own child who had died without him, for his destitute wife who was now a refugee in a foreign land, and for his other children abducted in France. Who was watching over them now? he wondered.

7

THE ELEGANT FRENCH resident had summoned the fat syndic to his study. They were sitting on either side of the deep walnut desk that stood delicately and with solidity on scrolled feet in front of the bookcase crowded with leather-bound works of law.

'Ever since the council ordered the deacons to remove the wretched fugitives, there have never been so many of them in Geneva, Sir,' said the resident. 'How do you account for that?'

'It is as I said, my Lord,' returned Monsieur Gallatin. 'Now that April is upon us and the winter eviction truce is over, there are more departures than ever before. But there are also even more refugees entering through the city gates.'

'What am I to tell the king?' said the resident, leaning forward and pressing his fingers upon his desk.

Sinking his chin into his collar, the fat syndic said: 'With all due respect, my Lord, you might tell him to stop sending imprisoned Huguenot nobles from his kingdom so that he may confiscate their fortunes.'

'It is not to confiscate their fortunes, Sir!' said the resident, holding up a correcting finger. He got to his feet, gesticulating as he spoke. 'It is so that their fortunes, or want of, may bring them round to their senses.'

'But for the vast majority it does not seem to be working, my Lord,' said the syndic, remaining wedged in his armchair.

'That is beside the point,' said the resident, pouting his lips and striding away from the desk toward the tall window draped in blue velvet curtains, neatly retained either side by braided tie-backs with golden tassels. 'They have been banished as enemies of the state, a punishment which, I might add, they have brought upon themselves. And I may add that it is working . . . to a certain extent.'

'Yes, my Lord,' said the syndic, whose heavy jowls drooped with his doleful smile, 'but the extent to which it is not working far outweighs the extent to which it is.'

'Some have abjured,' said the resident, turning in defence. 'I receive demands every day from people desirous to return to France. And indeed, the king has generously welcomed them back into his fold. What is more, they have even recovered their fortunes and estates without incurring any penalty.'

'And yet there are tens, hundreds of incoming fugitives, my Lord.'

'And you have been invited time again to rid this city of the king's disloyal subjects, especially those who have been here for many months.'

'I take it you are referring to the poor who have nowhere else to go.'

'Yes. Along with the profiteers and the beggars who have taken advantage of your bourse to obtain free meals and money on a daily basis.'

'If you could provide us with a list, my Lord, of those who

have wintered here along with their address, then we shall be able to cooperate as we have always done.'

'I gave you a list the other day.'

'We expelled every one of them, my Lord.'

'Then why am I told they are back again?'

'Are you certain it is the same people, my Lord?'

'Why, yes, my people tell me so.'

'Then we shall act again. However, as you well know, we have not the resources to check every person who walks through the city gates; it would hinder trade. And if that happened, we would have a revolution on our hands!'

'I could ask the king to send a battalion of soldiers,' said the resident eagerly.

'I would rather not, my Lord. If we did, the gentlemen of Bern would not be amused. They would certainly attack our city, or defend it, depending on how you stand. It would lead to war, which would not sit well with the king, I am sure, what with the Dutch threat on his northern borders, you know.'

The resident found himself at an impasse, and it was all the king's fault. It now struck him how much he hated his royal posting, and the wretched city with all the harassment and jeering behind his back, especially from the in-laws. With searching eyes, he said: 'Then, I repeat, what am I supposed to tell the king?'

The syndic had seen it happen before to other men. Roland Dupré had put up a good fight, but Gallatin could now clearly see the resident was near his wit's end. With a reassuring smile, and in his deep voice of reason, he said, 'That we are doing everything we can to oblige his subjects to leave Geneva, except, of course, those of noble birth he has expelled, who might want time to ponder whether they should return to their homeland.'

'Good Lord, I shall be glad to see the back of this place of perdition!'

'We are doing our best, my Lord,' said the syndic contritely.

A quarter of an hour later, alone in his study, Roland Dupré poured himself a strong cordial. Blasted Genevans, he thought to himself, blasted king, blasted de Croissy. It was like being caught between a rock and a hard place. He had had enough of this farce; the whole matter was becoming like a scene in a play from that Moliere fellow. And whatever had gotten into him, he, the king's representative, marrying a local Protestant girl? She had converted, yes, and he still did love her, but you could not convert the in-laws, could you? It was the king's fault for sending him to such a hapless place in the first place, where there were no Catholic ladies.

He had tried so very hard to play the tyrant, firm against adversity, but how long was one person able to row against the current? More and more, he found himself longing to flee, as much from his in-laws as from the city itself. The floorboards creaked under foot as he advanced to the tall window. To think, he had been a young man insouciant, full of spirit and ambition, and with a full head of hair, when he first entered that great courtyard door all those years ago. His stance had since acquired a slight stoop, his clothing had become heavier, and his periwig had grown higher and thicker, as like his king, he had moved into middle age. As he watched the fat syndic ambling towards the great wooden door, he hoped to God, for the sake of his sanity and his half Protestant children, that he would not be refused the commission in Florence.

8

'WHERE ARE THEY all headed?' said Paul, standing with his mother at the open window of their first-floor accommodation on Molard Square. Behind them, Jean Fleuret, Ginette's husband, was fitting a new beater to Jeanne's loom.

She was gazing at the crowd waiting at the port quayside, at the far end of the square. Judging by the agitation, the flat-bottomed ship was now ready to take on board another load of fugitives, mostly country folk by the look of their garb and their stance, and a few ladies and gentlemen of quality.

These first days of April sunshine had prompted a new surge of mass departures, and for the past week passenger numbers had swollen, which in turn had increased the morning hullabaloo rising from the market below Jeanne's window. She did not mind the noise. On the contrary, the proximity of her lodgings to the port never ceased to give her reassurance. The hundred or so refugees began to board with their bundles and baskets, bags and pouches, but no heavy chests. Jeanne wondered how they would all fit aboard.

'Further north,' she said to her son at last, 'Lausanne, Bern, perhaps as far as Berlin.'

'There's some that goes as far as Holland too,' said Jean

Fleuret, punctuating his words with another tap of the mallet. 'There,' he said, 'that should hold good and proper this time, Madame Delpech.'

Pulling herself back from her window view, Jeanne thanked him and moved back to her loom.

He said, 'I've replaced the whole beam part this time, good as new now.'

Jean Fleuret had kept his word which he had given when he, his son Pierre, and Paul found Jeanne depleted in a chair in her room with her loom in pieces. He had made makeshift repairs at first and then replaced each splintered part over the ensuing weeks.

'I can't wait to try it,' said Jeanne, pulling up her stool. 'And how is your work at the Bourse?' She had put in a word for him when the deacon had mentioned they were lacking a woodworker.

'What with the spring and more and more people flooding through the city gates, there's every day more deceased to bury. Be they dead from accident or disease, their next of kin bring 'em here, see? I s'pose they can't very well bury 'em along the wayside, can they? Consequently, I spend a good deal of my time putting coffins together. That's where the wood for the beam came from. And at this rate there'll be hardly any room left in the cemetery for the residents, let alone fleeing Huguenots!'

'Have you decided upon your plans?'

'Aye, we reckon we don't wanna be outstaying our welcome now that spring is well in full bloom. And what with the king's resident, I doubt very much I'll be able to get a proper job of my trade here anyway. So we're definitely planning on pushing north.'

'Yes, I see.'

'Will you and Paul be coming, Madame?' said young Pierre, who liked to talk as an adult now that he was on the cusp of adolescence.

'I cannot say yet, dear Pierre,' said Jeanne, with a motherly smile.

'Any news of your husband?' continued Jeannot Fleuret.

'Alas, none.'

'Your sister?'

'Neither. But I shall wait here if I am able to.'

'You do so much, you deserve something back. Let us pray good news is on its way, Madame Jeanne. As for us lot, I reckon we'll be leaving in a few weeks, soon as the nights become less chilly. My Ginette does hate the cold, she does. And I've said it before, you and the boy are more than welcome to join us. The more the merrier, that's what we say, don't we Pierrot, me boy?' The boy gave a resolute nod.

Jeanne did not want to go further north; it would mean moving further away from her children who were taken from her in France. But deep inside, she knew she might soon have no choice, whether her sister had arrived or not, for the authorities were becoming more insistent for refugees who had wintered in Geneva to move on. And if it came to it, she would rather go with humble people she knew, people who had been of mutual support, than with a crowd of passing strangers, even those pertaining to her former social rank. How she had changed, she thought. So she was glad to hear that the Fleurets would not be leaving just yet. It would give her time, time to receive news from Jacob, time, she hoped, for her sister, her brother-in-law, and her children to join her in Geneva. However, for them to arrive in May would mean they would have left in late March, early April latest, which was probably hoping for the impossible. Then again, Robert had means. They would be travelling by carriage, stopping at inns.

'Thank you,' she said.

'I reckon it'll be hard going, mind.'

'I know. Some people prefer to return to France, even if it means abjuring.'

'How I see it is as soon as folk see that Geneva i'nt so much a haven as a stopover, they realise life ain't so easy in exile, and travelling ain't gonna be no Sunday stroll neither!'

Jeanne knew full well what the carpenter meant. Though a welcome refuge, Geneva was not a viable place to settle, not without guild approbation—unlikely for a Huguenot, let alone a woman. She herself had already paid the price for stepping over the line. Since the incident of her loom, she had not returned to the master tailor's boutique. She did not want to see the employees gloat; it would only make her mad, and she would not be able to hold her tongue. So, she had not started a successful enterprise. No, instead, she had kept to making fabric exclusively for fellow Huguenots and poor fugitives—fabric which she either delivered to Ginette or to Monsieur Binet, the official relief fund tailor.

Jeannot Fleuret gathered his tools into a leather shoulder pouch, and under his arm he tucked a roll of Montauban cloth which Jeanne had handed him for his wife to perform her magic on. He then took his leave with Pierre. She told Paul he could go with them as far as the fountain on the square in order to fill the leather water bottle, but then he must come straight back up without dawdling with the vendors' children.

'Don't worry, Madame Delpech, I'll see him back,' said Pierre as the three passed through to the landing.

Jeanne returned to the window to view her son, Pierre, and Jean Fleuret emerging from the street door by the bakery, and heading for the fountain among the market crowd. She glanced to her left, where the last migrants were boarding the ship, and where a family was scurrying, each with a sack, to join the end of the queue. In all the months she had been residing above the bakery on Molard Square, she had never seen a vessel loaded with so many people. Hardly could she see a flat surface unoccupied. It was quite frightening, and to think that this was just the beginning of the season.

A good thing the wind is soft and the weather clement, she thought to herself as she recovered her seat at her loom. To think of all those people in the same boat, courageously moving to a new life, carrying the same grief of never seeing their hometown again, put her own remorse into perspective. Images came of the peachy brick buildings of Montauban, the clear view from the Quercy ridge over the flat, fertile plain that reached all the way to the foothills of the Pyrenees. Then she pictured her children playing at their country house in summer. But she pinched the bridge of her nose to halt the subsequent flood of misgivings, then began threading to give herself something tangible to focus on.

A short while later, she found herself hoping again that Jacob would be among the released Huguenots from the king's prisons, and wondered with excitement what life would be like in London, Brandenburg, or Amsterdam. In this way, she was able to weave her sorrows and joys together, and alleviate the ache in her heart.

A familiar knock at the door interrupted her escapade into

the future. She pulled down the beater of the loom and went to the door.

'Pastor Duvaux. I was lost in my thoughts; I didn't hear you coming,' she said after opening the door.

'I have a letter for you, Madame Delpech.'

Jeanne let him into the room and offered him a seat at the small wooden table. She knew he was as eager as she was to know the contents of the letter, and he did not look as though he was ready to let her open it in her own time. But it was only fair, she conceded. He deserved as much as anyone to know her fate, after all he had done to make her comfortable, and the lengths to which he had gone to integrate her into Genevan society, insisting every Sunday that she join him with his Sunday guests at his table. And they had after all formed quite a robust partnership, organising accommodation, food, and clothing for the newly arrived and the needy. He was entitled to sit down at her table now, as a partner, a friend, and her pastor.

She sat down on the other side of the table where he had placed the letter. She briefly examined the handwriting and opened the folded sheet of paper.

'I was hoping it would be from Jacob,' she said out loud. The pastor kept his silence as she proceeded in reading her sister's note to herself.

My dear sister,

I send you news which I will develop further in a subsequent letter, but I want to get this off to you as quickly as I can, for I am told the messenger is shortly to take to the saddle. R has been taken ill. I know this will come as a terrible blow to you, but I cannot express it any other way: I fear we will not be able to travel. I cannot leave him on his own. I am so very sorry, my dear sister.

It will bring you no solace to know that Lizzy still refuses to leave Montauban. She says she will not leave her sister's grave unattended, so it may be just as well we cannot travel.

Before becoming bed-ridden, R found out that J did embark for the Americas, either for Martinique or Saint-Domingue, we believe.

My darling sister, I will write with details of R's ailment later, but I do fear for his life. I pray to God every day that you and my nephew have found a safe haven. Your darling baby brings us much joy; the first thing she does in the morning is go to your portrait. My dear sister, you will not be forgotten.

Remember me to the pastor.

Your loving sister

Jeanne sat gazing into mid-distance, her eyes glazed over. She was not conscious of how long she was staring like this and was only brought out of it by the pastor's gentle insistence.

'Madame Delpech, Madame Delpech . . .' She felt a hand touch her forearm, and at last she acknowledged his presence. He was standing, pouring out a glass of *fine* from a bottle he had brought with him. 'Drink this,' he said, handing her the drink. 'It will bring you back to yourself.'

She raised the earthen beaker to her lips and took a sip of the liquid, which stung her tongue and then her eyes, but then left a warming glow in the region of her chest.

'Madame Delpech,' said the pastor, sitting back down opposite her. He wanted to reach out to the lady, but he could only touch her with his words. She looked suddenly frail, her brow pleated, her eyes searching. What did she see when she looked back at him? he wondered. He continued. 'Madame Delpech, whatever your troubles, please know you will not be alone here in Geneva. There is a way for you to remain here.'

She read the discomfort in his expression, and she saw he knew full well she had understood the meaning between his words. She gave a short nod, her eyes expressing gratitude for his caring. She knew too that his heart was sincere. The implicit insistence to remain in Geneva did not shock her either. In fact, it gave her some comfort. Her mouth twitched into a fleeting smile, the frail smile of a vulnerable woman who knew not which way to turn should her husband never be seen in this world again.

Bolstered by her faint encouragement—the encouragement testified by her non-remonstrance—the pastor decided to venture further onto a terrain he had often visited in his dreams, ever since Jeanne Delpech first sat down at his table, like it was her rightful place, in his deceased wife's chair by the tiled stove.

'Jeanne, please do not think me too forward or inappropriate. But if for any reason your husband became . . . lost . . . then I want you to know that I would be honoured if you would become my wife. No, wait, please.' He held out his hands gently as if to ward off any reproach. Now that he was in train, he had to go all the way. 'I do say it with honourable intentions, Madame. It would simply mean that you and your dear boy would have a home here in Geneva. It would mean that one day, you might be able to welcome your other children here. And it would mean that I would have a ready-made family to cherish, that my dear late wife was unable to give me.'

'Thank you. Thank you for your thoughtfulness, Pastor Duvaux,' said Jeanne, breaking eye contact. An awkward silence followed, neither of them quite knowing how to conclude. Then, seconds later, they were rescued by Paul clomping up the stairs with a pouch full of water. She rose to her feet.

The pastor had put forward his point, and the lady had not shown outrage or disgust, only slight embarrassment now that her son was on his way up. He knew enough about human nature to see she was reassured. Now he could leave her in the peace of her thoughts, and in the secret hope that— should Monsieur Jacob Delpech de Castanet not live through his terrible ordeal—he would stand every chance of taking care of the merchant's widow and children, whom he would cherish as his own.

That afternoon, Jeanne sat at her loom, weaving yarn recovered from used clothes. The act of weaving carried her away from her deepest fears for her husband, and threaded them into the fabric of a new pattern of thoughts. The new, albeit sad, notion that at least she would be saved from becoming a homeless wretch softened the pain of her sister's news.

9

GIVEN PROFESSOR BOURGET'S grand age and gout, Jacob took it upon himself to make evening calls at the slave shack over the ensuing weeks. He also accompanied the doctor in his general practice so that he might learn some of the professor's techniques and remedies. In this way Delpech was able to assist with burns, fractures, dislocations, and other wounds.

He brought down the child's fever by giving her barley water and oil of vitriol, as described in his medical book and confirmed by the professor. When she was up and laughing again, he made a point of dropping by no more than a few minutes at a time.

Elias Verbizier let him do as he pleased. After all, the Huguenot was doing him a favour by saving the girl. If all went well, in nine or ten years' time, she would be breeding home-grown slaves. A new generation of workforce that would not cost a sou, and would not have memories of Africa to distract them into lassitude and suicide. Moreover, soon the planter would stop importing worthless indentured male whites who had a limited term. Instead, to respect the race quota imposed by Paris, he would buy up white females only and get them to breed with the blacks. If only his old mother back in La Rochelle could see him now, he often thought; she always said he had a head for business. In the space of a generation, he would have a massive plantation and his own workforce of mulattos.

Jacob busied himself more and more with overseeing the slave workers. He could intervene when the slave drivers—some of whom were black Africans themselves, though of a different tribe—lashed out unnecessarily. And Verbizier again, at first, let him have his way.

However, after some discussion with Father Jeremy, it became apparent to the planter that this form of soft resistance was healthy neither for the plantation nor for the settlement. He sensed a wind of rebellion could well create havoc among his labour force, for even the indentured workers were beginning to talk back to their overseers.

So, after numerous warnings and efforts from both planter and clergy, it was decided that Jacob Delpech was beyond redemption. And now that the new mill and the wells were practically finished, he would have to be disposed of.

But that was easier said than done. Were he a rebellious, run-of-the-mill black slave or an indentured white labourer, it would have been as easy as putting a mad dog out of its misery. Article 38 of the Code Noir clearly endorsed it. *Fugitive slaves absent for a month should have their ears cut off and be branded. For another month their hamstring would be cut and they would be branded again. A third time they would be executed.* But Jacob Delpech was a Huguenot, and a gentleman.

Even Monsieur Dumas, the governor's lieutenant, was at ends with what to do with the shit-stirrer. The man was making everyone uptight.

'I know what to do, Sir,' said Captain Renfort as he and Father Jeremy deliberated over the matter with the lieutenant governor in his office.

'What is that, Captain?' said Dumas.

'Execution, Sir. Spaniards do it all the time. Takes away the rotten apple and decontaminates the rest by example.'

'We could have him on a charge of heresy if that's any help,' said Father Jeremy, eager to find a solution, it being nearly time for lunch. 'He has been blatantly divining in full sight of everyone.'

'He was searching for water, Father?' said Monsieur Dumas.

'Indeed, Sir, but it is still considered as witchery.'

'But you yourself have used one, Father,' said Captain Renfort.

Father Jeremy stared indignantly at the blockhead who was not getting the hint, and said, 'I am only trying to help, Captain!'

'I was thinking we could have him up for unlawfully assembling with that niece of his,' said Captain Renfort. 'I have a full report of their heretic movements and actions.'

'Yes,' said the lieutenant governor, pushing himself back in his mahogany chair, 'but that would mean burning him at the stake, as well as all those involved. It would stir up feelings.'

'I agree,' said Father Jeremy, raising an eyebrow slyly at the lieutenant governor, 'that's the last thing we want. There are far too many former Protestants here in the Antilles.'

Removing his hand from his chin, Monsieur Dumas said, 'I have an idea. Leave it with me.'

10

JEANNE SAT AT the sturdy kitchen table, cut out of a single piece of trunk. It stood solidly on trestles, and its edges were bevelled, the corners rounded. It perfectly illustrated the Fleuret family's abode and their nature, robust and effective, thought Jeanne.

She was half-turned towards Ginette, who was preparing flageolets in a copper pan at the sink, which was a hollowed-out stone slab with an outlet that channelled water through the stone wall. The fire smouldered and cracked in the deep hearth, and both women were rosy-cheeked, in the little cottage near the sawmill down by the river.

'You'll be eating with us, Madame Jeanne?' said Ginette.

'I wouldn't hear of it, what with all your preparations.'

'Preparations? Far as I can see, you're the one double-threading the buttons!'

'Well, it's no time to be giving you two extra mouths to feed.'

'Get away with yers. You ought to know by now no one escapes Ginette's kitchen without breaking bread and a warm bowl of stew inside of 'em! Besides, it's as much work for five as it is for seven!'

'All right then,' said Jeanne with a laugh, secretly glad to be with the Fleurets on their last day in Geneva. She had grown fond of going there to spin or to sew while Paul helped at the mill with Pierre. Ginette then changed the subject, as she often did to give vent to her thoughts.

'Do you really think Madame Rouget was a lady's maid?' she said, with large eyes.

'If she says so. Why?'

'Well, I think she was more a washerwoman. A lady's maid is chosen for her finesse, and Madame Rouget's got forearms like skittles. Haven't you noticed?'

Jeanne could only laugh. She would certainly miss their sessions and Ginette's exuberant talk about the church ladies.

'And what about the pauper?' said Ginette, pouring the washed flageolets onto a linen cloth.

'The who?' said Jeanne, already with a smile parting her lips.

'Monsieur Crespin. I call him the pauper 'cause he's got that scrounger's look about him.'

'Ginette! You are being unfair. He helps a lot, and he always takes the cloth from me so I don't have to carry it.'

'Yeah, does the same with my Jeannot, turns up to help just before lunchtime. That's what they do, you know, paupers, tramps, and profiteers. They make themselves useful just at the right time; then they get a free meal.'

'You are being harsh, Ginette. He used to be a woodworker, a cooper, I believe.'

'Jeannot says he's plenty resourceful and even useful, but a carpenter he's not.'

'Neither am I a proper weaver, and you might also say I've just turned up for a meal.'

'Get away with you!'

'Anyway, I'm just sorry it might well be our last together,' said Jeanne. 'There.' She placed the coat on a chair with a pile of other over-garments whose buttons she had reinforced. The humble abode with its functional furniture, and its bed alcoves in a bit of a shambles, might not be how Jeanne would have organised it, but it had Ginette's homeliness and her take-me-as-you-find-me feel about it. Jeanne then took up her own green coat and turned it inside out.

'And you and your boy, Madame Jeanne,' said Ginette, 'what are you going to do?'

Jeanne did not know what she was going to do. Her means to create revenue had been removed when the authorities had told her to sell her loom or risk having it seized. 'I am all at sea to be honest,' she said, scrutinising the stitching of the lining of her coat. 'Wait and hope. That is what I shall do.'

'That green coat of yours, I don't know how many times I've seen you darning it.'

'Strengthening it, Ginette.'

'Whatever. I will never forget the first time I saw it, like a song of hope, and I knew we would be all right. And I am not the only one. So, my dear Madame Delpech, if it don't bring you hope when it's been a ray of goodness for so many of us, then I say t'ain't fair!'

'I shall miss you too!' said Jeanne, pausing her needlework to look up with a smile.

'I s'pose it isn't bad at all at the vicar's, but if you choose otherwise, there's still time to come along with us.'

Ginette's empathetic nature lent itself to confidences, and Jeanne had confided in her about the pastor's proposition, which he had reiterated. Now that she had lost her loom, he insisted that she take up residence at the vicarage until news came of her husband, especially as she now only had the revenue from spinning. Jeanne knew the pastor's offer to be honourable and sincere; however, she had so far refused. Otherwise, it would be like giving up on her husband, and by the same token, on her children.

She said, 'As much as I would like to, I cannot leave yet.'

'You know,' said Ginette, 'you have to let go, my dear lady, let go of your departed child. She is with God now, is she not?'

Ginette had hit the nail on the head, as she so often did. It was true; Jeanne felt that going a step further than Geneva would be physically removing herself further from her living children left in Montauban, and her dear Louise's and Anne's graves.

Pouring the flageolets into the cauldron of ragout hooked over the fire, Ginette continued, 'Your children will be with you in spirit and in your heart, whether you are in Geneva or Siberia.'

'God forbid,' said Jeanne, trying to hide her emotion under a jest, but Ginette was not duped.

After replacing the lid on the fat pot, she turned around to face Jeanne and said, 'Distance won't keep them from your mind. That is how I was able to leave Aigues-Mortes. My dearly departed children are all alive. They are with God, they live in my memories, and they are also here,' she said, patting the top side of her left bosom.

'Thank you, Ginette,' said Jeanne, 'but you have your husband to urge you on. I do not.'

'But I still often feel insecure, and afraid. We know not where we are setting our feet. But whenever the dark thoughts come on, especially at night, I try to force them to one side, because fear is a gnawing demon. It will suck all the puff out of your sails if you let it, till you lose all will to move forward. So, I decided I wouldn't let it. I decided I'll always travel with hope in my heart and God as my guide. My dear Jeanne, do we have any other choice?' she said, suddenly overcome with emotion.

Jeanne put down her coat to one side, got to her feet, and took her friend in her arms. 'Are you saying I am weak, Ginette Fleuret?' said Jeanne with false comedy, to show she was not offended.

'Oh no,' said Ginette drying her eyes with her pinafore. 'You are the strongest woman I've ever met. You can make a golden cloak out of a cast-off robe, you can make order where there's chaos, and you are as brave as they come. No, my dear, but allow me to say that you are only human, and you may have felt weak at some stage. But you must keep striving forward in hope. I say only this: live in hapless hope and fall into despair, or help yourself and God will help you.'

'I admit it is not always so easy. At the moment, I know not if my husband is dead or alive.'

'He's alive and kickin' in your heart, is he not?'

Before Jeanne could answer, the door burst open and in walked Pierre and Paul, followed by the pauper carrying a basket of wood cuttings and cones.

'When you talk of the wolf, eh . . .' said Ginette in a low voice, while Jeanne cast her a look of reproach.

'Good day, Mesdames,' said the pauper cheerfully and smiled at Jeanne, standing with her green coat still over her arm. 'Monsieur Fleuret told me to bring these down to the house,' he continued. He then proceeded to pour his load into the basket at the hearth so that it would not be empty in case they were delayed. 'Have you heard? There's news of a ship lost off the shores of Martinique, all but a few lost to the sea, they do say.'

*

It was ridiculous, and totally out of character, but Pastor Duvaux had to know. The track lined with tender-leaved trees meandered round, and at last he could see the house near the mill, half-screened by a weeping willow. Paul playing in the distance with Pierre and his sisters, Rose and Aurore, confirmed what the baker's wife had told him, that she was helping the Fleurets down by the river. As he approached in his black soutane, he suddenly felt conspicuous and foolish, even though the children had not noticed him yet. He checked his step as if he had forgotten something.

'Turn back, you fool,' he said to himself.

But if he had been seen en route, how would he explain it if asked at church what he had been doing there? It wasn't as if he could present himself at another house either; they were few and far between on that side of the river. And the letter he had come to deliver to its addressee had travelled far. There was no reason that the news it carried could not wait another few hours. It now seemed obvious to him that the very act of bringing it so far out of his way made him look desperate. Yet he had to know.

He had thought up a story, to save face. He was on a visit to the Fleurets to thank them for their support; he had received the letter and thought he would take it along. That was the pretext that had driven his stride this far. But these people were not stupid. Where had he put his common sense?

He now admitted freely to himself that he had left it in his heart, for he was in love. And love was now so near. 'Stupid, stupid, silly old fool!' he told himself as he realised he could not take another step forward. He was about to turn back when there came a voice from behind.

'Ah, Pastor. What brings you so far this side of the river?' It was Jeannot Fleuret. He was carrying a pair of snared rabbits slung over his shoulder.

'Monsieur Fleuret, ah, you quite made me jump.'

'Going down to the house, are ye, Pastor? Madame Delpech is there.'

'No. Yes. As a matter of fact, I thought I would call in on yourself and your good wife, to thank you for all your efforts. I rarely get enough time at church what with so much toing and froing, you know.'

'I see, Pastor. Well, that's jolly nice of you.'

They began to amble down to the house.

'When are you leaving, Monsieur Fleuret?'

'Tomorrow, weather permitting. And that's if we can get on the boat.'

'Yes, I am afraid they do get packed. I have asked the syndic to lay on more.'

'Oh, they have, Sir. It's just what with the mild weather, everyone's got the same idea, haven't they? It was bad enough in April. But now, the days are longer and the nights not so cold . . . And everyone wants to get to Brandenburg before the grand elector pops his clogs.'

'Actually, I believe he has.'

'Oh?' said Fleuret. 'Are you the bringer of bad news, Pastor?'

'Oh no, I wouldn't let it worry you. His son is as

vehemently against your king as was his father before him.'

'Ah,' said Jeannot, reassured.

A few minutes later, they were met by the children outside the door. Jeannot opened it and offered the pastor to enter in front of him.

'Oh, Gigi, look who's come to visit.'

The two ladies inside had turned the moment the door was pushed open.

'Pastor Duvaux, what a surprise to see you here,' said Ginette. 'I expect you've come to check on Madame Delpech,' she continued. She did not keep her tongue in her pocket at all.

'As I was telling your husband, I was on my way here anyway to bid you farewell. Though it is true, the baker's wife did mention Madame Delpech might be here, I thought . . .' He paused as it suddenly dawned on him that this was neither the time nor the place.

Locking her eyes on him, Jeanne said, 'Pastor, is there something the matter?'

'Goodness gracious, no, not as such. You have received a letter, Madame, that is all.'

'Do you have it?'

'As a matter of fact, I do,' he said, bringing out the letter from his pouch. 'Thoughtless of me. I should have thought you might like to read it alone, in your own time.'

Jeanne had been waiting for this moment, had been praying for it. 'You can hand it to me here. We are with friends,' she said. She knew she might have to face up to a catastrophe. But if catastrophe there was, she would rather know sooner than later—and she would rather be surrounded by friends.

She took the letter. On focussing her eyes, she instantly saw it was not the hand of her husband. Her heart sank; neither was it the hand of her sister. A stranger's hand had written this. Was it to notify her of a tragedy? She closed her eyes, then slipped the knife Ginette handed her beneath the Dutch seal.

Inside the letter, she found another one which made her take her seat on the chair in front of the table. Again she slipped the knife under the seal. It was the seal of Jacob, the one he carried in his writing case. With her hand to her mouth to avoid the show of emotion, she scanned the first words—*Cadix, La Marie, Islands, London, when I escape* . . . These were the words her eyes stumbled over.

'Seigneur!' she said, 'Oh, Lord. It is Jacob. He writes from Saint-Domingue! He is alive!'

'Dear God, hope. There's hope for you, my dear,' said Ginette.

The pastor stood holding his hat, a forlorn smile of defeat on his face. 'That is good, Madame, but pray,' he said with feeling, 'what is the date on the letter?'

'It matters not. All I care is that it is his hand that ran across it. For all I know, he is already on his way to London,' she said, and took her son in her arms. 'That is where we must go!'

'But, dear Madame,' said the pastor gently, 'look at the date.'

'The twenty-seventh day of February.'

'Is it wise to travel now? I mean, without confirmation.'

'It is neither wise nor reasonable. But my dear, kind Pastor Duvaux, this is stronger than reason, it is hope! And to do nothing is to waste it, is it not?'

11

THE LIEUTENANT GOVERNOR of Leogane had spent a restless night being jabbed by mosquitoes, followed by a whole morning deliberating how to dispose of the Huguenot without rousing suspicions. In his agitation, he had scratched the bites on his inner thigh, making them worse. He was in no mood for compromise when he summoned Delpech and his niece that afternoon to his office.

'Sir, I have no explanation to give you.'

'But—'

'You are condemned to leave, or face a more serious charge!' said the lieutenant governor to the Huguenot, who was standing on the other side of his desk.

Did the man not realise he was doing him a favour? In fact, he was saving his bloody life, and that of his 'niece' to boot. He had enough on them to have them both roasted for heresy. However, Lieutenant Dumas prided himself on being a gentleman of honour, loathe to have more killings under his jurisdiction than was strictly necessary.

To the left of Delpech stood Marianne Duvivier. Behind them stood two soldiers waiting to escort the prisoners out.

Dumas opened the drawer in front of him and took out

three folded, wax-sealed letters, which he laid out one by one on his desk. Pointing successively to the handwritten documents, he said, 'These are your orders. One for the boat that leaves this night for Petit Goave. This, for passage aboard *La Charmante,* which will take you to Cow Island. As soon as you make landfall, hand this one to the commander of the island, Major de Graaf. He will arrange accommodation for you.' Dumas got to his feet. 'Take them. I wish you fair winds.' He nodded to his men to escort the Huguenots out.

'May the Lord be your guide, Sir,' said Jacob, picking up the orders and turning to Marianne, who was standing beside him. But she stood firm.

She said, 'Sir, have you news of my grandmother?'

Dumas looked levelly at the young lady who stood unflinchingly before him. She was clever, her clear voice was a model of articulate wisdom, and he was not insensitive to her becoming appearance. In truth, he was sorry to see her go. But Dumas was also a pragmatic man, and go she must, for she would never marry a Catholic, and so never bring forth new blood to the colony.

'Mademoiselle,' he said sternly, to stress his ascendance over youth and the fairer sex, 'you would do well to learn to speak when spoken to.' He knew it was the wrong thing to say the instant it slipped out.

'If I did, Sir, then I would never know what has become of my only family,' she said, indomitable as ever. 'Surely you can tell me if *La Concorde* made landfall or not. My grandmother is Madame de Fontenay of—'

'I know her name,' said the lieutenant governor, raising a hand to stop her discourse. It was typical of the young woman. Would she never let up? 'I have already told you, I will send news to you in due course. My word is as good as my bond. Now, good day to you, Mademoiselle, Monsieur.' With a lordly flick of the hand, he signalled again to his men to accompany the prisoners out.

*

An hour later, Jacob was standing in the study of the planter's residence. It was past five o'clock. The afternoon heat had abated. Monsieur Verbizier was holding, of all things, a *toise,* which was a measuring stick of the length of one toise, or six French feet. He was showing Delpech another one of his tricks which, he was proud to say, adroitly summed up his philosophy on life. He was determined to give the gentleman another demonstration of his superior reasoning and perhaps leave him wondering how the son of a rope maker had made a success in Paradise, and how Jacob, the son of a physician, now lived in poverty.

The long wooden stick was graduated with notches representing inches, of which there were seventy-two, there being twelve inches to a French foot.

'So, Delpech, if this toise represents a man's life and each inch a year, this is where you are in your life right now. Provided, of course, you live to seventy-two.' Verbizier planted a thick digit on a notch which corresponded to the forty-second inch. 'So, this part represents what life there is remaining to you,' he said, indicating the space on the rod above the forty-second inch.

'Fascinating,' said Jacob. 'It certainly puts it into perspective. Thank you for showing me, Monsieur Verbizier.'

'Not a great deal, you will agree. So you may as well make it fruitful, my good fellow. I hope you shall seriously think the matter over. It might help you see reason yet.'

'I shall, Sir, I shall. And I should hope you do too.'

'Do what, Sir?'

'Seriously think the matter over. Because if I understand rightly, this is where you are on the toise of life, provided you live to seventy-two, of course. For you could die of a seizure tomorrow; God only knows.'

Delpech placed an index finger six inches above where Verbizier had put his. Indicating the space to the end of the rod, he said, 'And this is how much time you have left to save your soul, my good fellow! Good luck, Monsieur Verbizier.'

A few minutes later, Jacob was setting off down the track towards the township for the last time, with his escort in tow.

*

As he marched ahead of his escort between the neatly laboured fields, flanked by luxuriant jungle vegetation, Jacob admired the dazzling view. Set against the westering sun and the beautiful teal-blue sea, it could well have been a tableau of Paradise.

However, on one side, there were rows of men hacking down cane stalks and stripping them of their leaves; women piling them onto carts; carts being hauled away by oxen. As Jacob passed, some slaves dared to cast their eyes his way. The white water diviner had been good to them. Jacob gave a half nod, but then a barrage of insults, like a bark of triumph, heralded the crack of the whip. Jacob halted, turned, and protested to the black slave driver, but through pure insolence, the man cracked his whip again as the armed escort pushed Jacob onward.

On the other side of the plantation, he saw women clearing away new land, building retaining walls and planting poles. Verbizier had told Jacob the plantation was set to double its workforce in just two years. But how? If, God forbid, everyone in the French colony had the same obsession with sugar, it would take the population of an entire country to harvest the crop and work the mills.

He passed the mill, where unspeaking workers were feeding the diabolical crushing machine with cane. What did they think of? Home, most likely. And like Jacob, they yearned for their freedom, to put meat in the pot for their families, to dance on fete days, to hear women sing and their elders tell tales of old. The liberty to recall their past lives—among buffalos, tigers, and giraffes in ancestral forests, vast plains and great watering holes—was the only sanctuary left to them. Their minds were their only escape now, Jacob realised, but for how long? In a generation, even these memories would be gone.

Verbizier's banning chatter and song while feeding the machine had not helped the workers focus their minds on their labour at all. More lives had already been lost. Was it any wonder that these men were accident prone? But were they? A downcast moment in the day, the slip of a hand, and their torment was over. How horrible. At least, on Jacob's advice, now the cane feeders were allowed to alternate with the ox driver to get them out of the seat of temptation. No, this was not Paradise.

A pretty domestic slave girl strolled wearily by him on her way up to the big house. She was carrying two dead hens in a basket. Though she must have been no more than thirteen, Jacob noticed her belly had grown considerably since he first came to the plantation. She used to be a favourite of Verbizier, full of smiles and bubbling with life. She glanced at Jacob for a fleeting moment, then at the soldier behind him, before casting her eyes downward and walking on.

He would miss the child. She had given him a cause in

this godforsaken place. She was walking again; she was brave. How long would she live before her smile was stolen from her too? Had his time here counted for anything at all? A few lashings averted, perhaps, but that was already in the past. Would these black men and women remember that a white man had not accepted their condition of servitude? Or would their bitterness and hatred for all white men grow in their hearts and in those of their children?

He wished he could say goodbye to the child, at least to leave a seed in her memory, in her heart. But his escort had strict orders. The Huguenot was to retrieve his effects and go directly to the port. He was to see no one.

But then he saw the child's mother. Monifa was working in the indigo field. As he passed her by, she raised her head, then placed her free hand over her mouth. She was twenty yards away from him. They locked eyes for a brief, telling moment. Then he looked straight ahead again. He did not want her to feel the tongue of the whip.

He passed parallel to the last well, which was protected by a circular wall, as they all were now. He had deliberately placed this one as close as possible to the slave quarters so that the women and children would not have to carry the water so far. But he knew their shacks could be shifted at any time as needs befit the expansion of the plantation.

He prayed inwardly that these people would find God's peace one day. Otherwise, what justice would there be in the world?

*

Two hours later, Jacob gave his first order to the skipper of the small cargo boat.

Huguenots were not allowed to congregate. But Madame Grosjean and Professor Bourget had braved the restriction to wave Delpech and Duvivier off. Marianne bade a tearful farewell. Jacob was about to offer the address of his house on the Quercy plain, all those leagues away. But then he remembered he no longer had an address to give.

'May God be with you, my friend,' said Professor Bourget. 'I shall watch over Madame Grosjean with Madame Colier,' he said to Marianne.

'And I shall watch over the doctor,' said Madame Grosjean, leaning on her cane.

Something in the surgeon's expression told Jacob he had resigned himself to his fate, that he would die here on the coast of Saint-Domingue, thousands of leagues from his homeland, like so many others. However, the esteemed professor seemed content with the consolation of the simple but jovial company of the old lady.

They embarked and cast off, waving as they left the township walls behind them, and sailed into the encroaching night.

The little vessel, rigged with a single sail, advanced slowly at first along the channel that led into the roadstead. Jacob scanned the shore to his left. Then he saw her. Lulu in her mother's arms, and Bono was there too, all waving.

Heavy-hearted but relieved to see them, he waved back. 'God be with you, my friends,' he called out. 'May God give you strength, Monifa, Bono, Lulu,' he shouted, waving harder. 'Goodbye. Goodbye, my friends . . . Goodbye, Lulu! Goodbye, Lulu!' They soon became a huddled shadow and were engulfed by the darkness.

This could well have been Paradise. But it was not.

12

WERE HE A Catholic, Pastor Duvaux would have made the sign of the cross three times over.

But he was not, so he closed his eyes and prayed to God to give the boat safe passage. At least they would not be going out in the middle; they would be hugging the coast, he thought to himself. He had been helping Jeannot and Cephas lug the baggage aboard.

The boat to Lausanne via Morge was packed mostly with French refugees and their spartan baggage and knapsacks. Below deck was already packed solid. Above deck, families were staking their claim to every flat sheltered surface while trying to take refuge from the infuriating gusts of wind that made the gentlemen hold on to their hats and pulled wisps of hair from under ladies' bonnets. Some of the travellers had already begun breaking their bread and slicing dried sausage, for it was already past midday. The departure had been delayed because of a dispute.

Those at the end of the queue had been told they would have to wait for the next boat. For a good number of them, that meant having to wait another three days. So, having no place to stay, they remonstrated and pleaded.

'All right, I can take a dozen more,' the captain had said, in spite of protests from regular passengers from Morge. 'Long as you don't complain about seating arrangements, cause there ain't none!' The captain had given a loud roar into the wind that rivalled the cries of gulls and gestured to his men to let the remaining passengers board.

'Why does she always have to carry so much?' grumbled Jeannot, lugging another bagful of provisions.

'For the children, who do you think!' Ginette called back.

The pastor opened his eyes. Amid the assortment of people in their diversified garb, he saw the distinct green coat of Jeanne Delpech again. She was approaching after arranging a corner for her things on the lee side. Her smile was intelligent, sublime, and resolute, he thought.

'You should be in Morge in about three days if this wind keeps up,' he said, picking up the thread of their conversation.

'I shall miss Geneva, and my little rooms,' said Jeanne, with a smile. 'And I shall miss our outings.'

The pastor simply bowed his head in acquiescence.

Jeanne continued, 'But now you must start your life anew, Pastor.' He gave a smile. He was glad she said it. She was implying that she knew that his feelings for her had brought to the surface emotions that his wife's death had nullified. It was like a benediction to live again.

'I have much to do, as you well know, Madame Delpech. Summer is soon upon us. And frankly, I won't know which way to turn now that I have no one to lean on.'

'There will be another to take up the flame, I am sure.'

'Not like you, though. But you are right to move on, my dear Madame Delpech.'

'Thank you, and may the Lord bring you happiness.'

He mirrored her smile and took her hand with thanks. The Fleurets and Paul joined her in their farewells.

'My goodness, I nearly forgot!' he said, reaching inside his cape. 'Here. You must take these; you will need them on your travels.' He had made out an attestation for each family, and one even for Crespin, to enable them to travel on without hindrance.

He disembarked, and waved and nodded to other passengers who had known him through the church. It was a lone man, however, who stood on the lake wharf, but a man with perhaps a new lease of life. An odd thought occurred to him standing there: he could never have become a Catholic priest.

The main sail flapped in the wind, the lake surface was full of watery humps, but the captain, to the general relief, ordered the moorings to be detached.

'I do wish this wind would ease up, though,' said Ginette, glancing dubiously at the sky while tucking wisps of hair beneath Rose's bonnet.

'I am sure everything will be fine, with God's grace,' said Jeanne, doing likewise to Ginette's other daughter, Aurore, while Pierrot and Paul stood leaning over the side, waving.

'Oh aye, I'm sure you're right, because I'm not particularly in any hurry to meet Him just yet, are you?' said Ginette with a little chuckle.

The dockers, with burly, weather-browned forearms, released the lines, and the flat-bottomed vessel carrying forty-three passengers was soon setting sail north-eastward.

*

Goodness knows what it must be like on the open sea, thought Jeanne, remembering how Jacob was loathe to travel over water, as she covered her son with a blanket. The Fleurets were huddled next to them, the youngest children sleeping upon sacking placed on the decking. A number of passengers had already felt the effects of the Joran that swept off the slopes of the Jura, and which bunched up the waves that made the boat roll.

They passed Versoix, which was French territory; then they sailed on to the waters of Coppet, where they anchored as evening encroached. The lamps were turned on above and below deck, and despite the constant pitch, folk lay down their heads to sleep. The wind, however, fell off completely after dark, and the whiplashes against the mast became nothing more than a rattling in the rigging amid the ghostly sounds of cracking timbers.

Clouds scurrying by in the grey light of morning, and the faraway sight of vineyards on slopes, were what met the voyagers as they rubbed sleep from their eyes.

'That be French territory, just over that ridge,' said one man, a merchant from Morge, nodding and yawning towards the distant hills.

'Too close for comfort, I say,' said Jeannot Fleuret, chewing on his pipe while sitting on the port-side steps.

The wind that obeyed neither man nor beast picked up, despite the merchant's promise that the Joran wouldn't blow till evening.

'Whoa, steady as she goes!' he cried out as the ship seemed to dip into a deep trough and rise up again unexpectedly. Over the ensuing half hour, the dreaded Joran did pick up dramatically and now sent powerful gusts bowling into the square sail of the vessel.

Jeannot and the merchant were still sitting on the port-side steps when all of a sudden, a gush of cold lake water sprayed over the rim of the boat. Jeanne, Ginette, and the children, who were huddled together still half in slumber, let out screams of alarm. Some of the passengers shot up onto their feet. But the mountain wind that skimmed across the deck in quick successive gusts knocked some of them off balance, causing them to slip over, which brought an explosion of nervous laughter from some of the onlookers. However, any mirth was immediately dampened as another wave bowled over the side of the boat, then another.

Very quickly the lower deck was ankle deep in water. From the sombre hatch, the sound of frightened people replaced that of grunts and groans. Jeanne moved back from the dripping rim and held on tightly to her son; Ginette followed suit and pulled her clutch together around her. Jeannot, who had pocketed his pipe and risen to his feet, looked around from the steps to catch the captain's eye.

'She's too heavy, man,' he hollered. 'She's too low in the water. Let loose some cargo!'

'Nobody move, and she'll hold,' bayed the captain at the bar.

But the impetuous merchant at Jeannot's side was quick to pull out a knife. The next minute, he was cutting into the tethers of a batch of barrels.

'No, stop him!' yelled the captain. Jeannot understood the immediate danger. It was the wrong side to lighten the load, but it was already too late. With the next dip into the trough of a wave, four barrels went rolling overboard, causing the boat to suddenly bank to starboard.

Jeannot staggered over to port side with the intention to lighten the load there to counterbalance the merchant's error.

But the slippery deck, the tilt of the boat, and the gusts of wind sent him bowling against the side of the vessel, along with the merchant and several other passengers. Then the boat was lifted by a rising mound of water. Those on port side slid to starboard, and with the further shift in weight, the unthinkable became imminent.

Jeanne, who had managed to lodge herself with Ginette and the children under the port-side steps, shrieked out: 'If we go over, hold on to something that floats, children, and don't let go!'

No sooner said than the mountain wind slipped under the flat-bottomed hull and seemed to catch hold. It began heaving the boat over, sending merchandise, passengers, and crew overboard into the cold, cold water. Screams of women and terrified cries of children echoed from the hatch leading to the lower deck.

In those desperate seconds, Jeanne could not decide if they should hold on and hope the boat would become right again, or let themselves slide to the side that was taking in water and attempt to grab hold of a cask. Then she saw the dinghy being released and Cephas Crespin leaping into it. But as the glimmer of hope presented itself, to her horror she lost hold of her son, who went sliding inexorably towards the starboard now under water. Barrels and parcels rolled and tumbled freely, some clobbering people, making them fall unconscious into the lake that was whipped into a frenzy by the erratic wind sweeping down from the Jura. Young Pierrot, seeing his friend go, purposely let himself slide across the deck in his pursuit.

Jeanne would have jumped after him too, but she knew Pierre, like his sisters, was used to jumping off the jetty in

Aigues-Mortes and knew how to swim. Pierrot managed to grab Paul by the scruff of the neck after they hit the water. A cask landed beside them, as under the force of the wind and the waves, the boat continued to capsize. The girls and the ladies went sliding to their fate amid screams of terror as people hauled themselves out of the hatch turned into a death-trap.

Jeanne could not swim. But as she instinctively reached for the water's surface, her hand caught a floating punt used to push the barque away from the quay. It barely allowed her to float, but it sufficed to let her break the water's surface.

'Paul! Paul! Paul!' she screamed out, as the ghastly sight of lifeless bodies bobbed amid the tumultuous waves around her. She could not die now, after all she had been through; did it all mean nothing? Her strength was failing her, and she began thinking that if her son had drowned, it would be easier to let herself go too rather than endure the agony of his loss. At least she would be with him. But how? How would she find him in heaven? In her confusion and fear, she cried out: 'God help me, please!'

Rising up with another great wave, she quickly scanned her watery surroundings again, and this time caught a glimpse, she was sure, of her son holding onto a cask.

She was about to call out despite the penetrating cold that froze her jaw muscles, but her throat suddenly tightened. She began to choke from an invisible force, until it pulled her out of the water and she saw the edge of a rowboat. She realised she was being yanked out, and like a drowning cat, she scratched for a hold on the boat until, with an unceremonious tug at her bottom, she was hoisted aboard. Moments later, looking up, it was the pauper she saw, who was now letting the sopping body of an inert woman slip back into the lake. Inside the boat, she saw a pile of coins and rings.

She pretended not to take in the scene and, catching her breath as another cold cloak of water splashed over her back, she cried, 'Over there, please, my son.' Cephas Crespin held her gaze a moment. 'Please!' she beseeched. Then he put his back into the oars, while Jeanne focussed her remaining force on shouting to her son to keep holding on.

Paul was holding Pierre with his arm under his friend's chin, while desperately clasping the cask with his other arm.

'Pierrot . . . got hit . . . help!' he cried out, desperately trying to keep his friend's head above the water.

The pauper approached, pulled Pierre, inert, half into the boat, and felt in his pockets. Jeanne anticipated what he was about to do.

'My God, don't you dare!' she growled.

'He's dead. No point.'

'You don't know that. Get him aboard! Get them both, I tell you!' said Jeanne, who quickly slipped off her ring.

'Take it!'

'I'll take 'em both if you give me your coat and everything inside it,' bawled the pauper above the din. Was it Providence that put it into his hands now? He just had to take it with all its weighted lining.

'Get them in first!' said Jeanne, with fire in her eyes.

The pauper hauled in Pierre, then reached for Paul who, the moment he hit the bottom of the boat, was out cold.

Amid the turmoil, Jeanne placed the lads front down on the bench in an effort to bring them round.

By this time, help was arriving in the shape of rowboats manned by villagers. They were fast approaching the capsized vessel. The pauper, without looking for more survivors, put his back into the oars under cover of the grey light of morning, and within fifteen minutes they were within wading distance to the stony shore.

'Now give it to me!' said Cephas.

Distraught at the boys, who would not respond to her frantic attempts to bring them round, Jeanne reached in her pocket and brought out a handful of coins. 'I have nothing more,' she said. 'Now help me get them to shore!'

'I don't mean your bloody silver, woman!' he said. 'Give me yer coat!'

'I have nothing more in it!'

'You ain't foolin' me, you toff!' The man then lunged for her. Screaming, she kicked and fought back, clawed at his face with what strength was left to her. His mutilated thumbs prevented him from getting a firm grip on her throat, so he thumped her hard. She fell back into the bottom of the boat.

'Get away from me!' she growled between gritted teeth.

There was only one thing to do to shut her up. He snatched up an oar, then clobbered her across the face with it, and again until she fell unconscious on top of her son and Pierre, her face covered in blood.

At last, he wrenched off her coat, scavenged around for his little pile of booty, then waded speedily to shore.

13

As THE SUN shone over the lake, having cleared the distant mountaintops, the pauper stopped in a pool of light.

He had climbed the wooded hill in order to cross the range westward, the shortest route into France. He had made good ground, and now he was rewarded by being able to settle in the first light of the sun, whereas the valley and port below were still in the dimness of a paling morning. It was a fitting start to the new day, a new life, bathed in golden sunlight. He brought out his knife. Might be better off keeping them sewn into the coat, he thought to himself, feeling the stones through the lining.

During the climb he had envisaged diamonds, sapphires, rubies, and emeralds. He took a deep breath of fresh morning air. Standing with Switzerland on one side with the lake below lit up like liquid gold, and France on the other side where the foothills rose into the Jura, he could already see himself mounting a magnificent steed. But first he would get himself a nice place to live. No, no, first, he would buy some fine clothes; he would dress as an alderman, he would need to look the part. Next he would go wenching with the finest. Then he would choose a place to live and get a wife, or perhaps the wife first, then the house, then the sprogs. That was the substance of his dream which had occupied his thoughts as he had climbed, for two hours solid, where neither horse nor cart could venture. There again, he would certainly need more coin than the measly amount he had collected, and how would he exchange the jewels without rousing suspicions? He put the thought to the back of his mind; it was but a minor obstacle. Was he not a resourceful man? Had he not obtained an attestation of good character from the stupid pastor?

He sat a while longer in the knowledge that he was untraceable, savouring the very moment that marked his change of fortune, from rags to riches. The jacket was of fine fabric, a little worn but still worth a fair price in itself, and cutting the silk lining was like throwing away good coin. So he started unpicking the thread at the seam, the very thread he had seen the Huguenot lady strengthen at the Fleurets' cottage down by the river. But then, with an irresistible urge to hold his fortune in his palms, he dug his knife into the lining and slit it carefully across the hem. His eyes widened as the stones tumbled to the ground. But they widened not in glee, they widened in shock and horror, and then narrowed in wrath. He let out a mighty roar from his tightened gut. 'Why? God! Is there no justice for a pauper? Jesus Christ!'

The stones his knife had let loose were just that, dull, lacklustre stones, devoid of any value.

*

Two days later, the death bells tolled over the little port of Nion. Thirty-eight people had perished; extra coffins had to be brought in from nearby towns in haste. The whole village had walked behind the coffins to the Protestant graveyard, where the deceased were laid to rest. It was a simple burial, in accordance with Protestant beliefs that they could not intercede on behalf of the dead for their entry into eternal life. No mass, no prayers, no superstitious ritual. They simply remembered.

'Your mother is in good hands,' said Jeannot to the boy after the funeral service. 'She will recover, but she must rest here. Tell her I have had to take our Ginette away from this place before the grief overtakes her, before I lose her too. You understand, my boy?'

'Yes, Sir,' said Paul, his face clouding over with sorrow. 'But I don't understand why Pierrot had to die and not me.'

The man and the boy were standing outside the tall house where Jeanne was bedridden. But for the rustling of birds in the trees and the trickle of a nearby fountain, all was calm— a calmness only broken from time to time by the distant snorts of horses in front of their carriages, on the adjoining road at the bottom of the lane. They were waiting to carry the surviving passengers on to Morge, the port town where the boat had scheduled to dock, and whence the refugees would take up their route northward.

'I know, Paul. I know,' said Jeannot, tears running into the cracks around his eyes. 'Now you listen here, my lad. Pierrot loved you like a brother, you know that.'

'And I loved him like my brother, Sir.'

'Well said, my boy. Remember, if you are the one who survived, it must be for a reason.'

'He will always be with me. Always, Sir,' said Paul, whose voice broke into a sob. Jeannot lifted the boy off his feet, and placed the lad's head on his powerful shoulder.

'Listen, my boy. You survived. Now you owe it to Pierrot to become a righteous man. Never forget to do him proud. You hear me?'

'I promise,' said the boy, controlling his sobs.

Jeannot put the boy back down but remained crouched at his level. 'Be brave, my little man. Look after your mother till I get back.'

'I will, Sir.'

'The doctor says she is over the worst. When she comes round, tell her we have gone to Schaffhausen. Tell her I will be back to collect you both when she is better.'

Getting up, Jeannot laid a gentle hand on the boy's mop of hair. Then he walked briskly to the waiting cart at the main lake road.

The boy wanted to see Ginette and Pierrot's sisters, but something prevented him from approaching the end of the narrow street: shyness, modesty, guilt perhaps. So he remained where he was, and watched the carriages from a distance roll away along the coast till they were screened by houses. He felt an urge to run down to the track as a horrible feeling of loneliness swept through him. But he did not want to be left alone in the road near the church where his best friend in the world lay six feet under. So he stayed in front of the house where his mother lay in convalescence, recovering from injuries that were caused, it was assumed, by a falling object. Though how she had managed to board the boat was very much a mystery.

*

On the wooded hill above the church, Cephas Crespin had a better view of the carriages. He watched the cortège rumble along the coast road, and saw the boy enter the house where his mother must be making a recovery.

Cephas was cold, hungry, and seething with ire. Enough niceties now, he thought to himself. He had come to claim his rightful reward, and it was all he could do to prevent himself from running down to the house and taking what was rightfully his, for saving the life of the bourgeois boy.

14

THE LITTLE BOAT arrived at Petit Goave the following day in the blue-grey light of morning.

'Would you like me to wait here with our effects while you find out about our passage?' said Marianne once they were standing on the landing stage. It was a pleasant place to be with the gentle sun on their backs, a clear view across the calm bay on one side, and the laboured fields and luxuriant island-scape on the other.

'Would certainly make sense,' said Jacob, looking about him further up the jetty which met with stone fortifications. 'But if looks are anything to go by, I think you had better stay close by me.'

He was referring to the little groups of matelots here and there who were already dozing, sitting, talking, smoking, and playing games of chance in the open air. These men, Jacob was to learn, were buccaneers recently in from a campaign.

However, it was not the robbery of their effects that concerned Jacob most, but that of Marianne's virtue. So they took up their things, which consisted of a canvas sack each and a small chest that Monsieur Bourget had given Jacob during his stay at Leogane. Inside it were instruments of surgery and vials of medicine that Bourget had in double.

They reported to the commander of the settlement, a certain Captain Capieu, who pointed out *La Charmante*, a small two-masted brigantine, which was sitting at the anchorage among other cargo ships, some being loaded, others offloaded. *'She's* a shallow-draft vessel,' said Capieu, 'ideal for hugging the coast out of the reach of Spanish frigates.'

They found the captain of the brigantine, a certain Francis Poirier. He was overseeing a couple of crew members loading barrels into a dinghy for transit to the ship. The captain, an affable, burly man in middle age, wiped his hands on his baggy slops, then he read their order for their passage to Cow Island.

'We'll not be leaving for a day or two, M'sieur,' he said. 'Still waiting for provisions from Le Cap, see. But there's nothing keeping you and your niece from making yourself comfortable on board if that be your pleasure.'

The longer Jacob could remain on firm ground, the better. So he gave thanks to the skipper and told him that Captain Capieu had already mentioned board and a place to sleep. As prisoners of the king, they were, after all, under his jurisdiction.

The following day, Jacob and Marianne walked by the fort that looked over the bay. The mist had cleared, and the view was picturesque and peaceful. With nothing better to do, they soon found themselves in conversation with three of the buccaneers they had seen on arrival.

It so happened they too were expecting provisions from Le Cap. Neither Marianne nor Jacob had ever met a buccaneer before, and as a matter of fact, these turned out to be most civil and affable.

They explained they had got good pay from a recent expedition, so good, in fact, that they were deliberating whether to go on privateering, or to follow the governor's petition for them to withdraw from service and set themselves up in a more tranquil occupation.

'You being a man of culture, Monsieur Delpech, what would you do with the loot?' said the man who had introduced himself as Thomas Leberger.

It seemed quite abstract to be here in this idyllic scenery, tranquilly being asked advice by men who were mercenaries and killers, although you would not necessarily think it to hear them speak as they did in earnest. Even so, Marianne thought that a tactful tone would be the best to adopt, but Jacob, faithful to himself, said, 'Well, I should put down my sword, take a wife, and follow a more Christian way of life, and repent for the sins I have committed.'

After a brief, uncomfortable silence which made Marianne's pulse throb, the man glanced at her, looked levelly at Jacob, and said, 'I'm a religious man meself. We always pray before battle, don't we, lads?'

'Yeah, and after our last victory,' said the man to his right, 'Raveneau got us singing out a Te Deum, didn't he?'

'Aye,' said the man to his left. 'Best look after your soul. You can kill a man, but you can't take his soul, can ya?'

'No, you cannot take a man's soul,' said Jacob, 'because it is your soul that determines whether you go to heaven or hell.'

'I can see you've got a smart head on you, Monsieur,' said Leberger. 'And that be exactly what I was thinking 'n' all. Just needed to hear it out loud, like.'

The buccaneer reached into a pouch inside his jacket and said, 'Here, take this as a token of my gratitude, Sir.' He ostentatiously handed Jacob a Spanish gold escudo, though what the man stalked in the tail of his eye was the niece's reaction.

Jacob was about to protest when Mademoiselle Duvivier, who had turned her head and was glancing into the bay, said, 'Is that the ship?'

Monsieur Leberger took a step towards her, so close that she could feel the heat of his suntanned body, and capped his eyes with a hand to reduce the glare from the sea. 'By the thunder of Neptune, I believe it is!' he said. Then, after a clap on the back from his mates, he cordially bid farewell, leaving Jacob one gold coin the richer, and Marianne all aquiver.

She seemed to stare out at the roadstead, still capping her brow with a hand, though the sun was behind her. But secretly, she was straining her eyes to watch the matelots as they hurried back along the quayside towards the township, to alert their other mates. Their smell, that of strong men, lingered with her a moment, as did their litheness. But then she shut them from her mind and followed Jacob's gaze over the roadstead where the cargo ship was dropping anchor.

They stood watching a good while as the crew offloaded the delivery of people and goods. The longboat was soon advancing at a good pace through the calm, dazzling water, carrying a small number of passengers, no doubt returning planters having bought provisions in Le Cap Français—or so thought Marianne and Jacob.

Delpech gave Mademoiselle Duvivier a gentle nudge as the longboat came closer. 'Marianne!' called a familiar voice, and the next instant, the young woman had shed her womanhood and, caught between tears and laughter, began running like a child to the wharf-side. The old lady, sitting beside a woman in her forties, was her grandmother.

A short while later, the girl wiped her eyes as she embraced her only relative, the witness of her identity, and her only link to her ancestry. She became filled with the irreplaceable love of generations, as her grandmother held her head to her bosom.

Was it an incredible coincidence? Or was it a noble act of kindness that brought them together again? Jacob suspected the latter, and he was now beginning to understand why, of all places, Lieutenant Dumas had sent them to Cow Island, the place where everyone knew ships stopped to water before continuing their voyage to Jamaica. Was it not to give them a chance to abscond?

By late afternoon, the brigantine was loaded, and the captain chose to sail out with the land breeze along the coast.

The evening below deck was spent in conversation, with the two parties sharing their stories under lamplight. Madame de Fontenay and her friend, whose name was Madame Charlotte Odet, were unaware of the shipwreck which many aboard *La Marie* had mistaken for *La Concorde*. However, Madame Odet recounted how the ship that brought her from France, *L'Espérance*, was indeed shipwrecked off Martinique. There were only forty survivors who were taken to CapFrançais, where not long after, *La Concorde* came to moor and delivered her load of Huguenots. The two ladies joined forces and formed a religious resistance. They urged everyone to refuse to join the Catholic Church and encouraged recently converted colonists to convert back.

'We supposed they could not put up with us any longer,' said Madame de Fontenay. 'And I knew you were further down the coast and hoped that was where we were headed. And here we are!'

It became apparent to the young woman now that her continual remonstrance had not fallen upon deaf ears after all.

'But why did the lieutenant governor not tell you about your grandmother?' said Madame Odet.

'I do not know,' said Marianne.

'I can only surmise,' said Jacob, 'that it is the policy of the government to separate families in an attempt to break their will. And in the case of Monsieur Dumas, being formerly of Protestant stock himself, he did not want to risk looking as if he would favour a Calvinist. I suspect he knew he would be doubly watched by the clergy.'

'Anyway, I am pleased to see my granddaughter looking so well,' said Madame de Fontenay, smiling at Monsieur Delpech and Marianne sitting opposite her. She sensed they had become close and was not surprised to hear of their uncle-and-niece act.

'Jolly good for you,' she said. 'I knew I could count on you, Sir, the moment I set eyes on you!'

It was a joyful reunion, only darkened by the horrible stories of brutality and bondage, and the fact they were still prisoners themselves. Jacob asked Madame de Fontenay what her intentions were now.

She said, 'I have decided not to think of tomorrow. Not to regret the past. Just to live life in the present, in the company of my dear granddaughter until I see her wed.'

'Grandmother!' said Mademoiselle Duvivier.

'You are nearly eighteen, my dear. It is that time in a woman's life.'

The old lady was certainly an inspiration, thought Jacob. She managed to battle on despite her age, having lost her family, home, and heritage. But his own situation was not that of Madame de Fontenay, and he could not share her outlook. As they tucked in for the night trip, he could think of nothing but a future day when he would be reunited with Jeanne and his children. He was as eager as ever to make his escape.

*

A few days later, they dropped anchor in front of Grand-Anse, a small village without defences that had been constantly harassed and plundered by the Spanish. Perhaps they did it, thought Jacob, in retaliation of French buccaneers such as Monsieur Leberger, who plundered and sacked Spanish townships on the great island of Cuba. Did these filibusters realise that while they were filling their coffers with stolen riches, the civilian population was losing their livelihood through no aggression of their own? But would they care? Probably not. It was becoming more and more apparent to Jacob that the New World was in fact a self-destructive society, centred on individual wealth and success. A world where barbarians could become masters.

A good number of these villagers mounted aboard *La Charmante*, in the hope they would be better protected on the fortified Cow Island.

There followed a hullabaloo of hoisting, packing, and securing what possessions they had before the brigantine was ready to take to the sea again.

'I bet you weren't expecting us lot,' said a man in banter from the group of colonists that settled near the Huguenots. They sat, squatted, or lay down as best they could among the ropes and barrels, baskets and chests, pieces of furniture, chickens and goats. 'I bet you ain't never been packed so close,' he said, which Jacob understood as being a reference to their normal respective stations in life. Or was he fishing to see if they were Huguenots?

'Oh, I find it rather cosy,' said Madame de Fontenay. 'One can even kick out one's limbs to their full extent!'

The man laughed out loud at what he took as fair banter from the old lady. Then he said, 'You might not see it the same way come this time next week, though, Ma'am.'

The Huguenots gave a polite and merry utterance, but said nothing of their five-month voyage packed like cattle. It was nonetheless a quiet victory to be treated as ordinary passengers.

It was clear by their conversation and the way they spoke that these folk must have been indentured workers, now freed of their bondage, looking to establish a new life for themselves. Now that the bridge had been established between the classes, conversation turned to planting and crop cultivation, and Jacob was glad to impart some of his knowledge to the man who had first addressed them. He was a smallholder whose name was Jacques Rouchon, thirty-seven years old and originally from Nantes. He said he might even cross over to Jamaica from Cow Island, which gave Jacob further reason to believe his deliverance was nigh.

It was the tenth of June, and they set sail on a fair wind along the coast around the southwest leg of Hispaniola. They arrived at their destination eight days later as a new dawn was breaking.

Upon landfall, as instructed, Jacob handed his third order to the commander of the isle, Major Laurent de Graaf, the notorious buccaneer.

15

A SUMMER HAZE filled the air with scent, and the pleasing buzz of a bee collecting nectar accompanied the visions of Jeanne.

She saw her daughters and Paul playing in a meadow knee-deep in grass and wild flowers, then the girls in their summer dresses, opening a stable door where Paul was making a hay camp with Pierrot. But the sky suddenly darkened. Then there was rain, torrential rain, a river, and a soldier with a stern stance. Fear stabbed her heart as the eyes turned to murderous rage, and she saw the pauper raising a cudgel above her as she placed herself in front of her son in the bottom of a boat.

'No, no!' she called out, and immediately a new light, soft and dazzling, came over her as beads of perspiration shimmered upon her brow. She opened her eyes, dazzled by colours, and she found herself in a snug wooden bed, in a room with flowers on the balconette. A large-boned woman was attaching a shutter so that it would not slam shut, and bees were dancing in the geraniums.

'Mother.'

Jeanne tried to open wide her eyes, which made her wince,

and cupping the side of her swollen face, she turned her head to see her son. He had leapt out of a chair and approached her. Under his smile, she saw a trauma, and she knew, even before tears welled in the boy's eyes, the tragedy of Pierre.

'You are to stay as long as it takes to mend your head, Madame Delpech. I have been given instructions.' It was the large lady who spoke the words in her slow Swiss accent, thickened by guttural intonations. She was evidently from the northern parts and introduced herself as the housekeeper.

For the next few days, the nightmares and the dizziness kept Jeanne mostly to her bed. It was not until she was able to dress and go down for dinner that she met her host.

As Paul led his mother from her room, she discovered a spacious house of solid build, timber-framed and clad in stone. The wooden staircase creaked as they descended. At its foot stood a tall, finely carved case clock that counted time peacefully. It sounded its pleasant chime as Jeanne and Paul entered the solidly furnished dining room, where a white-haired gentleman stood up and smiled on their arrival.

'Madame, you were brought here and now you are under my protection,' he said, after the pleasantries of introduction. 'And I might add, I am a good friend of Pastor Duvaux, who sends his kind regards but has had to remain in Geneva to carry out his duties. You are welcome to stay as long as you wish in my household, Madame.'

'You are most kind, Sir. I will repay you for your hospitality . . . and for these clothes,' said Jeanne. The housemaid had laid them out for her and explained that they had belonged to the gentleman's daughter, who had moved to another town with her new husband. He wanted her to have them.

'Shan't hear of it. I am but an old man, and I crave company. It is I who thank you, Madame Delpech. And your son is charming. We have been entertaining ourselves during your convalescence by playing chess. I might add, he has talent!'

Monsieur Gaugin was a jovial gentleman, an alderman with a scholar's stoop. At table over leek soup, he said, 'I am myself of French heritage; my father came here when he was still a child. So, my dear Madame, my forbears were in the same situation as you find yourself today. And I consider it a duty and a pleasure to welcome you here where my grandfather was welcomed, by none other than his future father-in-law!'

'You are most generous, Sir. However, I really must make my way north. First to Schaffhausen,' said Jeanne, taking care not to show the side of her face that was black and blue.

'My dear lady, are you sure you are fit to travel?'

'My wounds will heal. Those of my friend's are much deeper. She lost her son.'

'Yes, I know, a terrible tragedy for many. Well, the difficulty will reside in finding transport, it being the busy season in the fields, you know. Moreover, did Monsieur Fleuret not say he would be back for you?'

'I am not so sure he would leave his wife and children alone now. And I would not expect him to. We shall go on foot.'

'All the way to Schaffhausen?'

'Yes,' said Jeanne, touching Paul's head. 'Then on to London, if that is what it will take to recover my children with my husband.'

'In that case, I will advise you which route to take to

Schaffhausen. For it would be unwise to walk for long stretches after the fall and the knock to your head. We all wondered how you got it. Were you hit by a barrel?'

Jeanne realised that no one was any the wiser as to the pauper's appalling behaviour; her son had not then revealed anything, but had he seen? Not wanting to delay further, she decided to keep it to herself. What concerned her more was reaching Ginette. She could well imagine her pain at losing her only son.

The following day, Monsieur Gaugin brought good news. There would be a charabanc to Morge, from where he knew daily journeys were made northward. It would not be difficult to reach Yverdon. From there she should take the boat across the lake to Neuchatel.

*

Holding Paul firmly by the hand, Jeanne paced through the milling crowd at the lakeside port of Yverdon, to find out about the passage to the other side. Her eye was suddenly caught by a flash of green. She stopped to focus her gaze on a small group of ladies by the wharf chattering, their young children playing at their skirts. A shudder of horror seized her, and she grasped Paul more firmly by the hand.

'What is it, Mother?'

'Nothing. It is nothing.'

But Paul had followed her gaze to the clutch of chatting ladies and saw the reason for his mother's sudden anguish. One of the women was wearing her green coat. It had been cleaned and was adorned with a brooch, but it could not possibly be anything other than the one she had cherished. It was evident from the lady's hat and shoes that the coat did not suit her budget. She must have bought it at an old-clothes stand or from a stranger.

'I see,' said Paul, as his mother turned and instinctively glanced around her, as if searching for an invisible menace.

But the boy slipped his hand from her grasp and ran towards the lady. On approach, just six feet from where the brood of ladies was chatting, he deliberately tripped himself up—a trick he had learnt from Pierrot. As he went down, he let out a yelp.

'Ah, my knee! My knee!' he wailed out.

Seeing the lady she took as the boy's mother in simple but quality clothing, the ladies reacted to the child's cries, and one of them broke away to tend to the lad. It was the woman in green.

'You alright, my love?' she said while Jeanne was rushing over to him. 'He yours, Madame?'

'Yes, no, I'm his aunt. Always slipping away and finding trouble, he is,' said Jeanne, taking the boy by the arm to pull him onto his feet. But the boy still clutched his knee.

'Kids these days, eh? Well, he shan't be hopping away anymore today.'

'Come on, Jacob, now, please. I've told you before, stop running off. What will your mother say if I lose you?'

'Oh, mine's just as bad,' said the lady. Jeanne looked at the boy next to the woman, two inches shorter than Paul, who was standing beside her with a big-eyed grin and a naughty smile.

'Ouch, it hurts!'

'Serves you right, young man!' said the lady, siding with the boy's aunt. 'You ought to learn to do as your aunt says.'

'I'm taking him to see his grandparents. Travelling yourself?'

'Payerme. We are travelling to Payerme.'

'Well, Madame, I shan't keep you. Come along, Jacob, up you get. Thank you, Madame.'

'Ouch, stop pulling, my aunt,' said Paul, walking with a limp. 'It still hurts!'

'Oh, I am sorry,' said Jeanne, continuing in a low voice, 'I thought you were playacting.'

'That was the plan, but my knee landed on a cobblestone.'

'And to think I thought you were overdoing the acting!'

'So? Is it or isn't it?' said the boy.

Jeanne looked down at her son, and realised at that moment how very astute and adult he had grown. She realised she now had more than a son; she had a clever accomplice. In a low voice, walking as fast through the crowd as Paul's limp would allow, she said, 'It is. I recognised my threading where I patched it up under the arm.'

'Thought so.' Paul had justly sensed her anxiety. 'Was it stolen, then?'

At first Jeanne did not want to let him in on her secret. But given the turn of events, she led him away from the crowd to the side of the wharf, and told him briefly about the aggression that took place while he lay unconscious in the boat.

'I thought there was something awry. Monsieur Cephas was nowhere to be seen among the survivors. So you think he might be wanting to get what he thought he stole?'

'You can never be too prudent when it comes to individuals of that sort. And by the way, your name is Jacob from now on,' she said, keeping her voice down.

'Jacob and the coat of many colours!' said Paul, with a clever grin.

'Jacob Delgarde de Castanet,' said Jeanne a moment later, as she smudged and scraped the attestation—already subjected to soaking from the boat accident—on a stone mooring bollard.

*

The Swiss Confederacy had by this time become relatively organised. Not wanting people to linger too long, it had set up road and boat links which conveyed refugees onward in their trek north. In most places, the local inhabitants had become used to the continuous flow of travellers, and were in the main prepared to harbour passers-by for the night until transport was arranged.

A short while later, Jeanne and Paul stood in the queue for the boat from Yverdon to Neuchatel. Since the tragedy—especially as the captain had been publicly shamed and sent to prison—checks had become more rigorous and boarding more controlled, with priority given to Huguenot women, children, and old folk.

The agent studied Jeanne's attestation.

'It got soaked, Monsieur. I was on board the ship that capsized.'

'I am sorry, Madame, a tragedy from what have heard. I was just trying to decipher your name. I have been asked to look out for a lady and a boy, and you seem to fit the description.'

Jeanne gave her son's hand a light squeeze. 'I don't think so, Monsieur, what was the name?'

'Delpech.'

Jeanne tried to keep her face from revealing her shock as she said, 'Well, as you can see, I am Delgarde de Castanet.'

'Yes, that's what I was wondering. See, there's a water mark on Del—.'

'—garde, Delgarde.'

'Pity, would have saved you from travelling alone.'

How could the pauper have the audacity? thought Jeanne. But then again, he had fooled everyone once. There was no reason why such a conniving mind would not try to do so again.

'I assure you, it is Delgarde. Delgarde de Castanet.'

'Yes, I see, please take your place aboard, Madame. Next.'

16

SURROUNDED BY TREACHEROUS shoals and reefs, Cow Island was a perilous place for the unsuspecting captain, which, Jacob deduced, made it consequently more difficult to raid. However, for the knowing master and commander, it was a choice spot, a place to shelter and careen, which was doubly why Laurent de Graaf had made it his base, and all the more so now that his command of it had been officialised by the French governor of Saint-Domingue. It was for this reason that the group of freed indentured colonists had elected to establish themselves here.

The buccaneer, revered by the French and feared by the Spanish, did not look at all like the callous man Jacob had been expecting. He was very tall, blond, and with his goatee, there was something of the elegance of a musketeer about him. In fact, he was disarmingly charming and refused to let Jacob reside any place other than in his own house, which, he said, had enough room to accommodate the ladies, if they did not mind sharing.

'Well, Sir, I do not know what to say,' said Jacob as they approached the promontory where the house was perched. It overlooked the northwest bay and the little natural harbour below. Madame Odet, Madame de Fontenay, and Mademoiselle Duvivier were walking along with them.

'Then say nothing, Monsieur Delpech,' said the newly appointed major, who motioned to the ladies to enter the modest abode before him. 'Ladies. I pray you enjoy your stay here at Cow Island.'

It was a modest house with a tin roof, and yet it was more convivial than the residence of Monsieur Verbizier.

The following morning, as the sun was rising, Jacob was woken by hollering sailors, banging and rolling noises, and all sorts of hubbub coming from down at the cove where de Graaf's great frigate was anchored. From his whitewashed window, Jacob could easily see the tall, energetic figure of the young major, directing operations.

An hour later, on striding up to the house in front of which Jacob was now standing, de Graaf said, 'Ah, Monsieur Delpech, you must excuse me, I have urgent business at my plantation in Petit Goave.'

Jacob had acquired a certain empathy for the man, knowing from their talk of the previous evening about how he himself had been a slave in the hands of the Spanish on the Canary Islands. He no doubt inspired the same feeling of kinship in his men which made him such a charismatic commander to fight for.

'I hope there is nothing awry, Monsieur de Graaf,' said Jacob, glancing across the harbour. It was a beautiful morning over the limpid aquamarine bay, rimmed with immaculate strips of sand where coconut trees grew. And there was not a ripple on the water.

'Just routine,' said the buccaneer, 'nothing I cannot handle.'

He did not halt but followed his stride into the study, where he retrieved some rolled charts. Then, on his way back through the hall, he said, 'During my absence, an English merchant ship will call by here. Do not be alarmed. The captain is a friend of mine. Daniel Darlington is his name. He will be arriving from Saint Thomas.'

'An Englishman?'

'I trust I can count on you to give him a warm welcome on my behalf?' said Laurent de Graaf, with an eloquent smile.

This was clearly a tacit invitation to leave the island, was it not?

'You may indeed, Sir,' said Jacob with discretion.

'Good man,' said de Graaf, tapping Jacob on the round of his shoulder. 'And I am certain you will find him receptive to your cause.'

'Understood, and I must thank you for your hospitality, Sir,' said Jacob.

'You are most welcome. And, please do not think me pert, but I hope to find my house empty when I return!' The tall Dutchman gave a short bow, then continued out through the door. 'My regards to the ladies!' he called back. 'Oh, and there are men I have left in charge here. They are here to guard against outside aggression, but they have orders to leave you in peace.'

*

Within the hour, the famous captain had departed as he had planned. And over the coming weeks, several times a day, Jacob looked through the brass spyglass he found in the salon, in the hope of spotting the silhouette of a ship on the eastern horizon.

During this time, he also explored the islet high and low, in its length and breadth. He made sketches, read up on medicinal plants, and, having found a musket in a cupboard, went hunting with Jacques Rouchon, the indentured worker he met on board *La Charmante* at Grand Anse. Rouchon was jovial company, rustic but practical-minded; he was also a crack shot and an excellent trapper. During their hunting jaunts, he recounted the exploits of de Graaf, how the colossus had defended the coast of Saint-Domingue against the Spaniards from Cuba, and how he had made a fortune plundering their treasure fleet and settlements.

'Very clever man, de Graaf. Can speak to his men in four different languages, you know,' said Rouchon one day as they were resting on the hilltop. It offered an impressive view over the lush mangrove forest on one side, and the harbour inlet fringed with golden beach on the other. 'And shrewd with it,' he continued. 'Do you know why else he's so attached to this here island?'

'I should think because it is easy to defend, for one,' said Delpech, scanning the eastern horizon through his spyglass.

'And because of the sunken treasure!'

'Treasure?'

'Aye, down there somewhere be the treasure of Captain Morgan of Jamaica,' said Rouchon, motioning towards the inlet, which prompted Jacob to swing round with the spyglass. Rouchon then recounted the story of how the islet used to be one of Morgan's assembly points, where pirates from all around the Caribbean would come together and join forces before heading out on a campaign against the Spaniards.

'Then one day, while they were making merry and letting

off muskets and guns and what have you, a spark flew into the gunpowder room and blew up Morgan's ship! That weren't all. She took down with her the two captured French ships laden with treasure! Just think, it could be at the bottom of that there inlet.'

'Then why does nobody fetch it up?'

'It be cursed; not even Morgan can touch it. He came back for it only to wreck another ship!'

'But why would it be cursed?' said Jacob, who was less interested in Morgan's treasure than the moral of the tale.

'Because the explosion took with it three hundred men, most of 'em so sozzled out of their brains, they couldn't swim even if they knew how! Three hundred souls haunt that very cove. Makes yer shiver, dunnit.'

On another occasion, Rouchon admitted he had come to the island with the other colonists, just to see with his own eyes where the treasure might lie. But given the curse, and now that he had been and seen, he was finding the mosquito-infested islet too small. He was wondering if he should try his hand on a larger island, one far from Santo Domingo and the Spanish raiders of Cuba. And one place that sprang to mind was again the one he briefly evoked on the brigantine. It was Jamaica.

With a free rein on the islet and with want of what to do, both Rouchon and Delpech also lent a hand to the other colonists. They had settled on the southwest slopes on the other side of the freshwater pond, though still only a short distance from the northwest harbour.

The eastern part was mostly avoided. Being low-lying, it was full of unhealthy swampland infested with mosquitoes, the island's biggest blight. Since their arrival, the new settlers had, despite the stifling heat and the incommodious insects blown by the breeze, already built rudimentary accommodation, churned and turned over the soil, planted crops, and located the best places to catch the massive manatee—a native delicacy—and the wild boar that roamed freely on the big island opposite.

To pass the time, Jacob had acquired an interest in sketching. He found the island offered incredible diversity for such a relatively small area. It seemed moreover to bring him closer to God; it gave him an even greater appreciation of His intricate creation. These were times he preferred to be alone. But of late, he had invited Mademoiselle Duvivier to join him.

One of the guards, a young man of some vigour, in the absence of normal social boundaries, had become helpful, then amiable, then forward. And he now was in danger of becoming blatantly disrespectful, taking it upon himself to call upon the ladies morning and afternoon under the pretext of proposing his aid for anything they desired. It was becoming awkward. Private Guillaume Girard was a simple commoner but a guard all the same, and they were theoretically his prisoners. What was more, he tended to pass by while Jacob was on one of his jaunts.

Marianne going out sketching with Jacob had curbed young Girard's ardour. At least, so it seemed.

Marianne enjoyed sketching out in the field as much as Jacob did. And when he attempted to explain to her the rudiments of art, it turned out that she had a far greater talent for it than he had. At times she wished she could be in a place where she could enjoy the same rights as men, so that she could learn to become a proper artist.

It was while they were out sketching the mangrove forest one morning that Jacob at last spotted the English merchant ship. They collected their apparatus, borrowed from the house—a spoil from a Spanish settlement—and together they hurried back to break the news to the ladies.

*

That was almost a week ago. Delpech had hoped he would be on his way to London by now. He was gazing out across the cove where the merchant ship lay on its flank like a beached whale in the shallow water. He had heard vaguely about careening. Now he was seeing it with his own eyes.

The ship was lashed down by ropes that were tied to the masts at one end and wrapped around palm trees at the other. The sun had been up only an hour, and already shipmates were working alongside her in a row—a few standing in the longboat, others on wooden platforms—chipping away the barnacles and scraping off the seagrass and seaweed on the exposed surface of the hull.

Captain Daniel Darlington, a well-spoken gentleman, not yet thirty, had explained to Jacob that if they did not careen and repair the ship, they would be at a serious disadvantage if they came across a Spanish patrol or vulgar freebooters. As it was, his ship *La Belle* had only just escaped pursuit coming round Puerto Rico. The embedded weed and molluscs had restricted manoeuvrability and created drag that had considerably slowed her down. She had received damage at mid-port just above the waterline, before she could get away with all the sail she could make.

So it was time to fix her up and give her a smooth hull. They would have to replace any splintered or worm-eaten timbers, and caulk and shellac gaps between planks, before applying a coat of amber-coloured tar to the whole for optimum protection.

Once repaired, the vessel would have to be hauled out and floated, then ballasted, balanced, and loaded with all the cargo, tackle, water, and supplies that had been removed to make her lighter for hauling. The whole job would probably take a couple of weeks, the crew being no more than a handful of seafarers.

Jacob had waited three years to be set free. He would gladly wait a few weeks more rather than risk foundering at sea.

Moreover, Darlington was not heading for London as Jacob had hoped, but up along the east coast of North America, to the province where he was born of a Dutch mother and an English pastor. Mr Darlington had nonetheless assured Monsieur Delpech that it was easy to get a passage back to Europe from New York.

Daniel Darlington spoke some French and lent a sympathetic ear when his replacement hosts recounted their odyssey, especially—and this did not escape Jacob's attention—when Marianne spoke. During the first dinner at the house given in his honour, Marianne seemed to glow with inner contentment which made her even more poised, fresh, and beautiful. It was the glow of youth, of youth eager to shine, of youth in search of a soul-mate. The young captain was captivated by her metropolitan manners. She was as refined as porcelain, which made him feel at moments coarser than he really was.

He was nonetheless a wealthy man, and showed the spirit of nonconformist nonchalance common to men of means.

He was of the first generation of the English fledgling township of New York. And he was proud of it, although he would certainly not swear allegiance to the English crown, or to any other crown for that matter.

Upon that first dinner—Darlington would dine at the house every evening thereon—Jacob saw clearly that a mutual empathy had been borne between the young people. An empathy which neither he nor Madame de Fontenay cared to discourage.

After the arrival of *La Belle* in the natural harbour, instead of accompanying Jacob, Marianne took to sketching the ship being hauled and secured for careening, and the operations thereafter, Darlington ever at hand to explain each operation to her. Her grandmother was never far away, chatting with Madame Odet and darning or embroidering new coifs, while secretly reporting to each other any signs of first love.

So Delpech suspected why the previous evening, Mr Darlington had insisted that the two of them spend the morning hunting together. He now turned to face the young man as he strode up to the house from the harbour, kitted out with his fusil over his shoulder.

Daniel Darlington said, 'Please forgive me if I am a little late, Monsieur Delpech. I was just going over the hull with my carpenter. It seems there is more damage than we initially anticipated. Several more planks need replacing.'

'That is unfortunate,' said Jacob, standing with his leather pouch strapped over his shoulder and his flintlock musket at his side.

'Thankfully, however, our absent host is as far-sighted as he is courageous; he always has seasoned lumber lying around in the storehouse for such cases.'

'Good, it would not do to take in water,' said Jacob with a congenial smile, despite the extra setback. 'But come, let us be off, before the sun gets too high.'

The two men stepped off at a brisk pace in the freshness of the beautiful morning.

'Would you believe, I always water here on the way from Saint Thomas, and yet I have never ventured further inland than the port beach?'

'Then be prepared to see some delights of God's nature, Mr Darlington!'

They took a forest trail past swamps. And as they climbed the hillock to dominate the scenery, they spoke again about the news from England, fresh from Darlington's contacts in Saint Thomas. It was not what Jacob had hoped. James II was still trying to establish Catholicism. There was even talk of the Protestant clergy inviting the Dutch king to take his place. This could mean yet another civil war in England. Jacob might have to set his sights on Amsterdam instead.

*

'That is where you will find turtles and manatees,' said Jacob, pointing to the expanse of seagrass and remarking that it grew as lush as the meadows of Holland.

'My friend, de Graaf, must feel quite at home then,' said Daniel Darlington.

'Except that in Holland, there are no slaves, sugar cane, or buccaneers!' said Jacob.

'I have been to England and Amsterdam. I realise that it is a very different world from here,' said the young captain, showing he would not shy from a challenge. 'But here, it is a world where only the fittest can survive. It is a land of opportunity; almost any man can live out his dream . . .'

'Or nightmare,' said Jacob. 'Do you know how many human lives your cargo of sugar has probably cost?'

'No, Sir, but I suspect there is injustice in all man's endeavours, and that most people turn a blind eye.'

'So you agree with slavery?'

'I do not, Sir. I am wholly against it. And I might add that I intend to stop this commerce and settle down. For the past five years, I have been going to and from these mosquito-infested lands. I have been shot at and chased, seen my ship pillaged and three times almost shipwrecked, and I can count myself lucky, compared to many of my past acquaintances who are no longer of this world.'

Jacob was about to make a sardonic remark as to the wealth Darlington had acquired, albeit indirectly, on the backs of slaves. But this time, he held his tongue, for he suspected the young man was ready to disclose the real reason for their jaunt around the island. Besides, he was right about how easily people turned a blind eye to recurrent atrocities. Did Jacob himself not turn a blind eye to galley slaves when he was a bourgeois in France not so long ago? Had he not financed an unspecified cargo lost at sea with his legal colleagues when in Montauban?

In a less controversial tone, Jacob said, 'And what might you do, Sir?'

'I plan to invest in my hometown and build a family before this life gets the better of me too.'

'I was given to believe you were unattached,' said Jacob, who had decided to make it easy for him.

'Yes, Sir, that is so, but the time has come for me to take a wife.'

'Indeed.'

'Yes, Monsieur Delpech, which brings me round to why I have asked you to walk with me this morning. I would like to speak about your niece.'

During their evening meals, Marianne had continued to address Jacob as her uncle—she had become so used to doing it in Leogane that it had become an automatism, and it still brought her reassurance while upholding the boundaries of their relationship, for Jacob Delpech still cut an attractive figure.

So Jacob thought he had better set the young captain right. Casting his gaze away from the expanse of seagrass, he turned to Darlington and said, 'Well, wait a moment. I must put you straight about one thing—'

'With all due respect, Sir, please hear me out,' said Darlington, afraid that Jacob was about to nip his prepared rhetoric in the bud, and his affections with it. 'I know you intend to return to Europe. However, I have struck up a rare fondness for Miss Duvivier, and I believe it is, or at least I hope, it is reciprocated.'

'What does she say?'

'She has no plans for the future, which is why I would like to ask your consent to ask for her hand.'

'Are you not precipitating things somewhat, Sir?'

'If I wait, she may get used to the idea of going back to Europe.'

'Have you spoken to her about your feelings?'

'I wanted to ask her uncle his consent first, so that what I will offer her will be free of obstacle. I mean, not that I mean you would be an obstacle, Sir . . .'

'Indeed, I shall not,' said Jacob. There was really no point beating about the bush, and the truth was, Jacob and Madame de Fontenay had already spoken about the eventuality. It would be a godsend.

'But, Sir, I beg you,' said the young man, his face flushed with a sense of injustice, 'please hear me out before making a rash decision. I realise that you wish to rebuild your heritage in Europe, but . . . I love her . . .'

'I am afraid you have misunderstood, Mr Darlington. I said I shall not. I shall not constitute a hindrance,' said Jacob. A visible wave of joy spread over the young man's face. Jacob continued, 'If you both desire to create a life together, then you must. As long as she finds the comfort she deserves, and her grandmother is well looked after in her advancing years.'

'Oh, she will, Sir,' said the young man eagerly.

'Good. And by the way, I was going to say I am not actually her uncle. At least, not by blood, although I have looked over her as if she were my own daughter.'

It could not have turned out better, and Jacob was delighted for the girl and relieved to have the responsibility removed. The young man was strong, his father was a pastor, he had resources—the cargo alone would make him a rich man—and to be frank, her breeding would certainly refine any coarseness Darlington had acquired owing to his birth and New World way of life. And with her strength of character, he trusted that she would make Darlington see the senseless savagery of slavery. Yes, it could not have turned out better. And now he would be able to concentrate on getting back to his own family.

The sun was near its highest point, and the heat was already stifling, so they decided to turn back westward towards the natural harbour. As he turned, Jacob caught sight of a distant ship. On seeing it too, Darlington was seized by a sense of urgency, and in a falsely calm voice, he said, 'If she consents, I dearly hope you will give her away.'

'Before you speak of marriage, should you not get to know each other better first?'

'Of course, of course, I am jumping the gun. She must know where I live, meet my family. No doubt I have seen too many of my friends die too young. Life is not like in Europe, as you well know. Here you have to seize the opportunity before it passes you by.'

But fate would have it otherwise. Delpech would not give her away to Mr Darlington after all.

*

Earlier that morning, a little after eight o'clock, Marianne Duvivier emerged from the house, fuming.

She had hardly slept a wink all night, what with the heat and the mosquitoes buzzing around her ears, and then with silly, rambling thoughts of Mr Darlington. How dare he laugh at her efforts to speak English during dinner! His French was hardly the epitome of eloquence either. Although it did occur to her that she had a tendency to correct his grammar, often. But then why did he insist that his ship was feminine when the proper language dictated it to be *le* and not *la navire*? And yet he would not have it any other way.

And how dare Monsieur Delpech accept to take him on a jaunt without her, as if it were too dangerous. After all she had been through, honestly, she had faced more terrors than many a trooper! Did they really take her for a silly young girl? And Monsieur Delpech, of all people; she thought he at least was on her side. She might have all the inconveniences of her sex—her periodical discharge, the cumbersome layers of clothing that made a woman of quality ostensibly decent—but that did not make her inept. And to top it all, now squalls of wind kept upsetting her hair.

But she would not be compounded just because there was no man about. Besides, the days had become far too warm and sticky to stay indoors, even behind closed shutters. So after her coffee, she took up her sketching equipment and the little folding stool which Jacob had fitted with straps. And despite her grandmother's remonstrance—none too insistent, as the old lady had not slept either—she headed off past the swamp area to the hillock on the south side of the little island.

Three quarters of an hour later, she was setting up on the clifftop to finish her sketch of the farmstead huts which spread along the low ground in the distance. She unfolded her stool close to the ledge, where the sea breeze kept the mosquitoes at bay, and sat with her knees supporting her drawing.

By the time she had finished her landscape piece, the big golden sun was blazing high in the sky. It was sweltering. She stood up, capped her eyes with her right hand, and looked eastward. There was still no sign of the amblers, not that she was expecting them, of course, but in the distance, she could see the outline of an approaching ship.

Then she moved her gear back forty yards to the shade of the trees on the edge of the wood.

*

Private Guillaume Girard was twenty-three. Until a few days ago, he had high hopes of declaring his flame—a flame that still raged inside despite the arrival of the Englishman. In fact, now it raged even more fiercely, for it was also fuelled by the feeling of injustice and the power of jealousy.

Girard knew he was better-looking than the merchant captain, and more practical too, and yet the Englishman walked in with a hull full of sugar, and she practically fell at his feet. Girard saw her turn on her charm like a soft glow in a warm night, as she had done with him: a smile that any man would die for, and the way she let her hand lightly touch his arm so he just melted into submission.

For five weeks, he had been shadowing her. Normal enough; he had been given the job of keeping an eye on the Huguenots. The old captain of the garrison—which consisted of just a handful of men—knew too well you had to keep reports up to date no matter what your commander said, because commanders could come and go as quickly as the turn of the tide. And that meant keeping your eye out in case questions were asked.

What the old captain did not foresee, though, was that Girard would get a twinkle in the eye for Miss Huguenot.

The soldier now often thought back at how he had cherished every one of her smiles at the beginning of their "relationship". How she had encouraged their nascent camaraderie, asking him a multitude of favours, and each time he obliged unfailingly. Would you bring us some fresh water, Monsieur Girard? Could you fetch some wood for the stove, Monsieur Girard? Do you think you could possibly retrieve that coconut up there, Guillaume? What a bloody baboon he had been! What a lackey! And yet he had felt a real complicity grow between them. That is, until the old crow poked her beak in.

Nevertheless, he still had been able to observe her from

the woods, from behind the rocks, and at night from the top of the slope that overlooked her room. He had learnt her every move. He had even seen her piss twice. Once in her room, and another time out in the field during a sketching session. It had taken all his willpower to keep himself from appearing in front of her. A whore once told him that women have an extra sense that tells them when a man is watching. And that they watched men even more than men watched them. It was obvious, of course, but it was nice to hear it confirmed by an expert on human nature.

Yes, Mademoiselle Duvivier knew what she was doing all along. Of course she was leading him on. It was time to see how far she would go now that he had her alone at last.

*

Girard had been crouching in the cover of the woods, doing his job, spying on her. He was now leaning behind a group of trees, and stood there in hiding, liberated and eroticised as she approached.

Two minutes later, she was unfolding her stool; then she sat back to take in the view of the sea and the faraway ship. She was in a lethargic, dreamy mood, and was roasting hot. She proceeded to untie her corset from the front, and then slipped her hand inside to open and close her blouse in order to let out hot puffs of air.

She let her thoughts run wild, as she often did at this time of day. Of course she was still a virgin. But she knew about lovemaking; she had seen a horse mount a nag when she was eleven. The image often played on her mind, and when she saw a man, she sometimes found herself wondering what he was like. Despite her prayers, this longing would never go away completely, so she had learnt to live with it, and let herself flirt with the idea in the privacy of her mind.

She now pictured the handsome Captain Darlington, his lips, his regular teeth, and his large hands. She felt like a woman in his eyes; he had known her no other way. Would he or wouldn't he? she wondered. Then she imagined him nude and her head level with his chest, her hands exploring his body.

She tugged at the lace of her corset to loosen it further. Sitting astride the stool with her back arched, she softly squeezed her plump breast through the fabric of her blouse. She then looked left and right, and brought out both her breasts, one after the other, and felt the air on her intimate skin like a liberation.

He had seen her do this before. This time, he was closer than he had ever been; barely half a dozen yards separated them. But she had her back to him, and he could not feast his eyes on her breasts, which he knew were as plump as pigeons. He had to move a step closer.

A noise in the trees, a bird perhaps, made her start. She swiftly tucked her breasts back into her corset, then spun round to face the woods.

Behind the screen of vegetation, he held his breath.

'Who's there?' she said in a steady voice, for the sake of her own conscience. But then she really did sense someone was spying on her. She had experienced the sensation before.

'Who's there?' she repeated with her hand on her collarbone, her blouse still undone.

'You know who's here, Miss Marianne,' said a man's voice. The girl gasped. Private Girard continued, 'We're drawn together, you and me. And you need me as much as I need you.'

He knew when a girl was ripe to shed her virginity, and he stepped slowly forward till he appeared just a few yards in front of her.

'Stand back, Guillaume!' she ordered, fighting off panic.

With confidence and feeling, he said, 'We just need to hold each other.' He took another step forward and held out his hand. 'Just once.'

'Get back or I shall scream!' she said, pushing back the stool, and she began to draw back slowly.

'No one will know of our little rendezvous.'

'You are drunk, Guillaume! I shall report you to your commander.'

'And I'll tell everyone what you get up to when you're on your own. Admit it, Marianne, you need it the same as I do.'

'Get away from me!' she said, scowling at him defiantly. He lunged for her. She turned to run. But in her panic, she tripped over the stool.

He was soon on top of her, smothering her in the smell of male sweat and rum, holding her in his arms despite her battling to get free.

He flipped her over, sat astride her, and slapped her full on the side of the face to calm her down. It shocked her, numbed her for a moment.

Then she felt his hands fall on her breasts, bunch them up, and squeeze them till they hurt.

'Get off!' she shrieked desperately, struggling to break free.

Having given full vent to her voice, she screamed out again, and again. 'Help! Help! Someone! Jacob! Help!'

But Girard was determined now. Even if it meant throwing her off the cliff once he was done with her. The rocks would break her bones, and the sea would carry her body away. It would be an accident. He would arrange her equipment near the clifftop. The squalls could be strong and treacherous on that south-facing ledge.

She continued to battle and scream, so this time, he punched her hard. He clamped her neck with one hand as a warning. Then he pinned down her shoulders.

She lay still, her head seething. She did not want to be hit again. Neither did she want to pass out.

He then removed his right hand from her left shoulder to feel for the top of his breeches, and to lift up her dress. Clamping her down with his left forearm, with his right hand he cupped her crotch, in the firm belief that she was bound to succumb in the end, just like the other virgins that had gone before her.

Her fingers reached out and touched a hard, cold object the size of a fist. She took it in her hand, but hesitated.

If she hit him, he would be sure to throttle her. He was capable of it. His hands were immeasurably strong. But then she remembered the promise she had made to herself and to Jacob on board the ship from France. She had promised never to succumb to the sovereign force of the male predator. So she clenched the rock tightly and struck Girard's ear as hard as she could.

The blow knocked him off her. She shot up and bolted, screaming for help, up a natural embankment so she might be seen. Despite his bloody ear, he was up after her, as swift as a falcon, and pounced on her shoulders with all his weight.

In the commotion of the ensuing struggle, there came a loud shot. It made both victim and predator freeze for an instant. Private Girard then instinctively wrapped his arms around his prey, rolling her over.

'Move and I kill you,' shouted the voice of Daniel Darlington, from a distance of twenty-five yards. Girard got to his feet, lifting her with him so that she formed a human shield.

'She's a witch, Sir,' he shouted to Darlington. 'She has bewitched me like she has bewitched you!'

He whipped out his knife from its sheath.

'Do you know what she does when she's alone?'

Marianne felt his powerful forearm on her neck, so tight that it blocked her windpipe. But suddenly the pressure was released, and she sank to her knees, gasping for air. She hung her head while recovering her breath as Darlington ran up to her. The side of her face was heavily bruised, but she told him she was all right. She motioned for him to help Jacob, who was at present wrestling with the soldier twenty years his junior.

Delpech and Darlington had split up as they had come to the opposite side of the wood. They had taken different routes to increase the chances of one of them arriving in time to prevent whatever danger it was that had caused Marianne to scream. Darlington had come round the west flank first; then Jacob had appeared behind Girard, moments after the gunshot.

Girard and Delpech were now locked in a fierce embrace. Jacob had latched onto the soldier's arm to stave off the knife from Marianne's throat. Before Darlington could intervene, they both tripped on a rock that jutted through the turf, and they fell where the ground stepped down just a few feet.

Delpech rolled swiftly away from the soldier so that Darlington could pin the man down with his musket. But there was no need.

Private Girard got to his feet, holding his belly, his face suddenly sobered. He looked down at his hand which he had pulled away. It was covered in blood.

'My God,' said Jacob.

The soldier staggered a few steps before sinking to his knees.

'I loved her,' he said. Then he collapsed completely, face down on the patchy grass.

Jacob was quickly upon the young man, turned him over, felt his pulse. 'My God, he's dead,' he said in horror.

Darlington picked up the bloody knife, glistening on the grass where it fell. He wiped the blade on Girard's shirt and replaced it in the soldier's sheath.

'We must throw him over. He will be taken by the current,' he said, latching onto the body by the ankles.

'My God, man, you cannot . . .'

'His captain will want to know who killed him.'

'But he fell on his own blade, Sir. You bore witness.'

'Doesn't matter,' said Darlington, dragging the body towards the ledge of the cliff. 'I am an English American. You are a Huguenot. You will be placed under arrest, and sent to Leogane to face trial. What chance do you think you will have?'

'He is right, Jacob,' said Marianne, visibly holding back her emotion. 'I hate to say it, but he is right.' She was still in shock, but was herself surprised to find her thoughts lucid and practical. 'His death will condemn you. We cannot let that happen.'

'The man had been drinking. His disappearance will be put down to a tragic accident,' said Darlington, brandishing the soldier's rum flask. 'We will leave this on the edge. We have no choice, Monsieur Delpech. He is dead, and thanks be to God, you and Mademoiselle Duvivier are alive!'

The man's soul had left him, and it was true nothing would be gained by taking the body back; there was no family to mourn him here on the island. It would most likely be buried at sea anyway. So at length, after a short prayer, Jacob agreed to the Englishman's course of action.

The two men solemnly took the body by its wrists and ankles, carried it the rest of the way to the cliff ledge, then swung it twice and let go.

All three of them looked over the edge to see that Girard's body had landed in the shallows. However, instead of being swept out to sea, it soon became apparent that it was being washed to shore.

17

IT WAS AN hour past noon when the *Sally-Ann* put into the natural harbour to refill with water, venison, and a barrel of fruit.

The two-masted sloop, armed with six guns, was on her way to Jamaica. She displaced 120 tons, was manned by fourteen crew members—composed of a mixed bag of nationalities, led by a French captain—and was carrying a delivery of French wine and fineries procured from merchants in Martinique. Jacob could do worse than to pay for his passage aboard.

Darlington's ship would be flopped on its side for weeks to come, and Girard's body, beached on the south shore, could be discovered at any moment. Once the soldier was reported missing, the garrison commander would put together a search party. So, Jacob concluded, it would be foolish not to take the providential ride to freedom.

He would not be entirely alone. Jacques Rouchon, who knew his way around a ship and could tie knots, had paid his passage by joining the crew. Delpech had told him he lacked the patience to wait another few weeks for Mr Darlington's ship, laid up as it was, and that he must find a passage to

Europe to reunite with his family.

Rouchon had put Jacob's edginess down to the imminent departure when he said: 'Aye, Monsieur Delpech, sure as day follows night, yer bound to find a passage across the Atlantic from Port Royal.'

By early evening, the sloop was ready to slip out with the land wind. Thankfully, Girard's absence had still gone unnoticed. Jacob reckoned his mates were covering for him, thinking he must be sleeping off a drunken stupor somewhere under a tree.

It was a good easterly that blew, and the fat, gleaming sun still had an hour to go before it turned orange and sank into the horizon. Moreover, there was naught on Cow Island that could tempt the crew to pass the night there. Truth was, nothing could compare with Port Royal, and they were all eager as hell to get there.

Jacob, aided by Darlington, placed his effects with his medical chest into the longboat. Jacques Rouchon was there with another sailor, loading the last runlets of rum. Marianne, Madame de Fontenay, and Madame Odet were standing thirty yards up from the foreshore to see Jacob off.

A few hours earlier, Madame de Fontenay, informed of the accident, had said to Jacob, 'I encourage you to run with the wind and never stop till you reach your goal, Mr Delpech. We do not want to see you fall short now!' But the thought now entered his mind that it might be premature to abandon them all to the care of Mr Darlington, whom, after all, he hardly knew.

However, the young Englishman must have read his thoughts. Striding back with him towards the waiting women, in a confidential tone of voice, he said, 'Fear not for the ladies, Monsieur Delpech, nor for Mademoiselle Duvivier. I shall take good care of them. You have my word, Sir.'

'It heartens me to hear you say so. Thank you, Mr Darlington.'

'It is I who am indebted to you, Sir, for looking after my future wife!'

Jacob could not resist a friendly chuckle and said, 'I am glad you have found more than what you had bargained for on this voyage.'

Darlington said, 'By God's grace, I have found what I have been seeking for many a year! I have found my true love!' As they came within hearing distance of the ladies, he handed Delpech a card. 'Please, take this,' he said. 'It is my address, should one day you find yourself in New York. You never know.'

Jacob was satisfied, his mind put at ease. He was learning to let go of his country gentleman's reserve, and realising that here more than anywhere, it was important to quickly get the sway of a man. For in this world of pioneers, people continually resettled from place to place by trial and error, and came and went with the winds of conflict and changing frontiers.

It was not without a pinch of sadness that Jacob bade farewell to the ladies, especially his "niece". She had thrown a shawl over her head, to protect from the gusts of wind, but also to cover her swollen cheek.

Teary-eyed, she thanked him for his unrelenting attentiveness and said, 'Please do not worry on our account, nor on anyone else's. You must concentrate your efforts on finding your family now, my dear uncle Jacob.'

She was right; there was no time for guilt. Like her, he should put the whole tragic accident behind him. He must focus on his next goal: his return to Europe.

Marianne was standing beside Darlington now. Jacob noted with satisfaction that they already looked like a young couple. And there was a new and profound complicity between them. They shared a terrible secret.

18

THE CROSSING TO Jamaica usually took three days. Jacob took enough provisions for four, in case the wind fell off. Jacques Rouchon was mostly kept busy with the crew, which suited Delpech well, as he could traverse his moments of melancholy and seasickness in relative solitude.

For the first two days, they made excellent headway under a steady easterly. But as the third night fell, the wind became more erratic, and the swell began to grow. Despite his rising nausea, Jacob had at last managed to drift off to much-needed sleep.

His dreams weaved in and out of recent traumatic events, and he saw Private Girard's face as the man rolled over him, driven by a desire to kill. A horrid swirl in the gut and a loud cry suddenly brought him smartly out of his fearful slumber, and into the living nightmare occurring about him.

'Get the sails off her, mates!' he heard the captain roar, as his eyes were met with a flash of lightning that lit up the sky through the hatch above. Almost instantly, it was followed by a sickening volley of thunder.

Hand over mouth, Jacob staggered to his feet and made a dash towards the gun port. But the chaotic pitch and roll of the ship sent him tumbling backward, and he was sick over the deck. A heavy gush of cold water then burst through the hatch and washed the planks clean, leaving Jacob drenched.

'Mister Rouchon, check the hold!' he heard the captain yell out, before another wave came crashing down on the upper deck.

Jacob was clutching the capstan as Jacques Rouchon, soaked to the skin, came sliding down the steps on his way to the cargo space below.

'What can I do?' shouted Delpech, now rid of the nauseating ball in his gut. Amid the din of booming waves, Rouchon motioned to follow him below into the hold. Already it was two feet deep in sludge and water.

'Can yer man the pump?' he shouted.

Jacob read his lips in the dim light of a lantern and made a sign that he could if shown how. Rouchon gave a quick demonstration before letting Jacob take over the task. It stunk to high heaven of bilge, but he kept to his station and pumped unrelentingly through the darkness. It allowed more qualified hands to perform on deck, reef the mainsail, and point into the wind.

The swell raged with fury the night through; it was worse than anything Jacob had ever experienced. Then, with the dull light of morning that began to seep through the hatch, the storm began to abate. The inpouring of sea gradually ceased. However, after such a battering, the timbers now presented a multitude of small leaks. And there was worse to come.

*

The storm had petered away as quickly as it had risen up, and barely left in its wake a sigh to power the sails. What was more, with a closed ceiling of dense grey cloud, it was impossible to pinpoint the sun. They were temporarily lost. Lost, with hardly enough provisions to last another day, save for the fruit in a barrel standing on deck, now full of seawater.

By the fifth day, Jacob's own victuals had run out. The water was rationed to just a cupful doused with a dram of rum, every three hours. 'Barely enough to wipe the salt from your lips!' groused Rouchon.

On the sixth day, the biscuit ran out, and there was no more cassava bread either, most of it having been spoiled in the storm. The captain allowed a cask to be tapped to lengthen the water. So the diet was watered-down French wine, and tobacco which was chewed or smoked to deceive hunger and prevent exhaustion.

There is nothing worse for a matelot than a stagnant sea. The crew were soon on edge. The captain had to keep the most volatile of them from each other's throats by sending them on duties at opposite ends of the ship. One of these mates was called Harry, an English rigger with a scar from his left ear to his nose. He was short, lithe, and as nimble on the top spar as he was deft with a blade. The other was a big Dutchman by the name of Piet, who could throttle a man with just one hand.

Jacob realised that it would not take much provocation for these men to kill, and he was all the more glad for the company of Jacques Rouchon. The tension was palpable as the two newcomers to the ship sat on the gun deck, each on a cask, smoking their clay pipes. In a low, gravelly voice, Rouchon explained a seafaring custom. 'I think you should know, Monsieur Delpech, that in the extreme case of starvation, one man's life can be sacrificed to save many others. Straws are drawn and the loser killed, bled like a sow, and eaten.'

'My God, that is inhumane, Sir, it is criminal!' said Jacob in an equally low voice, to quell his surprise.

'It is the custom of the sea,' said Rouchon. 'And if it comes to it, Monsieur Delpech, be sure to keep a close watch on the straw-holder's eyes.'

'Why the eyes?' said Jacob, who took another sip from his ration of drink.

'Because this crew be thick as thieves despite appearances. They'll not think twice about singling out the newcomer by the simple bat of an eyelid.'

'What do you mean?'

Jacques Rouchon blew another hoop of smoke from his pipe and said, 'For example, three blinks from the holder could mean the third straw is the one not to take, get it? You gotta keep an eye out, Monsieur Delpech, if you don't wanna end up their next meal!'

'Unless you are the first to take the pick, which would mean better odds.'

'If you say so, Sir, if you say so. Though I'd rather watch for the count. Anything else might be tempting the devil.'

'Or putting your faith in God!'

However, two hours later, the wind picked up. The stagnant cloud began to break up, revealing rags of blue sky here and there. The captain was at last able to locate their position. They had slipped off the shipping lane completely. He estimated it was another two days to the Jamaican port, God willing.

*

On the morning of the nineteenth of August, seven days out of Cow Island, the *Sally-Ann*'s sails began to lose their tautness and to flap. By three in the afternoon, the wind had volt-faced. The sky in the west began to bulge and toss and to turn an angry purple. The captain knew—they all knew—that what they saw rapidly advancing towards them was the most devastating phenomenon known to the Caribbean. The Caribs saw it as a manifestation of Maboya, the evil spirit. And they called it *hurricane*.

Despite their thirst, hunger and fatigue, all hands aboard swiftly set to work preparing the sloop for the battle ahead. They fastened down gun port flaps, secured cannons, strapped down any loose gear, and prepared the longboat for quick and easy release in case an emergency launch should be required.

Their only chance was to abandon course, again reef the mainsail, and steer as close to the eye of the wind as possible. By the time the crew had finished striking the sails, the prow had become awash with huge waves crashing down on it. The sea, cold and frothing, had begun its demoniac dance with the wind howling like hell's hounds all around them. Then the captain gave the ultimate command to strike the reefed mainsail, and let the ship run with the wind and steer by the whipstaff. There was nothing more for most of the mariners to do than to take refuge below deck.

Jacob read fear in their eyes, something he had not seen on the previous occasion. Some prayed in earnest, others remained silent, but all sat with the mark of dread etched into their stern expressions. One mate next to him mumbled incantations.

'Course I believe in God, course, I do, course I believe in

God,' he garbled over and over again in French, so panicked he had not the presence of mind to think of anything else.

It came to Jacob how the apostles had feared the storm on the Sea of Galilee because they too doubted their faith in Jesus. Delpech took it upon himself to help the terrified matelot by reciting the Lord's Prayer at the top of his voice, so that anyone in any language could join in.

The timbers now screamed with every battering as if the ship would break in half, and men were soon rolling about like skittles. Piet, the Dutchman, fell and cracked his head on the cascabel of a cannon, but there was nothing anyone could do for the big man, out cold as he was on the planks. 'He'll not fall any further,' growled one mate.

Another gigantic wall of water slammed over the ship from port side, and another smashed into the hull. And through the howling boom came the appalling sound of splitting timber.

'She's breaking up!' shouted Rouchon from the hatch of the hold, before another great screeching of timber resounded throughout the whole ship. Every man fit to stand scrambled above deck, where the captain ordered them to the longboat on the starboard side.

At the same time, a gigantic roller reared up and snatched three mates near the retaining cordage. Another wave wrenched away the longboat, and Jacob saw it go scudding away into the great folds of the sea.

'The gig, lads, prepare the gig!' cried the captain.

Despite the terrible conditions, the small boat was positioned in minutes. In the short time it took to carry out the operation, the sea had ripped away planks, expanding the opening in the ship's hull, and she was beginning to list. Great rollers now beat over the sloop from every side, like glutinous fingers trying to pull her down, trying to prevent the men from escaping.

Another three men were swept away in one go as they were about to lower themselves into the gig. One of them was Jacques Rouchon.

But through the roaring elements, Jacob could hear cries for help. The planter had managed to latch onto a trailing line and was hanging on for dear life over the side of the ship. Delpech pulled and heaved the rope till Rouchon was hauled back on deck.

The timbers let out another appalling screech. Not a second was there to lose. The bosun and two other men were already aboard the gig when it came to Jacob's turn to climb down the cordage. He hardly had the force to stand, let alone grasp the rigging, but in a last push of strength, he clambered over the side.

'Hurry, man!' shouted Rouchon behind him. But Jacob had given all he had, and he lost his grip. He slid down the side of the hull. However, by good fortune, the small boat was heaved by the swell, and Jacob was able to use the hull to throw himself aboard, narrowly missing Harry the rigger.

The next moment, a huge mass of water clobbered the ship on her windward side and weighted her down further. There came another appalling crack—it must have been the keel. Rouchon jumped aboard the gig behind Jacob. The ship began to turn up her long bowsprit as her stern began to go under.

'Cut her away, man!'

'Wait!' shouted Jacob. 'There's still men aboard!'

But the flash of a knife appeared before Jacob's eyes. It

belonged to Harry, the lithe Englishman, who proceeded to cut the ropes that attached the gig to the ship.

The little craft was instantly whisked away over the waves as the 120 tonner turned up her nose, then slid downward like a giant sea monster.

*

Of the sixteen men who set out from Cow Island, only five had made it into the gig: the bosun, Jacob Delpech, Jacques Rouchon, Harry the rigger, and the tiller mate. Every slide into the deep trough of a wave seemed like it would be their last, and time after time, each man committed his soul to God. And indeed, had they embarked on the heavier longboat, they would certainly have gone under by now. But the gig just kept bobbing up and over the waves as good as a cork.

By first light, the steep watery hills began to roll out into smooth undulations, and the sea became navigable once more. The five men in the boat were already half-starved; they had no rations, and just enough water to last the day at a push. But they were still alive.

Jacob promised God that he would fight tooth and claw to survive his terrible ordeal, and live thereafter as living proof of God's grace. But all was not written, and as Jacob well knew, mortal danger lay ahead.

They put up the mast and opened the sail to steer the craft west by southwest, according to the reckoning of the bosun. They then sat or lay for the better part of the day, recovering from their sleepless night of bailing out the little boat.

Come sundown, they used the sail to collect rain water that fell in light showers during the night. But it was a dismal collection, especially compared to the sea miles they had sacrificed.

The following morning, with not a cud of tobacco left to chew on and hardly a drop left in their flasks, the question Jacob most dreaded was put forward.

'Custom of the sea?' said Harry, who then laid the only musket down on the bench beside him. His eyes blazed with the fire of desperation. 'There's one shot,' he said. 'Otherwise there's the blade.' He flashed his knife in the garish sunlight.

The men looked solemnly at one another. Only Jacob was truly horrified, as much at the prospect of being slaughtered as at the thought of seeing man eat man.

'No, wait,' he said. He then pleaded on the grounds that, according to the rule, all present must give their consent, and concluded, 'It is unchristian. It is sinful. I say we first pray to God for deliverance.'

'All right, go on then,' said Harry in all simplicity. 'Then we get to it. Right?'

Jacob reached for his hessian sack, still strapped over his shoulder. It contained two precious items, his medical book and his Bible. The latter he took out, opened the damp pages, and read in French from the Gospel of Mathew that spoke of the storm. Each word grazed his parched throat, but he persisted, translating the words as best he could into English. 'And his disciples came to him and awoke him, saying, Lord, save us, we perish. And he said to them, why fear you, you of little faith?'

During the prayer spoken in English, Harry cut off a piece of rope and untwisted the twines, which he sliced up into different lengths. He then looked up with a sigh of impatience bordering on fury as Delpech at last concluded,

'Dear Lord, we ask for forgiveness for our mortal sins, and we ask for forgiveness if we have lacked faith. We pray, oh Lord, for the safety of our loved ones far across the ocean sea. And for our lost brethren, so they may rest in heavenly peace. And, dear Jesus, we pray for Your grace so that we may be saved from the mortal sin of murder. Amen.'

'Amen,' said Harry, businesslike. He glared around intensely at each one of the group. 'Now we draw straws. Right?' he said. 'Right?'

The mates replied with a solemn *aye*, even Jacques Rouchon. While all eyes were on Jacob, the planter from Nantes discreetly motioned to Delpech with his two fingers to watch Harry's eyes. Jacob gave a short nod.

But Delpech did not take heed of Rouchon's suggestion. Instead, he quickly put out his hand to take first pick. At least this way, there was no chance of being cheated.

Jacob did not choose the shortest straw. It was poor Rouchon who, only recently freed from his indenture, was about to be bled like a sow. The thought was unbearable, but this was the custom which he had accepted.

Jacob nevertheless tried to make a plea for Christianity, but there was nothing doing. Even the bosun, who was normally a charitable man, had the look of someone possessed by an insatiable urge, like that of Private Girard just before he fell on his own weapon. It was the look of a bloodthirsty killer.

Jacques Rouchon, seeing his fate was sealed, burst into a parched but brazen chuckle. 'Come on, Harry,' he said, 'make it quick, and drink to my soul!'

He laid down his head on the gunwale, keeping his eyes wide open. Harry hungrily placed the musket near the planter's temple and waited an instant to get the timing right between the bobs of the boat.

'Wait!' shouted Jacob, quite agitated, which made the gig bob out of time. He was now pointing to the sky where a squawking gull came nearer. Fuelled by the sudden adrenaline, he got unsteadily to his feet and looked straight ahead. 'By God, it is land!' he declared. 'Land ahoy, I say. Land ahoy!'

'Sit yerself down, man!' said Harry. ''Tis the trick of the sea!'

The bosun held up a hand to pause Rouchon's execution while the tiller mate seized the barrel of the musket. Careful not to disturb the balance of the boat, the bosun also rose to his feet.

'That be bloody land all right, lads!' he croaked, 'or I'll eat my own boot leather!'

A feeling of fraternity instantly supplanted the feral instinct of survival, and the men now wept dry tears of joy and clasped each other heartily. Only Harry, who would have eaten his own mother, wore the sneer of disgust on his face.

Whether it was a miracle or due to the bosun's navigational skills, before long, not only could they see land, but the distant masts of tall ships that told them they had reached the port of Jamaica. They had made it to Port Royal! Commonly known as the wickedest town on earth . . .

19

THE TEAL-COLOURED waterways and the breathtaking views through the Swiss valley—with the lush plateau to her right and the foothills of the Jura to her left—brought Jeanne a measure of tranquillity.

Monsieur Gaugin's mention of her head injury on her travel document had allowed her to travel with Paul by lake, canal, and river, from Yverdon across Lake Neuchatel, over Lake Bienne, and then all the way up the river Aar to the pretty village of Brugg. They arrived late in the day. A gathering of villagers headed by the mayor, a benevolent man, greeted them as they disembarked.

'You are welcome to stay in our homes, brethren,' he said. 'You will find food and a bed for the night.' He gestured to the good people standing behind him, who offered bows and nods and utterances of welcome. Jeanne was feeling faint after the long journey, which surely could not explain what she saw next.

It was a face in the crowd that stared back at her. It was the face of the pauper. She wanted to shout out, but first instinctively turned to her son and clasped his hand. When she looked again, the man was gone, and it was a different face that looked inquisitively back at her. The next moment, faces were spinning around her, and Paul was kneeling by her side.

'Fetch some water,' said one lady, who had been travelling with her since Yverdon. 'You fainted, Madame,' she said. Had Jeanne seen the man who was responsible for the mark on her face and the bump on her head? Or was it the bump that was responsible for her vision of that man? Jeanne no longer knew what to think as she was helped to a bench.

'Now,' said the mayor, clearing his throat, 'I have a message for a certain Madame Delpech if she is among you.'

Fortunately Jeanne, seated by now, this time retained an outer composure as he asked again. 'Madame Delpech. Do we have a Madame Delpech among us?' said the mayor, sweeping his gaze around the group at the quayside. His eyes seemed to linger over Jeanne and her boy. Jeanne also looked around as if she were searching for this Madame Delpech to step forward.

'Oh well, if anyone comes across her, I would be most obliged if you would ask her to see me. I have been given a message for her to remain here in Brugg.'

The audacity of the wretch made her want to step forward and shout out her story: How the man she had just seen had clubbed her and left her for dead for the sake of her jacket, believing it contained gemstones. How he had gone through the pockets of the drowned people, and then thrown their bodies back into the water without knowing if they had expelled their last breath or not. But what proof did she have to lock someone away, even if they did find him? So she bit her tongue and kept the peace. It was written on her paper that she had received a head injury; they could well retain her.

Then what would become of Paul? Moreover, the aldermen of the village certainly had far more to worry about herding refugees northward than the imaginings of a French bourgeoise. No, she had kept it under her hat till now. She had already made her mind up that the less anyone knew of her story, the fewer chances she had of being tracked down.

Jeanne joined the small group of people queuing to be led to the tavern; most of them would have felt out of place in a bourgeois home. On their way to the tavern, they passed a wondrous clock above the city gate that captured the admiration of all. Set in a recess above it, the painted figure of a Swiss countryman brought much-needed merriment to the group as it came out and counted the hours on its right hand, like a living person. But as Jeanne turned her head again, a sickness in her heart replaced the fleeting gaiety as she thought she saw the pauper skulking away. Could it truly be that her mind was playing tricks on her?

*

Early next morning, she waited in the fog, wrapped in her summer shawl with the other refugees who had been conducted to the wharf. Four flat-bottomed riverboats, attached two by two, were waiting for them to board. The leading boats that would carry the majority of the passengers were headed for Basle by way of the Rhine; from there, the passengers would head north. The second two boats were scheduled to let their load of twenty or thirty passengers disembark at a landing stage a league's distance from Zurzach.

'Paul, come and say goodbye,' said Jeanne to her son, who was throwing sticks into the current just a couple of yards behind her. She smiled back at the lady with whom she had exchanged a few pleasantries during the previous day's journey, and who had come to her aid when she had swooned. The lady and her adolescent daughter were waiting to board one of the first two boats headed for Basle, from where they intended to travel to Brandenburg.

'It's the best season for travelling north, if that is where you're headed, Madame,' she said.

'Thank you,' said Jeanne, 'but really, I have to see a friend at Schaffhausen.' Jeanne regretted the slip as soon as it was out and instinctively turned to see if anyone was listening. There was no one; most of the crowd were advancing towards the boats. With a half-smile, Jeanne continued, 'I pray you find your sons and your husband.'

'Oh, I am sure they are in Brandenburg. I must admit, though, I am not going to enjoy the river ride, specially not this one, from what I've heard. I'd much rather travel by cart, and I'd gladly put up with all the bone-shaking as long as I had the firm ground beneath me, for I am like a brick to water, Madame.' So was Jeanne, but she did not say so.

'I am sure everything will be fine, Madame. With God's grace, you will get over it.' Again Jeanne regretted her slip of the tongue. Had she not said the same to Ginette before leaving Geneva? 'I bid you farewell,' she said, as the lady followed the movement of the crowd into the first two embarkations.

'Bon voyage to Schaff . . . Schaff . . . whatever you call it,' called the lady. Jeanne did not try to correct her. Instead, she waved back, then set about gathering her effects to board one of the other boats.

No more than twenty yards from the quayside, the leading pair of flat-bottomed boats vanished, engulfed as they were in the thick, morning fog. The clock eerily tolled six dampened chimes as the second pair of boats were pushed away from the wharf and floated into the swift current of the river Aar.

For two hours solid, the mist rolled closely along the water's surface. It was impossible to make out the opposite bank most of the time, let alone the boats ahead. And certain narrow passages gave cause for hearts to pound quicker and women to yelp as they clutched their broods. But the captain bore a reassuring appearance: his impressive moustache was as impeccably trimmed as the garb of his profession. He was mindful to forewarn in a tenor voice of any bumpy rides ahead, and soon, most aboard became inured to the rapidly flowing waters. However, a small incident came about that for Jeanne would have dramatic consequences.

By mid-morning, the mist had lifted, and the sun was warming rigid muscles. Paul, at the prow, was the first to sight the two vessels travelling just one hundred yards ahead. He yelled out none too soon, because shortly after the sighting, the leading craft slowed.

'What be the matter?' called out the captain in German across the water, as the trailing boats managed to overtake the leading craft at a wide part of the river.

The answer was barked back in the same language, and judging from the hand-talk, it became clear to the French speakers that the two leading vessels had become untethered. In fact, they had become entangled in floating branches and other matter. The captain of both leading vessels preferred to pull over at the nearest quayside to re-tether properly.

The overtaking boats slipped through the widening waterway without further hindrance and continued through the epic Swiss riverscape.

'Steady as she goes!' the captain called out, and German accents all around seemed to fall upon Jeanne's ear, now that they were moving deeper into German-speaking territory.

There was no call to be miserable in such a beautiful environment. But though she sat bathed in sunlight, from time to time, her face clouded over as her thoughts spiralled back to the recent tragedy. What she would say to Ginette she knew not, so she did her best to empty her mind, to just let the gentle heat of the sun soak into her tumefied face.

By high noon, they arrived at a landing stage, where they took their lunch of bread, cheese, pâté, and beer that had been packed for them by their generous hosts in Brugg. Led by guides paid by the confederacy, the group of refugees then trekked at an easy pace to the small town of Zurzach, which they reached by late afternoon. From Zurzach, Jeanne and Paul climbed on a charabanc that took them and a handful of other travellers to the village of Neunkirch. Here, they dined on broth and were given a place to sleep.

'How far is it to Schaffhausen, Madame?' said Jeanne to the good lady who was ladling the soup, and who spoke some French.

'T'ain't far, Ma'am,' she said, 'not more than a two-hour walk across the plain, but they've arranged a cart for you. Not tomorrow, of course, but the day after the Lord's Day.'

*

Doubt filled Jeanne's thoughts as she lay holding her son, in the large room where other travellers snored in their sleep.

Should she have travelled north with the vast majority of Huguenots? At least they spoke her language, whereas the Germanic utterances she overheard now made her nervous.

These people seemed good and kind, but when she overheard them laugh out loud that evening, it had almost seemed as if the jokes were on her. But she could not bear the thought of leaving the Fleurets with no manifestation of love, sorrow, loss, and condolence. If she had headed north, she would never have seen them again. She would forever regret not having reached out to them in their grief. But what if they were no longer in Schaffhausen? And why had they decided to stop there anyway, when everyone else was headed for Brandenburg, where the grand elector's successor had extended his welcome to Huguenots to settle in his province? Could it be that Jeannot Fleuret had found work there? Just a few hours separated her from the township, and from knowing.

'Why can't we wait for the cart?' whispered Paul an hour later as Jeanne, having found a quill, scribbled a thank-you note on the kitchen table.

'Because it would mean waiting another day,' she said, keeping her voice down. 'That's if we're lucky, what with the season. And what if the cart is delayed?'

She silently led the way out into the freshness of the breaking morning and strode onto the stony track, as though she had decided to embrace her fate. Paul knew there was no debate to be had when his mother got the bit between her teeth, so he trotted along beside her with his load on his back and a long stick that had served him well the day before, on the path to Zurzach.

'I hope they won't think us ungrateful, but we must press on.'

'I hope there are no bandits!' said Paul.

'Well,' said Jeanne, 'your father always much prefers to

travel by early morning when the day is new and fresh . . .'

'And when the riffraff has not yet stirred,' continued the boy, quoting his father by heart. 'But what about Monsieur Cephas?'

Jeanne checked her step as she said: 'What about him?'

'I thought you . . .'

'Saw him? Seeing things, more like,' she said, resuming her resolute gait.

'Didn't you see him then, in the crowd? I thought that's why you fainted.'

'No, my mind playing tricks.'

'Then that would make two of us,' said the boy, looking up at his mother with the frank gaze of his father.

'Oh, I see,' said Jeanne.

She pulled her shawl over her shoulders, held her boy's hand tight, and, with her stick in her other hand, dug into the earthen track that took them towards the gold and blue light of the nascent day.

*

Sometimes, Jeanne thought, you have to live in the present, for the here and now. It enables you to put distance between life's tides; it saves you from getting muddled in future plans and from worries that have not yet even emerged. So, for the time being, she let past and future fall into oblivion as she walked hand in hand with her son, along the path that narrowed from the open plain into thick woodland. She felt young again, like she did in her country home when she used to run through the long grass with her other children, back in the days when the world seemed so simple, when men had not given up their sense of Christian virtue for the malice of a king.

Paul, sensing the bounce in her step soften, tugged her hand, and they ran together as if they were siblings. For a fleeting instant, the boy saw his mother as a little girl, and that the little girl needed protection and love like every child.

A cart coming towards them on a bend in the narrow road made them resume a more orderly gait. It turned out to be a couple with their three children. Early birds, no doubt, on their way to church. It reassured her to know that other like-minded folk would soon be following in their tracks. Hats were doffed, smiles exchanged, and as soon as they were alone again on the forest thoroughfare, Paul resumed his playful pranks, running into the dense wood and leaping out at her.

'Paul, stop it now,' she said, but the lack of conviction in her voice only encouraged the boy. He played stalk the deer, running from tree to tree, trying to get as close as he could to startle her again. The boy needed this time for play, she sensed. After all, despite the young man already budding inside, he was still only a boy of ten. So she let him have his free rein and continued along the narrow path at a good pace, pretending not to see him.

Walking on her own, her thoughts meandered back to her deceased children. Ginette was right; Louise and Anne would travel with her always, because she carried them in her heart. It was liberating to know she could travel the world, and they would still be with her. Just because they had been called to God did not mean she was not their mother. She still had five beautiful children.

But first she must get to Schaffhausen to give her support to the Fleurets. Then she would head up the Rhine and travel across country to Amsterdam. From the Dutch port, she would cross over to London, where she hoped to reunite with her husband. Together they would somehow recover their children who remained in Montauban: Elisabeth, who must be a young lady by now, and sweet Isabelle, who was no longer a baby. That was what she must do now.

But what if Jacob had not made it to London yet? What if the Fleurets had left Schaffhausen? Had her innate optimism got the better of her judgement again? A movement in the trees made her look left, to the edge of the forest.

'Paul. Paul,' she said, striding into the vegetation that skirted the wood. 'Paul, come out now.'

There was a muffled call and a loud rustle, like that of a heavy animal.

'Paul, don't be silly. Come out now, please!' she said in the uncompromising voice of a worried mother. But it was a large form that emerged from the dark undergrowth which quickened her pulse. And it was accompanied by a coarse voice.

'You want the boy?' said the pauper, stepping forward. 'I want the stones, the precious ones this time!'

Jeanne, rooted to the spot, for a long second just stared at the sight of the man, standing on the edge of the forest with one hand over her son's mouth and a hunting knife gleaming against his soft, white throat.

'Cephas Crespin, don't you dare!' growled Jeanne in the voice of a mother ready to die to defend her child. At the same time, she flashed her gaze at her son and read determination in his eyes. She knew that he had no sense of the danger he was in. 'Paul, don't move!'

Too late. The boy sank his teeth into his captor's hand.

'Ouch! You little tyke!' yelped the pauper. Then he grabbed the boy by the hair, lifted him onto his toes, and pressed the blade against his skin. 'Give me the stones, or I'll slit his throat now!'

'All right,' said Jeanne, holding out her hands, as much for the pauper not to draw his blade across as to prevent her son from trying to break free. 'Paul, don't move, please, for me, darling,' she pleaded. She knew that it would take just a quick lateral slice, and her son would be dead.

'The bloody jewels, woman!' bellowed Cephas Crespin while the lad struggled and kicked.

'All right, all right,' she said, hand on her shoulder strap to remove her sack. 'Paul! Please, keep still.' But as the man tried to tighten his grip and slowly pressed the blade into the boy's throat, Paul jerked back his head, and stamped and kicked for all his life. 'NO!' screamed Jeanne. Wasting not a second, and remembering the man's maimed thumbs that prevented him from clasping tightly, she took up her stick and in one movement brought it down with all her strength onto his hand, knocking the knife to the ground. The pauper tossed the boy to one side. Jeanne stood holding her stick, ready for another swing.

'No you don't, Cephas Crespin, or I promise I'll . . .'

She swung back her stick, but he was inside her reach too quickly and grabbed her by the throat, making her drop it. He snarled: 'Or you'll what?'

Her only answer was to gouge at his ill-shaven face like a wildcat. He punched her to the ground, then dived on top of her. He thumped her in the gut, slammed back her head, and flipped her over so she lay on her belly. Sitting on her posterior, he wrenched her sack from her shoulders, almost pulling her arms out of their sockets. She screamed with frustration at being clamped down. She cared not for the sack but kept up her struggle to give Paul time to get back to the thoroughfare, where he might find help from people on their way to church.

Pinning her torso down with his knees, the pauper plunged a hand into the sack to make sure the stones were there. But a dull, heavy blow sent him sideways.

On the relief of the pressure on her nape, she looked round to see Paul standing there, holding her stick. Then the boy swiped away her bag from the pauper, who was cupping his right ear.

'Leave it, Paul!' she cried out before the man, still on his knees, lunged for it like a rabid beast.

Still in a daze from the blows, she scrambled onto her hands and knees and threw herself between the pauper and her son. She was not going to lose another child while there was still life in her. The pauper staggered to his feet and booted the boy, who fell to the ground winded, and then stamped his booted foot down on Jeanne's shoulder.

Amid the leaves and insects of the woodland litter, she saw her son lying on the ground where the pauper's knife had fallen. With a feral scream, she crawled desperately to reach him. Two powerful blasts of a gun were the last things she heard before closing her eyes.

*

Jeanne saw herself standing, pregnant, holding her two-year-old daughter in her arms, with Paul and his elder sister, watching the cows being led into Mon Plaisir meadow, which lay between the house and old Renac's farm. The meadow had been given over to pasture that year. The gentle warmth of the sun made her face tingle as everything became a blur.

Then her gaze met the soft yellow canvas of a moving cart, illuminated by the sun shining on the other side. Realising she was no longer in a dream, she turned her stiff neck. 'Paul,' she said. The boy was looking out into the moving landscape, where a river ran parallel to the track behind them. He turned towards her. In a calmed voice, she continued, 'Paul, my boy.'

'You are safe now, Mama,' he said as she gestured for him to move closer. She felt the twinge of her swollen skin when she brought his face to hers. But it did not matter. She just needed to feel the cheek of her child on her bare skin.

The cart slowed. Before Paul could give any explanation, Jeanne heard a familiar voice.

'We found her. On the road from Neunkirch.' She recognised the voice of Etienne Lambrois.

'And not a moment too soon neither, by God,' said the voice of Jeannot Fleuret.

'She's in a poor state,' said Lambrois as the carriage came to a halt. The flap was pulled to one side.

'My God, my poor woman,' said Claire. Slowly, Jeanne removed herself from the cart. She embraced Claire—Claire with her large bump. Then she was met by Ginette. The two women fell into each other's arms.

'My God, look at you. I shouldn't have left you,' said Ginette, tears in her eyes, 'but I couldn't stay . . . I lost my boy.'

'I know, Ginette, I know,' said Jeanne gently. 'That's why I came as soon as I found out.'

'But he's still here, isn't he?' said Ginette, touching her large bosom. 'Where I keep my other darling butterflies.'

'Yes, my Ginette,' said Jeanne, with her hand on her own heart, 'and he is here too.'

20

ON THE AFTERNOON of August 24, five haggard and thirst-bitten castaways staggered from their gig onto the boardwalk at North Dock.

The port town was only just rousing from its siesta as they paused outside Customs House. It was closed. So they proceeded opposite onto Lime Street, where a tavern or three showed signs of life. On the veranda of the first establishment, a group of pretty painted ladies were sitting on stools or leaning on posts. They were smoking, chatting, or just drowsily watching the world and his mistress go by.

'Hey, prince!' called one of the temptresses in accented English, but the five men did not even turn their heads. Instead they dived into the cool tavern opposite, where the sawdust was freshly laid, and they ordered beer, broth, bread, and a pipe of wine to begin with. Two hours later, only Jacques Rouchon, Jacob Delpech, and the bosun—whose name was Benjamin Fry—re-emerged to report the shipwreck.

It was past six o'clock. The street was alive now with walkers, lookers and drinkers, and labourers rolling barrels towards the dock. The colourful painted ladies of the bawdy house across the street were down to three and busy in banter with a disparate bunch of matelots, five or six in number. They must have come from aboard the tall ship newly moored in the bay, thought Jacob as he and his mates made their way back towards Customs House.

'Up there's the Exchange,' said Benjamin Fry, who nodded to a building up the street on the right where groups of merchants were in discussion. 'And further up's the governor's place.'

They were crossing Queen Street, which was lined with rum shops and half-timbered houses. It led to the lieutenant governor's stone-built mansion. Soldiers in red coats, darkies carrying baskets, and a whole array of ladies and gentlemen in fashionable attire created the colourful street scene. It did not seem so wicked a place as all that, thought Jacob.

'I wager that's where a buccaneer will fetch his letters,' said Rouchon, turning to Delpech with a cheeky grin. Jacob knew he was referring to letters of mark, which gave privateers a legal right to attack Spanish ships and settlements. They had spoken about them in the tavern where Fry and Harry had given a brief rundown.

But Jacob was no longer listening. In fact, he suddenly found himself struggling to even put one foot in front of the other. Must be the heat or perhaps the fatigue, he thought to himself as he wiped his brow.

They continued across the east-west road, bathed in sunlight, and strolled to the door of Customs House to report the shipwreck. Rouchon turned to say something to Jacob, but then checked himself and said: 'You all right, Monsieur Delpech? You look a bit green around the gills, I must say.'

'Ye—yes, thank you. Must be the effects of the . . . the . . .'

'Of the what?' said Rouchon.

But Jacob was unable to think: his mind was swimming; the words to describe his meal eluded him. He bent over and touched his knees to catch his breath, and he felt like he was standing aboard the *Sally-Ann* again. As he looked up, his eyes were met by a whirling landscape of sky, sun, and buildings. Then his legs collapsed beneath him.

Face up, the next thing he saw was a succession of talking faces. They belonged to Rouchon, the bosun, a soldier in scarlet uniform, and a big-bosomed lady in a flamboyant feathered hat.

'He's got the fever,' she said.

Jacob closed his eyes, and for a second, he saw his wife and his children playing in their country home in France.

'Just shows, doctors are as vulnerable as the next man,' said the bosun.

Benjamin Fry thought Jacob's medical chest—now at the bottom of the Caribbean Sea—had carried the tools of his profession, in the same way a tradesman carries the tools of his trade. Jacques Rouchon did not attempt a foray into English to rectify what he knew to be a misinterpretation, so the error stood. Indeed, it was even upheld by the medical literature found in Jacob's sack.

'It's a chance I've a spare room, vacated only this morning,' said the large and exuberant lady. 'If he has coin, you can bring him round.'

In Port Royal, reputedly the richest town in the English Indies, not only was every service the object of payment, but people expected to be paid in ready cash.

During Rouchon's numerous jaunts with Jacob on Cow Island, he had spied the bulge of Jacob's *bourse* under his shirt. So he was able to reassure the lady of Jacob's solvency whether he lived or died. His level of English, however, only allowed him to make three-word sentences that reflected his bodily needs, such as *we go eat, give me wine, you me go*, and so on. So the planter's gesturing was just as eloquent as his words when he said, 'Oh, coin he has, Madame!'

Mrs Angela Evens was a Welsh-born matron and the respected widow of a tavern keeper. With the sale of her husband's assets, she was able to purchase a relatively peaceful lodging house, just a stone's throw away from the graveyard.

Rouchon, with his forthright air, was convincing enough for Mrs Evens to hail down a man with a cart who had been delivering barrels of beer. She ordered the man, whose name was Isaac, to deliver the sick "doctor" to her lodgings. The bosun continued into Customs House to report the loss of the *Sally-Ann* and most of the mates aboard, while Rouchon followed Jacob, slumped in the handcart, to his new lodgings.

*

At the height of his delirium, Delpech dreamt a Catholic mob was coming to lynch him. But the hundreds of people streaming by outside his second-floor window were in fact returning from the funeral of Port Royal's most illustrious privateer, Captain Henry Morgan. The former governor of Jamaica had passed away on his plantation the day after Jacob collapsed. The clamour of revellers drinking and singing was enough to rouse the dead, and Delpech wondered at one point during the commotion for what reason he was lying in hell. He was not, of course, although the captain's after-funeral celebrations would later indirectly bring Jacob grief of a distinctly mortal nature.

Jacques Rouchon visited the stone-built, three-storey lodging house every day around noon, for the first fortnight of Jacob's distemper. During the first moments of lucidity, Delpech mustered all his strength to give the planter money to buy laudanum, to dull the pain in his belly and help him sleep. He had read that more than anything, a sick body needed rest to be able to resist the ailment and be cured.

He also handed Rouchon a list of ingredients with which to make a draught for the calenture. This consisted— according to *The Surgeon's Mate*—of barley, two gallons of freshwater, liquorice juice, cloves, oil of vitriol spirit for his ailing head, and a spoonful of rose wine to take away the bitterness. Along with the doses of laudanum, the resulting decoction was about all Jacob could take down during the initial stages of his illness.

At the same time, other elements were combining that would pin Jacob down far longer than his present calenture and dysentery. These elements included Jacob's taking laudanum, Jacques's meeting up with Harry, and Morgan's funeral that acted as a catalyst for vice in the shape of dice.

*

One Tuesday, a little over two weeks after he had collapsed in front of Customs House, Jacob at last was able to sit up and spoon down the chicken broth Mrs Evens had concocted specially for him. He felt alert now that he had not taken any laudanum since Sunday, having heard how easily it could take root in the seat of a man's desire.

He was looking forward to seeing Rouchon, who usually showed up around noon. But noon came and went, as did the night, and the next day, without a sign of the planter. By the following Wednesday, Jacob prayed nothing untoward had befallen his friend, and he got to mulling over their last conversation together.

'You have been most generous,' Jacob had said. 'You may well have saved my life.'

'As you have saved mine, I might say,' Rouchon had returned.

At the time, it had struck Jacob, albeit fleetingly, that Rouchon had not used the preterit, as one would on relating a past event such as the one on the *Sally-Ann*, when Jacob hauled the planter from the side of the hull. He had used the present perfect tense as if the event had just happened and was ongoing.

'Although I don't deserve it,' he had continued, ''cause I have dabbled in the vice of dice, Monsieur Delpech. And the worst of it is that I won at first! Now I wish I'd lost.'

He had then related how, on the night of Captain Morgan's funeral, he had run into Harry, who had taken him to a dicing house.

'But I swear to God, it is not a place for a poor planter, and I fear I must soon leave, Monsieur Delpech, before it is the ruin of me.' But Jacob had not realised how soon.

There was a knock at the door. Instead of Jacques Rouchon, in walked Mrs Evens with his broth, which was as good a consolation as any, now that he was recovering his appetite.

'There you are, Doctor,' she said, sliding the tray over his lap once he had managed to prop himself up against his pillows.

'Thank you, Mrs Evens. You are so kind.'

The French doctor was a charming man, and she was not

indifferent to his soft baritone voice and accent. But there were nevertheless practical matters to be addressed.

She picked up his bedpan, matron-like, and proceeded past a little round table dressed with flowers, to the window.

'It is a fine day, Doctor,' she said. Leaning her generous bust out of the window, she threw out the contents of the pan into the street below. Turning back into the room, with a smile she said, 'Now that you are back among the living, Doctor, do you think you can pay me?'

'Pay you?' For a second, Jacob was taken aback, fearing the lady had misread his intentions.

'For bed and board, Doctor,' she said affably. 'I can only go on feeding you if I have food in the larder, and for that, I'm going to need some rent.'

'Oh, yes, of course, Mrs Evens, forgive me. I err have still a light head.'

How naïve he had been to imagine she had taken him in out of the goodness of her heart. He asked her what he owed her.

'It's seven shillings a week for the room, and three shillings for board, and a further shilling for care, which amounts to four crown and two shillings for the two weeks past, or four pieces of eight if you prefer.'

It was a hefty price to pay, he thought, considering that an indentured servant cost twenty pieces of eight, and that was for a three-year term. Yet it was a small price to pay for still being alive, although had he known the cost sooner, no matter how weak he was, he would certainly have chosen to stay in a more "godly" establishment. For the opposite wall often let through the intimate sighs and the most eccentric squeals of ladies and gentlemen in the clutches of their primal passions. He told Mrs Evens he would have some coin ready for her when she came back for the bowl. She exited the room with one eyebrow raised and her nostrils flared.

Once Jacob had finished his broth, he took the key hanging from his neck and reached across to the locked drawer where he kept his valuables. He pulled out the drawer and grabbed his plump little *bourse*. But the instant he did so, he knew something did not tally. His heart sank as he tipped up the sack. His eyes widened in shock, then horror, as one by one, instead of twenty-eight gold louis, an assortment of farthings and pennies fell into his hand. His hopes of boarding a ship to Europe were dashed. Not only that, he now found himself in debt.

Ten minutes later, there was a knock at the door. Mrs Evens's large figure filled the doorway. She stepped into the room and looked down at the drawer still open, then at Jacob, whose gaunt face was an open book.

'I knew it. He's taken your coin, hasn't he, Doctor?'

Jacob gave a nod. 'I must see the governor,' he said with incredulity.

'With all due respect, you are in no state to go anywhere. And besides, your friend is gone.'

'Gone? Why did you not tell me?'

'Only just found out myself. My maid says she saw him hopping onto a ship to Lord knows where. He was with a man with a scar across his face.'

'Harry,' murmured Delpech, recalling how the English rigger had once nearly skinned the planter for his flesh, and then had introduced him to dice for the planter to be fleeced.

'I did hear he was dicing, and losing. It's commonplace round here, you know. They live it up and goad each other on till there's nothing left, and they're back in debt and having to put out to sea again.'

'So, as I am his creditor, I am also the loser.'

'The only one who really wins is the tavern keeper. That's why there are so many of them. You're still going to have to cough up, though, Doctor, if you'll pardon the expression.'

'Madame, I have no other means,' said Jacob, taking in the immediate implications of the theft.

'You might try looking in your jacket, and if that's not enough, you'll have to write me out an IOU, Doctor. I do believe you to be a gentleman true to his word,' she said, with one hand on her hip, the other hand pointing to his jacket on a hook behind the door.

'Yes,' said Jacob, remembering the gold escudo he had been given at Petit Goave. But it was only worth sixteen reals, or two pieces of eight. So he was obliged to make out an IOU.

*

By the end of September, Jacob had put some flesh back on his bones, and was strong enough to go for strolls around the town and its port. Being in Mrs Evens's debt had obliged him to remain in her lodging house. He had, however, moved to a smaller room on the third floor which consisted of four bare walls with a single bed and a chest of drawers. She treated him kindly and agreed to continue to give him board and lodging in exchange for IOUs, which, by the time he was able to stand and walk about, amounted to five pieces of eight. And that did not include her deceased husband's clothes that she insisted he wear, for she would not have a gentleman walk about town in tatters.

*

Thursday, 30 September, was no different than the previous days, except that, instead of wondering how he could pay his passage on board a ship to Europe, he found himself pondering over Mrs Evens's proposition.

She had offered to let him stay on at her house. She would forget his debt and even pay for his medical instruments so that he could practice from home. In short, she was offering him freedom from debt in exchange for marriage.

Despite it being a very fair deal, he knew in advance what conclusion he would arrive at. The tricky part was how to let her down gently. After all, she was his creditor and had his IOUs, which she could well sell to the highest bidder.

From the quayside near Fort James, where gulls were pecking into a pile of fish guts, he had a good view of the dockers unloading barrels from a ship. He might not have the means to work as a merchant, he once thought, but loading and unloading merchandise was something he could do. However, he had dropped the idea as soon as he found out that any menial work would barely bring him enough to live on, which meant it would take many years to pay back his debt. She really did have him over a barrel, did Mrs Evens.

As he unravelled the whole farce in his mind, it was becoming more and more absurd. She would not even believe he was not really a doctor, so set was she on her ideal. He now realised why she had not kicked him out when she saw he was penniless. She had seen him as a good client from the start. Then she saw the theft of his money as an opportunity to move up from being a Welsh tavern keeper's widow to a respectable French doctor's wife. And having once taken root in her mind, the notion had grown till this morning, when she popped the question.

'I want you first to think it over before giving me your answer,' she had said.

Not wanting to provoke her immediate disappointment and have her flying into a direction she might later regret, he had promised he would.

As he ambled down Lime Street among the fashionable gentlemen and stylish ladies, he realised that in this town, where fortunes were made and thrown away on the roll of a dice, anything could go. And he could be anyone. He could call himself a doctor and no one would object, because everyone here was also trying to be someone else. Even Mrs Evens, whom he suspected of once being an indentured servant, then a lady of lesser morals before becoming a tavern keeper's wife, could aspire to become a doctor's wife.

The whole town, with its assortment of pretty brick buildings, its shop fronts, taverns, and cobblestones, was in fact a sham of a civilised settlement. And its morals were no less shallow than its foundations, built as they were on a spit of sand. Its pretty façades hid the lies and vice and sin at its heart, which entertained wicked men like Harry and corrupted good men like Rouchon, the planter, who, having once felt the lure of easy money, might well die without planting a seed as a free man.

He continued up the cobbled lane, passed the fish market, and turned into York Street, which led to the church and was lined with fine houses. He stopped at a large dwelling as per his habit and knocked. It was the maid who appeared at the door. She told him that Mrs Evens would like the pleasure of his company for a cordial before he went up to his room.

*

'I have a surprise for you,' said Mrs Evens excitedly, after the initial exchange of pleasantries.

They were sitting in the lavishly furnished parlour, where the patterned wallpaper and gaudy window hangings were in the image of its exuberant owner. She was sitting on her two-seater sofa covered in red brocade, which catered amply for her skirts. He was seated on the edge of the French wing chair opposite her. A low marble-topped table formed a respectable barrier between them. Upon it stood a carafe of lemon drink, two glasses three-quarters full, and a tray of sweetmeats leftover from the great rejoicings of the birth of the new Prince of Wales, celebrations which had been postponed to September because of the burial of Captain Morgan in August.

From the side of the settee, she brought out a large leather bag. She said, 'Your new tools of your trade, Doctor.'

Decidedly, she had resolved to make it as difficult as she could for him to refuse her offer.

'Dear Mrs Evens,' he began, 'you have been my . . . my guardian angel, and I deserve not your continued err kindness. I have thought over your err fine proposition, however.' Her nostrils widened and her brow pleated with concern, which almost caused Jacob to lose his thread. He continued. 'However, I am sure you will not err be able to live with a man who betrays his own wife and children, would you?'

'For you, Monsieur Delpech, I would bear up,' she said bravely, and with fervour.

It was no good. He would just have to hammer it home harder to make her see clearly.

'But really, I must return to Europe, Mrs Evens . . .'

'Monsieur Delpech, you cannot. You cannot refuse me after all I have done. I have nursed you back to life. Fed you when you were delirious . . .'

'And I am, and err will be forever, in your debt,' he said, which he regretted the moment it was out.

'You are indeed, Monsieur Delpech. And here, there are laws. It is bondage for a man who cannot pay. You are aware of that?'

'I cannot lie to you. Neither can I betray my family, Mrs Evens. I do, however, sincerely hope we can be good friends.'

Friends. It was the word she dreaded most. She did not want a good friend. She wanted a husband, but not any drunken riff-raff that came ten to a penny in these parts. She wanted a man of culture who would accompany her in the increasingly refined circles of the town whose gentrification was well in train. Especially since the new governor, the second Duke of Albemarle no less, had brought his entire entourage from England. No longer did the swelling bourgeoisie want to put up with uncouth sailors and coarse pirates. And Mrs Evens had the means to enter the bourgeoning society; she just needed a gentleman for a husband.

Jacob's refusal was all the harder to swallow in that she had not even contemplated it. Moreover, she had opened up her heart, for she really did have feelings for this man whose voice and imperfect English made her heart tremble like she never thought it would again.

In her disappointment, she turned sour. Coldly and haughtily, she said, 'Then I have no alternative but to take the matter of your debt to Chief Justice Ellerson.'

*

Later in the afternoon, two royal guards came knocking at Jacob's door. He put his meagre possessions into his hessian sack and was marched, not to the courtroom, but to the deputy governor's sumptuous house. Delpech thought this odd, as he knew the house was being rented at present by the new lieutenant governor, none other than Sir Christopher Monck, His Grace the second Duke of Albemarle. Why would he be taken to see the chief official?

'I asked you here for two reasons,' said Sir Christopher. 'One, to allow you to pay off your debt in the quickest fashion possible so that you may regain your liberty. And two, for you to tell me your cure against the fever.'

Of late, the Duke had been suffering from a tropical illness that his wife and entourage feared would carry him to an early grave. He was only thirty-four. However, yesterday his temperature had dropped, and this morning he was in fine spirits and well enough to get up and dress. And there was nothing the Duke liked more than to dress—apart perhaps from good company and Madeira wine—which gave some cause for distress as one could not pile on layers of clothing in Jamaica as one did in England.

Nevertheless, standing with one hand on the diamond-studded knob of his beautifully gilded walking stick, the duke was still a feast for the eyes. Indeed, Jacob at present was filled with awe at the dazzling array of blue satin and gold tassels that seemed to outshine everything and everyone in the opulently furnished room. Lord Monck was certainly larger than life, taller too. The piled hair of his enormous wig and his high-heeled shoes with jewelled buckles meant that he towered over the Frenchman standing humbly before him.

It took a minute or two for Jacob to realise that a man was

standing on either side of Albemarle. To the duke's right stood Mr Ellerson, the chief justice, and to his left a young man twenty years Jacob's junior, with a serious demeanour and an intellectual brow. This was Doctor Sloane, the Duke's travelling physician.

Albemarle gave a brief glance to his right. Then, turning back to Jacob, he said, 'The chief justice tells me you cured yourself of the tropical illness.'

Jacob answered in the affirmative and gave a brief account of his concoction and how much laudanum he had taken.

'The body needs to be err unfatigued in order to be able to combat the illness with the tincture,' he said in a precise and pondered manner, so that his strong French accent would not hinder the comprehension.

'I agree, Doctor,' said Sloane with indifference, 'although that is nothing we do not already know.'

Though ruthlessly down-to-earth, Sloane's answer nevertheless gave Jacob instant relief. It meant he did not take Jacob for an impostor.

'If it is nothing we do not already know,' said Albemarle, 'then why have I not been advised to take some?'

'Because you have been advised to first refrain from entertaining, my Lord,' said Sloane uncompromisingly.

Turning back to Jacob with a grunt, the duke continued, 'And would you believe the local practitioner insists I take bird peppers in a poached egg, because, he says, parrots eat them when they are poorly? I ask you, do I look like a parrot?'

Jacob forced himself to say that he did not, despite the Duke's dazzling appearance.

'And what about my jaundice? It is of great discomfort to my wife. She tells me I have gone Chinaman yellow! And yet,

Doctor Sloane here refuses to bleed me. What do you make of that, Doctor?'

'With all due respect, my Lord, I would not bleed you either,' said Jacob, who sensed it would be unwise to go against the advice of the trained practitioner.

Doctor Sloane removed his finger from where it pressed against his upper lip, and gave a short nod of approval.

'I would take rest,' continued Jacob. 'For the body must be invigorated physically to be able to fight the fever. And I would take a tincture as my principal source of nourishment. No wine.'

During Jacob's conversations with Mrs Evens, she had often spoken about the duke's reputation as a party head. A reputation that had been confirmed to her by one of the many servants the duke had brought with him in his yacht from England. And a reputation embraced by the rich, fun-loving Jamaican colonists.

'No wine?' said the duke grouchily. 'Would your tincture help deafen my ears to these midges? I do not think so. Would it refresh my rasping gullet? Certainly not. I do declare that wine is the only beverage drinkable in this godforsaken place! However.' The duke turned to his doctor. 'We shall take you up on the laudanum.'

'You would also do well to take a Spanish hacienda rather than a brick-built palace, my Lord,' said Sloane. 'I am sure the French would never have built their governor's house in infernal red bricks in this climate.'

'Brick reminds me of home,' replied the duke. 'A white Spanish dwelling does not!'

Albemarle faltered an instant, then took three steps back and slumped into his strategically placed armchair. After a little fussing from the Lord Justice and Doctor Sloane, the duke called for his secretary to bring him his tincture of wine.

Once he had taken his restorative, the duke was able to recover his dignified posture with his hand on his walking stick, albeit now sitting down. He said, 'In order to avoid putting you under bond, I have purchased your debt.'

Jacob thanked him.

'I did consider keeping you with me. However, you are French. Furthermore, I happen to know a captain who requires a surgeon for his next voyage, so I have sold your debt to him. I believe it is for the best. There might be an element of danger, naturally—there always is aboard a ship. However, if the captain's campaign proves successful, you shall be able to pay for your liberty and have enough coin to set yourself up wherever you mean to go.'

Jacob was suspicious of the "element of danger". But when Albemarle asked him if he was satisfied with the arrangement, he said, 'If it is God's will, then it is also mine, my Lord.'

Delpech was nonetheless glad to be leaving the Jamaican port, steeped as it was in sin, vice, and disease.

The chief justice handed Doctor Delpech the leather medical bag that Mrs Evens must have cunningly sold with Jacob's debts. He then ordered the guards to accompany the freshly indentured surgeon-barber to the north dock for immediate embarkation on the *Joseph*, a seventy-ton sloop with eight guns and forty-six men under the command of Captain Brook.

As Jacob walked down High Street between his guards, he found himself thinking with horror that he had never cut off a lock of hair in his life.

The doctor was ferried to the ship along with a pirate,

detained between two other soldiers, who introduced himself as Captain Cox.

'What's your name and station?' snarled the pirate.

'I am Jacob Delpech, Sir. I have been appointed as surgeon-barber.'

'That's all right then, but you'll not be needing shears on this ship. A good sharp knife and a solid saw might come in handy, though!'

The pirate chuckled to himself and said no more.

21

TEN MINUTES LATER, Jacob and Captain Cox were climbing aboard the *Joseph*.

Men were heaving lines, scuttling up and down the rigging, and getting ready to unfurl sails. From his vantage point on the quarterdeck, Captain Brook gave Cox a short nod of approval. The pirate was led below deck with his wrought iron chest, which was lugged behind him by two mates. Captain Brook then looped his gaze down at Delpech, who was holding his sack over a shoulder and his leather bag in his hand.

'So you be the French doctor,' boomed the captain, who had a permanent snarl that made him look disgruntled at everything he set his eyes on.

Looking up, Jacob noticed he was hideously ugly with a pockmarked face, was of average height with powerful shoulders, and was clad, not in English uniform, but in a frock coat that must have once belonged to a Spaniard.

Although it went against his moral grain, Jacob had no choice but to play out his fraud to the full. 'Yes, Sir. Doctor Jacob Delpech at your service,' he said. The captain waved him up to the navigation deck.

As Delpech went to climb the steps, a crewmate scurrying down the port side stopped in his tracks. He held Jacob's gaze for an instant. Jacob had the shock of his life at the sight of the man, who then hastened towards the capstan. Although he was bearded and his hair was tied back in the fashion of seafaring rovers, this man could be none other than Ducamp, the dragoon lieutenant who had ransacked his home three years earlier.

Jacob continued to the quarterdeck.

'Indentured to me, you are now,' said the captain in a gravelly voice. 'And so as you know, all aboard this ship is equal and shall be treated as such, till death do us part.'

'Of course, Sir,' said Jacob, whose mind was still half on the bearded mate.

'And we share the rewards of the catch.' The captain rubbed his greying goatee as if he were evaluating an estimable beast. Then he said, 'And two hundred pieces of eight will buy you back your liberty!'

This was Jacob's second shock, and he had barely been aboard five minutes.

'There must be a mistake, Sir,' he said, shaken with indignation. 'I owed not a tenth of that sum.'

With impulsive scorn and sudden fury, the captain bayed, 'Are yer saying a doctor is worth no more than a slave or a swabber?'

'No, Sir . . .' said Jacob, searching for his words.

But before he could get another one in, the captain— whose rage died down as quickly as it had flared up—said in his resonantly deep voice, 'As I said, Doctor, we share the rewards of our toil with all aboard. And there will be plenty of coin to be made where we are headed. As surgeon-barber on this here ship, you are entitled to one and a quarter shares of any spoils of war taken along the way. Fear not, Doctor, I'm not asking you to go on the account.'

What could the man possibly mean? Jacob wondered.

Captain Brook now clasped Delpech in a comradely manner on the shoulder, but his attempted smile and fixed gaze, which were perhaps supposed to express fellowship, did not reassure Jacob one bit.

'Show Doctor Delpech to his quarters,' said the captain to Jacob's escort. Brook then turned and gave a word to his quartermaster—a thickset, bald, and bearded man named Blunt—who in turn shouted the order to haul up the large anchor.

As Doctor Delpech continued towards his quarters, he heard the bosun, whom Jacob had known as Lieutenant Ducamp, call out in French for his mates to start winding the capstan.

Jacob continued to a space at the front of the ship down on the orlop deck, partitioned on one side by canvas drapes. The dimly lit enclosure, ten feet square, was furnished with cabinets and shelves containing the various gruesome implements of his profession. They included saws, knives, pliers, extractors, and lines of bottles and jars of ingredients, no doubt left by the previous surgeon-barber.

He opened his medical bag, which contained drawings that showed the various operative stages of amputation and other modi operandi. This unexpected wealth of know-how bolstered Jacob's morale and allowed his mind to put aside the bearded face of Ducamp for the time being. He plunged into the fascinating diagrams and instructions, neatly drawn and written in English.

As the *Joseph* slipped out of the port under light sail, Jacob gave a thought for Mrs Evens. She had cared for him, given him food and shelter in the hope of catching a suitable husband. Then she had set out to punish him for not succumbing to her attentions. But he felt no animosity towards her, for had she not ultimately set him on the road to freedom, to England? At least, that is what he wanted to believe.

*

An hour into the voyage and two hours before sundown, there were footsteps outside Jacob's quarters. In walked the bosun.

There was no one else on the orlop deck, but Ducamp closed the sheet behind him anyway. The two men stood eye to eye, both as fake personas, and aware of the power they potentially held over each other. Jacob was not a doctor. Ducamp was not a French Huguenot seeking asylum on an English merchantman.

'You have changed, but I knew who you were the moment I saw you, *Monsieur* Delpech.'

He glanced at the instruments that Jacob had laid out on the table before him for study. But Jacob had already instinctively grabbed a dismembering knife.

'You have equally changed since we last met, Lieutenant Ducamp. When you ransacked my house.'

Ducamp stood calm and still. He said, 'For sure, I am a changed man, ever since I left the king's service. On this ship, see, we respect every man's creed, colour, and class. And there is no majesty, no bourgeois, just good men, and a right salty bunch they are too. I have not come seeking an argument, but to suggest that what happened in France, stays in France. So you can put down your knife before you cut someone.'

Jacob stared at the face that brought back memories of humiliation, of pain, and of his separation from his wife and children. And now it brought him news he had been dreading to hear, that he must be on a freebooting buccaneer ship.

'So, have we a deal, Doctor?' continued the bosun.

Jacob gave a reluctant nod, and said, 'I see now why the crew are not in uniform.'

'We're not pirates, if that's what you're thinking. We're on a commission to transport Captain Cox to the settlement of Virginia. From there, he'll take a frigate back to London with his spoils of war, so he can fulfil the contract of his amnesty. But we are not pirates.'

*

Delpech settled into his new role quickly and, to his surprise, without much queasiness. Apart from a splinter removal, a successful tooth extraction, and the treatment of a gunpowder burn, all of which earned him the respect of the crew, there was little to do during the first few days. He read extensively, prayed frequently, and prepared lotions to remove gunpowder from flesh and a decoction of wine vinegar to treat burns, should the need arise for them again.

Jacob was at first taken aback by the crew's apparent lack of unity in dress and naval rigour—they slept or lounged, some with legs interlaced, wherever they chose to lie on their mats or hitch up their hammocks. But he soon saw it did not seem to hinder the progress of the ship. And they did not drink excessively, nor was there any dicing for coin. These privateers, as they were known, seemed to Jacob's now more discerning eye competent enough in performing their tasks, which gave him some cause for reassurance.

The heat was bearable, food and drink were in plentiful supply, and the *Joseph* was making good headway. So far, the voyage was turning out to be, both in the figurative and the literal sense, one he could easily stomach.

He and the bosun managed to keep their distance from each other until the third day, when Jacob heard a sudden clamour above deck. It was mid-morning. He was reading in his cramped enclosure by lamplight.

He looked up from his book as someone scuttled down the steps from the deck above. A moment later, a young crewmate of slight build and with soft facial hair was standing in front of the canvas partition of the surgeon's quarters.

'Beg your pardon, Doctor, you are needed on deck,' said the young man, catching his breath.

'What is it, Steven?' said Jacob, putting his book to one side and getting up. He liked the lad, who was respectful, willing to help, and desirous to learn to read, which Jacob encouraged by setting him lessons in English.

'It's the bosun, Doctor,' said young Steven, accompanying Jacob towards the steps. 'I reckon he must have misjudged the distance sliding down the rigging. Don't think he's used to it. Rope burns yer palms, and when that happens, you come unstuck, and down you go.'

By the time Jacob arrived on the scene, Ducamp was regaining consciousness, though still lying where he had landed. He gave a loud cry as his arm collapsed beneath him, when he tried to push himself up off the deck.

'Broken collarbone,' said Blunt, the quartermaster.

'I don't think so,' said Jacob, inspecting the wound. 'Pray, help him to his feet, and bring him to my quarters. He will suffer less out of the sun.'

This was not entirely true, for already the surgeon's den was like a bakehouse. The truth was, Jacob strode back below deck not for the comfort of the patient, but to glance over his charts and literature on dislocation.

Ten minutes later, Ducamp was lying on a table in the privacy of the surgeon's quarters, where the injured limb was dowsed in camomile oil. Next, Jacob gave Ducamp a piece of cloth to put in his mouth, to keep him from biting off his tongue. Then he asked Steven and the accompanying mates to hold the patient down. Remaining aloof to the muffled grunts of agony, he pulled and worked the bone back into its joint until the bump of the bone had disappeared, and the patient was calmed.

Wiping his soaked brow, he turned to the men. 'Thank you, that will be all,' he said.

He proceeded to apply a cataplasm made of oatmeal to the bruised and tender shoulder. Next, he began binding it. Ducamp, relieved to feel his shoulder tightly bandaged, at last broke the silence.

'I thank you, Doctor,' he said.

'I am carrying out my duty, Monsieur Ducamp. That is all.'

'Look, you cannot blame me for the dragonnades. I was only carrying out orders, and frankly, it was one reason why I left.'

Jacob finished tying the knot. 'It is done,' he said. 'You are free to go.'

But Ducamp remained seated, and in a conciliatory tone of voice, he said, 'I kept your wife and your children from my men. I stayed awake to make sure they were not touched, Monsieur Delpech. See, my own lad would have been about your boy's age.'

Jacob took a cloth to wipe his hands, and in a voice of controlled patience, he said, 'My wife is now a refugee in a foreign country without resources, my children have been taken from her, and my young daughter is dead, Monsieur Ducamp.'

'I am sorry to hear that, truly, but I tried.'

Jacob did not answer.

Holding his arm, Ducamp got up from the table and crossed the floor to the canvas partition. As he opened the flap, he said, 'Listen. There's been a change of plan. And there may be fighting at some point along the way. If there is, stay close to me.'

The bosun exited the surgeon's den, leaving Jacob perplexed. His puzzlement was doubled that afternoon when, going by the poop deck, he overheard the pirate in a discussion with the captain over the destination of their voyage. Captain Brook wanted to head for the Gulf of Mexico; the pirate preferred the Bay of Honduras. Yet was this man not supposed to be on board as a detainee? It certainly did not appear so. Moreover, Jacob was not aware that the latter port of call was en route to Virginia.

*

On the fourth morning out of Port Royal, the lookout spotted land. Jacob was busy cleaning his instruments. Using his medical book, he was able to identify the many and varied gruesome tools of the trade for dismembering, cauterising, and bullet extraction. He climbed the deck steps to see for himself the distant island, dotted with palm trees. And with grim irony, he noticed crewmates here and there cleaning their instruments too, though theirs were made to maim and kill—cutlasses, axes, muskets, and pistols.

By the time the sun had shifted an hour past its zenith, they were putting into a commodious cove where another sloop was already anchored.

As the *Joseph* carefully ventured into the clear blue waters of the natural harbour, there came a gut-churning explosion that made Jacob wonder about the intentions of the moored vessel. But when Captain Cox, standing at the bow, removed his hat and swept it before him in a gesture of salutation, a great roaring cheer rose up from the other ship's deck.

Jacob's suspicions were confirmed. This whole commission was a farce planned in advance to free Captain Cox.

Ducamp's offer of protection now became clear, as did the captain's claim that Jacob would find means to pay off his indenture. They were about to go freebooting.

*

The following day, the crew emerged as fresh as bilge rats. If any Spanish *guardacostas* should come upon them now, Jacob knew they would be as good as pigs to the slaughter. He had remained on board, preferring his own company to revelling ashore with the mates of the *Fortuna*, who had recovered their captain. He also chose to turn a blind eye to their drunken antics along the beach with the fall of the evening.

What had he done to end up in this devil's lair? He could not for the life of him fathom why it had pleased God to lead him to bear witness to the devil's machinations. All he could do was continue to breathe through it, upholding his faith until God showed him the way to freedom.

After a sluggish start, the *Joseph* and the *Fortuna* left the island that Jacob had found out to be Caiman Grande. They set sail westward towards the Yucatan Passage, which would take them through the Gulf of Mexico.

As they sailed on to the south side of Cuba, the lookout sighted the distant masts of a lone frigate. The captain was with Doctor Delpech, who was treating his syphilis.

'What she be flying?' he asked Quartermaster Blunt, waiting on the other side of the canvas sheet.

'French colours, Cap'ain, and she be a biggen.'

Jacob had finished applying the mercury ointment to the captain's skin. Brook grunted thanks to the doctor, then went swiftly to the quarterdeck to scrutinise the French vessel.

Jacob was left wondering if being captured by the French navy could be the answer to his prayers. Could it be the lesser of the two evils? But then, it suddenly did not seem so bad to be committing fraud as a privateer's doctor. At least, it was something he would rather do than find himself back in a French prison, where he might well face execution. And besides, was he not doing goodness among these outcasts that society had disowned?

Then he remembered the treaty signed by James II and Louis XIV while he was in his prison in France. It meant there was normally no cause for hostilities between the two nations. There again, affairs in Europe did not seem to be of great importance in everyday dealings in these faraway lands, which Jacob now realised were very much a law unto themselves.

But Captain Brook did not turn against the wind to escape the French warship. Instead, with the prevailing westerly full in her sails, the *Joseph* veered north by northwest, closely followed by the *Fortuna*, to give chase to the massive frigate.

Leading the way at a steady ten knots, the *Joseph* closed the gap within a matter of hours. By late afternoon, it became clear that the French ship was heading to Isla de los Pinos, the large island off the southwest coast of Cuba.

As the buccaneers approached under English colours, the French ship struck her main sails and sat waiting on the south side of the *isla*. She was colossal, twice the size of the English sloop. Yet Captain Brook continued his approach.

Jacob stood nervously near the main mast, inwardly praying for his wife and children, that they might find peace and safety from their tortures, should he perish this day. And he hoped to God he would stand courageous at his station, should a battle arise.

The *Joseph*, which had cut through the waves faster than the *Fortuna*, was within gunshot of the brigantine's prow. As the English sloop slipped closer through the lapping waters, Delpech could now perceive the tall stature of the French master, standing on the quarterdeck with his back to the westering sun. He could only make out the French captain's outline, but it was enough for him to recognise the man who had lent him his house on Cow Island.

The sloop, having shortened her sails, was now within shouting distance.

'What brings ol' Captain Brook a roving in these waters?' called Captain Laurent de Graaf over the bulwark using a loud hailer. 'Hunting sharks, are we?'

'Aye,' barked back Brook, 'and it looks like we've found a ship full of 'em!'

De Graaf let out a loud laugh.

*

Within the hour, both sloops and the French frigate had weighed anchor at a musket shot from the south-facing shore of Pinos Island.

The Dutchman quit his ship with a mulatto and was soon climbing aboard the *Joseph*, where Captain Brook met him with a welcome. 'Young scamp still tempting the devil, is he?'

'Indeed,' said de Graaf, 'and it looks like I've found 'im!'

The two men clasped each other's shoulders affably.

As they strode to the captain's cabin, a familiar face caught the Dutchman's eye. De Graaf offered a civil nod of recognition to Jacob, then proceeded to the stern of the ship without a word. There, he lowered his head into the captain's cabin, where Captain Cox was already waiting. Crewmates crowded around the open door to listen in on the conversation. It was their democratic right.

*

Decidedly, nothing was made to be clear in this world where English privateers mingled with senior French officials. An hour later, feeling abandoned to his fate, Jacob looked up at the man who had just settled against the bulwark beside him. He said, 'It seems, Lieutenant, that you were right about the change of plan.'

'That's de Graaf,' said Ducamp.

'Yes, I have already made his acquaintance, in different circumstances.'

'I wager he wants us to join him on a foray on Cuba.'

'On land? But that would equate to piracy.'

'Not if he has a letter of marque for it. Cheer up, Monsieur Delpech, 'cause if he has, it means you can buy back your freedom sooner than you thought. Long as you don't get killed, that is.'

There was a movement of the crowd around the captain's cabin. Brook stepped out, followed by de Graaf, the mulatto, and Cox. The expectant crew gathered around them or climbed up the standing rigging. Jacob and Ducamp approached.

'I have here a letter of Marque and Reprisal,' said de Graaf, holding up a wax-stamped document, 'to punish our Spanish neighbours for their barbarism. And the more we are, the merrier!'

Captain Brook then roared out, 'Are we up to it, lads?' The whole ship rocked with a hearty cheer.

The Dutchman left behind his mulatto named Joe, captured on a previous coastal foray. Joe, a former Cuban slave, knew the coast waters well and would serve as guide, should the ships become separated. De Graaf then made his way along the deck, accompanied by Captains Brook and Cox. He stopped in front of Jacob, who was now standing by the main mast.

'Delpech?' he said.

'You know our doctor?' said Captain Brook.

'Indentured doctor,' corrected Jacob. He could only hope the Dutchman would not question his occupation.

'We met on Cow Island,' said de Graaf with a quizzical look. But without further comment, he walked on, climbed down to his boat, and joined his vessel.

The face-to-face with the Dutchman had been awkward. What more could Jacob have said in front of fifty pairs of eyes? He could hardly explain his circumstances, or complain about his lot. And would there have been any point, given that the man was part and parcel of this association of rovers?

22

THERE WAS SOMETHING bracing about being in the middle of a seafaring force, something that almost made Jacob forget the immorality of the imminent raid

It was early October. The Caribbean winds had become more variable, and the flotilla was tacking back along the luxuriant south-facing shore of Cuba. With time on their hands, the crew prepped their weapons or practised their aim with pistols and muskets. Jacob admired how these well-seasoned hunters invariably hit their marks, despite the pitch of the ship.

One afternoon on the main deck, the bosun insisted Jacob learn something of swordplay for the sake of his welfare, and consequently for that of the entire crew. But Jacob was not keen.

'At least learn defence, man,' said Ducamp, holding out a sword to the doctor. ''Cause neither Jehovah nor Neptune will stop a steel blade from running through your spleen!'

Albeit reluctantly, Delpech took the sword, which won him a resounding cheer from the crew. Their cheers abated, however, when he declared he would not kill a man. He had made it his duty to save rather than destroy life.

On hearing the cheer, Captain Brook had ventured out from his cabin. 'You'll soon get a taste for it, Doctor,' he said, swaggering up to Delpech.

An intimacy had grown between them after Jacob treated his syphilis, which consisted of applying a mercury ointment to his facial and genital sores. And, with scientific gravitas, Delpech showed all those infected by the painful disease how to rub in the unction.

Cupping a large hand on the ball of Jacob's shoulder, Brook said, 'Then before you know it, the smell of black powder and blood on steel will be the perfume of your dreams!'

'I very much doubt that, Sir, with all due respect,' said Jacob, whose new-found importance among captain and crew allowed him a certain liberty of expression.

The captain let out gruff snarls, which was his form of laughter. 'Kill or be killed, Doctor!' he said.

He then turned to Ducamp with a look of exasperation which told the bosun to make the man see sense. The doctor was too precious to lose.

Brook went back to his cabin, where he continued to extract navigation information from Joe the mulatto in exchange for kindness, food, and coin. Joe was already planning ahead.

Meanwhile, Ducamp turned to Jacob and said in French, 'He's right, you know. It's kill or be killed. And you best make up your mind now, because when you've a cut-throat in your face, it will be too late!'

*

Bound by language and culture, the two men very often sat together, smoking tobacco on a chest or on steps. Jacob had long since adopted the pipe. Even when not lit, it was invariably planted in his beak nowadays. For if smoking on land kept mosquitoes from his ears, at sea it kept the foul bilge waters from infesting his nose.

On one occasion, Jacob let the bosun steer the conversation to something that was clearly on his mind. He had been beating about the bush, especially now that Jacob read the Bible aloud to any mates who would listen—and many of the men did, including Quartermaster Blunt. Jacob sensed Ducamp needed to get something off his chest.

'You say you obey God's will, but so do Catholics. How do you know God listens to you and not to them?'

'God listens to all who have faith.'

'You sure? I've seen many a religious man, good and bad, Catholic and Calvinist, pray for mercy and be cut down by the sword, no different from any imp or scoundrel. Then nothingness. No cries, no lights, no ghost, just the stillness of death. But you haven't seen it yet, have you?'

Jacob had stopped hating this man who had brought calamity upon his family. So he obliged with a question. He said, 'You are angry with God, are you not, Lieutenant Ducamp?'

'Angry? Not angry. How can a man be angry at nothing? Because if there were something, then why did he let my wife and son be killed while I was away defending his religion?'

Ducamp's eyes watered slightly, surely from pipe smoke. It could not be from emotion, could it? Again Jacob helped the bosun empty his bile of bitterness. He said, 'How did they die?'

'Swept away by disease. When I went home, the place was bare and lifeless. No older than your lad, my boy was. A bright lad, and now just gone. Nothing left to prove they even lived.'

'The rendezvous is in heaven, Monsieur Ducamp. It is the only hope.'

'Heaven? Even if there was a heaven, how would *I* get in? I have sinned. I have killed, and I prepare to do so again.'

'The choice is yours, but you must make it now. For when the musket shot flies to your head, it will be too late. Remember, if you repent, you may regain God's love through Jesus Christ, He is our Saviour.'

'And why not through Mohamed or Yahweh?' said Ducamp, who had lost some of the bitterness in his voice now that he had got his story off his chest—now that he had made it clear to Jacob that he too had suffered the grief of loss.

'I will pray for you,' said Jacob. By offering to pray for the man, Jacob realised he was forgiving him. And he felt relieved of his own ball of bitterness.

The bosun gazed through the gun port towards the approaching shore of Cuba. He considered for a moment that it was inhabited by people he was conditioned to kill.

After drawing on his pipe, he said, 'Don't make sense.' Then he climbed the sun-filled hatchway to prepare for manoeuvres.

*

Laurent de Graaf knew the southeast coast of Cuba well. The previous year, he had defeated Biscayan privateers off Jucaro who had been commissioned by the king of Spain to track him down. But the coast was still frequently patrolled by the *guardacostas*. So under the Dutchman's lead, the three ships slipped into the cove of a cay located a few leagues from the mouth of the Cauto River.

The warm smell of the land, of trees and fresh flowers and vegetation, was once again in Jacob's nose as evening encroached. He had joined two hundred men or more ashore, sitting, squatting, or standing around a cluster of rocks where the three captains made their case.

De Graaf proposed to draw any patrolling Spanish ships away from the Cauto estuary so that the other parties could slip into the river mouth aboard longboats and canoes. From there, they could follow the river upstream toward the township of Bayamo, one of the richest commercial and agricultural settlements on Cuba.

Once de Graaf had dispatched any *guardacostas* ships, he would lead his forces along the Manzanillo land route, shorter and more direct than the winding river. The idea was to attack the township from both sides, north and south.

It would be a daring inland campaign for sure, one that had never been attempted, which was all the more reason to suspect the place would be full of complacent merchants and planters with coffers full to the brim. And according to Joe, the little mulatto, the township, having never been harassed, lay pretty much open to attack.

'I got a question,' boomed a great bull of a man who had got to his feet at the front. 'What if they get news in Santiago? You can bet your breeches a full fleet will come chasing quicker than you can say *rumbullion!*'

'Winds are against a ship reaching Santiago,' said de Graaf. 'It would take a week for a runner to get there by land. Then a fleet would take three days at best to round the cape. That gives us ten days to take the town and carry the plunder back to the cays!'

Captain Brook stepped forward, and with his usual gruff charisma, he roared: 'What you say there, lads? Are we here for plunder?'

The little cove was filled with a resounding *aye* and a thunderous cheer that shook flocks of colourful birds from their perches.

The buccaneers immediately set about making ready all the boats at their disposal—including those from de Graaf's frigate—which would carry them to pots of gold, or to their death.

*

De Graaf boldly sailed his frigate away from the setting sun into Spanish waters. Captain Brook waited. The first stars appeared, and an hour after that, there still had been no shot fired, which could only indicate that de Graaf had not encountered any Spanish ships.

Brook's boat led the way over the starlit water of the placid coastal shoals. Thirty men had been left behind to defend and manoeuvre the ships if need be. Jacob at first assumed he would be among them, but Brook told him his services would be needed in the field. Barely an hour later, the eight-boat flotilla reached the mouth of the Cauto River.

The estuary, which once thrived with contraband activity, was still. The massive flood of 1616 had altered the river's course. It no longer offered an easy link to the embarcadero where, back in the day, merchandise to and from Bayamo used to be loaded and unloaded. These days, merchants preferred the route by land, which had the advantage of running straight to the township.

Brook, with the help of de Graaf's mulatto, led the way

through the dark, winding waters of the Cauto River. Captain Cox, Quartermaster Blunt, and five other senior crewmates followed in silence, each commanding a boat containing up to twenty-five men who took turns to row against the gentle current. Jacob sat in the one Ducamp was given to command.

They paddled along in Indian file in the white light of the rising moon, which was three-quarters full. They kept to the middle of the river, well away from the banks where the odd splash announced the presence of crocodiles. On a few occasions, they had to carry their embarkations over the marshy ground to the next navigable portion, and took shortcuts across strips of land whenever the river snaked round on itself.

A new day was dawning by the time they reached the old embarcadero. Only twenty miles now separated them from the township of Bayamo.

The boats were swiftly and quietly lifted out of the water and placed upside down in the long grass along the riverbank. Standing on the embarcadero, Captain Brook surveyed the surrounding vegetation and the rough dirt track ahead with satisfaction. Then he swung his arm around the little mulatto's neck in a gesture of companionship.

'Well done, Joe!' he said with a paternalistic glow, and puckered a kiss on the mulatto's forehead.

Jacob could not help but notice the new twinkle in the captain's eyes that, since their first night out of Pinos Island, seemed to search for the mulatto whenever he was out of sight. It was the same look many a mate shared with his chosen partner. It might be difficult to admit, but Jacob knew it was the look of trust, and love. The mulatto looked up at his protector with gratitude.

But as they proceeded into the track surrounded by woodland, the captain soon recovered his sardonic snarl. After fifteen minutes of marching, he stopped.

'Hold it, lads!' he growled, holding up a hand to halt the movement of the group. Fifty yards ahead, the road was strewn with felled trees. Fresh sap still hung heavy in the early morning air. It was a barricade. Somehow the Spaniards had gotten wind of the buccaneers' approach.

Something moved in the tangle of logs and branches. A head, then a barrel of a musket became visible. The first shot went off, closely followed by a cracking volley. It was a warning shot. Brook, a cunning and quick-thinking fellow, wanting the Spaniards to think he and his men had taken heed, signalled to everyone to turn tail.

The Spaniards must have worked all night, thought Jacob, as he ran with the group back to the embarcadero.

'We can take 'em easy,' said Captain Cox, once Brook had assembled with the other chiefs on the bank of the river.

'Nah, man. They'll have set up ambushes all along the route,' said Brook. 'We'll be well knackered by the time we get through to the township.' He put a hand on the mulatto's shoulder. 'Joe'll show us the way through the woods, won't you, Joe?'

'Yes, Captain Brook, Sir, I show you what you want!'

'Good lad!'

Cox made no attempt to debate his case; he had seen Brook this way before.

Brook's plan was swiftly put to a vote, and then put into action. The advancing men took turns to beat through the vegetation so as not to dull their blades.

Their relentless march through woodland and thick

undergrowth at last brought them to the edge of a thicket north of the township, which was not open, as was initially thought. It was protected by a stockade. Between the wall of timber posts and the thicket lay a field that had recently been laboured.

To Jacob's disappointment, all these unexpected barriers did nothing to deter the fervour of the buccaneers who, on the contrary, now made no secret of their presence. They beat the flat of their swords with relish and howled like baboons, sounds which would instil the fear of the devil into any man or beast.

*

The mayor of Bayamo was Guiseppi de la Firma, well born, and like all Spanish nobility, proud of his heritage. So proud, in fact, that he added five extra syllables to his already many-syllabled name, making it Senor Guiseppi Alonzo de la Firma del Barro Bravo. Guiseppi was also an important landowner whose fields of cocoa and tobacco stretched far and wide along the south-facing slopes of the township. Needless to say, being such a proud man, he was very clever too.

It was his idea to impede the onslaught of the assailants by setting up ambushes. A devout Catholic, Guiseppi also had the luck of the devil, and it so happened that a company of cavalry was at present stationed in his town. They had been patrolling across the hills from Santiago to Bayamo as an exercise to train up cadets.

Guiseppi now peered through the stockade at the disorderly rabble of rovers lined up on the edge of the thicket. Their slaughter would be his proudest achievement and might possibly earn him a place in Spanish history.

*

Jacob was standing with Ducamp. Captain Brook was just a few yards away.

'Most likely take 'em tomorrow,' said the captain, 'soon as de Graaf shows up.'

It had been agreed with the Dutchman that they should wait until he sent word of his arrival on the opposite side of the township. They probably wouldn't even have to raise their hangers, de Graaf had said in jest, thinking of the surprise on the faces of the townsfolk when they found themselves surrounded.

But the chief of the Catholics had other plans. At his disposal, he had a company of young, brave cavaliers, a captain ready to do battle, and he surmised that the insolent bucks in the near distance must have already suffered ambush after ambush till they had been pushed into the woods. Their attempt at intimidation, a ruse to hide their fatigue, did not fool him.

So, urged on by the company captain, who was impatient to put his training to good use, and despite no news from the barricades, the mayor ordered his surprise force of cavaliers to assemble in front of the stockade. And he sent word to the soldiers stationed at the ambush sites to cut the rovers down as they retreated. Not one of the rovers should get away; all must be stopped, dead or alive.

*

The buccaneers' cacophony was silenced as the horsemen took their positions for the two-hundred-yard charge across the laboured field. Captain Brook's eyes widened with surprise, then narrowed with a sort of glee.

'What have we here, lads?' he roared. 'Looks like

playtime's come sooner than later!' The men hallooed and bat their swords, once again making a terrifying din.

The horsemen, three lines deep, began steering their steeds towards the horde. But the horde was already spreading out into a treacherous crescent.

'Make 'em count, lads!' hurled Brook as the buccaneers drew their muskets.

The rovers did not run to meet them on the battlefield; they were not prepared to meet swords travelling at forty miles an hour. Buccaneers did not fight fair like proper soldiers: they fought to win. So instead they took aim with their muskets, and they began picking off their prey with an almost nonchalant precision. By the time the cavalry had reached the middle of the field, a third of them had fallen, whereas not a buccaneer was wounded.

Jacob was at first mesmerized. From the edge of the wood, he contemplated the scene with a strange fascination as tens of determined young men were struck down on the squeeze of a trigger. He watched the buccaneer next to him take aim with one eye half-closed, and fire his musket. Jacob followed the trajectory of the shot, as if time were slowed down, and a few moments later saw it sink into the head of a young Spaniard who then tumbled backward off his mount.

The acrid smell of gun smoke and the rumble of fast-approaching hooves jolted his senses and made him remember his station. But precisely where was it that he was supposed to stand?

He scanned left to right, where scores of buccaneers were popping away with their guns. As the sun was becoming stronger, his reflex was to back into the wood, where he put down his leather bag at the foot of a tree.

The shooting suddenly ceased. The thunder of hooves and the snorting of beasts grew louder. Then Jacob heard the roar of Brook. 'Step back, lads! Back to cover!'

A cavalier barely twenty yards away blasted out in Spanish, 'Lascars! Stand and fight like men!' It was the Spanish captain. He must certainly have felt cheated, for the lascars were not playing by the rules at all. Instead they backed into the thicket while bringing out their cutlasses in order to parry the onslaught.

The caballeros nevertheless continued their course over the undergrowth and straight into the wood, swiping at everything that moved as they went. But the trees, though sparse in places, made their horses swerve and reduce their gait.

The rovers were not slow to seize their chance. They rushed the confused steeds as they turned, pulling down their riders to the ground where a heavy razor-sharp blade awaited them.

The battle quickly evolved into a mass melee. Jacob found himself standing alone amid the raging fracas and hellish commotion made by steel and the many contrasted roars of men killing each other. He stood by his bag like an uninvited guest at a ball. It seemed like everyone in the wood had gone into a frenzied dance, and he was the only sane soul among them. There were practically two rovers to every caballero, which meant that Jacob lacked a partner to dance with. Not for long, though.

A young cavalier on foot, tall, lanky, and smooth-skinned, appeared before him. This was the kill-or-be-killed moment Brook and Ducamp had spoken of.

Delpech drew his sword just in time to parry a blow. The

muchacho was visibly inexperienced, clumsy, and probably terrified. Maybe this was his first melee outing. Maybe he lacked the killer instinct that came naturally to some folk. Maybe he had not made that kill-or-be-killed decision either. He struck with wild, sweeping blows, leaving himself open to a poke in the ribcage. But instead of a lunge forward, Jacob backed off, parrying again and again, until his back came up against a tree.

Unable to move backward as the caballero continued his attack, Jacob could only dodge and stick out his sword. Delpech felt his blade run through flesh and muscle till it butted against bone. The young man dropped his sword in mid swing. 'Madre!' he cried in one short, horror filled breath. He then deflated like a pig's bladder, and fell to the floor as blood leaked out profusely from the perforation in his side. Jacob looked down aghast at the fallen lad lying on the thicket bed. He felt sick. He let fall his dripping sword from his hand.

'Pick it up, man!' yelled a voice from a few yards away. It came from Ducamp, who was deflecting a blow from his adversary.

But Jacob could not.

A mounted Spaniard charged out of the sun into the dusty thicket. He reared his horse and pointed his pistol at the bastard at the tree with the muchacho lying at his feet.

Delpech, paralysed, gritted his teeth in terror and shame. Then there came an almighty explosion from behind his left ear, and the next instant, the Spaniard's head jolted back with the force of a cluster of shot that peppered his face.

'Pull yourself together, man,' shouted Ducamp, now standing next to him with a smoking double-barrelled pistol, which he holstered.

Jacob suddenly drew his own pistol and without a thought fired. Ducamp turned round to see the Spaniard who would have lopped off the lieutenant's head, had Jacob not sent a shot into his chest first. Ducamp finished him off and continued the fight.

'Go with Joe!' commanded Captain Brook to Jacob, ten yards further along and visibly relishing every kill. Nothing seemed able to resist him as he wielded sword and pistols with equal delight and dexterity.

The mulatto who had appeared at Jacob's side led the doctor deeper into the woods, away from the killing zone, away from the chaos of bloodletting and the flashes of steel and powder.

The fight was short-lived, and in less than an hour, the Spanish, seeing their numbers drastically dwindle, retreated across the field running and limping, some bowed over on horseback. But the distance gave the buccaneers enough time to load their muskets and take aim. This was not fair either, the Spanish captain would have thought had he lived. Jacob too was sickened as through the trees he watched the escapees fall. Only a handful of Spaniards made it back through the stockade alive.

Jacob looked around, appalled at the carnage in which he had partaken. His gaze paused at the tree where his first victim had fallen. He then rushed toward him, armed this time with nothing but his leather bag, for he saw the caballero move. Jacob knelt down beside him in a pool of sunshine. The young Spaniard was breathing, and he was conscious. Jacob loosened his blood-drenched tunic so he could breathe more easily.

'No *quiero morir*,' said the soldier, grasping Jacob by the sleeve, as if by doing so, he would keep a hold on life. There was nothing Delpech could do except try to cover the wound. The rest was in the hands of the Lord.

But as he was rummaging in his bag, he felt a shiver. A shadow came over them, blotting out the sunshine. Delpech looked up and saw in horror a red-stained goatee, eagle eyes, and a short, curved blade smeared in blood. It came hurtling down and severed the lad's head from his shoulders. Jacob jerked back in disgust as blood spurted over his face.

'Wrong side, Doctor,' growled Captain Brook. 'Should be seeing to our lads!'

Jacob promptly threw up.

Any wounded or dying cavaliers were quickly dispatched in a similar fashion by blade. There was no sense wasting lead shot on an incapacitated foe. Brook would argue that it was only right to put them all out of their misery, nice and quick. And it saved the buccaneers from any vengeful encounters in the future. For as the captain was like to say: 'Dead men don't bite back!'

It was monstrous. It was inhuman. Jacob failed to find any justice in it. It seemed that all the lines that had so neatly structured his existence were becoming increasingly blurred.

However, Jacob's sense of survival enabled him to not dwell on the atrocities he had been part of. Instead he focussed on the buccaneers' wounds. These mostly consisted of deep cuts and slices into the flesh, except one mate whose intestines had spewed out from a lateral slash to his belly. Jacob recognised Steven, the lad who had come running into Jacob's quarters on the ship after Ducamp's fall from the rigging, the lad who wanted to learn to read and write.

Jacob held his head, stroked his soft young beard, and said

423

a prayer as the lad stared into the sun, until death took him. The doctor then laid down his head, closed his eyes, and moved on to the next injured sailor.

*

The buccaneers had spent the night travelling upstream. Once outside Bayamo, they had planned to rest while waiting for de Graaf to take up position on the south side of the township. However, they had been surprised to find not only ambushes that forced them to take a fatiguing detour through wild woodland, but also a timber stockade and a company of cavaliers whom they had virtually decimated. And all for just five dead and a few dozen wounded.

Brook had no difficulty firing them up for a last attack, to finish the job while Lady Luck was still with them.

A plan was swiftly devised and validated by vote. Two teams of half a dozen crack shots took up positions. They gave cover to a third group of about a dozen men who made their way to the gate with powder and axes.

Jacob watched them stealthily cross the laboured field where Spanish bodies lay strewn. They met no enemy fire. Soon after reaching the gate, there came a loud explosion from the stockade, then a series of quick, successive axe strokes on timber, and the great gate was flung open.

The whole horde of roaring, fearsome men stormed across the field without a shot fired at them and poured through the open gate.

The town had never once been worried by assailants, and there had been no need to erect a stone wall. However, the mayor had told the townsfolk to die rather than fall into the hands of the lascars. So they locked themselves in their houses and fired shots from their windows, causing the buccaneers to halt and take cover. But Brook had dealt with this kind of nuisance before; from experience, he knew it was an easy one to resolve.

He gave the nod to storm houses at the edge of town and pull out the women and children, who were hiding under tables and inside cupboards. Two men were captured. They were knocked about but not killed. These were not soldiers. Any able-bodied cavaliers would have fled—as would those at the barricades as soon as they got wind of events. Instead Brook sent them to the mayor to tell him he would slit the hostages' throats and burn down the town if they did not surrender.

The mayor, entrenched in his residence with his retinue, returned a note, saying he had sent horsemen to Santiago, that a Spanish expedition was already on its way, and that the pirates would be annihilated if they remained.

Brook did not order the hostages to be killed. Instead he ordered a party of buccaneers to creep up and throw smoke pots through the downstairs windows of the mayor's residence. By noon, the buccaneers had taken over the whole town.

*

Captain Brook, who had no time for women with their silly screams and petty demands, put Captain Cox in charge of selecting the finest maids. The captain of the *Fortuna* then had them ushered to the beautiful salons of the mayor's residence, where the ground-floor windows had been opened to give the place an airing from the smoke. Old hags, ugly nags, and their sprogs were locked inside the church.

Ducamp and Blunt took charge of conducting the Spanish men to the edge of town, where they herded them into two wooden warehouses used for drying tobacco and storing cocoa beans. When they were done, Brook walked up to the warehouse under Ducamp's charge. In his thick, gravelly voice, he ordered the town's councillors to stand before him.

Five podgy, affluent-looking men, sweating buckets, showed themselves at the open doors. Of them, Señor Guiseppi Alonzo de la Firma del Barro Bravo stood erect and said, 'There is expedition coming here from Santiago. You stay, you will be *matados todos, todos*. Leave now, and you will save your life.'

Brook grabbed the man by the lapels. He brought him up to his face and said in a low, seething voice, 'You better think carefully where you've stashed yer coin, then! It might save your poxy lives. Savvy?'

He put the man down, stepped back outside, and gave the nod to Ducamp to lock the warehouse doors, which was promptly executed among indignant complaints in Spanish that the place was already like a bakehouse inside.

While the Spaniards were being left to stew in their juices, a party of buccaneers set to work on what buccaneers traditionally did best. They built a long fire in the middle of the main square. And over the fire, they made an extra-long *boucan*—a wooden grill placed on wooden stakes—where they could roast vast quantities of meat. Other contingents of rovers went rummaging for drink and cold food to whet the appetite.

The methodical slaughter of animals, especially the pigs, would curdle the blood of the hardiest prisoner, thought

426

Jacob, who was busy patching up wounds. He imagined the anxiety the wretched prisoners must be going through on hearing the almost human squeals. But he realised too that this was all part of the ploy to instil fear in the hearts of the townsfolk, to make them loosen their tongues. It would leave them in a better disposition so that the buccaneers could steal away as quickly as they had come. However, Jacob could never imagine in a thousand years of Catholic purgatory what would happen next.

23

THE PLAZA WAS soon a festival of many merry men, tucking ravenously into a feast of maize and meat, washed down with wine and rum.

A few hours later, once the sun's heat had abated, many of them had taken quarters in houses with good beds; others were at the mayor's residence with Captain Cox. Meanwhile, on the market square, Captain Brook summoned the five Spanish councillors to the shaded side, where the buccaneers had assembled a cosy array of seating.

The Spanish gentlemen, drenched in sweat, were visibly disgusted as they were escorted into the square, past pools of blood where animals were racked, gutted, and carved up. After passing the boucan, where dogs were stealing bones and half-eaten animal parts, they found themselves facing the snarl of Captain Brook, who was lounging in a magnificent armchair.

'Jack Taylor, frow 'em somink to eat,' said Brook, turning to one of the men at the boucan.

The sailor lobbed each of the Spaniards a pork chop from a dish. But either the gentlemen were not good at catching, or they were not hungry. They let the pieces of meat fall to the ground. After each failed catch, Jack Taylor feigned disappointment, which made his crewmates laugh out loud.

'We do not eat with thieves!' said the proudest of them in accented English.

Brook let his left hand, which was holding a bottle, drop to the side of his armchair, and motioned with the other for the white-haired Spaniard to approach, which he did.

'You've had enough time to think, Señor,' said the captain warmly. 'Now, you tell us where you've hidden your treasure, and we leave you in peace. That's the deal.'

'I take you to be a pirate,' said the Spaniard with pride. 'The vassals of the king of Spain do not make treaties with inferior persons!' But he must have sensed his dignity might be contradictory to his health this time, because he added, 'Soldiers on horseback will have already arrived in Santiago. You have no time to lose. If you leave now, you can escape the armada.'

However, this show of bravado and generosity did not have the desired effect.

'Pin him down, lads!' said Brook, businesslike.

The accompanying sailors who knew what this meant kicked away the man's legs from beneath him, and held him face up on the ground. A roar of laughter rose up from the drunken sailors lounging around the boucan. They were glad for some entertainment now that their bellies were full.

'Now what say you?'

'Never will I bow to filth!'

'Make 'im eat his own shit!' shouted out one mate. After another swig of rum, Brook put down the bottle, then pushed on the armchair and sprang to his feet. As he did so, he reached for an axe that was leaning on the side of the

429

armchair. He swung it over his shoulder as if he were ready to chop wood.

An expectant silence fell around the marketplace that was turning orange with the late-afternoon sun. The surrounding flora filled the balmy air with sweet-smelling perfume that mingled deliciously with the savoury smell from the boucan. Captain Brook was now stomping around the captive held to the floor.

'Go now, *por favor*. Leave us in peace, and I will *personalmente* vouch for your safe passage,' said the Spaniard.

'We go when I say so, and that's when you've told us where you've hidden your poxy coin, man. *Entiendes?*'

'Never!' said the Spaniard, whose pride had got the better of him again.

In a burst of rage, Brook roared and cussed. He then swung the axe from his shoulder and, in a nifty loop, slammed it down on the Spaniard's forearm. The spectators let out a cheer of appreciation. The Spaniard let out a cry of horror. He clasped his handless arm, blood spouting out the severed end.

'That's what you get for slapping Captain Brook in the face!'

Brook tossed the axe aside and drew a pistol from his sash. He bent over the man still writhing on the floor, and grabbed him by the shirt front. He cocked his weapon and shoved it into his mouth. The captain then delivered one of his favourite catchphrases that never failed to captivate his audience. In a deep, seething voice, he said, 'If you don't feed me silver, I'll feed you lead!'

But the proud Spaniard, who prized honour and courage above all things, could not bow down to a *ladron*, a vulgar thief.

'Que el diablo te lleve!' he said, and spat in the captain's face.

From experience, Captain Brook knew that the first sacrifices sufficed to get what he wanted, and the quicker they were done, the better it was for everyone, including the townsfolk.

Brook pulled the pistol away from the Spaniard's mouth and slowly stood up, still pointing with the barrel at an oblique angle. With a strange fascination, he observed the fear in the man's eyes, then squeezed the trigger. The onlookers roared out in hilarity and disgust. There was a mess where the Spaniard's head had been.

*

Jacob, who was sitting with Ducamp, had fallen into a deep snooze. Having become inured to the buccaneers' cheers, he had not woken when the town councillors were marched onto the other side of the square. He suddenly woke now with the sound of the shot. He turned his head to the scene taking place forty yards across the square. He could not at first fathom what was taking place.

The captain was turning round the four Spaniards waiting in line. He said: 'Like the man said, amigos, we have no time to lose! *Entiendes?*'

With a disgruntled shrug, the captain put his pistol back in his sash with its "brothers," as he called them. He then picked up the axe and curled his finger at the next councillor.

'What's it to be, amigo? Silver for me, or steel for you?' This was another one of the captain's catchphrases, and the audience reacted accordingly. They were enjoying the show.

The man, in his mid-forties, with a paunch from good

living, was febrile, and had pissed himself. He made the sign of the cross and stepped in front of the captain.

'No *tengo nada*, Señor Capitán . . .'

Brook said not a word. He fondled the man's buttons with his razor-sharp blade, and popped them off one at a time.

'*Es la verdad. Solo soy médico.*'

'On the floor! Now!' shouted the captain. The man fell to his knees, holding his heart.

'My God!' said Jacob, appalled. He could hardly believe his eyes as he looked around for someone to react. But he only saw the engrossed onlookers, some drinking, others scoffing corn on the cob or meat, others just watching the show. Ducamp told him to keep calm and stay put.

'Lay him flat, lads,' said Brook, 'and spread him out!'

'Pwaah, fat bastard's shit himself!' said Taylor, which produced a few laughs and a crackle of applause as the fat man was thrown on his back. He began gasping for air, as though he were drowning. The spectators watched with bated breath. Taylor punched him in the face to make him lie flat.

'For the love of Christ, man, stop this insanity!' cried out Jacob, getting to his feet and breaking the unnatural silence.

Brook frowned and fired his bloodshot eyes in the direction of his interlocutor, who was moving towards him. Then the captain's eyebrows straightened.

'Ah, Doctor Delpech,' he said in a comradely tone. 'You wanna have a go?' He took a few unsteady steps forward to beckon Jacob closer. 'Sweet vengeance, Doctor!'

'I have nothing against this man or any other man here.'

'But he's a Catholic.'

'He is a Christian!'

'Come on, Doctor, five pieces of eight for every finger,

fifty for every limb. And if you manage to make the bugger talk, I'll pay your indenture twofold!'

The captain's eyes were glazed over, unblinking, as he made his offer in all earnestness. Jacob read for the first time in his life the look of a madman, rapt in his hellish folly.

'Come on, Doctor, what do you say?' he urged.

Captain Brook was always glad to initiate a new member to his ways, and what better draftee was there than a doctor? What greater stamp of approval could there be for his love of inflicting pain and death? Not a stronger emotion was there as what one felt upon seeing a man's last breath; a doctor should know that. And there was no greater feeling than that of being the instigator of such emotion as pure terror. It overwhelmed by far all others. It was better than sex with women. It was the purest emotion he had ever experienced. It was the animal instinct of the predator, the confirmation of the sovereign force of the dominant.

Jacob had never thought such extreme madness could exist except in hell. He realised he was the only pillar of righteousness around. Deep down, he knew he had to act, or he would be as good as part of it. His Christian duty was to interpose.

Quashing his fear, he stepped forward and said, 'Captain Brook, I beg you to come to your senses, Sir. I beseech you in the name of God, cease this cruelty and hate, or it shall be your demise, Sir.'

'Hate? Who said I hate 'em? They might be Spanish filth, but they've got coin, and lots of it. I can smell it. So how can I bloody hate 'em, Doctor?' said the captain, turning halfway to his audience, who laughed out loud.

'Sir, these men deserve human decency. I beg you to take

hold of yourself. There are other ways to win respect.'

Had this French doctor not administered the mercury unction that gave him relief from his syphilis, Brook would have ripped out his throat by now. Instead he roared: 'I'll show you respect, Doctor. I'll show you how to get it from these dogs!'

'NO . . . NO . . . Wait!' shouted Jacob as the captain took a step back. Then he swung round and raised his battle-axe high above his head.

The Spaniard wheezed in horror as the incensed captain hammered down the heavy iron blade between his ribs. There was a thump, a squelch, the sound of smashed bones, expelled air, blood, and other matter, and the Spaniard gasped for air no more.

The captain turned to the remaining councillors. He roared: 'Tell me where you've put the poxy coin!'

Ignoring Jacob's continued protestations, which Brook put down to fatigue and a mild case of hysterics, the captain ordered the next man to step out of the line.

'By God. How can you stand there?' hurled Jacob at the group of sailors he had prayed with aboard the *Joseph*. 'This man is mad,' he said, with a stern eye for Quartermaster Blunt, who was among them. 'In the name of the Lord, I beseech you, stop him!'

Ducamp now had caught up with Jacob, and, taking him firmly by the arm, he swung him round. In a low but resolute voice, the bosun said in French, 'Are you out of your bloody mind, Delpech? Your life is on a thread, man, and I won't let you lose it!'

Jacob said, 'You cannot be part of this. You cannot let this go on.'

'This is what the Spanish do, except they make it last longer. The captain puts on a show to force the others to talk.'

'Bosun,' called out the captain, twenty yards away, where his next victim was pleading on bended knee. 'Tell the bloody doctor he is upsetting our proceedings. Tell him to put a sock in it, for the sake of his health!'

'He's calmed now, Sir. Just not used to campaigning, Sir.'

As the bosun answered, the noise of marching boots made everyone's eyes turn to the south side.

'You can thank your lucky stars this time, Delpech,' said Ducamp as a mob came roaring into the square.

'I thank God,' returned Jacob.

It was the land contingent, headed by the tall figure of de Graaf.

Brook stood, legs apart, balancing the long shaft of the axe on his shoulder. As the Dutchman came nearer, Brook called out, 'You took your bloody time, man!'

'You were supposed to wait!' returned de Graaf, continuing his stride while his men flocked round the grill like vultures. They took meat while Brook's men handed them drink and threw more meat on the boucan.

'Monsieur,' intervened Jacob as the Dutchman came by him. 'Please, put a stop to this man's murderous folly. The town is won . . .'

'Take the man away, before I stop his yap!' hurled Captain Brook. Then he raised his axe with both hands and slammed the bloody steel blade into the blood-drenched earth by the side of the praying Spaniard.

The bosun again took the doctor by the arm, but to Ducamp's alarm, Jacob shook it free and continued: 'The town is won—'

Ducamp had no choice but to place his thick forearm around the doctor's neck. The man had already made his point. Now he was tempting the devil.

'Sun's turned 'is bloody brain, don't know his arse from his elbow!' said Brook.

De Graaf stopped and held up a hand. 'Let him speak,' he said.

Ducamp released his hold. Jacob put his hand to his throat where the bosun's arm had pressed against his larynx. He said, 'There is no need for callous killing. I beseech you, stop this torture. The town is won!'

Before the Dutchman could answer, Brook growled: 'We didn't come here for the bloody town, you soft prick!'

Then he turned to the Dutchman, who could now see the carnage. 'You know the score, Laurencillo. It's for the good of us all. Sacrifice a few of the bastards, and the rest will jabber, right?'

Meeting Brook head-on, the Dutchman said, 'Ned, I told you before, man, no bloody torture!'

Brook knew de Graaf's rage, and his short fuse for a fight. He was a big bastard too. Besides, the passion for butchery had left him; he had got his fill of killing for now. Any more would spoil the special pleasure it brought. So he just grunted his discontent.

'Apart from that, you've done a good job,' continued de Graaf, remaining pragmatic. 'Now leave the talking to me, and we'll be out of here in two days with enough coin to sink a bloody galleon!'

Without waiting for an answer, de Graaf lifted up the Spaniard by the arm. In fluent Spanish, he told the man to take him to the mayor.

'*El alcalde* is there, Señor,' said the Spaniard, pointing to the body parts of the first sacrificial corpse.

De Graaf looked back at Ned Brook with disgust and annoyance. Now, instead of one leader, he knew he would have to deal with several of the *regidores*.

'For crying out loud, man, you've blown the head off the bloody mayor!' said the Dutchman. Captain Brook simply scratched the top of his head.

De Graaf marched the prisoner over to the other councillors waiting in line. So that Brook could understand, he said each sentence in English, then translated it into Spanish to make sure the Spaniards also understood. He said, 'Tell your people to bring us their money and valuables. We want one hundred thousand pesos by nightfall tomorrow. Or we will burn the town and everyone in it down to the ground. We also want fifty cows and all the barrels of wine, tobacco, and cocoa in your storehouse. Be off!'

Jacob, who had followed in the Dutchman's wake, was wondering if burning a whole population alive was any better than Brook's methodical sacrifice of a few leading citizens. However, at least de Graaf's way gave the poor wretches a chance to come out of the raid with their lives and all their limbs attached.

The Dutchman turned back to Brook. 'Ned, man,' he said, 'I want you to string up the bodies so everyone can see the consequences of their stupidity. The mayor'll help his villagers see reason yet. We stumbled on soldiers along the way, got 'em all, but you can never be sure. We need to be in and out quick, man.'

24

HUNDREDS OF THOUSANDS of flies swarmed over the battlefield where the caballeros had fallen. Birds, dogs, and even hens were digging into the broken flesh. And now, with the evening temperature, mosquitoes began siphoning blood from the living. Except for the two bodies strung up on display, the town square became deserted as the buccaneers took refuge inside houses or at the mayor's residence.

The drunken orgy had resumed in the salons and bedrooms, where the most pragmatic women accepted that they would do better to lead the game rather than be taken by force. At least this way, they were able to choose their partners, and avoid the ones disfigured by syphilis.

But this separation of mind and body was beyond many of the womenfolk. This was the case for one young lady who found herself being carried off to a room by a bull of a partner, much larger than herself. In his frenzied desire, he flipped her petite body over and bore down on her from behind, clutching her hips, her shoulders, and ultimately, her neck. 'Come on, woman. It's like shaggin' a sack o' beans,' protested the thick-necked sailor before letting her fall, inert and heavy onto the bed. The man, who was no stranger to such an occurrence, headed off for some refreshment, leaving the girl for dead.

*

Jacob had taken possession of the doctor's house. All the injured mates and their partners had left the premises except one. The young man, a cobbler's son from Bristol, lay dying of his wound on a mattress thrown down in the room that must have been where the doctor practised his surgery. There were medical instruments neatly laid out, and jars and ointments on shelves. The patient had been delirious, then chatty, and now he was unconscious again. Jacob did not think he would last the night; his buddy had also died, so no one was there to comfort him. Jacob had bound up his open belly. There was nothing more he could do.

He wondered if the battlefield tactic of putting the mortally wounded out of their misery was not so cruel after all. However, at least this way, the man had time to repent for his sins and commit his soul to God.

The battle had made Jacob see the fragility of life, and its futility without hope of life after death. All those men were born to parents who had no doubt shed tears of joy on the day of their birth. They were all born with fair souls as children of God. But then they had become corrupt and conditioned by hatred. Did not fate have a hand in that corruption, for no one chooses their birthplace or their station? There again, every man who had been taught Christian values was responsible for his life choices, be he born a Spaniard, a Dutchman, a Catholic, a Protestant. But Jacob pushed these thoughts to the back of his mind. He did not want to go into an inner dialogue about the fairness of faith, not while he was still in the void after so many deaths.

The house was comfortable. He entered the study, which was filled with medical books and collections of animals and insects that reminded him of his own father's house. He wondered what had become of his mother and sister. He only knew that they had fled Montauban before the soldiers had entered his beloved hometown. But he did not want to think about it.

He opened a cabinet and started sifting through drawings and personal papers of births and deaths and suchlike. It took him back to his own house. He also kept his wife and children's birth certificates in a walnut cabinet. But he did not want to dwell on those memories either, preferring to take refuge in the present.

Suddenly he felt a presence. He turned his head from the sketch he was perusing to see a dishevelled-looking young lady appear on the threshold. She must have entered the house from the rear. The cabinet was on the same wall as the door, so she did not see him immediately. She looked dazed, her clothes were torn, and her neck was red and blue. She was pretty, though, and Jacob knew where she had come from. He dared not think what went on at the mayor's residence but still felt shameful for it. Then she saw Jacob's reflexion in the glass on the wall opposite. She turned to him with a gasp of surprise, though no sound came out of her mouth. Her expression turned to indignation, as if to ask what he was doing there.

'I was admiring the drawings,' said Jacob. 'Is this your house?'

She had been abducted and raped; she cared not who this stranger was. She only cared that he would not hurt her. He did not look as if he would. She was dying to sit down, to forget. But she remained standing, clenching the knife she had taken from the kitchen.

'My father's,' she said in Spanish. Jacob, who had studied Latin, found that he could understand Spanish fairly well.

There came loud voices from the street, drawing closer.

'And the melons, all soft and bulging like pigeons,' said a deep and joyful voice outside the closed shutters that led onto the street. 'You've gotta give it a go, man.'

'If we find her,' said a more fluty voice.

'She can't have got far . . .'

Jacob quickly crossed the study and opened the door that led to the surgery room. He nodded to her to enter quickly. She was unsure whether she could trust this man or not, but she had no choice. Moments later, there were footsteps in the hallway. Then two men staggered wildly into the brightly lit room.

'Oh, sorry, Doctor.'

'What do you want, Mr Griffiths?'

'Looking for a tart,' said a big fellow whom Jacob deduced to be one of Cox's crew.

'Right tasty 'n' all,' said the chirpy man called Griffiths.

'Well, you won't find a "tart" in this house. Only Mr Barret.'

Jacob prayed his patient would not wake up and give the girl away. In fact, he hoped he was dead.

'Oh, right. How is he then?' said Griffiths.

The doctor did not answer. He just left an awkward silence.

'Well, give 'im our regards, eh, Doctor?' said the big fellow. Then he turned to his mate. 'Come on.'

The men backed out of the room and left the house.

A few minutes later, Jacob opened the surgery room door. The young lady stepped out, still gripping her knife. She looked at Jacob with her big brown eyes, then said, 'My father is a doctor.'

'Yes,' said Jacob, 'I have used some of his instruments.'

'He was,' she said, correcting herself, 'he was a doctor, until someone put an axe through his heart.'

She crossed herself, then moved toward the hallway. At the door, she said, 'Your patient is dead,' and she went upstairs.

*

Señorita Ana rose at first light, the cleanest time of the day. The drunks and thieves would all be asleep. She had slept with her door locked, a chair wedged under the doorknob, her knife under her pillow, though she remained covered in her rapist's smell the whole night through. At last she was able to fetch some water up to her room and wash the sweat and scum from her body.

It was still early morning, and all was calm when she ventured out to find her mother, sisters, and brother, whom she knew to be locked inside the church.

The township was built according to the Laws of the Indies, which meant a rectilinear grid of streets was built around the plaza mayor. Ana now crept catlike under windows and wrought iron balconies that resounded with snorts and snoring of drunken raiders; now she darted like a gazelle across open spaces, until she came to the north side of San Salvador church. She scratched with a stone at the wooden door that was locked shut. At last someone scratched back on the other side, and she slid her note under the door. She wrote to her mother only that she had escaped. She made no mention of the horrible fate of her father, whose body she had encountered the night before as she crossed the square, after escaping through the window of the mayor's residence. In the darkness, she had been drawn to two figures, each ligatured on a cartwheel between two torches. Then she saw him full on, with a cleft in the middle of his chest. In a bid for her sanity, she had kept her mind busy with prayer.

Now she was desperate to know if her mother, young sisters, and brother were well. If they were dead, then there was no point praying for their safety. If they were alive, she would pray to the Virgin Mary and all the saints of the calendar to keep them safe.

In the torment of the night, wrapped in the smell of her ravisher, she had clenched hold of that hope of being in the bosom of her mother and siblings again. It was what kept her from thrusting her knife into her heart. Her youngest brother was only eight, her sisters three, six, and eleven. She realised she would not be able to face living again if anything had happened to them. She was their big sister; she loved them with all her heart, like a little mother. If they were gone, her life would no longer have any sense at all.

There was another scratch at the door. Then she heard a hushed voice that said: 'We are here, Ana.'

'Mother!'

'Are you well?'

'Yes, Mother . . .'

'And your father, have you any news of him?'

She could not lie to her mother, but she could not tell her that he was killed. He, who had settled his family in Bayamo because it was far enough from the coast to be a haven from rovers and foreign armies; he, who had wanted a refuge so his children could focus on their intellectual understanding of God's world; he, whose altruism, love, and knowledge were unremitting; he, destroyed by men who smelt like goats and cared for nothing but their own sordid gratification.

'The men are locked in the warehouses, Mother. And you, how are you?'

The silence lasted two beats too long, and Ana knew her mother suspected the worst. Her voice was on the verge of breaking as she said, 'We are bearing up, my dear Ana, but the heat yesterday was unbearable for many of us, especially the old and the toddlers. I fear for your sister. We have hardly any water left. I pray to God the raiders leave soon. I do not know how we can go through another day in here.'

*

Ana decided there and then to live for something greater than herself. Now that growing into a woman had lost all its value, she was prepared to be taken again to protect her cause, for she could not lose her virginity twice. She suddenly became aware of the power of the charms of her carnal envelope, of her smooth and shapely curves, of her plump breasts that had grown so quickly during the past year, and which even in ordinary times men could not keep from ogling. She could now understand those women at the residence who had spoken to her of setting aside her body from her soul. The Lord would not abandon her in sin. Did He not forgive Mary Magdalene?

Yes, her mind was made up: she would be a whore to save the children. But she needed to do it with one of the men who could open the doors of the church.

A little later, she redressed in her mother's bedroom. As she passed her hand lightly over her soft breasts, she prayed to the Virgin Mary, who would understand. Then she knelt and prayed to God that He would help her in the name of His son.

'O God, please be there,' she said to herself as she left her room. 'Please be there!'

*

Jacob did not sleep easily on the couch in the study. He had slept with one eye open, wondering where he could bury Barret and the others, then wondering about the girl. Was she all right? Should he go to her door? But how would it be interpreted? Would she be vengeful, stab him while he slept? Then his interrogations and fretting had followed into scenes of horror, scenes of butchery and slaughter, of the face of the lad he had stabbed, of himself paralysed, unable to raise so much as a finger, or call out, impuissant to prevent the slaughter of innocent people. Then he saw a knife, the girl. He awoke.

She was standing over him. She was clean, her dark hair was soft and silky and held back with red ribbon, she smelt of perfume, and she was wearing a dress that made her look like a woman. She was truly beautiful, as Spanish girls often are when young, and she offered a shy smile. But what did she want?

'You were shouting,' she said softly in Spanish, with a motion of the hand.

'Oh. Yes,' said Jacob.

'I want to thank you for last night.'

It took him a moment to clear his mind of slumber, to translate the words. After she said it again, he realised she was talking about the sailors who had come looking for her.

'I am sorry about your *padre*,' said Jacob solemnly and slowly in French, slipping in any Spanish words he knew. 'I am equally sorry for the *alcalde*, and for all this killing.'

'The mayor was not such a good man. My father was, though.'

'I am sure,' he said, getting to a sitting position.

Ana sat down on the edge of the armchair opposite, poised and arching her back. She was determined to get this doctor to act for her. But how did you go about seducing a man? She had seen some women do it during events in Havana, where her father once had his practice. They smiled, empathised, laughed merrily at stupid jokes, and gave looks. It was an art that she had no time to learn. So how did you get a man to just lie with you?

'Can I do anything for you, Doctor?' she said.

She immediately regretted saying *Doctor*; it made her offer sound medical.

But Jacob had been a man about town when young. The olive-skinned girl was very attractive, and he knew she was after something.

'You are safe here. There is no need for you to act, my girl.'

'Thank you,' she said, slightly embarrassed. But a girl, she was not, and she kept up her pose, which was not without some effect.

Jacob noted her fleeting frown of disappointment, but he could see too that she was resolute to get what she wanted. Did she want protection?

'Yes, you can help me,' he said, nodding toward the surgery room where Barret's body still lay. 'Is there a place where I can bury our dead, *los muertos?*'

'The churchyard?' she said.

'He is not Catholic,' said Jacob, who was suddenly aware how absurd it was to mention the man's religious denomination.

Ana realised that there was no point keeping up her charade; she would fare better talking straight. She knew not this man's intentions, but she was ready to risk all. Relaxing her posture, she said, 'There is a special place. I can help you, if you help me.'

As the pain returned around her pelvis, her hips, and her neck, she desperately told Jacob about the plight of the women and children locked inside the church.

Jacob listened attentively as the girl returned to her natural self, a serious, obliging, and beautiful young lady.

Using his hands and key words, he explained he would speak to the commander without delay. There was no reason why they should not be released and given refreshment. He would tell the commander that in return, the buccaneers could bury their dead in a proper grave. Brook would not care. But Jacob believed de Graaf to be of Christian principles even if he sinned like a heathen. However, the Dutchman would need reassurance that the bodies would not be dug up and fed to the crocodiles as soon as the buccaneers had departed.

'You must talk to Father Del Lome,' said the girl in her native tongue. 'He is strict about religion, but if he gives you his word, he will keep it. You must tell him about our agreement.'

*

Delpech headed out immediately to the warehouses down by the riverside. That was where he would find the padre. But on the way, he was hailed by a sailor whose mate had shot himself in the foot. Jacob was obliged to lead the man back to the doctor's house, where Ana was hiding upstairs. At first, she was alarmed, wondered where she could run. But no one climbed the stairs. She quickly understood that the men had come to be treated.

Jacob extracted the lead shot, cleaned and bound the wound, and sent the man hopping with his partner. As he headed out again, he saw the girl on the stairs. 'Please hurry,' she implored.

He passed by parties of buccaneers escorting townsmen to their stash, and groups of five or six taking to the saddle on Spanish mounts, to venture out onto the versant and plunder farmsteads.

By the time he reached the warehouse built along the Bayamo River, it was already sweltering. The padre, a man in his sixties, was manifestly in no hurry to meet his maker; he was relieved to be offered a chance to step out of the inferno.

As the priest spoke only Spanish and Latin, the councillor who had escaped Brook's sacrificial torture offered to translate into French. Jacob explained that he was an indentured doctor who wanted to help the people who were suffering in the church. The padre told Jacob where they buried non-Catholics, and agreed that, if Jacob could save the women and children from further suffering, he would leave the dead rovers in their resting place.

The councillor took the opportunity to give Jacob his thanks for his intervention on the square, and now for saving those in the church where his own wife, mother, and son were also held. He said that he was aware that the doctor had nothing to do with these villains other than being indentured to them.

'I promise to give a good account of you, Doctor,' he said.

This left Jacob perplexed. And as he walked briskly back through the elegant streets lined with whitewashed houses, he wondered if the man really thought the town would be rescued by his countrymen. It hardly seemed likely, did it?

*

Within a half an hour, Jacob was standing in the governor's library. The windows were flung open; the shutters were half-closed.

Valuables and coin unearthed from gardens, wells, cellars, and cisterns had been trickling into the library all morning. The three captains were lounging on the comfortable seating, drinking and smoking while crewmates sorted the piles of gems, silver, and gold into casks for easy transport.

'You have no experience of campaigns, Monsieur Delpech,' said the Dutchman. 'It was in fact on my command that they be locked up. We cannot let any women or children roam about freely.'

'But, Sir, I beg you. The most vulnerable among them will certainly die of suffocation or thirst.'

'They're locked up for a reason, Doctor,' said Captain Brook. Jacob turned to face his captain lounging with a bottle in one hand and one leg swung over the velvet arm of his chair. 'And that reason be their own safety!'

De Graaf said: 'These men are predators. Many of them have wild imaginations and untamed curiosity.'

'Some o' these boys'll try anything once!' said Brook.

Outside, horses were drawing up in front of the building. Their snorting could be heard through the shutters. Brook got up, and looking through the shutter, he said, 'Have you ever seen a dog shag an old nag?'

'God forbid, I have not, Sir,' said Jacob.

'I have,' said Brook. 'On campaign, anything goes. That's why we lock 'em up!'

'They will suffocate . . .'

There came a bustling and footsteps in the entrance hall. Then in walked five buccaneers with a black slave.

One of them said, 'Picked him up three miles east.'

'*De donde vienes?*' said de Graaf.

'Santiago, Señor.'

The buccaneer then handed the Dutchman a piece of paper on which was written a message to the mayor of Bayamo. De Graaf translated the message out loud.

'Dear Mayor,' began de Graaf, who then flicked up his eyes to meet those of Captain Brook. The latter gave an innocent shrug of the shoulders. De Graaf continued. 'Dear Mayor Guiseppi Alonzo de la Firma and the people of Bayamo. The fleet is on its way to Manzanillo bay. They come with their mounts, so relief will be with you within four days of sending this message. Instructions are to delay payments, or only pay small amounts, to delay the raiders as much as you can. Signed, the governor of Santiago.'

'When was it sent?' said Cox.

'The fifteenth of the eighth month of 1688,' read de Graaf.

'Two days ago,' said Brook.

Jacob realised now what the Spaniard in the warehouse meant about giving him a good account. Somehow, perhaps from a different messenger, he had been receiving news. But Jacob said nothing, for there was nothing to gain from another dead Spaniard and a fatherless child. And in some respects, the Spanish fleet being on their way gave Delpech some cause for relief. Provided the captains withdrew, it meant the horrors he had witnessed would cease. Wouldn't they?

'What's the plan?' said Brook.

'Assemble the men on the plaza.'

'What about the people in the church?' said Jacob, seizing the space Brook left for thought.

'Give them scraps from the boucan and water from the well. No fresh cuts; we'll need all the provisions we can get for ourselves.' He turned to a crewmate and said, 'Trev, go with the doctor, fetch Rob and Two-Fingers, and smash the church windows . . . from the inside.'

'Thank you,' said Jacob, who knew this was as good a compromise as he would get.

'Doctor,' said Captain Brook. Delpech turned to face him. 'Remember to bring the medicines, right?'

Jacob knew what he meant and nodded his understanding. He then left quickly to draw pails of water from the well and fill baskets with cooked leftovers from the boucan.

*

Over two hundred buccaneers assembled on the main square. Brook spoke about the intercepted message; then de Graaf stepped forward. In a raised voice and a measured, slightly ironic tone, he said, 'Lads, I see no point wasting lives and plunder on a confrontation that would serve no purpose, other than the pleasure of killing Spanish soldiers!' There was a loud roar of laughter, mingled with *ayes* all round.

Along with a good stack of booty, de Graaf had attained his objective of taking the inland township, which would send a warning to the Spanish that he could strike anywhere. They would from now on think twice before raiding the west coast of Saint-Domingue, which the French Dutchman was commissioned to protect. Brook, Cox, and their men had also made a nice fortune for services rendered while thrillingly navigating close to death, sometimes too close. So it was unanimously voted to get out while the going was still good.

De Graaf then sent five horsemen to give notice to the mariners back at Manzanillo Bay, to sail the ship westward along the coast to where the *Joseph* and the *Fortuna* lay anchored at the cay. The rest of the raiders would travel down the Cauto River, which flowed into the bay a good twenty miles up from Manzanillo harbour. From there, they would continue by boat along the coastal shoals, under the cover of night.

Two groups of six townsmen were "volunteered" from the warehouses for the employ of the buccaneers. Under escort, these men were loaded into carts and put to the task of removing the barricades along the road to the embarcadero. And they did not dally.

*

Later that afternoon, de Graaf joined Jacob, who stood with his Bible over the dead sailors. They lay side by side in hessian sacks at the bottom of a large trench. Ducamp had shown up along with five score of maritime desperados.

Captain Brook had stayed in the library with the loot. He

never went near a graveyard if he could help it, preferring burials at sea. Seeing his crewmates cramped six feet under only put him in the doldrums and made him feel bitter with thoughts that his life was destined to be short, riddled as he was with the pox. He would rather spend his time watching mulatto Joe dress in silk and pearls. Captain Cox had chosen to remain in the playroom, as he liked to call it, for a last fling with his favourite female company.

As agreed with the padre, the short ceremony took place on the burial ground reserved for non-Catholics. The factions of Christianity seemed more absurd to Jacob now than ever. Their rules seemed only to obscure the essence of religion, namely, belief in God and one's desire to be near Him by following the teachings of Jesus.

He had witnessed for himself how manmade religious rules only gave perfidious men a pretext to commit wrongness to the extreme, in the same way that absence of morality led men to commit unimaginable acts of cruelty.

Standing at the head of the pit, he read a passage from Matthew chapter V, which he had translated into English. He then turned his head to encompass the silent horde of rovers huddled around the trench from left to right. In a loud and resolute voice, he said, 'To live without God is to live without hope. And life without hope has no value. God brings meaning and morality to our lives. God. Is. Hope. Amen.'

He said it, of course, not for the dead, but for the sake of the living, in the hope that some of them would find the righteous path. His eyes settled for an instant on Ducamp to his right.

'Amen,' mumbled the horde of wayward sailors.

The slight breeze rose up from the north. The burial

ground was suddenly polluted with the nauseating stench of putrid corpses. It came as a reminder of the scores of Spanish soldiers still strewn over the field where death had been sown.

*

The rest of the afternoon and the early evening were mostly spent carting provisions and saleable barrels of tobacco and cocoa to the embarcadero. From there, the cargo was loaded onto the buccaneers' boats, as well as pirogues and canoes that belonged to Bayamo boatmen, which increased cargo and seating capacity.

De Graaf negotiated with the councillors, who provided thirty "volunteers" to slaughter animals on the square and salt the meat which was then loaded for transport. It was at least an escape from the stifling warehouse, and the *vecinos* carried out the butchery diligently and swiftly to be rid of their assailants by nightfall. If the rescue fleet commander accused them of not delaying the buccaneers sufficiently, they had the perfect scapegoat. They would put the blame on Señor Guiseppi Alonzo de la Firma, their proud and now faceless *alcalde*, whose morbid silhouette seemed to be bearing reproachfully down at them from his wheel. The governor of Cuba could hardly hang him for failing in his duty now, could he? Pity he had to die so atrociously, though, but then again, everyone had to die sometime, and anyway, he was old, and inflexible, and a tyrant. At least this way, his life was given meaning, and he would be remembered as a hero, instead of as an ignorant town official who had stupidly sent a battalion of cadets to their deaths. The doctor, on the other hand, was a tragic loss. He had not long since been coaxed to Bayamo from Havana to look after the townsfolk; the move had not provided him with the safe living they had promised. Nothing could be promised in this world where one day, the spectacles of Paradise filled you with wonder, and the next, a hurricane or a band of raiders could come and devastate your entire existence.

Jacob meanwhile busied himself by replenishing San Salvador church with water and what food he could salvage from the boucan. Now, when the rovers opened the door for him to deposit his pails and extra goblets, instead of hundreds of staring, frightened, wary faces, three ringless ladies stepped forward in dignified gratitude and took charge of the distribution. One of them was the doctor's wife, to whom Jacob had given a note from Ana on his first visit, to reassure them that the water was drinkable and the food edible, that they were not poisoned.

On leaving them for the last time, he told them he would pray to God to protect and deliver them. '*Adios, y vaya con Dios,*' he said.

The whitewashed buildings were now bathed in the orange glow of evening as he hurried back to the house where Ana was still hiding. The streets had taken on a frenetic air in the end-of-day gloom as beasts of burden, horses, and carts stole away with the last of the barrels. Jacob guessed the urgency was enhanced by the fact that no sailor wanted to be the last to see the ghostly chaos left in the wake of their rampage, or hear the spirits of the dead cadets as night encroached.

He passed the mayor's residence, where de Graaf, Brook, and Cox were standing outside, in discussion over the barrels of loot to be loaded for transport.

He crossed the plaza amid empty hogsheads, bottles, jugs,

and piles of offal. The glowing embers under the boucan, the torches planted to give light, and the mass slaughter of animals, lent it a hellish hue.

The morning would bring to the townsfolk the terrible realisation of what had hit them, thought Jacob. They would have to come to terms with the weekend of rape, "consented" intercourse, killings, desolation, and stolen life savings and harvests. Jacob felt debased and ashamed to be part of it, despite his efforts to alleviate some of the horror. How could he dishonour himself further by taking a share of the spoils? It was not like stealing from the Spanish silver fleet at all, which transported treasures pillaged from the natives of these lands. This was an ordinary township with ordinary civilians who had no quarrel with the commanders of war.

A short while later, he pushed the rear door of the doctor's house and gave five syncopated knocks on the study table to let Ana upstairs know it was him. He went to the surgery room and hurriedly took the vials he needed for Brook and his crew. Then he went back to the study and sat on the sofa where he had slept—he had been unable to snatch any sleep in someone's bedroom. He picked up the wooden cross he had placed on a low table. He glanced over the six acorns he had stood in a line on a strip of wool.

The cross came from his own study, plundered and ransacked during the dragonnades. The acorns, chosen for their size and painted with faces, were sent to him from his son, Paul, when he was in prison in France. These were the objects of his cocoon of protection that gave him a reason each day to go on. They represented heaven and earth, and all he ever wanted. And they brought him comfort when God seemed to turn silent.

He placed the cross in his leather bag, even though, with deep regret, he realised that his prayer said to the desperados at the end of the burial had already been forgotten. He began putting the acorns safely in a writing case which he first packed with the wool.

'Your family?' said Ana, who now stood before him. He had not heard her enter. Now that she was in a more conservative dress, he could tell she must be no more than fourteen, barely older than his eldest daughter, Lizzie. Yet she was sharper than most adults.

'Yes,' he said solemnly. 'Me, my wife, my daughter Elizabeth, my son, Paul, this one's Louise who is with our Lord and her sister Anne, and this one's the newest member of the family. I hope to see them all again.'

'I hope you do too.'

'All is not so well in France, my homeland.'

'My father used to say the same about Spain. That is why he came here.'

'Ana, I have had to take some of the medicine from your father's cabinet,' he continued, using his hands to give shape to his meaning. 'I am sorry, but I cannot do otherwise if I want to see my family again. You understand? Truly, I am sorry.'

'Don't be. It is nothing.'

'Of course,' he said, realising the insignificance of the act compared to the horror she had endured.

'My father would have gladly let you have the medicine you need,' she asserted slowly so that he could understand, which took Jacob by surprise. 'You gave me hope and morality when in my despair I was lacking. You could have taken what I had left, but you did not. My father would have liked you for that, and for what you have done to save the people in the church from thirst and the calenture.'

Jacob got to his feet. He took both her hands. He said, 'Keep your faith, Ana, and others will have faith in you. Take this as a reminder to keep your hope, and others will hope for you.' He placed the acorn that represented his precious Lulu in her hand. 'Small acorns grow into great trees, just like a tiny spark can light a beacon. I will pray that you become a tree of wisdom and a beacon of hope despite these atrocities, Ana. Your family will need you.'

Half an hour later, Delpech was riding on one of the last carts out. His heart sank as he left the devastated township and followed the dark road to the embarcadero, accompanied by the evening song of birds, the chirping of insects, and the howling of hounds.

25

DE GRAAF HAD invited Jacob to sit beside him in his boat.

'I regret you had to bear witness to the horrors of war, Monsieur Delpech,' said the Dutchman in a low voice, while stretching out his long legs as best he could. 'But you must realise, it is an eye for an eye in this world. And this campaign was in response to far greater atrocities committed against our people.'

'A Christian would turn the other cheek, Captain de Graaf,' said Jacob, lighting his pipe.

The Dutchman let out an indulgent chuckle; then he said as if in banter, 'Have you ever seen a woman impaled? Or men burnt alive at the stake for heresy? Have you ever seen children picked up by the ankles and thrashed against the wall until their brains spilt out? Have you ever seen a man slowly sawn from his genitals upward? This is what they do.'

Jacob suspected that de Graaf was trying to give himself a good conscience and a clever pretext to attack and loot an innocent town. But he knew better than to argue with a man capable of leading a band of butchers without shedding a drop of blood himself. Instead he said, 'I have seen what men of war are capable of, Sir, whatever their nationality. If you continue to meet violence with violence, when will it stop? It is a virtue to learn to turn the other cheek and pray for those who persecute you, is it not?'

'That may work, Monsieur Delpech, if the offender has read the Bible and shares its virtues.'

It was a fair point, thought Jacob, puffing at his pipe as images of Elias Verbizier reeled through his mind.

'Besides,' said the Dutchman, 'if we abided by those virtues, you would not be able to recover your freedom and pay your passage back to Europe, would you?'

'I will take none of it!' said Jacob.

Fatigued, de Graaf preferred to let it drop, and made himself as comfortable as he could on his Havana hide until it was his turn to take the oar.

As the canoe slipped through the black, brackish water beneath the star-speckled sky, Jacob settled with his pipe. However, though it gave protection from insects and the foul tang of sailors, it could not wipe away the killing from his memory.

*

Travelling downriver would normally take a good deal less time than rowing up it. However, each craft also carried part of the spoils of victory. So instead of crossing the strips of land where the river snaked round parallel to itself, the buccaneers preferred to ride out the bends even though it added precious time to their return journey. And the closer the river got to the coast, the more it coiled like a Cuban boa. Sometimes it took half an hour to get to a point that was no more than a stone's throw across a strip of land. But it was certainly less strenuous than heaving barrels of provisions, crop, and plunder through marshland.

At one point, however, the water became so shallow and full of fallen branches that they were obliged to pull into the south bank. Then they had to carry their boats and cargo the short distance through the swamped woodland to reach the next navigable stretch.

The men in the pirogue that brought up the rear had been sneakily swigging as they drifted downstream. Instead of carrying the precious cargo separately like the crews before them, they got the notion to heave high their pirogue with the barrels still in it to save the hassle of lugging them. After all, it was only fifty yards to the next strip of water, and there were ten of them to carry it.

It turned out, however, that as they advanced carefully in the paling darkness of predawn, the main hindrance was not the cumbersome weight, but the nature of the terrain. The marshy ground was strewn with roots. One of the men tripped, sending another over with him. The false steps caused the boat to dip and tilt. The barrels toppled over to the ground. The one containing plunder had not been capped and hooped—given that it was soon to be emptied—and its contents spilt over the marshy bed.

Brook, who loved loot even more than his mulatto, was walking with the boat in front. He turned and saw the barrel of treasure a foot deep in thick, muddy water. He roared out: 'By Jupiter, I'll cut your bloody arms off if you don't put that barrel as you found it!'

The guilty party urgently lowered their pirogue to the ground. As if to prove the utility of their arms, they proceeded to frantically recover the spilt treasure, feeling around in the cold, murky water for any coin that might have toppled out.

Three boats up, de Graaf looked back and immediately guessed what all the fuss was about.

'For crying out loud! The lot of you drunk or just plain stupid?'

'Should 'ave waited till daybreak before heading down,' said Cox in the next boat up, thinking of the extra time he could have spent in the library in Bayamo.

'And we'd be in worse lumber than a beached whale!' returned the Dutchman. 'Because the Spanish aren't stupid. They'd have also sent soldiers across the hills on horseback!'

'Oh, yeah,' said Cox.

'Just pick up the big stuff,' shouted de Graaf. 'We gotta make it down before the day breaks over the bay!'

They salvaged what they could, leaving behind a small fortune to whomever would one day dig into the mud on the south bank where the river was shallow.

They soon caught up with the pack waiting further downstream on the river's edge. The whole band of buccaneers then rowed the rest of the way without another hitch to the river's mouth.

In the grey light of a misty morning, the seventeen-boat flotilla hacked along the coastal shoals until they came to the cay. Quickly and under de Graaf's careful eye, they heaved and hauled the takings into the holds of the three waiting ships so they could weigh anchor before the sun dissipated their cover.

'Rendezvous on Pinos Island for the count,' called out de Graaf from the epicentre of the circle of men, after a brief consultation with the captains.

As the men broke away to board their ships, the Dutch captain turned to Jacob and said, 'Monsieur Delpech, I am sure Captain Brook would not mind if you rode with me.'

'Like hell I would. You ain't stealing my doctor, de Graaf. He's indentured to me, and he's an invaluable member of my crew!'

'Then I will pay the indenture in advance of the doctor's share with interest, and I'll throw Joe into the bargain,' said de Graaf, shrewdly addressing the captain's two most delectable sins, which had a stronger hold over him than the virtues of a medical man.

'All right then,' said Brook at length, 'but leave the medicine with me.' The doctor and de Graaf agreed.

Deep down, the mulatto, who was wearing hoops and a silk scarf, didn't know whether to laugh or cry to be so esteemed by his new protector and multi-ethnic family. But all in all, he considered the services due were certainly worth the wealth and freedom that he could look forward to, and one day soon, he might even be able to jump ship.

Poor Joe's manifest enthusiasm would surely have been dulled had he not been ignorant, thought Jacob, of the sailor's ailment.

26

DELPECH WAS SITTING at the captain's desk, in the handsome frigate built for a sea prince.

De Graaf had invited him to share his cabin and use whatever space he could find, except the great mahogany table, strewn with navigational instruments and rolls of charts, that stood in the centre. Elsewhere was richly furnished with silverware, a fine French *glace*, and a Persian carpet. Delpech had strung up his hammock near a writing desk which enabled him to corner off a personal area. As the morning light flooded in through the stern windows, he wondered how a man could be so elegant and considerate and yet so ruthless. It was true, however, he had not actually drawn a drop of blood throughout the campaign. In fact, Jacob believed de Graaf's presence had reduced life loss. Yet given the man's authority over these battle-hardened cut-throats, including the obnoxious Captain Brook, there could be no doubt as to the Dutchman's murderous capabilities.

The deck outside the half-open door was losing its eerie stillness as it became animated again with predominantly French accents. Going by their cheerful banter, the crew were returning from Pinos Island in even livelier spirits than they had left the ship, three hours earlier that morning. The reason for this, Jacob knew, was they had just received their share of the booty, worth over one hundred thousand pieces of eight, the price of a thousand slaves.

Jacob hadn't written a thing. His wooden lacquered pen case with its pastoral scene still sat unopened on the desk beside his Bible. He had been thinking a lot about his life, about his goal to recover his family, and about his spiritual objective.

He needed means to pay for his freedom and to return to Europe. Yet the Christian values to which he wholeheartedly adhered left him unarmed, and without resources to fight to recover his family. *Thou shall not steal!* And he had refused to take a share of the profit from the deaths, desolation, and robbery of innocent people. If he had, how could he qualify for a place in heaven?

A knock on the door brought him out of his introspection. *'Entrez!'* he said, turning round on his leather chair. His sunken eyes showed surprise when they met with the large frame of the bosun that filled the doorway. 'Ah, Monsieur Ducamp, have you jumped ship?'

The bosun advanced into the spacious cabin, whose wide array of stern windows offered an excellent view of the shore.

'Not yet, Monsieur Delpech, no intention of going north yet.' He was referring to de Graaf's imminent departure to Saint-Domingue, which meant circumnavigating the island of Cuba windward and included a detour northward to Nassau. 'I have come to give you this.' He held out a leather drawstring pouch.

Jacob got to his feet. Ignoring the bosun's outstretched hand, he said, 'I am sorry, I distinctly told Captain de Graaf that I would have nothing to do with such ill-gotten gain.'

'It's not loot,' said Ducamp. The pouch of coin made a jingling thud as he dumped it on the desk beside Jacob's Bible. 'It is payment for the belongings I sold from your house in Montauban!'

'I cannot become a profiteer!'

'It's coin I had before, and it is not negotiable. Would you deprive a man of his first step toward redemption, Monsieur Delpech?'

Jacob glanced at the money bag. Was this not an answer to his secret doubts?

'By the grace of God, take it, man. You deserve it. You have been a light of good and a ray of hope to many of us here. And I can assure you, I have never seen a bunch of cut-throats stand so still as when you spoke at the funeral. Some of the lads want to know if it was from the Bible.'

Jacob gave a curt nod. 'It was, Lieutenant Ducamp,' he said. He twisted his torso to reach for his desk. Turning back with his Bible in his hand, he said, 'Matthew chapter five. Take it, please.'

'You are a good man, Monsieur Delpech,' said the bosun, 'and good men deserve to be free!' Taking the book, he held Jacob's gaze for a full second, an instant of mutual understanding which said more than all their pleasantries.

'It is written in French, not Latin. It is God's will that all men may one day be able to read the word of the Lord, and examine their conscience for themselves.'

Jacob felt a fleeting movement of the heart as the big man's expression lost its grim, battle-worn mask of ruggedness, and he saw the lad standing before him, humbled like a son, and with a sheen of hope as if, at last, he had received a long-awaited gift. 'May it help lighten your burden, Monsieur Ducamp. And may God stay with you!'

'I'll say it again, you are a good man,' said the bosun. 'If God exists, may He protect you and yours, Sir.' He bowed, then turned without another word said.

Jacob followed him with his eyes and watched him lower his head back through the cabin door onto the now bustling deck, and climb down the rigging to the longboat to join the *Joseph*. He was taking the Book of God into hell, thought Jacob. There was hope.

Sitting back at the writing desk, Jacob pulled out a sheet of paper from the desk drawer, then he opened his pen case. Five acorn faces stared back at him. He arranged them on the desk on the strip of wool. He then prepared his pen, drew ink from the well, and began to write.

My Dearest Wife . . .

27

ETIENNE AND CLAIRE Lambrois had stopped at Schaffhausen. Situated on the Rhine at midpoint between Geneva and Brandenburg, it bordered the minor German states of the Holy Roman Empire. During their spring travels, Claire had become overly fatigued, and Etienne had decided to make a halt for a couple of days.

The young couple had been given hospitality by the First Consul of the Magistrature, Monsieur Rhing de Wildenberg, who was only too glad to entertain them and give vent to his love of French culture. He had completed his tour of France as a young man and spoke the language fluently. Claire and Etienne had initially planned to rest just a few days, a week at most, but during a conversation at table, Etienne discussed his future plans.

It so happened that Monsieur de Wildenberg had a son-in-law who was hoping to expand his woodworking business, given the new sawmills and the expansion of the wealthy township. 'So one thing led to another, and here we still are,' Claire had told Jeanne, while sitting with Ginette in front of the dwelling that Etienne had been able to rent. Situated close to a sawmill not far out of Schaffhausen, the squared timber-framed dwelling came with the added advantage of a large adjoining barn, useful for Etienne's carpentry activities. To everyone's contentment, it also now employed Jean Fleuret. It was the reason why Jeannot had headed directly for Schaffhausen instead of Brandenburg, Etienne having previously sent word inviting him to stop by on his travels.

During a discussion a little later, Jeanne learnt how the officials looking for Jeanne Delpech had not been prompted by the audacious pauper after all. As soon as the Fleurets arrived at Schaffhausen and informed Etienne and Claire of the boat tragedy, and that Jeanne was recovering in the village where Pierre was buried, Lambrois and Jeannot headed out in a cart to fetch her and Paul.

By the time they arrived in Nion, Jeanne had already left. Monsieur Gaugin explained to them her intentions, so Etienne sent out a message to officials along all the possible routes to stop her so that they could take her back to Schaffhausen by cart. But in Yverdon, they bumped into none other than Cephas Crespin, who told them that, not wishing to travel by boat, she had taken the land route through Payerme. This was confirmed by an agent of the Confederacy who had seen a woman in a green coat with a little boy.

'I assumed that green was a favourite colour of yours, and that you had naturally purchased another one of the same colour,' explained Etienne, over the dining table which stood in a separate room from the smoky cooking kitchen.

'We found the green coat, all right,' said Jeannot Fleuret, 'but on another woman!'

Lambrois said, 'When she described the person she bought it from as having mutilated thumbs, we immediately knew it to be the pauper.'

'And we knew something didn't tally righ' 'n' all,' said Fleuret, 'seein' as he'd sent us on a wild goose chase.'

Etienne explained how they hurried back to the track that Monsieur Gaugin had told Jeanne to take. They soon picked up the trail of a Madame Delgarde de Castanet. Lambrois, who knew Jeanne had a nobiliary particle after her name, had a gut feeling that they were on her path, which was confirmed when they asked at a pair of riverboats on the Aar if they had seen a lady travelling with a boy. By good fortune, a woman was able to tell them that she had travelled from Yverdon with a lady and a lad who had since headed to somewhere that began with *Schaff*, and that they had taken the road to Zurzach.

Lambrois and Fleuret ventured across country in the light of the moon, neither of them wanting to rest until they had found Jeanne and Paul. They arrived at Neunkirch a couple of hours after sunup and were directed to the place where Jeanne had left a note of thanks.

'There are too many coincidences,' said Jeannot with a glimmer in his eye. 'It can only have been an act of Providence that brought us to your aid in time, can it not?'

'Pity the wicked imp got away with your bag, though,' said Ginette.

Jeanne gave a contented smile and said, 'It is of no consequence. We are safe and alive, and we are here now among friends, aren't we, Paul?'

'Brave lad, too, taking on a full-grown man,' said Etienne, clasping the boy's shoulder blade.

'Aye,' said Jeannot, 'there be a courageous young man inside that heart of yours, me boy, that's for sure.'

'I did as Pierre would have done,' said Paul, with both hope and sadness in his smile. 'I am sure he was with me.'

*

Jeanne accepted to stay for the imminent childbirth. Lacking her mother, Claire was glad to have Jeanne at her side. She was reassured too that the Fleurets had decided that they could do far worse than to settle in Schaffhausen, where Jeannot would not lack work pertaining to his true trade.

One warm Sunday afternoon, Jeannot was sitting in the shade on the bench outside the kitchen, watching the children—Paul and his daughters, Rose and Aurore—playing in the meadow in front of the house. Jeanne sat down beside him.

'It is beautiful,' she said.

'Isn't it? He would have loved it here,' said Jeannot, rubbing the side of his big, tanned face. 'I do miss him. Can't help it,' he said, turning to her, his eyes glistening, his brow furrowed. 'I keep wanting to tell him I love him, but he's not there.' Jeanne placed a hand on his forearm, and pressed her fingers on his Sunday shirt. He continued, 'Why this sufferance, Jeanne? For what? For whom?'

Why indeed, she knew not. She too was sometimes given to ask: Why had her faith driven her from her beloved homeland? Why had her children been taken from her? Why did Lulu and now Pierre have to die? Had they not given enough proof of their faith? But she tried not to dwell on it, tried to live in the present and have faith in the future. It was the only way to move forward without the ground subsiding beneath her feet.

At length, she said, 'I do not know, Jeannot. But what I

do know is that your Pierre and my Louise are with Jesus, that one day we shall be reunited in heaven.'

Jeannot placed his hand upon hers. 'Thank you,' he said. A solitary tear ran down the creases in his face. 'I needed to hear it. It is my one hope.'

*

Upon the general insistence, Jeanne agreed to winter in Schaffhausen at least until she received confirmation of Jacob's arrival in London, for she still had no certitude that he had gone there, that he had escaped even. She and Paul would thereafter take to the road again in better health.

The glorious days of summer soon gave way to the autumn chill. But the early snows in October were as fresh and beautiful as the summer meadows were warm and picturesque. Through the church, the group of immigrants integrated into Schaffhausen society—facilitated by the First Consul and Etienne's professional connections, as well as a general willingness to embrace their new home. 'I never thought Etienne would pick up the language so quickly,' said Claire one day while feeding her baby by the fireside.

Jeanne said, 'Just goes to show what a pleasant environment and good people can do to boost your willingness to fit in, doesn't it?'

'Bit of a struggle sometimes, though, ain't it,' said Ginette. 'I don't know if I'm ever going to make 'em laugh in German one day.'

In spite of the cold, Jeanne and Paul had also settled into the ways of a Swiss country town. They marvelled at the annual sleigh races, with horses magnificently harnessed and attired for the occasion, and Paul enjoyed activities in the snow with new friends. Jeanne helped with Claire's baby, who was named Jeanne Lambrois, and also at church despite the language barrier. In this way, with much relief, she looked forward to some kind of stability during the harsh, cold months in the company of people she loved.

But one clear and icy-blue day, she received the letter she had been praying for. The men were at work, Ginette was at her new dwelling, and Claire was lying down after the baby's feed. Jeanne sat alone to open it in the kitchen, where chestnuts were roasting in the hearth for the children who would soon be back from the schoolhouse. The tall case clock counted time as she set her eyes on the letter and read:

My Dearest Wife,

I have encountered as many difficulties as atrocities, but by God's grace, having escaped my gaolers, I do believe my fortune has turned. I will not elaborate on the course of events that have enabled me to write this letter, but I am free, my dear Jeanne. I can imagine the torment you yourself have had to endure, and I long for the day when we shall be united again. So I will ask you, my dear wife, to join me in London, where I will meet you. I am told there is a Huguenot church there. That is where you will find news of my whereabouts, and you can be sure I will run to meet you as soon as I am given word of your arrival.

My heart beats for the day that will bring us together.

Your husband who loves you dearly, Jacob

Jeanne kissed the paper that her husband's hand had brushed, and then pressed the letter to her heart. She gazed through the kitchen window at the winter wonderland of snow and ice that muffled the ambient noises and gave off a blue hue, now that evening was encroaching. Of course, she was elated; of course, she must leave at once. But apart from the local pathways which town valets had sprinkled with sand, they were snowed in.

LAND OF HOPE

Book Three of
THE HUGUENOT CHRONICLES
Trilogy

PAUL C.R. MONK

1

'AFTER A NUMBER of setbacks, at last I find myself travelling aboard a merchant ship a free man. My only regret, my dear wife, is that I asked you to join me in London, since I am still on the other side of the world.

'As I sail along the North American coast to New York, where I plan to secure my passage to London, I have heard it said many a time that there is great unrest in England.

'I pray that this unrest between the Catholic king and his subjects does not turn to civil war, should William of Orange, as I have heard it suggested, claim the throne of England for himself and his English wife. Should war there be, I pray to God that you, my dear wife, and our children will find refuge, and that it pleaseth God to soon bring us together in this world gone mad.'

In cadence with the gentle pitch of the ship, Jacob Delpech lifted his quill off the paper, which he had placed atop a barrel of odorous ginger loaves.

He knew very well that the letter in all probability would not reach Jeanne before he arrived in the English capital. Nevertheless, setting down on paper his gravest thoughts gave him a vent for his regretted demand. He let the plume tickle the stubble beneath his nose as his cold fingers took refuge inside the sleeve of his fur coat, purchased off Chesapeake Bay, Virginia, from a gentleman travelling south.

The captain's roar above deck interrupted Jacob's train of thought. 'Lay low the mainsails, lads! Keep her easy, keep her well east o' them Oyster Islands!'

The base of the mainmast gave a groan as the crew set his orders into action.

Picking up the thread of his thoughts, Delpech glanced at the young woman opposite him, asleep on the floor in the dim light, her young daughter curled into her body and a cape wrapped around them both. The English ship he had boarded in Nassau had put into port to water and to trade in Carolina, where the woman had pleaded for passage. She had promised the captain that her husband would pay on arrival, he having ventured ahead some months past.

Jacob had since overheard her saying to a neighbouring passenger that she could no longer bear the midges and mosquitoes in Charles Town, having already lost two of her children to fever.

The captain blasted out further orders, and the sleeping huddle began to stir. Clawing her shawl away from her face, the woman found herself locking eyes with the gentleman opposite, and instinctively trying to decipher the meaning of his furrowed brow. Was there a good soul behind that stern, unshaven façade? She had previously decided to believe that there was, so she allowed the corner of her mouth to twitch into a half smile.

Before Jacob realised he was staring at the object of his inner conversation, he caught the searching, anxious look that accompanied the woman's timid smile. He offered a nod in greeting as he put down his quill and then returned his writing material and letter to his leather pouch. Suppressing his worrying thoughts, he strode to the steps leading to the upper deck, before social convention required that words be exchanged between them. His mind was crowded enough without having to dwell on other people's struggles.

As a man of southern skies, Jacob could never fathom why people had to submit themselves to the rigours of the cold northern winter when there was plenty of room down south. However, there he was, and thankful indeed for his warm overcoat as he stiffly climbed the mid-deck steps and showed his face to the breaking, dingy December morning. Raising a hand to the cold sea spray, he turned his gaze towards the ship's wheel, where there stood a heavily dressed man watching the crew tying back sails.

'New York Bay, Captain?' called Jacob, making an extra effort to articulate through the bitter cold as he climbed the few steps to the quarterdeck.

'Ah, M'sieur Delpech,' belched the captain, hat pulled down tight and greatcoat buttoned to the chin. Flicking his head to starboard, he continued with gruff geniality: 'Aye, Sir, that be Long Island. Gives protection to the harbour, see? And over there, that's Staten.'

Jacob's eyes now followed the captain's nod port side, where, through the thinning swags of mist, he perceived clusters of modest dwellings scattered along the coast, some already smoking from their chimneys.

After a moment's scrutiny, Jacob declared: 'No city walls there, Captain Stevens, far as I can see.' It was a statement carried forward from a previous conversation which had raised the issue of safety in these northern settlements. They had not only suffered Native Indian raids but, more importantly to Jacob, attacks by French forces from New France, whose leaders were keen to secure fur trade routes. Jacob wondered if he should have waited for passage aboard a ship headed directly to London from the Antilles, rather than jump at his first opportunity to head back to Europe via New York. But he had been impatient to remove himself from the treacherous pirate haven of Nassau, where Captain de Graaf had dropped him off.

''Tis also an island, Sir,' said a loud voice coming from Jacob's right.

Delpech turned from the seascape view to face the large person of Mr van Pel, a Dutchman who had long since settled in the flourishing trading post. He had climbed the mid-deck steps and now joined Jacob at the quarterdeck balustrade. He said: 'Folk of your persuasion have settled and built their homes there in the way of your homeland, you know.'

Where Jacob was from, houses were not made of stone. They were made of peach-pink brick, but he said nothing, just let the fleeting picture of the fertile plain where he was born flash past his mind's eye. He said: 'So they are French Protestants?'

'That they are,' replied the Dutchman, 'and Quakers too. No doubt you'll be able to find a plot there for yourself . . .'

'And a wife to boot, if that be your inclination,' added the captain, having sauntered over to join them.

'Oh, I already have a wife, Captain,' returned Jacob soberly, 'and my intention is not to stay here. For she and my children await my return in . . .' It suddenly occurred to him that he could not say with certainty where they were— London, Geneva, France? 'In Europe,' he finished.

The Dutch-built merchantman sailed at half sail on an even keel through the placid waters of the natural harbour. Within the hour, she was rounding the small isle that van Pel called Nutten—in reference, according to the Dutchman, to the thriving population of nut trees growing there. At last Jacob began to see through the patchy mist, thicker at this point, to the battery at the tip of the Manhattan trading post.

'New Amsterdam,' said the Dutchman in an ironic tone.

'New York, Sir!' blasted the English captain, placing a heavy, consoling hand on the Dutchman's shoulder before swaggering back up to his command station.

'I wouldn't be surprised if it gets another name change before long, though,' said van Pel to Jacob. Then, as if to plumb the depths of his counterpart's thoughts, he added: 'Or will it go back to being as it was?'

'Haven't the foggiest, my good fellow,' said Jacob, not without some pride in his mastery of the English language, acquired from his travels in the midst of the damnedest devils of the deep blue sea. But he preferred not to enter into a political debate. He did not need to let anyone know his deepest thoughts. Either side of the fence could lead to danger in these times of upheaval, he thought, what with the conflict with New France.

The ship entered smoother waters while Jacob leaned on the balustrade, trying to peer through the dissipating mist at the configuration of New York.

It was composed of a mismatch of Dutch-style buildings made of stone and brick, the windmill that presently stood as still as a sentinel on the west side of the promontory, and an assortment of vessels moored along the eastern side. Jacob thought it more reminiscent of the port of Amsterdam than anything English.

The merchant ship continued her course slowly into the roadstead to the east of the promontory. Leaning with forearms on the bulwark and loosely clasping his hands, Jacob was soon able to more closely make out the influence of visiting cultures and the resulting mix of architectural styles inserted between the crenelated Dutch-built edifices. It was an odd blend, he thought, as odd as the English brick houses built among the white-washed Spanish haciendas and one-storey houses of Port Royale in Jamaica. But this was the New World, after all, a new world he was growing accustomed to. It was a land of many nations where people were thrown together in the mutual hopes of a fresh start and a fair chance of success. He only hoped the sins of the Old World had not washed up on the shores of New York as they had done on the spit of land occupied by Port Royale.

Mr van Pel pointed out City Hall, where the battery was peopled with stevedores hoisting a winch, market sellers carting their produce, oystermen pushing carts, and small clusters of merchants who Jacob imagined were talking business. But if he could hear their muffled voices through the morning mist, he would find that the dwindling fur and tobacco trade due to border troubles was not the only talk of the New England township. The eighty-tonner lying at the wharf, just in from England, had not only brought linens, woollens, tools, and wine. It had also brought unofficial news of a probable invasion of England by the Prince of Orange and his Dutch army. Would the navigation rights now be reviewed to better suit the colonists' activities? Would New York regain its former status as a province? Would the Catholic king leave England in peace?

But even if he could hear the gossip, it would not have

clouded his mind much. His one thought now was to get back to his family; the world could go mad without him. He would take some rest on firm ground, before setting out on another gruelling voyage across the ocean on as solid an ocean-going vessel as he could find. And judging by the size of the English ship at the slip, he was relieved that he had found one that would do the trick.

As he scoured the harbour, it struck him that the colony settlement, though well established, was not exactly as large as Bordeaux or even Marseille. It would surely not be too much of a task, he thought, to locate Daniel Darlington, the Englishman in whose hands he had left Marianne and her grandmother.

He was keen to pay a social visit to the young lady he had watched and cared for during their detention and their escape from Hispaniola. It would tie a loose end in his mind and set him at ease to know that she had found comfort and satisfaction, that neither she nor young Darlington had been accused of involvement in the tragic accident that had caused the death of a drunken soldier, and had forced Delpech to part ways or face trial and execution.

A blast from the captain, followed by the thunderous clanking of running chains, brought the vessel to a timber-creaking halt. The ship came to anchor at a gunshot from Coenties Slip, situated at the mouth of East River. It was, according to van Pel, less prone there to oyster reefs than the Hudson River that flowed along the west side, all the way up to Albany.

The West Indies merchantman—with its delivery of molasses, rum, and ginger—would have to lay in wait for a loading bay to become vacant. But the captain allowed all the passengers to be rowed ashore. All, that is, except for two.

As the travellers excitedly brushed down clothes, straightened hair, and gathered their effects in the dim light of mid-deck, the captain motioned to a lady fastening her daughter's bonnet.

'Madame Blancfort,' he said, standing on the hatch steps. 'With all due respect, I'll have to ask you to remain aboard till yer husband comes to pay ya fare.'

Jacob, now standing at the ginger barrel where he had recovered his meagre effects, could not ignore the ball of indignation that surged in his chest. 'But Captain Stevens, Sir,' he protested, placing his leather pouch back down on the barrel of ginger. 'That is wholly unfair. She can hardly run away from the island. Indeed, I will vouch for her and her child.'

'Then I must ask you to do so with coin, Monsieur Delpech,' said the captain affably enough, though standing erect and formal to match the Huguenot's posture.

'It is all right, M'sieur,' said the lady in French. 'I will wait here. We have waited to come to New York for so long, another hour or so will do us no harm.'

'As you wish, Madame,' said Jacob, secretly relieved to opt out of the potentially embarrassing situation, for he did not have the means to spend his money needlessly. He really ought to learn to put the reins on his acute sense of injustice.

'But please, Sir,' continued the woman, 'if you would be so kind as to enquire after my husband. His name is Jeremy Blancfort. Please tell him his wife and daughter are here. He will come immediately, so please do not fret, Sir. What's an hour more compared to a month-long voyage?'

Delpech and the French-speaking wives of the other

families aboard assured her they would do as she asked and arranged to meet again in church. Then they proceeded to the upper deck, where they could climb into the boat which would take them to their new lives.

It occurred to Jacob that he would not have left his wife without monies to pay her fare, even if it were to scout for an adequate settlement. Was the husband not conscious of the dangers that could befall a lone woman? At least, he would not have left her entirely without means; for he had seen what became of penniless women in Port Royale. But then, was his situation so very different? Could Jeanne have suffered similarly in Amsterdam, in the hope that her husband would be able to pay her fare on arrival in London?

*

Half an hour later, Jacob Delpech was standing on the timber boardwalk of the cold and foggy wharf with his fellow travellers. These consisted of Irish, Dutch, German, and Huguenot individuals and families who had boarded the ship as it sailed from port to port up the North American coast. Some had relatives in New York. Others spoke of Staten Island, where they planned to purchase land now that their indenture was ended. Jacob glanced around at these hopeful colonists, all looking slightly bewildered. But it was a welcome change from the privateers, pirates, soldiers, and profiteers he had become accustomed to.

The sight of small parties of would-be settlers had long since become an integral part of the New York portscape, and welcoming them had been set up as a procedure. The patrolling town constable who came to greet them invited them to make their presence known in an official capacity, something they would need to do should they wish to apply for denizenship.

'City Hall is over there, Ladies and Gentlemen,' he said in a Dutch accent, pointing across the battery to a fine five-storey brick building. He then waved to a cartman to come and carry their effects while Jacob bade farewell to Mr van Pel.

'Godspeed, and good luck in your endeavours, Sir,' said the Dutchman. Then he sauntered, with stick in hand and sack slung over shoulder, along the wharf and into the busy market street with other returning passengers.

After being at sea for so long, climbing the sturdy stone steps of City Hall without having to counter any pitch or sway brought a secret feeling of security and permanence to more than a few. The petty constable, the cartman, the registration process, and the solidity of the building all enhanced the impression that this township, be it but a speck in the vastness of the American continent, constituted a sure foothold, made to last. However, they pushed the doors into a spacious lobby where furrowed brows and concerned undertones contrasted radically with any feeling of optimism.

They were met by a tall gentleman, in simple but elegant blue attire and a white frilled necktie, who spoke words of welcome in English.

'Sir,' said Jacob, making a slight bow, 'I am sure I will be forgiven if I speak on behalf of my fellow travellers in thanking you for your warm welcome. However, before we begin the process of registering our presence, I have been asked to enquire after a certain Monsieur Blancfort, Jeremy Blancfort.'

The gentleman looked squarely at the somewhat ragged

though evidently high-born Huguenot. 'I see,' he said in a subdued tone, as if to prepare the way for some bad news. 'A friend of yours, Sir?'

'No, Sir, I am but a messenger for his wife.'

'Ah, yes,' said the clerk, adjusting his horn-rimmed nose glasses. 'His wife in Carolina, if I am not mistaken. We wrote to her only last week.'

'She *was* in Carolina,' said Jacob. 'She is at present with her daughter on board the merchant ship that brought them here from Charles Town. She is waiting for her husband to liberate her of her debt to the captain, who requires full payment of her fare.'

'Oh,' said the clerk, raising a hand and pinching his chin, 'I am sorry to say, and equally sorry to inform you, that he has met with his maker.'

In truth, having seen so many deaths of late, Jacob was more irked than moved, for who would take responsibility for the poor woman without means now?

In a grave tone befitting the sad news, Jacob said: 'Did he leave any instructions?'

But before the clerk could answer, a red-haired woman stepped forward from the pack and said bluntly: 'Did he leave any money?'

Delpech did not have to turn to his side to recognise the voice of the Irishwoman who had been Mrs Blancfort's neighbour throughout the sea journey. Jacob was almost embarrassed at his own superfluous question, but relieved that someone else had joined the conversation.

'I regret he did not,' said the clerk. 'The money he had was used towards his burial.'

'If you don't mind me saying,' said the forthright

Irishwoman, 'surely to God it would have been put to better use sending it to his family! No use to a dead man, is it now? If you'll beg me pardon.'

The clerk paused a moment for thought, looked towards the wide staircase that resonated with the mutterings of voices and footsteps tripping down the steps. Then, looking back at the woman, he said: 'Well, er, what can I say? I can only hope she finds a new husband, Madam.'

'But she has a child,' said the woman.

'That is not an obstacle in these parts, you'll find,' said the clerk encouragingly. 'We lack children for the future of our colony. She will find a husband soon enough, and all the more so as she has living proof that she is not barren. Provided, of course, that she is not past mothering age . . .'

'No,' said the woman, 'she's certainly got a few more baby-making years in her yet.'

'There we are then,' said the registry agent with a note of triumph, as if he had solved the widow's problems.

The rest of the little group also seemed to be won over by Mrs Blancfort's hypothetical prospects, and let out interjections of relief. It became evident to Jacob that he was not the only one who had neither means nor time for another burden. Nevertheless, looking at the Irish lady, then at the clerk, he said: 'But someone is going to have to break the news to her. And what about her present predicament?'

'I suggest we deal with the matter once we have entered your names into the register,' said the clerk with a winning smile, while moving into step. 'Ladies and Gentlemen, now if you would care to come this way—it won't take long.'

Meanwhile, the approaching footsteps and male voices now resonated more loudly as a cluster of half a dozen men descended into the lobby.

'As I said, Sir,' continued Jacob, walking beside the clerk past the stairway, 'personally, I am only in transit. My plan is to travel to—'

But before Jacob could finish his sentence, a young man broke from the cluster of gentlemen dressed in long, sober cloaks and Brandenburgs. He stopped in front of Jacob and said cheerily: 'Why, it is! Monsieur Delpech, Sir, how good to see you again! I was not expecting you until next week.'

*

'I would personally welcome William as king,' said Daniel Darlington, who had been telling Jacob how he had been summoned that morning to City Hall to discuss the news just in of the possible takeover of England by the Dutch prince.

The two men were walking westward along Pearl Street, and now they crossed Fish Bridge that straddled the narrow canalised river where fishermen brought in their catch. Despite the foul stench of low tide, Jacob felt enlivened by the smell of land air, and by being in the thick of people going about their daily business. Turning to Darlington, he said: 'I only hope it does not end in war.'

'For the moment, I gather this is yet to be confirmed. And God only knows what has been happening across the ocean. But what really gets my goat is when England sneezes, we catch the flu . . . three months later! And I will add, Monsieur Delpech, that I find it revolting and insulting to be tutored by men who know not an Iroquois from an Abenaki Indian.'

The subject impassioned the young New Yorker, born and bred. But Jacob's polite smile made him see that he was preaching to the choir, and that he was probably guilty of being pedantic to a man who had just walked off a ship from Nassau. 'But here you are, dear Monsieur Delpech,' he said. 'Your presence brings a welcome change. Marianne has been so looking forward to seeing you,' he said as they continued along a narrow street flanked on either side by neatly arranged dwellings of brick, stone, and timber. A fascinating blend of cultures, mused Jacob, though surprised he was to encounter free-roaming poultry and pigs along the way.

However, in truth his thoughts were elsewhere, neither on the high spheres of European leadership nor on the gutter where the pigs foraged. His thoughts were with the woman and child on the ship. How easy it was to fall into debt and ruin, well did he know. But he did his best to tuck the thought away for the time being. 'And I shall be glad to see her!' he said.

'I dare say you will find her somewhat changed, though,' pursued Darlington with a secret smile. Jacob turned away as the young man coloured slightly, the very thought of publicising his intimacy in the street striking him. He touched his ear and let out a puff of vapour with a little cough. 'This is Broadway,' he then said as they turned into a wide thoroughfare. It led past the governor's residence and continued straight past high houses and walled ornamental gardens that had already suffered from the frost. 'Our house is not far from Wall Street,' said Daniel, pointing towards the wall that gave the street its name, 'precisely on the other side of the palisade outside the city gates. Too many rules and regulations to build a house of decent size within.'

They followed the broad thoroughfare through the city gate into a vast countryside that opened with a row of well-kept gardened houses to their right, and a pretty burial ground to their left. The rutted earth road, growing busy with country carters returning from market, rolled on through green pastures to the edge of a distant forest which, according to Darlington, populated the length and breadth of Manhattan. Jacob halted his stride to admire the distant haze of reds, greens, and golds. Sunbeams now shone between purple-bellied clouds onto nearby furrowed fields of dark brown that sloped gently up to a windmill, stationed on higher ground.

From the stillness of a solitary leafless elm tree came the *caaw-caaw* of a crow. A slight variation, thought Jacob, to the call of the ones that used to nest in the lime trees outside his country house in France. But still, the smell of the earth, of mushrooms, of the reinvigorating winter chill, all filled him with the same inner peace he used to experience in Verlhac. It was the smell of the northern hemisphere. It was the smell of home.

'Pleasant, isn't it?' said Darlington, tipping his hat to a carter and his wife as they passed.

'Indeed, Sir, indeed it is,' said Jacob amid the sudden chatter of jays from a cluster of trees in the graveyard. After another beat, Jacob said: 'Do you know how he died? Blancfort, I mean.'

'I do. I believe he contracted an illness,' said Darlington, moving back into step and inviting Jacob to do likewise. 'He was found one day dead in his bed. It was quite the talk of the town. Folk were fearful to know what illness it was that took him away. But it seems to have been a solitary strain.'

Solitary indeed, thought Jacob as they took a right onto a narrow hard-earth track. How cruel the accidents of life could be. 'But his wife and daughter are aboard the ship.'

'I expect the ladies will tell her. Better it be a lady, and I expect the town intendant will see to them. There is nothing you can do to bring the man back. He was buried two weeks ago. Anyway, here we are.'

Before them stood a large stone house, a charming two-storey building with a ground-floor section that jutted out on the right side as the visitor went in. Darlington pushed a wooden gate into the grassy court, where a goat was attached to a piquet to keep the grass trim. Cupping his hand to his mouth, he called out in a sing-song voice. 'Marianne! Madame de Fontenay! We have an important visitor! Marianne . . .'

A face soon appeared at the glazed window that looked out onto the elevated porch. Seconds later, the porch door was pulled open, and Marianne stood on the threshold bearing the bump of pregnancy, her searching eyes showing concern. She was closely followed by her grandmother, who stood as dignified as when Jacob had left her at Cow Island.

*

Marianne sensed Jacob had undergone traumatic experiences in the short time that had separated them.

Even before she had greeted him with open arms and set him down at the dining-room table, she had noted how gaunt he had become, and that the melancholy in his eyes had grown deeper. And she longed to reach out to him, to return the help he had given her in her times of need. Had he not protected her honour when she had been disarmed? Saved her life from a drunken soldier and put himself at risk of execution? How could she draw him out of his affable carapace?

492

'Before receiving your message, I expected you to be in Europe by now, my uncle,' she said, placing a cup before him and filling it with hot coffee to go with the fresh bread, goat's butter, and jam to restore him until dinnertime. They kept mostly to English for the benefit of Daniel.

Jacob appreciated her keeping up the uncle-niece act that they had played during their forced exile from France. He knew it stemmed from a genuine affection, but he recognised too her gift for unlocking unsayable secrets from the confines of one's memory.

He had caught her concern at his current physical condition in the pleat of her brow, before her smile broadened in an effort to hide it. It was the same pleat of concern he had seen when, while in confinement in Marseille the previous year, she told him he had only suffered a scratch to his eye when he had collapsed on being told of his daughter's tragic death. But the gash to his eye was deep, and she, with her grandmother, had helped it heal. And she had shined her gentle light when he dreamt of nothing but blackness.

But he was not going to recount to a young mother-to-be, over twenty years his junior, how he had been shipwrecked, taken ill, robbed, and sold to a privateer, and had sided with pirates to capture and ransom a Cuban township.

Turning his gaze from the glowing embers of the wide hearth, he smiled cheerily and said: 'I have had a tumultuous journey to get this far, but do not fret on my account, my dear niece. I am a little fatigued, but well, and I am here in one piece, and very glad to see you looking so well!'

But Marianne, obstinate as ever, said: 'Tumultuous journey, my uncle?'

He would have to concede some ground, so he said: 'Well,

in short, I became indentured as a ship's surgeon-barber to a privateer captain, although the term buccaneer would be more appropriate.' He let out a false laugh.

'My goodness!' exclaimed Marianne in an attempt to coax more out of him. But Jacob was not ready to say more.

After a pause for another sip of coffee, Daniel Darlington said: 'What was his name, Sir?'

'Brook, Captain Brook, and I wish never to hear it again.'

'I have heard the name before. I remember de Graaf mentioning it a few times. I have also heard since that he came to a bitter end . . .'

Jacob said nothing of de Graaf, the Dutch-French privateer turned major, who had in fact led the Cuban campaign, but who nevertheless had delivered him from servitude and helped him secure a passage northward from Nassau. But there was one man Jacob did want to know more about. He said: 'Do you know what became of his crew?'

'I do not.'

It was Ducamp who Delpech now wondered about, the faithless, battle-hardened lieutenant who he had left with the hope of redemption. But he feared yet another hope dashed, another fissure in his already weakened faith—not his faith in God, but in humanity. So he said nothing more on it.

Glancing sidelong at her husband, Marianne pressed Jacob's hand and said: 'You must stay here as long as it takes for you to get stronger, my uncle.'

Jacob was not aware that he needed to get stronger. Did he look so worn? He thought not. He just needed to be removed from his immediate past memories and to draw nearer to recovering his family. Was that so difficult to understand?

'There is no need to put yourselves out on my behalf. I shall stay at the tavern we passed in town and be off by the turn of the tide tomorrow, God willing, if not by the end of the week.'

'Ah,' said Darlington, 'the season here has been exceptionally clement so far, but I fear it is about to turn nasty for sea travel. You would do better to hole up until February, Sir. Moreover, I would be surprised if any ship sets out across the ocean before winter's end, Monsieur Delpech. So, please accept our hospitality, not because I owe you the lives of my wife and future child, but because I offer you my friendship, Sir.'

Seeing Jacob still on the fence, Marianne insisted winningly: 'I will not sleep knowing that my only living uncle is alone at a stranger's tavern!'

But it was the old lady, knitting in her chair near the fireplace with a cat on her lap, who at last won him over. Having spent her married life with a French officer, she well knew the look of a man who had been to war. And once all the battle fanfare was over and he was home with his family, she knew of the need to divert thoughts by day and ease nightmares by night, and of the impression of the futility of life, and of disillusionment with God.

'You will stay here, Monsieur Delpech, and nothing more will be said of your piratical adventures!' she said, flitting her eyes at Marianne and Daniel.

Marianne, who had absolute faith in her grandmother's wisdom and was not slow on the uptake, followed up by saying: 'Instead, I will tell you of our plans to build a new house further along the east coast with some French settlers from La Rochelle. Daniel agrees, don't you, darling?'

'The land is good there,' said Darlington, taking up his pipe, 'and if it allows my wife and her grandmother to feel more at home, then that is where we shall live. For I made a promise to a gentleman and a friend, that I would look after them, do you remember, Monsieur Delpech?'

Jacob gave a nod and a smile of approbation. 'I do, Monsieur Darlington, I do.' Marianne, standing between them with a hand on her waist, looked affably cross while her grandmother looked up with a sardonic grin. But before they could say anything, Jacob continued: 'And I believe my dear niece and her grandmother made a promise to look after a certain gifted but impetuous loose cannon in danger of losing his life at sea.'

After a moment's silence for the penny to drop, Daniel burst out into laughter. 'Oh, and they do, and they do,' he said in good fellowship. Then he slung his arm around his wife's waist and brought her to gently perch on his knee. Marianne patted him playfully on the head and topped off his coffee while her grandmother, after an eyebrow raised to Jacob in complicity, continued with her knitting.

'And by the way, I could do with some advice on land management, tobacco to be precise,' continued Darlington as Marianne took away his pipe. 'My guess is there'll be a large market for it, now that His Royal Highness has deprived us of the Delaware country against our wishes.'

He was referring to King James II's order which joined the province of New York to the Dominion of New England. It did not sit well with New Yorkers because it meant depriving them of their constitutional and property rights.

But Jacob was only half listening. His plan was still to leave for Europe at the first opportunity, and never mind the weather. Besides that, with all this talk of promises, a pang of guilt reminded him of one he had made recently. 'I would be glad to be of assistance if I can,' he said. 'But speaking of promises, the lady on the ship . . .' Jacob then explained about the poor woman's predicament to the female company. 'I do hope she has found accommodation,' he concluded.

'She will be cared for, I dare say,' said Marianne.

'You cannot lay down your cloak for every damsel in distress, Monsieur Delpech,' said Darlington.

'No, but I would not want my own wife and child to suffer such humiliation. Would you?'

'Well said!' exclaimed Madame de Fontenay in a confidential voice.

The New Yorker gave a slow, penitent nod of the head. His grey eyes then locked on Jacob's. 'Then I shall enquire after her,' he said with new conviction.

*

Jacob almost regretted watching Darlington—dressed in leathers, beaver hat firmly pulled over his head—mount his steed and canter off amid eddying leaves into the afternoon turned colder and blustery.

'He has to go back to town anyway,' said Marianne a few moments later, turning from the window, 'to meet some French acquaintances whom he promised to introduce to a friend who can assist them with the purchase of land. The land we told you about.'

'Oh, he's always hopping on his horse,' said Madame de Fontenay. 'It is one of the disadvantages of living outside the city walls.' Marianne shook her head in feigned exasperation.

Though far from what Marianne and her grandmother

had been used to in her mother country, Jacob could see that the young woman had certainly settled into home life and had made a cosy abode. French dressers, silverware and glasses in a rack, quality furniture, and rugs on the waxed parquet gave the place a positively French appeal that allowed Jacob to feel quite at home.

He sat in an armchair by the fireplace, cracking walnuts. Madame de Fontenay was still seated opposite and still wrestling with another dropped stitch. 'Over the strand and off the needle,' she muttered. It was something she had decided to take up in order to while away the winter evenings, especially now since she had a little someone to knit for. She told Jacob of their voyage from Cow Island, where Delpech had been obliged to leave them with Darlington. 'The last sea voyage I shall endure in this world—knitwise and slide across—and the next, God willing,' she said between stitches, with a mirthful glow in her eyes.

Marianne, meanwhile, anxious to show her command of home management, proposed to Jacob to set her maid to heating water for the tub, there being no public baths in New York. Jacob, despite the risk of bathing in winter, accepted her offer, remembering the polite turn of her head when they had embraced on the porch, and recalling his wife's heightened sense of smell during her pregnancies. Indeed, he admitted he must stink to high heaven, he said once the black servant girl had positioned the brass tub before the hearth.

'Don't worry, Martha is not a slave, Jacob,' said Marianne, reading his thoughts. 'She gets a wage, food, and a room next to Grandmother's.'

'As you can see, we have moved up in the world!' added Madame de Fontenay with a drop of irony.

'I would not, for a minute, imagine that you could become a supporter of slavery,' said Jacob, flinging a handful of walnut shells into the fire. 'But what about the plantation your husband spoke of?'

'Oh, I will talk him out of it should the notion blossom in his mind, and he will listen to me, have no fear.'

'And he certainly does that, all right,' seconded Madame de Fontenay. 'Why, he will do anything for her, just like my husband used to . . . in the early days. But slaves or no slaves, my dears, what is worrying is being so close to New France. It is bad enough living in the sticks with the wolves!'

'We are not living amid the wolves, Grandmother, rather the squirrels.'

'And the rats! And what if the French invade and capture Manhattan? What will happen to us?'

'That is why those from La Rochelle have chosen the east side, Grandmother. You need not worry, Daniel already told you. And we shall have a splendid house, more land, and people with whom you can speak in French.'

'Oh, I am past worrying about myself, my dear. The French and the Indians wouldn't roast an old timer like me, far too nervy,' said the old woman, as plucky as ever. 'And I am not worried about a splendid house either. I'm quite all right with Martha next door; at least she doesn't keep telling me how to knit properly! I was thinking about you two and the baby.'

'Daniel says there will be a boat moored in the bay in case we need to escape to New York, or to Brooklyn. Besides, if the French attack, which they won't, it would be from the west. They would come down the Hudson River from Albany.'

The old lady gave no answer. Instead, she placed a finger on her lips and nodded towards the opposite armchair.

Perhaps it was the coffee and nuts, or the warmth of the fire, or maybe something else, but Jacob at last had given in to an irrepressible urge to close his eyes. He had fallen into a snorting slumber, stirred only by the intermittent pouring of hot water from a ewer.

*

Half an hour later, he was transported back to his country estate in France, fields golden with wheat and orchards laden with fat fruit. He was standing in the reservoir he had devised for irrigation purposes, where his children and his farmhands sometimes bathed after a long summer day's picking.

He suddenly found himself standing underwater with a crowd of babbling people, fully dressed and having fun, bounding from the shallow lake bed to the surface. He looked around and saw his son Paul kicking away from the stony bottom with a gleeful smile. But as the boy reached the end of his thrust, the water's surface seemed to inch agonisingly further away.

'I need to breathe now,' Jacob heard the boy say calmly after landing back down on the lake bed, eyes beginning to bulge. Jacob seized him by the waist, thrust him upward, but again the boy only broke the surface with his outstretched hands. Jacob propelled the boy upward again with all his might. Again, only the boy's hands reached out of the water.

But suddenly, as the lad began to sink back down, an anonymous hand plunged into the water, clasped the boy's arm, and pulled him out of the lake.

The next instant, Jacob was standing on the grassy shore.

Paul was standing, eyes reddened, lips violet with cold, but alive. There came a sudden loud pop, and Jacob, fearing musket fire, threw his arms around his son protectively as a company of dead Spanish cadets came walking, weapons in hands, from out of the black waters of the lake.

'No!' cried Jacob. 'No! Go away!'

Jacob awoke to an insistent knocking at the lounge door.

'Are you all right, Monsieur Delpech?' called the voice of the old lady.

The fire crackled in the grate as he sat up in the bathtub in a cold sweat, burdened by thoughts of his wife stranded in London, burdened by the thought of the woman on the ship drowned in grief and debt.

'All is well, just fell asleep in the tub, ha,' he called out, surprised at the thickness of his voice.

*

The following morning, Jacob ached all over and could barely stand, let alone walk. The bone-chilling cold and muffled silence, the bleak light seeping through the window, and the echoey caw of the crow gave an atmosphere of stillness.

Half-frozen and trembling, he managed to slip his arms into his overcoat and stagger from the bedpost to the dresser near the second-floor window. His gaze fell upon a spectacular surprise. A glistening blanket of pure white snow lay over land, rooftops, and trees. He placed an eye to the cold brass telescope mounted on a tripod near the window box and pointed it towards the East River estuary. 'Good God,' he croaked to himself as a cold droplet dripped from his nose. 'The river has frozen over!'

2

'MY DEAR SISTER,

I pray this letter finds you in good health, and that you and my dear nephew have found satisfactory refuge with the good people of Schaffhausen. Your letter gave me much hope for your husband, but both Robert and I are of the opinion that it would be better to rest until the spring, before you travel to London to be reunited with him. Please write back saying you will, my sister. It will reassure me to know you are with friends in wintertime rather than on the roads.

'Elizabeth is becoming a fine young lady and misses you dearly. You must know that she would not follow your guide because, she recently confided, she could not leave her little sister in her grave, even less her baby sister Isabelle. She has indeed become a proper little mother and would make you proud.

'I know it must pain you to be so far from them, but, though Robert has pulled through his illness, I will not pretend that he will ever be strong enough to leave the country. However, a day will come, he is sure, when Lizzy and Isabelle will be able to join you.

'Meanwhile, he has been desperately trying to gather signatures of trustworthy men so that he may send you a bill of exchange. Although, as you can imagine, given the present climate, almost everyone he has approached would rather wait before committing their names and reputation in case they are discovered financing a Huguenot. It is preposterous, I do concede, but Robert is adamant he will get funds to you eventually. It is merely a question of time.

'I have enclosed a sketch of the girls as they are now. They were drawn last Wednesday 14th December. What merriment we had, and such a job it was to have Isabelle sit still long enough. But she did so when we told her she would be sitting for her mother, the lady in the painting.'

The sound of children's laughter brought Jeanne's eyes from Suzanne's letter.

She gazed out of her bedroom window at the undulating ice-crusted layers of snow that surrounded the house of her hosts. It sat outside the city walls, a daring decision for sure, but it meant paying fewer taxes and being near the sawmill. And besides, young Etienne Lambrois feared neither villain nor beast.

She watched Paul and a host of rambunctious children guffawing, running and sliding behind horse-drawn sleighs that were being conducted to the frozen lake at the end of the snow-covered track. A steady stream of villagers in boots and furs were cheerily walking or skiing down to join the crowd that had already gathered there. Today was a particularly special day, the last day of the sleigh races. Two of the

Huguenots would be racing in the final, and the honour of the seasoned Schaffhausen sleigh drivers was at stake!

Etienne and Jean Fleuret had repaired and made new a number of sleighs, two of which they had purchased for their own winter activities. They were at present driving them down to the lake around which the races had been taking place since yesterday.

Jeanne returned a wave to Paul, who was climbing aboard Jean Fleuret's sleigh, before glancing round at the wall above her pinewood dresser where the sketch of her daughters was pinned. She then reread the lines in her sister's letter that mentioned why Lizzy had refused to join her, and that she missed her mother, which gave Jeanne some consolatory reassurance. But of course, Suzanne could not say the same for her baby daughter, snatched from Jeanne's bosom when she was barely weaned. Isabelle, who would be a walking, talking child by now, would have no recollection of her mother to miss. Jeanne would be *the lady in the painting* at the top of the stairs, that was all. After mulling it over time after time, it now made sense to Jeanne that it could only be God's will for Lizzy to remain in her hometown, where she could watch over her baby sister and at least transmit some of the motherly love Jeanne had given her.

'Jeanne?' called an excited female voice. 'Jeanne? Are you coming?'

'Yes, yes, Claire. Be down in a moment,' returned Jeanne, getting to her feet and reaching for the winter cloak and muff laid out on her bed—her green coat of old no longer sufficing for the rigours of the Swiss winter. They had been given to her by a widowed burgher who had heard of her plight and brutal fall from wealth. But Jeanne had insisted on paying with earnings from her work. She made cloth for a master weaver anxious to learn the techniques taught to her by the French weaver in whose workshop she had been given refuge, before her flight from France.

Without friends, she thought to herself, where would she be now? How would she have survived the harsh northern winter? With a last glimpse through the window at the leaden sky, Jeanne pinned on her flat beaver hat and exited the room, thinking to herself that it would not be easy to give up a roof and her friends when the time came to leave.

*

Down at the lakeside, Jeanne, Claire, and Ginette joined the village folk standing in little clusters—now cheering as the sleighs sped by, now dipping their heads into their shoulders like the subdued crows perched in the tall, bare trees of the nearby copse.

The afternoon rolled on in high spirits, along with hot mulled wine and pleasant chatter, into the final race. Already chimneys on distant farmsteads were letting out wispy ghosts into the purpling sky.

'Beautiful, invigorating, and nose-nippingly cold, Monsieur,' said Jeanne to a burgher who had asked in French how she found their life in the north. Never once had she imagined she would one day experience such a spectacle, born as she was in a warmer clime. Only once had she ever experienced foot-deep snow in her native Quercy. She well remembered how quickly it became the curse of ladies' hems sullied in the ensuing slush.

Yet here in Schaffhausen, where for months on end it fell in places as deep as a maid was tall, folk took it in their stride, fitted as they were with fur-lined clogs to keep toes warm, and *raquettes* tied to shoes to keep them from sinking into the powdery snow. They carted goods on sledges and travelled on rough snow carts that gave a smoother ride than many a luxurious carriage, thought Jeanne, having ridden down to the edge of the frozen lake on one. The racing sleighs, however, were veritable works of art, feasts of the imagination with elaborately carved wooden figureheads of fantastic animals, griffins, naked savages, and wild beasts.

'Come on, Etienne!' cheered Claire as the magnificent pageant of horses and sleighs now approached the bend where the three ladies were standing near the bonfire. Jeanne and Ginette joined in with cheers of encouragement as the sleigh bells grew louder, along with the rumble of hooves and the thunderous swish of the runners. Etienne whooshed by, still holding second place, with dogs yapping at his horses' hooves.

'Go, Jeannot, come on, Paul!' called Ginette as Jean Fleuret's sleigh thundered by, cutting the ice in fifth place. Paul, sitting by his side, threw a wave to his mother as the vehicle flew by at a frightening speed.

The man and the boy had bonded following the loss of Jean's son Pierre, who had been Paul's best friend during their time in Geneva. It was not something Jeanne had wanted to encourage, for she knew how difficult it would be for them both when the time came to depart.

The ladies continued their chatter near the glowing embers of the log fire. Claire's baby, who had been left at the house with the maid, was teething. Ginette was coping with the death of her boy and was glad to be pregnant again. Jeanne spoke of her plans now that she had received a letter from Jacob, telling her where to join him.

'But what if your husband was dead? Where would you go once you got there?' said Ginette Fleuret, round and rosy-cheeked, cradling her large bust with her muff.

'Ginette!' said Claire in feigned reproach, her pretty chin raised, hands held together inside her fur muff. 'I dare say Jeanne has not thought of that eventuality.'

The contrast between the two ladies was almost comical, but Jeanne loved them both equally. If Claire were made of porcelain, refined and fragile, Ginette would be made of potter's clay, robust, rough, and solidly fashioned.

'Well, I think she ought to,' said the seamstress from Marseille, placing her chubby hand on her waist like a handle. 'I mean, if he has gone and popped his clogs, God forbid, where would she go once she got there?'

The question often reverberated through Jeanne's mind like the ever-present sound of carrion birds in the bleakness of winter. What if Jacob had died en route? What if all her prayers had been for nothing? But surely that would be too cruel. Yet, had she not prayed for the safety of her dear three-year-old daughter with the same fervour? Had she not prayed hard for weeks on end, and then seen herself running after Lulu in her dreams, seen her child wriggling from her belly-kisses, and then lying asleep in her arms as per her habit the minute they had begun a carriage journey to their country house? Yet, all the time she had been praying and feeling solace from her prayers, Lulu was dead, her soul long since elevated to heaven. Could her prayers for Jacob be just as much in vain? If they were, then she would rather remain here with her friends, and commit herself to the local language and customs.

'And if he were, my lovey,' pursued Ginette, 'we'd keep

you here with us. I've seen plenty a roving eye glancing sidelong at you, my Jeanne. You're still of marrying age, you know, and there be eligible men even in Schaffhausen!'

'Ginette!' gasped Claire, putting a hand to her mouth.

Ginette went on in a confidential tone. 'Take the widowed burgher . . . nice catch, sensible man . . . you'd bring some refinement to his household, my dear lady. And didn't he say he loves to speak French? A right chatter-mill an' all—'

'Ginette, shhh, you do go on,' said Claire, sensing Jeanne's discomfort.

'I'm only thinking out loud,' said Ginette, who knew, whenever Jeanne let her ramble on, that she was not far from hitting the spot.

'Thank you for your concern, dear Ginette,' said Jeanne good-humouredly, 'but sometimes I'd rather you thought inside your head!' There was no point in denying her deepest doubts that Ginette had a knack of bringing to the fore.

It did sometimes occur to her that it would be easier if her husband had perished. She would bear up to the fact. It would even make her life easier, for she could start over. But there again, who said life was easy? It was not, and Jeanne never had chosen the easy path. If she had, she would have pretended to forsake her faith; she would have kept her children. And Lulu would be alive and well, if she had forsaken her faith.

But what was a person without a soul? An empty vessel navigating life without a destination, without any hope of going somewhere. God was hope, and she hoped, nay, she firmly believed, that the final reunion was in heaven as Jesus had promised. How pointless living would be if there were nothing but blackness, and how terrifying.

'I am sure Jacob is still alive,' said Jeanne with confidence. Once again, she stood proud in the satisfaction that she had beaten down those dreadful demons whose sinful whispers sometimes came to prey on her. 'But you are right, Ginette. I cannot leave my friends again without prior knowledge of Jacob's safe arrival in London. It would not be fair on Paul.'

'No,' said Ginette, 'nor on my Jeannot . . .'

'But he is alive, I am sure!'

Ginette gave Jeanne a squeeze on her arm as the horses drawing the sleighs came cantering back in a thrilling, icy rush. Jeanne's momentary doubts made way for the exhilarating swish of the sleigh blades as Claire clapped and called out her husband's name.

'Come on, Etienne!' shouted Jeanne too as Etienne's horse took the lead coming out of the turn. Jean Fleuret and Paul were not far behind as the main pack, closing up the gap, entered the bend.

The fast and massive dogs were racing the horses again, a little too close perhaps for comfort, thought Jeanne, as one of the young dogs, fast and fearless, ran along Etienne's horse as if yapping encouragements at it to go faster. But then the rider just behind, taking advantage of the impetus of the bend, came hurtling fast and furious on the outside.

'How thrilling!' cried Claire, clapping her hands and cheering her man at the top of her voice. 'Come on, Etienne!'

But Jeanne, who had been watching one of the dogs pestering the horses' course, had stopped cheering. An instant later, her fears were confirmed when there came a terrible high-pitched yelp as the dog, who must have slipped on the ice, received a hoof to the head.

'Oh, my goodness!' cried Claire as the animal screeched and rolled across the track.

The Swiss driver close behind skilfully avoided the creature by an inch of its life. But Jeanne now wished he had not. For ten lengths behind, Jean Fleuret was also racing out of the bend, taking third place. Jeanne froze in fear, stopping her mouth with her hand. The dog lay in the path of Jean Fleuret's sleigh.

Ginette, standing beside her, let out a loud, guttural cry. Jeannot roared and pulled back the reins, in an effort to steer the horse away from the wounded dog lying in the way of the sleigh runners. But with the pack of racers being so bunched together, there was no place to go. This, after all, was a race of honour. The Swiss drivers, oblivious to the wounded dog immediately ahead, could not be beaten by French novices.

There came a short, appalling squeal, a thud and a horrible crunching sound as Jean's nearside sleigh runner hit the animal full on.

The impetus of the bend and the sudden shift in weight sent the inside sleigh runner flying off the ground. Jeanne saw, as if time were slowed down, the carriage rise up on one side and begin to keel over as the panicked horse continued its course.

Jeannot turned his head to Paul, now clinging to the wooden frame with both hands.

'Jump, Paul! Jump, now!' he screamed, knowing the whole thing would be a death trap should it flip over.

'My God, no!' cried Jeanne as she ran hard, suddenly in a cold sweat, and with a sickening, pounding fear in her heart.

Jeannot waited until the last moment to jump, until the boy had leapt clear, until the sleigh was almost vertical.

The big man landed solidly in the snow. He quickly got to his feet, while Etienne up ahead managed to take command of the panicked horse that gradually slowed, with the weight of the sleigh now top-side down.

Jeannot Fleuret was already at Paul's side as Jeanne came running up. 'Oh, my God,' he said. 'Paul! Paul, me lad!' With his large, leathery hands, he gently rolled the boy over.

Paul did not answer. The smudge of red snow where his head had lain face down, and the blood streaming down the side of his face from his scalp, bore witness to an unlucky landing.

Jeanne now threw herself into the snow beside her son. She put her head to his mouth. 'Dear God, he is breathing!' she said, trying to remain calm. 'He is breathing!'

Praying to herself that it was not just wishful thinking, she held the boy's head as the group of townsfolk made way for a middle-aged man, panting and puffing, who she recognised as the pharmacist. He was soon on his knees, and bending with gravity over the boy to check his arterial pulse.

3

JACOB DID NOT once think he was going to die in New York.

His plan had been to rest with friends a few days, then take the first good ship to Europe. But he had not accounted for the bone-biting cold of the New York winter, which forbade any Europe-bound travel until the thaw.

Neither had he anticipated his sudden illness, though when it struck, he knew from past experience he would just have to resign himself to inactivity until the strain relented. So he kept to his bed in the draughty upper-floor room, heated by a stove that infused the air with the fragrance of thyme.

But his soul remained in torment, caught in a mind-bending vortex of images of his wife and his children, of war and death, of blood-drenched blades and powder and steel. They intermingled like the swirling dance of snowflakes that continued to cover the fields and trees outside his window.

By the fourth day of his illness, he was able to sit up on the edge of his bed and stare at the wall. It provided him with a blank canvas on which to put some order to his crowded thoughts. But how to make any sense of it all with a Christian mind? he wondered.

He clenched his hands together and bowed his head in prayer. But he knew that nothing in earth or heaven could erase the visions of bloody battle, nor take away the grief of losing a child. Consequently, he could not bring himself to pray for the well-being of his family, for he could no longer bear any more disillusionment should tragedy there be. Instead, he prayed to God for his journey to continue, while at the back of his brain, his incessant incantation repeated: *They are all right, of course they are all right, they are all right . . .*

There came a knock at the door. 'Come in,' he said croakily, while the forefront of his mind was still focussed on ending his prayer with *amen.* He turned as the door was pushed open.

'Ah, Monsieur Delpech,' said Madame de Fontenay in her usual sing-song voice. She was followed by Martha, who gave a little curtsy like a proper lady's maid. 'We heard you had come back to the living. How are you?' pursued the old lady. She then turned to take the tray to let Martha make her way to the window, which the girl opened, and then pushed out the shutters set ajar to let in the purple-grey light of a cloud-laden sky.

'We have brought you some warm milk and honey.' Madame de Fontenay placed the tray on the bedside table. Martha, on the other side of the room, closed the windows again, then departed, leaving the door half open. 'She's coming along fine,' said Madame de Fontenay to Jacob, who smiled amusedly at the old lady's determination to keep up Old World standards. 'I used to bring milk and honey to my husband, you know, whenever his nightmares came on. It never failed to bring him a bit of comfort.'

Jacob did not quite know how to respond. Did his terrible dreams provoke shouts in his sleep?

'You mustn't feel ashamed, you know.'

'Oh, I hope my phantoms have not been disturbing you.'

'No, and they will become less tempestuous over time, and perhaps once you have recovered the comfort of your own home.'

'Come, we both know neither you nor I shall ever recover that, Madame,' said Jacob, who was not in the mood for niceties and make-believe.

'Ah, but I wasn't talking about your house, Monsieur Delpech; I was talking about your home. For you can make your home with your loved ones around you anywhere, can you not? Do they not say home is where the heart is?'

'Indeed they do, Madame de Fontenay. Indeed they do,' said Jacob, subdued and slightly guilty at his earlier bluntness. 'I expect you miss your former life, do you not?'

'Oh no, Monsieur Delpech. And there should be no room and no need for pity of things . . . shall we say . . . lost.' It was as if she had peeped into his thoughts.

He had not failed to notice that her attire was now more in keeping with a modest widow than a lady of the aristocracy. How humbling it must be to have fallen from living as a lady to an old settler. But he admired her courage and determination to make something good out of the ruins of her past life.

She went on: 'And to be honest, Monsieur Delpech, I have never been more content, never felt more useful in my entire life! Why, I would much rather be a helpful grandmother than a dead weight in my grand stately home in France. So, please, no pity, neither for me nor for yourself, if I may say so. We just have to get on with it, and start up home again. Don't you agree?'

'I do, Madame de Fontenay. Wise words, well spoken.'

'Bah,' said the lady, swiping her bony hand as though shooing away flies. 'I only wish there were more people around of my generation! And between you, me, and the bedpost, I would have rather preferred to live in a warmer climate, like Madame Odet. She got off the boat in Charles Town, you know. Had people she knew there . . .'

With the evocation of the Carolina colony, Jacob was struck by a thought that had been nagging at the back of his mind, an image of the lady on the ship and her young daughter. She had asked him to find her husband. He had not seen her since then; the news of her husband's death must have broken the poor woman, in debt as she was. 'I was going to ask —' he said.

But footsteps on the stairs, followed by the voice of Marianne, interrupted his train of thought. 'Grandma?' she called out.

'Oh, now look at us!' said the old lady to Jacob, a look of amusement in her eye. 'I would never have thought I would be caught in a gentleman's room by my granddaughter!' Then, calling out, she said: 'Here, my dear, I am with Monsieur Delpech.'

The next moment, standing at the open door with her hand resting on her bump, Marianne said: 'I am so glad you are on the way to full recovery, my uncle. We have made you some broth. Would you like it here or downstairs?'

'Thank you, that is most kind of you. I shall take it downstairs,' said Jacob, who then edged in the nagging question that had not left him since he fell ill. 'By the way,

Marianne, do you know what has become of the lady on the ship who lost her husband?'

'Yes, I do. The poor woman is to stand before the tribunal today. They are to decide what to do with her. Her only hope is that a gentleman steps forward to offer to take her as his wife.'

'Oh. Or else?'

'Daniel says her debt will be purchased for her, and she will have to pay back the town treasurer.'

'You mean the poor woman could well end up indentured all over again.'

'I am afraid so.'

'But she has only just finished her four-year term. Is it likely that anyone will step forward?'

'Daniel says nobody will.'

'Why not?' said Jacob, who, in his feeling of injustice, overlooked the non-negligible matter of love and compatibility. 'Are there not enough men seeking a wife and family? I thought that was the crux of the success of any colony.'

'No one will have her yet because of her husband's illness. And she has not been here long enough to be sure she does not carry the disease.'

'But she wasn't even here, and I am willing to vouch for her good nature.'

'But you have been ill, my uncle. It would be as good as a condemned man bearing testimony to a—'

'It would be unfair to send her back into servitude,' interrupted Jacob. 'I must get to the tribunal!'

'You are a good man, my uncle,' said Marianne, calmingly. 'But you cannot right all the world's wrongs.'

'No, but one should treat people in a Christian manner, and treat them how you would like them to treat you or your family.'

'I do understand, and I would go with you —'

'No, Marianne, I refuse to have you go out in the snow in your condition.'

*

Barely an hour later, Jacob was wading through the glacial morning air, crunching snow under his fur-lined boots despite the country trail having been recently shovelled clear.

Clad in a heavy waxed cloak, he pulled his beaver hat tightly over his forehead to give protection from the gusts of swirling snow as he headed for the city gates. The blustery wind carried the stirring howl of a pack of wolves from the other side of the distant windmill. He slipped and fell over. He picked himself up. He slipped again. He picked himself up again.

'Confounded stuff!' he grumbled under his breath, and wanted to kick himself for bothering about the lady on the ship, and got to thinking he would be better off if he were not a man of his word. But to renounce your true self was like scathing your soul, was it not? His was scathed enough already. Facing the thinning snowfall head-on, he did not hear the muted rumble of hooves behind him. When he saw the pony out of the corner of his eye, he slipped and fell again.

'Jacob, please, get in,' cried a voice from the closed two-person sleigh, driven by a caped and booted black man who tipped his hat.

Jacob scrambled to his feet again and climbed aboard.

'You should not be out in this weather in your condition,

my uncle!' said Marianne playfully.

'And neither should you, my niece!' said Jacob. 'I should like to accompany you back.'

'Ha! I am not ill,' returned Marianne, 'and baby is in the warmest place of all.' She called out to the driver: 'To City Hall, Joseph!'

Onwards they sled in the purple snowscape, through the city gate and down the icy thoroughfare Jacob knew now to be called Broad Street. It being weather to be indoors by the fire, they passed only a few handcarts and wagons, and pedestrians wearing native snowshoes, a fascinating invention, thought Jacob.

Within half an hour, he was kicking off snow stuck to his boots before entering with Marianne through the tall doors of City Hall. The lobby was surprisingly crowded with an array of people conversing in clusters. Going to court was visibly as good an activity as any in this weather, deduced Jacob, as he followed Marianne through the crowd, chattering now in Dutch, now in French, with some English thrown into the mix.

Daniel Darlington soon came into view, standing with a small group of gentlemen by the courtroom door. He greeted his wife with playful reproach for venturing out on such a cold day. Turning to Jacob, he said: 'And I was not expecting to see you here, Monsieur Delpech. Are you well?'

'Much better, thank you, Mr Darlington,' said Jacob. 'I was setting out on foot when your wife came along and refused to head back. So here we are. I hope I haven't missed the audience . . .'

Darlington needed no further explanation. He said: 'Actually, you are just in time, Sir. There has been a bidding of indentures and redemptioners this morning, and I believe your lady in question is about to pass. But please, let me introduce you to a good friend of mine.' Darlington turned to his right where there stood a man of wealth, visible by the cut of his cloth rather than ostentatious adornments. In middle age and of average height, he wore a rictus that could have equally been interpreted as a smile or a snarl, depending on one's disposition or circumstance. 'This is Mr Jacob Leisler,' said Darlington. 'He is in the fur trade.' To Leisler, he said: 'Monsieur Jacob Delpech de Castanet, gentleman notary, landowner, and merchant.'

Both introduced men gave a congenial bow.

'I heard about your tragic plight, Sir,' said Mr Leisler in a faint Germanic accent. 'You must know that here you are among friends.'

'Most kind of you, Sir,' said Jacob, who returned the thin smile, although he was not too keen about his "plight" being talked about in the city hall lobby.

'Indeed, I do believe there are well over a hundred Huguenot families here now, if not two hundred. Many of them originate from a place called La Rochelle. Where might you be from, Mr Delpech? I only ask in case I know of anyone from your hometown.'

'Alas, Monsieur is not from La Rochelle, Mr Leisler,' said Marianne, standing on the other side of her husband.

'I am from Montauban, Sir,' said Jacob, who did not fail to notice that the gentleman had made no hesitation in dropping the particle of his name. But the sound of Jacob's hometown, albeit in his own mouth, fleetingly rekindled his previous life in his mind's eye. That old life seemed like worlds away, standing as he was in a melting pot of cultures, in a fledgling city surrounded by a white wilderness, freezing fog, and wolves.

'No, I am sorry. I know of no one from there. I can, however, introduce you to the Rochelle contingent.'

'Thank you, Sir. However, my intention is not to remain.'

'Pity, because I believe there is a woman in need of a husband.'

It was clear to Jacob that he was speaking to a self-made man, quite possibly a diamond among his peers, but an uncut one at that. Jacob had an instinctive liking for him, though. He said: 'Indeed, I travelled along the coast aboard the same ship as she. And I can vouch for her kindly spirit, although I cannot offer my support in a matrimonial capacity.'

'Then let us see what the "grandees" shall make of the poor young wretch and her daughter from Charles Town!' said Mr Leisler as the crowd began filtering through the doors into the courtroom. 'We are going in.'

*

She stood before the court hopeful, not browbeaten. Her glance caught that of Jacob. Her features, set in defiance, suddenly cracked, and the pleats between her long oval eyes furrowed —a trait that reminded him of his own wife. Then she resumed her resolute pose.

The panelled courtroom of dark-wood partitions and balustrades was spacious and full to the brim, every inch of bench occupied. Aside from the tavern near the fort, the city hall was no doubt the best place for entertainment in town, given the weather, thought Jacob. The dead man's wife was the news of the moment and had attracted feelings of pity, especially as she had a child. Before she passed that morning, a new series of indentured servants and redemptioners off the ship from England had been paraded in to be adjudged. The dead man's lady was the pinnacle for the day's audiences.

'Madame,' said the presiding magistrate, leaning over the bar, 'you have been placed in custody on charges brought against you by Captain Benjamin Stevens, to whom you hold a debt of the price of your fare from Charles Town. After much deliberation, and given the fact that your husband had only recently arrived in the township, the only way out of your predicament will be for the town treasurer to purchase your debt.'

A wave of relief spread over the woman's face as she grasped the shoulder of her child clinging to her leg. The audience let out a sigh of satisfaction.

'However . . . as you have no sustenance, no immediate income, and no relations here in New York, the only way for you to reimburse the town for your debt is through the terms of an indenture contract.'

Groans and muffled protests arose from the benches.

'Your Grace,' beseeched the woman, 'I paid my dues in Charles Town already as an indenture servant for four years. It is that reason that brought us here to New York, to start afresh. My husband wanted to find some land so we could live off our own labours. I beg you, Your Honour, please don't make me go through it all again.'

It was the first time Jacob had heard the woman speak in English, which he thought she spoke impeccably well after four years of servitude in the English colony.

'Madame,' said the magistrate, 'I see no other means unless your future husband is willing to pay your debt.' The magistrate paused for effect, perhaps in the hope that a gentleman would step forward at the last moment. But no one did. For who would pay the woman's debt when she could come as an indenture? Besides, who was to say she would not bring her late husband's illness with her? Jacob looked on, beset by his inveterate sense of injustice.

Amid whispers and chattering in the audience, a French-accented voice suddenly rose up loud and clear: 'My Lord, Ladies and Gentlemen . . . with all due respect, you are asking this poor woman to pay her dues twofold and by the same token to double her burden. If there is any justice in this New World that respects the justice of God, then surely she should be given charity!'

'Hear, hear,' murmured voices from the audience.

The French voice continued: 'Through no fault of her own, her husband has died prematurely. I can personally vouch for her good character and sound bill of health, having voyaged with her all the way from Charles Town. Surely you cannot increase the poor woman's burden!'

The magistrates and the courtroom spectators of New York had just met Jacob Delpech. After a pause to take in both the newcomer and his discourse, a number of courtroom figures voiced their agreement, which led to a free-for-all debate between bench neighbours.

'Order. Order,' called the chief magistrate, who then turned to the newcomer still on his feet. 'Sir, someone has to pay. It is the law of our sovereign.'

The crowd let out unreserved boos.

'Order. Order! Let there be order!' called the magistrate.

The courtroom settled into silence again. The magistrate continued. 'Noises will not advance this young lady's plight. And you, Sir, please be seated,' he said, looking over his spectacle at Jacob. 'Unless you have a firm proposition to make.' Jacob sat back down while the magistrate reasoned: 'As an indentured servant, the lady will enjoy the benefits which include meat, drink, apparel, and lodging. It is the King's law.' The magistrate visibly regretted his last sentence as this time, an even greater roar of discontent rose up on the last two words.

'Down with the Jacobites!'

'Out with the Romans!'

Jacob was about to stand up again when a voice, gruff, confident, and bold, sounded from his left-hand side.

'My Lords . . . My new friend is right,' said the unmistakable voice of Mr Leisler. 'How can we create a new world, free for all, and free from the archaic laws of England, if we cannot even welcome those in their momentary passage of strife? Must we not found our society on equality before God and with the chance for all under His sky to succeed here, no matter what their social condition?'

'Hear, hear!' roared the crowd.

'Order. Order!' called the magistrate. 'Sieur Leisler, would you have the town's treasury pay for everyone's failure?'

'My Lord, the man came here for a month. I remember him well; he was full of courage and ideas. His only failure was his untimely death, and now you ask his spouse to pay?'

'Bend the rules for one, and we will soon be the prime destination for every unskilled labourer and convict from Europe! Is that what you want?' The magistrate, who visibly enjoyed an imposing presence, scanned the audience of spectators from left to right into silence.

Leisler, still standing, flourished a finger and said in a loud and confident voice: 'Then I will pay her fare, Sir!'

The audience gave a roar of approval while the magistrate held up his hand to silence them again. 'That is all very well, but who will pay for her sustenance, Sir? Or would you have her walk the streets with her child? Or work in the tavern?'

The French newcomer then stood up beside the woman's benefactor and said: 'If my friend will pay her debt, I will provide means for her until she is able to gain employment.'

The audience gave another almighty cheer. The woman, bringing her hands to her lips, looked across the room towards Jacob in gratitude.

'Then, Sir,' said the magistrate, 'you would still need to give her monies to see her through the winter, at the least.'

'That is indeed my intention, so help me God,' said Jacob, whose heart secretly sank as he said this. But how could he not practice what he preached?

'So she will find lodgings at the inn until other means become available to her,' said the magistrate with nonchalance.

'No, Sir,' said a woman's voice to Jacob's right. Jacob turned to Marianne beside him. 'The inn is notorious,' she said, rising to her feet, 'notorious for tripping women into sin for the pleasure of the stronger sex! I offer to employ her and give her board and lodging in my home. Provided my husband agrees.'

Daniel Darlington bobbed up in his turn. He said: 'I do, I do that. Whatever my dear wife says . . .'

The audience laughed along good-heartedly with Daniel's quip. So old Madame de Fontenay was right, thought Jacob, and what was more, her granddaughter's power of persuasion over her husband was apparently common knowledge.

4

WHAT WITH ALL the brouhaha in the courtroom, Jacob quickly became a familiar figure.

He was pointed at in the snow-clad streets of the town, and singled out with a nudge and a nod in the little French chapel down near the battery, where Huguenots came from all over Manhattan for the Sunday service.

Yet all he really wanted was to make for Europe, which the present winter freeze forbade. He knew deep down that it was just as well, though, weakened as he was by his many misadventures and recent illness. His body would probably not have stood up to the rigours of a gruelling winter voyage in freezing temperatures, should that have been an option.

So he resigned himself to assisting the Darlingtons with drawing up plans to settle around the bay —the bay which the Huguenots from La Rochelle had deemed exceptional enough to start a settlement there. Darlington's intention was to build a farm to cultivate primarily the lucrative tobacco crop that Europeans craved.

In January, Darlington and Delpech decided to take advantage of a window of fresh but cloudless weather. Having hired two good steeds and a packhorse, the two men rode out northward at the first gleam of dawn, with the intention of getting a look at how the land lay in the dead of winter. It was a twenty-three-mile ride along the Boston post road. After two hours in the saddle, Darlington halted his mount on the hoary crest of another wooded hill. The onward trail descended into an area of gently sloping land that converged into a bay. It was surrounded by a few leafless trees, snow-covered fields, and a litter of log houses with smoking chimneys.

'I give you New Rochelle,' said Darlington with a sweeping motion of his hand. 'You'll see, the land is good and fertile, and the fish are plentiful in the sound beyond.'

Jacob slowly scanned the humble beginnings of the new colony. 'Fine place for a settlement, I should say. Water, high ground for a mill, rich soil, and I wager there is plenty of game in the pantry!' he said, nodding towards the woods.

Onwards they rode, sinking between the fields where green grass and dark-brown earth broke through the thin veil of snow crust. 'As I said, the land was bought up by a lord in London,' said Darlington. 'A Lord Pell. Deceased now, though. So I asked Leisler to negotiate the purchase of six thousand acres on the Huguenots' behalf so they could become owners of their fields rather than leaseholders. He knows the nephew who lives in New York. A certain John Pell.'

'An enterprising fellow, this Leisler.'

'And a good friend. Gave me sound advice when my father and mother died . . . Came to New York as a mercenary soldier, would you believe. Son of a clergyman preacher like myself, and now he is one of the wealthiest merchants in New York.'

'Lady Luck has smiled upon him, then.'

'A little luck and a natural flair for spotting a bargain, I'd say. You may find him brash, unrefined, but he is a good fellow to the marrow, true to his word and as smart as any of the "grandees," as he likes to call them. And he's living proof that here a man can meet with success without a birthright, as I have seen in Europe. Why, pardon me for saying so, but some of your so-called elite are perfect imbeciles, frivolous, and so self-absorbed it is a wonder how folk there put up with them.'

'I will give you no argument there, dear Darlington! Indeed, your ways in these new lands have certainly opened my eyes.'

'Then I'll put it to you again, Sir: come join our ranks. Here a man of your calibre can aspire to great success. My word, you already have the affection of half the population of New York!'

'Ha! It is something I will certainly consider, once I have recovered my family.'

'I urge you to decide quickly, though; the best plots are already being snapped up. But come, there is a tavern where they give a good welcome to riders from Boston and New York, and I will introduce you to a few of the Huguenots. Then I will show you a handsome plot not far from mine. Overlooks the bay. Its south-facing slopes would make for fine farmland, I am sure.'

*

Back at the Darlingtons', the conversation over supper turned to preparations for the spring move and the promise Jacob had made to the Huguenots he had met in New Rochelle.

Learning of Jacob's fluency in English and his former training as a jurist in France, they had asked him if he would assist in linguistic and legal matters. With Jacob's help, they would be able to understand the full purport of Mr Leisler's negotiations for the purchase of the land from John Pell of Pelham Manor.

'I am delighted to hear you accepted,' said Marianne. 'It might sway the balance in favour of your becoming our neighbour . . .'

'Alas, it is not something I am able to contemplate for the time being,' said Jacob, seated across the table. 'I do look forward to making myself useful, however, at least until the thaw, when the first ship is ready to set sail for Europe.'

'If I may say something,' said Mrs Blancfort, looking up from the cauldron in the hearth.

Since her redemption from slavery, she had stepped into her new role as first maid with relish, taking over most of Marianne's activities now that the latter was great with child. All Mrs Blancfort needed now was a husband and a good stepfather for little Françoise, her daughter, who, as usual, was taking her meal in the kitchen with Martha. The notion occurred to her that the Lord may have put Monsieur Delpech in their path for that very reason.

'Yes, you may, Charlotte,' said Marianne, whose poised tone demonstrated her ease in the role of mistress.

'Well, as tragic as it may sound, Monsieur, how do you know your wife's still of this world?'

'Madame Blancfort! Really!' said Marianne, flabbergasted. It was not the way she had been brought up, for servants were not usually permitted to give their opinions unless asked. But this was the New World, and she knew, as did Mrs Blancfort,

528

that relationships were more brazen here, especially since the great majority of wealthy men were recently made.

'No, that is quite all right,' said Jacob, holding up a hand with a complaisant chuckle to show he was not offended. 'I will gladly answer. Indeed, I have oft-times been given to ask myself that very question.' He turned his gaze to Charlotte Blancfort, who smiled candidly back from her place at the hearth. The glowing embers and candlelight gave her complexion a pretty hue and made her large oval eyes glisten attractively. 'I do live in hope that I shall see my wife and children in the very near future. And it is that hope that will carry me across the ocean. There can be no other way.'

'Oh well,' said the first maid, 'it will be a pity to see you go, Monsieur Delpech, a good, strong man of resources such as yourself. A mighty good catch for a lady, if you don't mind me saying so.' She shrugged one shoulder with comic effect, which drew a ripple of laughter from the table, and then went back to dishing out bowls of salted pork and lentil stew.

It was the closest Mrs Blancfort could come to letting Jacob overtly know that she was available and willing, should he ever be inclined to take a new wife.

Jacob took no offense. There was no point in pretending that Charlotte Blancfort was not doing the right thing. If she was here, it was after all while waiting to find a husband.

Jacob said: 'Come, Madame Blancfort, I have no doubt a husband will come along for you soon. You are too young to remain a widow for long, and I am sure that when the fine season comes, the butterflies of love will again flutter in your pretty eyes.'

'Thank you, Monsieur,' said Charlotte.

'Uncle Jacob!' said Marianne, perhaps a little jealous.

'How romantically you sayeth loving things.'

'I have not always been middle-aged, my dear niece!' said Jacob, to which Madame de Fontenay looked up with a glint in her eye.

'Ah, and memory of a full youth is certainly the most comfortable pillow for slumber in old age. So fill it up, I say! Oh, how I used to dance the evening away . . .'

Amid the merriment, Martha marched into the room from the small lobby, nervously wringing her hands. The second maid fixed her eyes on Darlington and said: 'Sir. There's Mr Leisler come knocking at the door, he—'

Before she could finish her sentence, the visitor erupted into the room, with his feathered beaver still on his head. A blustery draught followed him in, making the candles flicker in their lamps and the embers glow redder in the chimney. All heads turned in unison to face him from the dining table that stood before the hearth, the ladies occupying the seats nearest the fire.

'Come in, my dear fellow, and pull up a chair,' said Darlington, standing to greet his friend. Meanwhile, at a nod from Madame de Fontenay, Martha rushed back to the front door to make sure it was properly barred.

After a short greeting all round, Leisler did as suggested, and, swiping his hat from his head, he said: 'Ladies, Gentlemen, please excuse this intrusion. I have important news of further developments in England. We have been given to believe that a Dutch fleet has indeed landed in England!'

'William of Orange at their head . . .' said Darlington.

'Yes, I received the news from a ship's captain, who heard it from an English merchant who had recently unloaded in Charles Town.'

'If this is true, it is reassuring news,' said Jacob. 'For if he takes the throne, it would mean Louis of France no longer has any sway over England.'

'I agree,' said Leisler, 'but it could also mean war, civil war, if James Stuart tries to resist.'

'What does Lieutenant Governor Nicholls say?' said Darlington.

'He denies any such tidings since no official news has reached his ears.'

'He is in denial!' said Madame de Fontenay, not afraid to vent her thoughts despite her heavy French accent.

'Not quite, Madame. For he has nevertheless given orders for the provincial militias to be on alert to protect the province for the king. King James, that is.'

'But what if James is no longer king?' said Marianne.

'Then the risk is that James will seek support from France,' said Leisler. 'And our trouble is, Jacobites are in power here and in command of our fort.'

'Not to mention our defences are in such a poor state of repair that even the wall would not constitute a major handicap for the French, should they decide to attack.' Darlington was referring to the French stationed in New France, further north.

'I never thought I'd ever hear myself say this of my own countrymen,' said Jacob. 'But if the French attack, then our goose will be cooked!'

'Quite,' seconded Marianne, 'for if they did, I fear we Huguenots would be put to torture before execution.'

'With all due respect, Ladies and Gentlemen, we shall see to it that French forces will never enter here!' said Leisler. Turning to Darlington and Delpech, he said: 'We must organise a secret safety committee should this news turn out to be true. I have already spoken to Milborne and a few others who would be prepared to take part. Because if New York becomes Catholic, we will all be done for!'

5

IT WAS RUMOURED in taverns and New York homes that the Dutch prince had succeeded in his invasion of England. Bolstered by the feeling of distrust of the Jacobite office holders, Leisler set about secretly planning the defence of the would-be Protestant king's values —values of liberalism and freedom of conscience on par with those of the people of New York.

Due to his knowledge of law and the English language — the go-between language of Dutch and French —Delpech became the ears and mouthpiece of the Huguenot contingent of Manhattan. Little by little, he began to feel a sense of duty towards his co-religionists. In fact, he began to feel in his element, in the faraway land where there was a sense that a new and fairer way of life was not only attainable, but in the making.

But the arctic winds had not yet brought any impartial news from England by way of merchant ships. Only a couple of large Royal Navy vessels had made landfall in the province so far that winter, and only a few droplets of information had leaked through to New York via Boston. What was more, the French were abnormally calm on the New France frontier north of Albany, as if they, too, were awaiting news. What could possibly be happening in Europe?

'Is this state of affairs not ridiculous?' said Darlington late one January afternoon, to a group of prominent New Yorkers brought together in Jacob Leisler's dining room. 'Here we are, waiting for the great powers that be to dispatch crumbs of information to determine our future! I say it is intolerable, Gentlemen. To think they have probably never even set foot on these lands!'

The small committee, which included Darlington, Delpech, Leisler, Milborne, and a few merchants, had gathered in the privacy of Mr Leisler's townhouse, a large and comfortable three-storey stone building veneered with kiln-fired brick and built when the town was under Dutch governance. Decorated with the bold splendour characteristic of Amsterdam merchants, the long, flagstoned dining room where the meeting was being held was adorned with beautifully carved *kasten*, dark-wood panelling, and thick drapes at the window boxes. The party of seven sat around the long dining table on high-backed chairs, a silver tankard in front of each of them.

Delpech had turned up with the intention of asking the ever-busy Leisler if he had made any progress for the Rochelle Huguenots. Sitting before the fire, he could not fail to admire the splendid array of weaponry displayed above the tiled mantel, which tallied with what Darlington had told him of the New Yorker's past in the Dutch army.

'Yes, but we officially belong to the Crown,' said Jacob's neighbour. His name was Jacob Milborne, a methodical Puritan approaching forty who worked as clerk and bookkeeper for a leading merchant. 'And we benefit from its protection. If we did not, then you can be sure that New York would soon be called New Orleans!'

'I do see your point, Sir,' returned Darlington, 'but that also means this town could just as easily be turned over to the French if that be the whim of the so-called elite of England!'

'I think not, my dear Daniel,' said Leisler. The host was sitting slightly back from the dining-room table in his favourite armchair, almost as an observer. He was holding a glowing ember with his pipe tongs, and proceeded to ignite the tobacco in his long-stemmed clay pipe. After drawing upon it twice, he pursued: 'I firmly believe the rumours of King James's demise, and every day I pray for its confirmation.'

'Then we should have to fend off the French anyway,' said Darlington, 'lest they damn us to popery!'

Reaching over to let drop the ember in the hearth and replace the tongs on a brass stand, Leisler said: 'We shall be in better hands if William asserts his wife's right to the throne and becomes king himself.'

'Aye, give me a liberal Dutch Protestant over an English Louis XIV anytime!' said Milborne.

'And we all know William's love for the French king!' The host's ironic remark brought a round of complicit chuckles.

'You can be sure he will send his soldiers to protect our livelihood,' said Nicholas Stuyvesant, the son of the former Dutch governor.

'And his taxes,' added Darlington.

'But if William steps in,' said Milborne, 'at least we shall recover our seal and the independence of our administration.'

'Nonetheless, Gentlemen,' said Leisler, 'Mr Darlington does have a point regarding the remote rule of these lands. As you well know, I am the German-born son of a French Calvinist. You, Sir, are from France. Both of you are of Dutch ancestry. And you, Milborne, are born a subject of His Majesty in Albion. Only Darlington and Stuyvesant here are natives of this city. Yet, I say we are all first and foremost New Yorkers!'

The gentlemen let out hear-hears all round, some lightly tapping the table. Even Darlington gave a nod of acquiescence.

Leisler went on: 'We stand united in our perspective on trade, in our tolerance and love of freedom of worship.' Then, sweeping his head slowly round to include Darlington, he said: 'But the fight for independence from remote powers cannot be for today! First, we must regain our seal and ensure New York will still be our home tomorrow. And for that, we need to be sure the Protestant monarchy will be respected!' Daniel was about to interrupt, but, raising his free hand, Leisler persisted: 'Please, Daniel, hear me out . . . Thank you. For what if our governor, Lieutenant Governor Nicholls, and the military and customs officeholders refuse to acknowledge a Protestant king? What if they side with the enemy, as will James Stuart should he be dethroned?'

'You are right,' conceded Darlington. 'A greater threat looms immediately over us. And I fear, as we stand today, there is no defence set up in case of French attack.'

'One might go so far as to say it could not have been planned better for an invasion,' said Stuyvesant, cocking an insinuating eyebrow.

Darlington said: 'I say we take control of the town. If we do not act—as you say, Milborne—this place may indeed be soon renamed New Orleans . . . I say we act now!'

'The people of New York are vastly behind us,' said Stuyvesant.

'Gentlemen, let us not be hasty, however,' said Leisler, holding his lapel in one hand and the stem of his pipe in the other. 'We must plan this wisely, so that when the time comes, we are able to take over the town without chaos, in the tradition of Stuyvesant senior. And at all costs, I say we await news of an official nature before we take the governor's residence.'

'I agree,' said Milborne, 'or else we risk being tried for treason, no less.'

'Mr Delpech,' said Darlington, looking across the table, 'I know you have come to see Mr Leisler on another matter, and I do not want to drag you into our problems, but what say you?'

What with an Englishman asking a Frenchman what to do in case of French attack, and a Frenchman seeking refuge in an English colony, decidedly, the world really had gone mad, thought Jacob, who, to be truthful, had been enjoying his mulled wine in his silver tankard. The alcohol and the heat from the mulberry-and-white-tiled hearth that crackled peacefully before him had lulled his senses. He now placed his hands composedly upon the table in front of him to give himself a countenance. He said: 'I would say . . . Mr Leisler is right to plan for such an important event, for the French would put any chaos to their advantage. As Mr Leisler's military background will have taught him, if and when the time comes, there must be swift action if we are to stay in control after the takeover. I would humbly suggest that plans be drawn up as soon as possible to prepare actions and designate defence parties, so that the interim commander will know exactly what to implement upon takeover.'

'The fort will have to be manned night and day,' said Darlington.

'We should have to strengthen the city walls,' said Leisler.

'And sufficient warning should be provided to those residing outside the wall should the threat prove imminent,' said Delpech.

'Indeed, we shall have to place sentinels and cannons at strategic outposts,' said Leisler, who then drew again from his pipe.

Seizing the moment, Jacob said: 'Speaking of which, Sir, if I may digress from the discussion just a moment, do we have news from Lord Pell with regards to the land purchase?'

'Ah, I do indeed, Delpech. I have received the first draft of the contract . . .'

'Excellent. I shall set up a meeting with my brethren to finalize land plots and boundaries. I have drawn up a list of no fewer than thirty names . . .'

Delpech said no more on the subject and let the more pressing debate carry on to its conclusion, which was to establish a plan of action by their next meeting.

6

JACOB THREW HIMSELF into his new toil. It enabled him to calm his frustrations born of the impossibility of achieving his own goal. His mind thus occupied, he was able to diminish the terrible nightmares that had previously made him restless at night.

He helped translate legal documents; became a go-between to express questions and answers between the Huguenot contingent and Leisler; and was a constant source of knowledge when it came to planning the new settlement, the construction of which would continue in earnest with the thaw. The position of the mill was his specialty, along with land irrigation. It was important to ensure that every plot had access to its own water supply, the value of which could easily have been overlooked in these months of overabundance of ice and snow.

Despite the petty disputes mostly relating to future property boundaries, Delpech found himself playing a pivotal role in the creation of the new township. It gave his life new meaning to be part of something greater than himself, and it was restoring his faith in humanity.

These planning sessions came to a head one day during a

meeting after church at the Darlingtons' house. The house was conveniently situated on the track back to New Rochelle. Every Sunday, Huguenots made the hike from their temporary timber country dwellings to New York. A Sunday service was given in the humble French chapel built by French refugees the previous year. For those who had already begun settling in New Rochelle, it meant a forty-six-mile round trek, one which they undertook every Sunday, weather permitting. The men and the heartiest women walked beside the rough oxen-drawn carts that transported children and those not up to the long march. Jacob stood in wonder the first time he saw the caravan wend its way to the gates of New York, singing one of Marot's hymns. The mere sight of them in the nascent light of a Sunday morning never ceased to lighten his own burden and double his desire to assist them in their installation. Though his compensation for his work was not of a tangible nature, it was priceless all the same. They enabled him to recover his bearings and mend his moral compass, damaged in the company of the buccaneers from Port Royal.

'It is but a slight hardship compared to the joy in our hearts of being able to worship God openly,' a man named Bonnefoy had said when Jacob had expressed his admiration after church. 'And what is more,' Bonnefoy had continued, 'what greater joy can there be in the knowledge that we are building the foundations for our children and our children's children, so they may celebrate God's love in a like manner, free from persecution!'

The meeting took place in the dining room after the service, as usual with the would-be councillors of the settlement, some of whom still resided in New York while waiting for the winter to pass. Those who had already begun settling in New Rochelle stayed behind, while the main caravan went on its way back so it would reach home before nightfall.

Marianne sat in for her husband, who was down at the quay, preparing a cargo of tobacco and sugar for the next ship to London. Besides, the meeting being held in French, he preferred his wife to be his ears and his mouthpiece. Madame de Fontenay sat cosily at the hearth with her knitting needles. 'In case things get out of hand!' she had said with a twinkle in her eye. 'Because I am not very good with them for much else.' Then she had given a sigh of despair at the tiny, oddly shaped garment she was trying to knit.

Jacob proceeded to translate a document, showed the settlers a draft of the plots, and noted down any questions for the ensuing exchange with Leisler. The meeting was coming to a close when Monsieur Bonnefoy, a leading tenor of the party in his early forties, popped the question that Jacob suspected would come sooner or later.

'Now, Monsieur Delpech,' he said, resting his clenched hands on the table before him, 'I have been asked unanimously by all those present, if you would care to stand as a member of the new council which, as you know, is to be made up of twelve aldermen.'

It was a heartening proposition for sure, and one that gave Jacob a profound satisfaction. But he knew that it also meant becoming a villager and putting his name down for a plot. Jacob placed his palms down upon the table as if to give himself extra balance. For well he might be tempted to leave his money in this new world, and keep only enough to pay for the voyage back with his family. At last, he said: 'I thank you for the offer, Gentlemen. Alas, as you well know, I cannot stay.'

'We do understand your position, Monsieur Delpech, but once you have recovered your family, you will need a place to settle, will you not?' Monsieur Bonnefoy then opened his arms to embrace the whole table to give more weight to his offer. 'Well, Sir, we should be most honoured if that place be with us.' Amid deep rumblings and hear-hears around the table, Monsieur Bonnefoy persisted: 'This can be your new home with like-minded people who value your moral fibre and your talents. You have given us your expertise freely and without restraint. Your place is among us. What say you, Sir?'

Marianne, sitting opposite Jacob, read the discomfort on his knitted brow. She knew how difficult it would be for him to commit to such an opportunity, and Jacob did not give his word lightly. She knew that leaving Europe indefinitely would mean leaving behind his dead children in their graves, and that two of his daughters might even still be with his sister-in-law, for all he knew. But his modesty forbade him from laying out his personal woes. And now that she had her own child in her belly, she could imagine the pain of having lost one. She glanced towards Madame de Fontenay by the hearth behind her for some tacit guidance. But the old lady simply raised both eyebrows in an expression that Marianne knew well. It told her to act as her heart told her to.

The young woman turned back to the table and, as poised as the men despite her youth, with an indulgent smile in her voice, she said: 'Gentlemen, I pray we show some patience. Perhaps Monsieur Delpech needs to allow the proposition to mature in his mind before committing to an answer.'

Monsieur Bonnefoy, good-natured, said: 'Oh, do not

worry yourself, Madame Darlington. We only beg for a preliminary reply so that we can allocate a place.' He then turned back to Jacob. 'What say you, Sir?'

Jacob had gone over the possibility time and time again, and the merchant in him told him he would do far worse than to pledge his return. Sure, it would be an exciting and adventurous new beginning, but could he honestly commit to a plot and a place as councillor? And how safe would this land be in two months, in two years? The threats were numerous: wild animals, Indians allied to the French, the English under King James, invasion from his own countrymen from New France.

'Sir,' he said, 'please do not think me ungrateful if at this minute I do not say *yes*.'

'But you do not say *no* either.'

'I should rather sleep on it and promise to give you my pondered reply when we meet next Sunday.'

It was a fair enough compromise, accepted by all, and one that would buy him time to weigh everything correctly in the balance.

*

Later that afternoon, Jacob sat alone with a handful of papers and his pipe in the small sitting room.

The coming events were exciting, and playing a major role in such an adventure as the birth of a township was something he was finding most gratifying. He was acutely aware, too, that a decisive moment in history was about to be played out in New York —that of the defence of the township as a free city.

Of course, he had planned to depart for Europe at the first

opportunity, but the merchant vessel, for which Daniel Darlington was preparing a shipment at his warehouse, would set sail for London via Boston, possibly extending the voyage by a week, maybe two. He had also learnt of another ship, albeit smaller, that was due to sail in early March, which was just a few weeks away. Given that this second option was to sail directly from New York to London, it would probably arrive in the English capital only weeks after the Boston ship. Not only would it mean less time at sea, but it would allow him to help tie up any loose ends with regard to the purchase of the land that would harbour New Rochelle. But what should he do about Bonnefoy's offer to buy into the township and take a role as alderman?

His mind was soon swimming again with indecision. 'Get a grip on yourself, man!' he said to himself. He slammed down the documents onto the little round table and gazed into the hearth, elbow on the arm of his armchair, hand cupping his pipe. Little by little —amid the calm of the crackling fire, the purr of the cat kneading the cushion on Madame de Fontenay's chair, and the discreet click of the bracket clock upon the walnut commode —he began to realise to what extent his mind had become overcrowded, submerged in matters that were far away from his initial goal, matters that had nonetheless also become important to him. For was his role not indispensable for a satisfactory outcome? Leisler, after all, was a merchant. Would he not try to price the land so he could make a handsome profit for himself when he sold it on?

But now, sitting with his pipe in the absence of the male party and the cacophony of preparations, he was able at last to put everything into perspective and, hopefully, hear a voice of reason through the commotion of his vagaries . . .

'Are you well, Sir?' said the maid, carrying a pewter tray full of cups, saucers, and a coffee pot.

'Ah, Madame Blancfort,' said Jacob, removing his pipe from his lips. 'Sorry, I was miles away . . .'

'I believe miles away is exactly where you ought to be, Monsieur Delpech,' continued Charlotte Blancfort, brash as ever, 'if you'll pardon me for saying so.' She placed the tray on the low table in front of the fire while Jacob sat agape.

'You know she is right, Monsieur Delpech,' said a lively voice from the doorway. Jacob rose from his seat to face Madame de Fontenay as she hobbled into the room. 'Take no notice,' she said with a nod to her cherry walking stick, 'hip giving me gyp. Good news for you, though. It's a sure sign that milder weather is on its way.'

'You cannot keep fighting everyone else's battles, you know, Sir,' said Charlotte. She then stuck out an arm to help the old lady to her chair.

Madame de Fontenay picked up the cat and dumped it on her lap as she sat down. 'There, lap warmer!' she declared.

'And perhaps, this is not your battle to fight, Jacob!' said the voice of Marianne, who walked in holding her bump with one hand and her lower back with the other. Her belly had grown considerably, and her face had become fuller. It occurred to Jacob how much her life had changed, and how she and her grandmother had taken it in their stride, just like Madame Blancfort, who now only had her daughter left of her family of five. 'At least, not at this time,' pursued Marianne. 'For your true fight is surely elsewhere, my uncle . . . many miles away.'

The ping of the bracket clock announced the time for

afternoon coffee, a ritual that the ladies had installed which broke up the monotony of the wintry afternoons. Charlotte Blancfort proceeded to lay out the cups and saucers while Martha and little Françoise brought in the sugar scraped into a bowl from a sugarloaf, and some gingerbread cookies on a pewter plate.

'Did you not say that you lived in hope of seeing your wife and children soon, Monsieur?' said Charlotte. It would have been deemed impertinent of a maid to speak to a guest of her mistress in this fashion. But Marianne knew she would not stay long before she, too, found a new home. Madame de Fontenay just smiled with an amused twinkle in her eye.

'I did indeed,' said Jacob.

'I only mention it,' continued Charlotte, 'because so did I live in hope, Monsieur Delpech. I boarded a ship with no means in the hope of joining my husband. But then I found out that hope alone ain't enough, is it? And truth is, I delayed too. Had I taken the previous ship like I was planning, I would have been able to care for him, and he wouldn't have died alone in his room, and we'd all be together today . . .' Charlotte bit her lip to retain her steely countenance.

'You mustn't let your hope wither away, though, Charlotte,' said Marianne comfortingly.

'Oh, I won't let it, Madame Darlington, thanks to yourselves and all your kindnesses.' Charlotte put on a brave smile that embraced Jacob as well as the old lady.

'You have plenty to hope for, Madame Blancfort,' said Jacob, while Marianne put an arm around her. 'And yes, I do see your point. You have to set your sights and keep to them . . . I admit, I myself . . . seem to have been somewhat swept off my feet.'

'The ship is due to sail in a few days, Jacob,' said Marianne.

'Yes, it has been constantly at the back of my mind. But I have been told there will be another next month, and direct to London, that one.'

'Charlotte is right. I would dally not if I were you, Monsieur Delpech,' said Madame de Fontenay. 'Bring back your family here, if that is your desire. But go and fetch them before it is too late!'

Jacob said: 'I shall weigh up the pros and cons of leaving so soon, I promise.'

Jacob, however, would not have to deliberate for long.

*

The following Tuesday, Jacob was back at Leisler's fine townhouse, going over the plotted map and the adjustments made during Sunday's meeting with the Huguenots.

On the way, he had noted a foretaste of spring: the first white flowers poking through the thin layer of snow on the pretty graveyard near the north gate; the wide sun-splashed thoroughfare in New York, busier than usual; and the animated market near the fort, packed with vendors, animals, and spindled carts. Jacob also noticed the rivers now flowed mostly free of ice.

Only the Huguenots who still resided in New York attended the meeting held in Leisler's dining room. Marianne, having already spoken with Jacob, had preferred not to attend, given her condition. The party had made good progress: their host was confident that they could get the ball rolling as to the signing of the deed, now that parcels had been drawn and confirmed. All that was required now was for Leisler to make the purchase from John Pell, who had agreed in principle to the sale of the six thousand acres.

The meeting had just come to a close. The attendees were looking through the tall rear window in admiration of Leisler's long garden, bare and hoary but orderly and attractive in the late-morning sunshine, when the manservant announced Daniel Darlington.

Not being one for endless meetings, Daniel had found a pretext to oversee the lading of his cargo down at the wharf at Coenties Slip. He doffed his hat on entering and said: 'Gentlemen, please forgive my intrusion, but I have, if not official news, at least important first-hand news from England.'

All present stared in silent expectation.

'Ah,' said Leisler. 'And what might that be?'

'William of Orange is King of England, Gentlemen!'

There was a short silence before the Huguenots fully took in the announcement, while Leisler stood in stupor, holding his chin.

Monsieur Le Conte, a tall, serious-looking man, taking the initiative, said: 'Zat is good, yes?'

'Indeed it is,' said Jacob. There was a release of tension in the room as the penny dropped.

Leisler, however, remained stern-faced. 'Who told you?' he said.

'A captain just in from Virginia.'

'Then we must act,' said Leisler, now poised for action. 'Gather as many people as you can at the tavern, Daniel.'

Within a few minutes, the Huguenot gentlemen were taking their leave.

Leisler asked Delpech if he could stay behind a minute.

'You know what this means?' said the merchant and

former soldier as the door closed behind the last gentleman from New Rochelle.

'Quite possibly war in one form or another, I'm afraid.'

'Yes, I'm afraid you are right, Sir, if it has not already started.'

'Good grief!'

'And knowing your circumstances, Mr Delpech, please do not think me curt if I take it upon myself to offer you some advice.'

'Fear not, Sir, it will be well received.'

'I am sure your compatriots would appreciate your staying to help administer the township, but if you are to leave, I strongly recommend you do so as soon as possible, Sir. You can take the next ship to Boston. From there, it will take you to London. This is my strong advice, Monsieur Delpech, for I fear the French will not be slow in setting up a maritime blockade.'

7

CLAD IN A waxed travel cloak, Jacob watched the clump of land at the tip of Manhattan become gradually enshrouded in swathes of fog.

Would he return to this New World, clement but cruel, so fragile and yet so resolutely defended by its new populations? It presented a chance indeed to start from a clean slate without all the backlog of centuries of warfare, conflict, and political intrigue. There again, could New York be on the verge of becoming embroiled in imported statutes, mentalities, and traditions?

Standing aft on the quarterdeck of the merchantman, he turned his eyes starboard to the misty shores of Staten Island, where many a Huguenot had braved the journey to make a new life. Another interminable voyage lay ahead of him, he thought while scanning the farmsteads nestled in the slopes, but one nonetheless made sweeter in the knowledge that it would take him to his loved ones. And should England not hold its promise, he might well be driven to risk one more voyage to this land of hope, where he had fellowship and connections, despite the inconveniences which were far from minor. The freezing cold winters were barely tolerable for a man from the Midi of France, and then there was the constant threat of French or native invasion.

The weather remained calm and the going slow for the first days of the ocean crossing. It went without incident until the second week out, when one morning brought the sight of a distant ship. By her colours, she was ascertained to be Dutch, a Dutch fluyt, and she was heading straight into their trajectory. After some debate, the merchant captain, a commanding fellow with a bellowing voice, decided not to change course. If the rumours were true about William of Orange taking the English throne, there would be no call for them to fight off a Dutch attack.

'And if the rumours are not true?' said Jacob, listening in the captain's cabin with the crew.

'If they are not, then she might well blow us out of the water, Sir,' said the captain with a genial chuckle. 'But fear not, if enemies they be, they would aim to take the ship and cargo for the merry sum they would make.'

'What if the flag is a decoy?' said Jacob, calling to mind his buccaneering days. 'What if they are privateers, Sir, or worse, pirates?'

'Ha, then we shall be ready to fly!' said the captain with a heartier laugh. 'And you, Monsieur Delpech, shall stand by the swivel gun ready to fire!'

Jacob did not know the man well enough to determine if it was part of a show of bravery to laugh off the danger, or if his apparent bonhomie indicated that he did not take the threat seriously. Either way, incredible as it seemed, on the whim of a monarch a friend could turn foe and aim to blow you to kingdom come. Surely there must be another way to govern countries?

He pondered Darlington's vision of forming an independent state with no king or aristocracy, where only men of talent were pulled from the rank and file to govern the people for the people. It sounded preposterous, for how could common folk know about international affairs and territorial rights? Yet, would it not be better to lay a country's future with a body of men rather than with just one man designated to rule by birthright?

The Dutch ship had the advantage of coming from Europe with knowledge of the latest developments and what alliances had been made. There again, things could be worse, thought Jacob; the fluyt could have been flying the black flag, or even worse than that, the French *bleu-blanc-rouge*!

By mid-morning, the two ships were just half a nautical mile apart. The sea was calm, the wind fair and in favour of the merchantman from New York should flight be the only option.

'The moment of truth approaches, lads!' called the captain. 'Stand ready to run with the wind!'

Jacob stood at the swivel gun and prayed he would not fail in his mission, that if the time came, he neither found himself with a yellow belly nor one filled with lead.

'The Dutchman still shows no colour for battle, Sir!' called the first mate, looking through his spyglass. It felt to Jacob like the very ship gave a sigh of relief.

Ten minutes later, both ships had reduced sail and hove to so that a brief verbal exchange could be achieved as they passed.

The captains gave a salute as their vessels arrived broadside starboard. With a speaking trumpet held to his lips, the Dutch commander called out. 'News from England. William of Orange is your new king! William of Orange is King of England!'

'Is there war?' called the English captain, cupping his hands.

'War with France! Beware of French frigates!'

'Is there civil war?'

'There is not,' called the Dutch captain as the ships finished passing each other and sailed onwards into the vastness of the ocean.

*

They were carried along on a favourable wind which made the going fair though the sea became rougher, and the ride more agitated. Jacob found little to do but introspect and try to plan his first steps in London. But then, an unfortunate incident came to drive all introspection away and filled his mind for the remainder of the voyage.

After a day of slack, the wind had picked up again, and the captain gave the command to sail under topsails with a single reef. The crew were in good spirits, and the captain's cat purred comfortably on Jacob's lap while he read his only books, glad to find refuge within his mind. All of a sudden, he heard a cry, a splash, then another voice yelling out: 'Man overboard!'

Delpech promptly brushed the cat aside and ran up the steps to the main deck. Crewmen were striking sails, others running down the length of the ship on the starboard side, their eyes peeled on the water frothing at the ship's timbers.

'There, man!' called a sailor from the rigging. The mate at the aft cast a line over the balustrade so that it landed in the sea, in the trajectory of the young rigger who had slipped from his perch. The drowning sailor threw out an arm in a desperate effort to grasp the cord that would save his life. But agonizingly, he under reached. The captain gave no order to turn back, and it was not expected of him either, for everyone knew that the lad could not swim. He went under once more in the wake of the ship and was seen no more.

The death silenced the crew's merry banter and left Jacob reflecting on the fragility of life, and the sailor's one chance to live or to die.

The sombre spirits were swept aside, however, a few days later, when death also threatened the lives of the bereaved. When the crew were getting to sleep in their hammocks and Jacob had just blown out his candle, there came a great crashing din as the ship became weighed down at the stern and raised at the prow. Seconds later, a deluge came gushing into the lower decks washing the men from their slumber.

It was swiftly determined that they had been hit by a huge wave that had rolled over the stern of the ship, sending great volumes of seawater into the hold. Jacob promptly found himself in a line under lamplight, rapidly passing buckets full of water to the next man while other crew members frantically worked the bilge pumps. All night long, they pumped and baled, fearful of the next great wave that Jacob knew from past experience would certainly sink the vessel. But the gigantic wave must have been a freak of nature, for although the weather was blowy, the sea was not as big as in a storm.

The following morning found the crew fatigued but in cheerier spirits. The drowned sailor was no longer in their forethoughts, thankful as they were not to be joining him in his watery grave.

The voyage continued with fair weather and Godspeed, these two incidents being the only mishaps along the way, but which nonetheless awakened Jacob to the risks of a possible return to the New World.

At the crack of dawn, after eight weeks of ocean travel, they were heartened by the sight of the English coast near Plymouth. But the wind dropped off, and with the current being contrary to travel, they were obliged to lie at anchor near the dunes. They weighed anchor again at nightfall only to have to drop it a day later. It was another ten-day wait before current and wind came favourably together to enable the ship to set sail eastward along the English coast again. She put into port in early April, some seven miles from London, where part of the cargo was due to be unloaded.

By now Jacob's nerves were frayed to the extreme, so close was he to the place that promised to reunite him with his loved ones. He dared not think who of his family he might find in the English capital, and who he might not.

Two days later, unable to wait any longer, he managed to gain passage aboard a small, single-masted fishing boat headed for Billingsgate harbour, which Jacob knew to be a stone's throw away from London Bridge.

*

Should have used small change, thought Jacob as the single-masted fishing boat made its way up the Thames by the light of a half-moon. He had reached into his travel purse and pulled out a silver dollar to pay for his passage to Billingsgate.

The fisherman, mid-forties with a weather-worn face, had peered with alert eyes at the man with a foreign accent. 'From France, Sir?' he had said in a chirpy, matter-of-fact way.

'I am French, indeed, although France is no longer my home.'

'Ah, thought as much,' the fisherman had returned with a satisfied glance to his young mate. 'An 'Uguenot, eh?'

Jacob had answered in the affirmative while the fisherman pocketed the silver dollar and brought out a farthing. Accepting the coin, Jacob had then taken a pew amid the baskets of fish near a heap of netting at the stern. The fisherman had then pushed away with the help of his young mate into the flood tide.

Now Delpech instinctively felt under his cloak for the bulge beneath his waistcoat where he kept his belt purse, of a good deal more consequence than his travel pouch. Turning his collar to the light easterly wind, he set to pondering that these men would be his foes had the King of France not made an enemy of Protestants. How preposterous was that? And he realised the fisherman's fleeting look of suspicion on hearing Jacob's accent was no less justified given that France was now at war with England.

The square sail was rigged close to the prow, and the gentle north-easterly breeze kept it taut while the boatmen steered or heaved with their oars. The star-speckled sky and the glow of the moon were light enough to allow navigation past the looming shadows of moored vessels. The elder fisherman at the helm kept up a running commentary designating the various warships, frigates, and prison ships anchored along the Kentish riverbanks. He also reassured his French passenger, telling him of a great many Huguenots having taken the same river trip to London Town.

'Come in the merchantman, did ya, Sir?' said the fisherman, hand on the rudder.

'Yes, Sir, I did. From New York,' replied Jacob, half turning on the plank seat to face his interlocutor. Why did he have to go as far as to mention the ship's provenance? He wished he had bitten his tongue. But the chirpy fisherman was infectiously sociable and probably knew where it had come from anyway. He was probably only making conversation, thought Jacob; it was the way of city folk.

'There's money in New York, ain't there, Sir?' said the fisherman's mate between two strokes of the oar. Jacob took the young man who was standing at the prow to be the older man's son.

'I believe there is,' said Jacob, then adding, as though to put the record straight: 'That is, if you are in fur or tobacco, and alas, I am in neither. And there is no lack of hardship, not to mention the risk of invasion.'

'And pirates,' said the fisherman's mate with cheeky malice in his voice.

'Speaking of which . . .' said the elder fisherman. Then he pointed in the dark to the north bank foreshore, at the silhouette of a rotting corpse in a cage attached to a post. 'Ole Jim Baillcy. Got caught as you can see; then he got tried, tarred, and strung up. Weren't a bad show, though, was it, Wil? We was there, and now there he is. Still sailin' in the wind, ha!' The fisherman doffed his hat. The gruesome cage returned a squeak as it swayed in the wind while the boat slipped by in the smelly black river.

Jacob felt a shudder down the spine as it suddenly occurred to him that the coin he carried could be misconstrued as proof of piracy. For he had no justification as to how he had come by it. Who would believe him if he said that it was reimbursement from the very soldier who had ransacked his home and sold his possessions in France? So he decided it was wiser to simply say, if asked, that the money came from his estate in France. It was just unfortunate, he thought, that the pouch that Lieutenant Ducamp had given him contained more silver dollars and pieces of eight than French ecus.

The nauseating smell of fish was attenuated now by the river sludge, now by the rich bouquet of the spring vegetation—vegetation increasingly interspersed with square silhouettes of buildings as they neared the city.

Barely an hour later, they were passing the Tower of London. It gleamed in the moonlight and stood as proud and square as he remembered it from the time when he spent a season in London with his father. Immediately before him loomed London Bridge, with its frothing waters streaming between the cutwaters below. He looked up at the assortment of towers, turrets, and tall houses, huddled shoulder to shoulder with windows all aglow. He wondered if they still displayed heads of executed criminals on spikes on top of the south bank gatehouse, a sight that had given him nightmares as a young lad, coming as he did from his provincial French town of Montauban.

But at last, here he was, sitting in the main artery of the great sprawling city. Now, he wondered, could he remember the way from the bridge to the French church he attended with his father all those years ago? That church had since burnt to the ground, the district north of the bridge no doubt modified. But he only had to find his way to Threadneedle Street, where, following the great fire of '66, he knew from his father it had been rebuilt on the same spot. The fisherman had not heard of the church, it not being in his parish, but could direct him to the street in question.

They rounded a dung boat from which emanated the

nauseating stench of offal and the filth of beasts that grossly overpowered the smell of the fisherman's catch. Fifteen yards further on, the little boat arrived at Billingsgate wharf, where the fisherman's mate cast a line around an oak mooring post. Turning to his wealthy Huguenot traveller, the fisherman said: 'Now, up the stairs and keep going till you come to Thames Street at the top, go left and carry on over the main thoroughfare leading from the bridge. That's still Thames Street. Keep going till you get to the Cock and Bull sign in Dowgate, then go right all the way up, and you'll come to a square where you'll find Threadneedle Street if that's where your church is . . . Place will have changed a lot though since you came 'ere last, Sir, when was it?'

'Sixty-four,' said Jacob, getting up to step onto the wooden boardwalk. Jacob gave thanks and bid farewell to the fishermen.

It was not yet nine o'clock, and there was still a crowd of river folk —merchants, fishwives, and market vendors — collecting and inspecting the last delivery of the tide. Jacob, still with the stench of fish and offal in his nose, was attracted by the savoury smell of pork and roast lamb. The sudden desire to eat, the need to confirm the fisherman's directions, and the proximity of the tavern drove him to push the door into the elegantly named Salutation Tavern. He kept his ears pricked in case he heard French spoken, knowing from the fisherman that many French people had fled across the Channel. But he quickly discerned that most of the patrons quaffing ale at this hour were riverside folk, for what honest gentleman would be out in a tripling house at this hour of the night? Nonetheless, the rush of voices and the warm smells of bodies, ale, and broth filled his senses, made him feel quite heartened by his arrival in London.

Once he had ordered a platter of sausages and oysters, he said to the alewife: 'I am looking for the French church on Threadneedle Street.'

After he repeated his question, partly due to the noise, partly due to his accent, the buxom lady said: 'You wanna cut across Puddin' Lane, my love, up past the butcher's and across into Great Eastcheap.' After further guidance from patrons who knew the area, he was left with a muddled set of directions different from those of the fisherman, which had already slipped his mind anyway. But as long as he was pointed in the right direction, he could always ask along the way.

He stepped back out into the dark and dank street, refreshed and relieved, as the night watchman gave ten of the clock and all well down by the riverside. He followed his feet through the tenement streets of Billingsgate, and through a miserable square that smelled of piss where ladies sang out their compliments in gay, flat tones. He hurried along Pudding Lane where butcher's carts left vile droppings of offal in their wake as they trundled down to the waste barges. The first drops of rain made him pull down his hat and sink his head into his collar as he passed dark alleyways —alleyways where the odd drunkard or vagrant lay crumpled and snoring.

Minutes later, his face glistened in the drizzle, that same fine rain he recalled from his youth when his father had come here to study medicine. But that was back in the '60s, just three years before the great fire that had ravaged the city and rendered this part of it unrecognisable. For where there had been wooden houses and winding lanes, now there were buildings of brick and stone, and straight lanes and narrow alleyways, no doubt, thought Jacob, to reduce the risk of a conflagration spreading should one flare up again.

On turning westward into a narrow side street, he suddenly felt a shadow encroach upon him. As he half turned his upper body, he was violently grabbed from behind. A thick forearm pressed against his larynx, and he was yanked to the entrance of a dark alley.

'Help! Help!' he cried out, struggling for his life. He was thrust further into the alleyway. The next instant, he felt a blow like a cannonball hurled into his gut that forced all breath, all sound, out of his lungs. He doubled over, his lungs taut and burning from the blow and unable to take in air.

His legs were kicked from beneath him, sending him crashing down and hugging the ground. Writhing for air on the hard paving, he then felt an immobilising weight in the small of his back while deft fingers flitted around his waist with a knife.

For the love of Christ, he did not want to draw his last breath here. He spewed out another cry for help with what air he could suck in.

Still wheezing for breath, he heard a baritone voice from a short distance call out: 'Oy! You two! Stop there!'

The weight of a knee was instantly released from his back, and he twisted around, now taking in short, painful gasps, to see the two robbers take flight. Then he heard heavy boots thundering closer.

'You all right, fella?' said the same baritone voice he had just heard.

Now getting to his knees in the light of the watchman's lantern, Jacob instinctively touched the cut over his eye where he had hit the ground. 'Thank you . . .' he said to the big watchman between pants. 'None the worse for wear . . .' The large-boned man helped him to his feet. 'God bless you, Sir,' continued Jacob. 'You may well have . . . have saved my life!'

'That may be, Sir,' said the watchman, 'but I would rather wager they scarpered because they had found what they were after!'

Jacob checked to make sure his travel pouch was still safe in his undercoat pocket. It was. But then he felt for the weighty lump he always carried around his waist. 'Dear God, my purse, they have stolen my purse!'

*

The following morning, in the bleak light of the breaking day, he was greeted by the pastor at the main door of the church.

He had spent the night waiting in the intermittent drizzle, wrapped in his waxed travel cloak which had kept his suit of clothes mostly dry.

After listening to Jacob's account of his origins and his recent encounter, the pastor, a man of advancing years with an academic stoop, took him to the sacristy. He introduced him to a French Londoner, a mild-mannered but forthright gentleman in his late fifties by the name of Samuel Clement. A former merchant, having fled to London when the crackdown on Protestants in France first began, he often acted as warden in these times of abounding refugees, and as a filter to sort the wheat from the chaff. He gave Jacob some water so he could wash the dried blood from his grazed face and hands.

'Had you taken a hackney,' said Mr Clement, handing Jacob some bread and soup, 'London would have reserved you a warmer welcome, Monsieur. It would have set you back one and six, but at least you would have kept your purse!'

'Monsieur, had I known where to get one, I may well have done the very same,' replied Jacob with an affable bow as he took the bowl.

A few hours earlier, he would have been annoyed at the remark that perhaps carried with it a note of scepticism as to the existence of such a large purse. But Jacob had already stamped out his raw anger during the night while waiting for the church to open.

He could have kicked himself for his lack of vigilance, for not taking a bed at an inn, and for having blunted his awareness with one pint of ale too many. That said, the aggressors must surely have known he was carrying Caribbean money, he had surmised, and had passed through his mind all the people with whom he had interacted: the fishermen, the alewife, the patrons of the tavern who might have heard his accent and seen him paying with New World coin; the stevedores who had directed him to the fishing boat in the first place. Or could it have been just a fortuitous encounter? There was little chance he would ever know.

Sitting in the sanctuary of the church as attendants entered to prepare for the Sunday service, he was able to feel at peace and to relativise. At least he no longer carried ill-gotten coin. The lump had literally been cut away from around his belly, like a malignant tumour. And apart from minor cuts and bruises, he had escaped unscathed. Was it not then a blessing in disguise? Not really, he thought to himself, for it left him back in the grips of poverty and starvation.

However, he had escaped with his life, and any sum of money lost would be worth the sight of Jeanne and his children now. He still had his travel pouch, and he would find work; his English had improved no end, thanks to his forced piratic dealings and his time in Jamaica and New York. Moreover, on a more positive note, at least he was rid of the shadow of an accusation of piracy that had loomed over him due to the unjustifiable provenance of his fortune.

'I propose we consult the register after the service,' said the pastor before the service began, 'unless, of course, you find your wife among us this morning.'

The congregation entered. Jacob stood inside the porch with Mr Clement. While the church official perfunctorily checked co-religionists' *méreau* —a token that people showed to prove they belonged to the Protestant faith —Jacob, standing two paces behind him, eagerly watched the faces pass in the hope of seeing his wife.

The church had stood on Threadneedle Street in one shape or another since the first wave of Huguenot immigration to London in the previous century. It had since become a port of call for French Protestants to enable them to establish links for a quicker and more intelligent integration in the capital of Albion, all the more complicated now that England was at war with Louis XIV's France.

The district where it stood had become a traditional place for Huguenot craftsmen such as watchmakers, silversmiths, and cabinet makers to settle. The immigrant population, who enjoyed a reputation for excellent craftsmanship, had brought with them their habits and customs as well as whatever they had salvaged of their wealth. The sumptuous new buildings in the vicinity of the church—buildings that Jacob had seen in the grey light of morning—attested to their prosperity. Jacob observed a generally well-heeled congregation which made him conscious of how shabby he must look.

His suit of clothes, purchased in New York, was stained; his stockings were mud-splashed, one torn. And his shoes lacked lustre, with one of them missing a buckle that must have come off during the mugging. However, it was plain to most that this man standing by the attendant must be a refugee from France—as many of them had been themselves—and he met not with frowns of disapproval but with sympathetic smiles, and often a handshake of welcome.

But Jeanne was not among them. No one had even heard of her, which was hardly encouraging, given her gregarious nature.

After the service, Jacob followed Pastor Daniel into the sacristy, where the service items were carefully stowed and ledgers diligently filed away on shelves and in simple, dark-wood cabinets.

'I am sorry,' said the pastor, shaking his head dolefully after looking through the register again. 'The name does ring a bell. However, no lady or child by the name of Delpech de Castanet has declared their presence in London, which does not necessarily mean she is not here.'

'Thank you, Pastor,' said Jacob, 'but I am afraid it does. For I specifically asked my wife to find her way here.'

Pastor Daniel gave a consoling nod. He moved to a different drawer and began running his fingers over a stack of letters, pulling one out every so often for a closer look, then inserting it back into the pile.

Jacob continued: 'However, that is to some extent a relief. I do not know how she would have sustained herself, as I had given her unsound advice, not thinking I would be held up in New York, and not taking into consideration winter snowfalls in her host country —'

The pastor meanwhile had pulled out another sealed letter. He adjusted his pince-nez on the bridge of his nose. 'Ah,' he said, interrupting Jacob's discourse. 'I knew I had seen the name somewhere.' The pastor then handed Jacob a letter addressed to Jacob Delpech de Castanet, in care of the French church on Threadneedle Street, London.

With sudden fear in his stomach, Jacob recognised Jeanne's handwriting. He now dreaded the news the letter contained.

'Thank you,' he said, taking a seat while studying the vermilion seal which showed the stamp of Jeanne's signet ring. Was she still in Geneva? Had their children joined her? Had the money he had left been sufficient? And what about Robert, his brother-in-law, who had abjured and remained in Montauban? Had he been able to salvage any of Jacob's wealth? Added to the anxiety, a feeling of guilt now weighed in Jacob's heart. Guilt for not having been able to provide for them, for being caught up in the affairs of New York, for stupidly losing his money to the planter in Jamaica, and now the money he had been given by Lieutenant Ducamp.

He broke the seal, unfolded the letter.

'*My dear husband,*

'*Your letter has given me great hope. However, I am unable to leave Schaffhausen where I have taken refuge, for the snows have fallen in abundance. I am advised to wait for the thaw, indeed until the month of April when it becomes warm enough to travel across country. But do not worry on our account as we are in good company, having found refuge thanks to the friendships we made in Geneva.*

'So much has happened that I cannot even begin to tell you, but I am sure your journey has been fraught with incidents, as has ours. I say ours, but I must tell you, it gives me great sorrow to inform you that as yet I have been unable to recover our dear daughters. Only our beloved son has been able to join me, and only thanks to his brave heart and resolute nature, something I am sure will not fail to fill you with pride. Our dear daughter Elizabeth has refused to remove herself from Montauban, preferring to remain with our dear youngest baby.

'Your mother is in prison, Jacob, in Moissac, and your sister also in prison but in Auvillar.

'But bear up, my dear husband, for with the grace of God, we will be together as a family again. So please do not let this news bring you down. But rather look forward to a future date that will bring us at last peace and happiness in each other's company and in our faith in the Lord.

'Your loving wife,
'Jeanne.'

8

JEANNE HELD HER breath an instant to steel her nerves as the post carriage bore down the towpath.

One side offered the deep greens of hillside pastures, tinged with the tender lime of bourgeoning deciduous trees, the other the spectacular force of the Rhine Falls. An apt image, she thought, of her present situation as she watched the flow of water sliding inexorably nearer to the ledge.

Would she land on the bubbling white foam below, or would she splash onto the rocks? Such was the indecision she felt now, even though there could be no turning back. She had no other choice but to once more exchange the comfort and security of dwelling with friends for the company of strangers and the hazards of the elements, in spite of her apprehension of water travel.

But no matter how strong the temptation of warmth and friendship, she always managed to shoo it away on recalling her prayer to God last December, when her son lay bleeding from his terrible sleigh accident.

As he had lain livid and unconscious in the soft, freezing snow, she realized at that instant that no mortal comfort could rival the desire for the well-being of her children.

She vividly recollected how she had prayed and promised to God that she would relinquish her own comfort for the well-being of her children and the life of her son. Ordinarily, she dismissed such demands on the Almighty —perhaps through a fear of disappointment —but what would her life be without her children? At times like these, she almost regretted not recanting her faith. But there again, she knew that without it, she would be no better than a tree without its heartwood, a hollowed trunk without spiritual fibre, and that would be worse than death, for it would be death without hope.

She turned her eyes from the sliding river waters and levelled them upon her son, wedged between Jeannot and Ginette Fleuret. Though saddened by the departure, he was nonetheless eager to reunite with his father, who had sent a letter confirming his arrival in London. She noted that his hair now covered the patch on his scalp that had been cropped to access the gash to the side of his head, which he had suffered upon his jump from the sleigh. It was Jean Fleuret who had carried the boy —so he would keep warm against his large body —back to the house, where the doctor was able to properly tend to him.

The morning sunshine was dazzling and the cold blue sky uplifting. 'It is as good a day as any to embark on a long journey, I suppose,' said Claire, sitting between her husband, Etienne, and Jeanne. She had finally succumbed to Jeanne's decision to leave with the spring instead of waiting for the more clement season of early summer, when most of the other Huguenots were planning to depart.

'My very thoughts,' said Jeanne, who, with a reassuring smile, removed her hand from her muff and grasped her friend's arm tightly. In times like these, Jeanne knew the younger woman missed her mother. Claire, always the emotive one, fought hard to keep her eyes from filling.

The wagon rolled on down the sloping track, taking them closer to the embarkation point, a stone's throw from the foot of the falls. Etienne Lambrois leaned over to address Jeanne and said: 'I only pray Louis's soldiers do not resume their forays into the Palatinate. Note, if they do, I shall enlist against them . . .'

'And that is another reason why we must depart now if we don't want our road to Amsterdam to be cut off from us,' returned Jeanne, as much to herself as to her friends. They had insisted on travelling the short distance to the river landing stage to wave her and Paul off.

An hour later, Jean Fleuret was carrying Jeanne's waxed linen knapsack onto the flat-bottomed boat. It was an unnecessary action, for it was not that heavy. But Jeanne sensed the rough-cut carpenter needed to vent his tacit emotions this way, to show his care in action rather than in words. He placed the bag carefully under the best seat in the middle of the rough-hewn cabin at the aft of the vessel.

He then joined the others on the wharf, where, behind the clusters of people giving farewells to the half dozen other passengers, stood barrels and packets of merchandise awaiting the next departure. The single-mast boat on which Jeanne and Paul were to embark was already loaded with barrels and parcels tightly bound and secured. The sixty-foot-long vessel was robustly made without finery. Once it had reached its destination, it would be sold for firewood.

'All aboard!' called the master boatman, an affable man of few words by the name of Fandrich.

Jeanne's heart suddenly throbbed with a profound regret at leaving her friends, perhaps never to see them again in this life.

The boom of the falls thirty yards upriver forbade any hushed talk. It was just as well because, at that moment, if a last offer to remain until June was dropped from her friends' lips, she might not have had the heart to refuse. However, neither Claire nor Ginette gave her that opportunity. Instead, they tacitly bolstered her resolve to depart, and let her go despite their longing to keep their merry troop together forever. So, sensing their friend flinch, they emboldened her with brazen words of love and encouragement as they embraced for the last time.

The moment soon passed, and the anguish on Jeanne's face no longer furrowed her brow as Etienne reminded her of the town whence she could take the route to Amsterdam. Yes, she was sure she would not have him ride with her. Of course, she would be fine, she insisted. Moreover, Etienne would be needed at the mill, and quite possibly in the regiments of Prussia, if the French attacked again.

'But a woman travelling alone, my dear Jeanne,' said Claire above the din, again keeping herself from pleading with her friend to stay, albeit for just a few more weeks.

'Worry not, Madame Claire. My mother is not alone,' said Paul in his important voice. 'I will look after her.'

'Well said, and I'm sure ye will, my lad,' said Jean Fleuret, with a large hand on the boy's shoulder. 'But we'll miss ye all the same,' said the carpenter, who had not the strength to resist taking the boy in his arms. 'Remember what I said to ye, my boy. I want you to grow up strong with the goodness in your brave heart intact. You hear me?' The boy gave a nod as the man ticked off moisture from his tear duct. 'You make me proud, Paul, you hear? And I will be proud to call our baby after you, should the baby kicking in Ginette's belly be a boy, that is!'

'And if it ain't, we'll call it Paula, so there!' said Ginette, ready as ever with a quip.

'All aboard, Ladies and Gentlemen, please!' cried the master boatman again. Jeanne and her son took their place amid the cargo, the crew, and the other passengers.

*

The boy sat by his mother, secretly clenching her hand as the rear boatman steered the vessel downstream in the easy-moving waters, the falls now but a distant haze of mist behind them. Just the two of them again, venturing into the unknown, but now their goal was to reach husband and father.

Jeanne had learnt to sit as still as possible, wrapped in her shawls, her hands in her muff, in the most comfortable position so that the pockets of air beneath her clothes remained undisturbed and were constantly warmed by her own body heat. In this way, she could sit like a mother goose, head shrunk into her plumage, offering as little exposure as possible to the elements as the meandering river carried them between forestland and bourgeoning orchards.

By mid-morning, thankfully, the sun was strong enough to warm the timber, which gave off the sweet smell of pitch. Jeanne shared provisions and polite banter with the other passengers, who, it turned out, were all on their way to Berlin. In this spirit, they passed under the covered wooden bridges of Rinaud and Eglisau, continued past Röteln, Kadelburg, and a quantity of huddled villages. Towards the end of the day, they pulled into the landing stage on the edge of Laufenburg, where they spent the night in a wood cabin on the outskirts of the castle town.

The following morning, as per usage, the three boatmen sent the boat empty of people down the short, impracticable stretch, strewn with rocks. The passengers joined the barque on foot a little further downstream, where they were allowed to take up their places.

Despite Jeanne's initial reluctance of the river journey, only once was there any cause for alarm. They were passing under the covered bridge of Rheinfelden, where the Rhine narrowed into a bend and suddenly became fast-flowing. The boat took a bad furrow of water and soon found itself caught in a swirl. Surprised, the three boatmen found themselves in a spin and hurtling towards the rocks broadside. The master boater roared an order that neither Jeanne nor Paul understood, though the tone indicated the urgency of the situation. Scenes of the horrific shipwreck on Lake Geneva reeled through Jeanne's mind as she found herself scouring the boat with her eyes for something to cling onto, should they capsize. But two of the seasoned navigators dug in their oars in unison to bound off the rock face, while the rear boater steered with his punt to straighten the raft as it rounded the obstacle.

All was re-established, with more fright than hurt, but then a parcel the size of a pillow had become detached and fallen overboard. Paul was nearest the packet. His reflex was to reach for it to save it from being taken with the current. He managed to get both hands on the string that bound it, but on lifting the waterlogged parcel, he was pulled off balance. Jeanne saw the boy about to keel into the water and managed to grab him by his breeches just in time. The lad brought back the packet with commendations from the crew. Jeanne, however, was not in a mood to cheer, and kept the boy within her reach for the rest of the day's journey.

By evening, they made footfall in the beautiful city of Bale, to Jeanne's great relief, for neither she nor Paul could swim if by misfortune they were dumped overboard like the parcel. She was more anxious than ever at the prospect of boarding the barque once again, and the night's sleep in a tavern had not calmed her fears this time. They had not been very fortunate whenever it came to boat travel, and taking no heed of the last episode would be irresponsible if they did not turn to a means of transport more favourable to their capacities. Would going on the water again not be refusing to hear God's warnings?

'But it is the fastest way. Etienne told you, Mother.'

'I know, but certainly not the safest!'

'It is if you consider marauders, wild animals, and soldiers, though. That's why he insisted that we stay with the boat till we reach Worms, where we are to pick up another vessel to Amsterdam.'

'That may be so, but I have had enough frights on the water, thank you very much. It would be different if we knew how to swim, but we do not. And even if we did, it would still be like battling an onslaught of Titans to fight against the current!'

'That is true,' conceded Paul, who understood perfectly well his mother's tacit reference to Pierre's death. Pierre, his best friend, Pierre, who could swim like an eel, and yet who had drowned like a trapped rat.

'We shall go by land the rest of the way to Worms, Sir,' said Jeanne to Herr Fandrich, the master boatman. 'It will take us a good deal longer, I know, but we shall endeavour to catch rides on northbound carts . . .'

She was standing in the nascent light of dawn by the embarkation point; the other passengers were boarding and taking their places of the day before. The half darkness of the spring dawn was quickly growing lighter, and Jeanne could now fully perceive the pleats on the boatman's forehead, and the look of concern under his eyebrows.

He lifted his hat and smoothed back his long, thinning grey hair. 'With all due respect, Madame,' he returned in perfect French, 'I would rather see a lone woman on my boat than think of her walking that road alone. I would not have my lady walk on her own, especially not in days as these, Madame.'

'You are kind, Sir. However, I am afraid I will have to take my chances and feel the earth beneath me with the Lord as my guide.'

'Alas, the Lord will not defend you against villains and soldiers, will he now?' said the boater. 'And what will I say to the gentleman who gave me instructions to make sure you arrive safely in Worms?'

'You will kindly tell him that to arrive safely, I have taken the land route,' said Jeanne, who realised she had painted herself into a corner. For seeing the boater's genuine show of concern, she realised deep inside that the dangers would be far greater travelling without company.

However, the boatman, who had dealt with many a traveller stricken with water fright, took a different approach.

'Madame,' he said, adopting a softer tone, and holding his

hat with both hands, 'I was not going to bring the subject up so early in our travels, but news has reached my ears since last night that would give you no choice . . .'

'What news?' said Paul, looking up intently into the man's eyes.

'The French have again entered the Palatinate,' said the boater, with a glance down at the boy before appealing to the lady. 'Even if you kept to this side of the river, it is highly likely that you would encounter French soldiers, or they you, Madame.'

The French entering the Palatinate was what had delayed her journey the previous autumn. Jeanne stood wordless as the boater filled the silence. 'They may well be going further into the Palatinate,' he said, 'but there will still be soldiers patrolling. And with all due respect, a woman with a French accent travelling alone with her boy can only mean one thing, can it not?'

'That we are Huguenots trying to reach the Dutch Republic,' said Paul.

'Believe me, I have seen their work: they have no pity. They will take you back to France if they spare your life at all, I fear, Madame. You may be well aware that soldiers are not tender souls.'

'I am,' said Jeanne.

'Then, please, take your place aboard, Madame. Besides, the worst of the rapid waters is behind us. The Rhine is an old, slow river from now on.'

'I see,' said Jeanne. 'Very well, I see we have no other option, as you say, Herr Fandrich,' she said with a slight bow, and proceeded with Paul to the landing stage, her fear of the soldier a good deal greater than her fear of the elements of God.

'And laddie,' said the boater, glaring at Paul, 'if you see a parcel fall overboard, you leave it for a boater to pluck out, eh?'

'Oh, that he will, all right,' said Jeanne. But her thoughts were already turned to the voyage ahead down the Rhine, where French soldiers were prone to cross.

9

PAUL SAT ON deck, eyeing the clutches of French soldiers posted on a bridge and patrolling the quays near Strasbourg.

'It's where the French troops crossed the river to take Philipsburg,' said the master boater in German. It was in response to the boy's question on the river's great width where it meandered past the Alsatian city. By consequence, it was also shallow in places, which made it a crossing point par excellence for French cavaliers to access the regions of the Palatinate.

Continuing in French as he pulled the oar, Herr Fandrich said: 'The scoundrels then advanced on Mannheim further north and razed it to the ground . . . They gave the people a week to get out, but they had no place to go, and right in the middle of winter too. So many of them were given refuge in Worms. Running out of wheat now, though. That's what this lot's for.' He nodded to the cargo of barrels neatly stacked in rows on their sides. 'Strange times these, lad, strange times!'

As the barque slipped along with the current through the slow, meandering river, he told the lad about the sack of the Palatinate commanded by the French king to burn down towns and villages. Mainz had been razed to the ground,

Heidelberg castle partially destroyed.

'Won't we get stopped, though?' said Paul, articulating his mother's fears.

Jeanne was sitting inside on the cabin bench, hidden from view. Crudely built at the aft-most part, the cabin also housed a latrine partitioned by a drape for the convenience of the ladyfolk, of which there was now only one. The others had disembarked to continue their journey by cart to Berlin.

Herr Fandrich said: 'No fear of that. Who would feed the people otherwise? The French might be villains, but they're not stupid. They need folk to pay their taxes, you get me?'

Jeanne felt relief once they had cleared Strasbourg. She could once again sit with her son in admiration of the passing vistas: now of pretty riverside villages and rolling hills of tender-leaved trees and blooming wild flowers; now of cultivated fields and lush green pastures where the land had been deforested.

The barque carried them at a steady pace through the wide and tranquil river that presented no treacherous traps along this stretch to the experienced Rhineland boatmen. They stopped for the night at the only inn of the monastery village of Leimersheim, just five miles short of the Philipsburg fortress which harboured a detachment of French troops. Though Herr Fandrich was authorised to transport wheat for the population, there was no point tempting the devil, so he had decided to travel past the fortified town in the early hours, before the officers were at their posts. He could always bribe a lower-graded guard if need be.

Early next morning, they came into view of the flat fields surrounding the citadel of Philipsburg, situated on the right bank. Jeanne braced herself on seeing neat lines of hundreds of canvas tents. She could hear the distant crackle of the camp kitchen fire and the faint banter of Frenchmen amid the distant bleating of lambs—lambs whose lives would most likely be short, she thought, judging by the number of mouths to feed. It was a wonder that the shepherd had not herded them away from the reach of the soldiers, but then she recalled what Herr Fandrich had said about the French policy of banishing the populace.

Yet it was a strangely picturesque sight to behold as the morning sun shone down on the encampment. Female camp followers were busy cooking in the field or scrubbing down by the river; soldiers were shaving, smoking, cleaning weapons, and tending to horses. Jeanne even felt a guilty pinch of pride at the orderliness of it all.

'Part of your king's army,' uttered Fandrich, seeing Jeanne at the cabin doorway contemplating the activity of the camp.

'Not our king's,' corrected Paul, who sat cross-legged on a warm stack of barrels.

'No, not our king's,' seconded his mother.

'No, of course, otherwise, you wouldn't be on this here boat, would ye?' said the boater with a satisfied smile. 'And besides, we are in conflict with Louis, not France.' She sensed his feeling of revolt. It was right for him to test her partiality, given the affliction her country's army had brought to this land. And she was right to implicitly recall her own predicament as another victim of the Sun King. It cleared the air.

'You are certain our passage shall not be hindered?' she said.

'Like I said, we are authorised to navigate,' said Fandrich. 'The king and his henchmen have no interest in civilians, apart from collecting their taxes.'

'What about the wheat?' said Jeanne.

'They will burn down our homes if by misfortune they deem them in the way of their defences, but it is not their policy to let the king's future taxpayers starve to death. But that said, I suggest you return to the cabin, Madame.'

The boater gave a short, reassuring nod, but Jeanne had been in a similar situation before. It had nearly cost her life in prison and cost her guide his head. But what else was there to do?

'Everything will be all right, with God's grace,' said Frantz, the boater's son, sensing the lady's scepticism. A lean and genial lad in his early twenties, he understood French but spoke mostly in German. Paul translated his words, to which Jeanne responded with a polite but straight smile. She had often said those exact words herself. She had said them before the shipwreck on Lake Geneva. She returned a nod to the boater, then turned to her son.

'Paul, come inside with me, please,' she said in a non-negotiable tone.

As they rounded a kink in the river, they were met with the fortress ramparts that stood before them, firmly implanted into the river bedrock. A little further along, the grim stone walls jutted out, forming a V-shape. The fortification extended at this point to the opposing bank. Jeanne and Paul, peering from behind the drape, did not require any leaps of the imagination to understand the fort's total dominance. The cannons strategically placed on the rampart walls could blast any vessel from the surface of the Rhine.

'Steady as she goes, keep her midstream, boys!' commanded

Fandrich in German in a confidential tone, as they slowly passed between the fortifications on either bank.

Jeanne sat back on the rustic bench, and twisted her torso to peer through a knothole in the timber wall to spy the land on the left bank. It was equally occupied by the army of her home country, an army which had become the object of her worst nightmares. She had come so far, and, given the choice, she would rather die on the Rhine than be dragged back to France.

Paul was peeking through the gap between the curtain and the door frame. 'Cannons on either bank,' he said in a low voice, keeping his mother informed. He was about to say something else when a deep voice, calling from the right riverbank, caused Herr Fandrich to shout out a reply.

'What is it?' said Jeanne, moving to the opposite side of the cabin to see through a knothole that Paul had previously punched out in a pinewood plank.

'There are two soldiers on horses,' whispered the boy. 'One's waving to pull us over by the bridge a bit further down.' Paul then kept silent in order to take in the boater's answer and to process it through his brain. Then he said: 'Herr Fandrich is trying to tell them he is carrying wheat, and that his family have been boaters for five generations.'

'Dear God,' said Jeanne, her face suddenly drawn and livid. 'I knew we should have taken the land route!'

The boater stepped to the cabin doorway. 'Stand back,' he said under his breath, then swiped the drape to one side and stood half inside the cabin, reaching for his leather pouch which Jeanne presumed contained his papers. 'Fear not,' he whispered. 'Just stay inside and say nothing. I will tell them you are my wife if need be, but do not speak!'

The helmsman steered the barque in the slow current towards the right bank. The soldiers followed downstream on horseback. Once the barque was ten or fifteen yards from the shore, the boater resumed the exchange in French in a genial manner.

'Ah, vous parlez français!' Jeanne heard one of the soldiers call out. Herr Fandrich gave an affirmative answer and reiterated his purpose and right to travel, saying so in broken French. It was an old trick to flatter the soldier and make himself appear dull and inoffensive.

Jeanne sat, trying to steady her nerves and consider what she might say should she need to play the part of the boater's wife. She knew enough German from her stay in Schaffhausen to deliver short, varied replies. If the Frenchmen did not know she was French, and if they did not speak German, she thought optimistically, there would be no reason to suspect her, would there? It was plausible enough, but what about the boater's son? He was old enough to be her brother. She now wished she could have planned for this eventuality beforehand; if she had, she would have suggested to Fandrich that she was his second wife and that Frantz was born of his first wife, now deceased. But she had succeeded in duping soldiers before. With the grace of God, she could do it again, couldn't she?

The lamb bleats grew louder as they approached the riverbank, and Jeanne could easily make out orders from the camp yonder in French.

'We do not contest your right to navigate, boater,' said the soldier who had initially called out. 'We have diverted you to warn you that you had better moor at the next landing stage downstream, or it will be at your own risk and peril if you continue on your journey this day.'

'Thank you,' said the boater politely. 'But I not have far to go. Only to Worms, Sir, so with respect, I take that risk.'

'Your cargo can surely wait, can it not?' persisted the soldier.

'I . . . I rather continue,' returned the boater, 'but thank you, Sergeant.'

'Please yourself!' said the soldier, who was not a sergeant but a corporal, which of course the boater knew full well.

'Thank you,' said the boater. 'Good day to you, Sirs!'

Jeanne could hardly believe her ears. She glanced inquisitively at her son, who just shrugged. Had she understood rightly? Were they letting them pass so easily? She placed a finger on her lips to keep Paul from speaking in case, in his enthusiasm, he wanted to explain. Peering through the knothole, she saw the soldiers bring their reins over to steer their mounts away. But then, amid blowing snorts from the horses, she thought she heard a mocking laugh, followed by an ironic comment from the other cavalier, a comment which gave her cause for concern, if not alarm.

'Did he say "enjoy the fireworks"?' she asked Paul.

'I didn't hear,' said the boy.

'I could swear that is what he said . . .'

*

The mention of the comment gave rise to debate, haste, and much concern—concern suddenly amplified when, an hour later, they were navigating towards the city of Speyer.

Built around a magnificent cathedral, the thousand-year-old city was set back from the Rhine by a floodplain and wooded meadowland that rose up gently to the city walls, or rather, what was left of them. Across the field, where squadrons of French soldiers were coming and going, Jeanne could clearly see beyond the tumbledown ramparts straight into the township, which before January would have been screened by stone.

'They wanted to torch the whole city,' said Fandrich as they came level to an inlet used as a river port, 'but the burghers managed to persuade them to limit the demolition to only the fortifications. See?'

'At least people's homes were saved . . .'

'Aye, my fear is they'll try to do the same to Worms—'

Before Fandrich could finish his sentence, Frantz, standing at the prow, let out an exclamation in German.

'God, no!' said Herr Fandrich, twisting his torso to face the east city gate.

Jeanne followed the direction of the young man's index finger with her eyes and instantly saw the reason for their interjections. On the grassy space between the port inlet and the river, horse-drawn cannons were being manoeuvred to line up their barrels towards the city.

'They've come back to finish what they started!' said Georg at the rudder, holding his forehead.

At the same time, Jeanne saw a cluster of men, women, and children near the river's edge, being shoved back from the landing stage.

'They're stopping people from crossing!' said Fandrich. 'Take the boy and crouch down inside the cabin in case they let loose a shot, Madame!' Then, turning to his crew, in the vernacular he said: 'Keep right of midstream, boys!'

They swiftly glided along, keeping their heads down as close to the gunwale as possible. They did not stop at the barks from soldiers who, busy with containing groups of pleading townsfolk, soon gave up trying to hail the boat down. Their ensuing warning shots only served to scatter the townsfolk as the boat continued its course on the far side of the river.

By late morning, they reached the sacked and plundered city of Mannheim, reduced to ruins and rubble. This was the demolished city Herr Fandrich had spoken about, and the reason for his voyage to fetch his cargo of wheat.

If ever Jeanne had felt self-pity during her ordeal, it was now banished from her heart as she envisioned generations of memories blasted out of existence. No longer did she feel that underlying pride on seeing the regiment at their camp in Philipsburg. It was shame and hatred she felt now for her people, so easily subjugated by one king, one law, one religion. She, Paul, and the crew alike stared wordlessly at the sight of total destruction and desolation in the sunny May late morning, now filled with flying insects and tweeting birds. The men had removed their jackets as the boat floated with the current, oars raised out of the water, past the ruins where women were bent over in search of odd pickings of what was left of their homes.

As the men rolled up their sleeves and began to dig into the water again, there came a distant, gut-wrenching, thunderous boom.

'Dear God, they're bombarding Speyer!' said Fandrich, looking southward. It was not long before his supposition was manifested by clouds of black smoke bellowing upward on the horizon behind them. 'I think that fireworks is indeed what you heard, Madame Delpech!'

'Alas!' said Jeanne as other sickening blasts followed.

They all agreed to refrain from halting for lunch and for the men to keep rowing until they reached Worms. While Jeanne cut the oarsmen's bread, cheese, and dried sausage, Paul handed them beakers of beer from a cask. They advanced fast and wordlessly. Could their hometown be on the list too? To be bombed like Speyer or torched like Mannheim? And if it was, what could three unarmed men do to prevent the attack of a whole army bent on methodical destruction? But no one brought that question up. The men only knew they had to get there as quickly as they could to be with their family in their ancestral hometown.

10

WHEN JEANNE HAD found out that Herr Fandrich's barque would be travelling to Worms, she could not help feeling that God had meant her to purchase her fare for that boat, rather than a later one.

Worms: the city of the diet where Luther reaffirmed his theses and maintained that salvation was by faith alone; the place where the first Bible was printed in the tongue of the common people. She had imagined herself spending a couple of days strolling with Paul through its lanes and worshipping freely in its churches, savouring the moments to carry with her in her memory. The very mention of the ancient city had given her new encouragement and the assurance that her onward journey would take her to a good place, a land of hope where she could rebuild her life. But her memory of Worms would turn out to be quite different.

It was reassuring to note that, as they approached the great city, there was no trace in the late-afternoon sky of smoke behind the screen of newly leafed trees. But as they emerged from the gentle bend in the river, Jeanne could not help raising her hand to her mouth in horror.

As in Speyer, demolition work had begun on the

fortifications that had been blasted or pulled down. Great breaches in the city wall revealed half-timbered dwellings, cobbled streets, and recalcitrant city dwellers who had refused to leave their homes and their possessions unguarded. Troops were assembled at various points: before the east gates between the river and the port inlet, and around the various towers and bridged entries. They were manoeuvring horse-drawn cannons and other machines of destruction.

'Dear God! They are going to torch the whole city!' said Herr Fandrich incredulously. He pointed to the firebombs stacked in a cart, close to the main Rhine entrance where soldiers were preparing their incendiary devices.

As they came broadside to the riverbank, a short distance from the port inlet, winding the rope around the temporary mooring post, Herr Fandrich said: 'Georg, Frantz, take the wheat downstream. We will be needing it now more than ever!' Then, turning to Jeanne, who stood at the cabin door, he said: 'Madame Delpech, once further downstream, you must make for the hills with the boy and join a caravan. The whole stretch of the Rhineland Palatinate will be plagued by the scoundrels! I fear you will have to continue your journey over land.'

'I thank you for getting us this far, Herr Fandrich. I am only sorry we have arrived to such a demonstration of brutality and—' There came an earth-trembling boom that resonated from the north gate. It was immediately followed by a loud, gut-churning chorus of human cries as the tower crumbled to the ground.

'My God! Father, you cannot enter the city now!' said Frantz, whose gestures were eloquent enough for Jeanne to understand his outburst in the vernacular.

'Would you have me leave your grandmother to be buried alive?' said Herr Fandrich, jumping ashore.

'But . . .'

'You know your grandmother, Frantz. She said she would not leave her home if the soldiers came, and you know how mulish she can be.'

'Mother would have persuaded her . . .'

'I hope so, my boy. But I need to be sure! Besides, there is something else I must recover, without which we are unlikely to recover from this tragedy. Now be off,' said Herr Fandrich, releasing the mooring rope from the post. In French, he said: 'Godspeed to you, Madame Delpech . . .'

Just as Fandrich was passing the mooring rope to Georg at the stern, a mounted officer, directing operations forty yards away, turned in his saddle and hailed Fandrich with the only phrase he knew in German: 'Halt! You!' Then, changing to French, he hollered: 'Halt the boat!' He shortened his reins and pulled back, and the horse set forth at a fair canter to the temporary mooring bay.

Realising the boat would never be able to cast off far enough to be out of gunshot, the boater told his crew to hold it and looped the rope back over the mooring post.

'You cannot enter the city,' said the officer, regardless of whether the men aboard could speak French or not.

'Sir, I return just, and I fear my mother still be in there,' said Herr Fandrich.

'Your mother will have been given ample notice, boater. The town is empty, I am telling you, and dangerous . . .'

Neither Jeanne, silently waiting in the cabin with Paul, nor Fandrich was duped. For the city of sixty thousand souls was located sufficiently close to the river for them to have previously seen through the breach in the wall civilians carrying sacks and carting belongings.

The officer persisted: 'And if anyone by obstinacy has remained despite our repeated warnings, then that is down to them, and may they commit their souls to God!' He flicked his eyes over the cargo. 'That wheat you are carrying?' he intoned on his high horse.

'It be that, Sir,' said the boater, despite his son's frown. But Herr Fandrich was also a seasoned trader and knew in his bones there was no point in trying to deny it. His idea from the moment the officer hailed him was to retain as much of it as he could and cast away as quickly as possible.

'For my soldiers?' said the officer.

'To feed the people, Sir,' said Fandrich without irony. There was no point in rubbing the Frenchman the wrong way. 'I . . . I have an authorisation.' Fandrich brought out a paper from his inner pouch and handed it to the officer. He knew the officer would not read it, it being in German, and if he could, he would see that he was reading nothing more than the boater's licence to navigate. 'But please allow me to offer you a couple of barrels. My men will unload them for you here and now, then depart.'

'One-half of what you have!' said the mounted officer.

'This is a town of sixty thousand souls, Sir, but I will give you a quarter.'

'One-third,' insisted the officer, who knew full well he could confiscate all the barrels, but which would also mean making out a report.

'One-third it is, but I will ask you to let me enter the city.'

The officer did not give the second clause much thought. 'Very well,' he said, apparently amused, 'but on your head be

591

it. And bear in mind that the fires will begin shortly. You will have to be quick!'

Fandrich gave instructions to Frantz and Georg to unload and then to continue downstream and keep the cargo hidden at his brother's until the way was clear to Osthofen. Of course, he could not know at this time that the small town had also been sacked. He then stepped to the boat cabin, swiped the drape to one side, and said boldly in German: 'Wife, make haste with the boy. We go now!'

The officer raised an eyebrow on seeing the woman and the boy appear on the open deck and climb out of the barque, but he nonchalantly turned a blind eye. There was nothing to be gained by needlessly bringing complications and other officers into the deal, and the wheat would make a tidy sum for such little fuss.

*

Half turning to Jeanne, Herr Fandrich said: 'I am sorry it turned out this way, Madame Delpech, but I did not think it wise to leave you in the company of soldiers.'

They were passing at a brisk step through the lesser of the northeast gates, unguarded and a stone's throw away from where Frantz and Georg had begun unloading barrels onto the wharfside.

'You need not apologize, Herr Fandrich,' said Jeanne, with her sack strapped to her back, one hand clutching her skirts and the other clasping her son's hand. 'It is rather I who am indebted to you,' she said, while dodging horse muck and a gentleman pushing a handcart.

'Once through the west gate, you must take to the forest, where you'll find others,' continued Fandrich without slowing. 'I will take you across the city. My house is on the way to the gate. But we must hurry!'

Unable to talk for want of controlled breath, Jeanne gave a nod, and, lifting her skirts further, she ran harder behind the boater, with Paul at her side. They hurried down the main thoroughfare of half-timbered houses, past a tavern and shops where shutters had been forced open, windows smashed, and interiors looted. It was surprisingly busy for a town that was supposed to be evacuated, she thought.

They passed countless city-dwellers of every social condition, and even entire families, scurrying towards the west gate, babes in arms and children in tow, belongings stacked and strapped onto handcarts. These were the recalcitrant few, those who had refused to leave their homes. Those who had been hiding in hopes that the soldiers would leave them in peace as they had done back in January, who had refused to believe that their thousand-year-old city would be razed to the ground in a single afternoon, as if its existence had no meaning. Seeing them scuttling through the streets brought back to Jeanne a childhood memory of when, as the River Tarn broke its banks, she saw tens of hundreds of moles scampering from their burrows in the grounds of her father's country house. Of course, it was not fear of water that had brought these people out of their hiding places. It was fear of fire.

Another loud, crashing sound blasted her eardrums from the north wall as another defence tower came down, and a new smell accompanied it. 'Smoke!' cried Paul. 'Look! There!' He pointed with his free hand in the direction of the appalling noise, at flames searing up above the rooftops a few streets away.

'Looks like they've started to torch Jew Lane!' said Fandrich. 'We must hurry!'

They crossed a square where a fountain idly spurted water into a basin. They rounded the church and slowed their pace at a crossroads in the thoroughfare, with the west gate barely a hundred yards in front.

The boater pointed to a street corner, at an abandoned cart that had a broken wheel. 'Wait here,' he said once they had reached it. 'You cannot come any further. My house is too close to the wall they are cannoning. My mother is practically deaf, and if she is inside, she will not have heard the extent of the destruction. If anything happens, you must run straight to the west gate, then to the forest. And stay clear of soldiers!'

In reality, Herr Fandrich suspected his mother would have at least felt the vibrations of the crashing towers, and that she had probably fled. But he had something else to recover, something he kept in a secret place that even his wife knew nothing about. It was his hard-earned savings and the gold florins from another age that his father had passed down to him before he died. He kept it all under a floorboard, just like his father had done before him. It was a nest egg for the family, should hard times fall upon them.

Jeanne gave a nod, then placed both hands on the cartwheel to recover her breath. She watched the boater run fifty yards down to the far end of the lane, where he entered a small house that stood in the shadow of a lookout tower.

A dubious place indeed, thought Herr Fandrich, as he entered his home for the last time.

Fanned by the gentle spring breeze, fire was raging higher and faster in the Jewish district and smoke could now be seen rising up in sectors to the south. Jeanne waited with Paul behind the broken-down cart in front of a bakery for what seemed an interminable length of time. Another great belly-churning boom resounded from the north wall while she anxiously watched the last few city dwellers in the thoroughfare running towards the west gate.

But in reality, it must have been no more than a few minutes before Herr Fandrich re-emerged into the narrow street, slinging the strap of a leather pouch over his shoulder. His mother was not with him. Jeanne could have screamed out to him to quicken his step. But to her utter dismay, after a pat to his head and realising he had forgotten his hat, he about-turned and doubled back to his house. 'Now what's he doing?' said Jeanne in exasperation.

He re-emerged thirty seconds later, this time to find a pair of troopers with torches exiting an alleyway a few houses up from Fandrich's. They sauntered cockily towards him.

Jeanne stepped back into the recessed doorway of the bakery, pulling Paul by the collar so he flattened himself likewise against the boarded-up door. Peeping around the edge of the alcove, she saw a quick verbal exchange between Fandrich and one of the soldiers. She could barely hear the sound of their voices in the background of explosions and falling bricks and mortar. But she understood by Herr Fandrich's gesturing that he showed neither anger nor exasperation as one of the soldiers passed his torch to his mate.

The trooper then approached Fandrich, pulled out a flintlock from his belt, and reached out with the other hand. The exchange had brought the soldier, who she could now see was bearded, parallel to Fandrich's front door so that

Jeanne's point of view was presented with his right profile. She saw Herr Fandrich instinctively covering his pouch with his right hand, shaking his head and smiling the same genial smile as with the officer at the wharf. But these men were not officers. The bearded soldier now standing three yards from Fandrich pointed the pistol at the boater's chest. There followed a short expletive, then a click and a cracking fizz. Herr Fandrich crumbled to the ground.

Jeanne watched, her eyes wide as Dutch guilders, as the bearded soldier bent down and pulled the leather pouch from Herr Fandrich's shoulder, lifting the limp arm as if he had just slaughtered a goat.

Jeanne placed her hands over her mouth to muffle the sounds of her horror. 'My God, my God!' she murmured with incredulity while the soldiers now entered what looked like a brief wrangle. The other soldier, who sported only whiskers, shook his head, passed back the torch, and walked to the alleyway on the other side of the lane. Looking left and right, the bearded trooper then followed his battle buddy into the alley which led to the Jewish district.

Numbed, trembling, and petrified, she pulled herself from the edge of the alcove and pressed her body back against the bakery front. She let herself sink down the door, her back remaining flat against it, until she was sitting on the heels of her boots. 'Dear God. Where are you?' she murmured, her eyes transfixed in the middle distance. Then she felt a tugging at her shawl, and two small hands alighted upon her shoulders. Paul gently shook her. 'Mother, Mother, come on, Mother. We cannot stay here!'

There came another thunderous crumbling sound, this time of bricks and mortar. A house must have caved in a few streets away. It shook her from her torpor, and she looked squarely at her son as the sound of marching boots filled them both with urgency and a new dread. Advancing a few paces into the main thoroughfare, through the dust and smoke she saw with horror a battery of field artillery filing in through the west gate, in a blurry stream of crimson and fire. Torches in hand, they were turning southward towards the cathedral.

She could not bear the thought of a confrontation with any soldier, let alone with an entire battalion. And what would she say if they were stopped?

But then, glancing in unison with Paul to her right towards what Fandrich had called the Jewish district, they perceived another route out. A narrow side street slanted off the main road to the city wall, or rather, where the wall had stood. For at the end of the backstreet, there was a gaping breach of fallen stone where she could make out the hazy figures of a few city dwellers climbing through it, fleeing for their lives.

The air was growing thicker with smoke blowing in from the houses ablaze at the north wall. But she realised that mixing with the fleeing townsfolk was their only chance of escape. She reached for her son's hand, and needing to reconnect with humanity, brought it to her cheek, cupped and kissed it before striding back to the corner to fetch her sack that she had taken off her back.

She took a last glimpse at Herr Fandrich, lying on the ground at the end of the lane. But to Paul's surprise, she just stopped and stared. 'My God!' she said, unblinking. She could have sworn she saw an arm move. It flexed again from where it had been dumped by the soldier and flopped to the boater's side.

'He must still be alive!' said Paul, looking up at his mother.

'Yes, and we cannot leave him there!'

'But what if they come back?'

Jeanne had grasped the principle of the layout of the city, which consisted of main thoroughfares with lanes running off them. These lanes were also criss-crossed by narrower lanes or alleyways just wide enough for a handcart to pass through. In the boater's lane, Jeanne now noticed two alleys that must give access to side entrances into yards and houses, tucked away within a block of buildings. She pointed to the one a dozen yards down from the crossroads where she and Paul were standing.

'That must run round to the alley further down, where the soldiers first came out,' she said. Then she looked down at her son and gave his hand a squeeze, and they made a dash across the mudded lane, neither seeing nor caring what they were treading in.

They followed the alleyway around the block of humble dwellings to the alley nearest Fandrich's house by the north wall.

The soldiers who had continued into the alleyway on the other side of the street were nowhere in sight. Jeanne and Paul scurried to Fandrich to find him drenched in his own blood, but still breathing. He let out a groan as Jeanne and Paul dragged him by the boots into the dark alley, away from the lookout tower that threatened to crush Fandrich's house at any moment.

'He's badly injured, and he's too heavy for us to carry,' said Jeanne, on her knees, inspecting the wound to the boater's bloody chest. She was back to herself, sharp and practical, and was thinking that, if seen, it would be plausible enough to pass themselves off as the spouse and son of this injured townsman. 'We'll need a handcart or something to carry him . . .' she said, turning back to Paul. But the boy was already running back down the alley. 'Paul, come back!' she called out in a loud whisper.

'Saw a handcart on the way,' said the boy, twisting his torso round to answer in an equally loud whisper. 'Won't be long,' he said, then shot off. She could do nothing else but let him go.

She was wondering how they would carry the boater over piles of tumbledown stone in a handcart when Fandrich half opened his eyes. He turned his head, and, in a faint voice, he said: 'Leave me . . . Madame, save yourselves now . . .'

But Jeanne's attention was elsewhere, and she put a finger to her lips as the sound of boots and French voices drew closer in the lane.

'Where's he bloody gone!' said one of the voices which, she presently ascertained, belonged to the bearded trooper who had shot the boater down and stolen his pouch. 'Told you, man! We shoulda thrown him into his bloody shack and torched it!'

'He's been dragged,' said the other soldier. The pair of them cautiously followed the trail of blood across the cobbles towards the alleyway, a few houses further up.

Jeanne had silently got to her feet, had backtracked down the alley a few yards, then had stopped at a high wooden gate, painted green. She silently tried the latch to find it open, pushed the gate to reveal a boater's yard.

From the entrance of the alley, the soldiers saw the body on the floor, five yards in. They caught a glimpse of a woman's hand as the green gate closed. 'You go through the house!' said the bearded trooper in a low voice to his accomplice before striding to the green wooden gate, where he paused for a moment. He stroked his moustache and lasciviously squeezed his chin with his free hand. Then he booted the gate open to reveal a yard that contained a handcart, ropes, and an array of hooks, short masts, and cordage. He also saw a handsome woman, no doubt the wife of the man he had shot, running to the back door.

Jeanne had her hand on the iron handle when she heard the sound of boots resonating in the corridor inside the house.

The bearded trooper to her rear slowly laid down his torch by the gate as if he did not want to frighten a wild animal.

Jeanne, on turning, noticed Herr Fandrich's leather satchel slung over the trooper's shoulder, and another larger, bulging bag as she eased her way slowly back into the court.

'You'll do, my pretty German maid!' said the trooper, moving slowly towards the handcart that stood between them. 'Don't be shy now . . .'

Knowing what he had done, knowing what he was about to attempt, Jeanne stood erect, superior, no longer wanting to hide behind a false identity. And in a controlled, fierce, and forceful voice, she said: 'You should be ashamed of yourself, young man!'

The trooper, momentarily taken aback by the woman's outburst in French, glanced over to his fellow looter, now standing on the step of the back door.

'Bet she's a Huguenot toff,' said the fellow looter.

'Are ya?' said the bearded trooper, looping the syllables in the direction of Jeanne, who stood, steely-eyed, in anticipation of an attack from both sides.

But the accomplice looter just chortled and said: 'We all know what happens to Huguenots, don't we? One good thing, though, she ain't likely to tell tales on us, is she?'

'What d'ya mean?'

'Come on, man, now's not the time. We got Jew Street to do before it burns. And she's hardly gonna be running into the arms of the captain, is she!'

'Oh, I ain't letting this one pass, colleague. I'll catch you up in a mo'. . .'

'Suit yourself, man,' said the fellow soldier, leaving his mate alone in the yard with the Huguenot toff.

The bearded soldier, with one sly eye on the dame, placed his musket against the wall, unstrapped his cumbersome bag, and let it drop to the ground. He could see her trying to figure out which way to run, her eyes flitting this way and that, but there was no chance of getting out; he had her cornered. It was cute, though, and all the raunchier given the fact he had never had the pleasure of a toff, let alone a Huguenot toff.

'You stay away from me!' growled Jeanne, and tried to think of something better to say to get him talking, to delay the inevitable. If she could make him turn around the cart, she could grab his musket. But then what? How did it work? Did you just pull the trigger? What if it wasn't loaded?

But the soldier was in no mood for playing cat and mouse. He had much to do, many houses to plunder, and he was not going to waste any more time. He just wanted to shoot his bolt and be done. So he feigned to approach slowly; then, in a surge of brute strength, he rammed the handcart against the fence, cutting off her escape route. He grasped her, pulled her towards him.

She struggled, beat his chest, scratched his beard as he

spun her round like a puppet and forced her face down onto the handcart deck.

He clenched her from behind, squeezed her pleasing bust, and latched onto her by the hips. Then, keeping a strong, firm weight in the small of her back with a forearm, he began lifting up her skirts.

She roared with rage, managed to wriggle free, twist herself round, and pull him to her so he could not get a swing in. She felt for his side, gripped his knife, pulled it out of its sheath. But he smiled a mischievous, lubricious smile, wrapped his hand around her slender wrist, and directed the knife to her throat.

'Just relax, duchess,' he said in a low, menacing voice, 'and everything will be all right . . .' He pushed her flat against the cart deck, nudged her thighs apart with his knees. But then, he keeled over.

She looked up at the space previously occupied by the bearded face and saw the butt of the soldier's musket, then the intense brow of Frantz as she dropped the knife onto the cart.

Frantz reached out a hand to her, fetched her up off the handcart deck.

'Thank you,' she said, brushing her skirts down. Bending over the soldier lying unconscious on the ground, she wrenched the leather satchel from over his shoulder. 'Your father's,' she said, handing it to Frantz. 'He is still alive . . .'

'I saw,' said Frantz, urgently turning back towards the yard gate where Paul was now standing. There was no time for awkwardness. After Jeanne persuaded Frantz to refrain from finishing off the soldier with his own flintlock, they directed their steps through the alleyways and backstreet to the north wall.

Frantz transported Herr Fandrich, still barely conscious, in the handcart. Within ten minutes, they were at the breach in the wall by the Jewish district. Frantz carried his father in his arms while Jeanne and Paul dragged the cart over the rubble to the other side.

By now, French troopers were torching the houses in all districts, throwing firebombs onto thatches and detonating mines. Townsfolk who had refused to leave were pleading with soldiers on foot and officers on horseback. But it was clear these men had a job to do and, ignoring the protestations, went about it in a businesslike fashion, no doubt to distance themselves from the calamity of their acts. A few who did answer the protestations more often than not did so in jeers and scorn, then set light to cloth and thatch, like they were taking pleasure in braving the forbidden but exquisite act of destruction.

Frantz, gritted teeth and bare arms hard as brass, wheeled his father behind Jeanne and Paul as they melded into the stream of townsfolk fleeing to the high ground among the trees. These were the ones who had not wanted to abandon their homes until the last moment. Now they marched onwards in silence, their ancestral city all ablaze behind them.

*

The appalling clamour of crumbling mortar, followed by the dreadful cries of people losing their heritage, had intermittently broken Jeanne's slumber that night under the trees.

Now the skyline over the city of Worms was paling. In an hour, it would be day. In an hour, the full horror of the destructive binge would no longer be an incredible nightmare: it would be a reality etched in their memories.

Already some folk were stirring; men stoking fires, women heating broth with whatever edibles they had been able to take with them.

As Jeanne sat back against a pine tree, Paul's head on her lap, she glanced round at Frantz, sitting by his father who was laid stretched out on rags. 'How is he now?' she said in a soft voice.

'Not different since the doctor dug out the bullet,' said Frantz, keeping his voice down so as not to wake the boy. He spoke in French, with scatterings of German when the French words eluded him.

'What did the doctor say?' said Jeanne. 'If he makes it through the night, he might recover, didn't he?'

'Yes.'

'He lost a lot of blood, though.'

'And he would be dead by now if it was not for you.'

'And so would I be if it weren't for you, Frantz,' said Jeanne, touching his forearm.

'You can thank your boy for that, ein gescheiter Bursche! He hailed us down as we were putting out, ran along the wharf yelling out till we heard him . . .'

'What will you do now?'

'Take him to my uncle's, where I think my family are. If he dies, I want him to be with family . . .'

'What can I do?'

'There's nothing more; this is not your war. You must continue westward as you started, Madame Delpech. I heard some folk will be heading that way on foot. Go with them to Bingen. Once past Bingen, you'll be safe. That is where the Rhine narrows into a deep gorge, and you will be able to travel safely by river the rest of the way.'

11

THREE DAYS AFTER the torching of Worms, Jeanne and the boy sat with blistered feet on the high ground overlooking the port town of Bingen.

It lay huddled around a knoll upon which stood a run-down medieval castle. Down by the riverbank, she could easily make out a horde clustered around the landing stage. A handful of French soldiers were supervising the Palatinate exiles who were queuing to embark on the next rivercraft.

She took a moment to contemplate the beautiful spring morning. Wild flowers stood all abloom in the meadow around her. Only the hum of flying insects and the distant clonk of cowbells interrupted the peace.

The previous days had not been too unkind either. Whenever it showered, at least she and Paul had been able to find shelter in a barn or among wide-leafed trees with the rest of the contingent they were travelling with. And being able to answer calls of nature in a timely fashion—without the embarrassment of having to hold oneself over a latrine at the stern of a moving vessel—by far made up for her aching feet.

She had a thought for Herr Fandrich. He had made it through the night. After sunrise, he had opened his eyes and, like Frantz, bid her and the boy farewell. She had insisted on helping them in their onward journey to their relation's house. But Frantz had urged them to move on with the group of folk who were taking to the road. And if experience had taught Jeanne one thing, it was to travel in company, the more the merrier, although of course there was nothing merry about these bedraggled exiles.

A great many of the townsfolk of Worms had remained in the vicinity with the intention of rebuilding their homes from the ruins of the inferno. But a whole host of them had decided they could no longer bring themselves to return to a charred home in the knowledge that, even if they rebuilt it like in '77, it stood a fair chance of being burnt down again. Such was the fate of those living in the Palatinate, straddled as it was across the contested river Rhine.

They had trekked across the hills of the Palatinate, passing haymakers agog and shepherds agape. Oft-times, they were able to shelter in barns where, since heifers and cows now stayed out at night, they had the good fortune to put their heads down on straw. Time and again, they witnessed the horrors of the French King's scorched earth policy. It left standing no building that could serve the armies of the League of Augsburg, and forced more devastated people to join the ranks of the exiled. And yet, the war had not officially begun.

It put Jeanne's own predicament into perspective. And now, as the vast majority of the forty or fifty fellow travellers had done, she put it to the far reaches of her mind and focussed on the present moment, the lovely and precious present, no longer giving a thought for the future.

Having kicked off her boots, she was now rubbing her

swollen feet. 'I can no longer put one foot in front of the other,' she said.

'Neither can I,' said Paul, who was sinking his bare toes into a lush patch of clover while resting his chin on his knees.

Jeanne looked down again at the Palatinate exiles that she had let go ahead. Word had got out that civilians were allowed to get away to the Low Countries. And sure enough, she had observed the crimson-and-blue-uniformed French soldiers letting the leading batch board a previous vessel.

'What do we do now, Mum?' said Paul, following her gaze. She turned back to him with a smile, a youthful smile. It always melted her heart whenever he called her "Mum" instead of "Mother," as convention dictated by his breeding. But here in the open countryside, there were no conventions, just the living, breathing, lazy air of burgeoning summer all around them.

'We have a choice,' she said, tightening her smile. 'Either we walk to Amsterdam, which means another fifteen days' trek. Or we risk taking the next boat.' Jeanne nodded back towards the port below them, where a large rivercraft was coming to moor.

'But there are French soldiers down there,' he retorted.

'Yes, but they will take us for civilians from the Palatinate. I don't think they will be much bothered about catching Huguenots.'

'But we can hardly show our papers, can we?'

'Neither can many of those we travelled with. We can say they were lost to fire.' Then, glancing down at Paul's feet, she said: 'Careful of the bees, darling. You don't want to get stung.'

*

The flat-bottomed rivercraft could carry at least fifty passengers, thought Jeanne. So it should be able to carry her, Paul, and the remaining folk waiting at the landing stage, where people from Bingen had provided food and drink.

They shuffled along with the queue. Jeanne counted five French soldiers controlling the embarkation. Two were barring the access to the gangway so people could pay and board in an orderly manner. They had set up a table behind which one of them was seated. Two more were keeping the queue in order. And another one was servilely assisting with loading bags and young children, and collecting tips. Though the latter had his back to her, his gait seemed strangely familiar. But in the anxiety of the imminent departure, she brushed the notion aside, put it down to nerves or coincidence. For who could she possibly know in the French army?

The uplifting babble and children's laughter from the crowd came as an antidote to the gloomy drudgery of the previous days. It was a cheerful interlude, a suspension of sadness, bathed in the comforting warmth of the sun. Psalms were sung in German, adding to the comfort and excitement of the "excursion" into the lowlands, to a new life. But Jeanne knew it would not be just plain sailing and, just as she had experienced before them, these Palatines would soon hit upon the harsh realities of integrating a new culture and language.

However, living life in the present enabled Jeanne to experience the benefit of these moments of solace. They helped her to keep going, thankful in the knowledge that the river would soon take them away from persecution for good. While standing in the queue, she had observed up front a number of Palatinate women alone with young children, passing without papers. It was confirmation that they would not require a passport as long as they paid the tithe.

She looked down at Paul, standing brave and ready to play his part. He had inherited her ear for accents, she mused. As he was so young, his brain had worked like a sponge in Schaffhausen, absorbing the new language with his comrades of play, a language of which she had only gained a rudimentary grasp. But at least they looked like any other Palatine traveller; their clothes, though of quality fabric, presented no finery. Paul wore a brimmed hat, and Jeanne had pulled her shawl over her head as had many of the women to hide against unwanted glances and the sun, though gentle it was.

'Der nächste, bitte!'

The syllables struck like a hammer, flattening her musings as the previous passengers, having paid, advanced up the gangway to board the riverboat.

She steeled her nerves, threaded her arm through the strap of her knapsack, and advanced with her hand on her son's shoulder to the landing stage gate. The soldier in a blue frock coat flipped his hand to prompt her to move more quickly. 'Schnell, schnell!' he snapped, in the assumption that this lady was a German Palatine like all the rest.

The other soldier, a young sergeant with a benevolent, moustached face, smiled upon her approach from the camp table behind which he was seated. But it was the older fellow, standing six feet tall with stubble on his chin, who quick-fired the questions in a gruff voice in German.

'For two?'

Jeanne nodded.

'Where you from?'

'Worms,' returned the boy in German.

The balmy-faced soldier noted the information in a logbook open on the table, while the older man told her the price to pay to board. She well knew this was illegal and unethical, but at least it meant these soldiers were more preoccupied with financial gain than with catching Huguenots. A lesser evil, perhaps, that would enable them to move on. She lowered her eyes to conceal her look of scorn as she placed the silver thalers she had previously prepared on the table.

'Papers?' continued the tall soldier in German. But his question, alarming though it was at first, quickly allayed any anxiety, for it was indeed a question. It was not an order to hand over a passport. Like some of the ladies she had observed before her, she simply shook her head.

'Lost in the fire,' said Paul in German.

'Can't she speak for herself?'

'Not since the fire,' returned the boy.

The soldier stared at them for an instant, then acknowledged the statement with a curt nod and told them the price for travelling without papers. This, too, was an abuse of power, scornful and illegal. Jeanne nevertheless unshouldered her sack and dug for the extra coin.

But as she lowered her head, in the corner of her eye, she caught sight of the servile soldier lumbering up the gangway. He was striding back in a syncopated gait to fetch another bag for which the previous family had paid a surcharge. A sudden surge of blood sent her heart pounding as she raised her hand to her mouth. The man had a mutilated thumb.

She flashed a glance at the other hand, only to see it also had suffered the thumbscrew. She now recognised the laboured gait of Monsieur Crespin. Céphas Crespin, who was also known to her as the pauper. The pauper who had gained her trust with the intent to rob her. The pauper who had abandoned drowning people at the shipwreck on Lake Geneva. The man who had attacked her, beaten her, and left her for dead. What should she do?

Buying time, with her back to the gangway, she made as if she was scouring her sack. She brought out an empty hand, looked the tall man in the eye, and shook her head. She grabbed her son's hand and prepared to leave, pressing Paul's shoulder for him to make haste. But the boy did not need a cue, for he had followed his mother's look of panic and also had seen the mutilated thumbs of Crespin.

'Hey, lady!' called out the balmy-faced sergeant. He pushed away from the camp table and hopped round to intercept her. 'Where you going?' he continued in French. Jeanne did not answer. Instead, she gave a curt shake of the head and continued onwards, back towards the queue.

The tall man by now had stepped over to translate into German. The sergeant affably insisted, 'Tell her she can pay in food, sausage, or whatever takes her fancy.'

Taking care to at least let the translation begin, she shook her head resolutely.

The boy looked up at the soldiers with purpose. 'We will see later,' he said.

'In that case,' said the sergeant to his subordinate, 'tell her she can take back her fare. We are not thieves, are we, lads?'

'What's up?' called out an oily, smiling voice before the translator could finish. 'Little lady got cold feet, has she?'

Jeanne recognised the all-too-familiar voice of Céphas Crespin, and he was lumbering up towards her.

She dared not turn around. Keeping one hand on Paul's shoulder in front of her, she pulled her shawl more tightly around her bust and head with the other hand.

'Where she from?' said Céphas Crespin, now standing between the table and the remaining queue of a dozen people.

'Worms,' said the translator.

At that moment, Jeanne felt a hand claw the top of her shawl and rip it from over her head to reveal her swan-like neck and her fine brown hair tied up in a chignon.

They might have been able to outrun the decrepit pauper, but there was no chance of escaping these young men, who were now joined by one of the troopers previously positioned to watch the queue.

She swung round. Her hairpin fell out and let tumble her miniature Bible. But it was no big deal; here, everyone was a Protestant. The soldiers let it lie where it was.

Jeanne looked Crespin squarely in the eyes. He had a full beard now that covered half his face, which explained why she had not made the connection on seeing him from a distance. She recognised his pockmarked cheeks all right, though, and the snarl on his upper lip as he smiled at her vacantly, without emotion or recognition.

'Can't pay the surcharge,' said the sergeant.

'Where she say she's from?' said Crespin, who was by far the oldest of the soldiers.

'Can't talk, but the boy says they're from Worms,' said the tall translator.

Céphas Crespin turned back to the lady. He then smiled his deliberate fawning smile of old, the smile he had perfected to gain her trust when carrying fabrics for her at the church in Geneva. Now it only filled her with disgust and scorn. And she loathed him all the more for pretending to give her hope that he had somehow not recognised her.

''Course she ain't paid,' said Crespin, keeping his eyes dotingly fixed upon her. 'She's a rotten, stingy Hugo!'

With a self-satisfied smile, he bent down to retrieve her miniature Bible, while the sergeant gave the nod to his subordinates to arrest her.

But Jeanne's hatred of this man bending down at her feet was all-consuming—this man who would have slit her son's throat for a bagful of booty. She was oblivious now to the men attending her as she screamed out, 'You evil wretch! You evil, obnoxious wretch!'

Slipping her arms free from the soldiers' hold, and mustering all her might, she delivered her boot into the pauper's smarmy face, into the scoundrel who would rather loot dead bodies than attempt to save drowning people. As he rose up, cupping his nose, she then kicked him between the legs. And again she kicked him as he staggered in agony until the soldiers, hampered by the boy and protestations of injustice from some of the exiles, at last managed to pin back her flailing arms and drag her away.

*

An hour after the riverboat had departed, Jeanne and the boy arrived by packhorse at a field encampment.

After enquiry, the sergeant was directed to the top of the camp, where the commander was inspecting the field guns. Young Sergeant David suddenly realised how ridiculous he and his crew must seem, escorting a woman and a boy. Camp followers looked on with amusement amid catcalls and hoots from soldiers cleaning their arms and playing dominoes. The escort seemed excessive. It reminded him of a time when he was out hunting for game one day and found himself with five other huntsmen, beating about a single bush to get a pheasant to come out and take flight. But he could hardly double back now.

He was beginning to loathe Crespin's influence, the easy coin made by cashing in on the exiles' desperation, and now the arrest of a Huguenot lady on foreign turf. It was not as if they could put her in prison. What would they do with her?

It gave Jeanne no joy either to hear the softer consonants and vowel sounds of her mother tongue as she marched along the alley of bivouacs, where soldiers and their ladies eyed her speculatively. How could her journey of escape end here after so much hardship? Paul would be taken from her. He would be brought up by Jesuits, who would end up hammering their dogma into his skull until they had cracked it like a nut. He would be broken, brought up to fight for the king, and die a young man on one of his battlefields.

The commander was in discussion with his artillery man where the field camp met a meadow of long grass and wild flowers. Sergeant David approached with his cortège. It comprised three soldiers, a corporal with a bloodstained nose, a young boy, and a fine-looking lady of noble carriage. The commander's curiosity was piqued enough for him to suspend his conversation. With a flourish of the hand, he granted permission for the young sergeant to speak.

'Monsieur le Marquis de Boufflers, Sir,' said the sergeant. 'We encountered no enemy, the only encounter being of a religious nature more than anything else, Sir.' Sergeant David then glanced over his shoulder to where Jeanne had been told to halt with the boy. They were flanked by two soldiers on either side.

With his foot on the carriage wheel of a twelve-pounder, de Boufflers placed an elbow on his knee and his chin on his fist. But before he could respond, the corporal with the blood-splashed nose stepped forward from the right flank of the female prisoner. 'Permission to speak, Sir,' said Corporal Crespin eagerly. He was not going to let this squirt of a sergeant fifteen years his junior get all the credit. 'I recognised the lady from my surveillance days in Geneva, Sir.'

'That is true, Sir,' said Sergeant David generously. 'There would have been no call to arrest her otherwise.'

'She is a Huguenot,' added Crespin, in case the allusion had escaped the marquis. He handed him the miniature Bible in support of his statement.

'Name?' said de Boufflers.

'Delpech, Sir,' said Crespin, 'Jeanne Delpech.'

'Countess Delpech de Castanet,' corrected the lady, standing erect. Inside, however, she was submerged in mixed emotions of fear and fury. For she realised she was standing before the very man who had caused the loss of her social position, the death of her child, the imprisonment of her husband, and the estrangement of her baby and eldest daughter.

She recalled her sister relating to her how he looked when he had first entered her hometown of Montauban. He had shown then, too, the characteristic arrogance and nonchalant flick of the wrist that pertained to the generation bred in the manners of Versailles.

'Where are you from, Madame?' he said in a polite fashion.

Jeanne stood proud but speechless before the architect of her sufferance.

'Come, speak up, Madame, we have not got all day!'

But still she stood tongue-tied. Then she felt a hand clasp the bun of her chignon, and heard the voice of Crespin. 'You've been asked a question —owww!' The last word was punctuated by a sudden cry of pain as the boy placed his boot in the shin of his mother's aggressor. The pauper turned and clobbered the lad, who promptly fell to the ground.

'Don't you dare!' said Jeanne, who was held at either elbow by the soldiers who flanked her. She shook herself free, then reached for the boy, who had picked himself up off the floor and was rubbing his cheek.

'Where are you from, Madame?' said the marquis more firmly, which made everyone remember their places.

'I am from Montauban,' said Jeanne, at last, having released her vocal inhibition. 'A place you know well, Sir.'

'Indeed, Madame. Wonderful town, too hot in the summer, though. But the people are understanding and most welcoming!'

Jeanne no longer saw the illustrious commander in uniform, but a churl being ironic in the most callous and unchristian way. She was suddenly inhabited by a rush of fury.

'You, you scoundrel!' she said. 'You take yourself for an honourable gentleman, but you, Sir, are no more a gentleman than this leech here!' She gave a flick of the head towards Corporal Crespin on her right and persisted, narrowing her eyes, in restrained wrath. 'You have ruined my family, invaded my home, taken my children, and sent my husband across the world. In the name of what saint or devil, I ask you!'

'In the name of political and religious unity, Madame,'

said de Boufflers, quick to follow up and removing his foot from the carriage.

'I am a Christian, Sir, and I am French!'

'But you are a Huguenot, Madame!'

'And proud to be so, Sir, like all the Protestants of this land. And know, Sir, you will never break my spirit; you will not break that of my son either. I would rather die and face my Lord and judge!' She felt herself succumbing to her anger, sliding dangerously out of control. So, standing firm, she shut her mouth, not because de Boufflers had held up a hand as if to stop an onslaught, but because she knew she must find a valid reason for this man of war and strategy not to send her back to France. He would be more irritated than moved by an appeal founded on emotion alone.

'That may be so, Madame,' he said with superior calmness. 'However, as you can imagine, I have other preoccupations than self-righteous Huguenots to think about . . .' He made a discreet gesture to encompass the line of cannons parked on the edge of the field camp.

'Then let us go,' said Jeanne levelly. 'You cannot take me back to France! Moreover, this is not French soil. You have no right to hold me here!'

'Sir,' said Crespin, slipping in with his insistent, droning tone, feeling that his revenge was slipping from his grasp. 'Shall I put them somewhere, Sir?'

'What, and mobilise three soldiers, Corporal?' said de Boufflers.

He was in a lethargic mood that afternoon. And he was weary of the scorched earth campaign, fatigued by the company of soldiers. He turned his head away towards the meadow of long grass and wild flowers, bathed in late-afternoon sunshine.

Although this lady did not look particularly fashionable in her modest garb, she did have breeding. She had character, too, and he liked a lady with character. It was what had attracted him to Madame de Maintenon. The lady was right; this was not officially French soil . . . at least, not yet. He could not argue with that.

He turned back to her. 'Countess . . .' he said with a nod, and tossed her Bible to her. But to everyone's astonishment, she visibly took this as a cue to leave. She grabbed the boy's hand and stomped clean off into the meadow.

'Sir? What shall I do?' said a baffled Sergeant David.

De Boufflers was gazing wordlessly across the meadow where the sunlight was lending the long grass a golden tinge, as the lady and the boy made a trail through it. *Delpech*. He had heard the name before; now he remembered. Delpech, of course, the merchant gentleman who would not renounce his faith, and neither could he shut his mouth for the life of him. He had sent the man packing to God knew where and used the little family as an example to those who might be tempted to convert back. And for all intents and purposes, it had been a success. At least, it had done the job during his appointment as colonel-general of the dragonnades. Anything else no longer mattered, for unity had been forged in France.

'Halt or I'll fire!' called out Crespin. He had understood from de Boufflers's previous remark that there could be no prisoners. In other words, some things in wartime were better done differently, and he had primed his matchlock musket with powder.

Jeanne, resolute, did not break her stride. She would not go back to France to spend the rest of her life in prison. And she would not allow her son to be broken. She clenched Paul's hand tightly as she heard the sound of a charge being rammed into the barrel of a musket. But she strode on through the lush green grass, amid the late-afternoon sunshine and insects all abuzz. She now locked eyes with Paul, who smiled back with a look of determination that told her he understood and accepted the risk. He reciprocated her squeeze of the hand.

The pauper cocked his match while de Boufflers still stood in contemplation of the lady and her boy. So this is where her destiny has led her, he thought, back into the wolf's mouth; how strange. Of course, he had experienced similar coincidences, and he knew that they meant nothing. This one, though, would make for excellent conversation material at court.

'Halt, I say!' called Corporal Crespin, who then blew upon the match cord to kindle the embers, and opened the pan, giving the smouldering cord access to the gunpowder.

'Sir?' said an anxious Sergeant David, who knew that Crespin rarely missed a target.

At last, de Boufflers raised his hand to hold the fire. But Crespin had pulled his arm sharply to his shoulder and had the boy nicely in his sights. The proud lady would live the rest of her life in remorse for the death of her son. It would teach her to play with a Crespin. And besides, he was only interpreting orders. So he squeezed the trigger nice and smoothly without the slightest jerk. But the instant he did so, a downward blow struck the barrel of the musket.

'Leave it, soldier!' said de Boufflers, letting go of the barrel as the countess swiftly yanked the boy into her path. She glanced back over her shoulder, then strode onwards with her son in front of her. 'She will not be broken,' said de Boufflers.

'But, Sir . . .'

'Let her go, man. Instead, pray for your own rotten soul lest you die on the field. Your section will be fronting the action in the morning!'

12

IN BEAUTIFUL AMSTERDAM, Jeanne was relieved to experience life without the constant threat of being pounced upon by French soldiers.

And the wait in the bustling merchant city par excellence had the advantage of allowing her and Paul to rest their sore and weary feet. They were staying at the tall canal-side house of a Huguenot who had made a new life there as a clockmaker. The Dutch, though austere in appearance, loved to spend their money on non-wearable luxuries, and his timepieces were much prized.

A methodical, clever, and neat man with a spiritual understanding of the universe, Monsieur François Barandon no longer regretted the fortune he had lost to the French royal coffers. He had moved on, and besides, his former wealth had certainly already been spent by the war-hungry king, whereas his new fortune, born of his own hard work and talent, was growing. The narrow house built over four storeys, its lavish furnishings, its well-stocked basement and loft, proved it.

'Dear Madame Delpech, I am certain that your husband, resourceful as he has previously proven to be, will no doubt turn his talent into silver again,' said Monsieur Barandon to

Jeanne one day. They were seated at table in the high-ceilinged dining room whose walls were beautifully painted with bucolic scenes and pictures of trees laden with fruit.

'The problem is not his lack of talent,' returned Jeanne, lowering her pewter fork, 'or his hard-earned knowledge, but the fact that laws learnt in France cannot be applied to foreign cultures as can techniques of time craft.'

'That is true, François,' said his wife, an impeccably dressed and robust lady in her mid-thirties with her fair hair drawn back into a coif. 'We should count ourselves lucky and thank God for the choices you have been given to make.'

'Does that mean that God has not helped my father, then?' said Paul, who should not really have spoken at all. But as his young mind evolved precociously due to events, he had begun to take liberties. The Barandons' young daughters, just a year or two younger, sniggered at his gall.

'Paul, dear!' said Jeanne, though finding it difficult to justify reprimanding him. He had been her travel companion, and she had come to treat him almost as an equal despite his age.

'The boy is quite welcome to speak his mind in this house, Madame Delpech,' said Monsieur Barandon with a reassuring smile. 'Come, lad, now's your chance to develop your argument, and we shall see if we can answer it.'

'Well, otherwise, he would have made Father choose a trade that would bring him prosperity in adversity, wouldn't he?'

'An interesting point,' said Monsieur Barandon, lost for words. Jeanne came to the rescue.

'No, Paul, dear,' she began in a condescending tone, 'it does not mean that at all. God has given us the liberty to make our own way through life, and sometimes life deals blows that cannot be anticipated. Otherwise, we would have left the country many years ago, as your father used to say we should. But what God has given us is the ability to strive on in adversity, and strive on we must if we love him, and we will be rewarded in life as befits our expectations. And for the time being, it is for our family to be reunited under the same roof.'

So I was right after all, then, thought Paul, who had begun to suspect that God was not playing fair at all. But he kept these thoughts to himself, for fear of upsetting his mother.

'Amen,' said Monsieur Barandon. 'And let us pray that your father will remain strong in faith to strive forward despite the odds life and the devil throw at him. And let us in the same way give thanks to God that I have the blessing here today of your company to remind me how the cards of life are not evenly dealt.'

That evening, Jeanne lay awake in the large feather bed, wondering how in the world Jacob could weave a livelihood in London.

*

Two hundred and sixty miles across the Channel, Jacob lay wondering how he could have fallen from grace so quickly.

He was forty-five today —forty-five and no place to call his own after having worked hard all his life. He had overcome hurdles of oppression time and again. Time and again, he had picked himself up, dusted himself off, and set forth on his battle horse, all to end up in middle age living in two rooms in a lowly district outside London. And to top it off, with no talent for the manual trades that Huguenots so often excelled at, he saw his remaining monies dwindling at an alarming rate in the horribly expensive English capital.

It was unfair, but to dwell on it would be to give in to self-pity. In the sallow light of a candle lamp, with a hand on the twinge in his back, he sat up on the edge of his rope bed that sagged in the middle. His eyes fell upon the little acorn faces—each representing a member of his family—lined up in a row on the straw seat of a wooden chair that he used as a bedside table. No, actually, he had not lost everything, he reminded himself.

He stood up and removed the straw tick mattress. Then he got down on his knees on the rough floorboards and reached for the straining wrench, a mallet, and a couple of pegs which he kept under the bed. These were the tools for tightening the rope that was threaded the length and width through the holes in the oak bedframe. Next, picking up the slack with the wrench and wedging the taut side with a peg, he began methodically tightening the rope that formed the bed base, pulling it hole by hole on alternate sides so that he could at least sleep tight. Then he put back the mattress and made his bed.

Feeling better for the exercise, he sat back on the edge of his tightened bed and picked up the book lying on top of his Bible on the chair. Monsieur de Sève had handed it to him the previous week at the coffeehouse behind the Exchange.

Jacob had met Philippe de Sève at the French church. A Huguenot from Berne, ten years Jacob's junior, he had lost his wife and their child in France during childbirth. He had arrived in the English capital a few weeks before Jacob. Both being of southern stock, they had formed a solid friendship from the start and rendezvoused every day at the coffeehouse on Birchin Lane, a five-minute walk from the church, where they could catch up on events in France and in England. They kept up each other's spirits, and made plans for a later date that would see them in partnership to take advantage of their Huguenot connections inside France.

Jacob flicked through the book. It was titled *The Compleat Soldier, or expert artillery-man.* On handing it to Jacob, Philippe de Sève had told him of Marshal Schomberg's defection from the French army, having refused, like so many veteran soldiers of his generation, to recant his faith. The duke may have been one of France's greatest generals, but he was too close to the grave to risk losing the way to eternal peace in heaven.

'Schomberg has laid down his sword to William and Mary,' de Sève had told Delpech that late morning in the crowded coffeehouse. It being pleasant and balmy, Jacob recalled the place being alive with chatter, laughter, and shouted greetings. The doors and windows had been flung open, though the sweltering air was still heavy with the fragrance of roasting coffee and tobacco smoke. Jacob and Philippe had sat head to head in a walnut booth so they could hear themselves speak, their hats and frock coats hung up on a wall peg above them. 'The king has commissioned him with raising an army, my dear Delpech.'

'Good Lord, is he going to fight against his king?'

'No, an English one. James Stewart is in Ireland, preparing to retake the English throne . . .'

'Not good. That would mean a Catholic king in England!'

'Precisely. That is where we come in, my good fellow, us and thousands of Huguenots like us. Schomberg is keen to enlist good cavaliers and men of quality. There is no reason why we cannot both put ourselves forward. I am told by

Monsieur Despierre that we would receive a lieutenant's salary. As much as seven pounds two shillings, my word!'

Jacob remembered choking on his pipe at this point during the conversation. He had spent many a restless night torturing himself over how to regain what he had lost, nay, how to provide for his family and pay his rent in the coming months. 'I should say any salary would be welcome,' he had said, wiping a moist eye and lowering his pipe.

'It is a godsend, Delpech. It stands to reason,' de Sève had returned with cheer.

Looking back on the scene now as he flicked through the pages of the soldier's guidebook, Jacob realised the pay was very attractive indeed when you considered that a carpenter only got one-seventh the amount. The new English king must be very keen to keep his new throne, and Parliament just as adamant to stave off a Catholic return, he thought. However, he did not think, as did his friend, that it was a godsend to send men to the battlefield, rather the work of the devil or higher powers on earth. But he had kept the notion to himself in the coffeehouse, there being many other Huguenots elated to fight against any allied forces of the French king—a king who had banished them from their own homes and confiscated their lands.

A leaf inside the guidebook fell from between the pages to the floor. Jacob bent down and picked it up. On it was printed a ballad titled "The Protestant Courage." Jacob read the first verse:

'Sound up the trumpet, beat up the drum,
Let not a soul be subject to fear,
Since the true pride of all Christendom,

Does against France in valour appear,
The courageous worthy seamen,
Does from all parts to London advance,
For England's promotion, they'll fight on the Ocean,
Against all the strength and power of France.'

The *power of France* could well be thought of as the dethroned English king, Jacob thought, as de Sève had argued. For was not King James financed by the coffers of Louis XIV, who was providing men and arms?

Jacob did not want to go to war against his own country, though. Neither did he want to kill or be killed. But Philippe de Sève had reassured him that they would not be on the front lines. And besides, it was out of the question to let a cousin of the despotic king plague the lands of refuge.

Jacob slid his legs onto the bed, now taut, glanced at the acorn faces on the straw chair, then snuffed out the candle, condemned as he was to go to war.

*

Philippe de Sève also rented a room in the timber-framed tenement building on the narrow, unpaved street east of Brick Lane. In fact, it was de Sève who had advised Delpech to take the second-floor rooms before they were snapped up, given the continuing influx of Protestant refugees.

The digs were spartan, the plaster between struts and beams was cracked in places, and the coarse timber floorboards at first made Jacob almost lose his balance. But the two rooms, one street-facing, the other looking out onto back yards of the new constructions, were spacious, cheap, and, being on the second floor, relatively well-lit.

It did not take long for him to spruce the place up and give it a godly sheen, knowing Jeanne could arrive at any moment. It was bad enough asking her to reside in the poor district outside the city walls; he could not expect her to live without the bare necessities as well. So, thanks to church contacts and the travel money which had not been stolen, for a good price he was able to purchase simple but sturdy furnishings: an unpretentious four-poster which came with a trundle bed underneath, a dining table and straw-seated chairs, an upholstered two-seater, a wardrobe with a glace, appropriate bathing equipment, and a three-panel screen for privacy. The church supplied him with crockery, covers, and bed linen.

It was cheap, and the area rough, but it meant he would not have to ask for alms from the Huguenot church to pay the rent. Like this, at least there would be one place where he could hold up his head, and keep up the pretence of bourgeois etiquette.

Jacob had paid his rent that morning to his landlady, a top-heavy, large-hipped lady in midlife who occupied the first floor with her cat and memories of her late husbands.

Mrs Smythe was far from being the pleasantest of Londoners Jacob had met. As de Sève put it, she was a paradox unto herself. She took their rent money with one hand and with the other was ready to shoo away all the aliens back to where they came from, to *fight their battles on their own turf*, as she liked to say. By *aliens,* she especially meant the French, who had brought with them their fancy dressmaking skills and silk-weaving techniques. 'Bless my soul, London is not the place it was!' she would blurt out whenever her eye caught sight of a passer-by in the Frenchified fashion.

Mrs Smythe owned the weaving workshop on the ground floor, which she had taken over after the death of her first husband, a weaver by trade of Flemish descent. She was beginning to feel the pinch of the influx of French weavers whose unparalleled mastery and extravagant variety could only previously be procured at much expense from the famous looms of Lyons. Lustring, velvet, brocade, satin, *peau de soie*, fine ladies' mantuas, corded silk called ducape, and fabric of mingled silk and cotton—all of the highest excellence—were becoming the new norm. By consequence, Mrs Smythe's plainer fabrics were fast going out of fashion, and she had reduced her workforce to just an aging part-time journeyman called Alf, an accommodating man of few words who ran errands, fixed the loom, and delivered the cloth to clients; Nelly, a seventeen-year-old seamstress whose parents had placed her with the childless widow of her second uncle once removed; and her good self.

Thankfully, she was able to rent out her upper-floor rooms for increasingly higher prices, paradoxically thanks to the workforce from across the Channel, which enabled her to balance her books. Like Jacob, having been driven out of home and country with little or nothing, these skilled refugees craved work and vied for lodgings in the cheap parish east of the city walls, currently under development for their accommodation. The allotted area was known as Spitalfields. And it was a stone's throw away from Mrs Smythe's house.

Jacob sat in the comfortable, albeit worn, upholstered armchair he had retrieved from a church acquaintance. He had put on the shoes he had waxed a moment earlier, and now sat staring at the wooden cross he had nailed to a support timber. He was feeling pretty low, wondering how on earth he could escape from the infernal spiral that had time and time again relieved him of his wealth. It was moments like these, when his mind was empty, that he found himself prey to his inherent bourgeois fear of becoming destitute.

But a familiar knock on the door brought him back from his thoughts and put a brighter tempo into his heart. He pulled himself up and stepped to the door, which he opened knowing full well who he would find on the other side.

Philippe de Sève was dressed in a black suit, a white lace collar, and white stockings despite the season. A black felt hat crowned his head, from which his natural cavalier locks cascaded onto his shoulders.

'Good day to you, dear fellow,' said Philippe, standing before the door. 'Magnificent start to the day!'

'A fair morning indeed,' said Jacob cheerily, closing his front door behind him.

'Let us hope it will bring us as fair news,' returned Philippe. They stepped to the narrow stairwell, so narrow in fact that Jacob had been obliged to use a long rope cast from the window to hoist his furniture inside.

Jacob knew full well what his friend was referring to. But Jacob's hopes were not at all focussed on the imminent announcement of their mobilisation. He hoped, as every morning, to receive news of Jeanne via the church on Threadneedle Street.

'I was wondering,' said de Sève as they continued down the rickety wooden staircase, 'do you think we are to wear our uniforms on the way there?'

'You mean to join the regiment?'

'Yes, bearing in mind that we are permitted to join them as we see fit. We are not obliged to leave with them from London.'

'Well, I suppose it would make us rather conspicuous,' said Jacob. 'On the other hand, it would make for a lighter pack if we did.'

'Fair point,' said Philippe. 'I must remember to enquire while you are at church. It will make a change from this suit I purchased from that Dutch puritan I told you about. Why, I verily feel like a condemned man.'

'Ha, wait till you get your first pay, my dear friend, though take guard not to overindulge in the colour such as myself. I do feel such a pillicock in this bright blue . . .'

Whenever they walked down the narrow and uneven staircase to the first floor, they normally hushed and trod carefully. But in the exuberance of the sunny morning after a week of summer showers, they both overlooked their habit until it was too late.

The landlady's front door cracked open. Then Mrs Smythe, dressed in her grey overdress, beige bodice, and white apron and bonnet, appeared overtly industrious with an old birch broom that had seen better days.

It was still early in the morning, and Mrs Smythe would not be down to the workshop for another hour. She looked haggard, her hair as lustreless as dried broomcorn. She had spent another sleepless night wondering how long she could hold on to Nelly, who was also her first husband's second niece once removed. Maybe she could let her go two days a week until more orders came in; it would not be long before the autumn winds reminded ladies of their winter wardrobe. But then, the girl might go and find work with the enemy.

On the other hand, why did she not just give up the ghost and rent out the workshop to the Frenchies? She would if she could, but she knew deep down that it was beyond her. It made her cringe and toss and turn in her sheets at the mere thought of it. The small outfit had been started by her first husband when they were young, her husband whom she had loved.

The two Frenchmen gave her good day as they made footfall upon the landing.

'Why can't you talk in English?' she said with her usual frankness and sardonic smile.

'We do, Madam,' said Jacob, smiling politely, 'but is it not normal to speak the language of one's homeland with a fellow countryman?'

'Get away with you,' she said, giving half a sweep, then stopping again as the gentlemen tried to edge their way past her. 'And how does anyone know you're not popish spies plotting against the king, then? We're not daft over here, you know,' she said with a fearsome glare.

Jacob paused a moment on the landing. With his arms crossed, he peered down into Mrs Smythe's clever but anxious eyes. Standing erect, he said: 'Then I invite you to follow us now, and you will see where we go every morning.'

'And where's that in English, then, if it isn't the coffeehouse?' challenged the landlady.

'To the French church, Madam, the Protestant church!'

'To the blimmin' church? Ha, why, bless my soul,' said Mrs Smythe, shaking her head incredulously. 'If my first husband could hear you now, he'd soon talk some virility into youse, all right. I mean, aren't you gentlemen supposed to be looking for work? Church is for Sunday, for heaven's sake!'

Did he really have to listen to this? He had remained as polite as humanly possible. Were he in a stronger position, he would give her a piece of his mind. But besides the fact that this was not his country of birth, he felt all the weaker because he had no revenue and therefore was not paying taxes. He had little doubt that Mrs Smythe suspected that it irked him not to be pulling his own weight. Or perhaps he was just being overly sensitive.

Refusing to enter into a fruitless debate, Jacob bowed his head and gave the woman a stern farewell. She swept after them as if to shoo them away, as they went bundling the rest of the way down the stairwell. She knew as well as they did that she could easily find other lodgers should the need arise, and fetch a higher price for the rooms given the increasing demand.

Philippe de Sève's riled glance to Jacob needed no words as they stepped into the street. Delpech pursed his lips and chased away a fat bluebottle. The city stench rising with the heat of the morning sun made Philippe turn his nose into his scented lapel. But at least the lane was dry, littered with splashes and turds thrown from chamber pots, but mostly dry. They passed by the open square of land, the tenterground, where already women were laying out their cloth tautly on the tenters. Philippe tipped his hat politely to one of the young ladies.

'Good day, Mademoiselle,' he said in French, which was no less common an occurrence nowadays than giving good day to an acquaintance in the streets of Pau. Indeed, the jabber that arose from such gatherings of ladies often resounded in French. The young lady gave a coy smile and a bow as she continued hooking her woven fabric tautly on the wooden frames, to keep it square and prevent it from shrinking.

'Would you have a twinkle in your eye for an apprentice weaver, de Sève?' said Jacob in a surprised voice, as they entered an alleyway where cats were lounging half in the sun, half in the shade.

'Are you afraid she might be below me, Jacob?' said Philippe in jest.

In fact, Jacob's surprise was only a half measure. He had experienced a similar egalitarian feeling of excitement in the new colonies. For the new refugees, London was a place where the usual social fences had not yet been erected and the customary exterior signs of wealth not established. Everyone was more or less in the same boat.

'In fact, I do fancy I might take a wife on my return, actually,' continued Philippe.

'And good for you, Sir!' said Jacob brightly. He had seen his friend on the wretched days when his loneliness made him haggard. For unlike Jacob, Philippe had no family reunion to look forward to; his loved ones were all dead, his solitude all-consuming. 'And would you be planning on becoming a rag merchant?' said Jacob in banter.

'Oh no, my dear fellow. We have our master plan.' Philippe said it in jest, but Jacob was nonetheless secretly reassured to hear it. Philippe went on. 'I dare say in a few years' time, Londoners will have as much choice of home-made fabric as in France!'

'And not only fabrics, my good fellow,' said Jacob, recalling the respected watchmakers and silversmiths he had met through the church. 'I dare say that soon, the only French merchandise that we shall be able to ship exclusively from France will be crops and wine!'

'And that is where we come in, Messieurs Delpech and de Sève, Merchants of London!' said Philippe with a flourish of the hand.

'And lucky it is for us that planters cannot bring with them our clement skies of southern France!'

At the end of a narrow alleyway, they came to the busy thoroughfare that met with Whitechapel Street from Hare Street and the open fields east of Shoreditch. This was the appropriately named Brick Lane, where cartloads of bricks were trundled into the city from the kilns in the fields.

'It will be an avenue from London all the way to the village of Hackney, according to some,' said de Sève as they crossed the rutted road, still unpaved at that end.

'I have no doubt it will,' said Jacob, 'considering the number of brick carts I have seen passing through here every day of the week; it is truly phenomenal. The city seems to gobble them up at an astounding rate! I am given to believe, too, that Spittle Fields will no longer be what its name suggests.'

'Spittle Court, they should rename it,' said Philippe, 'if the building petition goes through.'

There was business indeed in building houses made of brick, thought Jacob, amazed at the multiple opportunities that the monstrous city offered a man of means. But means is what he and de Sève lacked. So they had agreed to pool their earnings once they were decommissioned, with the aim of entering into business together.

'Bonjour, Messieurs,' said a gentleman, walking with his wife who Jacob recognised from the French Church. Both Philippe and Jacob gave a polite bow to the acquaintance and continued on their way westward. They took the route past the modest, pretty weavers' dwellings of Fashion Street, then along the old artillery garden until they arrived at Bishop's Gate Street. The wide thoroughfare was already heaving with streams of horse-drawn traffic, mostly headed cityward, and hawkers crying out their wares.

It was not long before they found themselves at their usual parting point under the sign of the Flying Horse Inn, near Bishop's Gate. A carthorse was drinking at the trough, others were lined up to carry their passengers into the city, and sedan bearers stood ready with their black chairs to carry their fares through the alleyways and backstreets where horse travel was forbidden.

'I shall meet you at the usual place, I hope with news of our leaving date, my dear Delpech,' said Philippe.

'It is a fine season to be going on a journey,' said Jacob. 'It will be a welcome change to get out into the fresh air of the countryside, I must say. Meet you at the coffeehouse later!'

The two men set out on their separate ways, de Sève heading westward towards the new artillery ground. Jacob continued through Bishop's Gate, down the wide and traffic-choked avenue towards Threadneedle Street as he had done every day since settling in Albion.

'Prithee . . . make way!' came a deep shout from behind as he entered the street in question. He niftily stepped aside to let strong-armed bearers carrying a sedan chair scurry by. Jacob watched it glide past him, no doubt on its way to the Exchange. It reminded him of his brother-in-law's account of how his wife was forced by brutes of the French army to spend the night with her newborn baby in one such chair. It was during the month of August, four years ago almost to the day. While she was in labour at her sister's, Jacob had been forced to serve soldiers who had taken over his own home. Had he known she would be thrown into the streets just two nights after the baby was born, he would have thrown down his life to relieve her. But by the grace of God she had endured, and escaped to the country. She had found a winter sanctuary in one of his brother-in-law's farmsteads. But come spring, her baby and children were wrenched away from her when she was forced into hiding to avoid imprisonment. Having since travelled across the world, would he have rather chosen to recant, now knowing the suffering and destitution his allegiance to his Protestant faith would bring to him and his family? He could not say.

The peal of church bells chiming in the hour and another hawker's cry prompted him to instead contemplate the city's awakening, to distract his mind from thoughts of his family and how they had been able to manage without him. He continued to remind himself that God had given him such trials for a reason, saved him from others perhaps to live to fight another day. Nevertheless, he had not expected to enlist one day to fight on a battlefield.

It was eight o'clock. The shuffle of people on the pavements thickened: well-heeled gentlemen heading for the Royal Exchange, labourers in working attire, and ladies with baskets on their way to Wool Church market. He was glad for the daily pretext for a foray into these more sumptuous streets, rebuilt after the great fire, a welcome respite from the district where he now resided. It was a well-hooved district and a testimony to the wealth of opportunity the city had to offer. If he could muster enough funds with de Sève to create a decent investment pot, he might well be able to build up his fortune again. He might well one day be walking with those merchants to the great temple of commerce, the Royal Exchange.

There was much to do beforehand, though. For starters,

there was a war to be won, and then there were the restrictions imposed on non-natives to be tackled.

At last he came to the new French church. The early-morning service being over, it was virtually empty. No sooner had he entered the cool brick building and bowed in reverence than he was greeted by the pastor.

'Monsieur Delpech, I was expecting you.'

Jacob's heart leapt—the pastor was hobbling excitedly towards him from the vestry, and he was brandishing a letter.

A note from Robert might bring him news of monies recovered; one from Jeanne would bring him the love he needed right now to go on.

Jacob took the letter. 'Thank you, Pastor,' he said. 'Thank you very much.' The old man gave a wordless bow and left him to the discretion of a rear pew.

Jacob sat forward, half closing his eyes. But he could not bring himself to pray that the contents would be good tidings. The news it contained was already written, and there was nothing any prayers could do to alter the facts.

He recognised Jeanne's elegant handwriting. At last he broke the crimson seal. Anxiously, he unfolded the letter. In the hunger for information, his eyes could not track whole sentences from start to finish, but singled out key words. They picked out 'Palatinate,' 'refugees,' 'Amsterdam,' 'ship,' 'London,' 'soon,' 'Paul,' 'August.'

'Dear God. Thank you, thank you!' he whispered as he sat back, the sheet trembling in his hand. He swallowed, steadied his nerves, then read the letter again sentence by sentence from start to finish.

*

638

Philippe could hardly wait for Jacob to take a seat opposite him.

'Schomberg wants to leave in early August while the weather holds,' he said excitedly. 'We are to attend training in uniform from tomorrow morning until we head for Wales for the crossing to Ireland.'

They were sitting in their usual haunt on Birchin Lane off Cornhill. Jacob had just paid his penny and ordered a bowl of the black, gritty drink that he took with a pipe to take away the bitterness. The exuberant chatter and chink of crockery made any discreet conversation impossible. But Jacob did not mind; he had his own news that he wanted to shout to the world.

'Yes, I heard. Bumped into Monsieur Lafont, who was on the way to the chophouse,' he said while the serving boy nonchalantly filled his bowl, pouring the thick coffee from considerable height. 'I only hope I see my wife beforehand!' Jacob's boyish grin broadened irresistibly into a wide smile.

Philippe, who sported a pointy beard, brought his pipe from his mouth. Wide-eyed, he said: 'Why, my dear fellow! Is she due in?'

Jacob gave a curt nod which allowed him time to quash the surge of emotion. 'Yes,' he said at last as the boy moved on to another table with his jug of coffee. 'I received a letter, says she's in Amsterdam, that she's getting the next ship to London.'

'Do you know when?'

'She says they are to embark once enough passengers have been accounted for. I imagine they could even be here in a matter of days . . .'

'Or weeks,' said Philippe, grasping the tail of his goatee.

'The only thing is, Jacob, we are to join up with the regiment in Wales in ten days.'

'Then we shall try to hold back as long as possible. Are you with me?'

'I am, Sir!' said Philippe, raising his cup.

'Good, then we shall go to the chophouse for lunch to celebrate!'

*

The following morning, Lieutenants Delpech and de Sève walked down the staircase of the Smythe tenement building, their boots falling heavily on the steps. Mrs Smythe, broom in hand, stood agape at her door upon seeing two dazzling soldiers dressed in pearl-grey frock coats and breeches, and white neck scarves and sashes. It was a uniform she did not recognise, for it was the uniform of the Huguenot regiments of King William of England.

'Madam,' said Jacob, tipping his felt hat as Mrs Smythe scuttled backwards through her door.

13

JEANNE AWOKE TO the insistent tugging at the hood of her cloak and the strident cries of gulls.

She cracked open an eye to see the dawning day filtering into the gun deck through the hatches, bringing colour to the huddle of fellow passengers. She turned her head to the caress on her cheek. 'We're in London, Mother,' said Paul in a low, excited voice. He had returned from above, where Jeanne could now hear shipmen scurrying about the deck in response to the orders heartily hailed in Dutch.

'Klaar voor de kaapstander!'

'We are coming to anchor,' continued Paul, his eyes bright and shining like two silver shillings as the folk around them—some propped up against posts and barrels, others lying willy-nilly upon the deck timbers—groaned into consciousness.

Blurry-eyed, the passengers began to gather their meagre belongings, some their yawning offspring, while bundled babies suckled at their mothers' breasts. People began looking around like alert stoats, wondering whether to abandon their places and make a move to the upper deck where the air, though chilly, was at least free of the foul smell of bilge water and the like. But their choice for the time being seemed to favour the latter, inured as they were to the stench of unwashed bodies, and sick and pisspots.

For Jeanne, the immediate relief was that of arriving safely to port, for the crossing had been rough at times, causing people to puke in unison. She had never travelled in a cargo ship over the open sea, and never had she been so fearful as when the boat had rocked and swayed far more than the craft on which she had travelled on Lake Geneva.

However, the general feeling of deliverance that accompanied the end of any seafaring voyage lay largely muffled under the anxiety of now facing the unknown, in a different language, and in a nation presently at war with their country of origin.

The clomping of boots descending steps diverted the voyagers' attention to the hatch, where a stout Dutch gentleman—the same who had shepherded them onto the ship in Amsterdam—hummed and clapped his hands together. 'Ladies and Gentlemen,' he said in accented French, standing on the second step from the bottom. 'Welcome to London Town. Please make your way above deck in order to board the wherries that will ferry you ashore.'

Jeanne shouldered the sack she had used as a pillow. Then, holding onto her son's hand, she followed the queue of passengers up to the main deck, where they were met by the soft, golden light of early morning.

Even the nauseating stench of river sludge and city offal did not quell Jeanne's amazement at finding herself suddenly in the middle of a great sprawling metropolis. Awestruck, she stood with Paul at the starboard balustrade. Her gaze passed along the north bank, where tall, shabby timber-framed dwellings and riverside warehouses touched shoulders with palatial buildings in the shimmering light of morning. 'That's the Tower of London,' said Paul, pointing to the white tower on their right. 'It's where they keep traitors before they are executed,' he continued, proud to impart knowledge recently acquired from a rigger as they had sailed up the Thames at dawn.

Jeanne slowly scanned the riverbank from the Tower, past Custom House to Billingsgate wharf, wondering how on earth they could fit into such a jungle of stone, bricks, and mortar.

'And that,' said the boy, motioning to his left as though he were announcing a theatre act at a fair, 'that is London Bridge!'

It was an extraordinary sight for a provincial lady to behold. What a pageant of light and fantasy, she thought, facing what seemed like a thousand windows reflecting the first rays of the sun. 'Why, it's a whole village on a bridge!' she said as her eyes followed the roofline. She marvelled at the hotchpotch of gables, turrets, and cupolas atop houses, many of whose first floors extended thrillingly over the water.

The boy pointed towards the south bank gatehouse. 'That end is where Papa said he saw heads on spikes when he came here with Grandpa,' he said, amused at the look of disgust on his mother's face. But thinking about it, she remembered that Jacob had indeed stayed in London as a young man, and probably could still speak the language. Her heart pulsated with a new ray of hope. Could this truly be the land of opportunity Jacob had spoken of?

The Dutch merchantman lay at anchor amid a flotilla of tall ships and small craft, waiting for a landing dock to be able to unload. Meanwhile, the refugees were brought by wherry to the north bank by the dozen. Jeanne and her son descended unsteadily into one such rowboat—used ordinarily to ferry Londoners the length and breadth of the Thames—and were soon being given a hand up the slippery stone steps before Custom House. It was August 14th.

Some of the passengers were met in an effusion of joy by friends or relations, who stepped out from the crowd waiting twenty paces back from the steps. They had been tipped off as to the arrival of the long-awaited ship by a church messenger, who had received the news that the vessel had entered the Thames estuary. Jeanne and Paul scanned the dock in the hope that their eyes would meet those of their husband and father.

A welcome committee of ladies and gentlemen stood to one side, ready to direct those without relations to temporary accommodation. Behind them, Jeanne recognised the faces of passengers who had been ferried ashore in a previous wherry. However, she was about to find out that she would not be joining them, that she would not need to count on the kindness of yet another stranger.

A white-haired pastor with a Genevan accent, holding a notebook and a graphite stick, opened his arms in welcome. He gave instructions in French that those without prior arrangements would be catered for and should wait with their fellow passengers until the wherries had transported everyone from the ship.

'But before you do,' said Pastor Daniel, 'please step forward if your name is on my list here.' The little party stood in expectation, with their effects at their feet. Both Jeanne and Paul continued to scan the crowd for late arrivals. In fact, they had not stopped scouring the scene since they descended from the ship into the wherry. But their eyes had still not found what they were looking for as the pastor's croaky voice read out his list of names.

'Monsieur Brocard . . . Madame Cazenave . . . Monsieur Dalençon . . .' he said, leaving a pause between each name for the owner to step forward. As of yet, no one had. He went on. 'Madame Delpech de Castanet.' Again he paused and looked up. But lost in the search for her husband, Jeanne was not sure she had heard right. Paul, who had not missed a syllable, tugged her hand, and they both stepped forward.

The priest gave a brief smile and motioned to them to stand next to him, then continued with his short list. After a few more names, it turned out that, of all the passengers, Jeanne's name was the only one on it.

As she stood by the pastor, she dwelt on why her name had been singled out, why Jacob had not come to meet them. Was he ill, or worse? She turned to Paul, whom she sensed was trying to decipher the pleat in her brow. She touched his cheek in a gesture of mutual comfort.

'Madame Delpech,' said the pastor some minutes later in French, having introduced himself as the pastor of the French church on Threadneedle Street. 'I have a letter for you from your husband.'

'Oh?' said Jeanne. 'Is there anything wrong?'

'Rest assured, Madame, nothing wrong, no.'

'Then why could he not meet us himself?'

'He had to depart, Madame. However, he has left you a key to your accommodation, which I will be only too glad to accompany you to, once you have registered and taken refreshment at the church.' Jeanne thanked him and tried not to let her disappointment show. But the pastor nonetheless sensed her confusion. He said: 'He was obliged to leave four days ago with his regiment, Madame.'

'His regiment?' said Jeanne, somewhat taken aback.

'Yes, Madame, he is a lieutenant in King William's army. I would not be surprised if he had already made landfall on Irish soil by now.'

14

STANDING BY THE campfire with his bowl of beef-and-pea soup, Jacob contemplated the lough, its calm waters shimmering in the dawn.

The stench of mudflats—populated with wading fowl—mingled with a hint of heather that wafted down from the emerald hills. And the acrid tang of black powder floated over the port town of Carrickfergus.

Jacob, like ten thousand other Huguenots would do, had answered the call to join King William's army. It gave the Huguenots honourable employment and allowed them to potentially cross swords with their persecutors. For word had got out that James II's army in Ireland was to be supplemented by Louis XIV's soldiers. The first challenge was to oust the deposed Catholic king's forces from the Protestant towns captured in the north. As the Jacobites retreated, they plundered settlements and villages, burning everything they could not take with them. It was the same scorched earth policy Louis of France had resorted to in the Palatinate.

It was August 28th. Jacob and Philippe were among the two-hundred-strong cavalry regiment that had disembarked six days earlier at White House, located between Belfast and

Carrickfergus. The former had been relieved of Jacobites, who had retreated southward upon the arrival of Marshall Schomberg's main army. The latter was still occupied by a pro-Catholic Irish garrison composed of one battalion and nine companies. Their mission was to slow the English army under Schomberg as much as possible to allow James time to rebuild his depleted army after his failed attempt to take Derry. Before retreating within the town walls, they had put flame to any building that might serve the Williamites.

Jacob took another sip of his savoury soup. Then he turned his gaze to the web of masts that stood like a hundred Protestant steeples upon the smooth and peaceful lough. Peaceful, that is, since Schomberg had ordered the royal ships to menacingly train their guns on the besieged castle, and since the Jacobites had raised the white flag.

But despite the surrender, it was clear to Jacob that the Catholic commanders had accomplished their mission. Not only had they delayed Schomberg's march south, they had managed to negotiate favourable conditions of surrender. The terms allowed the defeated garrison to "march out with flying Colours, Arms, lighted Matches, and their own Baggage . . ." What was more, the Jacobite invaders were to "be conducted by a Squadron of Horse to the nearest Garrison of the Enemy." In other words, until they were out of harm's reach of the Protestant inhabitants who might not like to see the instigators of their recent torment get away scot-free.

Jacob was among the horsemen selected to accompany the Jacobites the first few miles out of town. He gulped down the last dregs of his broth, then lit a pipe, thinking how odd it was that he missed his awful bowl of coffee at the coffeehouse in London. He was soon puffing away in protection against the smell of the last cartload of bodies that had rolled by. The last count was over one hundred and fifty men killed on each side, plus a handful of cows.

Around him, tents were being dismantled by gentlemen's valets. Through the gaping hole in the north wall, he could see the devastated town, strewn with debris and rubble, the tops of buildings blown off, and smoke still coiling into the balmy sky. He now gazed at the cloud of flies above the festering carcasses of the lead-peppered cows. They had been herded atop the rubble of the breach by the besieged soldiers in a desperate bid to prevent the besiegers from entering the town.

'Damn waste of good meat,' said Philippe, holding the reins of two horses as he came strolling up. He handed the reins of one to Jacob, who, not in the mood for banter, gave a thick grunt. It occurred to him that the same could be said of the cartload of dead men, who looked no less morbid and spiritless than the dead bovines. It was frightening.

Two hours later, Jacob and Philippe were waiting in their saddles outside the east gate with their cavalry squadron. Three hundred and fifty battle-worn Jacobites were marching from the castle with their wives, children, and camp followers in tow. To the beat of their drum, they marched up the ravaged street that was flanked by Schomberg's foot soldiers. Jacob saw haggard-looking townsfolk watching in dismay and anger. After sizing up the instigators of their living nightmare, many of them now hurled insults between the shoulders of Schomberg's troopers, who were letting the invaders get away with their flags flying.

At last, the dishevelled column of Irish Catholic soldiers approached the gate where the Williamite cavalry squadron were to take up their escort mission. Jacob looked around dubiously at his English captain, Sir William Russel.

Having delayed their departure from London in the hope of seeing Jeanne before leaving for Ireland, Jacob and de Sève had embarked from Highlake with an English cavalry regiment. It had been agreed that the two French lieutenants would join their Huguenot regiment in Belfast once the siege of Carrickfergus was over.

The captain gave orders for the detachment to split into two so that twenty-five horsemen rode on either flank of the Irish garrison. It all suddenly seemed to Jacob like a very tall order. Not the task of keeping the garrison in line, but the more delicate challenge of keeping the townsfolk from taking their revenge. It quickly became clear the population would carry their verbal attacks much further than the city gate.

'They should expect a rough quarter of an hour,' called Jacob in French to de Sève.

Philippe, a few lengths in front, turned in his saddle. 'Aye, they say you only reap what you sow, my friend! And I'd rather be up here than down there right now!'

The swelling crowd was clearly curious to find out what was going to happen to their former captors.

No sooner had they left the gate than the most vocal womenfolk marched up to the Jacobite column with verbal digs and hard pokes to provoke a reaction, until a horseman closed the gap and established order.

'Cavaliers, keep tight!' ordered the captain, cantering up and down the file of enemy soldiers. But gaps were inevitable along the line of horses, and the forays of verbal aggression continued.

The file continued their march to the beat of their drum

past the first houses, charred and gutted, that lined the road south outside the town wall.

Old Mrs O'Leary in a grey peasant's bodice and skirt, hair bound in cloth, was collecting her thoughts inside her roofless, burnt-out home where she had raised her sons. Gareth had died from the fever, and Edward was killed as he strove to protect their hometown from the invading Jacobite force. She was not prone to tears, old Mrs O'Leary. She was hard as toenails and not one to make waves either; ripples, rather, was the philosophy handed down to her from her French grandfather. *Little by little the bird builds his nest*, she used to say to her boys, who were hampered with the impetuosity of youth and lacking the guiding hand of their father, missing at sea.

In the void of her loss, she was thankful that Gareth had fathered a son. The toddler had been taken north with his mother to their Scottish cousin's in Ballymena. She was thinking that she might join them; the child looked so much like her Gareth. But her ears pricked on hearing the march of boots. And the accompanying outbursts suddenly pierced the bubble of her grief.

She turned from the blackened room where her kitchen had been, and looked through the burnt-out window. She then scurried to the threshold, where the wooden door was still half-hinged and open.

There she stood, hawkeyed, as though picking out her prey. A minute later, eyes all aglare, Mrs O'Leary stomped across the dozen or so yards that separated her from the passing Jacobite file. Mad-eyed and with a primal rage, she let out a visceral cry that made even the townsfolk start with horror. It did not form decipherable words, though the appalling sound was eloquent in itself. It expressed all the grief, pain, and anger of a mother who had lost her babies and the home she had brought them up in. It was a cry that needed no words, a cry that many understood, including Delpech and de Sève, between whose horses she had lunged towards the Jacobite column. They both searched in alarm for the source of such soul-wrenching sorrow.

Fingers curled into rigid dart-like claws, she charged at the soldier who had flamed her house. She reached for his face but only managed to scratch his neck and latch hold of his long hair. Turning sharply, he shook her off, clamped her upper arms and then flung her to the ground like a bundle of sticks. Two women came to her aid as, on her knees, she belched out her pain in a woeful wail, holding her belly like she was giving birth.

An eruption of voices and indignation rose up as a group of womenfolk broke into the file in a single body. They swooped upon the soldier like vultures, tore at his face, pulled him down. They then dragged him from the rank and covered him in blows from pounding knuckles and rough brogues on feet.

Philippe and Jacob managed to coordinate their mounts to push back the assailants. Meanwhile, the soldier was pulled back from the ground into the Jacobite line by his brothers in arms, visibly none too keen for a fight.

But the soldier made a sign that did nothing to lessen the tension. Instead, it spread the feeling of indignation as fast as the flames that had ravaged Mrs O'Leary's house. The crowd called for justice to be done, that the Jacobites be led away to be massacred, each and every one of them. But they were not. It soon became clear to them that their enemies were merely being conducted away from the scene of their crimes, as if they were on a church parade.

By the time they had marched a mile out of the township, the townsfolk had measured the cavaliers' willingness to intervene. It was clearly less fervent than the crowd's visceral desire for bloody justice. Justice for their destroyed homes, their dead husbands and sons, their diminished health through privation of food, and the disease-ridden tots that might not see the end of day.

Wild kicks began to hit home and isolated punches to fly. Jacob sensed as well as the Jacobite officers that just one spark of fury from the column would ignite an explosive reaction. Captain Russel sent one of the French cavaliers for reinforcements, telling him to leave discreetly and then fly like the wind.

The inevitable happened soon after Philippe's departure.

A soldier's wife reacted viciously as a Protestant fishwife stepped up and tugged her chignon from behind. Had the soldier's wife let herself suffer the dishonour and let the woman have her moment of satisfaction, then maybe she would have lost nothing more than a bit of face. But ferocious as a wildcat, she turned: 'Get off me, ya filthy faggot!' she screamed, twisting and clawing the air as her assailant went on pulling the chignon back, forcing the soldier's wife to her knees.

'Let her go or I'll let fly!' shouted her husband, holding his musket by the barrel as if he was about to use it as a bat.

But the fishwife sneered and pulled the woman's bun harder, making wide circles which made her scream louder and the onlookers laugh harder. The husband swung back his musket, but a burly Protestant stepped forward and snatched it from the soldier's grasp. The Jacobite let loose a punch. The Protestant whacked the butt of the musket handsomely round the soldier's ear. The Jacobite tumbled, a corpus of townsfolk surged forward as if on cue, and the fighting began.

The soldiers were better equipped to fight, but the townsfolk were angrier, their raw fury quadrupling their strength and desire for instant, bloody justice. They easily wrested the firearms from their former captors' hands. The Catholic commanders ordered their men not to draw their sabres, knowing that if they did, their own massacre would be inevitable.

The soldier's wife was now a plaything. Townsfolk of both sexes clawed voraciously at her shawl, bodice, and skirt, tearing them to shreds. Within minutes, she was on her hands and knees in the mud in nothing but her shift, trembling like a frightened bitch. Then her face was pushed down into the mud and the rest of her clothing ripped off in seconds, her body groped, her blood-stained bloomers held high.

The women went on the rampage against their adversaries of the same sex, to tear off their clothes, and give them back some of the medicine that the Catholic wives had dealt them in their own homes.

Sporadic fighting erupted all along the file. Even high-grade officers were set upon. The horsemen, unable to intervene with their arms, could only endeavour to separate the brawlers with their mounts. After another intervention, Delpech saw a soldier step out from the column and start making for the woods across the bog.

Damon Laverty had joined King James's army not just because everyone else had. In truth, he couldn't care less about who was in charge across the Irish Sea. All he cared about was pretty Maddy O'Flanerty, the baker's daughter, and getting some decent pay in order to fetch her hand. But he was not prepared to give his life for the sake of a king's throne. It was a good crack at first, but now he had had enough. And what was he going to say to his best mate's ma about her son Danny getting his head shot off by a cannonball?

He put it all to the side for the moment. The woods were close by, and if he could just sneak off while no one was looking, just like Jerry his other pal had done before the siege began, then he could be home in less than three days. Then he would do as his old man had told him to do: he would take to the oar and bring the fish to market like his forebears had done.

'Where you off to, laddie?'

Damon looked up. He saw two angry-looking men facing him. One of them was holding a dense, knotted stick that he was tapping into the palm of his hand. Damon turned to his right, only to face a woman standing impassively between two other men. He recognised her. She was the one he had to pull away from Danny while her husband was being held for clobbering a sergeant. The sergeant then had the man shot and his house torched.

'L-Look, listen,' Damon blurted out, sensing his life was in danger. 'I didn't shoot your husband . . . I . . . I could have aimed to kill, but I did not. I swear to God I aimed aside.' But his plea made no difference. This was not a tribunal. It was going to be an execution.

The sound of cantering hooves made the party turn in unison. A chestnut-brown horse came through the middle of the pack, carrying a soldier in grey uniform.

'Stand back!' cried out Lieutenant Delpech to the assailants.

'He's ours!' roared one of the men.

'Is retaliation what the Lord taught you?' returned Jacob sternly.

'Is plundering and burning and killing what the Lord taught them?' said the woman virulently. 'He killed my husband!'

'I didn't, I swear to God, I aimed aside!' said Damon desperately.

'Aye, we'll pay our dues in heaven or hell, as long as these bastards get what they deserve!' said one of the men.

'For the love of Christ,' said Jacob, maintaining a loud, commanding tone of voice, 'has there not been enough of killing?'

But since they were blinded by grief, humiliation, and anger, Jacob was sure these people would not let the man live. Turning and bending down to the soldier, he said sharply: 'Give me your hand now!' It was the only way of saving him from execution and the townsfolk from mortal sin.

Damon did not think twice. He seized the cavalier's hand and climbed behind him sharpish. In her hunger for revenge, the woman ran behind the horse for a few yards while shouting out: 'You dirty, filthy scumbag! Come back here and yer dead!'

Jacob cantered back to the main file where horses were screening the Jacobites from the furious, madding crowd.

Damon descended, back among his regiment.

Another woman cried out in indignation: 'You should be executing the bastards!'

'Whose side are you on, anyway?' shouted a man.

Trying to keep control of his shying horse, Jacob said in a loud but controlled voice: 'I am on the side of God!'

But the townsfolk were not impressed; they were not ready for a moral lecture. They had already seen too many men and women die through turning the other cheek.

The jostling crowd began surging like the ebb and flow of a swelling sea, and more and more Jacobites were being set upon, some dragged from their column to receive a beating. Jacob realised that someone was about to be killed, and that the first death would lead to a massacre, one way or the other, and he was in the thick of it.

But then a rapid movement entered the corner of his eye. He turned to see a scarlet coat, a blue sash, and a hand holding up a pistol midway down the line. A deep, gravelly voice called for order, but to no effect. Then a tremendous blast rent the air, sending birds from the surrounding woods into flight. The clamour died down as quickly as when Mrs O'Leary had let out her primal cry. Officers being manhandled were able to shake themselves from the grips of their assailants as an instance of total calm followed.

It was the old duke in person, Schomberg, sitting high and mighty on his large horse, a picture of dignity and conviction in his grey periwig and tricorne hat. He was holding up his smoking gun. Raising his accented voice, the marshal endeavoured to talk sense into the townsfolk. But the voice of the crowd soon rose up again, calling for executions, and protesting against the Jacobites being marched off without so much as being called to account for their dastardly actions.

Damon Laverty sensed that things were about to turn nasty again. The townsfolk had become a sinister mob. He had been saved once by a greycoat, but he knew that none of the other Protestant horsemen had much heart to impose order upon their fellow Protestants.

So, eyeing his previous pursuers and the vindictive woman now calling for immediate justice, again he decided to slip away. Taking advantage of the distraction caused by Schomberg, he backtracked discreetly through the file of soldiers. Then he dashed back the short distance to the approaching battalion of Williamites on foot.

Meanwhile, midway back up the line, Schomberg intoned with finality: 'Get back to your town, or face the consequences!'

At the tail end of the column, Jacob noticed other Jacobite troops following Laverty's lead, preferring to find refuge among their Williamite counterparts than to risk facing the mob.

But now fully aware of the battalion of redcoats on foot coming up the rear, the townsfolk stood back, some unclenching their fists, others lowering the arms they had snatched from their former gaolers.

Under the duke's command, the battalion on foot swiftly took control. They pushed the dishevelled Jacobites back into line, and forced the battered and bruised to limp onwards. Denuded wives were clad in coats to cover up.

In this way, the Jacobite column was conducted to a safe distance from Carrickfergus, the pretty port town they had left in ruin and desolation.

On leaving the Jacobites to their fate on their march south through the hills to Newry, Delpech turned to de Sève, who had ridden up to his flank. 'I wonder if any of those men will be held to account,' he said.

'God's justice will prevail,' said Philippe. Jacob still hoped it would. Philippe went on: 'I just wonder why we are letting them go only to return our fire another day!'

Jacob then saw the young soldier he had saved. He was marching in file with Schomberg's men. 'The world is an unfathomable mess,' said Jacob, and took refuge in his pipe.

*

Some hours later, on marching upon Belfast bay with his new brothers in arms, Damon Laverty got to thinking that he might even be able to find a way to join a ship and sail to the New World, where he had heard fortunes were made.

15

SITTING ON HIS chestnut-brown mount, Jacob said a silent prayer for the souls of the men whose bodies were being released from the hangman's noose.

Jacob sometimes wondered if Protestants and Catholics had forgotten they were Christian. But he knew the men's souls would be with God if they had faith, be they Protestant or Catholic. They would be judged on their life's deeds, not their desertion from the English army.

They had left Belfast the day before. Marshall Schomberg had recovered all of his army and had set the whole train of twelve thousand foot soldiers and two thousand on horseback on the road to Dublin. That was where James Stuart had set up his government, and where the bulk of the Catholic king's army was encamped.

The bodies were swung onto a cart waiting on the roadside outside the fort of Hillsborough. Jacob clicked his horse onwards.

Private Laverty continued to stare for a full minute after watching the grim fate of the Protestant deserters. He knew it was what awaited him should he get caught by his former brothers in arms.

For the time being, he had let go of his hopes of finding a ship to take him to the New World where fortunes were made. Instead, he thumbed the rosary deep inside the pocket of his new jacket that had belonged to a dead Williamite. It was what his mother had taught him to do as a boy, to pray to the Virgin Mary in times of trouble. He had seen men dangle before without giving it a second thought. But perhaps the unsettling sensation in his stomach was due to his feeling under the weather. It always made him feel down whenever he got a sniffle. He should have learnt to smoke a pipe like a sailor, he thought to himself; it settled the nerves, apparently, cleared away foul smells, and staved off hunger.

On horseback, Delpech discovered a beautiful land made up of lush green glens, wooded mounds, and pretty villages. But the further southward he rode, the more devastated the landscape became, Jacobite invaders having looted and torched entire townlands that were now empty of people.

With such a large army, the going was slow. They spent the night outside the deserted market town of Dromore. By the end of the next day, they had reached Loughbrickland, where they encamped on the side of a hill. The Huguenot cavalry regiments were allocated their own area so as not to stir up inherent rivalries between English and French troops.

Jacob was getting used to hearing French spoken all around him. It still seemed odd, though, to hear a Huguenot rejoice upon finding an old acquaintance or a distant cousin in the fields of Ireland. The main topic of conversation since leaving Dromore was the latest intelligence regarding the township of Newry. A key position on the road to Dublin, Newry was the last stop before the Slieve Gullion mountain that separated Ulster from Leinster and the plains of Meath.

'Berwick?' said Jacob to Monsieur de Bostaquet, an affable and forthright middle-aged gentleman turned soldier. Having fled France and relinquished his fortune rather than his faith, he had joined the Dutch provinces and crossed the Channel to England in King William's army. They were standing around the campfire, having just left their horses to pasture. De Bostaquet knew the ropes, gave guidance to the many gentlemen merchants who swelled the Huguenot ranks so they were more battle-savvy than they would have been. Jacob and Philippe appreciated his company.

'The Duke of Berwick,' said de Bostaquet, 'King James' natural son, from a second bed, but his natural son all the same, Sir.'

'I heard he has a reputation, this Berwick,' said Philippe.

'Indeed, already, one so young too. Not yet twenty if my memory does not fail me, and already given with passion to the practice of pillage and torching. One to watch, you might say,' added de Bostaquet with a hint of irony, 'and now the blighter is in Newry!'

On the news of Berwick's occupation of Newry, Schomberg pushed his army southward through the increasingly ravaged glenscape. The rare farmsteads Jacob passed had all been pillaged and torched. And with no one about to harvest it, the corn stood rotting in the fields. But worst of all, the weather turned bad: now a fine drizzle, now torrential rain.

By the time they reached the foothills of the Morne Mountains north of Newry, Berwick had retreated with his army, leaving a town in flames in his wake.

'Dear God,' said Jacob, looking down from the hills at the coils of smoke rising above the walled township. The place was clearly still ablaze. 'Why such gratuitous destruction?'

'It is exactly the tactic Louis's commanders employed in the Palatinate,' said Monsieur de Bostaquet, riding by Jacob's left flank. 'It is so we find nothing we can use.'

They clicked at their mounts and rode down into the town, where a few townsfolk were still fighting the fire with buckets. Only a handful of houses were still standing.

Schomberg was both moved and furious over the dastardly acts that Berwick continued to perpetrate. The marshal ordered a corps of horse to press onwards in an attempt to surprise the young scoundrel before he destroyed the township of Dundalk.

*

Damon Laverty's morale was in his boots. The weather was atrocious, the soup as clear as cabbage water, and the high winds kept blowing down his tent, which he would have to pitch all over again tomorrow. He should have stayed with his garrison and marched south; at least they were fed properly with solid portions of meat and a decent clump of bread to soak up the broth juice. He never seemed to make the right choice, though, either jumping in too early or not holding out long enough to reap the fruit of steadfastness. Was he really so fickle? That was what his mother often called him, fickle as the wind, and he was beginning to think she was right.

A troop on horseback passed by him. Soaked to the skin, he looked up from the stake he was hammering into the sodden ground, angling it so that it would stay in. He caught sight of the French cavalier who had saved him from a summary execution. He stood upright and gave a salute, for you never knew when you might need a friend. Then a treacherous gust kicked into camp, blowing a wet canvas flap into his face. It was all bloody unfair.

*

No sooner had they been served their bowl of watered-down broth than Jacob's party were called to saddle up.

Jacob's backside still ached from the previous stint in the saddle as he rode past the infantry camp, where he caught sight of the young soldier he had rescued. He had visibly defected, or deserted, depending from which side of the fence you looked at it. Delpech gave a nod to the soldier's salute. The lad looked so young, thought Jacob, or was it he who was getting old? He had noticed that people seemed to be looking younger these days, quite frightening to think about. Or could it be that, given the nature of the context in which he found himself, he was surrounded by an abnormally young population compared to normal everyday life? At any rate, he was consequently all the more glad for Isaac de Bostaquet's company. Hale and hearty in his mid-fifties, de Bostaquet was a tour de force and served as a source of hope—hope that it was not too late for Jacob to endure life's battles and raise his children to his family's former station.

The party rode on to the assembly point south of the town at the foot of Slieve Gullion mountain. There they joined Count Mesnart, Schomberg's third son, who was in charge of leading the detachment of officers to Dundalk.

*

Jacob, like every other cavalier, kept his aches and pains to himself. For they all knew that an epidemic could be looming on the horizon. Even as they rode past the infantry camp, Jacob had noted the chorus of splutterings and groans.

'In a word, camp fever,' said Isaac to Jacob as the cavalry train rode two abreast into the hilly terrain. 'You don't want to stay in camp too long, my good fellow. Avoid it like the plague!'

But Jacob soon found there were inconveniences that counterbalanced the benefits of being out on a mission. Lashing rain and gale-force winds constantly assailed the party in their arduous trek through the tricky, boggy tracks of Slieve Gullion. Neither Jacob nor Philippe had a cape. Their unwaxed jackets became heavy sopping weights on their shoulders. To add to the hindrance, the retreating Jacobite soldiers had taken care to smash river fords, which meant the horses had to wade through the cold mountain waters.

Philippe cursed the clap of thunder and the rain that now came down even harder as they crossed a mountain stream.

'There is one consolation, though,' said Isaac as they rode on through the night between the dark wooded slopes. 'Means there is less likelihood of musket attack.'

'That's true, because of the rain?' said Philippe.

'Ha, of course, a musket will not fire in the wet,' added Jacob.

'Indeed,' said Isaac. 'Gunpowder does not like water any more than we do!'

He was right, of course. For although Jacobite scouts were certainly following their progress, the Williamite detachment encountered no enemy vedettes, and they breached the hill of Faughart as the sun cracked through the violet clouds over Dundalk Bay. Jacob scrutinised the sky, as did others of the detachment. Then, with satisfaction, he said: 'There is no smoke!'

The cavaliers had battled hard against fatigue and the elements, but it had paid off. Now they rode into Dundalk town, saved from destruction and without a shot being fired. Young Berwick, having got wind of the cavaliers' approach, had given the order to flee during the night.

*

The unwalled town consisted of one long street that ran north to south from the tip of the Kilcurry estuary. The first task was to scour both town and surrounding country in search of provisions for the men and forage for the horses. Jacob and Philippe searched the deserted houses, but Berwick's army had already helped themselves. The two men could gather but a beggarly store of corn, hardly of any consequence for the cavalry detachment, let alone the main bulk of the army soon to arrive.

Thankfully, some hours later, as the main army marched down the hill, sopping and caked in mud, a patrol turned up with two thousand sheep, and the slaughter began.

Meanwhile, Delpech and de Sève dried their clothes and stole forty winks in a vacant house, relieved to find a bed, a hearth, and shelter from the howling wind and the rain. But barely had any notion of rudimentary comfort seeped into their tired minds and limbs than the call was raised again. This time, it was for officers to double back through the mountain to Moyry Pass to help retrieve the soldiers who had collapsed from hunger, fatigue, or illness.

Jacob saddled up with Philippe, Isaac, and the rest of the task force. Though the rain had ceased, eight thousand hooves and twenty thousand marching boots had turned the mountain trail into a quagmire in places. But within the hour, they had reached Moyry Castle, a rudimentary three-storey tower house that guarded the pass, and which at present gave refuge to the lame men.

*

Even though his limbs were as stiff as an old maid's, Damon Laverty could have kicked himself for joining their stupid war in the first place. And he had no inclination to leave the tower house, especially so late in the day. It was more than he could bear to pull his aching body away now from the drowsy heat of the fire crackling in the hearth on the second floor. The dry logs piled at the side of the fire had been a constant source of comfort. He had been looking forward to a nice warm night with a solid roof over his head, away from the relentless wind and dampness of camp life.

'Up you get if you want food tonight, soldier!' said the sergeant, a man chosen to stick with the stragglers for his stern but indulgent temperament, uncommon for a man of his station. A seasoned soldier, Sergeant Tatlock had seen many a comrade fall in the line of duty, and he knew most of this untidy lot would probably not live to tell their tales. Even so, his mission was to shepherd them into camp.

Damon now preferred to keep his own company, especially since the recent talk of Roman Catholics needing to be purged from the Williamite rank and file. It had filtered down to him that Schomberg had become increasingly wary of Jacobite sympathizers. Faced with a growing lack of resources, recruiters had not been overly cautious as to their recruits' religious backgrounds. Catholic soldiers had been told to show themselves. Those who had done so had not been ill-treated, for they were still soldiers of the English army. Many had been wrongly sent to Ireland and so were shipped off to fight against the French in northern Europe. Damon would have stood up likewise, but what if he was sent packing back to his garrison instead? He would dance at the end of a noose just like those Protestant deserters. Besides, he did not want to fight the French on the flats of Flanders. So he had curled up and kept himself to himself.

'Ow!' he croaked, on feeling a sharp dig in his butt.

'You're taking the piss, soldier! ON. YOUR. BLOODY. FEET! NOW!' roared Tatlock, which sent shock waves through the lad's skull. Not wanting another boot in his crack, Damon climbed slowly to his feet. He gathered his overclothes, hung out near the fire. He put on his breeches, jacket, and boots. Then he followed the line of fatigued and ailing men down the ladder to the chilly ground floor.

Twenty minutes later, they were assembled in the grey light of the afternoon in the cattle enclosure that surrounded the stone keep. From here, the feeblest were given transport, while the walking sick were met by their mounted escort, waiting to lead them to Dundalk.

It was a two-hour march to camp that would take three. Because of the deep, slippery mud left in the wake of the main army, the caravan took a different route where the ground would be firmer. But they came upon a swollen stream where the ford required a quick fix for the marchers to pass over.

Damon hardly had the force to stand in the chain, let alone pass on the broken stones for the next soldier to place. At one point, he lost his footing and found himself thigh-deep in cold, rushing water. The sergeant boomed his discontent. Then he said: 'Now you're in the bloody drink, soldier, you might as well wade to the other side and wait under the trees!'

Half an hour later, the men were marching over the stepping stones. Damon got up to join the line, staggering onwards in the muddy path in his sodden boots and breeches as if he were dragging nine-pound cannonballs attached to his ankles.

'Close up the rear, soldier!' roared the sergeant. But, unable to carry himself any faster, Damon lagged behind. Then he saw one of the horses up ahead swing round. The next moment, a hand was thrust before him.

'Give me your hand!' said the horseman to the foot soldier.

Damon recognised the French lieutenant.

'Yes, Sir, thank you, Sir,' said Damon, his foot in the vacated stirrup, quite chuffed that his salute back at Newry camp had borne its fruit. The saddle was warm, and the horse's hide made excellent leg warmers.

'Your name?' said Jacob.

'Private Laverty, Sir.'

'Well, Laverty, do not drop off, do not fall off, and we will be in camp an hour before sundown. A bowl of mutton stew will be waiting for you.'

'Thank you, Sir,' said Damon, heartened by the prospect of meat.

They spoke briefly about the terrain, the uncommonly wet season, and what the Irish soldier's father did for a living.

'How old are you, Laverty?'

'Eighteen and a half, Sir.'

'Oh,' said Jacob, taken aback at such a young age.

'Aye, same age as the Duke of Berwick, I am told, Sir,' added Damon in as virile a voice as he could muster, which was not difficult given its croakiness.

'What would your mother say about you being in the English army?'

'That I'm a heathen, Sir,' said the lad spontaneously; he regretted it the moment it came out. So he hastened to add: 'But I'm not, Sir. I believe in God as much as the next man.'

'That is good,' said Jacob. He did not ask if the lad was of Protestant or Catholic ancestry.

On they rode, falling silent the rest of the way, Damon fighting against the desire to sleep. He was a stocky lad, and normally resistant to the elements, having spent many a rough day on the water fishing with his da. But it was different out at sea. For a start, there was always something to do to keep your mind alert. And his da never went out twice, only once every day, except in stormy weather and on the day of the Lord. 'Otherwise, you'll not give your body time to flush out all the chill,' his da would say to his mates, who were sometimes tempted to go out on a second tide.

And then there was always the reward of the catch, and the thought of his ma's stew and a blazing fire to chase away the damp inside. Damon could hear her nightly refrain: 'Remember to thank the Lord and his Mother for your safe return!'

'Here we are,' said the French lieutenant, pulling on the reins of his mount. Jacob was glad they had arrived, what with the lad's coughing in his back.

Evening was encroaching. Fires were lit amid the clusters of men, bivouacked in a field dotted with trees that looked over Dundalk Bay. It lay before Kilcurry River and was strewn with soldiers' clothes hung out to dry on trees and on lines. Not all the tents had been erected, which Jacob took to mean that they would not be staying long.

'Grab yourself some stew,' said Delpech, pointing towards the camp mess, where camp followers were dishing out food to a swarm of men.

Damon roused himself from thoughts of his soft feather bed as he let go of the rosary buried in his pocket. Groggy-headed, he thanked the Frenchman and climbed down. He had forgotten his body was stiff, his ankles still weak, as he swung his right leg back over the horse's rump. On hitting the ground, he stumbled backwards and fell on his butt.

'You all right?' said the French lieutenant.

'Aye,' said the lad, 'I'll not fall any further!'

Getting to his feet, he instinctively felt his jacket pocket. A look of alarm spread across his face.

Jacob saw, in the half light, at the same time as the soldier, a wooden rosary lying in the mud where the lad had fallen.

'I'm not a spy, Sir,' said Damon.

'I don't doubt you,' said Jacob, who thought the lad to be sincere. He had spoken of his home like any homesick soldier. Not an ounce of disdain against Protestants came out of his mouth, even though Jacob had laid a few rhetorical traps. 'But keep it inside your pocket, eh?'

Jacob was not against Catholics, and he appreciated that some people needed material rituals to connect with the Lord. He rode off to put his horse to pasture, and to let the lad recover his rosary. He thought nothing more of it.

16

JEANNE WAS DRAINED after trudging with Paul from the spinning wheel maker's shop in the late summer sunshine.

They had hiked through the interminable streets of Whitechapel and up Brick Lane. In her life, she had never seen so many people in one day. It made her wonder where they all lived. It was also both surprising and reassuring to hear French so often spoken as they had approached the weaver district where she had her digs.

Back in her rooms, the excitement of her purchase was such that she found the strength to laugh and dance around it with her son, and at the risk of making the floorboards creak. The spinning wheel would bring in enough revenue to sustain them, even if it meant long hours of repetitive wrist-aching activity. But it was a price she was willing to pay if it rendered her free from the alms. And through the church, she had already met tailors and dressmakers who would be willing to take her yarn.

She poured two glasses of lemon water from an earthenware jug while Paul eagerly put the spinning wheel together. But then, as she contemplated how the light fell in the room, a cloud darkened her brow at the recollection of the landlady's glare on the first-floor landing. Mrs Smythe had opened her door as they had passed. Standing with her back arched on her threshold, arms cradling her large bosom, she had looked frowningly upon them as they carried a stool and spinning wheel parts.

'Bonjour, Madame,' Jeanne had said, holding the stool and the spoked wheel. She could have kicked herself for not remembering how to address a person in English. The landlady had knitted her eyebrows, tutted, then stepped back into her rooms and closed her door.

Jeanne had only spoken to her once before, just over a week earlier, through the old pastor who had translated the rules of the house upon her arrival. Those rules made no mention of a spinning wheel, though perhaps she ought to have at least informed the landlady first. Jeanne remembered the look of disapproval when she had expressed that she did not know English yet. She did not see herself now fumbling like a child for words she could not translate and trying to mime out an explanation. So she had not said anything. She realised, however, she would have to learn the fundamentals of the language quickly if she was to get by.

It wasn't as if she had purchased a cumbersome loom that might require a licence, though. And besides, she had learnt her lesson in Geneva, and could not afford to pay for a loom only for it to be smashed. But a spinning wheel: every home had a spinning wheel . . .

*

Next morning, Jeanne rose with the lark and went to fetch water from the well.

She went early, while Paul was still sleeping, so she would

not have to queue. Not because she was pressed for time or did not want to see people. No, by going early, at least she would not have to foolishly avert eye contact. For she felt embarrassed at not being able to even fumble for a greeting in the vernacular. Of course, she had spoken with people at the church a number of times, but everyone there spoke to her in French. Moreover, having lost all her capacity to communicate in her usual simple elegance, she was now totally bereft of her standing and dignity. Snobbishly, perhaps, she did not want people to think she was inferior, and she could hardly wear a sign on her back telling people she was born a countess.

The night had been stifling, and now the wind had picked up, blowing thick, dingy clouds from the east. It felt like it was going to rain. She passed by a square where linen was blowing in the wind on the tenterhooks. The way was familiar to her now, and she had previously seen that this was where cloth was stretched and hung out to dry. As she approached the well, her heart sank on seeing two ladies, one short and pudgy in middle age, the other a young maiden, slim and lithe. The young maiden gave the older lady good day as Jeanne arrived. Jeanne smiled and nodded.

Marie-Anne Chaumet was a spirited maiden, born in Lyons with a natural smile. She had arrived in London with her aunt and uncle and was apprenticed to a French weaving house whose owner also originated from Lyons. Her youth allowed her to take life one day at a time and worry neither about the past nor the future.

'I hope it's not the end of summer already,' she said to the lady in her naturally perky voice as she looked up at the heavens.

'Oh, you are French!' responded Jeanne, in her normal, restrained bourgeois voice, though not without a note of cheeriness. She was nonetheless glad to set the tone.

'Marie-Anne,' said the younger woman, neither impressed nor put out by the bourgeois accent. She knew that most Huguenots were no better off than she was, and this lady was no exception. Otherwise, why would she be fetching water herself? She went on. 'But they call me Mary around here, though,' she said.

Jeanne presented herself with her nobiliary particle, something she usually dropped, it being overly long. But here, alone as she was, she might only get one chance to make known her identity and true station. Then, fearing class isolation, with a smile she said: 'But Jeanne Delpech will do.'

Marie-Anne spoke of her learning to become a weaver at the house of Dublanc, once a fine house with a solid reputation for quality work in Lyons.

'I have just purchased a spinning wheel myself,' said Jeanne, before realising how lowly it must appear she had fallen.

'You, Madame?' said Marie-Anne.

'My . . . my husband is at war,' said Jeanne, which was explanation enough.

'It has taken the best of them,' said Marie-Anne, with a momentary droop in the mouth as she recalled the young man who used to give her the eye. But it soon passed, and, smiling, she said: 'Anyway, there's always a demand for cloth, but weaving is where the money is, Madame, and that's what I want to be. Then I shall marry a weaver. Can you weave?'

'I can, actually. My speciality is thick cloth.'

'That's good; it'll soon be the season for it. I'm sure you could get employment.'

That was precisely what Jeanne wanted to hear, and it confirmed her decision to purchase a small loom. She would put it by the south-facing window that overlooked the back yards. But would she be within legality if she got one? She would ask at the church. If the maiden's employer was allowed to ply his trade, then why couldn't she? She would specialise in the cloth of Montauban and perhaps a few fineries. She would be no match for the master silk weavers, but at least she could earn a better living than from spinning.

'I was actually thinking of getting my own loom.' Jeanne wondered if she had said too much to this infectious young maid. But she was relieved to find someone to converse with in her native tongue. 'However, I must learn English first. Do you speak any English, Mademoiselle?'

'I should hope so. I've been here for two years, Madame,' said Marie-Anne; then she added: 'You need not worry. Just get mingling with the ladies here. It'll soon rub off on you. Some of them prattle on whether you understand them or not. You'll soon pick up the lingo.'

'You must be very clever,' said Jeanne. Marie-Anne had never thought of herself as clever before; she grinned. Jeanne went on. 'If only I could get the first words to help me enter into conversation, it would help. But I still don't know how to give someone *good day*, let alone say *métier à tisser*. And how do they distinguish between the formal and the informal *you*?'

'Oh, they don't. They just say *you* as in *Good day to you, Madam*. So, no complications there. And the word for *métier à tisser* is *loom*. Loo-oo-oom.'

'Loo-oo-oome,' said Jeanne, finding the word funny, and was unable to resist a spurt of laughter.

'There, easy!' said Marie-Anne, laughing with her. As they walked together back towards the tenterground, Marie-Anne told her the English terms for such words as *yarn* and *cloth* and *bucket of water*, the last of which Jeanne already knew from her son, who had picked it up. If she could pick up patois while living in hiding in France, and some German when in Schaffhausen, then there was no reason why she could not learn the language here, especially if this was to be her son's new home and her place of work.

'Good day to you, Madam,' said Marie-Anne in English as they parted company at the tenterground.

'Good day too yoo, Mademoiselle,' said Jeanne.

The town was beginning to wake, and so would Paul. *Loom, yarn, water*, said Jeanne to herself, in cadence with her march past dogs barking at a cat, vendors pushing handcarts, and masons carting bricks and mortar into the city. She felt lighter despite the gathering clouds overhead and the extra weight of the water pail, and she was resolute to learn the vernacular. She would write to Jacob to bid him to return, and she would find out the law regarding weavers. She did not want to pay for a loom for it only to be smashed. But perhaps the guilds were not as stringent here as in Geneva. Perhaps the demand, given the size of the population, was much greater.

*

She tried to step lightly as she climbed the rickety staircase of the tenement house. Not that it would have made any difference. For the landlady had been keeping an ear out for her and opened her door as Jeanne set foot on the landing.

Mrs Smythe had been thinking. In fact, all night she had

been tossing and turning, as much because of the new lodger as because of the prickly heat. She had a profound sense of duty, did Mrs Smythe, drilled into her from an early age by her father, a corporal who had served under Cromwell. She was now faced with the duty to report potentially unlawful activity under her roof. Spinning for home use was one thing, but what if the lady was planning on spinning as a business? There again, the French lady seemed well-to-do, her French husband had gone off to fight in William's war in Ireland (she had checked the uniform), and she did not offer superfluous smiles like some of the desperate wretches just over from France, who then stole her clientele. But a French woman potentially spinning for money in her rooms—whatever next? A loom, perhaps?

But Mrs Smythe also had a head for business. So she had thought up a line of attack that would satisfy her sense of duty and perhaps revive her enterprise. The question was, did the woman even know how to weave? She had decided to find out.

The French lady returned her nod as she stood on her threshold, trying to crack a smile, which she knew did not become her, so she did not try to push it too far. 'Madame,' she said. 'I see you have purchased a spinning wheel.'

'Madame?' said Jeanne with a guarded smile at the landlady, who looked perfectly insincere. 'Sorry?' she added. It was one of a dozen words she had picked up since her arrival.

'A spinning wheel! You are a spinner!' said Mrs Smythe, trying her best to get through to her. But visibly, the woman couldn't understand her arse from her elbow. 'A spin-ner. You

'. . . spinning wheel,' she said more loudly while drawing a wheel in the air.

'Ah,' said Jeanne. 'Ze spinning veel.' She could hardly pretend she did not have one. And she saw her hopes suddenly evaporating. No matter, she thought; she would use the money she had set aside for the loom to find other lodgings where she could keep her wheel and retain her meagre independence until Jacob returned. 'And . . . vat . . . ze spinning wheel?' she continued, failing miserably to make a proper sentence. She could not help feeling a fool, unable as she was to construct the simplest of questions. So she rinsed her mouth with a spluttering of French in an attempt to recover some form of dignity.

'No, dear, in England we speak English!' said Mrs Smythe.

Jeanne put down her pail and crossed her arms. She was not going to be bullied by a lowly English matron. 'Vat you want? Madame?' she said curtly.

But Mrs Smythe cracked another smile, wider this time so that it frankly pleated the corners of her mouth. Then more gently, she said: 'Come, Madame. Please, come with me.' She closed her door behind her and stepped across the landing. *I'm not gonna blimmin' eat you, my dear*, she thought to herself on seeing the French lady's eye of defiance. 'Come, Madame, have no fear, leave the water here. No one will take it.'

Jeanne wondered what on earth she wanted. The landlady beckoned her to follow her down the rickety staircase. She was evidently making an attempt to be civil, so Jeanne followed on down to the ground floor, where Mrs Smythe showed her into a weaver's workshop. It was full of labelled shelves of reels of yarn, patterned fabric draped along the back wall, a great loom that took up a quarter of the space, and a dressmaker's workspace with bowls of buttons and reels of ribbon arranged by colour. The landlady pointed next to the loom. 'Spinning wheel,' she said.

Jeanne nodded. She wasn't stupid; she understood the first time. But she was nonetheless surprised to see the set-up and could now understand why the woman might be concerned about the potential competition. Too bad, thought Jeanne; she would find new lodgings. 'Yes, and loom!' she said, pointing to the large machine.

'Do you know how to work it?' said the landlady, forgetting her gesturing. Then she raised her voice while doing invisible actions with her hands. 'Can. You. Work. Loom?'

'Me work loom?' said Jeanne, cottoning on at last. 'Yes. I do loom and . . . er . . .' Jeanne stopped short of saying she would move on because she did not know how to say it. But then, Mrs Smythe's mouth broadened into an uncommon smile as she clapped her hands together under her chin.

'Good. Madame Delpech, you work here on this loom? For me, yes?' Was the woman offering her a job? 'You work your spinning wheel afternoons. And here in mornings, you work the loom, yes?' said the landlady, gesturing to the loom, then to the ceiling as she spoke.

With further insistence from Mrs Smythe, Jeanne at last gathered the deal. She would be able to keep her spinning wheel to spin yarn in the afternoons and work mornings on the loom at the workshop. At least it would keep her within the bounds of legality while she learnt the language, and she would not have to pay for a loom which might end up smashed anyway.

To Mrs Smythe's joy and relief, the French lady gave a

short, definite nod of acceptance.

Mrs Smythe had her French fineries. The Smythe workshop was back in business!

Jeanne had only been in England over a week, and already she had a job. But how much would she be paid? She would ask Marie-Anne the going rates. But more worryingly, what would it be like to work under her landlady?

17

IT SOON BECAME clear to Jacob that the army would not be pushing directly to Dublin as Isaac de Bostaquet had first suggested.

'Apparently, the supply ships that were supposed to put in at Carlingford Lough are encountering contrary winds,' said Isaac to Jacob and Philippe the morning after their arrival. He had just walked back up to camp from the town where the old marshal had set up his headquarters. The three Huguenot cavaliers were standing outside their mess tent, where de Bostaquet's valet was hammering home pegs. Jacob had advised that the tent stand in the sea breeze to chase away bad air whenever the sky hung low.

'I only hope we don't dig in for long here,' said Jacob, scanning the marshland to the east and the swollen river to the west. 'We might be well-protected from enemy attack, but there is little defence against the bane of bad air!'

Not only lack of provisions plagued the Williamite army. The outbreak of disease en route was growing worse, and already, numerous deaths had been registered.

The next day, parties of cavaliers were sent to scour the countryside for food. Jacob rode with Philippe and de

Bostaquet to Carlingford, an hour away in the saddle at a good pace, in search of reserves and for news of the supply vessels from Belfast. The morning was clement, the tide was out, and the bay lay placid as they set out along the damp track that ran through heathland, gorse, and heather. 'I had no idea there were so many,' said de Sève as they cantered along half a dozen flatbed carts carrying the deceased and the sick. The sick carts were also headed for Carlingford, where a hospital had been set up inside the stone castle by the lough.

Once in open country, they could have been anywhere, far away from disease and conflict, thought Jacob as they cantered on at an even pace. 'Don't know about you, Delpech, my good fellow, but the less time I spend in camp, the better,' said Philippe, letting out a chuckle. His spirits had lifted now that they had removed themselves from the dingy scenes of camp squalor and strife.

As Jacob nodded in agreement, his eye caught a puff of smoke in the distant foliage past Philippe's right ear. It was instantly followed by a crackle of shot. Philippe's mount let out a horrific squeal of agony as its legs gave way in full canter. 'Enemy attack!' roared Jacob, shortening the reins to regain control of his frightened steed.

'Over there!' trumpeted Isaac up ahead. He pointed to the higher ground to the left, where a flash of Jacobite redcoats had launched their mounts into full gallop. 'After them, gents!' hollered Isaac. 'We have the advantage of loaded pistols!'

'Philippe's down!' shouted Jacob, but Isaac had pushed his horse into a thundering gallop in the direction of the fleeing Jacobite vedette of three dragoons. Now riding close to his horse's mane, a primal instinct suddenly took hold of

Delpech, overwhelming his initial desire to ride back to his fallen friend.

Pistol in hand, Delpech charged ahead like the wind, pushing his horse in the mud-splattered tracks of de Bostaquet's mount. But the enemy had a head start. And visibly more familiar with the mountain terrain, they knew where exactly to pass through the boggy patches and increased the distance that separated them from their pursuers.

Isaac led the chase for a minute more. But after losing eye contact, he then raised a hand, and with the other pulled on his reins to halt.

They gave a mutual nod, and then swiftly doubled back to the ambush point, where they found de Sève's horse lying panting, frightened, and helplessly in pain on the ground. Philippe was sitting, one leg stretched out, by the animal's head. He lowered his pistol on the party's approach and placed his hand on the horse's neck, now uttering sounds of comfort in an effort to calm the horse down.

Jacob dismounted and handed his reins to Isaac, who remained in his saddle to keep a lookout.

A cavalier's horse is more than a steed. It is an ally, a loyal friend that will run through hell, carry you despite hunger and fatigue until it drops. Philippe's feeling for his mare was no different. She had carried him when he was fatigued, had taken him through the mountains, across rivers, through mud and rain. He continued to speak to her, calming her nerves, until she laid her head flat on the ground, blood streaming from her eye, her leg clearly fractured. He passed his loaded pistol to Jacob. Jacob knew it would take a hard heart to kill one's own horse. Delpech returned a solemn nod. He took position near the mare's head, Philippe's pistol in one hand, his own in the other. 'All right, Rosy, girl, all right,' said Philippe, then gave Jacob the nod. Jacob fired twice into her skull.

'Better make tracks out of here!' said Isaac, breaking the short silence after the birds had flown and the horrible echo had died down. Struggling with his leg, Philippe managed to climb behind Jacob to finish the run around the mountain to Carlingford Town.

*

The seaside market town had suffered the same fate as Newry. Sacked, torched, and deserted, it provided no sustenance except for some oatcakes that they took from a few breadless inhabitants. In return, Jacob gave them the whereabouts of Philippe's dead horse, which they could cart back to Dundalk camp for a handsome reward and food.

'We will catch up with you on the road to Dundalk, once we have taken our fellow to the castle hospital,' said Jacob, translating for Isaac.

The three Huguenots proceeded to the waterfront where there was still no sign of supply ships. Philippe by now was unable to walk on his swollen ankle, which Delpech, after a brief diagnosis, suspected to be fractured. So the next stop was Carlingford Castle, where they could leave Philippe in the qualified hands of the medical staff.

The great room where medieval banquets were once held by day and where castle dwellers used to sleep by night was now occupied by the battle-wounded from Carrickfergus and, since yesterday, by the first casualties of the fever from Dundalk.

'Straw, blankets, and two bowls of gruel a day,' said Jacob, once Philippe had been given a spot among other French patients.

'Wonderful, I shall be living it up!' quipped Philippe, who spluttered into a cough.

Isaac stood shuffling from foot to foot, impatient to hit the road. For one, he detested hospitals; it was after all where most men died. Secondly, he was anxious to return to camp to warn the approaching sick convoy of roaming enemy vedettes. Although now with hindsight, he suspected the musket attack to be an opportunist strike by a straggling patrol.

'Cheer up. This could mean the end of the war for you, my dear fellow,' said Jacob to Philippe. 'There's a good chance they will send you back to England!'

'What for?' said Philippe. 'No one awaits me in England, except Mrs Smythe for her rent,' he joked. 'I shall stay here until I can walk. Then I shall hitch a ride back to Dundalk on a cart.'

'That's the spirit,' said Isaac. 'I will send you some moor rabbit. The soldiers eat them; not much meat but tasty all the same.' Then he stepped forward with bonhomie and gave Philippe a farewell pat on the arm to prompt their departure. They were yet to catch up with the local folk sent to recover Philippe's horse before the bloat set in.

*

Over the next couple of weeks, Jacob took part with Isaac and other officers in foraging missions, escorting dragoons into the surrounding fields to harvest hay and corn, which they rolled up and tied to their mounts. There had been brief visual encounters with Jacobite vedettes who, though they sometimes harried them in their toil, as yet had not ventured into armed conflict.

Every day Jacob returned from the field, he noticed a new development in the construction of the camp. Still unsure of his officers' true alliances and of the ill-trained Williamite army, Schomberg had decided not to advance on Dublin straight away but to dig in at Dundalk until his supply chain was secured and his army better trained. Earthworks were built, entrenchments dug, and batteries established at strategical points from the southern tip of the main street to the northern encampment on the other side of the Kilcurry River. Tents were gradually replaced by huts and barracks built from felled trees. And on each return, Jacob noticed the fever spreading with increasing ferocity.

One day, having harvested as much as their allotted field had to yield, they rode back into camp earlier than usual. Jacob was struck by the sight of tens of carts heading out on the road to Belfast, each transporting a grim load of dead soldiers. He cast a look of incomprehension to Isaac, who looked equally dumbfounded and sickened. Surely, had there been an assault, they would have heard the cannon fire that sounded the alert and bade their urgent return. But Jacob concluded that the guns had remained silent, for there was no hint of the acrid smell of gunpowder in the air. The entrenchments presented no damage, men around the camp yonder were being drilled as usual in the techniques of battle, and most of the horses were still in pasture, some sheltered in their newly made huts.

'What has happened here?' called out Jacob on approaching a cart driver.

'Camp fever, Sir,' replied the Irishman glumly. 'Dropping like sheep, they are. At this rate, ol' James won't even need to attack.'

The unhealthy spot, the atrocious weather conditions, and weeks of undernourishment had leagued in a tripartite force to assail the Williamite army, bringing not the bane of war's hellfire, but the scourge of disease. Soon, hundreds of men were dying weekly, hundreds more falling ill, while every day, Schomberg said his prayers in the local church. And in his indecision, he delayed any move forward. Needless to say, Jacob was glad to be in the saddle, and glad too that he had left Philippe in the healthier sea air of the castle by the lough.

*

The camp was divided by regiment and nationality. But old animosities rankled and tensions still grew, exacerbated by the rumour of a Catholic conspiracy within the ranks. And what put more oil on the fire was James Stewart's offer of a pardon to Williamites willing to defect to the Jacobite army—an army well fed, paid in real money, and provided with bedding and shelter from the oncoming sickly season.

Damon Laverty had grown ill. Even so, if there was a way to get back to his regiment and then be sent home without the risk of execution, he would have jumped at the chance. But Schomberg gave the order for no unauthorized soldier to venture out of camp upon pain of death. And he rewarded with money for every deserter or spy apprehended dead or alive.

One afternoon, Sergeant Tatlock came to Laverty's tent and ordered the private to get his carcass down to the bridge, where carts would be waiting to take the sick out of the godforsaken camp. Damon wondered if he could make it without shitting himself again as he laboriously pulled on his knapsack. Off he trudged with a horde of walking sick, withered and sallow. 'Jesus,' he thought, 'if the boys attacked now, we'd be done for!' But lacking the energy to carry the thought any further, he plunged his hand into his pocket and fingered his rosary beads.

*

The late September sky had opened up, offering a respite from the previous weeks of dismal weather. Jacob had been in the saddle since daybreak. His foraging party had been sent into the Carlingford-Newry mountains, the land south of Dundalk being now out of bounds, with the Jacobite army having seized the bridge over the Fane.

Delpech was standing in a field where his party of twelve were harvesting corn. He had advised that they cut from the top of the slope, the dominant side, where it was drier and easier to hack the stalks that grew in little mounds in sets of three or four. But even in the rare sunshine, it was still a hard graft. The razor-edged leaves could slice bare skin, so it was wise to keep covered all over, right up to the chin. But no one complained, really; at least they were being useful, and were out of the cursed camp. And there were perks to the job too. They had just had lunch, a proper lunch of cooked corn on the cob and fresh rabbit roasted on the spit, dowsed with a skinful of ale.

The men had risen from their meal and, under Isaac's command, had scattered across the field to their allotted patch. Jacob could now hear the rhythmic sound of the chopping of corn stems that punctuated the song of swallows, catching insects fleeing the massacre.

'Another hour, lads!' Jacob heard Isaac call out.

He continued to cast his eyes over the valley from the south-facing mountainside while peeing against a tree, one of a cluster that flanked the cornfield. From here, he had a clearer view over the valley and distant hills, not unlike the view from the Quercy ridge of his homeland, where the great plain stretched to the foothills of the Pyrenees. These Irish folk certainly knew how to work their land, he mused as he contemplated the patchwork of fields, some divided by low stone walls. It was all predominantly of deep greens, beautiful under the patchy blue sky, which made it all the more difficult to believe how men could confine themselves to the squalor and damp of an unhealthy encampment. But such was the madness of man in his folly for war. Jacob's horse nickered as if to agree with his wandering thoughts.

During his lunch break, Delpech had read the letter again from Jeanne asking him to return to England. It had put the spring back into his step and restored his hope, knowing she had made it to London. According to Isaac, there would likely be nothing more than a standoff between the two armies before the bad season prevented military manoeuvres. The ground between them offered no firm battlefield, only marshland which would bog down man and horse.

'If we go into winter quarters, you might get winter leave,' Isaac had said.

Jacob finished peeing while his horse, holding its head high, snorted its unrest more loudly. 'Easy, boy,' said Jacob, patting him on the neck. 'What's the matter . . .'

Then the source of his steed's fright came into earshot. A dull drumming quickly grew into a thunderous rumbling of hooves.

'Enemy attaaack!' he heard someone cry out from across the field.

Jacob's foot was in the stirrup when the first shots were fired, closely followed by more musket shots and the cries of men.

Now in his saddle, Jacob could see a dozen Jacobite attackers bearing down onto the harvested part of the cornfield. Their brandished sabres now shimmered like scythes in the late-summer sun. They had already emptied their pistols into the furthermost foragers caught by surprise.

With his loaded pistol at the ready, Delpech quickly pushed on to the field where his fellow cavaliers were mustering. Some were only just mounting, having run to their horses tethered in the shade of the trees.

They cried out in unison: 'A l'attaque!'

Jacob pushed forward with half a dozen Huguenot cavaliers to meet the assailants, who were mercilessly swiping at the men still running back from midfield. Isaac, who should normally have been in his saddle, had two enemy horses on his tail. Jacob broke from the pack, brandishing his pistol. He steadied his posture, held his breath, and gave fire. On the impact of the ball, his target fell from his horse. Isaac, meanwhile, dived to one side, narrowly escaping a beheading.

All about, the foraging party were retaliating, many of the attackers now fleeing under fire, having spent their shot.

Bearing in mind his poor performance when wielding his sabre during his brief training, Jacob decided to dismount. Besides, his first-ever encounter on a battlefield had been on foot with buccaneers in Cuba, and, having seen them annihilate a Spanish cavalry unit, he had more faith in their ways than in those of the army.

'Stay on your horse!' shouted Isaac. But Jacob had already swung his leg over.

The fallen Jacobite was already on his feet, blood seeping from the musket ball Jacob had planted into his left shoulder. But with the adrenaline of conflict now pumping through his veins, Delpech no longer envisaged the man. He now only saw the target. The choice was clear, kill or be killed.

The Jacobite, a burly veteran, visibly felt the same way. He charged. Jacob parried. After crossing swords three times, Jacob could now feel his strength ebbing away under the weight of each clash, the last of which resulted in a cut to his cheek. Again the Jacobite thrust forward; again Jacob parried. But this time, recalling his buccaneer training on the deck of a ship, he stuck out a foot as his assailant passed, knocking him off balance. The Jacobite swung round erratically, too widely. Jacob deflected the blow, leaving the adversary's guard momentarily open. With no time to think, Delpech thrust his curved sword deep into the belly. He pulled out his blade. Blood streamed out, the man went down—it was horrible. But there was no time to dwell.

'Your back, Delpech!' cried out Isaac on the approach of hooves to Jacob's rear.

As he instinctively crouched, he felt a sharp thud cut into his left collarbone. Then he rolled to the ground in a muddy pool as the horseman's blade swished an inch over his hatless head. Glancing around to take stock, Jacob managed to get to his knees as the horseman manoeuvred for another attack. But for the life of him, in the slippery mud, Jacob could not get to his feet. Facing the charging horse, he would certainly be hacked, if not trampled, to death. But then he heard a loud blast behind his right ear. Looking round, he saw Isaac holding a smoking pistol.

'I knew I had it somewhere,' he said as the wounded cavalier veered off his trajectory.

Isaac hurried to Jacob's flank and gave him a hand to help him to his feet. But the horseman had visibly not had enough. He pulled his horse around for another charge.

Recalling how the buccaneers had retreated into a thicket in Cuba when faced with a mounted attack, Jacob hurled out: 'Back to the corn!'

'The stalks won't stop a horse,' shouted Isaac as they backtracked to the uncut corn a dozen yards further down.

'No, but they will break its course!'

Their backs were against the corn stems when the cavalier came coursing upon them at full gallop, holding out his sabre with his right hand. Jacob knew that, if held with a firm wrist, at this speed it could slice through a man's neck cleaner than a falling axe. But the cavalier had no choice but to pull on his reins as he approached the corn stems, breaking his steed's momentum.

Unable to use his left hand to pull the cavalier off, instead Jacob slashed at the enemy's left leg while Isaac deflected the horseman's sabre strike. The Jacobite let out a roar of sudden pain. Isaac swiftly pulled the man down to the ground and put him to death.

*

The skirmish had finished as quickly as it had begun. While Isaac searched the dead cavalier, Jacob staggered up the slope, where his previous victim lay crumpled in a pool of blood and mud. On the far side of the cut field, dead foragers lay by their shocks of corn. The wounded were being tended to.

Exhausted and clutching his left shoulder, Delpech fell to his knees, his thoughts numbed as he looked into the sky. The power to muster a prayer escaped him. So he simply watched the sun shimmering between the clouds.

After a few minutes, he felt the warm muzzle of his horse at his left cheek. As he fingered the trailing reins with his left hand, he glanced down at his red jacket, sopping wet and brown with mud. He removed his right hand from his hacked shoulder, undid two upper brass buttons, and found his white shirt sopping and crimson. 'Dear God,' he said. He had lost a lot of blood, but somehow he felt appeased in the sun, and he did not feel like paying attention to it.

But Isaac soon arrived to bring him round from the shock. Professional and efficient, he fastened Jacob's shoulder and left arm with the sash of the dead Jacobite. 'It'll keep your arm still. You don't want to be losing any more blood,' he said.

'How many?' said Jacob, nodding to the bodies on the far side of the field. They were now being loaded onto their mounts.

'At least five good men,' said Isaac. 'Come on, we'll get you properly strapped up at camp first . . . then off to the hospital.' Isaac gave Jacob a leg up so he could hoist himself into the saddle.

The dead foragers were attached to their horses along with their day's shocks of corn, and the party rode into the valley back to camp.

*

Upon their arrival, a convoy of merchant carts was rolling out with their daily quota of dead from disease.

The sick were climbing unsteadily onto more carts that Jacob assumed were to take them to Carlingford hospital, where he too would be headed once he had recovered his effects. But first, he needed his wound to be properly bound, the ride back having loosened the sash and caused more blood loss.

On passing the line of sick soldiers, he picked out a familiar face, youthful but pasty and sickly. It was plain to see that Private Laverty was beset with fever.

'Come on, come on, a warm place and some grub await youse at the hospital, lads!' shouted the sergeant, to encourage the men to climb aboard the carts faster.

As Damon heaved his aching body into the flatbed cart, he lost his grip and slipped. He instinctively brought his other hand from his pocket to catch himself. As he did so, his rosary tumbled out and landed in the mud. Suddenly awakened by his inattention, Damon glared round quickly, then made for his communion beads, the beads that had kept him attached to God amid this inhumanity, to the Virgin Mary in the absence of his mother, to his home amid the squalor.

Behind him, Private Davies looked twice. In his delirious state, he could hardly believe his eyes. What should he do? All Catholics had been ordered to show themselves following the foiled conspiracy to infiltrate the Williamite camp. He had been warned there might still be Catholic spies among them. Davies remembered the marshal's orders: those who did not show themselves would be treated as spies and executed.

If he called the sergeant, Laverty could be hanged. Davies did not want his mess mate to be hanged, and he did not think he could be a spy either. So what should he do? He turned with his lips pursed as Sergeant Tatlock came marching down the line. But as he did so, Davies saw the barrel of a pistol in the corner of his eye suddenly being thrust forward. It belonged to the Dutch soldier behind him.

Jacob saw it too. As Laverty reached for his beads, he looked up and caught the French lieutenant's alarmed eyes.

'NOOOO!' blasted Jacob.

There was a loud detonation that covered Jacob's cry. Damon fell to the ground, clutching the item that had helped him bear up to the inhumane conditions. It would now be the item that would condemn him as a spy after death and declare innocent the puller of the trigger. But Jacob knew Laverty was no spy. He was just a homesick lad.

'Dear God,' said Delpech, 'this is madness . . .' Then he blacked out and fell from his horse to the ground.

18

DELPECH HAD BEEN meaning to get to Carlingford Castle to see Philippe, but foraging duties had taken up all his waking hours, and the weeks had passed.

Jacob, of course, encountered no good Catholic nuns to cater for the sick at the castle, as he would have in his native France. The Protestant religion forbade them. It rejected the notion that wealthy men could gain God's grace by providing cash endowments to charitable institutions. However, the doctors and surgeons could at least count on female camp followers and a few wise women to dispense basic care.

With his prior knowledge and experience of battle wounds and despite the lack of laudanum, Jacob insisted that the deep slash to his shoulder be first investigated and thoroughly rid of any cloth drawn in by the blade before being cleansed in rose oil. After the harrowing and painful experience of being stitched while held to a chair, a carer dressed the wound. She then bound the arm so that the catgut suture would not come loose.

He felt calmed as the body's natural painkillers kicked in and the carer finished working around him. He was sitting, eyes half closed, when an older matronly carer stepped into his field of vision.

'Monsieur Delpech, your friend is still here,' she said as the younger carer finalised her knot to secure his sling. Jacob looked up and nodded curtly to shake the sleepiness from his mind. The lady continued. 'I will show you to his place.'

'Thank you,' said Jacob. 'I think I know where he—'

'He has been . . . moved,' she said with solemnity.

A few minutes later, the matron was leading the way through the great room along an alley of hundreds of ailing men lying on straw ticks. Jacob slung his bag over his good shoulder as he passed the soldiers in various stages of the contagion. Its onslaught had already taken more lives than the whole of the Irish campaign put together.

With his free hand, he instinctively covered his nose from the stench of human faeces, and thought to himself that at least Private Laverty had been spared agonising in this foul place. It was small consolation, which nonetheless helped him stave off his raw feelings of injustice. But there was nothing to ward off the guilt he felt at the death of his five comrades in the field. If he had told them to start cutting the corn from the bottom rather than from the top of the slope, the assailants might have thought twice about attacking. For they would not have had the advantage of the downward slope.

'Monsieur Delpech,' said the matron in a discreet tone, after turning towards Jacob as they walked on. 'I must warn you, he has been very sick.'

'Sick? He came here for a broken ankle!'

'We believe he had already contracted the flux before his arrival. For it took hold the day after you left him here.'

'But that was over two weeks ago, Madam. Why was I not informed?'

She explained that, besieged by the illness, they lacked

time, resources, and space.

There was no point in discussing it further. He knew he would have been hard-pushed to make time for a ride to the hospital anyway.

'How is he now?'

'Very poorly.'

'Oh,' said Jacob, alarmed at the gravity in her face.

'Frankly, each day, we are never sure if he will make it through the night . . .'

She then stopped at the end of a line of sick soldiers. She gestured with her hand to an inert form lying on the floor and covered over with a blanket. They exchanged discreet nods. Then she left Jacob to it.

'Philippe,' said Jacob. The body beneath the blanket moved when Jacob bent down and gently nudged the shoulder with his free hand, the other being bound up under his frock coat. Delpech pushed aside a bowl of untouched gruel, got down to his knees, and sat back on his heels. The patient's limp hand slowly pulled back the blanket.

'Philippe?' said Jacob softly, barely able to hide his horror and grief. It was a rat-faced, beady-eyed man with a scraggly beard that glared back at him.

'Jacob, my good fellow,' said Philippe, his voice faint and hoarse. He had lost a lot of weight. His complexion was sallow, his skin sagging, and his eyes were sunken in their sockets. When he pushed aside the blanket revealing his upper body, Jacob saw he was but a pale reflection of the fine-looking man he had been in London. 'You . . . you should not have come,' he said, barely louder than a whisper.

Jacob said nothing of the wound that had forced him to visit the hospital, and he felt a pang of guilt. 'I would have come sooner,' he said, 'had I known you had been taken so poorly.'

Philippe went on. 'I am glad to see you, though, my friend.'

For want of anything better to say, Delpech gave news of the stalemate in Dundalk and the supply ships that were at last arriving from Belfast. But Philippe's misty gaze seemed to register no engagement. He just stared vacantly back at Jacob.

'Are you drinking? You must drink,' said Jacob.

Philippe shook his head once. 'Can't. All goes straight through . . .' He swallowed with difficulty, then continued. 'Listen, Jacob . . . I . . . I will not have made much of an impression on this earth . . . I fear my tracks will soon be erased. But you, my friend . . . you have a wife and family. Get out, Jacob . . . Leave this godforsaken place . . .' Philippe's voice was drying out. He paused again to muster more breath and gulped in an effort to lubricate his vocal cords.

'We shall both leave here,' said Jacob. 'Messieurs Delpech and de Sève, Merchants of London, remember?' But Philippe, not listening, went on with his discourse.

'I was wrong to bring you here . . .'

'We both came to earn a living and to fight for our beliefs, Philippe. And to prevent the spread of religious intolerance.' Jacob could not help feeling that his voice lacked conviction.

Philippe held up a feeble hand: 'Promise you will leave here, and I will die a peaceful man, Jacob.'

'You are not going to die, Philippe . . .' said Jacob. But Philippe looked desperate, and Jacob suddenly realised that a miracle was unlikely.

'No, listen . . .' said Philippe. 'My only solace now is in

heaven . . . with my dear wife . . . and our infant.' Philippe struggled to swallow. Jacob suddenly feared the worst. He took his friend's hand. Philippe went on. 'But I don't know what . . . what heaven will look like. Do you know, Jacob?'

For a moment, Jacob was lost. Then he remembered his Bible. He let go of Philippe's hand, then brought out his Bible from his sack. He opened it at Revelation. He read: 'Then the angel showed me the river of the water of life, bright as crystal, flowing from the throne of God and of the Lamb through the middle of the street of the city; also, on either side of the river, the tree of life with its twelve kinds of fruit, yielding its fruit each month. The leaves of the tree were for the healing of the nations. No longer will there be anything accursed, but the throne of God and of the Lamb will be in it, and his servants will worship him. They will see his face, and his name will be on their foreheads. And night will be no more. They will need no light of lamp or sun, for the Lord God will be their light, and they will reign forever and ever.'

Philippe reached out a hand. Jacob clasped it. Philippe said: 'Read it again, Jacob.'

*

The epidemic in Dundalk claimed the lives of over six thousand men, one-quarter of the Williamite army posted there. Philippe de Sève was buried at a Protestant church, like many Huguenots whose French names were chiselled into headstones planted in the Protestant graveyards of Ireland.

Jacob was not given immediate leave. Even a soldier with one good hand could be part of a cannon crew should the need arise, and resources were running desperately low. But Schomberg's battle plan was still not on the table. So

Delpech, against his friend's advice, put his medical experience to good use in the castle hospital that desperately lacked hands to help relieve the sick and the wounded.

19

Mrs Smythe was sure that if her first husband were still alive, she would be at the head of a house of half a dozen looms by now.

What he lacked in business acumen, he made up for in know-how. They had made a good team, for he had the talent to learn quickly and would have nailed the French techniques if someone had shown him. If only he had not slipped off a wherry and drowned, drunk as a lord, in the River Thames.

Since that fateful day, she had managed to navigate many a rough passage without him. More recently, she had weathered the French invasion of weavers by letting out her upper-floor rooms. She had survived the storm, and now she was raring to fight back.

Her new French employee was stringing whole sentences together. Nelly, her seamstress and second niece once removed, was learning how to set up a loom in the French fashion. And the weather was not likely to get any warmer—last night had been the coldest in November so far—which was all the better for business. Ladies would be requiring those new overcoats and suchlike they had been putting off due to a hitherto clement autumn.

But since yesterday, the leaves had fallen from trees in Spittle Fields and the old artillery garden. The freezing chill now had London firmly in its grip. By consequence, the tailors that Mrs Smythe supplied would be confirming their orders at long last. But not content to sell woollen, linen, and felt fabrics, she now wanted to get on to the fineries she had secretly dreamed of producing in the Smythe weave room, ever since the French invasion began. Her plan was to offer her clientele what they craved. In other words, the finest that Lyons could offer, and at very attractive prices.

It was early Monday morning and still pitch-black outside. She had prepared her workshop the day before so that her workers could not resist embracing her plan. She had purchased end reels of silk at a good price to use as a trial run. It would be pointless spending out on thread if no one could turn it into brocade, velvet, satin, or *peau de soie* . . .

If her plan worked, in time her deft little seamstress would take on the heavier cloth, leaving Madame Delpech to take the beam of a new loom.

The place was all aglow. She had lit a few extra lamps, which made the silk thread shimmer even more beautifully. And she had got the wood burner crackling earlier than usual so that the chill would be chased from the room come daylight.

The seamstress entered first as per her habit, for Mrs Smythe detested a late start. She allowed an exception to the rule, however, for the French lady who would invariably sail through the door like a breeze without so much as a word of excuse. But Mrs Smythe had learnt to keep the peace for the sake of good working relations, and generally made an extra effort to force her pout into a thin smile. But this morning,

Madame was even later than usual, and pushed the door a full hour after sunrise.

Jeanne thought it pointless to sit down at the loom until it was light enough for her to see properly. And sometimes, the London sky was so dingy, she could hardly see properly even at midday. On those days, she would have to get the girl Nelly to do all the setting. With such a lack of bright light here, was it any wonder that weavers in France had the edge over the English when it came to colour? Not to mention that the windows here should be bigger, not smaller, to let in more light. Nevertheless, she was becoming used to the changes of life and the gloomy London sky. She had purchased warm second-hand clothes at the rag market at Petticoat Lane, and had managed to get Paul into the school at the Huguenot Church on Artillery Lane, a ten-minute walk from their rooms.

But she still had not gotten any news from her husband since early autumn, when she received a letter from him that spoke of his wound. As an enlisted officer, he had been obliged to remain at a place called Lurgan until the decision was given to end the season's war campaign and go into winter quarters. He had hoped this would mean getting leave to winter in England. She had written back to him, bidding him again to quit the army. She would rather live frugally with her gentleman merchant than receive a widow's pension. She had refrained, however, from mentioning that her daughters were still not with her.

The only news she had received since that last letter was through Mrs Smythe. She had been informed by the army that Monsieur de Sève would not be returning to her lodging house.

Jeanne had kept going, living on her meagre revenue, which she knew through Marie-Anne she could greatly increase if she offered her services to another employer. But working in the same building meant she would at least be accessible for Paul should he need her, and be there when he returned after schooling. And this morning, she had remained at his bedside, stroking his forehead, for he had come down with a nasty cold.

'Ladies,' said Jeanne in greeting as she entered the room that was noticeably warmer than usual. 'It is so cold this morning. I cannot believe it!'

Mrs Smythe struggled not to mention the lateness of the hour. She must retain her superior calmness, for Madame Delpech had already shown an ugly turn of temper on a number of occasions. Especially on one occasion, when Mrs Smythe tried to impose an extra hour of work during lunch. Jeanne had stormed off in a huff and would not return to work until two days later, narrowly averting a commercial catastrophe with one of the clients.

'Ah, Madame Delpech, have you noticed anything—apart from the lateness of the hour?' she said, which she immediately regretted, and tried to cover up the slip of the tongue with a benevolent smile.

'My son vas poorly zis night,' returned Jeanne as she scoured the room, smiled to Nelly, and noticed the shiny columns of silk thread. She took her seat at the loom.

'Well, I hope he gets better quick. Now, Madame Delpech, I have purchased the silk we spoke about last week so that you may start practicing on small items such as—'

'But I am sorry, Madam, I told you. I do not know about ze silk.'

Of course you don't, my sweetie, thought Mrs Smythe. She cracked another smile and went on: 'But you can learn, can't you?'

'How I learn?' said Jeanne, who never asked to become a silk weaver in the first place. 'I do not want.'

'Come, Madame Delpech, you are French. You must know something of silk. I suspect you are hiding your true colours again . . .'

'I do not do silk,' said Jeanne, more insistently. But her limited command of the English language turned her insistence into something bordering on rancour.

'While you are in my employ, Madame, you will have to learn!' said Mrs Smythe. She would not be talked down to by an employee who, what was more, lived virtually free of charge under her roof.

Jeanne's English had come along to allow her to express the bare necessities, but it left her without linguistic defence when it came to a verbal battle. Moreover, she now found herself physically trapped. For it would be unwise to move at the beginning of winter. 'I am not a silk weaver, Madam!' she said as her only defence.

Mrs Smythe's plan was going awry. She had hoped her good humour and the effort to purchase the beautiful silk thread would have incited the French woman to go the extra mile to satisfy her employer. Did the woman not have any professional pride? Nevertheless, Mrs Smythe was not done yet. 'Madame,' she said, trying to calm the tense atmosphere, 'I am prepared to increase your hours and pay.'

'It will make not difference,' said Jeanne. 'I am not qualified to do silk!'

'Ah, but if it is the London guild you are worried about,

Madame, we are outside their jurisdiction. Why else do you think your countrymen have settled here outside the city walls?'

That was interesting to know, thought Jeanne. But even so, she would not be whipped into doing something she could not do properly. 'No, I say, Madam!' said Jeanne with finality. 'Now, I must go to my son!' She got to her feet and sailed out, head poised, into the half light of the freezing cold staircase.

*

Paul was sleeping open-mouthed. Jeanne wondered what she would do were she without him. He opened his eyes.

'Don't worry, Paul. We shall be out of here once I have found somewhere. We shall move to a nicer place.'

The boy sniffed and wiped his nose on his cuff. 'We don't have any money,' he said in his indomitable voice of reason. Then he sneezed.

Jeanne sat down on the four-poster rope bed; then she lay her head down beside him. She decided she would not return to the workshop. She would not work in any workshop. She closed her eyes, and fell into a comforting sleep.

*

There was a knock at the door.

Jeanne awoke to a glacial room, the wood burner having consumed its fuel. The tip of her nose was cold, but it was warm as toast in bed with her son, snuggled under the covers. She got up and covered over Paul, who groaned and sneezed.

'Yes, I am coming!' she called out in French in answer to a more insistent knock. She straightened her shawl and

708

pinned back her hair, then opened the door.

'Madame,' said Mrs Smythe, standing on the landing with her big overcoat on.

'Madam?' Jeanne returned.

'I fear there has been a misunderstanding.'

Jeanne let the landlady stand on the threshold and looked levelly into her eyes, her head slightly held back. 'You mean?'

'I mean I would be much obliged if you returned to work. There is an order for your woollen fabrics. I am willing to overlook the silk until I find someone qualified to weave it, which should not be difficult as I will be offering lodgings with the job.'

'Ah,' said Jeanne, who guessed where the landlady was leading. It was surely a preamble to her eviction, was it not?

'Now, concerning your rent. Knowing your current circumstances, I have refrained from bringing it up.'

'Rent?'

'Yes, Madame. Your husband only paid for your first three months of accommodation here. So from August to the end of October. He said the money would be sent to you as part of his pay.'

Jeanne recalled the letter from Jacob, in which he briefly explained that his pay was in arrears, but that he had been told it would arrive shortly, and that money would be sent over to her.

The truth was that the Huguenot soldiers had not been paid for months. It was not considered urgent. They would hardly abscond; they had nowhere to go. Jacob had been able to borrow money for his own needs, but had no means to get any monies to his wife.

Mrs Smythe went on. 'In a letter from your husband, he

asked me to allow him extra time to pay the rent. Well, I have kept my word, but the fact remains . . . your husband is in a dangerous line of work, is he not? All the newsletter reports are not good, and dare I say it, for all I know, he may even have gone the same way as Monsieur de Sève. For all I know, I may well get a message from the army like the one I got for Monsieur de Sève. Then what?'

Jeanne remained proud, unmoved, and dignified despite the turmoil inside and the freezing cold draft whirling up the stairwell.

Mrs Smythe went on. 'I am sure you are aware there has been a massacre due to camp fever. Now, you are six weeks in arrears, Madame. But, I am prepared for you to pay it back in instalments. That is, as long as I am able to count on your continued services to cover all the incoming orders. At least, until I have found a replacement for you.'

Jeanne realised Mrs Smythe was playing her trump card. But Jeanne also knew that Mrs Smythe was desperate to complete the orders, so she remained silent and let her suffer a little bit more.

'What do you say, Madame?'

'I say it is unfair,' said Jeanne at last.

'On the contrary, I have been very fair in saving you from the burden and strain of this debt. However, you will understand, I have a business to run, and a lodging house in high demand. Why, rents in the neighbourhood are going sky-high; the lands are being snapped up for building. You will not find a more spacious set of rooms for the price! Put yourself in my shoes, Madame.'

'I say it is unfair because you pay under the market rate!'

'Oh, so have I not been fair in employing you despite your

lack of knowledge in silk? Weave silk, my fair lady, and I will pay you more!' Jeanne, putting her fist on her waist, was about to reply, but, holding up her hand, Mrs Smythe forestalled her. 'Nonetheless, Madame . . . Nonetheless, I will up your rate by a penny.' Mrs Smythe then pulled out a slip of paper from her pocket and handed it to Jeanne. 'Here, Madame Delpech,' she said affably, 'here are the details of the rent in arrears.' Jeanne took the slip. Mrs Smythe continued. 'May I leave it with you, Madame? I hope I can expect you downstairs tomorrow morning to fulfil the orders.'

The landlady turned to leave, then checked herself. 'Oh, and how is your son?'

'Recovering, thank you, Madam,' said Jeanne. Then she slammed the door shut, harder than she had intended.

*

Jeanne would not be walked over and exploited by a lowly workshop keeper, she thought, quite snobbishly, a trait that had nonetheless carried her above the lowly emotion of self-pity.

Through her church contacts, she told herself she was bound to find her own clientele. She had heard stories of Huguenots, from silversmiths to weavers, finding their feet and excelling in their endeavours, so why couldn't she? The London population was clearly open to the fashion and techniques brought from France, despite the war. And now she knew that being outside the city walls meant she would not be subject to London guild rules.

But what to do about the rent in arrears? She simply did not have the ready cash to release herself from Mrs Smythe's debt. She was not alone, though. She would go to the church. She would seek advice from Pastor Daniel. If he had no answer regarding the legality of Mrs Smythe's proposition, at least he could put her in touch with someone who could help her.

It was bitter cold, and a flurry of snow covered the walk to the church on Threadneedle Street. This was the mother of Huguenot churches in and around London, where, like all Huguenots in the area, Jeanne had been registered, and through which Jacob sent his correspondence. It was also where she felt most in phase with her true nature, which made her suspect what a snob she really must be. For the Huguenots in this district belonged mostly to a higher class of craftsmen than those of the church on Artillery Lane, who were mostly cloth workers.

At every turn of a corner, Jeanne never ceased to marvel at the maze of endless lanes and streets, not to mention the array of means of transport that conveyed people through them. The moment she stepped through the city gate, it all felt both grandiose and belittling. And it made her realise that she was really a country girl at heart after all.

Catholic and Protestant bells rang out in unison as they had once done in France. Jeanne had long since noticed that people did their business whatever your creed or confession here, unlike in today's France, where a foreigner was a stranger and being a non-Catholic was a crime punishable by death or a life at the oar. And to think, Jeanne used to believe that this kind of intolerance belonged to a time when people still wondered whether God had made the world flat or round. But it was happening today in her home country, whereas here, in this city of business par excellence, the religious freedom transcended the society, opening avenues and offering opportunities.

The south-facing church steps were glistening in a pool of sunshine that had melted away the night's frost. She pushed the small side door into the church, where a choir was practicing. She said a prayer and then marched to the sacristy, where she gave good day to Samuel Clement, the warden.

'I fear Pastor Daniel is out, Madame Delpech,' said Mr Clement affably. 'But if you have come about the letter, I can give it to you.'

'A letter?'

'Yes, from the army, I believe,' said Mr Clement, turning to a neatly placed pile of correspondence.

The mention of a letter from the army wiped away Jeanne's thoughts of her present dilemma as she feared the worst. A moment later, Mr Clement handed her the letter in question, sealed with the stamp of the army. She took it with solemn thanks and said she would open it later. She could not take another setback just now.

'Are you all right, Madame Delpech?' said Mr Clement.

Jeanne assured him she was fine. She thanked him again, told him to give her regards to his good wife, and walked out of the house of God. It was not a place to face her disillusionment.

Numbed by the shock, she took to walking the streets of London. A thin film of ice had formed over puddles in shaded streets where the pavement was uneven. Her feet took her down towards the river, where no tall buildings would oppress her. How she longed for open fields; how she missed the great sun-filled plain where she was born, where she had been so happy. Why is happiness such a perishable thing, she wondered, and so difficult to preserve?

She soon found herself at the riverside by Dowgate Dock,

near Three Cranes Stairs. Only the buildings on London Bridge to her left blocked her view. She felt faint for lack of something inside her. She sat down on a bench and watched the boats and wherries carrying passengers wrapped up for the cold, back and forth across the Thames. She sat with her thoughts amid distant cries from stevedores and dockhands, fish wives and merchants as the old river continued its course before her under the leaden sky.

What should she do now? she wondered. How could she go on if the letter she was holding announced that Jacob had succumbed to his wounds or had contracted the terrible camp fever? Either way, crying about it would not help her situation. So she just sat there, gathering her thoughts.

'Madam. Nice day, innit?' said a cheery male voice beside her.

It was a warm voice, and a word of kindness would not go amiss right now. She glanced to her right and gave good day and a guarded smile to the gruff-looking gent, who had taken it upon himself to take a seat beside her. She did not want to appear a snob.

'French?'

'Yes, Sir.'

'I like a bit o' French,' said the man, with a crafty leer. Jeanne was not sure she understood right. He continued. 'How much then, eh?' Jeanne then looked at him in shock and horror. 'Come on, my lovely,' coaxed the man, sliding closer. 'How's about sixpence for a grope and a suck?'

Jeanne stamped to her feet, but he grabbed her arm.

'Only askin', ain't I?' he said in banter. Jeanne shook her arm from his grasp and scurried away with his barking laugh in her ears.

God, she thought, had it all come to this? Prostitution or the life of a labourer in a weave room?

The bells of St Paul's rang out behind her as she turned eastward onto Thames Street. She reflected on the possible missed chances God had laid in her path. The chance to recant, for example. Had she done so, she would still be in her beloved Montauban. Had she abjured, she would still have her children about her now, warming themselves by a well-fuelled fire. She would have lived in disaccord with her convictions, but maybe that was the price to pay.

Had she refused the path of abjuration out of pure selfishness?

If not, then for what? For the sake of religious freedom? For the right of every man and woman to follow their beliefs and their intimate convictions? For the right to walk through the doors of the church of their choice? For the right to denounce the Catholic one-thought regime, appropriated by unworthy men who created chains of power and worshipped their moneymaking schemes? Who had immorally attached their laws and political aspirations to the teachings of Christ?

Jeanne slipped on a puddle on Fish Street but managed to recover her balance. She continued on her train of thought.

True, she would still be in Montauban, but the world would be condemned to a one-thought regime if she, Jacob, and people like them had not resisted the temptation of choosing the easy path. That was all very high and mighty, but what now?

She suddenly wondered if her outlook on life was all wrong.

'Madam. Madam!'

Jeanne turned around at the call of an approaching lady.

She stopped walking to let the young woman catch up with her.

'You dropped this,' she said, handing Jeanne the sealed envelope.

'Oh, thank you, Madam.'

'I know how important they are,' said the woman, who was forthright and rosy-cheeked, neatly dressed but not expensively so. She went on. 'I had one myself. My husband's a military man, too, you see.'

'Oh, I . . .'

'Cheered me up no end, so I do know how you'd feel if you'd gone and lost it . . .'

'What do you mean?'

'Ah, have a look inside, and you'll find out, Madam! Go on, open it!'

Jeanne paused a moment. The woman had a friendly face. She had run after her with the letter. She had received one like it. And it had made her happy.

At the woman's insistence, Jeanne removed her gauntlet gloves, which she held under her armpits, then broke the seal. She found it hard to decipher the English handwriting at first. She then brought her cold fist to her mouth as her eyes glistened in the freezing air.

'There, see, payment for officer's wives!' said the lady, underlining the words with her gloved forefinger.

Jeanne could hardly speak. She suppressed the impulse to cry, brushed her eyes, crushed her cold, red nose with her palm.

'Thank you,' she said to the young lady. 'Thank you!'

'Don't thank me; thank your ole man, my love. You just have to take it to the payment desk, and then you'll get what's owing to you.'

20

JEANNE STOOD BY the warp frame in the workshop.

She was wearing her thick woollen shawl over her shoulders to keep the cold and damp from her aching back, and was showing the seamstress how to set the warp. But though the girl was helpful and pretty, Jeanne found her not very bright and sometimes impertinent.

'All right, Madame Jeanne! So it's over and under and up to the top,' said the seamstress, trailing her finger over the corresponding pegs.

'Yes,' said Jeanne, trying very hard to keep calm and patient. She had already explained this part ten times to her.

Jeanne had paid her rent in arrears and agreed to carry on weaving on Mrs Smythe's loom in her frugally heated workshop for a raise of a penny, although she still had not received it. And now, with the run-up to Christmas, the orders had increased to such an extent that she was obliged to forfeit her own spinning and work the loom in the afternoons too. She had been working full days for weeks now, only able to get to church on Sundays. She felt like her world was shrinking, now reduced to her rooms and the workshop. She had received no more news from Jacob, and neither had she heard from her sister in France, now that the war prevented correspondence between the two nations.

'Over and under in form of an eight, Nelly. It is not so difficult,' said Jeanne in her heavy accent. But at least she was making sentences.

'All right, Madame Jeanne,' said Nelly, 'keep your hair on. You don't have to shout about it!'

'I am not shouting. But you must open your eyes, Nelly. You make mistake, you start again!'

'Well, I can't help it if I'm no good with machines, can I?'

'But do you want to be a weaver or no?'

'I'd much rather marry one, if you don't mind me saying! And my feet are blimmin' freezing. Ain't yours?'

Jeanne was losing her patience, and Nelly was losing her concentration again and becoming saucy.

Nelly did not appreciate being told what to do by someone who did not even speak properly. She might have been someone where she came from, but they didn't want her, did they! 'Anyway, I've got these dresses to do . . .' said Nelly, who was fed up with the French lady's moods. She was nice at first, but now she just kept talking to her as if she were a dimwit, which she was not, because dimwits don't know what they want, do they? And she most certainly did, especially since she met the gentleman the other day, when Madame Jeanne had stomped off upstairs in another one of her fits as she often did.

He was a weaver in his mid-twenties, not very tall but good-looking with long, wavy hair, just like the dead soldier who used to live upstairs, and he had smiled at her.

Mrs Smythe had introduced him to the seamstress and shown him the loom where Jeanne normally sat.

'I am purchasing a newer one. It should be assembled by next week,' Mrs Smythe had told the young man slowly and deliberately. After repeating it, and using her hands to convey what she was getting at, he had returned an irresistible accented grunt of comprehension. 'Ah, bien, monté . . . la semaine prochaine,' he had said. He was French, too, and only spoke a little English, which, with hindsight, Mrs Smythe saw as an advantage. It meant that she would command any linguistic exchange.

This weaver was young, male, and attractive, and Nelly had got to dreaming of a possible romance, unless old Aunt Smythe got in before her. But she knew deep down it was only her sense of jealousy playing tricks on her. Besides, now past mothering years, Mrs Smythe had already been through three husbands. She was only concerned with her business.

Now that she had broken in one foreigner, Mrs Smythe was ready to take on another. In fact, it had become crucial that she do so, what with the French lady's high-flown attitude, not to mention her lack of silk weaving expertise. And besides, a rebellious element could put her whole business at risk, especially now that orders were coming in fast and furious. She could not allow the momentum to slack. If she delayed the Christmas orders, she would be roasted. No one would ever trust her again.

So she had decided to invest in a new loom. While enquiring about prices and delays at the loom maker's, she had bumped into this Monsieur Chausson, a weaver's apprentice from Tours, no less. It did not take much to imagine what the mere mention of a weaver from Tours could do for her good name and business.

She had been planning on purchasing the loom after the

end-of-year festivities, once her suppliers had paid her. But sometimes, you had to think on your feet and know to snap up an opportunity when the good Lord put one in front of you, because they did not come often. So Mrs Smythe had been down to the loom maker's that morning and had left a down payment, which was not an easy thing for her to do, since parting with money was something Mrs Smythe hated more than anything.

'Afternoon, ladies,' she said on entering the workshop, which lacked the familiar rhythm of the loom, a music Mrs Smythe loved more than any other.

'I thought you'd have finished setting by now. C'mon, get a wiggle on, ladies, let's get beating!' she said in a sing-song voice, punctuating her order with a clap of the hands. It was the refrain Jeanne detested most, loaded as it was with patronising superiority.

How she could have kicked herself for letting the woman get the better of her. She suppressed the impulse to stamp her foot and turn on her heels, for there were orders to honour. Instead, she smiled wryly and said in the politest voice she could muster: 'It would be easier if we had not so cold, Madam. There needs more wood on the fire.' But after only four months in the English capital, she had not mastered intonation as well as she would have liked. It came out like a demand.

Mrs Smythe had just handed over the first part of a small fortune to the loom maker. She was not in the mood for self-restraint. 'Madame, no matter how much wood goes up in flames, if you are not active, then you will always feel the cold! And besides, too much heat makes one sleepy, and I cannot have you delaying further on the orders, or they will never get done, will they!'

'I give you more hours than we agreed, Madam,' said Jeanne. 'I have kept my word, but you not. You said my pay would go up!'

'I also said, Madame, that I would have to be paid myself before I can become extravagant with pay!'

'Extravagant? You pay a lower rate than everyone!'

'Huh! Weavers are ten to a penny nowadays, my dear. It would seem all the world would be a weaver!' said Mrs Smythe, leaving the rest of her thoughts implied. But she knew she must not push it too far, for there were orders to be completed by Christmas Eve, which was in little more than a week. 'Until then,' she continued in a more temperate tone of voice, 'I promised to keep the rent at the present rate, which works out the same as an increase in pay, does it not, Madame?'

'No,' said Jeanne, standing erect. 'It removes my freedom of choice! And that, Madam, is why I am here! And you did not say you increase the rent!'

'Offer and demand, Madame,' said Mrs Smythe with a winning smile. 'But look at it this way: if the demand went down, then so would the rent!'

Jeanne was fuming inside. Did this woman think she was dumb? She would not be condescended to, and all her pent-up anxiety and fury began to boil over, which brought out her accent even more when she said: 'In zat case, I shall return to my veel, Madam!'

'You shall do no such thing if you want to keep your job. You will resume your loom!' said Mrs Smythe, emboldened by the knowledge that she no longer had to walk on eggshells, for Monsieur Chausson could easily step in for the moody French tart.

Jeanne had had enough of being talked down to by a lowly penny-pincher. She had had enough of this cold, damp place, of having to slip out and rush through her market purchases instead of enjoying the friendly banter of the vendors. She had had enough of having to refuse invitations from church acquaintances. She had fled her country in the name of religious tolerance. She was not going to forfeit her liberty to act in the very country that was fighting a war in defence of that tolerance, a country that had renounced Catholic domination, torture, and burnings at the stake for the freedom to choose.

'Then do it yourself!' she said.

'Oh, I won't need to!' said Mrs Smythe as Jeanne stomped past her to the door, which she pulled hard behind her.

Mrs Smythe was momentarily tempted to run after her. But then she remembered she did not need to. She would find the young weaver that very morning. She would tell him he need not wait for the new loom, he could start tomorrow, and that the job came with a room.

21

JEANNE STOOD BACK and admired her son, dressed in his new suit.

She had dug out a blue velvet coat, waistcoat, breeches, blue stockings, and buckled shoes at the second-hand clothes market and had altered the garments to fit properly.

It was Christmas morning, and rare sunshine flooded the apartment, setting off the lively colours. She was pleased with her handiwork and her attempt at fitting him out in clothes she thought more in keeping with his lineage. She fastened his thick, black woollen travel cloak beneath his chin, kissed his forehead, and placed his tricorn hat on his little head.

Then she put on her own heavy cloak over her beautiful oxblood boned bodice and beige woollen skirts. Her white linen neckerchief protected her bosom from draughts, and she had attached white linen cuffs for the special occasion. Next, she pinned her wide-brimmed hat over her coif and pulled on her embroidered gauntlet gloves of soft beige lambskin.

'How do I look?' she said to Paul.

'Like a countess,' he returned approvingly. 'Shall I go first to check that the coast is clear?'

Over the past week, he had served as her stairwell scout. And so far, they had not bumped into the landlady. Jeanne did not want to be asked to work in the workshop again. She had felt guilty at first about abandoning her post, but then was shocked at how quickly Mrs Smythe had replaced her, almost as if she had set her up to leave so the new weaver could make a start.

Jeanne did not want to stir up tensions, for, though she could hardly bear being under the same roof as Mrs Smythe, she knew she must wait until the cold snap was over to find new lodgings. In the meantime, she had kept mostly to her spinning wheel, venturing out to the market for provisions less frequently than before as, given the cold, she could conserve edibles in the larder for longer. Paul had been on hand to fetch up water and faggots for the wood burner.

'No, we shall go down together,' she said. She could not keep putting off an encounter. Anyway, the workshop would be closed.

As they descended the creaking stairway, they could hear the knocking of wood on the landing below. It could only be Mrs Smythe, sweeping before her door. Jeanne could hardly turn back, and besides, she would have to confront her at some stage.

'Madam,' said Jeanne as the landlady looked up from her sweeping. 'Happy Christmas, Mrs Smythe.'

Mrs Smythe cracked a smile which contrasted with her frosty frown, and returned her lodger's season's greetings. She sniffed and feigned not to notice their high-class garb.

'By the way, Madame Delpech,' she said, standing prim and proper behind her broom. 'I should inform you that the new weaver will be moving in shortly now that the previous lodger, the northerner, has moved on.' She was talking about a discreet northern man who had rented the room above Jeanne's while he was in London. Jeanne had only ever seen him once, busy as she was at the time in the workshop downstairs.

'Thank you,' said Jeanne, who longed for the day when she would announce her move to another abode.

'So he'll be settling in Monsieur de Sève's old room. That poor friend of your husband's who died. Have you any news, by the way?'

'No, I have not.'

'May the Lord help him in his plight,' said Mrs Smythe, trying to be nice.

'Thank you,' said Jeanne, guardedly. Jeanne sensed the woman was leading up to something. It was clear she had deliberately formulated her chat to bring it round to Jacob so she could fish for news.

'I should also let you know,' continued Mrs Smythe, 'I have purchased another loom, better for silk. The other one will be needing a weaver, though, should you be inclined . . .'

'Thank you, Mrs Smythe, but I am sure you will find someone to work it for you,' said Jeanne, desirous to curtail the conversation. By saying it out loud, she had at last made intellectual and psychological closure. She was relieved to imply that she would never work for the landlady again. She felt better, suddenly serene for it.

'I am sure I will,' said Mrs Smythe as Jeanne stepped across the landing. 'Especially as the job comes with rooms!'

Jeanne gave Mrs Smythe good day while pushing Paul onwards to continue down the last flight of stairs.

It was a beautiful and frosty morning. Bells were ringing

out across London as they directed their steps to the Huguenot church on Threadneedle Street. They had set out earlier than usual to make sure they would get a place in a pew, although Mrs Clement, the warden's wife, did say she would save them places next to her and her husband.

Jeanne exchanged nods, bows, and Christmas greetings to acquaintances as they entered the church, already two-thirds full of finely yet soberly dressed Protestants. A far cry, thought Jeanne, from the gaudy fashions in France. Mrs Clement gave a sign, and Jeanne and Paul took their places.

The minister preached most excellently on Luke 3, she thought. But Jeanne soon let her attention drift and her thoughts ramble, and prayed for her husband's safe return should that please Almighty God. Then she got to pondering over Mrs Smythe's remark. She had said that the weaver job came with accommodation, but there were no other rooms available if the new weaver was taking the one recently made vacant. Jeanne concluded that it was a thinly veiled threat. Either she resumed her work at Mrs Smythe's loom, or she would be thrown out on her ear. Whatever the legality of the situation, it meant Jeanne would have to act quickly. For she was adamant this time: she would never set foot in Smythe's workshop again. It was bad enough knowing that the woman slept in the room beneath hers, let alone sharing the same air under her haughty stare.

After the service, she and Paul joined Mr and Mrs Clement along with Pastor Daniel and half a dozen other acquaintances for Christmas dinner at their house in neighbouring Soho. Jeanne was surprised to find a handsome neoclassic town house, three windows wide and three storeys tall. It was set back from the street and entered through an elegant white portico. Decidedly, Mr and Mrs Clement had done well to have fled France with their fortune intact before the troubles in France had begun. Jeanne felt a pinch in her heart at realising she could well have done the same, and been in a similar situation now with her husband and children around her at this Christmastime.

A gentleman who Jeanne knew by sight but had never officially met was introduced to her as Monsieur Jacques Rulland. An English gentleman of French ancestry, his father had moved his English wife and their family to London from La Rochelle back in '48 after Cardinal Mazarin, in an effort to curb Protestantism in the port city, founded the bishopric of La Rochelle. A mature and prosperous man in his early fifties, Monsieur Rulland possessed a weaving house and had been a widower since the previous year, when his wife succumbed to scarlet fever. He had the rigid allure of an Englishman, and spoke French with a slight English accent, pleasing to a French ear. It occurred to Jeanne that this was how Paul might sound and appear in years to come, the gentleman having left France at the same age as her son.

After the usual badinage, the topic of conversation at table inevitably turned to the Irish campaign, the fear of James Stuart's return to the throne, and the determination of the new Dutch king and the English people to retain their freedom to practice the religion of their choice. It was common knowledge that Jeanne's husband was fighting in Ireland, and she appreciated that they had not limited the conversation on her account. After the mention that there would be no more advancements made during the months of winter, in her calm and poised voice, Jeanne said: 'I only hope and pray I get my husband back. Though I am proud he has embarked on the fight to stave off intolerance.'

'And so you should be, dear Madame Delpech, and so should we all!' said Mr Rulland quite spiritedly in his quaint English accent. 'And so should his son, my word!' he continued, placing a benevolent but frank eye on Paul, a cue for the boy to speak.

'I am, Sir,' said the lad forthrightly. 'And I hope to follow in his footsteps.' This took everyone by surprise, coming as it did from an eleven-year-old, and no one less so than his mother. There had been no soldiers in her family, and she secretly hoped there never would be. But not wanting to belittle him, she held her tongue.

'And whose side would you fight on, my lad?' said Mr Clement.

Paul sensed this was an important question, especially as it was asked by none other than one of the men who let people into church. 'Why, that of freedom of conscience, of course!' Mr Clement gave a thin-lipped smile of appreciation while the table gave a round of hear-hears.

Mr Rulland raised his glass. 'To the birth of our Lord Jesus and freedom of conscience!'

After dessert, they retired to the spacious, high-ceilinged parlour with crystal chandeliers, where Mrs Clement and her daughters led the singing. Then they merrily played blind man's buff. Jeanne laughed so hard, it brought tears to her eyes and made her cheeks hurt. It surprised Paul to see her so merry. In fact, he did not recall ever seeing her in such a frivolous state.

After the fun and games, a collation was served.

'Madame Delpech,' said Mr Rulland, who was sitting opposite her in a wide-winged armchair. Jeanne was seated on a canapé. There was a low table between them with a tray of mince pies, and Mrs Clement sat in her poised and affable way next to her. 'I have been given to understand you have a talent for the loom. Surprising of so fair a lady, if I may say so.'

Both piqued and flattered at the suggestion that weaving was below her, Jeanne said: 'Surprising, perhaps, but it has stood me well, Sir, and helped me pay my own way.'

'I see. If I may be so bold as to ask, who do you weave for?'

'Actually, I am contemplating acquiring a loom of my own, for the wage I earned at my previous employer was ridiculously low compared to the going rate.'

'I see. So you are without a loom for the moment?'

'I am, Sir. But I have my spinning wheel to keep me going. I should have to move to new lodgings before I install a loom.'

'Madame Delpech says she would very much like to learn silk weaving,' prompted Madame Clement.

Jeanne explained: 'I have been given to understand there is a more lucrative market in silk cloth.'

'Indeed, there is, Madame,' said Jacques Rulland. Then, licking his lips as though turning over words in his mouth, he inched forward in his seat and said: 'As a matter of fact, Madame Delpech, silk is one of my workshop's specialties. Should you be seeking employment, albeit temporary, I should be glad to have you aboard. If you know how to use a loom, then you will learn silk weaving quickly enough.'

'Oh. That is most kind of you, Monsieur Rulland. However—'

'Please,' said Rulland, sensing the prelude to a rebuff, 'there is no hurry for an answer. But please, do dwell upon it, Madame.' He brought out a visiting card and handed it to her. Jeanne thanked him kindly and promised she would.

From the other side of the room, Mr Clement stood up and suggested a last game of blind man's buff, to everyone's delight.

Rising with her counterparts, Jeanne felt a warmth in her heart with the assurance that should Jacob, alas, not return from Ireland, she need not remain a lonely widow for very long. And then, as the very thought of becoming Jacob's widow sunk into her slightly fuddled mind, she clasped Paul's hand and inwardly prayed her husband would return to her, that they would live again as a family.

*

Jeanne had had a delightful day in the bourgeois comfort at the Clements' house in Soho.

Now she felt like a countess as she was driven through the streets of London, through Bishop's Gate, up the busy thoroughfare, and through the narrow streets past Spittle Field. How easy it was to fall back into manners of old, she thought. It felt right. She was once a wealthy countess, after all.

But of course, it was all a sham. Tomorrow, she would be dressed in her common grey petticoats and bodice. Tomorrow, she would be carrying water to her rooms. Tomorrow, she would be lighting faggots, opening windows to let out the smoke, and stuffing rags into gaps to stop up the cracks in the wood burner. If it was sunny, she would be spinning at the window; if it was overcast, she would be spinning by the stove, in spite of the dim light. But that was tomorrow.

Today, she was a French countess, dressed in elegant

simplicity, wrapped in her warm travel cloak, riding through the streets of London in a carriage paid for by a gentleman acquaintance. Mr Rulland in his enthusiasm had even promised to take her for a bucolic ride into rural Hackney, come springtime. Naturally, she had declined; it would not be correct to accept to go on such an outing with a gentleman unless they were accompanied. But she noted that he had not been put out and suspected that he would arrange something with the Clements.

People glanced up at her as the carriage trundled through the crowded poor districts. Paul was gripped by the view out the opposite window; how strange it was to look at his play area from the height of the carriage. It looked shabby, and he felt ridiculous in his best bourgeois clothes. What would his street mates think?

They turned left onto Brick Lane, where the road was bumpy, frozen solid into furrows. A knock on the roof interrupted Jeanne's sumptuous thoughts. It was accompanied by the jangle of harness bells as the carriage came to a halt.

'Maman, we are here,' said Paul.

'Brick Lane, Madam,' called the driver.

Jeanne asked the driver to pull up past Brown's Lane. He did not need to see where they lived. After descending, she felt the shock of passing from Soho to Brick Lane, and suddenly worried she would be taken for a wealthy bourgeois who had lost her way. She clenched her cloak around her and hurried along with Paul to the tenement building.

But a few minutes later, they were thankfully climbing the stairs to their rooms. It was getting dark already, and there was a warm glow coming from the door ajar on the landing above. It was accompanied by the sound of scraping, as if furniture was being moved.

As Jeanne turned the key in the lock, someone came bounding down the stairs. It must be the owner of the pile of linen that had been left on her landing, she thought.

'Oh,' said a male voice as Jeanne half turned to face the stairs. She saw a young man with cavalier curls. He bowed. 'Er, I am . . . Monsieur Chausson,' he said, fumbling for words in English.

'You can speak in French,' said Jeanne levelly.

'Ah, good, that's a relief,' he continued. 'I am the new weaver, Madame . . .'

'I see. And I am the old one,' returned Jeanne, unable to keep a sardonic twitch from creasing her brow.

'Oh, I would never have guessed,' said Chausson, with a fleeting glance at her attire. 'I . . . I have been admiring your work, Madame. But if you don't mind me asking, why did you stop?'

'Shall we say . . . discordance,' returned Jeanne. The word just popped out of her mouth; she did not mean it to refer to any difference of social class, but it seemed so apt for many aspects of her life now.

'I can well understand that,' said the young weaver. He then explained he had been a journeyman since his arrival from Holland, though he was originally from Tours, where he had been an apprentice. 'I shan't be here long, though, a stopgap until I get to grips with the language. Then I'll get my own premises and a loom of my own,' he said. Jeanne wondered if Mrs Smythe and the seamstress would let him get away so easily. Without further discussion, he picked up his pile of linen and bid her and the boy season's greetings and a good evening.

A few moments later, she sat down on her bed, her dress discordant with her surroundings, her education discordant with her situation, and stared at her spinning wheel, discordant with her breeding. But had she any other choice than to be what she was not? At least she had not betrayed her faith and deepest convictions. Paul came and sat on the bed beside her.

'Mother,' he said, 'what will you do if Papa does not come back, like the gentleman implied?' She looked at him as his eyes welled.

*

Jeanne worked through Christmastide and into the New Year, her orders keeping her busy, keeping her mind from becoming wayward. For she had been thinking of her future options, whether Jacob returned or not.

She could take up Mr Rulland's job offer, or wait to purchase a loom once the cold snap was over and she had found new accommodations. The second option would give her freedom from subordination. However, it would also mean living life to the rhythm of the loom beater. But the encounter with the French-born English gentleman and the ride in the carriage also allowed her to realise that she was not as old as she sometimes felt. She still had her breeding and could still attract a husband of quality. And she still had a good few childbearing years ahead of her yet. Should she have to remarry, she knew it would be hard to build an unbreakable bond of love such as the one she had enjoyed with Jacob. She would have to build instead a strategic alliance for the sake of her future, to save herself from the loom and to give her children a station in life that she had forfeited by not recanting her faith in France. Someone like Monsieur Rulland, who had known true love and would have more pragmatic expectations, might be a prime choice.

Sitting at her wheel, she gazed out at the barren yards lit up by rare winter sunshine, as her ears pricked to the sound of heavy masculine footsteps on the stairway. The new weaver returned to his room every day at lunchtime. No doubt to escape the oppression of Mrs Smythe, thought Jeanne. She had left him to his own devices, had exchanged neighbourly greetings whenever they crossed on the landing. He looked the part and seemed to be getting on well, especially with the girl. On returning from the market, Jeanne often heard gales of laughter coming from the workshop and overheard the seamstress correcting his English. The girl was apparently showing a better frame of mind with him than she had done with her. And Jeanne had once heard a soft giggle and two sets of footsteps creeping up to his room. It was looking as though young Nelly would catch herself a weaver after all. And why not? She was pretty; she would teach him English; they would make a complementary team when setting up business.

Their alliance made sense, as had hers with Jacob. Jeanne born into a noble family, he a wealthy notary, and they had made a beautiful family, shattered by the folly and intolerance of the Catholic Church and a king.

The steps halted outside her door. She turned on her stool with sudden alarm on the second rap. 'I'm coming . . .' she called out as she stood up. Crossing the room, she tucked her fringe beneath her bonnet. Dear God, she said to herself, closing her eyes, bracing herself for the dreaded news she had been half expecting. But as she stepped forward, the doorknob was turned. The door flung open. There stood not one but two people. Paul in the arms of his father!

Jacob stood wordless on the threshold as Paul scrambled to the ground.

Dumbfounded, Jeanne stopped in her tracks, four yards from the door, and let her hands drop to her sides. Jacob, thinner, rugged, and dressed in a grey military overcoat, was barely recognisable as the middle-aged, portly merchant-planter she last saw nigh on four yours ago. Attired in a simple grey dress, wisps of hair escaping from beneath a white bonnet, Jeanne stared intently with her pale blue eyes.

'Jeanne?' said Jacob. She realised how she must look to him; he had never seen her in a cloth maker's garb. 'My dear Jeanne,' he continued. Her eyes studied the soldier's uniform, then his face. He had a scar on his right cheek, half covered by his beard of two weeks.

Paul tugged on his father's thumb, and Jacob stepped into the room. 'I expect you are hungry,' said Jeanne.

'I expect you are angry,' said Jacob.

Jeanne shook her head. His eyes conveyed to her his deepest regret and told her he realised all she had suffered. She bowed her head into her knuckle; then she lunged towards him. He took a step forward and met her grasp with his embrace.

'I am here now,' he said, kissing her forehead, then her cheek, then her lips.

Paul said: 'I will go and fetch some more wood.'

'And some beef!' said Jeanne, cheerily, wiping away her tears of joy as the boy flew out, closing the front door behind him.

She turned back to Jacob. 'Our daughters . . .' she began.

But he put a finger on her lips.

'I know. Paul told me.'

She guided him to the room next door, removed his greatcoat, then his jacket, his smell invading her senses. 'Does it still hurt a lot?' she said, on sensing him flinch at the touch of his left shoulder.

'Not anymore,' he said. He scooped her up like a newlywed and carried her to the rope bed, where he had thrown his hat.

*

Jeanne caressed his bosom with her palm, then ran her fingers lightly over his left shoulder, softly exploring the deep red scar in his flesh.

'It still hurts.'

'It twinges. Still cannot raise it above my head, but I should rather count myself lucky. Half a span further, and it would have been my neck . . .'

She placed an ear to his chest so she could listen to his beating heart. 'I missed you. I missed us, Jacob,' she said as he caressed her hair. Then she raised her head as a sudden thought pierced her mind. She said: 'You are not going back.' He touched her temple lightly with his right hand but remained wordless. 'Jacob . . . Jacob?'

'The war is not over, my Jeanne. I must return when the campaign resumes. But we'll have time to work things out.'

Jeanne sat bolt upright, her steely eyes glaring at him with indignation. 'Jacob, don't you dare! I have been through hellfire and heartache to follow you here. We have to get our children back and build a home. For the love of Christ, you will not leave me again, Jacob Delpech!'

Jacob was both moved and reassured by her passionate outburst. She loved him, and he felt it in his heart. Nevertheless, trying to reason with her, he said: 'Jeanne, my dear beloved wife, I have thought of nothing else since I left Belfast. All the way, I have been tossing it over in my mind. But—'

'No, Jacob, no excuses! You will not leave me here in this horrid place! I can't anymore . . .'

'Wait, Jeanne, hear me out,' said Jacob, gently catching hold of her hands. 'You are right, and we have much to do. But the truth of the matter is . . . I need a wage.'

'I have heard it said at church that some soldiers will be allowed indefinite leave with a pension equivalent to half their normal pay. We shall move away to somewhere cheaper. We have never been city people, Jacob. We shall find a place in the country, near a port.'

Jeanne sat up straight, her ample breasts moving freely under her shift. She was still a beautiful woman; her hips were wider than when they first met, but she had maintained her figure.

He reached over for his jacket, slumped on the chair, and pulled out a pouch from his inner pocket.

'The truth is, my pay is in arrears. My partner is dead. This is my only treasure, my dear wife.'

Jacob reached then for the tray on which Jeanne had served him bread and cheese. He placed it upon the bed between them and rolled five acorn faces from the pouch onto it.

'These are what have kept me going, and they are frankly all I have left. I shall not stop until we are all together, Jeanne! Even if it means going back to war!'

Jeanne locked eyes with her husband. She read desperation and determination. He read compassion and resolution as she said more softly: 'You will not have to go back to war, Jacob . . .'

She jumped off the bed. He watched her hips swaying gracefully as she moved across the room to fetch her great cloak. She then skipped back and sat on the edge of the bed with a knife and carefully began unstitching the cloak's lining, the chill in the air making her nipples point under her shift.

'What are you doing?'

'Wait, and you will see,' she said.

He was thinking to himself how he had missed her body when she pulled out her hand from the lining to reveal a small leather drawstring pouch, one which normally carried change. Without a word, she untied the mouth. Then she poured not loose change, but diamonds and pearls, rubies and emeralds next to Jacob's acorns. Amazed, he recognised the diamonds, the pearls, and the gemstones that had been set in her ancestry jewels, her diadem, the necklace he had bought her . . .

'Why, you clever, clever lady!' he said joyfully, his hand meeting hers.

Jeanne explained how she once nearly lost them, how she had constantly sewn them into her coat, her skirt, her bodice, changing places lest someone suspected their presence. She told him about the horrid pauper who stole her coat, thinking her jewels were inside the lining, then how he had followed her and stolen her bag, leaving her for dead. She spoke about her life in Geneva, her stay in Schaffhausen, and her escape with Paul through the war-torn region of the Palatinate.

'Now, Jacob. You shall not go back to war. We have both

been through enough wars. And we have means to find a home for your acorn family!'

He placed the tray beside the bed and wrapped her in his arms as they heard footsteps, deliberately loud on the stairs. Jeanne quickly whipped her shawl around her shoulders as the latch was lifted and Paul entered the room next door.

He put down the basket of wood and placed the slab of beef on the table. Responding to his mother's call, he entered the bedroom where he looked coyly but contentedly at both his parents in the bed in the middle of the day. His bashful smile broadened when his gaze fell on the tray. Upon it, he saw the gemstones. Among them, he saw the acorn faces he had made all those years ago in the farmhouse where he stayed with his mother and sisters. He wished they could all be together now.

22

AMID THE SEETHING melee of fighting men, Jacob suddenly remembered to never leave his flank exposed. He swung round desperately, wildly clashing sabres as another determined assassin came upon him . . .

'Jacob. Jacob, darling. You were having one of your bad dreams . . .'

They came less frequently nowadays, but when they did, he felt drained of energy and at odds with himself, as if his soul had been scathed. Then, as always, he remembered he had killed a man. In fact, he had purposely killed twice. Once in the woods of a Cuban township when he shot an assailant in the chest, and once with his sword in a cornfield in the Carlingford mountains that overlooked Dundalk Bay.

He cracked open his eyes at the caress of a calming hand on his greying temple. Jeanne knew his nightmares came especially when he was agitated over something. She too had spent a wakeful night, unable to get to sleep under the weight of her regrets.

'It'll be all right,' she said as he held her hand an instant on the side of his face.

A few moments later, Jeanne jumped out of bed and threw

on a brocaded robe over her nightgown. Jacob eased his legs over the edge of the bed while she folded back the interior wooden shutters, then pulled open the window that looked out onto the emerald hills south of Dublin. The deep green scenery always had a soothing effect on him, whatever the weather, especially after a nightmare. Jeanne enjoyed the view, too, for it was the colour of hope.

There came a soft knocking at their door.

'Come in, my boy,' called Jacob, having recognised his son's footsteps in the corridor. He told himself he must kick the habit of calling him *my boy*. He was a young man now, after all.

Paul pushed the door into the bedroom, where morning light flooded through the window that his mother was closing. She turned to face him with an anxious furrow on her brow. He was already dressed in his uniform, not grey as he had remembered his father's to have been, but Venetian red. 'Mother, Father,' he said. 'A messenger has come. The *Sapphire* is in the roadstead.'

'Thank you, thank you, dear Lord!' said Jeanne, clenching her hands.

'But the tide will be out, so might I suggest we head out for Ringsend?'

The village of Ringsend was located on the estuary of River Liffey, a mile from Dublin, and barely a couple of miles from their house. It was where ships could ferry urgent goods, messages, and passengers when faced with contrary winds, or if the tide was not favourable for an entry into Dublin harbour.

'Should I get the messenger to tell them to unload the barrels as well, Father?'

'No, Paul, the wine can wait, my boy,' said Jacob, slowly half turning with a hand on the base of his back. 'The barrels can be unloaded in Dublin. Ouch . . . I only wish I hadn't put my blasted back out.'

'Serves you right for trying to lift one on your own! Honestly!' said Jeanne, in mirthful rebuke. Jacob realised her playful tone was a vent for her deep relief. The ship was in!

'Oh, it wasn't so much the barrel as my blasted shoulder giving me gyp; that's what put my back out.'

Jacob had been laid up for two days already, but at least he was able to sit up and walk now.

'I can go on my own if you prefer, Father,' said Paul.

'Oh no, my boy, much better today. But I shall let you take the reins, though.'

Paul said he would have the carriage ready in half an hour. Then he took a step back into the corridor and closed the door behind him.

A robust young man of eighteen, bicultural and bilingual, Ireland was now his home. He had been schooled by a master in the new Huguenot town of Portarlington and was destined for a military career in the British army, albeit against his mother's wishes. But Jacob still hoped to bring him over to the family business.

It was May, the year 1698, twelve years after the dragoons invaded Montauban and ejected Jacob, Jeanne, and their children from their home. After William of Orange had chased James Stuart from Ireland, Jacob was among the loyal Huguenot officers who were awarded a pension which equated to half his normal pay. Like many Huguenots, he was invited by the English Crown to settle in Ireland, where the cost of living was cheaper. They had been settled in their new home since '92. Around the same time, he had also received an invitation from friends to settle in New Rochelle. But Ireland was closer to France, and Jeanne had never lost hope of seeing her daughters again. 'As long as there is a breath in me still, I shall hope,' she would say.

Jacob's pension was barely enough for a family to live on, even in Ireland. But from the proceeds of the sale of Jeanne's jewels, Jacob was able to build a house a mile south of Dublin from the ruins of an old farm. He had since managed to build up a small trading nexus with the help of his late brother-in-law, Robert Garrisson, and former business partners now settled in Amsterdam. There had been ups and downs with cargo lost to the French and rough weather, but Jacob had long since learnt to hedge his orders by not putting them all in the same ship. The small business had kept him going.

The house that they called *Les chênes*—translated as The Oaks—was a far cry from the château Jeanne and Jacob Delpech de Castanet had left behind in the south of France. It was of simple construction, with large windows and spacious enough with five bedrooms, three good chimneys that also served the upper floor, flagstone flooring in the kitchen, and solid oak floorboards elsewhere.

Despite his back pain, Jacob was particularly joyful this morning, and pleased by the knowledge that the ship at anchor had brought his first delivery of barrels from France safely to port. Since the Treaty of Ryswick, signed the previous autumn, so bringing an end to the Nine Years' War, business was flourishing. The Channel had become a less dangerous place, now that trade had resumed with France.

However, trade was far from being his main concern today

as he sat contemplating the early-morning sunshine breaking through the clouds, flooding the distant hills here and there in a golden sheen. It was not the warm, vibrant sunrise he used to love in his homeland of southern France, but it nonetheless brought him an inner peace.

'Are you sure you don't want to come to the landing stage?' he said to Jeanne, who was doing her toilette at her dressing table behind a three-fold screen.

'No, Jacob, there will need to be extra room for baggage, and besides, who will look after Pierre?' Of course, the maid could look after their youngest, but Jacob said nothing, suspecting that she wanted it to be like a homecoming.

*

The mackerel sky, strewn with longer rags of blue, brightened the deep greens here and there of the surrounding fields. Little Pierre, Paul's six-year-old brother, jumped off the swing attached to the oak tree upon the sound of an approaching carriage.

'Mother!' he called out from the front door. 'They're here!'

Having removed her apron and left her culinary preparations to her maid, Jeanne now stood, wringing her hands on the threshold.

How could she explain her flight from France, leaving her daughters for the sake of her faith? In their eyes, was she not the mother who had abandoned her children?

Paul pulled on the reins, and the open carriage slowed to a halt at the bottom of the garden, a stone's throw from the front door. Jacob climbed stiffly down, then gave his hand to his eldest daughter.

Elizabeth had felt overjoyed and strangely humbled to find her father waiting for her at the windswept landing stage, along with her brother Paul, a young man now, and so fine in his military frock coat and boots.

Neither she nor Jacob spoke about what had become of the townhouse, the château, the estate, and the farmland. Before his death the previous winter, Robert had made it clear in a letter to Jacob that there was no possibility for Protestants abroad of recovering confiscated land and property.

Neither did they speak of religion or of his daughters' forced Catholic upbringing. Instead, they spoke about the difficulty of leaving France, of the long voyage and how Aunt Suzanne had insisted on having her manservant, Antoine, chaperone them to the ship in Bordeaux.

'She has become more fretful since Uncle Robert passed,' Elizabeth had said. 'Thankfully, she still has Cousin Pierre, and us . . .' After an awkward pause, she had said: 'Father, you do know that I must return to Montauban?'

Jacob recognised the steely resolution of Jeanne in his daughter's eyes. He had said: 'Fear not, my dear daughter, I have not asked you to come here to deprive you of your free will.' She was contented, but what about her mother?

Isabelle, overawed at meeting her father and brother, sat with her hand in her sister's. Jacob let her get used to him in her own good time. He trusted the knotted threads of the past would all become untangled in due course.

But other long-harboured worries assailed Elizabeth as they had made their way between laboured fields and meadows with gambolling lambs to the house in the country. She had had her reasons for refusing to leave France all those years ago, for letting Paul go with the guide instead of herself. But was it really to remain with her sister? Or was it through self-interest and preferring the company of her friends in Montauban? She had nevertheless taken it upon herself to become her sister's surrogate mother, albeit not realising the role would last so long. It was one reason why, at twenty-five, she had so far refrained from marrying, even though she had not lacked suitors, especially with the Delpech patrimony thrown into the marriage portion. And would her mother forgive her for wanting to return to her hometown after this visit? Would she forgive her at all?

Jeanne recognised Elizabeth in the body of a poised, pretty, and refined young woman as Jacob helped her alight. Then she instinctively turned to take the little girl's hand in a motherly fashion.

It suddenly occurred to Jeanne that she must look a great deal older than the lady in the painting that the girl had grown up with.

After a moment of unblinking hesitation, Jeanne marched forward, her hand to her mouth. But then emotion got the better of her self-restraint, and she ran like the wind as Elizabeth burst into tears and opened her arms unreservedly. Mother and daughter fell into each other's arms.

Moments later, Jeanne was at last holding the baby, now a girl of eleven, snatched from her breast in one of France's darkest and cruellest periods of intolerance.

*

Half an hour later, while Elizabeth, Paul, Jacob, and Jeanne chatted excitedly in the lounge before dinner was served, Isabelle played with her younger brother on the swing under the oak tree. She thought it all very strange, being an elder sister and having parents. Yet somehow it all seemed to fit, like a torn tapestry stitched back together.

Also in

The Huguenot Connection series

The Huguenot Connection trilogy ends here, but the Huguenot series continues with MAY STUART which features some of the secondary characters encountered in the trilogy.

MAY STUART

Port-de-Paix, 1691. May Stuart is ready to start a new life with her young daughter. No longer content with her role as an English spy and courtesan, she gains passage on a merchant vessel under a false identity. But her journey to collect her beloved child is thrown off course when ruthless corsairs raid their ship. Former French Lieutenant Didier Ducamp fears he's lost his moral compass. After the deaths of his wife and daughter, he sank to carrying out terrible deeds as a pirate. But when he spares a beautiful hostage from his bloody-minded fellow sailors, he never expected his noble act would become the catalyst for a rich new future.

May Stuart is a standalone novel set in the world of the thrilling Huguenot Chronicles trilogy. If you enjoy unlikely romance, period-authentic details, and rip-roaring tales of redemption, then you'll love Paul C.R. Monk's tale on the high seas.

What readers are saying:

"A most enjoyable, uplifting read."

"Great story of a woman with other ideas of her future."

"I loved this book just like I loved his Huguenot Chronicles. Entertaining, and so well written, that the characters come alive with realism."

MAY STUART is available from Amazon and high street bookstores.

ABOUT THE AUTHOR

Paul C. R. Monk is the author of The Huguenot Connection historical fiction trilogy and the Marcel Dassaud books. You can connect with Paul on Facebook at www.facebook.com/paulcrmonkauthor and you can send him an email at paulmonk@bloomtree.net should the mood take you.

GET *BEFORE THE STORM 1685* AND EXCLUSIVE MATERIAL

Building a relationship with my readers is one of the best things about writing. I occasionally send newsletters with details on new releases, special offers and other bits of news relating to my historical fiction series. You can get a **free copy of my novella** *BEFORE THE STORM 1685* by signing up at BookHip.com/FSZRFG

Thanks for reading,
Paul

BY THE SAME AUTHOR

In The Huguenot Connection trilogy:

Merchants of Virtue

Voyage of Malice

Land of Hope

Also in the Huguenot Connection series:

Before The Storm 1685 (prequel)

May Stuart

Other works:

Strange Metamorphosis

Subterranean Peril

ACKNOWLEDGEMENTS

My special thanks go to Marc Bridel, secretary of the Huguenot Society of Switzerland, who welcomed me in Payerne and gave me invaluable information about the Huguenots in Switzerland. My supportive advance reader group gave me feedback and extra eyeballs once those of the editors' had passed over the manuscript. My thanks also go to my mother and brother who were a constant source of encouragement while writing this trilogy. Finally, I thank Florence Monk, Anthony Monk, Dylan Monk and Lloyd Monk, who allowed me my nightly escapades into my study and gave enthusiastic advice when it came to publication.